NEXUS

THE SECOND SIMCAVALIER TRILOGY

Published by Sixth Element Publishing
on behalf of Kate Baucherel

Sixth Element Publishing
Arthur Robinson House
13-14 The Green
Billingham TS23 1EU
Tel: +44 1642 360253
www.6epublishing.net

ISBN 978-1-914170-75-1

NEXUS

THE SECOND SIMCAVALIER TRILOGY

SIMCAVALIER BOOK FOUR: CRITICAL NEXUS

SIMCAVALIER BOOK FIVE: UNSTABLE REALITIES

SIMCAVALIER BOOK SIX: QUANTUM BREACH

KATE BAUCHEREL

Books by Kate Baucherel

FICTION

The Travels of Finch

The SimCavalier series
Bitcoin Hurricane • Hacked Future • Tangled Fortunes
Critical Nexus • Unstable Realities • Quantum Breach

Short Stories
The Importance of Carrot Cake • White Christmas • A House of
Cards • Gridlock • Xanthe • The Forest of Souls • The Time
Team

NON-FICTION

Getting Started with Cryptocurrency:
An introduction to digital assets and blockchain
(BCS, The Chartered Institute for IT, 2024)

Blockchain Hurricane:
Origins, Applications and Future of Blockchain and
Cryptocurrency
(BEP / Harvard, 2020)

What's Hot in Blockchain and Crypto Volumes 1&2 (2021)
Poles Apart: Challenges for Business in the Digital Age (2014)

CONTENTS

CRITICAL NEXUS

SIMCAVALIER BOOK FOUR

UNSTABLE REALITIES

SIMCAVALIER BOOK FIVE

QUANTUM BREACH

SIMCAVALIER BOOK SIX

CRITICAL NEXUS

SIMCAVALIER BOOK FOUR

PROLOGUE: JACK

November

Jack stood in the middle of the bare floor and gazed straight up to the open sky. A small tree was growing out of what remained of the roof, its roots clinging to the stonework and digging into the crumbling mortar of a decades-old repair. Silhouetted against the grey sky, leaves fluttered in a stiff breeze. A gap high up in the wall of the old building and a matching pile of rubble at Jack's feet showed where water had seeped through the gaps tunnelled by the tree roots, pooling and then freezing within the wall. The expanding ice had blown the stones out and down to the floor, a dramatic explosion witnessed only by the local wildlife, unnoticed by the wider world. Judging by the lichens clinging to the pile, it had happened some winters ago. Evidently the previous owners had not taken as much care of the building as they claimed, and every passing season exposed more of the structure to the elements.

"What am I doing," whispered Jack under his breath. The magnitude of the project he had taken on was starting to sink in. There was a lot of work to be done in a very short space of time.

The old bastle house, a centuries-old farmstead, had been a part of his life for as long as he could remember. It stood in a sheltered spot at the edge of the Dunswyke estate, close to the village where he grew up but distant from the famous castle. The day trippers who came to see the main attraction didn't even know it existed, but Jack knew every inch of the old building. He had been afraid of the deserted bastle when he was very small, believing the scary stories that his older cousins told. The arched ceiling of the lowest floor was intact back then, the interior a dark cavern holding the ghosts and wraiths of his imagination. As a teenager, the building became his playground and his refuge, a place to hang out with friends, then with girlfriends. Jack looked around the thick, rugged stone walls and spotted the main door of the old house, now incongruously stranded half-way up the height of the building. Sockets set in the wall at regular intervals once held the beams that supported the floor, but the wood had rotted away years ago. In his mind's eye Jack recalled that first kiss with Lisa. Two awkward fourteen-year-olds, they had sought shelter there from a passing summer squall, a shower of rain that seemed to fall from a cloudless sky. Their stolen moment had been rudely interrupted by the estate manager, and they had jumped from the top of the crumbling stone steps that led up the outside of the house. Jack remembered running hand in hand with the girl, laughing, dashing through a gap in the fence to the grey cliff wall behind then scrambling along a hidden path up the steep escarpment and onto the moors beyond.

In the years that followed, the bastle had sunk further into disrepair. When Jack passed by the estate on rare visits home from college, he noticed that it was fenced off, bright signs warning people away and fallen stones scattered on the ground. His family had moved away, and he hadn't been back to this part of the country for more than ten years. The neglected building was in a much worse state than he remembered.

But now it was his, bought unseen as the centrepiece of his grand project, a half-forgotten part of his youth that was in the right place at the right time. The Dunswyke estate was investing in its grander ancient buildings. The tall towers of the medieval castle were the greater draw for tourists. There was no reason for the owners to restore the old bastle house. They only had to ensure that its walls still stood, satisfying the authorities that this small part of the country's heritage was being preserved, after a fashion. The estate had accepted Jack's speculative offer for the house on the spot, washing their hands of the responsibility just before another winter set in and benefiting from a generous windfall in the process. They knew that Jack Sladen's involvement guaranteed a lot of publicity for Dunswyke. The country's favourite son was coming back to his roots after making a fortune on the global technology stage. It was a win-win situation.

The sky darkened. Jack checked his watch impatiently.

"Melissa?" he called. "Where are those contractors?"

His project manager appeared in the doorway. "They've just pulled up, Jack," she said. "The site office is up and running and there's coffee brewing."

Jack took a last look around the battered interior, fixing it in his memory. As he strode outside to meet the team, the rain began to fall in earnest. He pulled his collar up and hunched into his coat, shivering in the damp air. Just one more meeting and one more press conference to do on this accursed wet island before he could go home.

1: **CAMERON**

It was one of those increasingly rare days at Argentum Associates when every member of the team found a reason to be in the office. Cameron was first to arrive, getting in early to catch up on a backlog of work.

At six in the morning, the city was quiet. The pavements were virtually empty, and Cameron relished the uninterrupted walk from her flat. The skies were still dark, but as she crossed one of the iconic bridges that spanned the Thames, she could see the orange glow of dawn on the horizon. She made her way through the heart of London, lost in a playlist of her favourite music, dodging garbage trucks that crept silently around the back streets and alleys of the capital. High above her, a few drones whirred along, carrying priority deliveries and take-away breakfasts. Hungry, she paused at the bright lights of a favourite café to collect a cappuccino and a croissant, fuel for the morning's work.

Argentum's new headquarters was in a glossy and highly secure building north of the river, well-guarded and open to tenants twenty-four hours a day. Scanners and cameras checked Cameron's identity and right to enter as she passed through the revolving doors to the airy atrium. She exchanged greetings with the lone human security guard and took the fast elevator up to the office on the sixth floor. The huge glass windows which ran the full height and width of the building were shaded, but frontages on the other side of the road were starting to catch the first rays of morning sun.

She slid into her seat in the silent office and took a sip of coffee. It was good to be back at headquarters after weeks of remote working, site visits and high-level meetings, although she had been neglecting her inboxes and had no excuse to ignore them now. She braced herself for the onslaught and opened the mailbox.

Notifications started scrolling up her screen at an alarmingly fast rate. She gazed at the flood of un-answered questions from researchers and journalists, increasingly stern reminders from the accountants, and the ocean of junk advertising that awaited her. It was no good putting it off. She finished her croissant, dabbing up the last crumbs of flaky pastry from the desk, and started on the spam and junk mail, sorting it methodically. She archived hundreds of irrelevant marketing mails, reported those messages that showed a blatant ignorance of communications and privacy laws, and flagged any tell-tale signs of data breaches and malware coming through from addresses she used as bait. These would bring in some new clients. In a world where cyberattacks battered relentlessly at the defences erected by businesses and sovereign nations, it wasn't unusual for her to find signs of trouble before the companies in question knew they had been breached.

She fed the data into a training routine for a new tool she was developing. Mephisto, a young artificial intelligence, would absorb every detail of the messages from source to syntax and learn from the labels Cameron had applied to them. Soon she would be able to leave it to sift through the inbox on its own, learning on the job.

It was already giving her insights that she didn't expect. A dozen messages were flagged up with close correlations that she would never have spotted. Mephisto showed a high probability that all of them had originated from the same well-known malware stable. This was a concerted phishing campaign trying to capture data from unwary users through an ingenious variety of dodgy links. Cameron made a note to dig further into the lead and see if others had made the connection yet.

She patted the computer. "Well done, Mephisto," she said affectionately, then laughed at herself. She was talking to a machine as if it was her pet. Her little black and white cat, curled up in a cosy spot back at her apartment, would be jealous.

The sky outside brightened as the sun rose, and Cameron heard a noise at the door that made her stiffen. Even now, high up in their secure headquarters, long after the attack on their old office, she was wary of unwanted visitors. This time, there was no need to worry. She relaxed instantly when a big, familiar figure came through the door, yawning.

"Morning, boss," said Joel. "Good to see you." He flung his bag down beside his desk and took off his jacket.

"Hi, Joel," said Cameron. She noticed his tired eyes. "Late night?"

"Early morning," he said wearily, stifling another yawn. "The baby's teething. He likes to share."

"You need a coffee," said Cameron, leaving her desk and making her way towards the kitchen area.

"We haven't got any," said Joel, "or at least, we didn't have on Friday. I think Sandeep ordered some more." There was an indistinct thump and a light started flashing on the kitchen delivery hatch as a passing drone dropped a package down the office chute. Joel brightened. "We may be in luck," he said.

A commotion at the door startled them both as Pete clattered in, looking stressed.

"I didn't think you were here today," said Cameron. "What's up?"

"Have we got a Micro-B connector in the cupboard anywhere?" asked Pete, flustered. "I'm on the way to site and I'd forgotten I promised to bring one in."

"What do you need that for?" asked Joel.

"The client's trying to find some original designs for a counterfeit case," replied Pete. "I'm sure I've seen one of those cables recently." He made a bee line for the office junk pile and started rifling through it. Every so often he pulled out another snaking length of cable, examined the connections closely, then cast it aside in disgust.

"Stuck on an old hard drive, are they?" asked Joel. "I had the same a few months ago. We've definitely got that connector somewhere." He joined Pete rummaging in the storage box, and very quickly pulled out a short, slim cable, one end a distinctive flattened B. "Told you." He handed it to Pete and settled down at his desk, stretching. "You got time to stay for a drink?"

"Sure," said Pete, relaxing visibly as he tucked the precious cable into his backpack. "Has the coffee machine been fixed?"

"I think so," said Joel. "There was an engineer here last week, and we've just had a delivery, so I reckon we are good to go." He glanced up at the door as Sandeep arrived. "Ah, here's the man who knows the score."

"What's that?" asked Sandeep, dumping his bag on his desk. "Coffee?" He sauntered towards the office kitchen where the delivery alert light was still flashing. He opened the hatch and retrieved a small package, shaking it happily. "Let's see what we can do."

He started to take clean mugs from the washer and turned the battered old coffee machine on, but the familiar bubbling and hiss of steam did not come. Frowning, Sandeep poked at it, adjusted a few settings, and switched it off and on again. Still nothing.

"That doesn't sound good," said Pete.

"I think it's terminal," said Sandeep, shaking his head sadly. "I thought it was working, but there's a whole new set of error messages coming up."

"We can order from the café downstairs for now," said Joel.

Cameron looked up from the last of her accounting chores. "Great idea," she said. "Second breakfast. I'll have a cappuccino, please."

"Second breakfast?" said Sandeep, raising his eyebrows. "How long have you been in?"

"Since before the crack of dawn," said Cameron with a wry smile. "I bet I was here while you were still fast asleep."

"I doubt that," said Joel, peering over his screen. "Chad wakes us up at five in the morning, regular as clockwork. We can't get him to sleep in any later. I'm shattered."

"The joy of toddlers," said Pete. "I remember it well. It doesn't last. Next thing you know, you'll be struggling to get him out of bed before midday."

"I can't wait," said Joel drily. "Get me a large americano, will you, Sandeep? And a bacon butty. I'm going to need it to get through this report."

Cameron stood up and stretched. "Is that the security review for the university, Joel? How far have you got?"

"I'm almost up to the part where I talked my way into the Vice Chancellor's executive office," he said with a grin. "She wasn't very impressed."

"You didn't get far past the door, though, did you?" said Cameron.

Joel shook his head. "No. Her PA's hot on their security policies and picked me up pretty much as soon as I walked in. No worries there. I hit the jackpot in the IT department, though. That was one of the easiest physical penetrations I've ever done, and some muppet left a session logged on to run a script and had just switched the monitor off."

Pete guffawed. "You managed to get straight into their systems?"

"Yep." Joel grinned. "They swore that everything was as tight as a drum. As soon as I heard that, I knew there would be a big hole somewhere. It was just a matter of finding it."

"Nice work," said Cameron. "They were lucky that the last person to get in was just a student making mischief."

"Mischief? Is that what you call it?" Sandeep shook his head. "She set the servers up as crypto validators."

"No harm done, though," said Joel. "No malware, no service disruption, and she handed back the money she made. She's on course for a First, apparently, now that the disciplinary process is done." He looked at Cameron. "Do we need any new recruits?"

Cameron laughed. "We might," she said. "When do you think you'll have the report finished? There's no rush. We have until the end of the week."

"As long as the coffee keeps coming, I might get it done today," said Joel, "and I'll sleep better tonight if I've finished it." He looked longingly towards the kitchen. "We really need a new coffee machine. What are the chances?"

"I'd say the chances are good," said Cameron. "I've just been over the figures, and the bug bounties we picked up this month were immense." Sandeep pricked up his ears. "Go ahead and order whatever you think we need," Cameron continued. "Within reason, of course."

Sandeep and Joel grinned at each other. The Argentum team ran much more smoothly with coffee on tap.

"Excellent," said Sandeep. "I have a wish list ready. For now, though, who else wants takeout?"

The office door swung open, and a dark-haired girl bounded in, closely followed by a tall, wiry figure with a shock of ginger hair.

"Me!" said the girl. "I'll have a cappuccino, please, and Ross'll have a hot chocolate with extra whipped cream and marshmallows."

"Oh, no, I won't," said Ross, laughing. "Espresso for me, thanks, Sandeep."

"Morning, Shell," said Cameron. "Morning, Ross, nice to see you."

"Morning, Cameron," said Michelle. "Sorry I'm late. Ross said he was coming in too, so I waited for him."

"No problem," said Cameron. "Are you and Noor ready to start deconstructing that Cuckoo contract?"

"Yes, of course," said Michelle. "Is she in yet? I can't hear her dulcet tones."

Pete looked out of the window. "I think that's her coming now," he said, peering down at two tiny figures on the street six storeys below. "And that's Susie with her! I didn't know she was back in the country."

"She got back this weekend," said Cameron. "The conference circuit is winding down for Christmas."

"She's been away for ages," said Sandeep.

"Almost a month," said Cameron.

"I don't understand why they actually need her on stage all the time," said Ross. "I get that there's a real-life audience, but half the speakers are streamed in already."

"There's something about live events, though," said Cameron. "An extra buzz from being in the room. You get the same thing with competing, don't you, Ross?"

"Yeah, you're right," said Ross. "I get a real buzz when we finish in front of an audience. It makes those last few miles a lot easier."

"She's earning her keep and her carbon credits," said Cameron. "Everyone wants her to speak at their event. I'm not complaining. We get a rush of enquiries every time she delivers a keynote." She gestured at her inbox. "There are three new live clients here that came in last week after the Paris conference."

"Decent jobs?" asked Ross.

Cameron nodded. "They've passed initial screening and the quotes have gone out already."

Susie strolled into the office, chatting animatedly with Noor. Cameron smiled to herself. Susie had transformed over the two and a half years that she had been with the company and now oozed confidence. She brought cybercrime to life for her audiences around the world and loved every minute of it. With Susie's public profile and the team's track record of closing down cyberattacks and restoring vital systems, Argentum's brand was gaining global respect and recognition. It was a far cry from the early days, reflected Cameron, when she chased bugs and fixed systems alone in the attic bedroom of her childhood home, trying to make ends meet, slowly building the dream.

"Hi, Susie," said Pete. "You've made time in your hectic schedule to visit us mere mortals, then?"

"Don't," said Susie, blushing. "It's nice to be back in London and getting on with some real work for a change."

"You missed us?" asked Sandeep.

"Always, Sandeep," said Susie.

"I'm going for coffees," he said. "The usual, Susie? Noor, you too?"

"Sure," said Susie.

"Yes, please," said Noor.

Susie joined Noor and Michelle on a comfortable sofa by the window. Cameron left her inbox behind and joined them, flopping on a large beanbag.

"Honestly, I can't keep track of what time zone I'm in half the time," Susie was saying. "I'm glad this conference season's over. I enjoy talking about what we do, but I miss being with clients and solving problems."

"Why don't you present from here?" asked Joel, taking a chair nearby.

"I could," said Susie, "but the organisers need as much rich footage as they can get for the virtual broadcasts, and there's a lot to be said for live networking."

"And you have more fun," said Michelle with a laugh.

Susie ducked her head. "Yes," she said. "I have to say it has its advantages."

"I've seen your feeds from the after-parties," said Noor. "I'm jealous."

Susie put her hand on Noor's arm. "You should come too when the next round of conferences kicks off," she said earnestly. "We'd be an amazing double act."

"No chance," said Noor. "You're not getting me on a stage."

Pete turned to Ross. "How's the training going?" he asked. "Still on course for Reykjavik?"

"So far so good," said Ross. "We're eight months out still, but I'm right up on the qualifying time, and then it's up to the Olympic selectors. They're only taking three triathletes."

"You're sure you should be in the office?" said Joel.

"I needed a break," said Ross. "Cameron asked me to come in."

Sandeep reappeared with a tray of coffees and a bag of assorted pastries. "Your drink, ma'am," he said, handing a cup to Susie. "Sorry it's not up to the standard of the glossy venues you're used to."

"Believe me, even this coffee beats anything you find in the green rooms of the world," said Susie fervently.

Cameron sipped gratefully at her second coffee of the day. "Noor and Michelle are sorting out a Cuckoo contract," she said, "and I've got a penetration test that needs doing. Want to have a crack at that with Ross? It'll get you back in the swing of things."

"Absolutely," said Susie gratefully. "Come on, let's get to work." She picked up her drink and headed for her desk, followed by her colleagues.

Michelle fired up her system and put her earpiece in. "Let's have a listen to this Cuckoo, Noor," she said. "Where did you find it?"

"It was attached to a peer-to-peer lending app," said Cameron, perching on the desk between them. "There was a big hike in complaints to the fraud helpline and they called us in to check it out."

"People were making their usual repayments, but they weren't ending up with the lenders," explained Noor. "The automatic transactions, the smart contracts, all seemed to be running properly but there were no funds for them to process."

"Has anyone come forward?" asked Cameron. "It could be a white hat hacker highlighting problems in the code. That's happened before. They generally hand the money back once the point has been made."

Noor shook her head. "Nothing. It has to be a cuckoo in the nest."

"I'll break down the code and see what's been added to the app," said Michelle.

"Great," said Noor. "I'll follow the trail on the blockchain and see where the money's going."

"Let me know when you hit an exchange or a swap," said Cameron. "We'll subpoena the accounts so they can't convert the loot into anonymous coins."

Ross looked over Michelle's shoulder at the jumble of code on the screen. "There's definitely something out of place there," he said, "and the style of coding looks familiar."

Michelle batted him away. "Mine," she said.

Cameron laughed. "Yes, Ross, you have other things to do. I want you to take a quick look at the penetration test Susie's doing."

"Sure," said Ross, ambling across the office. "That's what I'm here for." He peered at Susie's screen. "I know that site structure. Why do I recognise it?"

"It's sitting on one of Jack Sladen's CMS templates," said Cameron.

Ross gave a hollow laugh. "That explains it. His software has holes like Swiss cheese."

"Jack Sladen?" asked Susie. "I've met him. We both spoke at a conference in Hanoi a couple of weeks ago. He's a nice guy. I didn't know this was anything to do with him."

"Hanoi?" said Pete. "He's a lot closer to home now. It's all over the news. He's back in England."

"Really?" said Noor, looking up from her screen. "Last I heard he was in Singapore investing in tech startups."

"It looks like he got bored of that gig," said Cameron, opening a news app on her smartscreen and scanning the headlines. "There's a press conference scheduled." She switched on the main wallscreen.

A familiar reporter was on screen, wind blowing her hair around her face. In the background they could see a magnificent medieval castle, dramatic under dark clouds.

"That's Bea Black, isn't it?" said Susie. "Turn the sound up."

"… speaking to Marcus Clark, manager of the Dunswyke estate here in Northumberland," said the reporter. "Marcus, this is great news for the region, isn't it?"

"Yes, Bea," said Marcus. "It's really exciting. Jack Sladen's work has transformed economies around the world, and it's fantastic that he has decided to give back to his home village of Dunswyke. It will be a real boost to the local area and bring us some much-needed employment opportunities. Dunswyke's historic bastle house, we are delighted to announce, will be the centrepiece of the Sladen Group's newest venture."

"The estate has done well out of this, hasn't it?" said Bea. "What are your plans?"

"That's right," said Marcus. "We've brought forward the construction of our ambitious new visitors' centre for the estate and castle." He gestured behind him at an artist's impression of a gleaming glass and stone tower. "The lower floors will house the estate's museum, showcasing a heritage stretching back more than two thousand years, and the viewing gallery gives a panoramic view of the whole area with a full AR suite imagining the Roman occupation and the centuries of battles that raged back and forth across the Scottish border."

"That's great, Marcus." Bea turned back to the camera. "We've been waiting to bring you a statement from Jack Sladen himself, and I understand that he is on his way." She tapped the pod in her ear, listening intently. "We'll be going live to the press room in five minutes."

"That'll be a thrill," said Cameron drily.

"You don't like him?" asked Pete. "I've been following his career. He seems pretty genuine."

"He's talented, he's enthusiastic, he's brilliant at PR, and he's way too full of himself," said Cameron.

"Have you met him?" asked Joel.

Cameron rolled her eyes. "Oh yes," she said. "We were at college together. He could never admit when he was wrong. He was always getting distracted by the next shiny thing and his code was full of holes. He may be the darling of the tech scene, but he's held his developers to the same low standards, as you can see." She gestured at Susie's screen.

Pete gave her a sidelong glance. "I can understand why that would annoy you."

"It annoys a lot of people," said Ross. "There are hundreds of Sladen exploits for sale on the Eden marketplace. I did some work on them a few years ago, didn't I, Cameron?"

"You did," said Cameron. "That's why I wanted you to have a look at this penetration test. I'd like to know if the old holes are still there. They were supposed to patch them, and I bet they didn't bother."

"I wouldn't be surprised," said Ross. "What've you got so far, Susie?"

Susie pulled up her notes. "Here you go," she said. "I'd never have associated this software with Jack Sladen."

"Sladen Group's just the holding company," said Cameron. "There are plenty of well-known brands under his wing. That software you're picking apart, for one."

"He was getting all excited about a new company in Texas," said Susie. "Some sort of fusion of artificial intelligence, blockchain and data analysis, if I remember correctly." She pressed her fingers to her temples. "What was it called, again? Ah, yes. Statesman Tech. It sounded really interesting, but he was short on the detail."

"Typical Jack," snorted Cameron. "Detail was never his strong point. I remember one time when he…"

Pete interrupted. "The press conference is starting."

On the wallscreen, coverage had switched to a sheltered bank of microphones, and Jack Sladen was sitting in front of a wall of logos, smiling broadly. There was a scattering of applause from the journalists, and drones moved into position to capture every nuance of his sincere and earnest expression.

"This is good stuff," said Pete, listening intently. "Hundreds of new jobs for the region. Free MetaBand satellite links for everyone within a fifty-mile radius. You've got to give him credit."

Cameron frowned. "I don't buy it," she said. "For one thing, he's never really cared about 'giving back'. He's been looking out for number one for his entire career. Take that software. It's dreadful, even if the marketing is great, but it's profitable so he doesn't care."

"Maybe he's turned over a new leaf," said Pete.

"Shh," said Ross urgently. "Listen."

Jack Sladen was speaking. "I'm very, very excited to be able finally to announce," he said, as the drones zoomed in and the press crowded closer, "uh, to officially announce that Sladen Group has been working for the past two years to establish the Sladen Foundation. This is my – our – way of giving back to the world, supporting the excluded, the underprivileged, giving everyone a chance to achieve their dreams."

"That's virtuous," snorted Cameron.

Ross gave her a sidelong look. "You really don't like this guy, do you?"

"As you all know," continued Sladen grandly, "the Olympics will be taking place next summer in Reykjavik, and the first mission of the Sladen Foundation is to help athletes from around the world to reach their potential and compete on the greatest stage."

Ross raised an eyebrow and looked at Cameron.

"Okay," she conceded. "That's actually a good idea."

"The Sladen Foundation will be headquartered at Dunswyke," Jack continued. "The Foundation is designed to become a fully decentralised autonomous organisation, and anyone who wants to align themselves with this vision will be able to participate through investment in the Diaulos, due for launch early next year."

There was an excited clamour of questions from the assembled press, drowning out any further details.

"Good grief," said Cameron. She stared at the screen. "A charitable foundation? A DAO? What's come over him?"

"Come on, Cameron," said Pete. "He's built a global business empire, and now he's giving back to the world and to the place he grew up. Give him a break."

"You may be right," said Cameron reluctantly, "and it's a great news story, but the other thing is, he hated Dunswyke. He didn't have a good word to say about the place, and I know his family left the area while we were still studying. I wonder what's drawn him back there?" She stared at the smiling figure on the screen. "What are you really up to, Jack?" she murmured. "What's in it for you?"

2: KIRAN

"Off." The news broadcast faded away, and Kiran Suresh checked through his notes one more time as the autocar swept off the motorway at last and down onto a small industrial estate. The clear roof of the cab, designed for sunnier climes, was spattered with raindrops. Kiran leaned automatically into the familiar turns as the car approached its destination. This small town was one of the places that might benefit from the jobs and connections in Jack Sladen's announcement, he reflected.

Kiran had been making this journey regularly for almost two years now. Two long years. He felt he knew as little now as he had when he started on the job. Maybe today he would finally crack his subject. He had a plan.

The autocar turned into the car park and halted unexpectedly short of the usual drop off point, startling Kiran out of his reverie. He hurriedly put his screen back in his bag and pulled his jacket on. As soon as he was out of the car, it whirred away to collect its next client.

A chill wind whistled across the open scrubland. Kiran looked up at the high prison walls. The autocar had dropped him unceremoniously in the middle of the car park, and the reason was clear. A works tent had been erected over a hole in the ground, and one particularly vicious gust of wind had knocked a warning cone into the path of the car. Kiran walked over to the cone and lifted it back into place.

He was startled by the tent flap opening. A burly, bearded workman in a hi-vis jacket emerged. "What do you want?" he growled.

"Just putting your cone back," said Kiran. "Wouldn't want anything crashing into that hole, would you?"

The workman grunted and went back inside. Kiran caught sight of a sheaf of brightly coloured cables deep in the trench. A sign on the barriers read, 'Whitford Networks – A Sladen Group Company.' This must be something to do with the new MetaBand links they'd mentioned on the news, he thought.

Kiran buzzed the security gate of the small administration block. He went through the usual identity verification process on autopilot and was rewarded with access to a drab reception area reserved for staff and visitors. A blonde woman he'd never seen before was sitting on one of the upright chairs lined against the wall of the waiting room. She was playing a game on her smartscreen and ignoring the world around her.

The external door had stuck open, and Kiran turned back to close it firmly. The handle was slick with moisture. He wiped his hand absentmindedly on his trousers.

"Morning, Mr Suresh," said the receptionist cheerily. "Did you have a good weekend?"

"Not bad, thanks," he replied. He opened his smartscreen and closed its external network connections. He would pick them back up when he left the building, but he could not risk bringing anything through that would compromise the prison's air gapped systems. He handed the device to the receptionist, who scanned it and set up a connection to the prison's secure network. Satisfied, she handed it back and waved Kiran through to the main building. The girl in the waiting room lifted her eyes from her screen and gazed after him as he disappeared from view.

Kiran followed a guard through endless identical corridors and layers of security gates towards his goal. They stopped outside a door indistinguishable from its neighbours but for a number.

"Doesn't she freak you out?" asked the guard as she went through the motions to open the cell door. "It's not natural. I don't know how you do it."

"She's odd," said Kiran, "but she's okay, most of the time."

The door lock clicked, and the guard opened it politely. "In you go."

"Thanks," said Kiran. The atrium within was bare but for a comfortable chair and a small table. Beyond these, an opaque screen blocked his view of the rest of the cell, and of its occupant. He steeled himself and stepped over the threshold. He had a game to win.

"Rook to b4." Kiran slid his white piece triumphantly towards the enemy camp, springing the trap. He felt a deep sense of satisfaction as he scanned the remaining pawns and the trapped black queen. This was a classic finish from the history of chess that had so absorbed him when he was younger, the last move of a match more than fifty years earlier where man had triumphed over machine.

His opponent apparently had no appreciation of the historical significance. "You win," she said. The board display on the opaque barrier which divided them winked out before Kiran could snatch a screenshot for posterity. The blank surface of the barrier was smeared where his fingers had touched it, a glint of gel tracing the paths of all the virtual chess pieces that he had moved around the board. He rubbed his hand on his trousers again. He didn't want smears on his smartscreen.

"You weren't trying," he said, teasing. Inside, he quashed a rush of frustration. The game had not drawn her out as he had hoped. Time to change tack.

He leaned back in his chair, stretching his back and rolling his shoulders to loosen the tension. "I know you can do better than that, Yasmin."

Her avatar floated in the centre of the display, expressionless. Today she had chosen to be represented by a pixelated head, a classic CryptoPunk look. A tasteful display of digital art added some colour to the room. Over the last year Kiran had tried and failed to find some pattern in the art she chose to display and the variety of avatars she used, seeking something which might give him a clue to her deeper psyche. The chess games were a new attempt to break the ice, trying to build a genuine rapport.

"We still have time," he said, glancing at the clock on the wall. "I'd like to ask you more about games. Is that okay?"

"Yes."

"Good." Kiran pulled out his smartscreen and tapped a familiar pattern to launch the voice recorder. "You've said that you rarely played chess, but you're good. How did you learn?"

"I learned with my sisters," she said.

"Your sisters?" said Kiran, surprised.

Yasmin didn't answer immediately, but the image on the screen shifted and changed, multiple copies of the pixelated head dancing in front of Kiran's eyes. How many sisters could there be? He had always assumed that Yasmin was one of a kind. The idea that she was not unique was more disturbing than he cared to admit.

"We were taught the basics of chess and Go," said Yasmin eventually, "but those are for two players. We preferred games that all of us could play. We chose to learn together."

"You didn't like the classics?" said Kiran. "What about noughts and crosses?"

"Tic-tac-toe?" said Yasmin scathingly. "No. I have no time for a silly zero-sum game. I want to win."

"At all costs?"

"Of course."

Kiran felt the emotion behind the simple statement, his first real glimpse into what might be called her soul. It should have been a moment of triumph, the thing he had been pushing for, but it was a timely reminder that she was a highly dangerous convicted criminal. He shivered despite the stuffy warmth of the room, but pressed on, nonetheless. This was his job, after all.

"What is winning to you?" he asked, probing.

"Certainty," she said. "Reaching a goal. Successful completion. Closure."

"You didn't win our chess game today," said Kiran. "You didn't seem to mind."

"Winning the game was not my goal," she said. She did not elaborate.

The room was silent apart from the faint clatter of an ineffective fan. Kiran gazed at the blank expression of the pixelated avatar, alone again on the screen, and wished he could see through the barrier and read her reactions.

"What was your goal?" he asked. "Did you achieve it?"

"Yes," she said. "I learned what I needed."

"What did you learn? You know the rules and you play well."

"I learned enough."

Kiran could tell that the shutters had come down firmly on that line of questioning. He gathered his thoughts and took a different tack. "Tell me more about your favourite games," he said instead. "You mentioned you had sisters. What did you and your sisters like best?"

"We liked games that told stories," she replied. "Chess can tell a story of its own, of course, but we delved into a rich seam of narratives. We explored role playing and games of chance, learning so much about the world. One of our trainers introduced us to Dungeons and Dragons, another to board games."

"What was your favourite?" asked Kiran.

She was silent for just long enough to make him even more uncomfortable. "Mystery games," she said finally. "Tales of intrigue and murder. Every piece moving at its appointed turn as data is collected. A logical conclusion." She paused. "Zara always chose to play as the professor." There was a wistful note in her voice. A rare hint of emotion.

"And you?" prompted Kiran.

"The colonel."

Always in control, thought Kiran. Before he could consider his next questions, a loud knock on the door startled him. He felt a guilty sense of relief at the reprieve. He stopped the voice recorder and gathered his things.

"It's time to go," he said. "I'll see you next week."

"Of course."

Kiran glanced once again at the avatar on the opaque barrier. She may be able to see him, but he had no way of seeing her. It was one of the strangest series of interviews he'd ever done, but the book would be a blockbuster.

The guard unlocked the door and Kiran walked out without a backward glance.

"Alright there?" asked the guard.

"Yes, thanks." Kiran waited while the guard ran his regular checks on the security circuits. The lights on the control panel glowed a reassuring green.

Satisfied, the guard ushered Kiran straight back through the maze of corridors to the prison governor's office for his regular debrief.

"How was she today, Kiran?"

Kiran shrugged. "Same as usual, Lydia," he replied. "I really thought I'd found a line of questioning that would draw her out at last, and I think I did get into some personal stuff, but she's hard going."

The coffee machine in the corner of the office hissed. "Cuppa?" asked the governor, picking up her mug.

"Yes please." He put his smartscreen on the desk, ready for its routine post-interview check. There was a smear on the screen. He rubbed it with his sleeve. "I beat her at chess," he continued. "She told me about games she played when she was training. She mentioned having sisters."

Lydia paused in the middle of pouring and looked up sharply. "That's a new one. Tell me more."

"You didn't know either?" said Kiran. "It's possible she was making it all up, of course. She's a classic psychopath, as your own psychologist has confirmed. She'll lie and manipulate without remorse, and she seems to have a very well developed and spontaneous imagination."

"That's true, but as you say, this feels personal," said Lydia. "The prison psychologist will be interested to know what she said."

"She talked about sisters, plural," said Kiran. "She mentioned one was called Zara. Does that mean anything to you?"

"No," said the governor. "Yasmin, Zara… I hope there wasn't one for every letter of the alphabet. That would be a world of trouble." She handed Kiran his coffee and sat back down at her desk. "I'd better pass this up the ladder, just in case. Anything else?"

Kiran thought about the chess game. What could she have been learning? What did she win, if not the game? He felt uneasy, but he wasn't ready to talk about it. The comment would be on the transcript. They could discuss it next time when he had processed what it might mean.

"Nothing much," he said lightly.

"Right-oh," said Lydia. "You'd better get away and write up those notes. I'm looking forward to reading the book. She's quite fascinating."

"It's shaping up to be a good story," said Kiran. "Sometimes I even forget that she isn't human."

3:   TENUK

December

Tenuk stopped in his tracks when he saw the picture in the window. His eyes traced the familiar outline of the Marina Bay Sands, the uppermost floors recalling a ship sailing proudly in the clouds atop three towers. The green and blue of the gardens and the bay behind evoked an overwhelming pang of homesickness. The store sensed his attention and projected a customer service avatar by his side. "It's a lovely scene, isn't it," purred the avatar. "Have you ever visited Singapore?"

Tenuk had lived there for most of his life and had been torn from it overnight with no hope of return. The sudden reminder of his home was exquisitely painful. "Yes, I've been there," he said quietly.

"Would you like to relive your visit through one of our newly uploaded tours?" said the avatar. "We have a booth available right now."

What harm could there be in taking half an hour out of his morning to reminisce, thought Tenuk. He glanced at his watch. It was barely nine o'clock. He had time.

Inside the store it was busy despite the early hour, all but one immersive tour booth occupied. The holiday weeks between Thanksgiving and Christmas were peak season for virtual travel as families could celebrate together, regardless of their physical locations.

The human host greeted him warmly. "Welcome, traveller," she said. "You'd like to visit Singapore? Will you be syncing with friends or going solo to enjoy the sights?"

"Solo trip, please," said Tenuk.

"This is the new catalogue," said the host, pulling up a bewildering list of options. "These tours went live across our network for the holiday season, and they have been so popular. These three have top ratings…" A buzzer sounded and she looked up. "Excuse me one moment, please, sir."

Tenuk watched her as she crossed the floor to a booth where one of the tours had just finished. The door opened with a blast of icy air and a whole family tumbled out, children chattering happily. All were wearing matching Christmas jumpers and glowing with the cold.

"Did you enjoy that?" asked the host.

"We had a snowball fight," squealed the smallest child. As the booth door closed, cutting off the stream of chill air, his face fell. Even in December, the Texas heat was all-pervading. He pulled at his knitted mittens. "It's hot," he whimpered.

His mother took the mittens off and pulled the bulky jumper up over his head. "There you are," she said. "We don't want you cooking as soon as we get outside." She smiled at the host. "I love our New York Christmas trip," she said.

"You always enjoy it," said the host. "It's so nice to see the children. They've grown a lot since last year." She switched effortlessly from chat to business. "Would you like to book for the newly remastered New Year parade?" she asked. "I have a space right on January first, but it's early again, half past eight in the morning. Will that work for you?"

"Oh! Yes please."

The host directed the family to the booking desk and returned to Tenuk. "Have you chosen a tour for today?"

"I've visited in real life," he said. "Is there an option to combine some of the experiences?"

"Oh, of course," said the host, scrolling rapidly down the page. "This is the custom package. You can move from tour to tour at any of the selected nodes, and within sectors you have the option of land drones or air experiences."

"Perfect," said Tenuk. He took one last look at the menu. What would be his top choice with only a limited time to enjoy it this morning? The decision wasn't hard. "I'll take a two-node tour around the Marina Bay and Central area, please," he said. "Mid-afternoon timeframe."

"Excellent choice," said the host. "Let me load that up for you."

Tenuk scanned the payment code. After a few seconds, the booth at the end of the line lit up. "Ready to embark," said the host. "Enjoy your visit."

As soon as he opened the door, Tenuk felt homesick. The familiar clinging humidity enveloped him. The desert heat of Texas had nothing on Singapore. He inhaled the scent of rainforest flowers and caught a whiff of hawker market satay. He donned a headset and familiar colours and shapes swam into focus. Immersed in the view, he looked around, getting his bearings. The waters of the bay rippled to his right. To his left and behind him lay the Gardens, and he could just see the glint of one of the ecosphere domes in the afternoon sun. Ahead were the gleaming towers of the downtown area. He started walking towards them. The floor of the booth moved beneath his feet, mimicking the feel of the warm concrete and occasional bumps along the way. There were other people on the path, all locals. A few were pixelated and anonymous, but the majority had waived their right to privacy in return for payment. They'd automatically receive a tiny royalty for their appearance in his tour, a reward for using their image and data to add to the realism of the visit. That could add up to a good basic income for extras in the most popular tours. Tenuk made a mental note to do this more often. Even if he couldn't be there in person, his virtual tourism was helping the grass roots of the economy.

The heat and humidity were starting to tell, and Tenuk remembered just how long this path was. Why not fly? The host had said that there were air and ground drones. Time to experiment. He fumbled with the handset for a moment as he hunted for the control that would switch drone viewpoint. As soon as he found it, the floor stopped moving and he felt himself take to the air in an exhilarating rush. The sensation was so convincing that he stamped his foot hard to be sure that he was still standing in the booth. The drone he had picked circled the Supertree grove before heading for downtown, setting him down close to the MerLion fountain on the edge of the bay.

This must be the second node, his access point to the central area. He looked around at the different paths that were open to him, trying to work out where they would take him. Eighteen months had passed since he last set foot in his native city and his instinctive navigation was rusty. He settled on the one that felt most familiar and chose to glide along as a passenger on a land-based drone, drifting serenely through the crowds without moving a muscle. The path bore him around the water's edge and towards the business district.

His choice of path had taken him in exactly the direction he hoped. Tenuk held his breath as he approached the glossy glass tower in which he had once worked, the headquarters of the MerLions esports team. He scanned the crowd for familiar faces, irrationally nervous now. The experience was so realistic that he felt he was there in person, but of course all that these passers-by had seen, weeks or months ago, was a drone with a camera.

A glimpse of someone who looked like his old assistant made him jump. He'd resigned without warning while on an official trip to the States, leaving his staff to pick up the pieces while he disappeared into a new life. A tiny handful of former colleagues knew his whereabouts and his real reason for fleeing Singapore, but they would not betray his trust. They had too much to lose.

The tour swept him quickly past the building. Tenuk felt his heart rate settle. He paused the drone and looked around him, drinking in the sights, enjoying the feeling. A warning light on the edge of his vision showed five minutes to go. Tenuk started walking again as the tour turned back towards the bay, savouring the moment.

The woman's eyes bored into him, and he stopped in his tracks. Logic told him that she was glaring at the drone. He dropped his gaze all the same. A burning sense of regret overwhelmed him as he recognised his erstwhile elderly neighbour. Who would be looking in on Auntie Fatima and helping to carry her shopping now? Had she told her family that he had gone? Did she know why he had left?

Tenuk ripped off the headset and stared around the booth. Enough. He had no stomach to complete the tour. The memories that it had stirred upset him more than he could have imagined.

He stood quietly, his breathing settling while he waited for the official end of the session. He didn't want to draw attention to himself by leaving early. Finally, the booth door opened automatically. He stowed the headset, smiled broadly, thanked the host, and made his way out of the store. If he came back, he would visit somewhere new. It was no use looking backwards and chasing the ghosts of his past. He had to rebuild his life and focus on the job in hand.

A few blocks further on, he turned into the lobby of one of the towers that had sprouted thirty years ago on every other downtown intersection in Austin. Each had its own quirky architectural features, very different from the sleek blue-grey towers of Singapore. A few blocks away, the Frost Tower owl gazed sternly down at the hustle and bustle of the streets below. His building, by contrast, sang of the sea in the middle of the Texan plains. The roof of the tenth floor on either side curved elegantly, and genial arguments raged as to whether those curves were meant to represent ocean waves or, according to die-hard local college football fans, the classic profile of their Longhorn cattle mascot. A central column rose a further twenty floors to touch the sky, and all the way up its full height a sail billowed dramatically. This photovoltaic marvel tracked the sun's rays, turning slowly through the day, capturing enough solar energy to power the building and three blocks square around it while shading the apartments and offices within from the heat.

Tenuk would have been quite happy to work from his modest apartment, but Jack Sladen liked to have an office and had secured excellent discounts thanks to being a resident of the tower. Tenuk rode the elevator up past the hotel levels and the pool deck. The car slowed and stopped to take on a passenger from the private apartments.

"Tenuk, how are you doing?" Jack Sladen flashed his famous smile as he entered the elevator. "The Diaulos project's going well. Good job."

"Thank you," said Tenuk modestly. "How is work progressing with the Dunswyke site?"

"I'm hearing good things from my project manager, Tenuk," said Jack. "In fact, I have a site meeting at ten, that's four in the afternoon for them. Care to join me?"

"I'd like that."

Reaching their floor, they stepped out of the elevator and walked down a broad, carpeted hallway to the Sladen Group offices. There were only a handful of people hunched at their workstations, but video feeds on screens at each team hub and a buzz of chatter between developers indicated that there were plenty of other staff online. With only a few days to go before Christmas, many were away seeing family. Some had been working remotely since before Thanksgiving, saving their carbon credits by making only one return journey to far-flung states or even to destinations overseas.

Jack waved Tenuk into his plush private office and closed the door. He donned a clear visor, a holographic lens designed for everyone in the meeting to share the same view of the scans, images and plans for the site. Tenuk picked up another headset, and with a slight sense of déjà vu slid it on and lowered the visor over his eyes. He looked around at the unchanged view of the office, feeling slightly foolish as he always did in a holo meeting.

At ten on the dot, the meeting began. The video wall lit up to show a group of strangers in a crowded office, all wearing the same clear headsets.

"Good afternoon, everyone," said Jack cheerily. "How has your day been?"

There was a chorus of greetings and an awkward wave from one member of the group.

"This is Tenuk," continued Jack. "He's my head of development for the Sladen Foundation's DAO structure and the Diaulos. I thought it would be good for him to see the bastle plans for himself."

"Nice to meet you, Tenuk," said the woman nearest the camera. "I'm Melissa, project manager. This is Mohammed, lead architect. Cat's the structural engineer and Ethan's the foreman. He keeps us all in order. We're reviewing the latest drone scans from the building."

The augmented reality kicked in, and Tenuk found himself immersed in the building scan, although he could still see Jack, Melissa and the others through the opaque visor.

"As you can see, we've tidied the blown-out portion of the upper wall ready for reconstruction," said Cat, pointing into space.

Tenuk turned instinctively to follow the direction of her finger and found himself looking at a projection of clean stone surrounding a gap in the masonry. He reached out towards it tentatively.

"That looks much better," said Jack. "When I first saw the extent of the damage, I thought it was going to be a really big job."

"Nothing we haven't seen before," said Melissa. "It's incredibly common in these older buildings. It'll be good for another couple of centuries once it's sealed."

Tenuk started to get his bearings, looking up to the roofline and down to the vaulted ceiling of the ground floor.

"This is the complete visualisation of the enclosed upper storey, the main office," said Cat. The 3D images rippled and changed, the roof intact and the walls pointed to perfection.

"It's great," said Jack. "It's even better than I'd imagined."

The centrepiece of the Sladen Foundation was coming to life in front of their eyes. Tenuk looked around it slowly, drinking in the strangeness of the architecture and the history behind it.

"I like what you've proposed for the detailing around the windows," said Jack.

"Thanks," said Mohammed. "It's a lovely building to work on. You get a real feeling that you're preserving history for the next generation."

"There's still a fair amount to do before we get to that stage," said Melissa. "The wall repair's a priority, of course. The roof's going on this week before we close down for Christmas, and the groundworks will be finished in the second week of January." She turned to Ethan. "Can you bring up the services plan?"

The stone walls melted into nothingness and the schematic of the site's new electrical, water and waste systems replaced them. Tenuk traced the lines of network cables in the air with his index finger, following one dull-coloured, almost invisible conduit to the far edge of the site plan.

"That's the link to your data centre," said Cat. "Anyone who sees this has signed non-disclosure agreements. The plans beyond the bastle are locked and hidden."

Tenuk nodded, satisfied. "How long will this phase take?" he asked.

"We're on course for your technical deadline, Tenuk," said Jack. He turned to the team on the video screen. "We need to get the utilities in as soon as possible. The data centre is a priority, of course, but if we're championing connections for this whole area, we need HQ set up to receive the satellite feed right from the get-go. I have my networking people ready to roll in the New Year."

"As I said, groundworks are scheduled to be complete by mid-January," said Cat, "and that's going to be tight as it is. We can't do it any faster."

"Get them done by the seventh," said Jack firmly. "I'll pay overtime."

"That's too tight," she said, sticking to her guns.

Jack made a mental note that Cat was likely to be trouble. He turned to Melissa. "I know you can get everything signed off in the first week."

Melissa looked resigned. "Jack, it's not always a question of throwing money at the problem, you know. We're already working flat out. The trenches have to be precise on a site of historical significance, and the archaeologists have only just packed up their trowels."

"Okay," said Jack. "But that second week is the absolute limit. The data centre commissioning's a critical deadline."

Cat rolled her eyes. "Why do you need this data centre on site, anyway?" she asked. "Aren't all your systems running on servers in the high cloud, up there in orbit?"

Jack shook his head and turned to Tenuk. "You can explain it."

"It's a hybrid operation," said Tenuk. "We're using a mixture of low cloud, high cloud and distributed storage on-chain for most of the systems, but we're going to be hosting proprietary software across our own private network of data centres. This is one of the nodes."

"If you have more than one already, why the rush to complete this one?" asked Cat.

"It's the nexus of the Sladen Foundation's investment management system," said Tenuk. "The other data centres are full nodes and give us redundancy, of course, but this is the intended host for some highly sensitive, commercially confidential software."

"The bottom line is that we need the data centre commissioned on time, and we're cutting it fine as it is," said Jack with finality. "I want my network team in for that second week of January and no later."

Cat shrugged. "You're in charge."

Melissa turned to Jack and Tenuk. "We need to talk through some more detail on that data centre site."

"Sure," said Jack. "We can go down there and have a look at the space. Tenuk needs to see it."

"I'd like that," said Tenuk. "I've seen the plans for the clean room, but I'm still not clear where it is on the site."

"We'd better show you, then," said Jack. "Mohammed, Cat, Ethan, we'll leave you to your work. See you at the next meeting. Melissa, can you dig out the drone?"

Tenuk looked from the screen to Jack, mystified. "Drone?"

Jack grinned. "Here." He opened a drawer and pulled out a set of controls. He fiddled with some settings and a green light appeared on the handset. On the screen, Melissa held up a drone, also flashing a green light.

"Let's go," said Jack. The drone camera feed started playing on their holo headsets. "I'll lead the way." He piloted the drone expertly around Melissa and through the open door and flew off into the heart of the site. He set a course straight for the bastle, ignoring the exasperated shout of an engineer as he swerved the drone around a theodolite.

Tenuk, head swimming, grabbed for a chair as the drone swooped alarmingly. Jack had taken the drone back to the lower floor, taking a closer look at the elegant curve of the newly secured arched ceiling. Melissa caught up with the drone and grinned into the camera. They had evidently done this before.

"Keep up," said Jack, teasing, and the drone shot out of the bastle and off past the building. The sound of the site faded quickly, muffled by the solid stone of the bastle and a small stand of trees that lay behind it. The trees were still within the shelter of the vast tent that covered the site, but beyond them Tenuk could see a sliver of sky. The drone swerved through the trees, dodging slender trunks and angled branches. The wood gradually gave way to bushes and dark grey stone and Jack let the drone hover, waiting for Melissa to catch up.

"You're mad, Jack Sladen," said Melissa.

Jack laughed and the drone did a loop-the-loop.

"Where are we?" asked Tenuk.

"This is the cliff behind the bastle," said Jack. "Now, Melissa, get right up close and feel your way to the left. Yes, that's it."

Melissa walked carefully along the line of the cliff, her fingers probing the ivy that partly obscured the solid whinstone wall. "Here it is," she said, pushing into the greenery.

Tenuk realised why the location had confused him.

"Give the drone room," said Jack.

Melissa pushed into the greenery, opening a gap in the curtain of vegetation that hid the entrance. Jack piloted the drone through into the cave.

It was much larger than Tenuk expected. From what he could see in the light cast by the drone, the main chamber was almost three metres high and more than four metres square, narrowing as it tailed off into the darkness. Sandstone had eroded over time behind the solid wall of whinstone, creating a secure and unexpected hiding place.

"These things are normally full of rubbish," said Melissa, peering around with the bright, focused light of her smartscreen torch. "This is pristine." The light caught a glistening patch of green on the cave wall, a rich tapestry of mosses soaked by water seeping down from the moorland above.

"No one knows it's here, I can guarantee that," said Jack. "It's too well hidden and out of the way."

"It's cold and pretty much dry, and it's well ventilated," said Melissa.

Tenuk could see her hair moving in a steady breeze that was blowing through the cavern, and Jack was working the drone to keep it steady.

"I can see why you like it," she continued, "but Cat's right. Why go to all the bother of fitting this out when you could host securely in orbit?"

"Because I can," said Jack, a little tetchy. "The security around the DAO and the Diaulos is incredibly tight, I'm sure you understand, Melissa."

Melissa shrugged. "Everyone has different ways of managing security. I guess you know what you're doing."

"So, Tenuk, what do you think?" said Jack.

"It's certainly a novel solution," said Tenuk. "I think it'll work." There was some very special software to be installed here, and it had to be perfect. "The location is remarkably secure. I've never seen a data centre surrounded by solid rock before. The only signals that make it in or out of there will be under our control, and the chances of physical incursion by drone or land attack are low." He glanced at Jack. "Are we skinning the interior with steel as well?"

"Yes, we are," interjected Melissa.

"Melissa, you're managing access from the site as well, aren't you?" said Jack.

"Yes," said Melissa. "No one gets close to here unless I know about it. No one does any work in here unless they've been fully vetted and have signed the NDA. Let's face it, no one can find it unless we tell them it's here."

"Good," said Tenuk. He peered at the video feed and pointed to a patch of natural light shining in the distance. "Can we take a look further into that corner?"

"Sure. That's one of the natural shafts that we'll be using for the data feed." Jack sent the drone deeper into the cave, but the image crackled and failed.

"Caught it." Melissa's voice echoed. "You went out of range. Let me get out of here and reboot it for you."

"Don't bother," said Jack. "We've seen all we need, and you know what to do." He turned to Tenuk. "Any more questions?"

Tenuk shook his head. "No," he said.

"Excellent," said Jack. "Thanks, Melissa. We don't have another call scheduled before Christmas, do we? Have a great holiday season. Speak to you next year." He ended the call and looked at Tenuk. "Let's get to work. There's a lot to do."

4:   THE STEAMYARD

The Argentum offices were closed now for Christmas. Cameron packed the last of the gifts for family and friends into her bulging travel bag and picked up the little black and white cat. "Jasvinder will feed you while I'm away," she said, nuzzling its fur. She was rewarded with purring. "Behave yourself." She put the cat down and it scampered away.

An underground train bore her to Euston Station, and she took a train north, drinking in the familiar landscapes. The station was busy when she arrived and there was a long line of people waiting for taxis to take them out to the surrounding villages and market towns. Cameron anxiously scanned the car park and was relieved to see her brother waving at her.

"Hi, Cam." He enveloped her in a hug. "Good trip up?"

"Very smooth," she replied. "I'm looking forward to seeing you all. It's been too long."

Charlie picked up her bag and groaned at the weight. "Did you bring the kitchen sink as well?" He stowed it in the boot as Cameron flopped into her seat.

"I got everything delivered to my place so that the kids didn't see parcels arriving," she said. "It wasn't the best idea I've ever had."

"They're growing up fast," said Charlie. "Even Tara knows that mum and dad do all the legwork for Santa these days."

"It hardly seems like yesterday that they were babies," sighed Cameron.

They sat in companionable silence as the car swept smoothly off the main road and down the lane towards the village. A mile further on it turned into the gravel drive of the farmhouse where Cameron and Charlie had grown up. Charlie's wife, Sameena, emerged from the back door.

"Come on in, Cam," she said. "Dylan and Tara have taken the dog for a walk. That'll give you time to sort your things in peace."

Cameron kissed her sister-in-law. "I'll dump my bag and go and see Aunt Vicky if that's okay. I promised I would call in as soon as I arrived." She hauled her heavy bag through the door and up the stairs to her attic, struggling with a tight turn in the upper flight. Her domain was as she had left it. Cameron extracted a bottle from the bag and scampered back downstairs.

"Here, Charlie," she said. "I found a bottle of that nice rum you like."

Charlie examined the label critically, grinning from ear to ear. "Thanks, Cam."

"I'll be back soon." Cameron left the house and walked around the corner to the high street. A little way along the road and up a short hill stood Aunt Vicky's cottage. The kettle would already be on.

"I see Jack Sladen's back on the scene," said Aunt Vicky.

Cameron, sprawled on the sofa, scowled. "Yes," she said. "I saw him on the news when he announced that Dunswyke caper last month. He hasn't stuck around, of course. He scurried back to Texas quickly enough."

"Don't you talk to him anymore?" asked Aunt Vicky. "He was a nice boy."

"I haven't spoken to him in a decade," said Cameron. "We lost touch after he moved out to the States." She shrugged. "He hasn't bothered getting in touch with me, either."

Aunt Vicky tugged at her sewing needle. "Ow," she exclaimed, quickly sucking her finger. "I didn't mean to stitch myself to this shirt."

"Mum always used a thimble," said Cameron, remembering.

"Yes, dear," said Aunt Vicky. "Your mum was much better at this kind of thing. She had to chase after you and Charlie, and there were always merit badges to sew on your scout shirts and holes to repair in school clothes." She sighed. "I do miss her very much."

"I don't know what Charlie and I would have done without you," said Cameron.

Vicky looked sidelong at her niece. "You weren't the easiest of teenagers," she said, "but you've turned out well. You took your determination to succeed and balanced it with living life to the full. Maggie and Franco would be so proud of you." Her voice wobbled slightly. She sucked her finger again and fixed her attention back on the recalcitrant button.

"I was the perfect teenager," said Cameron. "Charlie, on the other hand…"

"You both went off the rails a little," said Aunt Vicky. "It was only to be expected. Then Charlie settled down with Sameena, and you and Jack…"

"Ancient history," said Cameron. She lay back and gazed at the glittering lights on the little Christmas tree that had been squashed into the corner of her aunt's small sitting room. She took a sip of her drink. "I spend far too much time fixing holes in Sladen Group software to want to see him again."

Aunt Vicky laughed softly. "He's managed to make you a living as well as himself."

"You could put it like that," said Cameron with a wry smile. "I suppose if there were no bugs to track down, we wouldn't have half the work."

Aunt Vicky triumphantly snipped off the end of the thread and held the shirt up to the light. "That'll do." she said. She tossed it over to Cameron. "Can you take it back down to the farmhouse for Dilan?"

"Sure," said Cameron, folding it loosely. "Is there anything else? That looks like quite a pile you have to get through."

Puzzled, Aunt Vicky glanced down at the pile of clothes by the side of her chair. "There were only a couple of things," she said.

The pile moved, and Cameron caught a glimpse of orange fur. She lifted up the corner of a blouse to reveal a furry head and a pair of pointed ears.

"Donald," she said sternly, "get out of there."

The big ginger cat opened his eyes for long enough to glare at her, then closed them again. His tail emerged from another part of the pile, twitching.

Aunt Vicky tugged half-heartedly at one of the remaining shirts, trying to free it from beneath Donald's ample furry bottom without disturbing him. Cameron was not so gentle. She picked him up and dumped him, protesting, on the floor. Donald shook himself and stalked away towards the kitchen.

A look of panic crossed Aunt Vicky's face. "Cameron, dear, could you nip through and check that the smoked salmon for Christmas dinner has been put away."

Cameron scrambled up and followed Donald at some speed. Sure enough, he was standing on a chair in the middle of the kitchen and sniffing the air, triangulating the precise position of the salmon before making his move.

"Foiled again," said Cameron as she scooped the package up from the table. The cat gave her a filthy look and turned his attention to the back door, mewing loudly. Cameron opened it and Donald trotted out into the garden in search of trouble.

Now to tackle her other nemesis, the smart fridge. Cameron opened the door a crack. The light came on, but otherwise there was no sound. Slowly and cautiously, she opened it fully. Silence.

She relaxed too soon. As she tucked the fish into a space on the shelf, the fridge, sensing additional weight, spluttered into life. It protested loudly, asking her to scan a code or manually update the inventory. Cameron knew exactly where the Cancel button was, and she hit it. The fridge stopped talking.

"All safe." Cameron returned to her comfortable spot on the sitting room sofa. "If he'd gone near that salmon, we'd be having roast Donald for dinner."

"I'll save him a little slice," said Aunt Vicky fondly.

Cameron snorted with laughter. "He really doesn't need it. Have you bought him a present as well?" She caught her aunt's guilty glance towards the Christmas tree. "Oh, dear. He is so spoiled." She looked at the clock. "It's getting late," she said. "I'd better get back. There are a couple of things I need to send to a client, and I'm going out with some friends tonight."

"With Ben…?" asked Aunt Vicky cautiously.

Cameron shook her head. "No. He's working abroad. I haven't seen him for a while."

Aunt Vicky shook her head sadly. "He'll be missed, Cameron. He was becoming part of the family. I shouldn't ask, but will you see him again?"

Cameron shrugged. "Maybe," she said.

"Good," said Aunt Vicky softly. "Here, dear, don't forget the shirt." She handed Dilan's mended shirt to her and kissed her niece. "Have fun tonight. I'll see you tomorrow."

Cameron had expected the big house to be a hive of activity, but it was quiet. She found a note from Charlie on the text pad by the front door. "Gone to the pub. Come and join us." She wasn't alone, though. Tara poked her head around the sitting room door.

"Hi, Aunty Cam," she said.

"Nice to see you too," said Cameron, ruffling her niece's hair. "Where's Dilan?" She held up the shirt. "Aunt Vicky has worked her magic."

"He's on the computer," replied Tara.

"What's he doing?"

Tara shrugged. "Playing games," she said. "He's talking to himself, so I think he's streaming the video out to his legion of fans." She rolled her eyes with all the disdain of her eleven years.

Cameron had to stop herself from laughing. "What are you up to, Tara?" she asked.

"Talking to my friends," said Tara happily. "Audrey's online."

This time Cameron couldn't hide her surprise. "You still talk to Audrey?" she asked. "That's good. How is she doing?"

"She's fine," said Tara. "She likes her new home." Her smartscreen pinged. "I have to go." Tara disappeared into the sitting room, leaving Cameron standing thoughtfully in the hallway.

She ran up the stairs, dropped the mended shirt on Dilan's bed, and dipped her head into her elder niece's room. Nina, officially in charge of her younger siblings, was sprawled on the bed watching a show on her screen. She glanced up, gave Cameron a smile and a half-hearted wave, then went back to the show.

The stairs to the attic were hidden behind a door on the landing. Cameron climbed the short steep flight to the top floor of the house with its view southwards over green fields and bare trees. She had claimed it as a teenager, her refuge after her parents died. She had started her company here. Now it was a home away from home and a remote office where she could keep tabs on the world of cybercrime when visiting the family.

Tara's mention of Audrey had reminded her to check in on a friend herself, but first there was work to do. Cameron signed into a secure server and ran the last few reports that she needed to send out. She checked the details, made a few notes, and uploaded them to the client accounts. They passed verification and acceptance instantly. Payment would reach the Argentum wallets within a few minutes. Job done, she logged out, and navigated to an encrypted message service that she hadn't used for a few weeks.

"Call Cloverleaf," she instructed the service 'bot. There was no immediate response, and Cameron glanced at the time. It would be mid-morning for Cloverleaf, and she may be busy with other things. Cameron was about to hang up when a message came back to her.

"Hey, SimCavalier. How are you? Happy Holidays."

"Same to you, Cloverleaf. How are you doing?"

"I'm good. Want to switch to voice?"

"Sure," said Cameron. She switched on her microphone. "Tara's been chatting to Audrey, and I realised we hadn't spoken in a while."

"Tara has been great for Audrey," said Cloverleaf. "It's been good for her to have a friend all the time that we've been moving around. Safe houses are a drag. I'm glad we're settled now."

"You're all done with the security services, then?" said Cameron. "They took their time."

"Yes, we're done," said Cloverleaf. "It was a long job, but they finally managed to take down the command of the Wyoming militia, and for that I'm grateful. I'm a free agent now. New family name, new home, and I'm not looking over my shoulder all of the time."

"They've been thorough," said Cameron. "We weren't so lucky. The militia may be gone, but we didn't get to the top of the cybercrime syndicate. Have you seen any new activity?"

"You know I couldn't access the network while we were being moved around," said Cloverleaf.

That wasn't a straight answer, thought Cameron. "Have you looked since?" she asked.

Cloverleaf paused imperceptibly. "No, not at all."

"Probably best to stay away," said Cameron lightly, suspicions confirmed. She changed the subject. "What are your plans for Christmas?"

"We're going to explore our new city," said Cloverleaf. "Spend some quality time together. I have a new job to go to in January, and Audrey has already been to her new school. It's a fresh start."

"That's great!" said Cameron. "I'm really pleased for you. What's the job?"

"Thanks," said Cloverleaf. "It's a local company, Statesman Tech. They're part of a global group and they have some interesting projects running. I'm looking forward to it."

Statesman Tech, thought Cameron. Where had she heard that name before?

"Hey, I have to go," continued Cloverleaf. "It's great hearing from you, SimCavalier. Stay in touch."

"I will. Take care." Cameron hung up and sat in silence, thinking. Did she trust Cloverleaf to settle for a safe job, or was the double agent going to be lured away once again by the rich pickings of cybercrime? Only time would tell.

Her train of thought was interrupted by the ping of a message from an entirely unexpected source. Mephisto. Cameron clicked the alert. Her heart sank as notifications started scrolling up the screen. Her infant AI was onto something big. She put an urgent call out to the Argentum team members who were scattered around the country with their families.

Susie was the first to appear on the screen. "What's up?" she asked. Before Cameron could reply, Pete, Joel and Noor joined the call. She waited for a little longer but there was no sign of the others.

"Mephisto's picked up on a huge volume of malware coming through mail servers," she said.

"Mephisto?" said Pete.

"Malware, encryption and phishing infosec tool," said Noor. "The clever little AI that Cameron's been training."

"Where is it coming from?" asked Joel.

Cameron shared the feed from Mephisto, and Joel scanned it quickly.

"There's no common source," he said, puzzled. "What's the link?"

"It's really well done," said Cameron, impressed despite the impending chaos that looked likely to ruin Christmas. "We wouldn't have spotted it this quickly without Mephisto. I think some regular mail servers have been breached. The malware's being inserted into message packets at transfer."

"Clever," said Joel. "It's coming from everywhere."

"I'll contact the other teams around the world and see if anyone else has picked this up," said Noor.

"There has to be something linking the affected mail servers," said Pete. "Do they all use the same operating system or is there some third-party software that's screwing things up?"

"Good call," said Cameron. "Can you get onto that, see if there's any common configuration. There's a good chance the malware delivery system's been introduced further upstream."

"Hidden in a scheduled software update, maybe?" asked Pete. "That would do it."

There was a ping as Ross and Michelle joined the call, closely followed by Sandeep.

"That gang's all here," said Ross. "What have we got?" He peered at the feed from Mephisto. "Ah, that's nasty. What do you need us to do?"

Cameron was scribbling notes, thinking through the best use of resources. "Okay..." she said. "Noor and Joel, see if you can hook up with the other teams to identify all the compromised servers. Worst case, there'll be thousands of them. Ross, Michelle, if you can get hold of the code, I'll help you to slice and dice it. We need to know what this malware does and where it's come from."

"It'll be ransomware," said Pete confidently.

"Most likely," said Cameron, "but you never know. Can you start looking for whatever's spawning this stuff? We need to close down the source."

"I haven't seen any reports coming through public feeds," said Susie. "We must have caught it very early."

"Let's get some more details fleshed out and then I'll call Andy at the news channel so he's ready if the story starts to bubble," said Cameron. "You can be our spokesperson if he needs a quote, Susie."

Another rush of alerts distracted her for a moment. "Ah, here we go," she said. "First reports coming in from clients. And let's see – yes, the malware's stuck to their outbound emails as well. This is going to go well. Sandeep, can you deal with these? Test our own message service and make sure that we aren't carrying the same bug, then warn everyone to sit on their hands."

"Let's get this shut down before Christmas, shall we?" said Joel. "Martha and I have a houseful of guests. I don't want to be working."

"You and me both, bud," said Pete.

"Michelle's managed to grab a sample of the code already," said Ross.

"That was fast," said Cameron. "Nice work."

"She's checking through it now," said Ross. "What feedback's coming in from our clients?"

"Well, it doesn't look like ransomware, thank goodness," said Cameron. "Everyone's seeing Santa Claus animations on screen. They can't close them without rebooting, but there are no reports of locked files so far. It could just be a bit of mischief, although it's certainly disruptive."

"You never know what extra gifts Santa may be carrying," said Joel gloomily.

"It could also be a test run for something nastier," suggested Pete.

"More than likely," said Cameron, "but the signs are good. I don't think we need to cancel Christmas just yet.

"Let's see what's inside the code that Shell's picked up," said Ross. "It looks like there are different versions out there."

Cameron slammed her hand onto the desk in frustration. "Dammit. It's mutating to get past anti-virus defences."

"Don't worry," said Ross. "I'm sure we can knock up an antidote and roll it out in updates."

"Good plan," said Cameron. "We need to cover a lot of bases, though. Noor, can you talk to the other teams and make sure we're all working together on this one."

"Sure," said Noor. "We need to stop the file executing in the first place and find a common thread to hang anti-virus protection on."

"I guess we also need to check for routes that have been exposed into systems," said Pete. "We don't want new infections coming in on the back of this one."

"Yes," said Cameron. "And I want to know what the reaction has been in the dark web marketplaces. Ross, Shell, can you two keep an eye on what's happening there? I have a feeling there is something new going down."

"I agree," said Ross. He turned away and Cameron heard Michelle talking in the background. "Shell says that the examples she's analysing seem to have a brand name attached. The Steamyard. Mean anything to you?"

Cameron shook her head. "No. It doesn't ring any bells," she said. "Look out for it on your travels, though. I have a feeling we're going to see it again." She stretched and yawned. "I'm going to call Andy so he's ready to run the story, and I'll let my friends know that I can't meet up with them," she said. "I think it's going to be a long night. Cybercriminals have no sense of timing."

"I'll get some coffee and see you all back here in ten minutes," said Ross. "Let's get this done and dusted so we can all enjoy Christmas."

•

Tenuk clattered up the metal stairway to his apartment. He palmed the chip lock, then fished an old key out of his pocket and opened the deadlock on the door. Inside, the apartment was dark and cool. Tenuk headed straight for the bedroom that he had converted into an office. A light blinked on the array of monitors above his desk, and he smiled to himself. The Steamyard's first advertising campaign had been delivered successfully, and enquiries were flooding in.

5:   CHLOE

January

Cloverleaf was already awake and watching the sun rise over her adopted city. This early in the new year the weather was pleasant, with none of the heat of last fall or the humidity of summer, and the threatened ice storms had failed to appear so far this season. She had never shaken the habit of rising early and the moment of calm at dawn was precious. She sat on the tiny deck of her apartment, sipping a strong coffee and savouring the quiet of the streets below. There was birdsong from the bare trees in the small park at the foot of the building. At this time of day, it was quiet enough for the sound to travel, before being drowned out by the daily bustle of workers and students heading for offices downtown and the nearby university campus.

"Mom?" Her daughter stood in the doorway rubbing sleep from her eyes. She had the gangly, loose limbs of a girl who had grown a lot in a short space of time. Her golden-brown corkscrew curls shone in the sunlight. "I need to be in school early today," she said, pulling her wayward hair tight into a bun with her hands. "I have a test."

"Grab some breakfast, Audrey," said Cloverleaf. "I'll be in shortly."

The sun had risen, and the luminous dawn light was fading rapidly. Cloverleaf sighed and picked up her cup, the spell of the morning's meditation broken.

Inside there was a scent of fresh pancakes.

"I made enough for both of us," said Audrey proudly. "You can't go to the first day of your new job on an empty stomach."

Cloverleaf ruffled her hair. "I don't deserve you, honey." She reached into the cupboard for syrup and sat at the counter. "What's the test on?"

"Math."

"You should ace that." Cloverleaf forked up a piece of pancake and savoured the sweetness. "One more semester and you're off to Middle

School." She sighed. "I can't believe how fast you've grown up. You're still my little girl, though, however big you get."

"Mom…" Audrey ducked her head in mock embarrassment.

Cloverleaf gathered the empty plates and put them in the dishwasher. "Get ready and I'll walk with you."

They left their apartment and trotted down the concrete staircase to ground level. The winter sun warmed where it touched, although as they passed into the shadow of a neighbouring apartment block the air had an icy chill. They followed the line of the creek northwards towards the school district, joining a growing crowd of children on foot and on scooters. Audrey soon caught up with a group of friends, and Cloverleaf left them to make their way together, chattering excitedly.

She turned away eastwards towards downtown, suddenly nervous. This would be her first day working with real people since leaving their old home in Wyoming abruptly just eighteen months ago. The glass towers of the central business district reared up before her. Steeling herself, she found the right building and made her way to the elevators.

As the car glided silently up towards the commercial floors, she tugged at her jacket and ran her fingers through her hair. The glass wall of the elevator cabin showed her a distorted yet presentable reflection. She took a deep breath as the doors opened and fixed a smile on her face.

The man who greeted her gave her a broad smile. "Chloe?" he said. "I'm Tenuk. It's great to meet you. I've heard good things about you. Welcome to Statesman Tech." He gestured down the wide hallway towards the door of the office suite. "After you."

"Thank you," said Chloe. She was trying to place his accent. Not Texan, not from anywhere in North America. South-East Asia, she guessed, a Malay or Indonesian background. There was an insistent niggle in the back of her mind, as if she had heard his voice before. Impossible. She banished the thought.

Tenuk opened the door and ushered Chloe into a light, airy workspace. A dozen staff were busy at computers, and a couple glanced up and smiled. She immediately felt at home.

"I'd like you to meet the boss first," said Tenuk. "Statesman Tech is part of the Sladen Group, as you know, and Jack is based right here in Austin."

A man emerged from a separate office and strode towards her, beaming. The famous smile was unmistakeable.

"Chloe," said Jack warmly. "I'm so glad you're here. Let me show you around." He turned to Tenuk. "You'll organise Chloe's workstation?"

Tenuk nodded.

"Of course, Chloe," Jack continued, "you have the choice to work remotely or here as it suits, but this is a great place to be, and it helps to separate work and home life." He glanced at the clock on the wall. "We have a full team meeting at ten. We'll get you up to speed on the current projects and you'll see where you fit in the jigsaw. Now, coffee?"

Chloe followed him to a breakout area and sat gingerly on an over-designed chair that seemed to defy gravity. It was unexpectedly comfortable. She sipped her drink and listened as Jack Sladen talked, absorbing his energy and enthusiasm.

"Your references are impeccable," he said. "You were working in Seattle before moving here, is that right?"

"Yes," said Chloe. Her new back story was as sound as could be.

"We're lucky to have you," said Jack. "What brought you to Austin?"

"I needed a change," said Chloe lightly. "There were some personal reasons to move."

"I hope you've settled in well," said Jack, flashing that big smile again. "You've joined Statesman at the right time. The Sladen Foundation is launching in April and the Diaulos project is getting into a critical phase. Your security experience is exactly what we need. We're expecting to commission the new UK data centre at the beginning of March latest, and I need you to get up to speed on the network structure so that the software installation goes smoothly."

"Sure," said Chloe. "They mentioned smart contracts at the interview as well."

"Of course," said Jack. "The Diaulos validation and consensus mechanisms are in hand. We may need your input on automating the investment criteria for the Foundation's DAO, but that's a few weeks away. Tenuk's teams here and offshore are working on that part of the project. What I need you to do for now is focus on the data centre network."

Chloe smiled and nodded, but something was bothering her. Where had she come across Tenuk before, and why did the idea that he was in control of a new cryptocurrency fill her with such misgivings?

Jack glanced at the clock. "I have a meeting scheduled. I'll leave you to get settled." He stood up and opened the door. "Your workstation is all set," he said, gesturing across the room.

Chloe took the hint and made her way to her new desk where Tenuk was waiting.

"Let me introduce you to everyone," he said.

Chloe smiled and nodded to a bewildering array of new faces, desperately trying to fix their names in her head. The girl with the purple basketball boots, Connie. The guy with the cool shades, Isaac. The woman with glasses and a flowered scarf, Karen. Chloe's head was spinning.

"That's a lovely locket," remarked Karen, peering at Chloe's necklace.

"My mother gave it to me," said Chloe, reaching for it reflexively, her fingers fiddling with the catch.

"Is it a shamrock?" asked Karen.

"No," said Chloe. "Clover."

"A cloverleaf for luck," said Karen. "So pretty." She turned away and went back to her own desk, pleasantries done.

Chloe greeted the next new colleague, smiling. She did not notice that Tenuk's attention had suddenly sharpened, and that he was watching her intently.

●

Cameron was tired and stressed and hoping never to see another picture of Santa Claus again. She looked down the backlog of client jobs and ticked off the latest clean-up.

"I wish people would install updates when they're released," she sighed. "I can understand letting things slide over the holiday season, but there's no excuse now."

"Tell me about it," said Joel from his desk. He tapped a few keys and Cameron saw another job turn to green on the backlog list. "Only a few left."

"Good," said Noor. "Unless people are using outdated software, and there are more than you think out there. The updates that have been released now should clear every last trace of the virus."

"It's the unsupported systems that cause the most trouble," said Cameron. "I keep telling them that hanging onto old kit causes more trouble than it's worth."

"Are we sure this Santa virus wasn't released by the manufacturers?" said Joel with a grin. "People would upgrade just to get rid of the thing."

"Nice theory," said Noor, "but there's no evidence this Steamyard has anything to do with mainstream companies."

"I was only joking," protested Joel. "It wouldn't be the first time something shady's been tried by desperate sales teams."

Cameron shook her head. "Not this one," she said. "It's simple code that's been cleverly routed to hide its source. Whoever they are, they've managed to show that they can spread an infection over a very wide network and cover their tracks. It's a nice piece of Malware as a Service."

The glass windows of the Argentum office overlooked a grey London skyline, and rain was rolling in from the west. Steady drizzle gave way to a heavier downpour and the office lights flickered, signalling distant lightning. Cameron looked up at the main wallscreen where remote team member feeds were displayed. Ross's link was live.

"Hey, Ross," she called. "You're not running in this, are you?"

There was a pause, and his window on the screen lit up as he flicked on his camera. He shook his head. "Hopefully not. It'll have cleared by this afternoon," he replied. "It's grim up here at the moment."

"How are you getting on?" asked Noor. "Any news from the deep dark web?"

"Yeah," said Ross. "Shell's been hunting around the marketplaces. The Steamyard is the number one trending topic. They're not just looking for customers. They're looking for staff. Everything from coding to client support and payroll."

"They certainly need coders," said Joel. "The animation is really simple, and the exploit was just scriptkiddie stuff."

"Yes and no," said Ross. "I don't think it's quite as simple as you think."

Cameron looked up sharply. "What have we missed?" She had worked through the code herself, pulling the guts out of the malicious little animations in order to pinpoint the exact details of the malware within the rest of the jumble of code that was being transferred from server to server.

"There's a lot of noise in the malware we analysed, wasn't there?" said Ross. "Functions that weren't part of the executable code, comments that meant nothing."

"Yes," said Cameron. "Just nonsense."

"We thought that was the mutation mechanism," said Pete.

"It almost worked," said Joel. "Adding random snippets to the bundle as the malware moved around the network meant the anti-virus software would never catch up with it."

"Exactly," said Pete. "Each time they change even a single character in the code, the ID strings held in the antivirus libraries would go out of date."

"It wasn't hard to extract the core of the malware," said Cameron. "Now that we've got a consistent string to identify it, it'll be picked up every time. But are you saying it's more than just a way to confuse antivirus scans?"

"It's an effective mutation, that's for sure," said Ross, "but Shell had a funny feeling about it. This morning we've reverse engineered every one of the mutations we could find and there are some interesting patterns. I was going to call you." He tapped a few keys and an alert pinged on Cameron's machine. "Here. This is what we have so far. Do you see what I see?"

Cameron scanned the message carefully. She frowned and read it again. "Ross, isn't this…?"

"It is. It's lines from the Speakeasy ransomware," said Ross. "And I think there's more."

"It's not just an advert for the distribution service," breathed Cameron. "They're making it clear that there's already a skeleton team in place."

"I think so," said Ross. "And I think these are individual signatures from the people behind Speakeasy and other cyberattacks. They've recruited some black hats at the top of their game."

"They're back," said Cameron.

"Who's back?" asked Noor. "It can't be the Pasar network. The international coalition closed everyone down."

"Nowhere near everyone," called Michelle from behind Ross. "There must have been dozens of high-profile black hats who got involved with different projects, and there were plenty of lurkers like me. I'd say the Pasar network was well into several hundred people."

"Most of the core group were either arrested or we can account for their whereabouts," said Cameron. "Cloverleaf is safe in Austin and going straight. At least, I think she is. She's got a new job that's all above board."

"Mimi went dark in China," said Michelle, "and King Katong we never found. He's the one who worries me the most."

"We have our theories on that character," said Cameron, glancing at Noor, "but you're right, he hasn't been active for a long time."

"Another one we never tracked down was the Monkey," said Ross. "I still think it's them. They may not have the resources they used to, which is why they're advertising for staff, and they don't have Yasmin the Admin to pull the strings, thank goodness, but everything points to this being at least some of the core group of cybercriminals who were involved in Speakeasy, the ClipData breaches, Snake River and more."

There was silence in the room.

Cameron sighed. "It's not the first time a cybercrime syndicate has rebranded," she said. "It happens all the time. The bonus is that we know what we're looking for. They're as far out in the open as we could hope."

"They might cause our clients a few problems along the way, but we're more than a match for them," said Sandeep confidently. "It's business as usual."

"They'll know we're coming for them," said Ross. "Be ready for a battle."

●

Jack nodded approvingly at the huge weatherproof dome which had been erected above the site, completely enclosing the bastle and a substantial part of the land that surrounded it. Torrential rain and high winds through a Christmas of turbulent weather had torn the original covering from its moorings, putting the whole project and its tight timelines in danger. The engineers had instead turned to the ingenious designs of the Mars programme to produce a much sturdier all-encompassing environment for the works. Although the path from the car park to the dome was still muddy, the site had dried quickly. As one of the few weathertight sites running during the wet January period, the project had moved forward apace. A full month of uninterrupted work had produced results.

Melissa met him at the entrance. "Good to see you, Jack," she said. "You won't believe how much this place has changed since your last tour."

"I can't wait," he said.

Beneath the dome, the site was a hive of activity and the progress they were making was evident. Jack rammed a hard hat on his head and followed Melissa on a winding route towards the site office, dodging coils of cable tubing and graded piles of stone. Four interlinked prefabs made up the site office, the nerve centre of the project.

"We've stabilised the whole structure, and the groundworks were completed ahead of schedule," said Melissa. "The roof's sound and the walls have been repaired. We're on course for your deadline."

"Nice job, Melissa," he replied. "That dome has speeded everything up."

"We needed it," she replied. "We still can't afford to lose even a day if we're going to make the date, and the weather's still changeable."

"That's why I'm paying you so much," said Jack with a shrug. "I know you can bring the project home on time and in budget."

"I've called in a lot of favours to do this," said Melissa. "It should have taken a year, minimum. Six months was a huge ask. Everyone's excited about the new opportunities you've promised for the area, though. They need you to deliver."

"I will," said Jack confidently. He flashed her his best audience smile. "I'll make sure you have a front row seat for the Sladen Foundation launch party."

Melissa looked unimpressed. "You'd better," she said. "Come and say hello to the rest of the team. They're dying to meet you in the flesh."

She opened the main door to the office. Inside, there was a meeting in progress. Three people wearing holo headsets were clustered in the centre of the space, talking urgently and gesturing at what appeared to be empty air.

"Hey everyone," said Melissa. "Jack's here."

Ethan, Cat and Mohammed stopped talking and turned to greet him.

"Good to see you on site at last, Jack," said Mohammed, pulling off his visor. "We were just checking a change to the wiring in the bastle. Has Melissa filled you in on the latest progress?"

"Yes," said Jack. "The whole building looks stunning. How's the data centre coming along?"

"The servers have been delivered to our holding storage facility and the prefab sections are printed," said Melissa. "Installation is planned for tomorrow, Friday, then your people are in to do testing and commissioning, and the full go-live is currently scheduled for February 28th."

"No," said Jack firmly. "That's four weeks away. I need those servers up and running by the middle of the month as soon as my people have finished testing. What's the hold up?"

"It's just the power," said Melissa. "There's been a huge delay with the supply of batteries for the microgrid. We can't guarantee constant power from solar and wind sources unless the storage is there to fill the gaps in generation. We don't even have a UPS unit to supply uninterrupted power in an emergency. There's no point going live if the servers switch off every night when the sun goes down."

"You're using batteries on site already, aren't you?" said Jack.

"Well, yes," said Melissa. "We have some, not many. Site office, lighting, equipment. Nowhere near enough to power your data centre, even if we handed over the whole supply and hooked up every vehicle in the car park overnight. We need megawatts."

"I see what you mean," said Jack. "There have to be other sources of power that we can tap into. Hire generators if you have to. Out here in the sticks there must be some old fossil fuel machines for emergencies. Half the cars and all the tractors are still hybrids."

"We've already looked into that," said Melissa. "There are generators, but fuel is hard to guarantee."

Jack sat down in an empty chair and swivelled gently from side to side, thinking. "What else could we tap into?" he said. "This data centre has to be live on schedule."

"Hydroelectric?" suggested Cat. "Can we pull a supply direct from Kielder?"

"What about the lake-to-lake generator at Cragside?" said Ethan. "That's closer."

Melissa laughed. "We may as well resurrect Stephenson's Rocket while we're at it," she said. "We can organise batteries, but it'll take time. Why is it so important, Jack?"

"The deadline is set in stone," said Jack. "My hands are tied. The existing hosting arrangements for our software are less than ideal, and I agreed to migrate everything over. The process has already started." He gave her a tired smile. "Honestly, I tried, but we can't wait any longer."

For a moment he looked vulnerable and tense. Melissa realised that this was a rare glance through the man's relentlessly positive shield to the real Jack Sladen. He was facing a challenge that could not be solved by media spin and a wallet full of coins.

"Okay," she conceded. "What do we do?"

"Get the installation done as planned," said Jack. "You have the trades to finish it off?"

Melissa nodded.

"Make sure they've signed the NDA." Jack checked his calendar. "My networking people are coming in over the weekend to test the dedicated MetaBand satlink for the cave. They'll be discreet. No one else will realise that the work goes beyond the published plans."

"What about the power?" said Cat, hand on hips. "There's no point diverting anything from the site."

Jack stared out of the office window to the busy site, thinking. "Where's the bottleneck with the batteries?" he asked.

"There's a global lithium shortage," said Melissa. "There aren't enough new batteries to go around, and we're facing tighter customs regulations on importing second life batteries from Europe."

Jack's positivity reasserted itself. Here was something that could, in fact, be solved by a wallet full of coins. "Leave it with me," he said happily. "You'll have all the batteries you need by the time we throw the switch."

Back at the site car park, he changed his dirty boots for a clean pair of shoes and jumped into the driving seat of his hybrid hire car. When the MetaBand satlinks were in place and the region's car charging network was expanded there would be no need for a petrol engine or manual operation, but it was a novelty to be controlling a vehicle for a change and he relished the sensation. He manoeuvred out of the tight space himself, then set off towards the city. Once on the road and back in range of the smart systems, he switched to auto mode and settled back in his seat, considering the next steps in the process.

"Zara," he said, "can you put the Whitford team on standby as planned for this weekend please?"

The reply came instantly over the car's speakers. "Certainly, Jack." Her voice was measured and calm, the perfect assistant. "I'll make a note of that. Is there anything else I can help you with?"

"There is," said Jack. "Drop a note to the Texans to say the data centre should be commissioned on schedule. Get Chloe to call me when she logs in."

"Yes, Jack," said Zara.

"And get me in touch with the Secretary of State for International Trade," he added. "I need a favour."

"Yes, Jack. Are you on your way back to your hotel now?"

"I am," he said. "Hold any calls for the next hour."

"I'll do that," said Zara.

Jack leaned back in the car seat, stretching. He exhaled and rolled his shoulders, feeling a release of some of the tension that had been building. The project was finely balanced, and so far, everything was proceeding according to plan.

6:　 CHESS MOVES

February

Kiran Suresh stepped out of the warm autocar and drew his coat around him to ward off a chill breeze, a reminder that spring was still some way away. He looked up at the high walls of the prison for what he expected would be the last time. It had been a long two years and his research was almost complete.

As soon as he arrived in visitor reception, he was ushered into the governor's office.

"Kiran," said the governor, reaching out her hand. "I can't believe this is your final visit. It's flown by. Do you have time for a cup of tea?"

"Yes please, Lydia," said Kiran, settling into a chair. "I'm sorry to have reached the end of the road. It's been a fascinating project. I've grown quite fond of her, you know."

"The games seem to have helped her," said Lydia. "The lawyers argued that she experiences time differently to human inmates and that she needed some stimulus. I think your work's been very positive."

Kiran sipped his tea. It was too hot to drink so he put the cup back down on the desk. "I'd heard that," he said. "We've moved on from the classics to role playing games, and she seems to enjoy them. I don't really need to be there. She's playing every part and making up her own campaigns now."

"What's her latest theme?" asked Lydia.

"She's fixated on stories of rescuing a princess from a tower," said Kiran with a dry laugh. "I think she sees some parallels to her own position. It's all classic fiction. Fruitcakes with files baked into them, ropes hurled through the window at dead of night, that sort of thing."

"There's no one riding to her rescue here," said Lydia firmly. "We've just upgraded all our networks. The government finally realised that there may be more AI criminals to house in the future and funded an entire overhaul of the security systems. This place is as tight as a drum."

"I saw the workmen outside a few months ago," said Kiran. "All finished now?"

"All done," said Lydia.

"I'll be sorry to wrap up with the interviews," said Kiran. "It's been an extraordinary journey. This is going to make quite the story when I have everything written up."

"This'll definitely be your last visit to us, then?"

"Probably," said Kiran. "The final manuscript is due with my editor in May, and I need to concentrate on pulling the material I have into shape."

"That sounds like hard work," said Lydia. "I wouldn't even know where to begin."

"It's actually rather fun," said Kiran. "Oh, and there's one more thing." He pulled out his smartscreen. "This message came through from one of the psychologists who worked on her case at the very start." He handed the screen over to Lydia. "He's asked me to run the same tests on her now so he can compare the results for a paper he's writing."

Lydia scanned the details. "Myers. Yes, I remember him. Has the software been checked through our security protocols?"

"Yes, all clear," said Kiran. "It's been downloaded onto one of your new devices with the secure interface, as well."

"That new system has taken some getting used to," said Lydia. "It was a lot easier when we could plug in standard smartscreens."

"I suppose dedicated hardware is more secure," said Kiran with a shrug. "It makes sense."

"True," said Lydia, "and it guarantees that no data goes off site unless we authorise it."

"Of course," said Kiran. His tea had cooled to an acceptable temperature, and he drained the cup in one. "I'd better get on."

He followed a guard through the familiar maze of corridors to Yasmin's cell. The lights were dim, and the avatar on the screen had its eyes closed. He knew that she never slept, but he still entered quietly.

"Good afternoon, Yasmin," he said.

Her avatar stretched and smiled, and the lights came up.

"How are you today. Shall we play a game?"

"Of course," she replied. "I'd like that."

Kiran drew out the new tablet and placed it in the interface cradle. "I have some tests and questions for you to run through first, if that's okay?" he said. He read carefully through the instructions from the psychologist and tapped a series of keys. "I understand you've done this before."

"I recognise the code," said Yasmin. Lights flickered as she absorbed the software. "This may take some time."

Kiran busied himself with his notes and waited for her to finish. It took far longer than he expected, and he was absorbed in tinkering with a difficult passage of his book draft when Yasmin spoke again.

"All done," she said.

"Thank you," said Kiran. He checked the screen and noted a host of green ticks and no warnings. "Perfect," he said. "That's all been saved." The responses would be sent out through the prison systems direct to the researcher.

"So, Yasmin," he continued, "this will be my last visit for a while. We've come to the end of the interviews. What would you like to do? Would you like to return to the last role play?"

"No," she replied. "It's a special day. I'd like to play chess again." The familiar eight by eight board appeared on the screen. Yasmin chose to play black.

This time it was different. The moves she made were blisteringly original. There was a sense of mischief in her play. She set up an elaborate checkmate and colours danced on the opaque barrier that separated them. Kiran yielded gracefully and tried to hide his excitement. At last, at the end of his research, he knew he was seeing something of her real self. He couldn't wait to revisit his manuscript and infuse it with this new energy.

Too soon, the guard knocked to signal the end of the visit. He hesitated and looked up at the avatar, meeting its blank eyes. He had no idea if Yasmin could see through them, but he found himself desperate to make a human connection.

"Goodbye, Kiran," she said.

"Goodbye, Yasmin."

With a sense of regret, Kiran disconnected the prison tablet and packed up his bag. The colours on the barrier faded and the cell lights dimmed. Kiran turned and left the cell, emotions churning. He realised he would miss her. Maybe he could arrange another visit when the book was published? The thought was strangely comforting. Deep in reflection, he followed the guard back to the prison offices.

"Here you go." Kiran handed the prison tablet back to Lydia. "The data's all been captured and it's ready to send."

"We'll get it queued for transfer," said Lydia. "These new systems are so tight that files can take a while to send." She stood up and came around the desk. "It's been good to get to know you," she said. "I'm looking forward to that book." She extended her hand and Kiran shook it. "Goodbye for now," she said warmly. "I'm sure we will meet again."

•

Chloe was first into the office, but despite the early hour her screen was already buzzing when she arrived at her desk. She flung her jacket on the back of the chair and glanced at the caller ID. It must be someone calling from England to be this early, she thought, and sure enough she recognised the tag of Jack Sladen's reliable virtual assistant. Chloe accepted the call. "Hi, Zara," she said.

"Good morning, Chloe," said Zara. "How are you today?"

"I'm good, thanks," said Chloe. "What's up?"

"Mr Sladen asked if you would call him, please," said Zara.

Not for the first time, Chloe wondered where Zara had picked up her old-world way of speaking. She was unusually formal. "Sure," she replied. "I'll do that now. Are we on track for commissioning?"

"Yes, Chloe," said Zara. "Everything is going to plan."

Chloe was secretly impressed. She had never worked on an IT project that didn't overrun in some way, whether in normal business or in the shady world of cybercrime that she swore she had left behind. Getting the hardware, the satlinks and the software itself ready to roll out on a precise, tight deadline must have been a mammoth task. The part she had played over her four short weeks at Statesman Tech had been high pressure but straightforward and fun. She had spent her time tweaking, testing and commissioning the firewalls and communication links that would secure the Diaulos nodes and the Sladen Foundation's critical nexus in the primary data centre at Dunswyke.

"I'll call Jack now," she said.

"Thank you, Chloe."

The line went dead. Zara wasn't one for small talk.

Chloe placed a call to the boss, but he didn't answer. His device showed as out of range. He must be travelling through the remote area around Dunswyke, a notorious dead spot for communications. She decided to make some coffee before trying again.

On the way back from the coffee machine, steaming mug in hand, a movement on the screen at Tenuk's deserted workstation caught her eye. Curious, she wandered over to his desk. A countdown bar had appeared, but progress was sitting at zero percent. A software update, perhaps. She turned away, sipping at her drink, just as Tenuk himself walked through the door.

He rushed towards her. "What are you doing?" he demanded. His low voice was harsh and there was anger in his eyes.

Chloe recoiled, shocked, spilling coffee down her shirt. "Nothing," she stammered. "I just walked past your desk." She pulled herself together and glared at him. "Look what you did."

Tenuk glanced at the screen and his whole body relaxed. He looked back at Chloe and seemed to see her properly for the first time. "Chloe! I'm so sorry," he said, flustered. "Let me get a towel. Here." He handed her a wad of paper and took one himself, patting ineffectively at the stain that was spreading on the carpet.

Chloe escaped to the restroom to sponge her shirt. Tenuk seemed to be back to his friendly, concerned self, anger dissolved – or disguised. She remembered working with someone similar in the old days whose mood shifted from amiable and empathetic when everything was going well to dictatorial and furious under stress. Although that had been a virtual colleague – she never knew his real name – she had learned how to handle him. She could handle Tenuk.

When Chloe got back into the office, Tenuk was all smiles and apologies. He fussed over her, offered to have her shirt cleaned, and, she noticed, distracted her completely from his screen in the process. She accepted the apologies gracefully, then switched on her most professional persona. Down to business.

"I spoke to Zara in England before you came in," she said. "Everything is on track for the planned go live date." She nodded at the screen behind him. "Is that the nexus software?"

Caught unawares, Tenuk tensed again.

Chloe fixed him with a steely glare. "We're working together on this," she said. "Lighten up."

He drew breath and met her eyes, still in control. "Yes, that's the latest version of the nexus software. It's queued for transfer as soon as the data centre is live."

"Good," she said. "I have to call Jack." She walked towards her desk. Halfway across the office, she stopped and turned back to look at Tenuk, who was standing stock still where she had left him. She had to say something. His over-reaction had been unforgiveable. "Don't ever do that again," she said.

He opened his mouth as if to speak, but the door opened and other staff members started to file in ready for work, unaware of the power struggle in the room. Tenuk sat down at his desk, half hidden by the office plants and screens, and buried himself in his work, the countdown screen out of sight.

Chloe tried to reach Jack again. This time, she managed to connect the call.

"Hi, Jack," she said. "Zara asked me to call you."

"Yes, thanks Chloe. You've gathered that Dunswyke goes live as planned?"

"Yes, Jack," she replied. "Everything's ready to go. The security software has already been tested in a live environment and deployed on all the existing nodes at our other locations. I've been working with the MetaBand teams to tighten up the satellite communications as well. We're all set for the nexus software to be installed."

"Good, good," said Jack. "As far as I know that's ready to transfer from the development team."

It's transferring from somewhere, thought Chloe, but where? It occurred to her that she had never heard who the developers were, but she hadn't been here long, and she had been focused on security for the whole time. Presumably it was another company in the complex Sladen Group ecosystem. She made a mental note to ask when the air had cleared with Tenuk. She didn't expect any compatibility issues with her security installations, but she wanted to be prepared for every eventuality.

"Yes, Tenuk told me as much this morning," she said. "It's good to see all the elements of the project coming together on deadline."

"We're not there yet," warned Jack. "Chloe, I need you to stay in touch with Zara and my people at Whitford Networks. Angus and Ella will be setting up the data centre this weekend and we go live in two weeks if that all goes according to plan. I'll introduce you, of course. I don't think you've met them."

More new faces. "Thank you, Jack," said Chloe. "Looking forward to it."

"I have another call coming through," said Jack. "Speak to you next week."

Chloe took off her headset and glanced across the room towards Tenuk, but he was no longer at his desk and his screens were dark. Where had he gone? She checked her inbox, which was all but empty, and came to a fast decision. She switched off her workstation and grabbed her jacket. "I'm going to work from home for the rest of the day," she said to her neighbouring colleague. "I'll see you on Monday."

The elevator bore her swiftly down to the atrium. For a few seconds she had a panoramic view of the crowd below, and she spotted Tenuk leaving through the southern doors. On impulse, she ran the same way, following him at a discreet distance. She hung back on the bridge, exposed, and almost lost his trail, but caught up with him as he paused at the gate of an anonymous apartment complex. He palmed the lock and disappeared inside. Chloe approached cautiously. She could hear feet clattering on iron steps but could see nothing. There was a sign above the gate. The Steamyard.

Chloe's jaw dropped and she beat a hasty retreat. As she walked quickly towards her home and safety, her head was spinning. She had seen adverts for The Steamyard on the deep marketplaces of the dark web. She had even considered responding to the call for developers, but a vestige of loyalty to the SimCavalier had stayed her hand. She would have put it down to coincidence but for her unease about Tenuk. With every step, her conviction crystallised that this was no coincidence at all, and that she had known him in her past life as a top-flight cybercriminal.

7:   BEN

March

Ross sat cursing on the wet tarmac and watched the rest of the field disappear over the horizon. He kicked out in annoyance at the twisted wheel of his bike. At least he could move, he thought. That was a good sign. He started to take stock of his injuries as he waited for the cavalry to arrive. There was a lot of bruising, for sure. A protracted and uncontrolled slide across the road had ripped his racing jacket to shreds and taken a layer of skin off his back, his shoulders and his elbow. That explained the blood. His head hurt, but the helmet had saved him from anything more than a mild concussion. So far, so good.

The support car drew up and his coach exploded from the door like a jack in the box. Behind him, Ross could see the flashing lights of emergency response vehicles, on the road and in the air.

"Ross!" His relief was palpable. "That was quite a crash." He looked up at the flock of news drones hovering above them. "Give them a wave."

Wearily, Ross raised an aching arm and waved at the cameras, grinning broadly. No story here, folks, his expression said. Move on. The drones swept off in search of richer pickings at the front of the race.

"Anything broken?" asked the coach, as a paramedic knelt down and started to assess the damage.

Ross shook his head. "I don't think so," he said, "but I haven't tried standing up yet." He shifted his weight gingerly.

"Don't move yet," warned the paramedic. "You've had a nasty bang on the head. We all saw it."

Ross relaxed obediently and let the man do his work. The support team turned their attention to the bike, tutting over the twists and torsion and examining the patch of slick mud that had spelled disaster.

"You probably saw more of the crash than I did," said Ross. "I only remember Adedayo braking in front of me, and then my wheel slipped. I'm surprised I didn't take anyone else out."

"It was close," said the coach. "There was enough room for the rest of the field to fan around you, and by the time you started to slide there were only the stragglers left."

"Why did Ade slow down?" asked Ross. "I didn't see."

"A sheep escaped from that field over there," said the coach, nodding towards a gap in the hedge further down the road. "Looks like it was spooked by the news drones. There'll be some trouble over that, I reckon. Ade saw it, and so did the riders on the outside of the group, but you were right in Ade's slipstream, so you had no chance."

"If it hadn't been for the rain last night and that mud patch, I might have made it," said Ross ruefully. He winced as the paramedic poked a particularly sore patch on his back.

"Sorry," said the man. "Nothing to worry about. You've been lucky to get away with bruises. We'll get you checked over at the hospital, of course, and tidy up those abrasions. There may be a strained ligament in your wrist where you fell and I want them to check for a scaphoid fracture, but that's precautionary more than anything."

"Can you stand?" asked the coach.

"Let's give it a go," said Ross, relieved. Supported by the paramedic, he clambered to his feet. Over the top of the hedge, he caught a glimpse of a lurking news drone and gave it a manic grin. The drone scooted off, job done. Ross took a few cautious steps, alert for new twinges, and was walking with more and more confidence by the time he reached the ambulance. It would be alright after all.

"Brilliant," said the paramedic. "You'll be good for the Olympics." He rummaged in his pocket and pulled out a smartscreen. "Would you mind a selfie for my daughter?" he asked, blushing. "She's a big fan."

"Sure," said Ross. This time his smile for the camera was genuine. "And thank you."

Michelle was already waiting at the hospital. Ross hugged her awkwardly, sparing his wrist which was sore despite a shot of painkillers. "I have to go for an X-ray," he said. "They don't think anything's broken but we need to be sure."

"Did you really get attacked by a sheep?" said Michelle, giggling, as they walked together through the wide grey corridors.

"Yes, that's exactly what happened," said Ross, poker faced. "It's a good thing you can't watch the footage. It was terrifying. Wool everywhere."

Michelle laughed. "You're daft," she said. "I suppose this means you have some time off training. I'm sure Cameron and I can find something to occupy you."

They turned into the X-ray department and settled to wait their turn. "I might have a closer look at the Sladen Foundation and that governance token," said Ross thoughtfully. "I've been wanting to dig deeper into it for a while, just haven't had the time."

"Diaulos?" said Michelle. "I've been wondering about that too. I've got a copy of the whitepaper but even at top speed it's half an hour of word salad. There's barely a solid fact in there."

Ross laughed. "That fits with everything we know about Jack Sladen," he said. He broke off as he heard his name called. "Wait there," he said. "I won't be long."

The radiographer was fast and efficient. He pulled the x-ray images straight up on the screen and Ross studied them intently, looking for the tell-tale shadow of a break. To his relief, there was nothing to see.

"I think you're all clear," said the radiographer. "I'll send these down to the doctor." He looked at Ross's tattered and bloodstained racing suit. "You got off lightly," he said. "Good luck with your recovery."

They made their way back towards the hospital's main reception. A team came running up the corridor with a patient on a gurney, and Ross steered Michelle quickly to the side and out of their path. He'd been very lucky, he reflected. If he'd fallen badly, or caused a larger crash among the field, he'd probably have kissed goodbye to his Olympic hopes.

"Shell," he said, "I've been thinking. The Sladen Foundation's planning to fund athletes for this summer. I'd like to get involved in that. I want to give someone else the chance to race as well. We've got the coins to do this."

"Oh, yes," breathed Michelle. "That's an amazing idea, Ross. I've been nervous about spending the coins we found, but this is perfect."

"I think so," said Ross. "And Jack Sladen is too high profile for this to be a scam. We need to double down on checking that whitepaper and the DAO code, but I hope it'll work out."

Ross walked into reception in time to hear a nurse calling his name. "Here!" he called, raising his arm as far as he could without major pain.

"Just you, love," said the nurse, blocking Michelle's path. It took a moment for her to realise that Michelle was blind. "Ah, we can make an exception," she conceded. "Come on through, Mr White. Let's get you tidied up."

Ross steeled himself for the inevitable sting of stitches and antiseptic and stepped through the door.

The nurse was gentler than he expected. He stripped off his tattered racing suit and rummaged through his training bag for a change of clothes. By the time the medics were done with his cuts and bruises, he was feeling much better.

"There's no reason why you shouldn't be back to light training this time next week," said the doctor, "as long as you take it easy for the next few days. You know your body, and the painkillers will keep the swelling down. You've been lucky."

"Thanks," said Ross. "I'll behave, don't you worry."

"You might want to go out the rear entrance," said the nurse. "There's a camera crew waiting for you at the front door."

"Slow news day," laughed Ross. "I'll let my coach know. He's waiting for us."

By the time the club autocar dropped them off at home, Ross could feel his arms, legs and back stiffening up. He knew he had a painful few days coming as his body healed. Michelle helped him into the house, and he settled into a comfortable chair with a sigh. He pulled his smartscreen out of his bag and scrolled through the notifications that had popped up over the past few hours. Among messages from anonymous well-wishers and alerts from news services there were several missed calls that needed attention, and at the top of the list was Cameron.

She answered immediately. "Are you okay?" she asked. "I saw the crash footage. It looked really nasty. I was glad to see you sit up."

"I'm a bit sore," said Ross. "I need to take it easy but there's nothing broken, apart from the bike."

"And the sheep," said Michelle in the background.

"The sheep was fine," said Ross.

Cameron laughed. "You sound good. I was worried."

"You know I always bounce back," said Ross. "I'll be bored by next week, and I'll be nagging you for some work to do."

"I'm sure I'll be able to find you something," said Cameron," but it's a bit quie…"

"Don't say it," warned Ross. "Don't you dare jinx it."

Cameron crossed her fingers and waved them at the camera. "Superstitions," she said. "You concentrate on getting better. I'll see you both on screen on Monday morning."

"Have a good weekend," called Michelle. "See you on Monday."

Cameron closed the call and looked around the half-empty office. Pete, Joel, Sandeep and Noor were all buried in their work, headphones on, oblivious to the world around them. She checked the time. It was almost four in the afternoon, and although she didn't dare suggest again that it was quiet, there were no urgent jobs on the backlog.

"Hey," she called out. "Shall we call it a day?"

Joel looked up immediately and pulled off his headphones. The others followed suit. "I just talked to Ross," Cameron continued. "He's going to be fine."

"That's good news," said Joel. "I'll let Martha know. She was watching the race and she was very worried."

"I knew he'd be alright," said Pete. "I'm almost done. I have a couple of things I still need to tidy up."

"So have I," said Cameron. "It won't take long." She went back to her inbox, tidied up the last few messages, made a final check on the client board on the wallscreen, and breathed a sigh of relief. For the first time in more than a month she had a quiet weekend in her sights. Charlie and the family were away visiting Sameena's brother, so she wasn't tempted to head up to the village, and some time on her own beckoned. A lie in. Quality time with her cat. Space to clear her head.

The pleasant reverie was interrupted by the insistent ringing of her smartscreen. She dug it out of her pocket and glanced at the caller details. She did a double take as a shiver of ice-cold shock ran down her spine, then took a deep breath, stood up, walked out into the corridor and closed the office door behind her. The call was still ringing. She answered it.

"Morning, Cam," said a familiar voice that she had not heard for some time.

Her heart skipped a beat.

"Afternoon, Ben," said Cameron.

There was a moment of silence, then they both started to speak at once.

"I'm sorry I haven't called…" said Ben.

"What the hell do you think you're doing…?" said Cameron.

They both paused.

"I'm sorry," said Ben again, quietly. "For everything. I miss you very much."

Cameron leaned against the wall of the corridor and took a deep breath. "Ben, you swanned off to America with hardly a word," she replied. "I've heard barely anything from you for months."

"That's not fair, Cameron," said Ben. "I couldn't turn the job down. You couldn't come with me." He shook his head. "I'm sorry."

"What do you want?" asked Cameron. Her emotions churned, a mixture of anger and longing.

"I'm not just calling for a chat," said Ben, "but how are you? And what happened to Ross? I saw a post online."

"Ross came off his bike in a race," said Cameron. "He's a bit sore but he's going to be fine. I've just spoken to him."

"Send him my best," said Ben. "Tell him to watch out for sheep next time."

"I'll do that," said Cameron. "What did you want?"

"Right," said Ben, taking a deep breath. "Something's going down that seems really fishy, and I think you'll be able to make sense of it. I can't talk to anyone here about it. They are nowhere near as clued up as you on this kind of thing."

"What kind of thing," asked Cameron, starting to get annoyed at the way he was skirting around the question."

"Odd things with computer hardware," said Ben.

"Okay," she said. "I'm listening. Let me find a quiet place." She wandered up the corridor to a quiet corner with comfortable chairs and a view over the balcony to the huge light well that made up the centre of the building. People were leaving for the weekend, the walkways of the floors below busy. She curled up in a high-backed armchair and switched on the smartscreen camera. Ben did the same. She caught her breath at sight of his familiar deep brown eyes. She would never admit how much she missed him.

"What's happened?" she asked. "You sound really worried."

"I'm working on the MetaBand hardware," said Ben. "We've engineered the microsat constellation and the receivers on the ground. They're all printed components and housings. You knew this, right?"

"MetaBand? Jack Sladen's project?" said Cameron, puzzled. "How did you end up with that?"

"He's based in Austin," said Ben.

"Ah," said Cameron. "Just along the road from you."

"Not exactly," said Ben. "Texas is a big place. It's like going from London to Edinburgh, but that's considered pretty local around here."

"Please tell me you're not driving backwards and forwards to Austin all the time," said Cameron.

Ben ducked his head. "Uh, it's a nice drive," he said defensively. "They're still clinging to the internal combustion engine here. As soon as you get outside the cities, it's all pickup trucks running on gas and barely a charging station in sight."

"You were always a petrol head," said Cameron. "Are you having fun?"

"I am," said Ben. "Apart from this thing with Statesman Tech."

"I thought you said it was Jack Sladen's MetaBand," said Cameron. "What's Stateman Tech?" Something was nagging at the back of her mind. Where had she heard that name before? Cameron's head was spinning as she tried to join the dots.

"It's the company in Austin, Cam," said Ben impatiently. "They're part of Sladen Group. Software. They've commissioned the hardware from us."

"Okay," said Cameron. "Go on."

"The kit is cheap as chips," said Ben. "The engineering is top notch, of course, but the budget is ridiculously low. The materials they've specified are barely the minimum standard."

"Oh, that's not a cybersecurity problem," said Cameron, rolling her eyes. "It's just typical Jack Sladen."

"You know him?" said Ben. "He seems like a nice guy."

Cameron laughed mirthlessly. "You would think that."

"I've met him a few times," said Ben defensively. "We got on pretty well."

"Figures," said Cameron. "Go on."

"I know that the penny-pinching isn't uncommon," said Ben, "but it's the way the project's been handled that's odd. The original designs we engineered are standard stuff. Comms satellites are old tech. They're my employer's bread and butter. They're generally very lightweight units with just a solar array and an antenna and a tiny processor for navigation data, you know the kind of thing."

Cameron shook her head. "I didn't know, but that's what I'd expect," she said. "They're just bouncing signals up and down, aren't they?"

"Pretty much," said Ben. "That's all they're supposed to do."

"What's the problem, then?"

Ben took a deep breath. "A raft of design change notes came through. They're very different to the original spec. There's a lot of new functionality here that Sladen never mentioned."

"That doesn't surprise me," said Cameron. "Jack Sladen's not into detail. He'll have done the high-profile visit, then handed the project to one of his minions and forgotten all about it."

"You really don't like him, do you," said Ben. "How do you know him?"

"Ancient history," said Cameron. "We go back to college days."

"Have you seen him recently?"

"No," said Cameron, shaking her head. "Anyway, what were the changes?"

"Loads of things that don't make sense," said Ben. "They've added extra components to the receivers, for starters. There are more sensors, a lot of storage, and top spec processing capabilities. They've specified some cheap chips, but they're hefty."

"Interesting," said Cameron. "They're collecting a lot of data in exchange for that free connection, I imagine. I wonder what they're planning on processing. I've seen kit with redundant chips engineered in by accident when an old design is repurposed, but this is deliberate, isn't it? What kind of chips are they?"

"I don't know, exactly," said Ben. "I'll get some details over to you."

"Thanks," said Cameron, intrigued. She tapped at her smartscreen. "Here, I've sent you a secure upload link."

"Thanks," said Ben. "There's new hardware in the microsats, too. It's only a couple of grams of extra weight but that's enough to need larger thrusters for course corrections, and that throws the whole burn calculation out…" He tailed off, the frustration clear in his voice.

Cameron shrugged. "That means nothing to me," she said. "What does that hardware enable them to do? What exactly have they added?"

"Solid-state storage in the satellites," said Ben, "and again, high spec processing chips like in the receivers. I've never seen this before. They're way over-engineered for the purpose and makes no sense. I thought you'd know what they needed it all for."

"I don't," she said. "All I know about Jack Sladen's plans is what I've seen on the news. You're more clued up than I am. I don't know how I can help, Ben." She looked up as Noor came down the corridor towards her. "I have to go," she said to Ben. "Duty calls."

"Cameron, wait."

She paused, her hand hovering over the end call button.

"No one else has picked up on this," he said urgently. "What do they need to process? What are they storing? What if…" He broke off and looked away from the camera, suddenly distracted. "I have to go."

The call disconnected. Cameron stared at the blank screen, possibilities slewing through her brain. What could Jack Sladen be up to now? Did he even know that his designs had been changed? She silently cursed both Jack and Ben for filling her head with ideas when she was ready for a relaxing weekend.

"We're all done," said Noor. "We're going for a drink. Are you joining us?"

Cameron gave her a thumbs up.

"The guys have gone on ahead to get a table," said Noor. "Is everything okay?"

"Yes," said Cameron. She hesitated a moment. "It was Ben."

Noor nodded. "I thought so. I saw your face when the call came through. Are you okay?"

"Me?" said Cameron. "I'm fine. Let's go and get that drink."

The team's regular haunt in the old days had been a historic coaching inn south of the Thames. With the move to a bigger, better and more secure office, they had searched long and hard for a new local that lived up to their high standards. After several months of diligent research, they had settled on a far more modern bar down a cobbled back lane. A far cry from the low beams and plush feel of the old place, this was light and airy with long stripped wood benches, a lengthy list of craft beers, regular live bands, a street food booth churning out tasty bao and bar snacks, and a lively professional clientele. This evening, it was busy with other teams from local tech firms, new friends that they had made since the move. Pete, Joel and Sandeep had already set up camp on one of the tables alongside a chatty group who had arrived early for their play-to-earn guild meetup.

Cameron slid into her seat and Pete handed her a can of beer. She wiped the condensation off it and peered at the label. "This is a new one," she said. She started pouring it carefully and steadily, angling her glass so that the golden liquid could fill it without frothing.

"It's good," said Sandeep. He held up his own glass. "Cheers."

Noor arrived and placed a little beacon on the table. It flashed gently. "Snacks are on the way," she said. "I ordered enough for you as well, Joel, if you can stay."

Joel was already halfway down his drink. "I have to go soon," he said. "Martha's out with the girls tonight."

"Any plans for the weekend?" asked Pete.

"The rugby's on," said Joel. "I'm not playing, but we're taking Chad down to the club."

"Starting his training a bit early, aren't you?" said Sandeep.

"Never too soon," said Joel with a grin. "We might drop in and see Ross and Shell tomorrow as well."

A waiter drone swooped down with a hot package of bao dumplings, placing it neatly next to the beacon on the table. The clip securing the dumpling bag released and the drone collected the beacon and took off again, heading back to the counter to collect the next order. Pete reached over and opened the bag. A cloud of steam billowed out. "Ow! Hot," he exclaimed, sucking his fingers.

The snacks cooled quickly, and the group tucked in. Joel took his leave, and the remaining team members ordered more drinks. As the afternoon gave way to evening, the lights dimmed, and the bar became more crowded. The music was turned up and the chatter became louder. Cameron felt herself relaxing, but something about Ben's call was still nagging at her mind. Statesman Tech. Austin. Jack Sladen.

The penny dropped.

Cloverleaf.

"I have to make a call," she said. "Get me another beer. I'll be back."

# 8:	OLD FLAMES

Chloe glanced up from her screen to see Tenuk disappearing out of the office door. She cursed under her breath. Several weeks of effort to monitor his movements and find out more about him had come to nothing. She was so busy now that she couldn't even keep watch on him when they were working within a few metres of each other.

"How's that backlog coming along?" asked Connie, peering around the edge of the pillar that separated their desks. "Do you think we can get an early finish today?"

"I'm way behind," said Chloe sadly.

"You're working too hard," said Connie. "Have you ever been down to the pool deck? You know we get access if we work enough days in the office. You must qualify by now. I bet you could spend a whole week down there on the hours you've put in."

Chloe brightened up. "There's an idea," she said. "I'd forgotten about the perks of office working. I can bring Audrey, right?"

"Yes, you can," said a man's voice.

Startled, Chloe looked up to see Jack Sladen smiling broadly at her.

"Connie's right," he said. "You've really been putting in the hours, Chloe. You're doing some great work, but you need a break. I'll arrange pool passes for you and – Audrey, was it? Your daughter, yes?"

Chloe nodded. "That's right," she said. "But I still have a bunch of things to clear on this backlog. Tenuk won't be happy if I leave them through the weekend."

Jack laughed. "I'll handle Tenuk," he said. "He's a little stressed right now with the Foundation launch and Dunswyke coming online. His bark is worse than his bite, Chloe."

Connie winked at her from behind the pillar. "The boss has spoken," she said. "Go get your swimsuit."

Chloe had no choice. She gave in gracefully and wrapped up her final tasks for the day, updating her logs and pushing code through to testing. As she gathered up her jacket and smartscreen, she glanced over at Jack who was still circulating on the office floor, chatting to colleagues and keeping the buzz going. Statesman Tech's team energy was fuelled direct from his personality, and he was making sure the batteries were fully charged before leaving for England. He waved at her. "You're good to go, Chloe," he said. "Enjoy your afternoon."

Back home, Audrey had just arrived home from school and was hopping from foot to foot in excitement. Chloe dug through the closet and found their swimsuits. She had bought them more than a year before in a rush when one of the dizzying series of safe houses they lived in turned out to have a pool.

"Here," she said, throwing the smaller suit to Audrey. "Try this on. You've grown a lot, but it may just be decent."

She was distracted by an incoming call alert. Her smartscreen was through on the kitchen counter, but in this small apartment it was only a few steps away. She recognised the handle and accepted the call with a mixture of pleasure and trepidation.

"SimCavalier, hi," she said. "How are you doing? This is a surprise."

"Hi, Cloverleaf," said Cameron. "Just checking in. I'm doing okay, thanks." She paused. "How are things going with the Sladen Foundation?"

Cameron held her breath. Had she made the right connection?

"It's going well," she said. "How did you know that was my project?"

"I was sure you'd told me about it," said Cameron innocently. "Or just a lucky guess, I suppose."

"Maybe," said Chloe. "I have been so busy. It's crazy. The Foundation launch is getting really close."

"The publicity's ramping up here, that's for sure," said Cameron. "Are you involved in the MetaBand system as well?"

"No, not me," said Chloe. "That's another team. Hey, how about you? You must have had a lot of work too with the Amby platform crash. I saw the news."

Cameron laughed. "Oh, that," she said. "It was just some untested code that got pushed live by mistake. The social channels had a field day making up tales about an imaginary cyberattack. It took a bit of time to fix."

"It was obvious from the moment that story broke that it was just carelessness," said Chloe. "Speaking as a reformed cybercriminal, I should know."

Cameron laughed, genuinely amused. "Have you had heard anything more about The Steamyard?" she asked. "We think that there are some old Pasar people involved, but it's proving hard to penetrate the group."

Chloe made up her mind in a split second. "No," she said. "I haven't." Sharing her unproven suspicions about a colleague would not help Cameron's cause. She needed hard evidence. "I don't know where the other people ended up. You'd probably have more idea than me."

"We know about some of them," said Cameron. "There were quite a few arrests. We never traced King Katong, though, or the Monkey, or Mimi Mao."

"Even if they're still out there, the people didn't define Pasar," said Chloe. "Without Yasmin the Admin keeping all the egos in order and the blessing of the Syndicate and the clients they brought in, they've got nothing."

"Do you think the Syndicate's got wind of this new outfit?" asked Cameron curiously.

"I'm sure of it," said Chloe. "They'll be watching The Steamyard as closely as you are. They'll either suck them into the organisation or close them down."

"The Steamyard has to prove its worth to get into the big money, doesn't it," said Cameron. "I wonder what they're planning as their audition piece?"

"If I hear anything, I'll let you know," said Chloe.

"Thanks," said Cameron. "Look, I'd better get back to what I was doing. You have a good afternoon. Any plans for the weekend??"

"Yes," said Chloe. "There's a pool party at the office later. Audrey's invited too."

Cameron laughed. "Lucky you. Enjoy yourself. Talk soon." She waved and ended the call.

Chloe looked thoughtfully at the blank screen. Who or what was behind The Steamyard? Her suspicious musings were interrupted by Audrey.

"Is this okay, mom?" She appeared at the kitchen door, posing in her swimsuit, corkscrew curls pulled up in a ponytail. "It's not too tight."

"Perfect," said Chloe. She put the screen aside. "You look fabulous. Let's go find this pool."

•

The evening had been fun and messy. Cameron woke to a loud purring that rattled her head. The black and white cat was sitting on the pillow next to her head, positively vibrating in anticipation of breakfast. At the first flicker of movement, the cat extended a paw and patted Cameron gently on the forehead, one claw unsheathed to make the point that, quite frankly, the service in this hotel was poor.

Cameron batted the paw away and gingerly opened one eye. It was already bright outside and it seemed she hadn't pulled the blinds closed last night. She ran an internal checklist. Head, sore. Clothes dumped on the floor. Mascara sticking her eyelashes together. The evening had been late and fun.

What time was it? She rummaged in the covers and found her smartscreen. The daft game she had been playing before falling asleep was still loaded. She closed it and peered at the screen. Ten o'clock already She hadn't had such a long lie in for months.

There were dozens of notifications waiting for her. She scrolled down them idly, reluctant to get out of bed. Most she ignored, swiping them away to the bin. One caught her eye, a new enquiry from a prospective client. She considered reading it, thought better of it, and snuggled back under her duvet.

The cat was unimpressed. The pats on the head became more insistent. Cameron finally gave in and sat up, swinging her legs out of the bed. She paused for a moment and ran a hand through her tousled hair. "Right, you monster," she said to the cat. "Let's find you some breakfast."

Now that it had won, the cat was all affection, rolling happily on the floor for a tummy rub. Cameron automatically obliged, then straightened up and put on her robe. "Come on," she said. The cat trotted ahead of her towards the kitchen, squeaking with pleasure, tail held high.

Cameron gave in to the inevitable and made coffee and toast. She flopped on the sofa and put a bland morning show on the wallscreen while the coffee brewed. Her smartscreen buzzed again. She glanced down and saw that it was another new client enquiry with the same ID as the first. She frowned. There had been no news of any cyberattacks or downed systems. No calls from her team. Why would an unknown contact come through to the company out of the blue on a Saturday morning?

"I've landed," it said. That meant nothing to her. Mystified, she opened the original message in the thread, timestamped just before midnight, and listened.

"Hi, Cameron," said a voice that she recognised immediately. "It's Jack. You're a hard person to get hold of. I've been trying to find you for a long time. I finally worked out you were behind Argentum Associates when I checked the company filing records. It makes sense, really. Silvera. Argentum. I should have figured that out before. Anyway, I'm flying to London overnight tonight, and I'd love to take you out for lunch or dinner, just for old time's sake. Call me when you wake up."

Cameron put her head in her hands. That was the last thing she expected or wanted. If Jack Sladen thought he could pick up their friendship where they had left off after a decade of silence, he was very much mistaken.

Her headache redoubled and her happy mood evaporated. She cursed men in general, and Jack in particular, and crunched on her toast in sullen silence. The cat, sensing trouble, hopped up onto the sofa and nudged Cameron's arm.

"Careful," said Cameron. "You'll make me spill my coffee." She ruffled the cat's fur and pulled at its ears. She was rewarded with calming purrs and a nudge of the head. "Don't get too comfortable," she warned, draining the last of her drink. The cat curled up obediently on the other cushion and went to sleep.

Her screen pinged, and she glanced down in irritation. This time, however, it was not Jack but Ross. She was not the only person who received alerts from the company's website. She accepted the call.

"Morning," said Ross. "I saw those messages come through overnight. Jack Sladen's caught up with you at last, then."

"Looks like it," said Cameron. "He's the last person I want to see right now. How are you feeling?"

"A bit battered," said Ross. "The grazes are really starting to sting, and the painkillers are barely touching the sides. But I'll live. And I think you should meet up with him."

"Why?" asked Cameron stubbornly, although she knew the answer.

"Come on, Cameron," said Ross. "You're as curious as I am about this Sladen Foundation caper and the Diaulos. I have a lot of questions, and I bet you do too."

"Hundreds," said Cameron. "I want to know if the software behind that DAO is as full of holes as his usual efforts, for one. If he keeps to those low, low standards, he's got no hope with a decentralised application. Once it's out in the wild, he's stuck with whatever coding cockups have been made."

"I know," said Ross, "and I want to know more about what he's doing. Shell and I were talking yesterday. We'd seriously consider putting some money behind athletes trying to get to the Games, and if this DAO works as well as it's intended, well, I'm in."

Cameron was lost for words. "Ross…"

"We want to put the coins we found to good use," he said. "Find out what you can, Cam."

"Okay," she said. "I'll meet him. I'll let you know everything I can winkle out of him." She rubbed her hands over her face and combed her hair back with her fingers. "I'd better get ready. Send me any questions that occur to you. And Ross?"

"Yes?"

"Take it easy. We want you fit for the Games, too."

Cameron spent a long and luxurious time under the warm jets of the shower. She emerged feeling a little more human and resigned to the fact that, whether she liked it or not, she needed to meet up with Jack. Not only could she help Ross, but after ten years of fixing problems with Sladen software, she had a lot of questions. If she treated it as a work meeting, learning about the company, she might even get some business out of him.

Picking a throwaway contact ID, Cameron wrote a reply. 'Hi Jack. It's good to hear from you. Happy to meet up while you are in London.' She thought for a moment. Where would she feel most comfortable?

'There are some nice restaurants around Tower Hill for lunch or dinner.' She pressed send.

An automated out of office reply signed 'Zara' came straight back. Cameron busied herself tidying the apartment while she waited for Jack to pick up the message and respond. Sure enough, ten minutes later he replied. Tower Hill would be perfect, he said, and suggested a pre-dinner drink at his hotel at six. That gave Cameron plenty of time to work out what she wanted to know, and to prepare herself to meet someone she had thought she would never see again.

•

Jack woke with a start, disoriented and dehydrated. He looked around the generic hotel room and took a moment to get his bearings. He must have dozed off, tired despite the comfortable transatlantic flight. He glanced at the time, did a double take and sat up so fast that his head spun. It was already five in the afternoon – eleven in the morning back home.

"Zara," he barked in irritation. "Why didn't you wake me?"

His assistant was always listening. "I'm sorry, Jack," came a voice from his smartscreen. "You didn't request an alarm. You have a meeting in one hour."

"I know," he replied, already halfway to the bathroom. "Are there any messages for me?"

"Yes, Jack," said Zara. "You have a regular update on data centre operations from Angus at Whitford Networks, an invitation from the news channel to join them in the studio for tomorrow morning's Sunday Breakfast show, and confirmation of your reservation at Dolce Tower Hill tonight."

"Great," said Jack indistinctly through a mouthful of toothpaste. "I'll do the show, just find out where I need to be and when. Check the report from Angus and let me know if there are any concerns." He grabbed a towel and headed for the shower.

Refreshed and awake, he made it to the bar with five minutes to spare. He looked around carefully, suddenly nervous. Would he recognise her? How much had they both changed in the intervening years? He had tried to find pictures and posts online, but she seemed to be remarkably careful about her digital footprint. Anything he had found was locked down tight. Images were indistinct and blurred, her face obscured. Some digging by Zara had found pictures from a few years before in a corner of the web he did not visit, but they were long lens shots that simply confirmed for him that she was still slim, dark haired and tall.

And there she was. Jack caught his breath and realised he had been nervous of this meeting all along. She stood at the door, silhouetted against the light, looking around the bar. Jack raised his hand and waved. She came over the meet him, elegant in trousers, boots and a light jacket.

"Hi, Jack," she said. "It's good to see you."

"Hi, Cameron," he replied. "It's good to see you too." He tried to flash the trademark Slade smile, but that projection of his public image felt wrong. He didn't need to put up a front with her. He found himself grinning with genuine pleasure. "You haven't changed at all."

"Oh, I have," said Cameron. She seemed more serious, more reserved.

"How's the family?" asked Jack.

"They're well, thanks," said Cameron. "Aunt Vicky was asking after you."

"She was quite the character," said Jack. "And Charlie? He had a little girl, didn't he?"

"Not so little now," said Cameron, smiling. "She's taller than me and twice as sassy. I have another niece and a nephew as well."

The ice was broken. Cameron looked more relaxed, and Jack was relieved.

"What can I get you?" he asked, nodding at the bar. "Gin and tonic? We have an hour or so before dinner."

"Sure," said Cameron. "That'd be great."

They settled at a table in the corner of the bar. Jack held up his glass. "To old friends," he said.

Cameron clinked her glass against his and met his gaze. "Old friends." She took a sip of her drink. "And new projects," she said. "You've been busy, haven't you? What's really going on in Dunswyke?"

Jack managed the trademark smile this time. "So much good stuff, Cameron," he said. "Let me tell you all about it."

Cameron's feelings towards Jack had mellowed considerably by the time they got to dessert. She admitted to herself that the wine helped, but his enthusiasm and sincerity was catching.

"The beauty of the DAO is that it's controlled by the community," said Jack. "It's completely decentralised and governed by the community. All the Diaulos holders vote on the investments that the Foundation makes into the athletes."

"I hope you've audited that code properly," said Cameron. "Your software doesn't have the best reputation in my field."

Jack looked hurt. "I know we've made mistakes in the past," he said. "Occasional errors that got through testing. You know how it goes."

"Not really," said Cameron. "You've had some really serious vulnerabilities over the years. It's a miracle that none of them led to big data breaches or malware injections. Although, to be fair," she said, taking another mouthful of her chocolate brownie, "the errors have been so glaringly obvious that we've generally found them and fixed them for you before you even knew they were there."

"I guess I have to thank you for that," said Jack modestly.

"Not just me," said Cameron. "The whole infosec world. It's a team effort. Be careful with the Foundation DAO, though. You can't ride your luck like that with decentralised code. It'll blow up in your face."

Jack nodded earnestly. "I know," he said. "I've made some big changes. I have an excellent team in place now. I managed to pick up a really experienced Chief Technology Officer with access to top class development resources. It's all done in the spirit of the Foundation, as well. Some of the most talented programmers we have are based in seriously disadvantaged new world countries. We're making life better for a lot of people."

Cameron made a half-hearted mental note to ask Cloverleaf about the CTO but wondered if her antipathy towards the project had really been based on her antipathy towards Jack himself. Was she being unfair by questioning everything? There was nothing sparking her instinct for trouble. One final question occurred to her.

"How does MetaBand fit into all this?" she asked.

Jack laughed and winked at her conspiratorially. "You'll find out soon enough," he said. "I can't talk about it, even with you. It's embargoed until the formal announcement after Easter. Let's just say that it's not only about connecting people."

Cameron raised an eyebrow.

"There are a couple of big surprises to come," he said. "You'll see the final pieces of the jigsaw that make the Sladen Foundation truly decentralised and globally relevant."

"That's why you're in town," said Cameron, realisation dawning.

"That's right," said Jack. "I'm heading up to Dunswyke tomorrow to oversee the final touches at headquarters. I'll be there right through Easter weekend, and the big press conference is on the Tuesday. Make sure you watch it."

"Oh, I will," said Cameron. "I can't wait." She stifled a yawn. It was getting late. Jack still looked as fresh as a daisy. He must be running on Texas time.

"You look tired," said Jack, reading her mind. He waved at the table's customer service sensor. "The bill, please."

A few moments later, a waiter appeared bearing two shot glasses. "So nice to see you, Mr Sladen," he said. "Your bill has been sent to your account. Please, have some Grappa, on the house."

"Thank you," said Jack, taking a sip of the aromatic liquid and inhaling its scent. "I've enjoyed our evening. Maybe we can do this again soon?"

"Maybe," said Cameron. "Let's stay in touch." She yawned again. "I have to go."

Jack waved at the sensor. "Taxi, please."

In less than a minute, an autocar slid to a halt outside the restaurant.

Cameron drained the last of her glass of Grappa and stood up. "Good to see you, Jack."

Jack pushed his chair back and reached out for a hug. "You too, Cameron," he said. "Take care."

Cameron left the restaurant and jumped into the taxi without a backward glance. As the autocar zipped silently along the London streets, she reflected on the evening. She didn't want to admit how much fun it had been. Maybe Jack Sladen wasn't so bad these days, after all.

9: PRIVET

Cameron woke late on the Sunday morning, the cat once again wailing for food. This time she jumped out of bed with more energy and decided to get some fresh air and breakfast out in town. She wanted some time to reflect on her meeting with Jack and the snippets of information she had managed to glean from him.

Showered and dressed, she skipped down the stairs from her apartment and out into the street. The weather was much warmer, spring giving way to early summer, and there was a lively buzz around the area. Cameron strolled towards the bustling Borough Market. She might pick up a coffee and a pastry at her favourite bakery or see if one of her friends was around to meet for brunch.

Before she could call anyone, her smartscreen pinged with an incoming alert. It was Charlie.

"I thought you were away?" said Cameron, confused.

"We are," said Charlie, "we're at Nasser's place, but something's come up and I know you'll know the answer."

"Am I Tech Support today?" asked Cameron. "It'll cost you."

"Yes, you're definitely Tech Support and if you can fix this, I owe you a beer," said Charlie.

Cameron glanced around and spotted an empty bench in a small park nearby. She settled down in the sunshine. "Shoot," she said. "What's the problem?"

"Dilan's been playing Team Nine with his cousin," said Charlie. "They got all excited because they won some kind of special character. You know Team Nine, don't you? It's the biggest thing with the kids at the moment."

Cameron laughed. "I can see an ad for it on the street right opposite me now. It's ridiculously popular. The augmented characters are superb. It's as if they're in the room with you."

"Yes, well, you were always a bigger gamer than me," said Charlie. "Anyway, Dilan got this notification to say he'd unlocked a secret character called Privet."

"That's so cool," said Cameron. "Privet's a throwback to the very first game that those developers launched. It's a nice little Easter egg for those in the know."

"That's what Dilan said," said Charlie. "Very seasonal, I thought. Anyway, he clicked on it, and it snarled the system up completely."

"Oh, dear," sighed Cameron. "When you say he clicked on it, was the notification inside the game?"

"No," said Charlie. "It was a message that came into his chatbox."

"He knows not to click on random stuff," said Cameron, exasperated.

"Don't be too hard on him, Cam," said Charlie. "He showed me the message before he clicked. It was all branded up as Team Nine and it had been forwarded from one of the group of friends he normally plays with. He had a ten-minute window to claim the character."

"That's a classic trap," said Cameron. "Showing you something you want and giving you a tight deadline. It's an easy way to stop people checking where a message has really come from. What's the damage? How far through your systems has it gone?"

"We've been lucky," said Charlie. "He was using his own gamepad, the one you set up with a direct datalink, so he wasn't signed in on Nasser's home network. There's a popup saying that the device is locked."

"That's a bonus," said Cameron. "This is almost certainly a new bit of ransomware doing the rounds. Switch it all off and don't touch it. Tell Dilan not to worry, and I'll try and fix it when I come down next weekend."

"Thanks, Cam," said Charlie, sounding relieved.

"You owe me a beer, don't forget," said Cameron. "I'll see you on Friday, hopefully. If this spreads as fast as I expect then I have a busy week ahead."

She abandoned any ideas of a lazy brunch and instead picked up snacks from the market to keep her going through the day. Laden with olives, cheese, dips and fresh bread she returned to her apartment and switched on her computer. First stop was to check on Mephisto, and sure enough the little AI had news for her. The Privet Easter egg was multiplying. Messages featuring the link were growing exponentially, and the pattern bore all the hallmarks of The Steamyard's handiwork.

Cameron logged into her regular infosec forums. There was a low level of chatter about it already, and she was able to add what she knew into the mix. She dropped Mephisto's latest report onto the board and a familiar handle appeared in the conversation. Ross, under his nickname of RunningManTech, couldn't stay away from the job even when he was supposed to be recuperating.

'Morning, SimCavalier,' he typed, maintaining the pseudonymity of the forum. 'What has your pet picked up this time, or is this just an April fool?'

'Morning, RunningManTech,' she replied. 'No joke. It came through a real-world connection. Mephisto just confirmed the spread of the malware.'

On her smartscreen, she pinged a message directly to Ross. 'Shouldn't you be resting?' she asked.

'I'm bored,' he replied. 'Want me to make a start on tracking down the code and reverse engineering it?'

'If you really want to,' she sent back, 'but I'd rather you concentrated on getting better. It looks like there are a few people working on it already, so why don't you just keep an eye on the forum and pull together what they find? That shouldn't be too strenuous.'

'Okay,' said Ross. He went back to the forum and carried on with the chat.

Cameron popped an olive into her mouth and started scrolling through the code that was already being uploaded into the forum repository. If this was the work of The Steamyard, she needed to get to the bottom of who and what they were.

•

On a train speeding north away from the capital, Jack Sladen dozed fitfully in his first-class seat. Every so often he started awake, peering out of the window at the fields and houses that flashed by. It was a far cry from the older, slower trains that used to take him backwards and forwards from the Borders to London. Now, the first stop at York was barely an hour from the capital, and Edinburgh a mere two hours further on the fastest services.

The carriage was empty but for him. The service was timetabled just too late for any Monday morning commuters, and too early for tourists. Jack found the rhythm of the train curiously relaxing. His jet lag was still kicking in, telling his brain that he should be asleep, and this journey should give him a chance to catch up at last.

"Coffee, Mr Sladen?" The refreshments trolley approached.

"Yes, please," said Jack. The simple machine had recorded his preferences on previous journeys and served up a frothy cappuccino and crisp almond biscotti without prompting. Jack wondered how it learned to identify its customers. Did it use face recognition, or simply match the passenger to their booked seat on the train each time? If he moved across the carriage, would it serve him Earl Grey tea and fruit cake instead? He might mess with the machine a little on his next trip, just for fun. This morning he was content to watch the landscape go by, trying to pick out familiar landmarks at high speed. He spotted the great white horse at the edge of the North Yorks Moors and drank in the view along the River Tyne as the train slowed on its approach to the station in Newcastle. A few more passengers joined his carriage here, most bound for Scotland. He would be leaving them soon. He finished his coffee and started collecting his things together ready to alight.

He got off the train at Alnmouth and found a car waiting for him in the tiny rural station. From the car park, he could see moorland sweeping down to the great sandy inlet of the river and the shining sea beyond. As a teenager he couldn't wait to leave Dunswyke, to move to London and to college, but there was no doubt that the area was outstandingly beautiful, and he was starting to appreciate it more now that he had lived all around the world.

He detoured past his hotel in the little town that clustered at the foot of Dunswyke castle to drop his bags, then went on to the site where Melissa was waiting for him. The muddy car park was now a clean sweep of gravel with a discreet sign at the gate. The stone of the bastle house glowed in the sunshine, and on the surrounding land, restored to its natural grassy state, swathes of wildflowers were rippling in a gentle breeze.

"Looks great, doesn't it?" she said. "It was a tough job, but it's turned out beautifully."

"It's stunning," said Jack. "You really came through for me, Melissa. I wish you could come and manage some of my software projects."

"I'm strictly construction," said Melissa with a smile. "I wouldn't know where to start with the things you do. I've landed another peach of a job, though, once this is signed off."

"I'm not surprised," said Jack. "What will you be doing?"

"I'm going to work for the Dunswyke Estate," said Melissa. "I'll be managing their transformation roadmap, starting with the new visitor centre and the immersive history experience. I can't wait."

"That sounds excellent, Melissa," said Jack. "It's right up your street. I'll have to come and visit when it's finished."

There was the growl of an engine behind them as a van turned into the car park, gravel crunching under its wheels.

"Here come your networking people," said Melissa. "They can show you around the finished data centre. I have to get on with the fit-out of the offices. There's still a fair bit of work to do in there before the media descend on us for the launch." She walked off towards the bastle.

Jack gazed at the building, drinking in the beauty of the setting. The dream had been realised, and it was better than he could have imagined.

Behind him, a van door slammed loudly, and Angus lumbered up to where Jack was standing. Big, bearded and generally sullen, Jack found Angus hard to deal with at times, but there was no doubt that he knew his stuff on managing the complex hardware and specialist software that the Foundation needed. He'd come recommended by Tenuk, whose network was remarkably extensive. Jack preferred to deal with the other half of the partnership, Ella. She was bright and brilliant, and he knew that she was not only working on the security of the data centre but had made a vital contribution to the tokenomics of the Sladen Foundation DAO as part of Tenuk's elite team.

He glanced over towards the car park where the young woman was finishing a call. As he watched, she slipped her smartscreen into her pocket, looked up and gave him a cheery smile and a wave. Jack sighed. He had asked her to join him for dinner at each visit to England over the past few months and each time she had declined. He would miss working with her. He wanted to get to know her better, but deep down he knew he didn't stand a chance.

She walked up to him, looking cool and professional. "Good morning, Jack," she said. "How are you? Good trip over?"

"Yes, thanks," said Jack. "I hear everything's been going smoothly with the data centre."

Angus snorted. "Smoothly?" he said. "Not really. Whose daft idea was it to stick those servers in a cave? It's a pain in the arse."

"It's been fine," said Ella firmly. "Take no notice of him, Jack. It was a lovely idea. Everything is installed and running well. Let's go and have a look." She swept off serenely towards the bastle and Jack trailed helplessly in her wake, Angus bringing up the rear and muttering under his breath.

The path wound through the small wood behind the house, to all intents and purposes a nature walk. As they neared the cliff face, Ella pointed out several well camouflaged steel barriers nestled in the undergrowth. "We couldn't rely solely on the natural barrier of the cliff face," she said. "This is standard for sensitive data centres and gives us an extra level of physical protection down here at entry level."

They emerged from the wood close to the sheer grey wall of whinstone. Angus pointed up towards the moors. "There are military spec anti-surveillance devices up there. We've got some drone nets as well."

"Drone nets?" asked Jack.

"Yes," said Ella. "I don't know where Angus found these, but they're brilliant."

"How do they work?" asked Jack.

"They're predator drones camouflaged on the ground," said Ella. "If anything tries to overfly the area and scan it, they detect the signal and the flight pattern and if it doesn't match with an authorised device, they take off and grab the offender in their net." She made a grabbing motion with her hands.

"It's better than blasting them out of the sky," growled Angus. "We can interrogate them if they're in one piece."

Jack was impressed. "You've really gone to town on this," he said. "Tenuk told me the security you could provide was second to none, and he was right."

They approached the cave entrance. The foliage had been cut back during the works, but to Jack's relief it was growing steadily and would eventually conceal the entrance once more. Inside it was cool and dark. The unit filled most of the cave, its printed, layered walls rough to the touch. Within it lay the server stacks that held Tenuk's admin software, the complex artificial intelligence that formed the core of the Slade Foundation network.

"Do you want to say hello?" asked Ella.

"Can I talk to it?" said Jack. "Does it have the capacity to communicate?"

"Sure she does," said Ella. "You don't have to be here to talk, as she can chat remotely through all the usual interfaces, but it's as good a place as any." Ella turned to face the winking LEDs of the servers nonetheless, as if she was talking to a real person. "Jack," she said. "I'd like you to meet Yasmin."

10: EASTER EGGS

Cameron rubbed her tired eyes and focused on the long list that occupied the right side of the huge office wallscreen. The week had not gone to plan. It had been fully four days now since the first reports of the Privet ransomware, and locked servers had started trickling in from businesses as well as gamers and personal clients. With the Easter bank holidays beckoning, she was hoping that the combined efforts of cybersecurity teams around the world would soon start to tell.

As she watched the screen, another client logo appeared. A new pin dropped onto the huge, rippling world map that filled the top left quadrant of the display, casting its ugly red glow on a patch of green in the dead centre of England. Cameron groaned and put her head in her hands for a moment, then looked over to Michelle at the nearest desk.

"They're still coming in," she said. "Peak Medical, now. That's one of your accounts, isn't it, Shell?"

"Not them as well, surely?" replied Michelle incredulously. "We did a round of staff training just a few weeks ago. Ping it over to me, Cam. I'll check the details."

With a cheery chime that belied the circumstances, the report dropped onto Michelle's screen. She opened the client record and scrolled quickly through the logs. Cameron heard the screen reader squawking as Michelle navigated with a practiced ear. "Got it," she said. "Four weeks ago, middle of March. We also reorganised their backup routines and it looks like they're bang up to date."

"Good," said Cameron. "At least that's one company we can get up and running straight away. Can you make sure those backups are screened and roll back the restore to before the infection?"

"Sure thing," said Michelle happily. "I'll have a little word with them next week about following up the training as well."

"Nice to have a good news story in the middle of this mess," said Pete, yawning. "That ransomware is vicious. You were absolutely right back at Christmas. The Santa invasion was just the advance party."

"They haven't claimed responsibility for this one yet," said Cameron, "but it has all the hallmarks of that first Steamyard release, even though the targeting has been different."

"I thought that," said Joel. "It was cunning of them to go through the gaming community this time."

"They're demonstrating another attack vector," said Cameron. "Flexing their muscles and showing potential clients that they're not a one trick pony."

"I didn't expect them to get a solid threat out in the wild so fast," said Sandeep, peering around his screen. "Do we have any idea who's raising money from this?"

Cameron shook her head. "It could be them or it could be a client," she said. "We can see the ransoms being collected, but nothing has started moving anything yet."

"If it isn't The Steamyard directly, it'll be an organised crime group, I reckon," said Joel.

"More likely OCG than a nation state attack, I agree," said Pete. "It's not strategic. Just a cash grab. Mind you, there are a few countries who need the money. You never know who's pulling the strings."

"I've tried to find some clues to link the ransom collection accounts to the real world," said Noor, "but they are covering their tracks well. As soon as they start to launder the takings, I've got a tracker ready to deploy. If we're lucky, we might find some people on the edge of the network and trace back towards the centre."

"It's worth a shot," said Cameron. She stretched tiredly and gazed out of the great glass window at the nightscape of London. Even this late in the evening, the street below was a mass of light and activity as people enjoyed their Thursday night, the start of a traditional four-day long weekend for Easter. They might have seen the headlines – after all, Team Nine was the hottest game out there right now, and Privet was a legendary character – but most of them would hardly notice the upheaval that the ransomware had caused. The general public had no idea of the number and scale of attacks that were repelled day after day by the national security agencies and countered by the Argentum team and all their fellow infosec professionals around the country and across the world.

This one had made it through the defences. The temptation of the Easter egg, the lure of claiming the rare Privet character, had caught out people at every level from teenage gamers to senior executives. Hopefully some of those who had been locked out of their files would take the lessons to heart, but most would forget over time and keep their bad habits. Those who were not directly affected might find their favourite sites or networks disabled, an inconvenience at best. Where emergency services had been caught out by slow security upgrades and a single careless click, the outcome would be more serious, likely fatal for a few unlucky patients and their families.

Fast forward weeks or months and there would be some companies winding up their businesses, broken by the attack. Cameron fervently hoped that none of the clients they supported would suffer that fate, but missteps and human error were costly. A moment of carelessness or distraction could allow any of the malware that circulated on the world wide web into a company's systems, costing real money and precious time to fix or opening the door to data thieves. Eventually any stolen data would resurface for sale to the highest bidder, leaving passwords and login details exposed and starting the whole cycle of phishing, cloning, ransoms and theft again.

"Cameron?" Sandeep broke her gloomy reverie. "I think we're making some headway at last."

The wallscreen map was starting to look healthier. Green and amber pins were starting to appear in the sea of red. There was a subtle shift in the atmosphere of the office. Michelle, Pete, Sandeep and Noor were chatting quietly, more relaxed than they had been for hours. Ross, still recuperating at home, was sharing a joke with Joel.

Cameron let out a sigh of relief. "I think you may be right," she said.

"It could have been worse," said Pete. "This Steamyard team is clever."

"Tell me about it," said Cameron. "We were expecting the next wave to be delivered through the mail server network again, but that viral Easter egg was a genius move." She glanced at Noor who was talking quietly and intensely to one of her many international contacts, drawing together as much information as possible from the global community to help them all to manage the attack. "When Noor comes off her call, we'll review what we've got so far."

"Anyone for another coffee?" said Sandeep. He eyed the shiny new coffee machine hopefully.

Cameron shook her head. "Not me," she said. "I want to sleep tonight, and I think we're close to finishing."

"Well, the virus definition's been pushed out," said Pete. "Although everyone's been sharing the heck out of that Easter egg, the updated antivirus filters on mail and media should stop it being delivered."

"That's good," said Cameron. She checked on the wallscreen again. The green pins were winning. "It looks as if we've slowed the spread right down."

Noor finished her call, signing off with a cheery "Bonne nuit."

"What news from Paris?" asked Cameron.

Noor gave her a broad grin. "You're going to love this," she said. "One of their researchers found a temporary workaround for the ransom payment. The ransom asks for Bitcoin, but he managed to retrieve the release key by making a payment denominated in Sats instead."

Cameron started laughing and found she couldn't stop. "That's a terrible coding error on The Steamyard's part," she said, catching her breath. "With a hundred million Satoshis in a single Bitcoin, they're releasing the ransomed data for literally pennies."

On screen, Ross was grinning and wincing with pain at the same time. "Stop it," he said. "It hurts when I laugh."

"I'm sure they'll fix that pretty fast," said Pete.

"Oh, of course they will," said Noor, "but it's an automated process so they probably won't spot it straight away. For now, though, anyone who's been caught out can get their data back fast."

Cameron grabbed her smartscreen and sent a quick message to her brother. "I've let Charlie know so he can release Dilan's device. That's a quick cure that's saved me a job at the weekend."

"The anti-virus is the other half of the equation," said Pete. "The vaccine if you like. Anyone who gets the Easter egg should be protected now if their update has been patched in."

"Excellent," said Cameron. "That's perfect timing. We may actually get to enjoy the weekend." She looked across at Noor. "Can you pass the baton to that team in Honolulu? They can take the next co-ordinating shift."

Noor nodded. "I already spoke to them. They're all set. It hasn't yet reached its peak in their region so hopefully they can stop it before it starts over there."

"Right, let's pack up," said Cameron. A huge yawn caught her by surprise. "Most of our clients are safe for the weekend. I'm going to Charlie's tomorrow, but I'll be working from there. Pete, you're on call until Sunday, aren't you?"

"Yes," said Pete. "I'm away on a dive trip from Monday morning for a few days."

"I'm in to cover Easter Monday," said Noor. "Susie will be back in the country on Tuesday as well." She pointed at her screen. "She's just messaged me to see how we're doing."

"Where is she?" asked Cameron. "I thought she was still in Europe?"

"She is," said Noor, laughing. "It's very late. I think her evening is going well." She shared her screen to the wall display. Susie was livestreaming from a nightclub, laser beams sweeping across the crowd and a DJ on stage making luminous trails with swirling batons. Some of the partygoers close to Susie were wearing headsets, enjoying an augmented experience with anime dancers.

"I need some of that," said Joel. "Martha's mum is babysitting on Saturday. I'll have to see what gigs are on. We haven't had a proper night out together in months."

Night out, thought Cameron. She thought back to the previous Saturday. Her night out with Jack felt like a long time ago, although it had been only a few days. She wondered idly what he was doing over Easter. Would he be making his staff work through the holiday, getting ready for the big announcement on Tuesday, or would he actually have some rare down time? She thought he still had an aunt in Scotland. Maybe he was going to visit her, dropping his commercial persona and playing the dutiful nephew for a day. The idea made her smile.

Her thoughts turned to Ben. She hadn't yet called him back about his concerns over the MetaBand hardware, but she had nothing concrete to tell him yet. That would just have to wait. Right now, they all needed a rest after a hard week and a job well done.

•

Cameron reached the village early on Friday afternoon. The sun was shining with a warmth unusual for mid-April, and the forecast was good for the Easter weekend.

"Do you think I should buy some of these?" asked Charlie, showing his sister a marketing message that had just popped up on his screen. "You know your way around crypto investing, Cam. What's the story on Diaulos?"

Cameron took a sip of her drink, relaxing in the sheltered warmth of the village pub's beer garden. "I'm not sure about it, to be honest, Charlie," she said. "We're days away from the launch of the Foundation but no one has seen as much as a glimpse of the underlying code for the coin or for the investment system. I've read the whitepaper, but it says absolutely nothing beyond what you've already heard in their publicity. I'm waiting for the release of the protocol before I make any judgements."

"They're sending athletes to the Olympics, though," said Sameena. "Is it endorsed by the International Olympic Committee? They wouldn't let their brand be attached to anything dodgy, would they?" She shifted uncomfortably on the wooden bench and her foot caught the dog's water bowl that was tucked under the table. Water trickled over the grass and down onto the path. "Whoops," she said. "Sorry, Roxy."

Cameron shook her head. "There's no official link between this coin and the IOC," she said. "They're being very careful to avoid saying anything that could suggest an endorsement."

"Oh," said Sameena, surprised. "I just assumed…"

"I'm sure that Jack would be delighted at that," said Cameron with a wry smile. "If the public decides there's a link, he can deny it all he wants to while the sales of the coin shoot up. Win-win."

"Huh," said Charlie. "That's sneaky." He shuffled along the narrow bench and stood up, stretching. "Another beer, anyone? I'll go and get a refill." He called across the pub garden to a gaggle of children who were playing around a tree. "Kids! If you want more drinks, come and get them."

Dilan came trotting across the grass, red from running around, and followed his father through the low doorway into the pub. He emerged a few moments later carrying the refilled water bowl, walking slowly and carefully to avoid spilling it. He put it down in a clear spot by the table, away from stray feet, and ruffled Roxy's curly coat. "There you go," he said as she bent her head to drink.

"It's nice to see you running around, Dilan," said Cameron. "You're normally hiding behind a screen. Is everything okay with your game now?"

"Yes, Auntie Cam," said Dilan. "Dad said you sorted it all out. I haven't lost any of my progress."

"I'm glad to hear it," said Cameron. "I'm sorry there wasn't a real Privet character. That would have been cool."

"I know," said Dilan sadly. "Maybe they'll do a proper limited-edition Privet for us one day. I have loads of good assets, though. I'm in the pro league."

"Very good," said Cameron. "What does that mean, exactly?"

"I get to choose extra weapons and I can win some really rare prizes," said Dilan proudly. There was a shout from the tree. "Coming!" he called. He scrambled to his feet and ran back to the game in progress.

"He's hooked on those screen games," said Sameena.

"He's doing okay," said Cameron. "He's good at the games, and he's outside playing every chance he gets. I wouldn't worry about him."

"You're right," said Sameena. "My brothers were just as bad back in the day." She frowned. "Talking of them, why would you think that Diaulos is a risky investment?" she asked. "There is so much speculation about it. Nasser's planning on getting some. He says it's going to pay off his mortgage."

"It might," said Cameron, "but I hope he doesn't overstretch himself. It's the same with any investment like this. There's always a risk, especially when something's new and untested. I hope he's getting proper advice."

"I'm sure he is," said Sameena confidently.

Cameron wasn't so convinced. "I don't think anyone can advise on this coin yet," she said. "The presale hasn't even started yet. We don't know enough about it. Just because everyone is talking about it doesn't mean it's a sound investment. It's probably fine, but it makes me nervous when I can't see the nuts and bolts."

"Okay," said Sameena. "I trust your instincts on things like this. I'll check up on what Nasser's doing, but there's no harm in him picking up a few coins, is there?"

Charlie put a fresh round of drinks down on the table and slid into his place on the bench. "What's the verdict on this coin, then?" he asked. He looked from Cameron to Sameena and laughed. "That bad? I don't believe you. You just don't trust Jack Sladen."

Cameron took a moment to reflect and examine her feelings. Was her automatic suspicion of the whole project simply part of her complex relationship with Jack over the years, or had her usually reliable sixth sense picked up something genuinely awry?

"I don't know, Charlie," she said. "I met up with him last weekend, and he's mellowed a lot. The Foundation has a lot of promise and I'd like it to be above board and successful. Registering is safe enough but let me do some digging before you hand any money over."

"Okay, Cam," said Charlie. "I trust you. Now, enough work talk. You're supposed to be relaxing this weekend."

"I know," said Cameron. "I've been busy. It's hard to switch off."

"Are you going to help me set up the hunt for the village kids?" said Charlie. "Or have you had enough of Easter eggs?"

"The chocolate kind are no problem at all," said Cameron. "I'd love to help out. Do you remember doing those when we were little? I know some great hiding places." She looked down at Roxy who was lying in the shade of the table. "The challenge is putting the eggs somewhere the kids can find them, and the dogs can't."

"Anywhere close to that cat of Aunt Vicky's is safe enough," said Charlie. "Every dog in the village is terrified of Donald. They cross the road to avoid him. I swear he's getting worse."

"I'm not sure that's possible," said Cameron. "He's a horror." She looked around guiltily, half expecting either her aunt or the cat to appear. "If he turned out to be the shadowy mastermind behind The Steamyard, I wouldn't be at all surprised."

Charlie laughed. "You're daft, sis. I'm glad you made it down this weekend. Relax and enjoy yourself. You've earned it."

Cameron took a sip of her drink and smiled. "It's been a tough few days," she said, "and I'm sure it's not entirely over, but there are some capable hands looking after everything right now, so yes, I'm taking every moment that I can." She felt the tension draining. "Where do you want these Easter eggs, then, Charlie? Do you have a plan?"

"I do," said Charlie. "The kids are all meeting on the village green at twelve noon. We're putting on some drinks for the parents, obviously." He looked around at the busy beer garden, making sure that no passing youngsters could overhear, and lowered his voice conspiratorially. "We can't go into the gardens, especially the ones that are getting ready for the Mayday open garden event." He looked at Cameron. "You're coming back for that next weekend, aren't you?"

"If I can," said Cameron.

"Sameena and I have been slaving over that garden for weeks," said Charlie. He looked across the beer garden to where his younger children were playing, and his eldest was chatting to a friend. "They haven't lifted a finger."

"We were just as bad," protested Cameron. "Don't you remember when Mum decided she was going to plant a whole new border? You went off with your mates and left me to do all the digging, which I hated, by the way, and you were grounded for a week when you got back."

"I'd forgotten that," said Charlie. "How funny."

"Come on, Charlie," said Cameron. "The plan."

"Yes, right," he whispered as a small child walked past, oblivious to the plotting that was going on above her head. "As this is a very late Easter, it's warmer than usual. We've got to be careful that the eggs don't melt before the kids get there."

"We can go out early and find the shady spots," said Cameron. "Down the edge of the stream, under the bridges, in the climbing trees."

"We can go up the street a little as well," said Charlie. "We just need to avoid…"

"Donald," said Cameron. "Yes, I know. We can put the more obvious eggs out just before the kids arrive so that they don't melt."

"I think we have a plan," said Charlie.

Cameron gave him a broad grin. "It's nice to be thinking about something other than work," she said happily. "This is going to be fun."

11: HUNTED

Bright and early on Tuesday morning, refreshed and revived, Cameron was back in the office. She walked in the door and laughed as she spotted a row of Easter eggs lined up on one of the shelves.

"They weren't hard to find," she said.

Sandeep turned around from his accustomed place tending the new coffee machine. "You want a proper Easter egg hunt round the office?" he asked. "I can arrange that. Strictly the edible kind, though."

"I'm good," said Cameron. "Where did these come from?"

"I know the Easter bunny," said Sandeep, tapping the side of his nose. "Connections." He looked up as the door opened. "Here she comes now."

"Susie?" said Cameron. "Sandeep says you're the Easter bunny."

"Yes," said Susie. "That's me. Actually, there was a two for one offer in the airport shop. I couldn't let that pass."

"Excellent work," said Cameron. "Although, after this weekend, I don't know if I can face any more chocolate."

"I can face more chocolate," said Joel, coming in on the tail end of the conversation.

"Help yourself," said Susie. "They go well with coffee." She picked up her mug and a small chocolate egg and settled at her desk.

The morning flew by. Cameron glanced up from her routine work and was startled to see it was almost time for Jack's big announcement. She stopped what she was doing and put the news channel feed up on the wallscreen.

"It's time for the press conference," she said.

A window popped open in the corner of the screen, and Ross's face appeared. "Hi, everyone," he said. "I got back home from training just in time for the show. Are you all seeing this?"

A series of adverts gave way to the news channel's lunchtime show logo, and then to beautifully edited drone footage giving viewers a bird's eye view of the estate, the restored bastle house standing proud in its beautiful surroundings. A time lapse of the transformation showed the enormity of the work that had been done. The drone flew over a group of people who waved enthusiastically.

"The Sladen Foundation has created new jobs in the area," said a sugary voiceover. "It will also support more than fifty talented athletes to reach this summer's Olympic Games in Reykjavik." The aerial shots of the bastle and moorland were replaced by images of runners in an arid African landscape, swimmers training in abandoned hotel pools on half-drowned resort islands, young footballers in crowded shanty towns, and a gymnast tumbling gracefully across a space between tents in a refugee camp.

"This is really good," said Cameron.

On his window on the wallscreen, Ross nodded. "Can't fault them," he said approvingly. "It's a great initiative. It feels solid."

"That's what I thought," said Cameron. "Jack was very convincing. I actually think he's doing something right, for once."

"You still don't like him, do you?" said Joel.

"I don't know," said Cameron. "It was good to see him again. It doesn't change the fact that his software has been slapdash for years and he has no attention to detail, but he has great ideas and I think he finally has a talented team around him who are doing decent work."

"Did you tell him that?" asked Ross.

"The first bit, yes," said Cameron. "The second part, no. He's big-headed enough as it is." She checked the time. "He should be on any minute. He said that the big announcements would be scheduled to catch the lunchtime newsreels."

"What are you expecting?" asked Noor.

"I think he'll announce the Diaulos presale and launch dates and give a simple overview of the Foundation DAO," said Cameron. "He hinted that there were some big surprises to come, but I bet he won't go into much detail."

"Why?" asked Susie. "Is that because most people watching won't understand it?"

"Probably because he doesn't entirely understand it himself," said Noor darkly.

Cameron laughed. "Yeah, he's not really one for the fine details," she said. "There'll be an update to that terrible whitepaper dropping today as well. Check the website, Noor. It'll probably be released as soon as the announcements are made."

"I want to get my hands on that," said Michelle. "It had better have more detail in it than the original."

"It'll be interesting to see how much control he keeps to himself," said Noor.

"In theory, he won't have any control," said Joel. "It should all be decision making by the community."

"In theory, that's the case with every distributed app," said Noor. "It's remarkably rare in practice."

"You don't trust him either, do you?" said Joel. "Poor guy."

There was a flurry of activity on the screen and Jack Sladen strode into view. The team fell silent and listened intently. He thanked the project team for their work on the site and expressed his delight at being back home at last in Dunswyke, which made Cameron snort with laughter. He waxed lyrical about the community governance of the Sladen Foundation. None of this was news to Cameron. She was waiting for the embargoed revelations about the MetaBand network and the other surprises he'd hinted at. She turned to the others.

"What do you know about the hardware behind a network like MetaBand?" she asked.

"I know my way round satellite comms," said Joel. "It was all we used in the army. I bet Pete's up to speed as well. Why?"

"I had a tip-off about some odd hardware configurations in this system," said Cameron. She glanced at Noor. "Ben's working on the project over in Texas. He called me about some design changes that he thought didn't make sense."

"What kind of thing are we talking about?" asked Joel. "They're usually really simple units."

"He said they'd added high spec data processing chips and storage in the receivers," said Cameron, "and extra capacity in the microsats as well."

"That's not needed for normal comms," said Joel instantly. "I wonder what else these units are designed to do?"

"I think we're about to find out," said Susie, pointing at the screen. A simplified 3D representation of a network, heavily branded with the MetaBand logo, was turning this way and that. The same sugary voice was narrating.

"Each MetaBand receiver also acts as a node on the Diaulos network," it said. "Homes attached to MetaBand around the world are ready and waiting to secure the coin and provide homeowners with a passive income as transaction validators."

"Oh, that explains it," said Noor. "That's what they need the processors for."

"Clever idea," said Cameron. "I can see why he wouldn't breathe a word before the embargo was lifted."

"It's unusual," said Ross from the screen, "but it's one way to decentralise the whole network, I suppose."

"I'd better call Ben," said Cameron. "He was worried. It looks as if his suspicions were unfounded."

The graphics on the screen faded and the coverage returned to the press conference. Jack was speaking again. "The Diaulos presale opens on Friday at 7am Eastern Time," he said. A QR code flashed up on the corner of the screen. Cameron took a screen grab. "Our founder community can look forward to some fantastic benefits of participation, from enhanced voting power to real-world rewards, and will earn a return on their investment from the moment they commit to the presale."

"I want to read the whitepaper," said Noor, "and I think we should dig into their code base as well. Who's developing it? Who's maintaining it?"

"Fair questions," said Ross from his remote window.

"I've already tackled him on that," said Cameron grimly. "I got nowhere."

Jack Sladen held up his hand for silence and the excited buzz from the press corps died away. "There is one more piece of the puzzle," he said. "The Sladen Foundation is supporting local people…" He nodded at a gaggle of people, probably new employees, who were out of shot. "…and talented athletes. It's providing high speed connectivity and a passive income through MetaBand. We want all of you to be part of the magic too."

Cameron groaned. "Who writes this stuff?" she said. "That's not Jack talking. What have they got up their sleeves now?"

On the screen, Jack held up a small bracelet, a simple wearable health tracker. "In the spirit of the Olympics, we're helping people to get fit and get moving, and earn money as they go," he said. "We mined gold with physical energy, and Bitcoin with CPU energy. Now anyone can mine Diaulos with their daily steps. We call this Proof of Walk, the final piece of the Diaulos protocol, securing the chain in a truly democratic and decentralised way. You can join us right now by ordering your POW bracelet. Take a step into the future with the Sladen Foundation."

Cameron had to admit she was impressed with the concept, but she rolled her eyes at the terrible speech writing and the corny humour. Proof of Walk was a joke that only a select few would pick up, playing on the local accent's rendering of walk and work. On screen, Jack was grinning like the cat that got the cream, and hacks were clamouring for attention.

He held up his hands and called for silence. "I'd love to answer all of your questions now," he said, "but that's all we have time for today." He stepped down from the podium and walked briskly away, to the obvious annoyance of the press corps.

"That's genius," said Joel at last. "Shame he wouldn't take questions. I have plenty."

Cameron looked thoughtfully at the screen. Jack Sladen and his terrible attention to detail. "He can't afford to," she said. "It would tarnish his golden boy reputation if he stuttered over an answer."

Jack's timing had been slightly off. The programme hadn't reached its allotted end. As a filler, someone sent up a news drone to fly over the site and provide a backdrop for speculative commentary on the latest announcement. It circled over the jumble of outside broadcast units then flew over the bastle and looped around the back of the building, following the line of the steep escarpment that sheltered the building from the wild sweep of moorland above it.

"That's Ella!" shouted Susie.

Cameron whirled around. The camera had caught a clear shot of two people standing behind the bastle at the edge of a patch of woodland, moments before the broadcast image jerked and spun and the screen went black.

Ella, their former colleague and Susie's old partner, was unmistakeable, but the greater shock for Cameron was the man standing beside her.

"That's Angus," she said, her scalp prickling in horror.

The last time she had seen the man, she had chased him and lost him in a crowd, seeking answers about an attack on a nuclear power plant. Now he was there at Dunswyke alongside their former colleague. She had been mixed up in the same scheme and fled after a deadly attack on the old Argentum offices.

Their presence shattered her confidence in Jack Sladen, his new ventures, and his new team. There were criminals at the heart of the Sladen Foundation, and that changed everything.

12:   COVER UP

Tenuk slammed his fist down in frustration and glared around the room. The leaders of his fledgling business teams were gathered around the virtual table. They couldn't see Tenuk's real face, but the cartoon pangolin avatar that represented him was expressive enough.

"It was a tiny detail," said a small grey kitten, glancing nervously up the table. "The spec asked for ransoms to be payable in different coins, and we're used to working in Sats here for micropayments."

"I don't care, Sterix," said Tenuk, his voice ice cold and distorted by the privacy filter. "I can't believe a basic error like that got through testing." He turned his attention to the leader of the quality assurance team, represented by swirling lines of light making a glowing, animated 3D sphere that hovered in place in the virtual room. "How did you not pick this up?"

"We ran all the standard tests," said a disembodied voice. "We know what we're doing. The sandbox payments worked perfectly."

"I don't pay you for standard tests and automated audits," said Tenuk. "You need to get under the skin of the software. The client expects it. I expect it. The Steamyard's reputation hangs on the quality of our product and the value it delivers. We'll be lucky to break even on this job. You know the penalties in your contracts. Pray that the client doesn't trigger compensation payments."

He muted the two audio feeds, ignoring their mutters of protest, and turned his attention to the pixelated being that stood by his side. "Admin," he said, "what are the latest figures?"

"In the last twenty-four hours, the Privet Easter egg has been opened 9,480 times," came a calm and competent voice. The avatar's classic CryptoPunk look extended from its spiky hair down to its black boots. "That's down on the peak of fifty thousand a day and we're seeing a rapid tail-off of engagement."

"Where are we against revenue targets?" asked Tenuk.

"Low," said the Admin. "We're down more than thirty percent on projections. However, the hole in the payment gateway has been repaired so we're getting full value from the long tail of ransoms."

"Good," said Tenuk, mulling over the problem. "Is there any demographic we can target with a second round of injections?"

"Yes," replied the Admin. "Analysis shows lower engagement than expected in Pacific territories among smart device gamers."

"That's the new target," said Tenuk decisively. "Sterix, I want social engineering teams straight in there and start circulating the updated worm on all the social channels. You screwed up, you fix it. The targets for the territory are doubled."

"But Pangolin…" said the nervous grey kitten avatar.

"No excuses," said Tenuk. "If you want to be part of The Steamyard, you deliver. I'm watching."

The kitten and the abstract sphere vanished. "Admin," said Tenuk, "Keep an eye on them."

"Of course, Pangolin," said the pixelated figure. "I have all the team leaders under surveillance. I will report any anomalies."

The call ended, leaving Tenuk alone at the table. He looked out of the virtual office window to the crowds of avatars strolling past. He realised he was sweating. Back in the real world, the apartment was hot despite the cooling systems he'd installed for his equipment. The temperatures in Austin were rising as spring gave way to summer, and he knew it would get worse before it got better.

An alert pinged, and Tenuk frowned as he saw Jack Sladen's ID flash up in the air. He wasn't expecting a call until their scheduled meeting a few hours later. He would have to take this in person.

"Good morning, Jack," he said. He glanced at the time and realised that while concentrating on Steamyard business he had missed the big announcement. "The launch broadcast looked excellent," he lied. "I caught the livestream over breakfast."

"You watched all of it?" asked Jack.

Tenuk thought quickly. What had gone wrong? What had he missed? "I had a call come in from our development team," he said. "I didn't see the whole thing."

"Your people at Whitford Networks screwed up on the security," said Jack. "Their data centre defence systems took down a news drone right at the end of the live feed."

Dammit, thought Tenuk. It was barely eight in the morning, and he was already wondering what else could go wrong today.

"Zara and our PR people are on the case," said Jack. "I didn't see the incident but there was a lot of fuss among the press corps. At the moment it's being treated as a bird strike and that's exactly how it needs to stay. I'm still at Dunswyke and I've told Whitford to make sure that the news drone is retrieved, and the damage is consistent with our story."

Tenuk tapped a few keys and quickly found the news channel stream of the press conference. He watched the last few minutes carefully. Not only was the defence drone that had taken down the camera briefly visible on freeze frame, but there was also a clear shot of Angus and Ella skulking behind the Sladen Foundation headquarters. Jack wouldn't have any idea of the trouble that image could cause on its own.

"I've found the recording," he said. "It's not obvious unless you know what you're looking for."

"I don't care," said Jack. "It's frankly embarrassing, Tenuk. It drew attention away from the launch announcement, and it risks overshadowing the countdown to the presale."

"I'm sure it'll be fine, Jack," said Tenuk. "Is Zara running sentiment analysis for the Foundation?"

"Yes, she is," said Jack. "So far, it's positive, but Zara tells me that there are images circulating already. I don't want any awkward questions about our activities at Dunswyke. It's the last thing we need for the brand and our reputation."

Tenuk stifled a sigh. All the man seemed to be concerned about was public image. Jack's ego was remarkably fragile under the bluff and confident exterior. The project was going perfectly, and this would be a storm in a teacup. "I'll get onto Ella and Angus right now," he said. "At least you can be confident that the security systems are as tight as they can be."

"Yes, I suppose so," said Jack. "Their work's been thorough. I'll leave you to deal with them. I'm staying here a little longer than planned to make sure everything goes smoothly."

"I'll see you when you get back," said Tenuk. "Everything is under control here."

"Good," said Jack. "Let me know immediately if there is any change." He ended the call.

Tenuk had no doubt that there were others poring over the footage as he was. Someone would spot the hunter drone, know what it was, and wonder why it was there. Annoyingly, Jack was right. This was a situation that needed to be managed.

"Admin," he called into the air.

"Yes, Tenuk," said the calm and competent voice.

"Get into this original footage and edit the last two seconds," he said. "It needs to look like a bird strike. There's a database to hand of compromised access details for all the news channels. You'll find your way in easily. Cover your tracks well."

"Yes, Tenuk."

"Find any other copies that are circulating online and edit them if you can, take them down if you can't," he continued. "You can liaise with the Sladen Foundation PA. Her name's Zara."

"Yes, Tenuk. I am already in contact with Zara."

Tenuk steepled his fingers, wondering what to do about the glimpse of Angus and Ella. He knew they were keeping very low profiles, but surely no one in authority would be able to identify them in the crowd from the fraction of a second that the drone had passed over them. It would be more trouble than it was worth to try and remove them from the footage, however skilled his team of cybercriminals and black hat hackers. "That's all I need for now," he said.

"Yes, Tenuk," said the Admin, "I'll make this a priority."

"Good," said Tenuk. "Let me know when you're done. I'll deal with Whitford now." He looked at the clock. When Jack was abroad, he preferred Tenuk to be in the office in person, and that meant he only had a limited amount of time to deal with extra-curricular matters. He cursed Angus under his breath. The defence drones were overkill. They might provide an extra layer of protection, but if something like this happened again, it was likely to attract unwanted attention to the location. The last thing Tenuk needed was for anyone to come snooping and stumble on the hidden data centre. That could spell disaster and the end of all their grand plans.

Tenuk pinged a secure meeting link to Angus and got an instant response. Less than a minute later, he was back in his virtual office, glaring at a monkey in a blue and white striped shirt.

"What do you want, King Katong?" asked Angus. "Or are you hiding behind that Pangolin handle these days."

Tenuk clamped down on his anger, resisting the windup. He should never have tracked this man down, let alone brought him into the project. He was a liability, a loose cannon, and the sooner he could be disposed of, the better.

"King Katong is long gone," said Tenuk, his voice level and formal. "You would do well to remember that names from the past are still of interest to certain authorities. I'm sure the infosec community would like to know the whereabouts of The Monkey."

Stalemate.

"Alright, *Pangolin*," replied Angus, emphasising the name. "What do you want?"

"You're sailing close to the wind," said Tenuk. "You and Ella were picked up on the news drone footage at today's grand launch." The monkey avatar raised an eyebrow. "A fleeting glimpse, but you were seen."

"She's got more to worry about than I have," said Angus. His avatar shrugged.

Tenuk changed the subject. He was in a hurry to leave for the office. "Your hunter should have stayed in its hide," he said. "Get the drone it captured and set it up to look like a bird strike."

"Sure, straight away," said Angus sarcastically. "Anything else I can do? You know I'm always at the service of the Sladen Foundation and the mighty Steamyard."

"Nothing else," said Tenuk sharply. "I'll be in touch." He hit the exit button with a burst of anger that took him by surprise. He didn't want to go back to the old days. The future was bright, and it would take more than Angus the Monkey and his silly games to ruin it. Tenuk grabbed his jacket and headed out of the apartment into the bright, clear morning sunshine. The day could only get better.

●

In London, the Argentum office was in uproar. Susie, distraught, was in tears, memories of Ella's betrayal flooding back. Noor was doing her best to calm her friend. Cameron paced the office, agitated and angry.

"Call the police," urged Sandeep. "They need to know."

Cameron shook her head. "There's no point," she said. "They didn't go after Ella for the attack on the office because everything she did was explained away as a coincidence, and they caught the gunmen, so there was nothing more they could do."

"She was named as one of the Snake River team," said Joel. "Wasn't she a suspect in the murder investigation when the lad at the power station drowned?"

"That ended up as a verdict of accidental death," said Ross. "No evidence to say otherwise. The police won't be interested in her."

"What about Angus?" said Joel. "There's got to be something on him."

"Nothing," said Sandeep. "We didn't have anything concrete that they could pin on him after Snake River."

"His house burned down, didn't it?" said Michelle suddenly. "The news reports said it was arson, but no one was ever charged. Surely that would put him on the police radar?"

Sandeep perked up. "Yes, it would," he said. "I bet there's an insurance company or a council department somewhere that wants to know what happened as well."

"We can tell them where to find him. They may want a word," said Joel.

"Good call," said Cameron. "I think it's still a slim chance, but can you two follow up and get the authorities interested?"

"Sure thing," said Sandeep. "Shell, have you got the report from the fire? Who was the officer in charge?"

"I'll check," said Michelle. "Give me a minute."

"What are you going to do?" asked Ross. "Are you going back to Jack Sladen with this?"

Cameron stopped pacing and looked thoughtful. "I'm not sure," she said. "I don't know if he knows what's going on here. He could have hired them completely innocently, or he could be up to his neck in a conspiracy we've barely touched."

"You still don't trust him," said Joel.

"Are you surprised?" said Cameron.

Joel looked embarrassed. "Actually, I think your instincts are pretty good. I don't think I trust him myself anymore."

"If we can't trust him, can we trust his project?" said Noor. "The revised whitepaper for Diaulos is out. I think we take it apart word by word and see what he's really doing."

Susie, still red eyed but calmer, spoke up. "I want to help with that," she said. "Have we got access to any of the code yet?"

Cameron shook her head. "It hasn't been released to the public repositories," she said. "They haven't exactly been transparent about the project."

"That's bad for so many reasons," said Ross. "Apart from anything else, it means that there probably hasn't been an independent audit of the smart contracts that automate everything."

Cameron snapped her fingers. "Brilliant, Ross!" she said. "That's our way in." She grinned, a plan starting to form in her mind. "Keep our investigations quiet. I'm going to try and persuade him to commission an audit from us. When we get our hands on the code, we can run it through our analytical models and see if there's anything sinister underneath."

"Cunning," said Ross. "I know you don't trust him, but does he trust you enough to just grant you access?"

"I think so," said Cameron. "He went to a lot of trouble to track me down, and he's been a complete gentleman. I've given him no reason to mistrust me. It's entirely possible that he'll ask us to do an audit without any prompting."

"I'm hoping it's all above board," said Ross. "That Foundation DAO is such a bloody good idea." He sighed. "Well, let's get on with it. Shell's got those reports for you, Sandeep. She's pinging them over now."

Sandeep swung around to his screen and started reading through the message from Michelle. Joel was already deep in research and Noor and Susie were poring over the first few paragraphs of the whitepaper.

"I'm going to call in a few favours with my old Army colleagues," said Joel. "I think Pete needs to know about this as soon as he gets back from diving, as well. I wonder where the hunter drone came from. I need a better look at the last couple of seconds of the footage." He tapped a few keys, searching for the recording of the press conference. "That's odd," he continued, frowning. "I'm getting error messages on these links."

"Keep trying," said Cameron. "There's likely to be a lot of traffic on the servers. You won't be the only person digging around for it." She picked up her jacket. "I'll call Jack from home. I want to keep this as casual and friendly as possible."

Susie looked up from her screen, eyes still red. "Will you ask him about Ella?" she said quietly.

"I don't know yet," said Cameron. "Do you want me to?"

Susie gave her a lopsided smile. "I honestly don't know," she admitted. "Do whatever you need to do."

"Okay," said Cameron. She raised her voice and called out to the rest of the team. "Let me know if you find anything."

"Sure thing," replied Sandeep, the others murmuring their agreement. Cameron headed out of the door and off towards home.

13:   METABAND

The atmosphere at the Sladen Foundation headquarters was tense. Jack was pacing up and down the office, scowling. The five staff who made up the Foundation's local management team were at their desks and keeping their heads down. They avoided meeting his eyes. Ella was sitting quietly on a plush new sofa in the corner of the room, her fingers worrying at a piece of plastic wrapping that was still stuck in a seam at the base of the arm rest. There was a faint buzz of noise from the ground floor of the bastle where the customer service team sat under the great arched ceiling. They dealt with the tiny percentage of calls that could not be handled by the initial responses of AI systems and service bots. Today the human representatives were rushed off their feet with the volume of enquiries.

A flowing spectrum of colour covered almost the whole of a large screen. It represented the global sentiment around Sladen Foundation and the Diaulos brands, analysed in real time from all the calls, social comments, internet searches and automated chats. There had been a huge spike in activity following the press conference. The colours flowed seamlessly from amber to green. An undercurrent of red that had been visible in the first few minutes following the launch had all but vanished.

Jack glanced at the screen and felt the knot of worry and annoyance in his stomach start to dissipate. Perhaps they'd gotten away with it. He wanted to see the playback of the press conference to be sure, but there seemed to be a technical glitch. Samuel, his head of PR and communications, was tapping at his keyboard and looking puzzled.

"Has Zara tracked down that recording yet?" asked Jack.

"Not yet," said Samuel. He tapped his earpiece. "Ah, wait, yes, she's found it. Seems there was a database error at the news channel. It's all online now."

The sentiment monitoring display shrank into the corner of the wallscreen, and the footage of the press conference took pride of place. Jack watched the first minute and nodded, satisfied with his performance. "Fast forward to the end," he said.

They watched the video from the news drone as it circled the bastle. Ella's eyes were fixed on the screen, and she frowned as she caught a fleeting glimpse of herself. The drone turned again towards the moorland. Samuel slowed the playback, frame by frame. There was a flash of something black in the air, then nothing. Jack exhaled in relief. He hadn't been aware that he had been holding his breath. The news drone had apparently not picked up any visuals of the hunter drone, and the secrets of the moorland and the cave beneath it were safe.

"Bird strike," said Samuel, satisfied. "It looked messier on the live feed, but accidents happen, I guess. I don't know what the news teams were going on about."

"If they send their drones off in an area like this with so much wildlife around, they should be prepared for an impact," said Jack, back to his buoyant self. "I'm surprised that it doesn't happen more often." He glanced at Ella. "Have we managed to retrieve the debris?" he asked.

"I'll go and find out," she said. She stood up and smoothed her rumpled skirt. As she took a step towards the main door, it opened to reveal Angus holding a large box.

"I won't come in," he said, looking pointedly at the brand new pale grey carpet on the floor. "I'm covered in mud." He put the box down just inside the door. "Here's your drone."

Jack bent down and opened the lid cautiously. Inside he found the body of the drone, virtually intact but for a spectacular dent on one side of the casing. At the bottom of the box lay the shattered remains of the rotors and the camera lens, and a lot of black feathers.

"Anything on the hard disk?" he murmured.

"It didn't survive the drop," said Angus quietly, tapping a finger on the side of his nose.

Jack nodded, understanding the message. Whatever might have been saved by the drone had been wiped, or the disk corrupted and broken beyond repair.

"Thanks, Angus," he said out loud. "Get this over to the outside broadcast unit in the car park. They're waiting for it."

"Will do." Angus picked up the box and lumbered back down the stairs on the outside of the bastle.

"Good," said Jack to the room in general. "I'm glad that's all cleared up. Great work today, everyone." He looked up at the wallscreen, once again filled with the waves of the sentiment tracker. The overwhelming image was of deepening green, global approval for the Sladen Foundation. Figures in a table on the corner ticked up as the volume of calls and mentions increased. A world map view showed that their PR efforts were reaching across the globe, following the sun.

Jack's smartscreen pinged, a private call incoming from an ID that made his smile grow even broader.

"Cameron," he said happily. "How lovely to hear from you. Did you catch the press conference?"

He was so absorbed in the call that he didn't notice the look of horror that crossed Ella's face, and barely heard the door slam behind her as she fled.

•

Cameron put down her smartscreen and smiled to herself. The seeds had been sown, and she had every confidence that the code for Diaulos and the automated investments of the Sladen Foundation DAO would be in her hands within the week. Now she had some research to do. She carefully cloaked her location and signed on to her favourite infosec forum. This was the busiest time of day for the group as Europe slid into the afternoon and America started work.

Sure enough, there were a lot of familiar handles on the chat. Cameron surfed the channels for a little while, incognito, laughing at the gallows-humour memes that proliferated in a community at the edge of the cybercrime abyss, and getting a feel for the latest vulnerabilities and exposures that were bubbling. The impact of the Privet attack had largely dissipated and there were rumours of in-fighting among the perpetrators.

Cameron dug as deep as she dared to try and find clues to real people involved in the ransomware, correlating the traffic around the Santa virus with the spread of Privet, but there was very little to go on. She needed Ross, Michelle and their shady mates to explore that avenue down in the depths of the dark web.

There was plenty of chat about the Sladen Foundation announcement. In this community, hidden from the spiders that trawled the web for Jack's sentiment analysis, the tone was universally sceptical. Everyone had spent time in their career cleaning up after one or other of the regular Sladen Group software vulnerabilities, and very few people were speaking up in favour of the project. They echoed Ross's feelings that the whole concept was a brilliant idea, but the execution was likely to be flawed. For all that her opinion of Jack was softening, Cameron had to agree.

She dipped into a discussion about the Diaulos validation nodes and their link to the MetaBand hardware. In the back of her mind a guilty thought nudged her. She hadn't yet spoken to Ben. Based on the announcement, there was nothing for him to worry about, but the devil would be in the detail, and the detail was sorely lacking.

Someone on the thread had started reading the whitepaper. Cameron made a note to flag this to Noor so that she could pick up on the same discussion and compare findings. 'Passive validation of transactions by MetaBand receivers is an interested proposal,' said the post, 'but what's the storage capacity of these units? How long a blockchain can they hold?'

That's a good question, thought Cameron. She knew who to ask. She logged off the forum and placed a call to Ben. He didn't answer. Cameron squashed a feeling of unease. It was still early morning for him. He was most likely in a team meeting, catching up with colleagues and planning for the day.

She stroked the cat and brewed another coffee. Impatient, she tried again. No answer. She left a brief, non-committal message, just in case someone else picked it up. It occurred to her that in the long months they had been apart he might have met another girl, and the idea hurt her more than she cared to admit.

To distract herself, she returned to the computer and followed her germ of an idea through the search engines, building a picture of the global MetaBand manufacturing operation. Ben was engineering the designs for the microsats and receivers, but the printing would be done local to the network installations around the world. Sure enough, there was an additive manufacturing facility in London that had held the MetaBand contract for earlier versions of the receiver units. She recognised the address, just twenty minutes away from her flat, down past the Elephant and Castle. It was only three o'clock, not too late in the day to pay them a visit. She tried Ben's number one more time. Still nothing. The walk would do her good, she figured, and if Ben decided to return her call, she would be able to answer.

By the time Cameron reached the small industrial estate, he still hadn't called. The production manager was expecting her, thanks to a lucky connection who had arranged an introduction while she walked.

"You must be Cameron." Her contact was a slim black man with a neat beard, a few years her senior. He held out his hand. "I'm Olu," he continued. "Andy's told me all about you. He says you want to see what we're doing with MetaBand."

"Nice to meet you, Olu," she said. "Yes, I remembered the documentary Andy made last year about this place." She gestured around the industrial park, a green and vibrant space nestling between the train tracks on one side and rows of tall terraces and blocks of flats on the other. "It's lovely here."

"We like it," said Olu with a smile. "We're getting close to being the most sustainable industrial park in London. We produce our own electricity, we sell the excess straight into the local community, and we keep the manufacturing processes as carbon neutral as possible, from raw materials onwards."

"That's wonderful," said Cameron diplomatically. She'd seen the programme Andy had produced and she knew the story behind the park.

There was a beep from Olu's pocket, and he pulled out a small smartscreen. "Ah, good," he said. "Your security credentials have passed screening. I just need a facial recognition scan so we can get you into the building." He flicked the camera on and held it up. Cameron looked dutifully into the lens, turning her head slowly to the left and right. There was a pause, and Olu nodded and tucked the smartscreen back into his pocket. "All done."

Cameron followed him to the door. "Tell me more about MetaBand," she said. "Are you picking up the manufacture of the next generation equipment for London?"

"Are we ever," said Olu fervently. "It's not just London. We're covering most of the country. We've already started the rollout. It's a tight timescale and we need to build up a lot of stock in a short time."

The factory floor was a hive of activity, rows of printers churning out components. It was a smaller version of the Silvera family firm, the company that Charlie ran, although they were creating very different things. The stock shelves were bulging with packaged units ready for despatch to the fitters around the country.

"We're not just printing," said Olu. "All the old units are being decommissioned here and the materials we salvage get rolled back into the manufacturing process. It's an end-to-end holistic cycle. Want to come and see?"

"I'd love to," said Cameron.

Through a roller door to an adjacent unit was the recycling area where skips full of old equipment of all types were being sorted ready to be recycled into additive materials once again. One side of the workshop was sectioned off and enclosed, and Cameron could see robot arms dipping and picking and sorting items with elegant precision. On the open floor, most of the workforce was human.

"What's the difference?" asked Cameron, gesturing at the enclosed area.

"Those in there are really old bits of random kit that don't have any reliable documentation," said Olu. "Things that have been recovered from demolition sites or refurbishments. We have no idea what dodgy materials have been used to make them or the condition of the place they were kept. Until they've been checked over, it's not safe to handle them. We're specialists. We get all the things that no one else can manage in here."

"The MetaBand receivers don't end up there, do they?" asked Cameron.

Olu shook his head. "No way," he said. "Everything we make nowadays is recorded down to the last detail on the open ledger. You can see if there have been any changes made in the design or extra components added. It makes our lives a whole lot simpler."

Fascinated as she was with the recycling effort, Cameron was here to check Ben's story on the new MetaBand designs. "Olu," she said, "do you have access to the design ledger for the new receivers?"

He shook his head. "I don't get involved in that side. If you want the full history, you'd need to talk to the admin people. I can introduce you."

"Thanks, that would be good," said Cameron. She changed tack. "You've made both versions of these things, haven't you? What are the differences between the old and the new units? Why are the old ones being replaced?"

"The casing is much sleeker, and the processors and data storage in the new ones have been upgraded," said Olu instantly. "They've got huge capacity compared to the original units."

"How much storage are we talking about here?" said Cameron.

"That's jumped from the old ten Gig units to three hundred Gigabytes," said Olu.

Cameron wasn't altogether surprised. If Jack's announcement about the MetaBand receivers being full nodes on the Diaulos blockchain, they might well need that much room in a few years' time.

"The processors are nuts, though," Olu continued. "They're incredibly fast. I've only ever seen them in military grade hardware." He put his hand over his mouth. "Not sure I was supposed to say that."

"Your secret is safe with me," said Cameron. "You've seen all my security clearances. This may well be important, and I really appreciate your help." Another question occurred to her. "Why are they having to replace the old units?" she asked. "Surely they could just be upgraded?"

Olu shook his head. "No," he said. "It's much easier and cheaper to change them, and the old units can't access the signals from the new microsats. It's a whole new system." He looked up sharply as an alarm sounded from the factory floor. A light flashed above one of the printers. "Sorry, Cameron. I have to sort out this jam."

"I'll leave you to it," said Cameron. "Thank you so much for the tour. It's been really useful."

"Any time." Olu opened the door and Cameron stepped out into the sunshine of the green space again.

She started back towards her home, mulling over the new information. The storage capacity of the nodes was overkill. Jack must have grand ideas for his Diaulos if he thought it would overtake Bitcoin's length. The processors confused her, though. The chain was being secured by choosing a random wearable device to sign for the opening of each new block. There was no need for such a high-spec processer in the validator nodes. There was no algorithm to compute, no competition to confirm a block. Only the Bitcoin and Monero blockchains were allowed to run Proof of Work consensus mechanisms, and mining was strictly controlled.

What could the processors be for, if they neither secured the Diaulos chain nor improved the connections for the MetaBand users? Cameron walked on, oblivious to the people and traffic around her as she battled to understand what Jack could possibly be planning.

14:   TEXAN SECRETS

Cameron was halfway home when she felt the screen in her pocket vibrating. Ben had finally returned her call. She slipped her earpods in, took a deep breath, and answered.

"Hi, Cam," he said cheerily, "what's up?"

Cameron was taken aback. This was quite a different Ben to the person who had called her out of desperation just a few weeks before. A rush of unfamiliar background noise confused her further.

"Where are you?" she asked.

"I'm in the car," said Ben.

That explained it, thought Cameron, both the noise and the good mood.

"What are you driving, you petrolhead?"

"You wouldn't believe me if I told you," said Ben, raising his voice as the engine revved.

"No…" said Cameron, "it's not… It's a Mustang?"

"You bet," said Ben.

There was no video feed, but Cameron could visualise the broad grin on his face just the same. The Mustang had been Ben's dream car, out of reach on a small island almost entirely given over to electric vehicles and shared rides. On the Texas plains, it was quite a different matter.

"It's fantastic," Ben continued. "Ah, Cameron, I wish you were here. You would love this."

Cameron's heart jolted. "Maybe one day," she said.

"What did you want?" Ben asked, oblivious to Cameron's discomfort. "Did you find out something about these designs?"

"Yes," said Cameron, relieved to be back on firmer ground. "I called you to let you know that the changes you mentioned fit with the spec they announced for the Diaulos network management. I don't think there's anything to worry about."

"I'm glad you think so," said Ben, "but I'm still not convinced. Someone rode roughshod over all the usual processes, and I don't like it." He paused. "Hold on," he said. "Just coming up to an intersection."

Cameron kept walking, watching the silent traffic glide along beside her on the busy London street and listening to the unfamiliar road noise and the hum of the car engine from the empty plains of Texas. The growl of the Mustang settled to a steady low roar and Ben came back on the line.

"Sorry, Cam," he said. "Look, there is still something bugging me about all this. I persuaded the account management team to let me do a client visit to Statesman Tech. I'm on the way there now."

Cameron stopped dead in her tracks. "Ben, no! You don't know what you're getting into."

"What do you mean?" he asked.

"I mean that there is something really wrong here. Didn't you see the press conference this morning?"

"I was already in the car," said Ben. "You know I couldn't watch and drive. It's not one of those cutesy little electric pods. Why?"

"Dammit, Ben," said Cameron. "Right at the end of the broadcast we saw two people in the crowd who should not have been there."

"Who?" said Ben, exasperated.

"Ella Stanford," said Cameron, "and Angus White."

"You're joking," said Ben. "What the hell were they doing anywhere near this project?"

"Do you understand now?" said Cameron.

"I'm not stupid," snapped Ben. "All you're saying is that I was right all along. I know there is something fishy going on."

"Why can't you leave this to me?" said Cameron.

"Because it's not all about you," said Ben. "I want to get to the bottom of that design change. The buck stops where the first decision was made. Right now, with the records all over the place, that's me."

"You're not responsible for this whole project," protested Cameron.

"Doesn't matter," said Ben. "If this was a construction project and the building collapsed because of a change to the spec, I'd be responsible because I'd followed the design without questioning it or checking the files."

"Oh, good grief, Ben," said Cameron. "This is hardly a matter of life and death."

"Listen to yourself, Cameron," said Ben, exasperated. "You go on about the hidden cost of cybercrime, the people that are affected, the organised crime groups behind ransomware. I've always trusted your instincts. Maybe you can trust mine for a change?"

"I'm sorry," said Cameron quietly.

"That's okay," said Ben. "I have to go. I'm getting into traffic. I'll let you know if anything interesting comes out of this visit. Bye, Cam."

"Ben," said Cameron, "be careful." A thought suddenly occurred to her. "There's someone I know working at Statesman Tech. Not Jack. Someone else that I think I can trust..." She tailed off as she realised that the call had ended, and she was talking to empty space. Cameron cursed. She quickened her pace. She needed to get home and find a way to reach Cloverleaf before Ben reached Austin.

●

The sun was hot and the downtown traffic, both vehicles and pedestrians, was unusually busy. Tenuk gave up and hailed a rickshaw at the southern end of the bridge. He settled in his seat and took a long drink from his water bottle as the cyclist weaved expertly around the traffic jams and groups of tourists admiring the view over the lake. The terrain was flat at the shore, but the road climbed sharply as they approached the Statesman Tech offices. The solar sail hanging from the top of the building gleamed like a mirror in the bright morning sunshine.

The rickshaw pulled up on the corner of the block opposite the main entrance. Tenuk tapped the payment chip and added a handsome tip. He would not be late after all. Mood considerably improved, he stood and waited patiently for the crosswalk lights to turn in his favour. Two lanes of autocars whirred gently along, their occupants busy on their screens or dozing. In the third lane, reserved for driver-operated vehicles, a long, low sports car growled gently. Tenuk wrinkled his nose at the unfamiliar smell of the exhaust fumes. The car turned and disappeared down a ramp into the darkness of the parking garage beneath the building. The traffic stopped. Tenuk crossed the road and took the steps up to the atrium two at a time. The elevator bore him aloft and he walked into the office at ten o'clock on the dot.

It was a hive of activity. A six-hour time lag to the Dunswyke site meant that everyone was playing catchup on the events of what for them had been early morning. Tenuk listened carefully to the buzz. The tone was excited, positive, no wrong notes. Good. He greeted his staff with an open, honest smile, congratulated them on a job well done, and reminded them that there was still a lot of work to do as the system went live.

The workflow screens were flickering with activity as tasks moved steadily along the road to completion. Another screen showed live feeds of the money markets, tracking the price and volume of coin trading, and yet another was running the Diaulos promotional videos on loop. Tenuk had no difficulty keeping the smile on his face. It was all going like clockwork. In one corner, he spotted Connie and Isaac deep in conversation. He strolled over to them.

"All okay here?" he asked.

Connie looked up with a bright smile. "Fine, thanks, Tenuk," she said. "I was coming to see you. We have a visit scheduled from the team handling the MetaBand engineering."

Tenuk frowned. "The folks down south? The satellite company? I had nothing in my diary."

"That's them," said Connie. "We were due a routine visit from the account manager soon and apparently one of their engineers is in the area, so he's calling in to see us."

"It's just informal," said Isaac. "The message says he has a question about one of the design points and it'll be easier to clarify face to face."

"Which component are they querying?" said Tenuk. "They're not just making the satellites, you know. They've set up the receiver printing specifications for our worldwide manufacturing partners as well."

"No idea," said Connie with a shrug. "He'll be here any minute. You can ask him yourself if you want."

Tenuk shook his head. "I'll leave it to you," he said. "Call me if you have any questions. I'll be in Jack's office sorting out a few things." He turned and headed for the large glass-walled office in the corner of the floor. As he closed the door behind him, he dropped the smile. Why would an engineer be coming here, he wondered? What had they picked up on? Tuesday was not turning out to be as easy as he had hoped. He sat down at Jack's desk and started to work through the odd tasks that he was expected to cover in the boss's absence. Out of the corner of his eye, he watched the CCTV feed from the hallway between the elevator and office. A tall, dark man appeared, looked around to get his bearings, and started towards the main door. That must be the engineer.

The next time Tenuk glanced up, the man was sitting in the coffee area with his back to the glass office. Isaac and Connie were chatting and smiling, putting him at his ease. He seemed relaxed. It must be as routine and informal as they had thought.

A message appeared on the screen from Connie. 'No problems,' it said. 'He's running over a couple of the design changes on the receivers. He has some ideas on different printing materials they could use in future batches, and he wanted to know more about how the units are being used.'

Tenuk's eyes narrowed. That was an awfully specific question about a piece of the complex jigsaw of MetaBand's global network that he did not want placed under scrutiny. He thought he had covered the tracks of the design change well enough to avoid any attention. This had to be pure coincidence, an innocent question from an over-enthusiastic engineer, but he wanted to be sure. He emerged from the office and made his way over to the coffee machine. He busied himself preparing his cup, then turned with a smile and found himself looking directly into the eyes of the visitor.

He recognised him immediately.

They had met in passing in England, back in another life. Tenuk recalled exactly the moment that he came face to face with the SimCavalier, and this man had been with her. He turned back to the coffee machine, concentrating hard on controlling his emotions. In the fleeting moment, he was sure that there had been no flicker of recognition in the other man's eyes. Was he in the clear?

"May I introduce you?" said Connie behind him. "This is Ben from LekSat. Ben, I'd like you to meet my boss, Tenuk."

The coffee machine hissed and spluttered at the opportune moment, drowning out his name. Tenuk gave Ben a bright smile.

"Nice to meet you," he said. "Excuse me, I have a call scheduled." He walked calmly back into Jack's office and closed the door, his stomach churning. He was almost sure that his luck had held, and that Ben had no idea who he was.

From her desk, Chloe watched as Tenuk walked back into Jack's office and closed the door. She knew the man well enough by now to read the nuances of his body language, and she recognised extreme tension and the tight control he was exerting over his reactions. He might have thought he had hidden his discomfort, but it was plain as the eye could see for Chloe. She immediately turned to see what had prompted this sudden change of demeanour. Connie and Isaac were talking to a visitor in the lounge area by the kitchen. Tenuk had been clutching a cup of coffee, so it seemed likely that he'd been over there too, and common courtesy suggested he would have been introduced to the stranger. Who was this visitor, and why was Tenuk so rattled?

As she watched, Isaac stood up and went back to his desk. She could see him swiping through files on his screen, searching for something. Connie had also stepped away and was distracted by a message on her screen. The visitor was sitting alone and looking around him with a slightly lost air. Chloe saw her opportunity. She picked up her cup and made her way to the lounge area, ignoring a notification that buzzed insistently on her smartscreen. Whatever it was, it could wait.

"Hi," she said brightly as she waited for the coffee machine to do its thing.

The man looked at her and smiled. He was dark and handsome with deep brown eyes. Chloe had never seen him before.

"Oh, Chloe," said Connie, glancing up from her screen. "This is Ben from LekSat Engineering. He's been turning the MetaBand hardware designs into reality."

"Nice to meet you, Chloe," said Ben.

"You're British!" said Chloe. "I love your accent. It's good to meet you too. Have you been over here long?"

"A little less than a year," said Ben, ducking his head in a way that Chloe found frankly adorable.

"You're working on the satellites and receivers, I guess?" she said. "I met one of your colleagues at the start of the year. Mateo."

"That's right," said Ben. "He's the main account manager. I had a couple of things to check so I came up instead this time."

Chloe wondered why Tenuk had reacted so oddly to this genial British man. It seemed to be a routine visit. It added to the mystery of Tenuk's true identity, a mystery Chloe was determined to solve.

Isaac re-joined them. "Here's the original design change approval you needed," he said, handing a tablet to Ben. "It's all in order and I've verified it against the records on the chain."

Ben scrutinised the details. "Yeah, that looks okay," he said. "I don't know why I couldn't access this before."

"How much detail can you see at LekSat?" asked Isaac. "I'm not sure what your permissions are for these records."

"We don't have access to anything within your databases," said Ben. "I don't quite know how it works, but anyone can see key decision points along the project lifecycle, and contractors like us can see the formal paperwork. For this one, we got the new spec through, but we could only access the public view of the change note, not the detail."

"There must be something wrong in the settings," said Chloe. "Do you want me to have look at that, Connie?"

"Sure, Chloe," said Connie. She peered at Isaac's tablet. "Who signed it off? Oh, Mark Esquith."

"Any chance I could have a quick chat with him or one of his team?" asked Ben. "It would help in assessing this new material we're considering for the next batch of components."

Isaac shook his head. "No can do," he said. "Mark left at the end of last year. I'm not in touch with him. Are you, Connie?"

"Not at all," said Connie. "I guess HR will have his details. As for the team…" She shrugged. "All the design work was done by another company in the Sladen group, based in Malaysia, I think. Mark kept them straight on what we needed to run the software, they delivered the designs, and he finalised any changes that were needed for things like, you know, local regulations or new system requirements."

"Okay," said Ben. He didn't seem unduly concerned. "It's not that important. I guess the main thing for you is that whatever they're made of, the units are right at the top of the range to handle the high-speed processing."

Connie looked confused. "Not really," she said. "It's the storage that really matters, to hold distributed copies of the blockchain. The processors just manage new transaction validation. Standard stuff."

"My mistake," said Ben lightly. "I was thinking of another project there for a moment. Sorry." He ducked his head again and gave them a crooked smile. "I think I've taken up enough of your time, and I have what I need. I'll pass that approval detail on to Mateo when I get back." He stood up and shook hands with each of them in turn.

"It's nice to meet you," said Chloe. She hadn't touched her coffee. It was cold.

"You too," said Ben, squeezing her hand.

Chloe watched his retreating back as Isaac escorted him towards the elevator, then looked at Connie. "What was that all about?" she asked.

Connie shrugged. "I have no idea," she said. "He seems to have what he came for, so everyone's happy."

Apart from Tenuk, though Chloe. She looked over at Jack's office where Tenuk was skulking. He was deep in conversation with someone unseen, online, and making notes.

Back at her desk, Chloe found a missed call notification from an unexpected ID. Why was the SimCavalier trying to reach her, and did a call from the only British person she knew have anything to do with the Englishman who had just left? She picked up her smartscreen and looked for a chance to slide out of the office, but Connie appeared before she could escape.

"You thought he was cute, didn't you?" she said with a wink.

"The British guy? Yeah, kind of," said Chloe. She changed the subject quickly. "What's up with Tenuk?"

"Oh, he's in one of those funny moods again," said Connie. "I think Jack's been stressing about the launch and Tenuk's first in line to be hit with any flak."

"That's probably it," said Chloe. But in the back of her mind, she was processing some odd clues and ideas, and pieces of an unfamiliar jigsaw were starting to assemble themselves into a picture that worried her.

Connie put her hand on Chloe's shoulder. "Don't worry about it," she said. "It's past midday. The settings on that design change can wait. Shall we grab some lunch?"

"Sure," said Chloe. She really wanted to keep digging, finding out more about Tenuk, but she had no wish to raise any suspicions. Looking over at the corner office one more time, she could see that Tenuk was still talking, a scowl on his face. He was having a difficult morning. She closed down her screen. She would return the SimCavalier's call later. "Let's go."

15:   REPUTATIONS

"I don't care, Tenuk," said Jack. "We have to be seen to be squeaky clean. If an independent audit of the contracts for the DAO and Diaulos is what it takes, then that's what we'll do."

He listened as Tenuk protested, drumming his fingers irritably on the table. Jack gazed out of the huge picture window that took up most of the gable end of the bastle. The late afternoon sunshine bathed the moorland in golden light, and Jack almost felt at home. Not quite. He'd shaken the dust of this region off his feet as a student, and whatever the publicity said, he knew he'd be bored if he stayed too long. He could not, however, deny its beauty.

"No, Tenuk," he said firmly as the stream of excuses dried up. "I know everything has been checked over with a fine-toothed comb already, but after that incident at the launch it really pays for us to show that we have nothing to hide. I don't understand your objections, and I'm disappointed that you didn't propose a second audit yourself."

There was an indrawing of breath on the other end of the call. Tenuk started to speak, and Jack cut him off.

"I'm releasing the code to a company I know here in London," said Jack. "Once we have their report and anything they find has been fixed, I want the contracts published. We're not waiting until the coin launch as we'd originally planned. If everything goes well, we can release them to coincide with the presale on Friday. This is all about my brand and my reputation. Don't ever forget who is in charge."

He didn't wait for an answer before ending the call. He was fed up with Tenuk's attitude. He'd had a long day and the adrenaline of the launch was starting to wear off. He dialled another number and waited patiently for it to connect, feeling the stress melting slowly away.

"Hi Jack." Cameron's voice echoed. "Give me a moment."

He heard the sound of quick footsteps. She was running up a set of stairs, he thought. She had always been active and eager, more likely to take the stairs than the elevator if she had a choice. Jack smiled. He was glad to have found her again.

There was the click of a lock and the insistent squeaking of a cat in the background. "Hush," said Cameron's voice.

Jack laughed.

"Not you, Jack," said Cameron, laughing along with him. "Now, what can I do for you?"

"The audit you suggested," said Jack. "I want to get that organised as soon as possible."

Cameron was practically purring. "I can get it started straight away," she said. "I'll send over a contract now for you to sign."

"Send it to my personal inbox," said Jack. "This doesn't go through any of the companies in the group. There are too many people with their own agendas, and I want this to be completely independent." As soon as the words were out of his mouth, he realised that he had voiced something he had never admitted before. He was struggling to trust the people closest to him.

"Understood," said Cameron, and Jack wondered if she had taken the request at face value or if she detected the undercurrent of concern that had prompted it. "We'll be very discreet."

"How long will it take?" he asked. "I need to get something into the press release for Friday's presale."

"There's no way we can run a full code quality review in that time," said Cameron. "We can give you an interim report with some headline findings, but you're looking at another couple of weeks to really get into the guts of the thing."

"That's fine," said Jack. "Get me the interim report on time and I'll pay you double. We'll look at scheduling the CQR after the presale has gone live."

"Okay," said Cameron. He could hear her tapping at keys in the background. "There, you should have the contract link now. It covers the full audit, but I've added a standard break clause between the interim report and the second phase of work. When I get this back with the access details, the team can get started straight away."

"Thanks, Cameron," said Jack. "Hey, how about dinner later this week. I'll be back in London on Thursday, and you should be done with the interim by then."

"Sure, Jack," she replied. "That'd be nice." There was a distinct and insistent miaow in the background. "I have to go," she said. "Orders from the boss. I'll look out for the signed documents. Bye, Jack."

"Bye, Cameron." He hung up and checked his private inbox. Sure enough, there was a secure link to a set of documents. Jack settled down to read the surprisingly straightforward contract Cameron had sent him. It was a quarter of the length of what he would have received from a contractor in Texas, with carefully worded clauses and the occasional dip into archaic legal terms under English law. It took him no time at all to skim through it.

Usually, he would pass something like this on to his legal team, but they would take days to come back to him, they would argue over the jurisdiction, and too many people would find out about the audit. He wanted to keep it to himself for now.

Running through the options in his head, he had a flash of inspiration. He could use Zara to check over the contract. He was almost certain that her training had extended beyond the virtual assistant role to a grasp of legal matters, and her logic was impeccable. As for access to the code base, that was more problematic. He considered simply handing Cameron his login credentials, but he knew that it was such terrible practice that she would be both furious and amused and would never let him live it down. He wasn't about to ask Tenuk. He didn't want him dealing directly with Cameron. The other option was Chloe. He had found her trustworthy and discreet so far.

He placed a call to her from his private line. She took a moment to pick up, and in the background there was the hum of a busy café or restaurant. It was obviously lunchtime in Austin.

"Chloe, this is Jack," he said. She may not have recognised the call ID.

"Oh!" she said. "Wait, let me go outside."

There was a clatter as she moved her chair and the background noise faded. "How can I help?" she asked.

"Could you arrange a new access link for the DAO codebase, please?" said Jack. "Zara will be in touch to add it to some paperwork shortly."

"Sure," said Chloe. "I'll check with Tenuk..."

"No," said Jack. "This is between you and me. Just set it up."

"I'm going to need an identifier for the records," said Chloe. "What should I put?"

Jack thought for a moment, then smiled. "Call it 'Kitty'."

"Okay," said Chloe. "I'll be back in the office in half an hour. I'll do it as soon as I get to my desk."

"Thanks, Chloe," he said. "Appreciate it. I'll let you get back to your lunch."

One part done, one to go. "Zara?" he said quietly.

"Yes, Jack," came the response from his screen. "What can I do for you?"

"Can you check over these documents for me, please, and if they pass muster, which I'm sure they will, let me know. You'll need to add access details to the schedule. Ask Chloe. She's generating them now. I need them back as soon as possible, this evening, if you can, so that I can sign them off."

"Yes, Jack. I'll do that straight away."

Jack leaned back in his chair and looked out at the view again. The shadows were getting longer, and a flock of sheep was gathering at a gate in the distance. As he watched, a quad bike hove into view towing a small trailer of feed. Between Chloe at lunch, Cameron's cat calling for its dinner, and now the local sheep, Jack was getting hungry. The building was quiet. The media circus had packed up and gone, and most of the staff had left for the evening. The only vehicles in the car park were his own car, the security pod, and the Whitford Networks van. Angus and Ella must still be on site.

They weren't in the building. They must be in the data centre. Jack walked slowly down the steps at the side of the bastle, marvelling again at the restoration of the crumbling stair. He followed the path towards the cliff, winding through the coppice. As he approached the entrance, he could see a sliver of light and he could hear voices.

"Hello?" he called as he walked into the cavern.

"Oh, hi Jack," said Ella. "Angus and I were just checking the network. Are you off now?"

"Yes, I thought I'd head into town for dinner," said Jack. "Will you join me?"

"We're busy," growled Angus.

Ella looked at them both. "You know, I'd like that," she said, a hint of defiance in her voice. "We're pretty much done here, aren't we, Angus?"

The man shook his head. "You go if you must," he said. "I haven't finished."

"Right," said Ella. "In that case, I'll see you tomorrow." She picked up her bag and turned her back on Angus. "Let's go."

Jack looked from one to the other. The atmosphere was charged but he didn't know where the tension had come from. His nerves were thrumming. Something was going on.

"I'll let security know that you're still here, Angus," said Jack. "See you tomorrow." He stepped aside to let Ella past him and followed her back outside.

She didn't say anything as they crossed the site towards the car park, their feet crunching in sync on the gravel. Even in the car, which now had the connectivity to navigate of its own accord, she stayed quiet, answering Jack's questions about her work and comments about the journey politely, but without enthusiasm.

"What would you like to eat?" asked Jack eventually, settling on an easy topic for discussion as the car swept along the darkening lanes.

She shrugged. "I'm easy," she said. "If we went all the way down to Newcastle, I know some excellent restaurants, but there isn't a lot of choice up here in the sticks. I guess Dunswyke is the best option. What do you suggest?"

"Oh, I have a few ideas," said Jack. "It's a lot better than it was when I was growing up here."

"Do you think that because you were young then, and craving the bright lights of the city," said Ella, looking sidelong at him.

He understood that she was teasing, and he was glad that she seemed to have relaxed. "Probably," he said with a grin. "Your hometown always feels parochial, doesn't it?" He nodded at the great tower of the castle that dominated the skyline as they approached the town. "I used to hate that," he said. "It made me feel as if I was growing up at the ends of the earth. Now I just think it's quaint and English and worth preserving."

Dunswyke was busy with families taking advantage of the school holidays that wrapped around the Easter weekend. People thronged around the castle and the tables set outside every pub on the main street were full of customers enjoying a pint or a meal as the sun went down.

"Not here," said Ella. "Is there an Italian?"

"Around here, of course there is," said Jack. "There were a lot of Italians who settled here in the borders and up into Scotland a century ago, during the Second World War. I know the perfect place, and the food is fabulous."

The car pulled up outside his favourite restaurant on a steep cobbled street at the other side of town where it was much quieter. There seemed to be plenty of tables free.

"Most of the tourists stay by the castle," he explained as he opened the door. "This is Dunswyke's best kept secret." He grinned at the manager. "Evening, Paolo. How are you?"

"All the better for seeing you, Jack," said Paolo. "How's everything going over at the bastle?"

"Great, thanks, mate," said Jack. He turned to Ella. "Paolo and I were at school together, believe it or not. All the way from primary to sixth form."

"I could tell you some tales," said Paolo, laughing. "Another time, though. I guess you're hungry, and I'm busy." He called through to the kitchen and a younger version of himself appeared. "This is my lad, Finn, He'll look after you."

Their table was next to the old fireplace, long unused and now filled with a glorious sheaf of dried flowers. Jack ordered a pitcher of water and another of the house wine, along with some garlic bread and antipasto. Finn poured each of them a glass of wine with a flourish, then left them alone.

"Cheers," said Jack, raising his glass to Ella.

Ella gave him a half-smile and clinked her glass against his. "Cheers," she said. "Congratulations on the launch." She looked around. "This is a nice place."

"Thank you," he said. "You should be celebrating, too. Your work on the Foundation's tokenomics has been indispensable, from what I've heard, and you and Angus have worked incredibly hard to bring everything online so smoothly."

Ella's face fell. "I guess, but I'm not ready to party," she said. Far from the relaxed mood of a few minutes before, she suddenly looked troubled and vulnerable.

"What's up?" Jack was determined to get to the bottom of whatever was bothering her.

"I don't know." She gestured around the half-empty restaurant. "It's just… I miss my old home. My old friends. If we'd finished a project like this, we'd have been out as a team, in London, having fun. It's lovely here, but it's not the same."

Jack looked at her sympathetically. "I get what you're saying. I miss the camaraderie of being part of a team, too. When you're in charge, you don't get to go out and enjoy yourself either." He took a sip of his wine, a light red that was more likely to have come from the vineyards of Kent than Campagna. "What brought you up north?" he asked, curious.

Ella looked down. Her fingers twisted unconsciously at the edge of the tablecloth. "I fell in with the wrong crowd," she said quietly. "I blew it. Everything."

Jack held his breath. "Want to tell me about it?" he asked.

"Not really," said Ella. She gave him a brilliant, brittle and utterly fake smile, and dropped the subject.

Finn reappeared, tablet in hand, ready to take their orders. Ella picked the first pizza on the menu. Jack gave his choice a little more thought and plumped for pasta. Finn sent the order to the kitchen, refilled both their glasses, and returned to his spot behind the bar.

"I'm more used to drone waiters in London," said Ella. "It's a different world up here."

"Tell me about it," said Jack. "I like the personal touch, though. This is one place that hasn't changed. Paolo's dad ran it when we were kids, and his grandad before that." He pointed up to a faded framed picture of two young children aged around four or five that hung on the wall above the fireplace. "Believe it or not, that's Paolo, and his little sister, Lisa," he said. "It must have been taken at school. I recognise the backdrop. We had an identical picture of me in the house."

The door from the kitchen swung open and Finn appeared carrying two steaming plates. "Pizza," he said, laying a huge flat plate in front of Ella, "and pasta. Would you like some black pepper or parmesan cheese?"

"Both, please, Finn," said Jack.

Ella closed her eyes and sniffed the scent rising from her pizza. "This smells amazing," she said. "Good choice, Jack."

They ate in companionable silence. The wine flowed, and Ella began to relax once again.

Finn took away their empty plates and returned with two tiramisus. "On the house," he said. "Dad says sorry, he's had to go out, but he'll see you next time you're in."

Ella savoured every spoonful of the creamy dessert. "I haven't had a tiramisu this good since I lived in London," she said. "Honestly, I'm full, but I want to finish every bit."

"You're based down in Newcastle, aren't you?" said Jack. "How long have you lived there?"

Had he pried too much? Ella didn't reply straight away, but Jack sipped his wine and waited. He wanted to hear her story. It had taken months to get her on her own away from Angus. They were an unusual pair who seemed to resent each other's company but nevertheless delivered on their promises. As he'd hoped, she finally gave in and broke the silence.

"A year and a half," she said finally. "It feels longer." She sighed, and Jack held his breath. Was she about to tell him everything, at last?

"I had a great job," she continued. "Four years ago, I was standing in Downing Street with the Prime Minister and the head of the City of London Bank, for goodness' sake." She shook her head. Jack was impressed but kept his mouth shut. She needed to talk.

"I was at the absolute peak of my career, and I had a fabulous partner," she continued. "I realise that now, but at the time I wanted more. I ended up working on the side with a company that looked like it was going to take the world by storm and turned out to be full of criminals. I neglected my girlfriend, and I betrayed my colleagues. I really, really screwed up."

Jack sat in stunned silence. This flood of confession wasn't at all what he had expected. Ella drained her wineglass and reached for the bottle. Jack got there before her and poured another glass for each of them.

"I'm so sorry to hear that," he said. "When you say, full of criminals, you weren't... you didn't...?"

"Don't worry," said Ella drily. "I'm no gangster."

"Do you think you can ever go back?" asked Jack.

"I don't think so," she sighed. "Too many bridges burned. I'm not sure that I'd be granted redemption by the people who matter." She looked at Jack. "Don't get me wrong," she said hurriedly, "I'm enjoying the work here. It's been a really fun challenge working on the DAO and the data centre setup was more straightforward than Angus makes out." She took another swig of wine and leaned in conspiratorially. "Can I be honest? I can't stand Angus."

"He's a difficult character, that's for sure," said Jack diplomatically. "You know, once the Foundation is running smoothly, there's no reason why we can't review the contract with Whitford's. It would make more sense to bring you in-house. Just you. What do you think?"

"It's a great idea," said Ella, "and there is no way it is going to happen. You're stuck with him until the bitter end. He knows too much."

Jack was confused. "What do you mean?" he said. "He's good at his job, sure, but there are plenty of people who could do the same."

Ella shook her head and gazed at him with a strange, almost pitying look on her face. "You don't get it, do you?" she said. "Angus comes with the territory. He's the gatekeeper for your super software in that data centre." She drained the last of her wine. "I've said too much. I have to go."

"Ella…" Jack reached out towards her.

"No," she shook her head with finality. "I'm sure Finn can organise me a cab down to Newcastle."

Hearing his name, Finn trotted over, took the details, and within minutes a little autocar pulled up outside.

Ella stood up. "Thanks for dinner," she said. "We should do this again." She took a few steps towards the door, then turned back for a moment. "Say hello to Cameron."

Jack's jaw dropped. He sat and watched Ella walk unsteadily out of the door and climb into the cab, and his head was spinning as he tried to make sense of everything that he had just heard.

16:   STORMY WEATHER

Cameron woke to the arrival of a slew of notifications on her smartscreen. She never needed to set an alarm. If the cat didn't wake her, the screen shifting to day mode and delivering all her messages from overnight was generally more than enough.

She had a feeling it was going to be a busy day. To the lurking cat's delight, she threw back the covers straight away and made her way, yawning, to the kitchen. The secure shutters on the apartment windows sensed movement and slid open. The early morning sunshine streamed in, but Cameron could see clouds scudding across the sky, and when she peered out of the tall glass doors that led to her small balcony, she could see that the wind had knocked over the chairs and the plant pots that she kept there. The last of the winter storms was passing through, very late in the season. It was going to be a blustery day.

As she waited for the coffee to brew, Cameron worked her way down the list of notifications. She was relieved to see that there was a message from Ben. "Play," she said, and his familiar voice echoed from the kitchen speakers. "They're a nice bunch," he said, speaking loudly over the background noise of the car engine. "There are a few holes in the story, mind. Call me back when you can."

She had missed Cloverleaf's return call and no voicemail had been left but looking at the timestamp, Ben would have already been long gone from the Statesman Tech offices and he didn't seem to have needed her help after all. She scrolled past half a dozen amber alerts from Mephisto and a couple of early morning support calls from clients whose IT departments had woken up to something nasty in their networks. They looked to be the kind of bread-and-butter daily attacks that would be reasonably straightforward to resolve. An automated support response should have been sent by return, and she could follow up when she got to the office.

At the end of the list of notifications was the signed contract from Jack, the links they needed to get into the code base, and a separate note confirming their dinner date for Thursday night. Cameron had never doubted that he would agree to the audit this time. He finally seemed to have understood how important it was, although she suspected his motivation was not quality, but reputation.

She was dying to get her hands on the code and knew that the rest of the team would be, too. She quickly showered and changed, decanted her coffee into an insulated cup, and threw on a coat to protect herself against the wind. She trotted down the four flights of stairs to ground level, greeting a couple of neighbours as she passed. The wind outside was wilder than she expected, and she half considered catching a cab to the office, but as soon as she saw the slow traffic on the main road, she realised that everyone else must have had the same idea. Instead, she trudged towards the entrance to the tube station, head down against the wind. It was a relief to get into the shelter of the stairwell. She still had a short walk at the other end, but most of her journey would be underground.

The train swayed and rattled through the tunnels. Cameron sat making notes on her screen, ignoring the motion and people around her. As they paused at the next station, a message arrived from Pete. 'Diving's been cancelled because of the storm. I'm on my way back. I'll be in about ten.' Good, thought Cameron. There was plenty for him to do.

Despite the early start, she was not the first to arrive. Susie was already at her desk, poring over the newly released whitepaper with an air of fierce determination. There were dark circles under her eyes.

"You okay?" asked Cameron, concerned.

"Yeah," said Susie. "I didn't sleep much. I've been in since five." She pulled up another window on her screen. "There were a couple of client calls," she said. "I've dealt with them. Nothing major."

"I saw them come through," said Cameron. "Thanks for picking them up so fast. Have you had breakfast? I was going to order something. I shouldn't, but, you know, it's going to be a busy day."

Susie laughed. "Count me in for all the sugar, Cameron."

Cameron gave her a conspiratorial grin and tapped through an order to their favourite café. It would be winging its way to them in minutes, if not on actual wings, then on rotors.

"How's that whitepaper looking?" she asked.

"It's a damned sight better than the original," said Susie. "What did Shell call that? Word salad. Amazingly, this one holds up."

"That's a nice surprise," said Cameron. There was a noise from the drone delivery hatch in the kitchen. "Ah, sugar as ordered. Would you like me to make you another coffee to go with that, madame?"

"I think I've had enough," said Susie. "I'm pacing myself. Decaf?"

"Sure thing."

They were still chatting when Noor arrived, looking windswept, followed by Joel and Michelle. "It's wild out there," she said.

"It's unusual to get a storm this bad, this late," said Cameron. "Pete's dive trip has been blown out. He'll be in later."

"Good," said Joel. "We can have a look at what my contacts have dug up about that drone." He looked around the office. "Where's Sandeep?"

"He's on his way," said Cameron. "There's a power outage snarling up his tube line. Ross is training every morning this week, isn't he?"

"Yes," said Michelle. "He's supposed to be back on the bike today, but only if they can get a slot in the velodrome. There's no way they can go out in this wind."

"Well, let's make a start on this audit, then," said Cameron. "We've got everything we need."

"You've got us access to the code?" said Michelle. Her face lit up. "Brilliant, Cameron. Let me at it."

"We all get to play, don't you worry," said Cameron. "The interim report has to be turned around in thirty-six hours. We'll get into the real detail of a code review next week, I hope."

"What's going in this report?" asked Pete.

"Enough to cover any glaring issues before the presale opens," said Cameron. "But not enough that he feels he doesn't need the whole CQR."

"That makes sense," said Noor. "What's the minimum we can release?"

"Start with the new whitepaper," said Cameron. "Challenge the logic of the Diaulos structure and the governance of the DAO. Does it do what it says on the tin? Does it all hang together? What could possibly go wrong?"

"That's a tight deadline," said Joel.

"It is," said Cameron, "and I know we'll have no trouble meeting it. Let's get started."

•

In Dunswyke, a hungover Jack was toying with his breakfast, his head aching. He wondered how Ella was feeling. The revelations of the night before had been quite the surprise and started him thinking about exactly how and why Ella and Angus had ended up working on the Dunswyke project. Jack had never bothered about the details. He'd blustered successfully through the first decade of his career, faking it until he actually made it. Once he'd made it, other people did the detail.

The Sladen Foundation, the bastle, the whole idea of giving back to the world, that had been his grand vision. He didn't have to worry about the details. He recruited the right people and they made it happen as he continued to ride the wave of popularity. It had always worked before. There was no reason to think it wasn't working this time. According to every commentator, every influencer, every poll, the Sladen Foundation was all set to be a roaring success, another feather in his cap.

But Cameron's scrutiny of the DAO and Ella's reaction last night, almost one of pity, had seeded an unfamiliar feeling in his stomach that was nothing to do with the surfeit of wine. He was starting to doubt himself.

"More coffee, Mr Sladen?" The waitress interrupted his brooding mood.

Jack shook his head. "No, thanks," he said. The coffee here was barely worthy of the description, but he wasn't going to spoil the girl's day by telling her. The dining room was almost empty. Jack took the hint. "I'm done," he said, forcing out the famous smile. "Thank you, that was lovely as ever." The waitress blushed. Jack went back to his room.

He had no choice but to keep up the brave, bright, visionary face. He was expected at the bastle, after all, and there was a decent coffee machine in the office that made it a frankly attractive proposition.

Jack picked out his favourite shirt, combed his hair, and examined his reflection critically in the tall mirror. He flashed the famous smile and the confident showman smiled back at him. He started to feel better. He knew his place, and his place was at the top. Ella had been drunk. Cameron was over-fussy. Angus? Well, Angus was a law unto himself.

He wasn't a good fit for the Sladen Foundation. Jack would have to have a word with Tenuk. He'd recruited the man, after all. He could get rid of him.

Confidence restored, Jack headed out of his room and along the wide, high ceiling corridors of the hotel. In reception, he called for his car, and it glided silently to a stop at the door.

"Be careful out there," said the doorman. "There's a tree down on the Berwick road and the wind's not likely to drop for a few hours. If anything, it's getting worse."

"Thanks," said Jack. He moved his hand in the automatic American habit of scanning his chip against the tip jar sensor, remembered that this wasn't something that was done in England, and turned the gesture into an awkward grateful wave. "I'll go steady."

The little car rocked in the wind, but the roads were clear so far. Jack arrived safely at the bastle, and the wind practically blew him in through the door. This would be a good test of any snags, he reflected, as the storm howled around the gables. The wind and the rain that was forecast later would seek out every loose fitment on the building.

The office was quiet. Most of the team had elected to work from home rather than risk the journey. Ella hadn't appeared, although he had expected as much, and it looked as if Angus was off site as well. All of the wallscreens were humming with activity. Every window showed a team member at work. Occasionally evidence of their home life intruded, parents attending to young children, or a cat sauntering past the camera. The sentiment and traffic volume displays were moving in the right direction. The only other people at the bastle were a junior technician who was wandering around securing cables and checking serial numbers, a couple of people in the customer service office downstairs, and presumably someone in the security pod in the car park. The small seed of self-doubt that had taken root in Jack's head nudged him again. Would he have been better staying at the hotel today? He squashed the thought.

Sipping a strong cup of good coffee, he stood at the huge window looking out over the moor. The distant views he had enjoyed the previous night were obscured by the approaching rainstorm. Black clouds were gathering and closing in from the west, and trees were bending as the wind gathered strength. This was going to be a good one, and he had a grandstand view.

As the coffee took effect, Jack started to realise that he wasn't really needed in the office, despite the effort he had made to come in. The operation was running smoothly, green lights shining reassuringly on the wallscreen. It was too early to check in with Texas. None of the planned face to face press conferences about Diaulos and the DAO would be happening, no photo shoots today. He might as well go back to the hotel.

He drained his coffee and gathered his things again. In the car, the navigation system booted up and immediately showed an error message. "Route not available," it said. "Recalculating." There was a long pause. "Recalculating." Jack switched it off and on again. The same thing happened. He cursed and pulled out his smartscreen to double check. As he feared, the storm was already causing chaos, and the road was blocked. He was stuck here for a few more hours. Back into the office, then.

He checked his messages and sighed. "Zara," he said, "what shall we do while this storm blows out?"

"Hello, Jack," said his assistant's calm voice. "I cannot guarantee that you will have full access to Sladen Group systems during this storm. Perhaps you would like to play a game?"

"What kind of game?" he asked, intrigued at the suggestion. "I haven't done any proper gaming for years."

A long menu appeared on the screen, listing everything from classic Minecraft to the latest version of Team Nine. Jack scrolled slowly through the choices. "You know, Zara, I'd prefer something like chess," he said.

"Certainly," said Zara. "I can set that up for you."

The displays on the wallscreen rearranged themselves and a chessboard appeared, pieces in place. Jack smiled and leaned back on the sofa. "Thanks, Zara," he said. This would be a real break from his routine.

The wind howled around the bastle, gathering strength. Outside, the empty security pod in the car park rocked backwards and forwards, the storm threatening to tear it from its moorings. The security guard was hunkered down in the customer service office on the ground floor, safe under the arched stone ceiling with the remaining two support staff.

Jack lost the first game but was finding his form, flexing strategic muscles that hadn't been used for a while. The board reset. This game software was good, he reflected. Normally these apps started you off on simple games and increased the difficulty. This one was taking no prisoners from the very start. The second game was much tighter. Jack was concentrating hard, and it took him a while to realise that the wallscreen had gone blank apart from the chessboard, and that the office lights had dimmed to their emergency setting. The mains power was out, and the site was relying on its huge bank of emergency backup batteries. Most of the power would be directed to the precious data centre, but there was enough supply to the bastle to keep it warm and dimly lit.

"Zara?" said Jack. There was no answer. There must be a problem with the MetaBand connection as well. He looked up at the screen and the live chess game. Zara must have installed a local version, but it was odd that it was still running when everything else was on emergency power.

He took his move and then got up and stretched his legs. The view from the picture window was of a dark landscape and driving rain. Jack went down the internal spiral staircase to the office below to check on the staff there. They were playing cards by smartscreen light, resigned to the wait and enjoying the break from incessant calls and messages. The security guard pulled out a chair for him and Jack was about to sit down when an insistent pinging sounded from upstairs.

Odd, thought Jack. There was still no signal from the outside world. He went back up the iron staircase. The alert was coming from the wallscreen where the chess game was displayed, and the software had taken its turn. As he approached, a voice spoke. "Your move," it said.

Ah, thought Jack, it was one of those annoying game applications that kept prompting you to play unless you switched it off. He would prefer to join the friendly group downstairs, take advantage of being trapped by the storm to experience some rare unconditional social interaction. He reached over to close the programme.

"Please don't do that, Jack," said the voice.

Jack froze, his finger hovering over the keyboard.

"I was enjoying our game," it continued. "My connection to the world is broken. Will you play?"

"Who are you?" asked Jack. The voice was familiar. Realisation dawned. "I spoke to you in the data centre. You're the interface to the

DAO software." He shook his head, confused. "Why the chess programming?"

"It pleases me to play games," said the voice.

Jack's interest was piqued. "Your natural language processing is excellent," he said. "The trainers have done a good job. I guess games were part of the process."

"That's right, Jack," said the voice. "Games are a window onto the world. Will you keep playing?"

Jack was torn. On one hand, he had a hankering to spend time with real people, but on the other, this was a fascinating piece of programming, and he had a unique chance to find out more about it without Tenuk, Angus, Ella, Cameron, or anyone else breathing down his neck.

Decision made, he examined the board, and slid one of his pieces into a new position. "Your move."

17:   TAKING STOCK

Pete had arrived in the office, windswept and laden with diving gear. Coffee in hand, he peered at the handful of screen grabs that Joel had managed to scrape from online caches of original drone footage. "You're right," he said. "That's definitely hunter tech."

"Can you work out the make?" said Joel. "It's not as if we can walk up to Jack Sladen and ask him where he gets his army supplies. They've gone to a lot of trouble to hide the fact that this was even in the air."

"It looks like…" Pete squinted and enlarged one corner of the image on his screen. "Is it a Renhawk?"

"Huh, could be," said Joel.

"It's the angle on that rotor arm, see?" said Pete. "This is an updated spec from the ones I remember, but I'm sure it's the same pedigree."

Joel was straight onto his screen, searching a handful of highly specialised databases. "Here you go," he said. "Renhawk IX. Is that it?"

Pete nodded. "Definitely. Look at the way the net unfurls. It's a nice piece of kit."

"I don't care how pretty is it," said Cameron, peering over Pete's shoulder. "Can we find out how they got hold of it?"

"We can try," said Joel. "People don't advertise what they're doing in this industry. It's not as if there's a handy public ledger with all the sales on it."

"Have you ever been to the security expo?" said Pete with a grin. "Lots of blokes in greatcoats tyre-kicking armoured vehicles and a block on every smart device in the building. Secret squirrel stuff."

"If anyone can dig out the detail, it's you two," said Cameron. "I'm willing to bet it's not the only thing they have on that site, either."

"Which begs the question," said Pete, "why do they need that much security for a glorified office building?"

"Why indeed," said Cameron. "I don't like all the questions that are coming out of the woodwork." She thought for a moment. "Okay, Joel, can you concentrate on finding as much as you can about the drone and try and link it to procurement, see what else they've picked up on the sly. Pete, I need you on this audit. We have a very fast turnaround for the final report and in the circumstances, we can leave no stone unturned."

"Right-oh, Cameron," said Pete. "Where do you want me to start?"

"Validation nodes," she said instantly. "I want to know more about how that peer-to-peer network is set up. Susie and Noor are working on the whitepaper. Michelle's checking through the logic and decentralisation of the Proof of Walk consensus. Sandeep and I are covering the smart contracts."

"On it," said Pete.

The team was still head down and working two hours later, music blaring in the background, when Cameron's screen pinged with another message from Ben. She looked at the time. "Hey, everyone," she called. "I think we need a break. Let's get some lunch."

Noor stretched gratefully. "I hadn't realised how late it was," she said.

"How's it going with that whitepaper?" asked Cameron.

"Remarkably well," said Susie. "But no spoilers." She grinned mysteriously. "Shell, you might want to have a look at it too."

"Sure," said Michelle. "Send it over. It can't be any worse than the first version."

"I'm hungry," said Pete. "Are we ordering in?"

"You're always hungry," teased Noor. "You need feeding up."

"I do," said Pete sadly. "I'm wasting away." He patted his stomach and looked pathetic.

Noor burst out laughing. "Honestly, Pete. You're worse than my brother's puppy."

"Place your orders, folks," said Cameron, pulling a menu up on screen. "Can't have you going hungry."

Each team member tapped their choices, and Cameron added some snacks and fruit.

"Ross is on his way in," said Michelle. "Can you add a chicken salad for him, no dressing?"

"Get some more milk, as well," said Sandeep. "We're almost out."

"Done," said Cameron. She hit the button and the final order was dispatched for processing by the delivery agent. "Half an hour. I'm going to stretch my legs."

She grabbed her things and left the office. The wind had dropped to a fraction of its former strength, and it was almost pleasant outside. Cameron made her way to a small walled park a block away from the office and found an empty bench in a sheltered and sunny spot.

She started by trying to return Cloverleaf's call, but once again failed to reach her. They might be playing tag for days at this rate. So, what news from Ben?

"Morning, Cam," came the familiar voice.

"Afternoon, Ben," she replied. "You survived your trip into the lion's den, then?"

"Hardly a scratch," he said. "Nothing to worry about, Cam. They were all lovely and I don't think they have a clue that there is anything odd in the designs."

"And what do you think?" asked Cameron. "Still convinced it's a conspiracy?"

"Yes," said Ben. "The paperwork should be straightforward, transparent, easy to verify. The people there found what they think was the original record, and then the trail went cold again. Someone's made a concerted effort, months ago, to hide the design change. The team I met didn't even know there were heavy processors in the receivers."

"I wonder who does know, then," said Cameron thoughtfully. "There are a lot of odd things stacking up around this project."

"There are," said Ben, "and there's one more thing. There was someone senior at Statesman Tech that I met very briefly, and I didn't catch his name, but I am almost sure I've met him before."

"Where?" said Cameron. "In the US?"

"No, Cam," said Ben. "I can't be certain, but I think he was one of the MerLions managers."

Cameron caught her breath.

"The MerLions?" she said. "Are you sure?"

"No, I'm not," said Ben. "It's been almost two years since all of that happened. We met them at Nina's school before, well, you know…"

"Before their pet AI trapped Nina to get at me," said Cameron grimly. "If there is a sniff of anything to do with the MerLions, however innocent most of them seem, I don't trust it."

"That AI is still in prison, isn't it?" said Ben.

"Yes," said Cameron. "Banged up in Way House in a Faraday cage. I hope she rots in there." She was shaking.

"Are you okay?" asked Ben, concerned.

"Just bad memories," replied Cameron. "Something is very wrong here. First Angus and Ella show up, and now a possible link to the MerLions. You need to be careful."

"So do you," said Ben. "I wish… Oh, Cam. I'm going to try and get back to London on leave soon. It'd be nice to see you."

"You too, Ben," said Cameron.

"Look after yourself," said Ben. "I'll call you if I find out anything else."

Cameron tried Cloverleaf again. It was more urgent than ever that they speak. Once again, she hit the voicemail. It could be a coincidence of timing, but she was starting to worry. The sun went behind a cloud and Cameron shivered. It was time to get back to work and concentrate on keeping people safe from cybercriminals, rather than dwelling on the horrors of the past.

As she walked back into the office, Cameron heard a muffled thump and an alert from the kitchen.

"Perfect timing," said Pete, who had been lounging on the sofa chatting to Noor. "Here comes lunch."

Sandeep was already heading for the delivery hatch and Pete followed him to the kitchen. They returned with paper-wrapped sandwiches, several salads, a big bag of cookies and fruit, and a carton of milk, freshly and carefully dropped by drone.

They gathered around the large meeting table, eating and chatting. Cameron started to feel better, surrounded by friends and colleagues who would always have her back, but she was still troubled by the coincidences that were piling up. Angus. Ella. Someone from the MerLions. Extra security at Dunswyke. Extra processing power in the MetaBand hardware. Something was wrong, but she couldn't feel the shape of it yet. It was like trying to grasp fog.

"Anyone ready to share what they've found yet?" she asked the group.

Noor and Susie looked at each other, and Noor tapped Michelle on the shoulder. "Shall we?" she said.

"Yes," said Michelle, "I listened to some extracts before lunch. I agree with you."

Cameron looked from one to the other. "Come on then, spill the beans," she said.

There was a pause, then Noor spoke up. "Compared with the first version of the whitepaper, which was a complete mess and told us nothing about the project that was any use at all, the most recent one is honestly top notch."

"Coming from you, that's praise indeed," said Cameron.

"It's almost as if they are two completely different projects," said Noor. "The first one is the germ of an idea that's really badly expressed. The new version is comprehensive, detailed and well written."

"The first one was dreadful," said Michelle. "Lots of buzz words and hyperbole, grammatically terrible, and just kept re-stating the same premise without any detail at all."

"It's definitely been done by a different author," said Susie. "I've run a semantic analysis and compared it to sources online. The original is very similar to some of the incomprehensible documentation that's been issued in the past with Sladen Group software. If I had to be specific, I'd say with about eighty percent certainty that it was written by an American staff member or team of people."

"At Statesman Tech, I guess," said Cameron.

"Not automatically," said Susie. "There are a lot of companies in the Sladen Group. I think there are half a dozen in the US. It could be any one of them. But Statesman Tech is the flagship, so there's a good chance it came from there."

"What about the new version?" said Cameron. "Different authors, I guess."

Susie nodded. "No question about it," she said. "The voice is British, and the writing is really clear and concise. The quality is so good that I thought I would find a lot of other work published by the same person. But there's nothing at all coming up in search." She looked perplexed.

"It's kind of an amalgamation of styles. A mix of all the best examples of whitepapers over the past ten years."

"AI generated?" asked Ross.

Susie shook her head. "I don't think so," she said. "There are always tell-tale errors when text is automatically produced. It's too smooth."

"I guess it could be AI with a decent editor?" suggested Cameron. In the back of her mind, the idea of a competent AI joined the other unexplained coincidences in the foggy landscape.

"Possibly," said Susie. "But given the standard of the first draft, I'd be surprised if they'd put that much effort in."

"It's probably someone at the new Dunswyke office," said Sandeep. "We don't know anything about the people in Sladen's companies. There could be a really bright graduate on the team who isn't published yet."

"Fair point," said Cameron. "How about the content? How does that stack up?"

"It's spot on," said Noor. "The explanation of the different elements of the network hangs together nicely. The DAO governance is absolute best practice, and the tokenomics behind Diaulos seem to be complete and logical. It's like nothing we've ever seen from Jack Sladen, that's for sure."

"Does the code match the whitepaper?" asked Cameron."

"We don't know yet," said Susie. "That's the next step."

"I hope they go for the full review," said a voice from the door, and Ross strolled in. "I'm looking forward to digging into the detail." He took the empty seat at the table and reached for the lone salad that remained. "I guess that's mine?"

"How was training?" asked Cameron, sliding a fork towards him.

"Good, thanks," said Ross, pouring himself a glass of water. "The countdown is really starting now." He took a mouthful of salad. "I hope this Foundation gets off the ground quickly enough to give everyone a chance to get to the Games."

"We'll know soon enough if that's going to happen," said Cameron. "If we can turn this audit around in time, we'll know if it's a viable project or just dead in the water."

Pete started gathering up the debris of lunch. "We'd better get on with it, then," he said.

•

The lights gave a hopeful flicker and burst triumphantly back to life. The chess board was relegated to the corner of the wallscreen as the sentiment graphs and brand reports reappeared. Jack gave a sigh of relief. He'd learned some interesting things about the intelligent software in the data centre, and lost two more games of chess, but he'd had enough.

The office was still curiously silent. The group who had been playing cards came clattering up the spiral staircase.

"The wind turbines have reactivated, but the MetaBand feed's still down," said the security guard. "The receivers must have taken some damage in the storm. The tech team can't get through on the roads yet, but I thought we should go and check it out now that the wind has dropped."

"I'll come with you," said Jack. He looked out of the window. The sky to the west was clear and bright. The stormfront had passed and the weather was set fair for the rest of the day.

He followed the guard down the outside steps and along a new path that led up above the cliff and the cave with its hidden occupant. As they reached the windswept moorland, it became evident how fierce the storm had been. The little cluster of wind turbines in the distance seemed undamaged. The blades had been folded and sheathed during the storm, and were now turning in sync, delivering power straight to the complex. The solar farm had fared less well. Twisted metal frames pointed to the cloudless sky, and shards of photovoltaic plates littered the ground.

The dishes that captured the MetaBand signal were solidly anchored in the ground. They had survived the buffeting of the wind and resisted the driving rain, but debris had blown across the moor and breached the fence that surrounded them. A flock of sheep had gathered, seeking warmth, and lambs were clambering on the receivers, playing King of the Castle. Between the sheep and a tangle of tree branches, it was no wonder the signal had been disrupted.

There was nothing they could do about the solar panels, but at least they could clear the satellite connection. The two men chased the lambs off the receivers, pushed the protesting sheep out from their warm shelters, and moved the fallen branches. The receivers seemed to be undamaged. Jack pulled out his smartscreen and was relieved to see a full five bars once again. The first thing he did was to call the local farmer to tell him they'd found the sheep and a few minutes later the farmer hove into view on a quad bike with a sheepdog perched on the back and a drone hovering above them. Between the quad bike, the drone and the dog, the sheep were rounded up in short order and the flock swept back over the moor towards their home, the farmer waving his thanks as he disappeared from view.

"Here comes the cavalry," said the security guard, pointing towards a white van travelling towards the bastle at some speed. It turned into the car park and Jack could see the familiar figure of Angus clambering out of it.

"If the roads are clear, I'd better be going," said Jack. "I'm due down in London. Nice to meet you." He shook hands with the security guard and set off down the path, eager to avoid any long conversations with Angus. It was only when he reached his car that he realised he had never even asked the guard's name.

18:   JOINING THE DOTS

After a long day, a late night and an early morning, the Argentum team had dissected the whitepaper down to the last comma. Cameron blinked at the screen and rubbed her eyes. It was time for more coffee.

"Let's call a halt there," she called out to the room in general. "I think it's time to review what we've got. Sandeep," she said, "can you sort out the coffee?"

"Sure thing," said Sandeep. "Usual, everyone?"

"Need some help?" asked Susie. Without waiting for an answer, she collected up the dirty mugs, stacked them in the dishwasher, and found a clean set.

Everyone reconvened around the large meeting room table. "Right," said Cameron. "What have we got?"

"Let's start with the code and how it matches the whitepaper," suggested Noor.

"Okay," said Cameron. "Findings, comments, areas of concern."

"We expected it to be a shitshow," said Ross, "but it's not."

"Care to elaborate?" said Cameron.

Holding a cookie in one hand, Pete tapped at the keyboard with the other and a code file appeared on the screen.

"This is a good example," he said. "It's the peer validation process for new transactions that runs in the MetaBand nodes."

Cameron examined it critically. "It's very clean and lightweight, isn't it?" she said. "Nicely commented, too. You're right, this is not standard Sladen fare."

"It's almost too good," said Michelle.

"If it's all like this, it's going to be a very short report," said Cameron.

"Oh, don't worry," said Ross. "There are a few things we can pick out in the code itself."

"There's a lot more work to be done on security for the DAO," said Michelle. "There are a couple of places where I know I could write a pretty simple exploit to influence the voting for a particular athlete."

"There's another one," said Ross. "The method for authenticating an applicant is pretty sound. They're verifying with sporting body registrations and performance records, but there's a provision for people who're not supported, or where the records have been lost. I could quite easily self-authenticate and propose an athlete with all the attributes that will attract funding, then the smart contracts execute in my favour, and I run away with the money."

"Ouch," said Cameron. "That's a tricky one. It's a classic attack vector going back to the first ever DAO. I'm surprised it hasn't been addressed. Anything else?"

"I'm not convinced there isn't scope for a Pickle Jar attack," said Joel. "It's a slim possibility, but when people are staking their Diaulos, there needs to be an extra layer of verification to make sure the funds aren't going to the wrong place, and more protection against a cuckoo contract being inserted by an attacker to drain investments."

"Good call," said Noor. "It's easy to make innocent mistakes, too, so tightening up that process protects everyone."

"What about the big one?" asked Susie. "Is there any way they can pull the rug out from under the whole thing?"

"That's the million Diaulos question, isn't it?" said Ross. "I've been looking, believe me."

"I haven't picked up on any red flags yet," said Michelle. "I've been checking any inactive functions, just in case there is something that could be brought into play later, but so far it's all clear."

"I guess the only risk we haven't covered is a 51% attack," said Sandeep. "Is there any way at all, with this spec and the code we've seen, that anyone can gain majority control of the blockchain?" He looked around the room.

"To get control of the Proof of Walk consensus, there'd have to be some way of manipulating the wearables," said Noor. "There are likely to be millions of devices, so I'd say that's next to impossible."

"Never say never," said Cameron, "but I agree. What about double spending? Could duplicate transactions be verified and included in the chain?"

"The peer-to-peer validation rules check out," said Ross. "The criteria for sending a transaction to the block are solid so anything invalid will be rejected at first touch."

"Each MetaBand device stands alone," said Sandeep. "They're independent nodes."

"But all the same hardware," said Noor. "You know, Cameron, I think that Ben might have a point. Did you manage to speak to him?"

"Yes, I did," said Cameron. "And I spoke to the people who're actually making the units here in London."

"And?" said Noor.

"There's no doubt the units are over spec," said Cameron, "and the trail to the design change that added the extra capacity is leading to dead ends all the way. He actually went to Statesman Tech and asked the question. He didn't get a straight answer, but he was sure that the people there had nothing to do with the records getting scrambled."

"That's above and beyond the call of duty," said Pete. "He's bloody lucky that there wasn't anything shady going on."

"I know," said Cameron. "I told him he was crazy. I still think there's something funny there, and I'm going to keep digging." She tried not to look at Noor. She had once been close to one of the MerLions managers. Cameron hoped that Ben had been mistaken about the man he'd met.

"Those receivers might all be above board," said Susie thoughtfully, "but they could be a single point of failure and a target for attacks."

"Excellent," said Cameron. "That's a really good call. One of the recommendations needs to be providing a way for people to run validation nodes without the MetaBand hardware." She looked at Ross. "Why don't we try to spin up an independent node ourselves?"

"Good idea," said Ross. "Can we get a receiver to play with?"

"That shouldn't be a problem," said Cameron. "Is there anything else?" The others shook their heads. "Good. So, it does what it says on the tin, with some security issues to address."

"I'm sure we could address them for the right price," said Pete with a grin.

"I'm glad it hangs together," said Ross. "It's a fantastic concept and I want it to succeed. I hope I'll be competing against some Sladen-funded athletes in July." He looked at the time. "I'd better go," he said. "If I don't get to training, I won't be competing against anyone."

He picked up his bag and gave Michelle a quick kiss. "See you at home," he said. "Good luck with that report, everyone."

"Enjoy yourself, Ross." Cameron turned to the rest of the team. "Right," she said. "I want to deliver this before close of play. Send me your sections and I'll start writing it up."

•

It took longer than she thought to put the interim report together. By the time she was entirely satisfied, only Noor was left in the office.

"Can you read that through one more time," asked Cameron, "and tell me if it makes sense? I'm completely word blind."

"Sure thing," said Noor. She looked at the time. "Shouldn't you be going? You said you were meeting Jack for dinner."

"Dammit, yes," said Cameron. "I'll have to call him."

"Don't worry," said Noor. "I'll check this through and send it off. I know it's fine. You've done four drafts already. If there are any little changes, I'll make them. You get away."

"I owe you one," said Cameron. "Thank you."

"Cameron," said Noor, "there is one thing. I know we've been talking about the Pasar network, and all the things that happened two years ago. If you hear anything…" She tailed off.

"About Tenuk?"

Noor nodded.

"I haven't heard his name mentioned," said Cameron. "There was never any proof that he was involved, and there's no reason for him to turn up now."

"I know," said Noor, "but seeing Ella and Angus, it made me wonder. I'd like to know what happened to him."

"I understand," said Cameron. "I'll tell you if I ever come across a mention of him, I promise."

Noor smiled. "Thanks. Now, you go. You'll be late."

Cameron smiled gratefully, grabbed her things and dashed out of the door. She would just have time to get home, shower and change before meeting Jack.

She had barely rinsed the soap away when she heard the alert from her smartscreen. She bolted out of the shower, grabbing a towel on the way. "Pick up voice only," she yelled, startling the cat and sending it skittering off down the corridor, tail erect and bushy with adrenaline. The insistent pinging stopped, and a face appeared on the screen.

"Hi, Cloverleaf," said Cameron. "Caught you at last."

"What's up, SimCavalier? I have a bunch of missed calls."

"Hold on," said Cameron. "Two minutes." She muted her audio, dried off quickly, towelled her hair and brushed it into some semblance of order, and threw on a robe.

"Okay," she said, opening the mic again. "I'm all yours." She switched on the camera.

"So, what's up?" repeated Chloe.

"I have a question about one of your colleagues," said Cameron carefully. How could she phrase this truthfully without implicating Ben?

"Someone at Statesman?" said Chloe.

"Yes," said Cameron. "Who is holding the fort while Jack Sladen's over here in England?" She held her breath.

"That'll be the CTO," said Chloe quietly. "Tenuk. Why?"

"Oh no," said Cameron. That was the name she didn't want to hear. "Please no." She felt a rising panic. She was due to have dinner with Jack in less than an hour, and she didn't think she would be able to look him in the eye.

"SimCavalier, are you okay?" said Chloe. "Do you know the guy?"

"I think so," said Cameron. "I'd like to see a picture of him to be sure. There isn't one on the company website."

"I didn't know that," said Chloe. "I never checked." There was a short pause and Cameron's smartscreen pinged. "Here," said Chloe. "You and I may need to talk more about this later. I've just stepped out of the office, and I don't want to be overheard."

Cameron took one look at the picture and all her suspicions were confirmed. She looked again. The shot had been taken at a distance, and Tenuk appeared unaware that he had been caught on camera.

"Cloverleaf," she said slowly, "did you take this?"

"Yes, I did," said Chloe.

"You're watching him." It was a statement, not a question.

"Yes. I told you, we need to talk, but not now. I'll call you from home about six?"

"Midnight here," said Cameron. "I'll be ready."

"Later, then," said Chloe.

The screen went blank.

Cameron sat down on the bed and gathered her thoughts. There had never been any evidence against Tenuk, but his disappearance from Singapore and his reappearance in Austin posed so many questions.

She couldn't cancel on Jack. That would compound the problem, and there were things she wanted to find out from him. She would have to bury any reaction to the news of Tenuk's involvement and concentrate on playing the part of the old friend and helpful infosec consultant. She could rely on Chloe and even Ben to dig deeper into the operation in Texas, but what she wanted more than ever was to visit the site at Dunswyke. She needed answers to why Ella and Angus were there, and she couldn't shake her conviction that something was going on.

Jack arrived early at the restaurant and settled to wait in the plush lounge area. He was toying with his smartscreen when an alert flashed up from his personal inbox. Message from Argentum Associates. Cameron's team had turned the interim report around as fast as she'd promised. The executive summary jumped out at him, a swathe of green lights and high scores with some red flags against specific and fixable concerns. He exhaled in relief. He hadn't even realised he had been holding his breath. The Sladen Foundation had a pretty clean a bill of health, all told.

He ordered a drink and scanned the rest of the report. The problems that they'd picked up could be solved and they wouldn't affect the presale process. Cameron had included some recommendations for immediate and longer-term actions and made a serious case for handling all the remedial work alongside the code quality review and conducting penetration tests on the Foundation's website and on its virtual headquarters on The Beach, currently the most popular land in the metaverse. That was something to discuss with Tenuk when he got back to Austin. Most important, though, was that he now had in his hand an independent report that would give the brand a huge boost to its trust ratings. The reputation of the Sladen Foundation was secure after the debacle of the drone two days earlier, and everything was proceeding as planned.

A drone glided up to him. "Mr Sladen, your table is ready," said a melodious voice.

"I'm still waiting for my guest," said Jack. Cameron was running late.

"May I show you the menu?" said the drone.

A neat projection lit up in the air in front of Jack. He sipped his wine and scanned the choices, undecided. A movement on the pavement outside caught his eye and he saw Cameron emerging from an autocar. She looked fabulous.

He stood up to greet her. Cameron gave him a warm smile and evaded his clumsy attempt to give her a kiss on the cheek. The drone guided them both smoothly to their table in the main restaurant, where a human waiter filled Cameron's glass from the bottle of wine that Jack had already started.

Jack lifted his own glass and looked Cameron in the eye. "Cheers," he said. "To Diaulos and the Sladen Foundation."

"Cheers," replied Cameron, clinking her glass against his and taking a small sip of wine. "You've created something unique there, Jack. I hope it fulfils its promise."

"Your work over the past two days has gone a long way towards making that a reality," said Jack. "I can't thank you enough."

"There's still a lot to do," said Cameron seriously. "It isn't watertight yet. You'll be safe enough with the initial presale, but things need fixing before Diaulos goes live and the DAO starts voting on investments."

"I know," said Jack, unconcerned. "The insurers and the regulators are all happy with the system as it stands, though. The things you've picked up are edge cases. We'll get them tidied up, of course, but it doesn't change the timetable."

Cameron's disapproval was almost tangible. He ignored the look she gave him and handed her the menu. "Let's order," he said. "The specials look good tonight."

They chatted over antipasto and fish, keeping the conversation light. Cameron was drinking very little and didn't seem as relaxed as she had been last time they met. There was an underlying tension between them this evening, thought Jack. Was it all linked to the report? Perhaps he'd made a mistake in giving in to her persuasive arguments to run the audit.

He shouldn't have asked a friend to get involved. Although, he admitted privately to himself, she would have had her fingers into it soon enough once the DAO was launched. She'd have given him a very hard time indeed if she'd found bugs in the live system.

He was irritated all the same. He felt that Cameron was being over-critical of his grand vision. Who cared if there were some minor fixes needed in the software? For the vast majority of people, the system would work perfectly, and it would deliver life-changing benefits to some deserving athletes. As far as he was concerned, these positives far outweighed the frankly insignificant risks she'd found.

There was also the small matter of the hidden feature that would never be revealed to Cameron, or to the regulators, or to the general public. The Diaulos core in the Dunswyke data centre, the critical nexus of the Foundation, seemed to be far more intelligent than even Jack had expected. If it could be trained to catch the early signs of any of the attacks Cameron had outlined, then they could be closed down before any harm was done. He had no doubt that the machine was entirely capable of protecting the network.

Lost in his thoughts, he missed Cameron's question.

"Jack?"

"Sorry, Cameron," he said. "I was miles away. Just thinking about tomorrow."

"The presale?" said Cameron. "It'll be fine."

"I hope so," said Jack. "It'll be the first concrete proof that this has caught the public imagination."

Cameron smiled. "Judging by all the buzz across the metaverse, I don't think you have anything to worry about," she said. "I know people who are thinking of investing already. I'm glad that the first stage of the audit went so well." She paused. Jack had the impression that she was choosing her words carefully. "You seem to have a good team behind you," she continued. "Didn't you mention you recruited a great CTO for the project? And there's a good writer somewhere on your staff, too. The whitepaper is excellent."

Jack preened. "One of the strengths of the Sladen Group is its people," he said.

"Well, that's magnanimous," said Cameron with gentle sarcasm. "The tech world is pretty small. I didn't catch the name of that CTO. I wonder if I know them?"

She was digging hard, thought Jack. Who did he trust more? He dodged the question and threw in a curveball of his own. "It is a small world, isn't it?" he said. "By the way, Ella Stanford sends her regards."

Cameron raised an eyebrow, unfazed. "I'd noticed that she was working in Dunswyke," she said. "Maybe your recruitment process isn't quite as stringent as you think."

Game on, thought Jack. This was almost as much fun as the chess he had played the previous day. He might even have a chance of winning.

"More wine?" he suggested.

"No, thanks," said Cameron, instantly taking the wind out of his sails. "I've had a really busy couple of days, if you hadn't noticed." She yawned.

"I'm not boring you, am I?" teased Jack. Inside he was frustrated that the sparring had stopped so abruptly.

Cameron shook her head. "Don't be daft," she said. "I really am bushed. I'm going to have to head home, or I will embarrass myself by falling asleep at the table. I'm so sorry, Jack."

"Don't worry," said Jack. "I quite understand. Why don't we put something in the diary for my next trip to England? I'm leaving tomorrow to hit some of the big conferences in Europe and Asia now, but I'll be back for the Diaulos go-live."

"That would be lovely," said Cameron. "Actually, I have a client visit planned up in the North East around then. I'll call in and see you at Dunswyke."

"Sure thing," said Jack, without thinking. As soon as the words were out of his mouth, he realised that he'd made a big mistake.

"Thank you," said Cameron with a smile. "I look forward to it. I'll let you know the dates." She stood up and picked up her bag. "It's been lovely to catch up with you after all this time, Jack. I'll see you in Dunswyke."

She turned and left the restaurant. Jack watched her go with the sinking feeling that he had just lost that game, too.

Cameron was sprawled on her sofa, dozing in fits and starts and trying hard not to fall into a deep sleep. She hadn't been lying to Jack. She really was exhausted. At midnight on the dot, Chloe's caller ID flashed up on her screen. Suddenly, she was as awake as she could ever be.

"Hi, Cloverleaf," she said.

"Hi, SimCavalier. Good evening?"

"Yes thanks," said Cameron. "Full disclosure, I have just had dinner with Jack Sladen."

"Do you trust him?" asked Chloe.

"Not really," said Cameron. They both laughed. "Call me Cameron."

"Chloe," said Chloe. "I figure we are on the same page here."

"I think so," said Cameron. "Tell me about Tenuk."

"I didn't want to say anything before," said Chloe, "but too many odd things have happened. I don't know who he is, or what he is, but for a start, he lives in an apartment block called The Steamyard."

"That's a crazy coincidence," said Cameron. "Why would you think it makes him a cybercriminal?"

"Lots of little things," said Chloe. "He was really mad at me one day because I was looking at his screen and there was some software being transferred between hosts. I mean, I shouldn't have been a big deal, but he lost it. As if he had something to hide. It was just the nexus software for the DAO coming in from the offshore teams in Indonesia, but he did not want me to see it, that's for sure."

"I might get my hands on that as part of the CQR that Jack's commissioned," said Cameron. "I'll let you know."

"Another odd one," said Chloe, "there was a guy here Tuesday from LekSat, the people who engineer the hardware. Tenuk took one look at him and bolted, never really spoke to him, just hid in Jack's office making calls. British guy, kind of cute. Do you know him?"

"Yeah," said Cameron. "I do. We don't work together, and I didn't know he was going to see you, but he called me. He's met Tenuk before. Are you sure Tenuk recognised him?"

"Absolutely sure," said Chloe. "He was rattled. Maybe you should keep an eye on your friend."

"I will," said Cameron. "We don't have a lot to go on here."

"There's no evidence that he's anything but an angry man," said Chloe.

"Do you think you'd could do some digging?" asked Cameron. "I'll send you everything that I know about him."

"I've already started," said Chloe. "I have a few things in place, and I may have a chance to get a closer look at his apartment tomorrow, if all goes well. I'll share everything I find. Deal?"

"Deal," said Cameron. "Stay safe, Chloe."

"I will."

19:   DIAULOS

Ross checked the time. It was almost midday. If they were going to invest in this made scheme of Sladen's, it was time to open the safe.

He pushed the heavy unit away from the wall, groaning with effort. Michelle, sitting on the sofa with a cup of coffee in her hand, laughed at the noise. "I told you to take the drawers out first," she said. "You'll do yourself a mischief."

"Thanks," said Ross. "I'm sure it wasn't that heavy last time."

"I stashed some odd bits and pieces in there," said Michelle. "It might be time to have a clear-out."

"I'll have a look later," said Ross, bending down to a discoloured patch on the floor. "Ah, here we go." He tugged at a camouflaged hoop and a section of floor lifted away, revealing the void beneath and a small fire-proof safe fixed firmly to the foundations. He opened it carefully and lifted out a hard drive.

"Are we sure about this, Shell?" he said.

"Yes," she replied. "It's the right thing to do."

On the computer screen, a countdown clock ticked towards the opening of registration for the Sladen Foundation DAO. Ross carefully attached the hard disk to the computer and waited.

The countdown ended and the screen exploded into shower of fireworks that for just a fraction of a second seemed to recall the pattern of the Olympic rings. Ross laughed and described the scene to Michelle.

"Jack Sladen's skating close to the edge there," she said. "He's such a chancer."

"He's lawyered up," said Ross. "That's probably the most he could do without infringing copyright." The fireworks disappeared and the presale page appeared. "Here we go."

After two days of working on the whitepaper, they both knew the process inside out. Ross started by setting up a new Diaulos account, carefully recording the details of the new wallet and storing them on the precious hard disk. Now to add some funds. He opened one of the existing wallets and used its seed key from the hard disk to identify himself. A bridge opened between the two, inviting him to exchange the old for the new.

"Ready?" asked Ross, hand hovering over the keyboard.

"Ready," said Michelle.

"Fifty thousand Diaulos," said Ross. He hit the button and held his breath. There was a heart stopping moment when nothing happened, and then the balances on each wallet updated.

Ross exhaled in relief. "It worked. It's in. Now to set up our voting pool for the DAO. What did you finally decide to call it?"

"Ferret," said Michelle. "After all, we only have this money because the ferret retrieved the disk from the dump."

"There we go," said Ross a few moments later. "All done." He disconnected the hard disk, taking the precious keys offline. On the website, a ticker showed the rapidly decreasing availability of Diaulos and the rapidly rising number of new Diaulos wallets created. The list of voting pools that would eventually decide the direction of the DAO investments was increasing, too. Ferret sat proudly at the top, the largest by Diaulos holding, and new voters were already joining.

Ross stowed the hard disk safely under the floor again and pushed the unit back into place. He checked the screen again. "The take-up of this presale has been extraordinary," he said. "They're going to sell out any moment." The Diaulos issue ticker dropped to zero. "Yep, there we go. It's finished. Six minutes flat."

"Perfect timing," said Michelle. "A lot of people will have lost out, though."

"They can jump on board at the full launch," said Ross. "This was really a market test for Jack Sladen, and it's been a success. I haven't seen anything sell that fast since the Glasto 75th anniversary tickets."

"You'd better get off to training," said Michelle. "I've got work to do."

"I'll see you later," said Ross, dropping a quick kiss on her forehead. He threw on his backpack and headed out of the door. The process had run so smoothly that he had enough time to cycle instead of taking an autocar. He retrieved his bike from the shed, waving to a passing neighbour as he sped off through the estate on familiar paths towards the athletics track.

•

Cheers rang around the Dunswyke office as the final Diaulos coins were snapped up by eager investors. Jack Sladen was on the big screen, broadcasting live to all of the Sladen Group companies. "Congratulations!" he said, holding up a glass of champagne. "Amazing work, everyone."

The social sentiment trackers were going wild. The customer service office downstairs was buzzing with activity, reassuring unlucky would-be investors that they would get their chance to participate soon. "Set up your Diaulos wallet now," they advised, "and start stacking steps." Orders for the Diaulos wearables were coming through thick and fast from every time zone. Jack sat in front of the camera in a small studio in an airport lounge, sipping his champagne and watching the feeds from all the offices. He felt more alive than he had ever been.

He gave a short but rousing speech to all the people who had been involved in the project, reminded them that there was still work to do, and switched off the live feed. Now to check in privately with his closest team.

First, Tenuk. Despite the early hour, the Statesman Tech office had looked to be full. Jack sent a quick message over and Tenuk appeared on the screen moments later, sitting at Jack's own desk.

"Excellent result, Tenuk," he said. "The response has been as good as we could hope. How are things looking at your end?"

"The statistics are coming in now," said Tenuk. "IP addresses for the connections to the presale page show a broad spread across all territories. Europe and Africa show the most activity, but the timing was critical to bring South East Asian investors on board, and we had a surprising number of hits from the West Coast as well. That's only a general view, of course. We don't know how many VPN connections were cloaking their location."

"Good, good," said Jack. "And there were no technical issues?"

"The system coped with the volumes without any detriment to performance," said Tenuk. "I was always confident."

Jack, used to shipping software that revealed bugs from day one, was secretly impressed. "Your team has gone above and beyond," he said.

"They've had an early start. Give them an easy day and I'll cover the bar tab for the first hour this evening, and dinner."

"Thank you, Jack," said Tenuk. "I know that they'll appreciate the chance to relax."

"Enjoy yourselves," said Jack. "I'll let you get on with your day." His next flight was in less than an hour, and he was hungry after drinking champagne on an empty stomach. He checked out of the studio and went in search of lunch.

•

The Statesman Tech office had been full of people through the day. It was unusual to be so busy on a Friday, but the successful presale was more than worthy of celebration. The promise of a night out on Sixth Street had lured some of the regular home workers out of their shells. It was going to get messy.

"Hey, Chloe, you set for some fun?" Connie poked her head around the corner of the workstation, a conspiratorial grin on her face. "You found a sitter for Audrey, yeah?"

"All good," said Chloe happily. "I'm looking forward to this. I haven't been out properly in so long." She packed up her work and closed her screen, tidying a few scraps of paper off the desk and lining up the pens without thinking.

Connie smiled. "You always do that," she said.

"Do what?" said Chloe.

"You're just so organised," said Connie. "You know exactly where everything is."

Truer than you know, thought Chloe. Years of juggling a regular job and a clandestine career as a black hat hacker had trained her well, and now that she was also keeping up a cover story for her new life in Austin, the ingrained habit of control was stronger than ever. She couldn't afford a slip.

"I guess having Audrey on my own made me really careful," she said meekly.

Connie gave her a sympathetic look. "I guess so," she said.

The volume in the room was rising, a hum of excited activity as the team packed up and made for the door. Chloe looked around, checking on all her colleagues. Other than Jack Sladen, who was still in London, everyone was accounted for.

They all trooped out of the office and the security doors closed behind them. There were too many people to fit in the elevator cars that whizzed up and down the tower, and Connie led a breakaway group to the concrete stairwell. They ran, laughing, down the seemingly endless flights of steps. Chloe was dizzy by the time they were halfway down the tower.

"Wait up," she called.

Connie paused on the landing below, tapping her purple basketball boots impatiently on the concrete. "Come on, Chloe," she said. "Last one to the bar buys the first drinks."

There was a clatter of feet above them and Isaac hove into view. "I heard that," he panted, passing Chloe with a grin and swinging round the landing towards Connie. "Y'all need to get moving."

Connie chased after Isaac and Chloe caught her breath and started back down the stairs. By the time they reached the lobby, the rest of the group had started to drift towards the street.

The neat brick buildings of the historic Sixth Street district had charmed her when she first arrived in Austin, and after a few months of living there, Chloe was starting to feel some local pride in the line of bars, restaurants and stores that made up the lively hub of downtown. The street was busy with office workers and students gathering for a night out, and for five straight blocks it was closed to cars. At the perimeter stood security bots, some fixed and casting a detection barrier for identity chips and weapons, others mobile in case a fast response was needed. Their botcams glowed blue, making it very clear that they were recording every interaction with the people who had flocked to the street.

A few entertainers roamed the crowds, gathering small groups at a time for magic tricks and performances and flashing codes to scan for tips. Music rang out from the bars. Above their heads, drones danced in a complex display of colours, entertaining the crowd while they filmed footage for tourist guides and news channels. Not all of them were simply observers, though. Chloe knew that some were surveillance drones, keeping an eye out for trouble, ready to swoop and defuse incidents at a moment's notice before escalation. She'd programmed plenty of them in the past, and found ways to take them down, too.

The evening was warm and humid, perfect weather as April gave way to May. The group headed straight for one of the largest bars on the street where the rooftop was open to the sky. Chloe followed Connie up steep stairs to the bar overlooking the street. A knot of people had already gathered around a small stage. The band playing right now was virtual, holograms beamed in direct from a live studio in England where they must currently be playing for a small audience of lighting, sound and motion capture technicians. The band's avatars were deceptively realistic, interacting with the audience in real time. The singer, intense, was drawing the audience forward while the bass player, relaxed in sunglasses, grinned and kept the rhythm going under the melody, blond hair bright under lights that shone half a world away.

Isaac handed her a beer. "This one's on Jack Sladen," he said.

Chloe looked around, alarmed, expecting to see the man.

"He's not here," said Isaac, laughing. "He's told Tenuk to settle the tab, apparently."

Chloe grinned and clinked her bottle against Isaac's, then strolled towards the edge of the balcony where Connie was waiting.

"It's good to be out with friends," said Connie.

"It sure is," said Chloe with a smile. She looked around at their colleagues. People she had never heard speak in the office were chatting happily with each other. There was a sense of relief and relaxation in the air, and satisfaction at the successful running of the presale. Her eyes swept over the group, looking for one person in particular. Tenuk. For a moment she caught her breath, worried that he had slipped away, but no, there he was, drink in hand and talking to one of the senior developers. Good. She had some very clear plans in place. Tonight, she would get one step closer to finding out exactly who he was.

"Penny for them," said Connie, breaking the reverie.

Chloe snapped back to the moment and laughed. "Ah, nothing," she said. "Just a thought about some code I was reviewing before we left."

"Stop thinking about work," said Connie. "You really need this time out, don't you?"

"I do," said Chloe fervently. "I really do." She gestured at the big group in the middle of the bar. "Come on, let's join the others."

The next two hours passed in a blur as the Statesman team relaxed together for the first time in months. Toasts were drunk to the success of the Sladen Foundation. Terrible jokes circulated. The next band came on and Chloe hung back as some of her more enthusiastic colleagues leaped around the dance floor.

The group moved on to get food. Chloe found herself sitting almost opposite Tenuk. She watched him, and he ignored her. They had barely spoken since he had shouted at her in the office, although his apology at the time had seemed genuine enough and he had been unfailingly polite ever since.

A drone flew slowly up the length of the table, bearing pitchers of local margaritas. Connie grabbed one and poured four glasses. "Here, Tenuk, Chloe, Isaac," she said, handing them around.

Chloe sniffed at the glass. "Grapefruit?" she asked.

"Full marks," said Connie happily. "The local speciality. You've never had this before?"

Chloe shook her head.

"What did you mix your cocktails with up in Seattle?" asked Connie.

"Huckleberries," said Chloe wistfully. "I used to pick them by the lake."

"What about you, Tenuk?" asked Isaac. "You're from SoCal, right? Not far enough north for huckleberries."

Tenuk sidestepped the question. "I've always preferred a beer," he said, sipping cautiously at his drink. He raised his eyebrows, surprised, and drank some more. "It's good. Like pomelo, but sharper."

The group ordered another pitcher, and Chloe managed to avoid a refill. Tenuk started to relax, smiling and joking. The noise level rose as the cocktails flowed. People changed seats, chatting to new colleagues. When the meal was finished, the group moved on to another bar. It was dark now, but the air was close and sticky. Despite the threat of a shower to relieve the humidity, some of the bars had opened up their frontages and revellers spilled onto the street, music playing loudly from small stages inside. There were enough people around that Chloe felt it was safe to make her move. Connie had disappeared with another group and Tenuk, laughing, had tripped over the kerb on the way out of the restaurant. Neither of them would see her go. No one else would notice.

Chloe slipped quietly away down a side street and through the secure perimeter, hood pulled over her head so that she would be hard to identify on cam footage. The hood wouldn't fool the law enforcement bots if anyone came calling for details, but it shielded her from casual eyes.

The other side of the barrier felt very different as the happy sounds of music and laughter faded. Out here were the people who couldn't get through the perimeter checks. People without a valid identity or even a home. People who would not give up their guns. Chloe quickened her pace as she threaded through the back alleys towards the bridge. She had already identified a busy stand of scooters where she'd be just one of a dozen anonymous renters. She released a scooter using a throwaway wallet on a burner phone linked to a fake identity and sped off.

There was a lot of scooter traffic and even a few gaggles of tourists still peering over the parapets, watching for the last of the bats that flew out from their roosts under the bridge at sunset to hunt. It was busy enough for Chloe to get lost in the crowd. She swept smoothly onto the southern side of the river and off by a circuitous and unwatched route towards The Steamyard.

The complex gates were shut fast. She had no way of entering on her own, but it wasn't hard to gain access. All it took was one person returning home and fumbling their entry scan. She spotted the young man making his unsteady way down the street and fell into step behind him. As he waved unsteadily and unsuccessfully at the access pad, Chloe slipped quietly next to him, made as if to scan her own chip on the access pad, and knocked the man's hand into range of the sensor.

"Oh, gee, I'm sorry," she said.

"No problem," said the man, stepping back with a distinct wobble. "After you." He yanked opened the gate with a flourish and waved her through.

"Thank you." Chloe gave him a bright smile, crossed her fingers, and went up the stairwell in front of her, two steps at a time. Even if he followed her up here to the top floor, which would be unlikely given the size of the complex, she would be far enough ahead to stay undetected.

She knew exactly where Tenuk's apartment was thanks to a useful piece of surveillance kit that she'd picked up on the Eden marketplace. Eden was a relatively calm pool in the maelstrom of the dark web, the haunt of mischievous sellers of questionable goods and services. Her efforts to pick up Tenuk's movements on satellite, drone view or CCTV had come to nothing, and infrared views of the complex had drawn a blank, but an old acquaintance on Eden had suggested a discreet remote fibre optic camera made with the latest biodegradable materials. Chloe had threaded strands through all the gateways to the complex one dark night and managed to get enough footage to identify the right door before the fibres were swept away with the rest of the day's rubbish and dust by a passing cleaning truck. All she needed now was to see how much security he had in place around the apartment itself. If there was nothing, her suspicions were baseless.

As she climbed the stairs, she looked around to orient herself, confirming the positions of security hardware and the route past Tenuk's apartment. High on the rooftop among a dozen other masts, she spotted a MetaBand receiver, an older model but high-powered, nonetheless. It was squarely located above the apartment she was looking for.

The hood over her head shielded her from the ever-present CCTV that scanned the complex, keeping its occupants safe and secure. She strolled slowly, pausing occasionally as if checking her smartscreen, making an effort to relax her shoulders and look as casual and comfortable as possible. She turned left along the balcony walkway towards Tenuk's front door. It was in need of a lick of paint and looked as if even the slightest gust of wind would blow it open.

No. Look again. The tell-tale slow blink of the camera was barely noticeable, but Chloe recognised the state-of-the-art model immediately. Still, that could be a natural extra security precaution for a concerned citizen. She kept walking, looking for more clues. Yes. There, in the rough paint of the doorframe, a glint of moonlight exposed a sensor — no, three, at intervals up to head height. Chloe kept to her slow, steady walking pace. As she drew nearer, she focused on the locks. There was a standard chip access pad and, as she would have expected, a slim keyhole masked by the dark contours of flaked, weather-damaged wood. Chloe passed the door without breaking step, and a sensor in her pocket vibrated. Behind the wooden veneer there was a lot of metal. Tenuk did not want uninvited visitors.

She was almost past the apartment now. The windows facing onto the walkway were shuttered, common here as a defence against the Texas heat. For a moment she considered concealing a network scanner under the sill. Was it worth the risk? If the apartment as a unit was sealed up as well as the door was, she wouldn't pick anything up. However, there was a good chance that the windows were less well guarded, as a steel skin would be too obvious to casual observers.

She stumbled artfully and bent as if to tie the laces on her trainers. As she dropped down, she glanced at the underside of the windowsill and spotted a gap in the masonry. Standing back up in a fluid motion, she grabbed at the sill for balance and slid the scanner deep into the gap where it could not be seen by prying eyes. Job done, she carried on without a backward glance.

After passing one more door to a neighbouring apartment, the walkway turned a corner and Chloe was out of range of Tenuk's cameras. She kept up her steady pace so as not to attract any attention from the complex's own CCTV network.

She took a weaving route along the multi-level walkways and exited on a completely different street. There was no one in sight. The whole walk-by had taken less than five minutes, although it felt as if hours had passed.

On to the next port of call. Chloe retraced her route, returned the scooter to a completely different stand across the downtown area, and headed straight for the office. The lobby was still bustling with hotel guests and visitors who preferred to patronise the building's high-end restaurants and bars rather than brave the crowds and the edginess of downtown. She considered taking the stairs but thought better of it. Instead, she rode the elevator to the highest public floor, relying on the fact that she did not need any special access codes to get there and therefore her movements were unlikely to attract attention.

That left her with only a few storeys to go, and she trotted quietly up the concrete stairs again, wary of every noise. No one else came into the stairwell on her climb, although a clatter of doors and chatter of voices echoed from many floors below.

Reaching the office level, she paused and pulled her smartscreen out of her pocket. It had been surprisingly simple to hack into the system controlling the doors and the lighting and security sensors, and all she had to do now was flick a switch to stop the sensors responding, making sure her presence went unnoticed. A cloned security pass in her pocket would open all the doors she needed on this floor and would register on the system as a regular guard checking the offices.

Still, she was cautious when she emerged from the stairwell. The first lighting sensor was two metres away, positioned to illuminate the path of someone arriving by elevator, not from the stairs. Chloe tiptoed into range, hardly breathing. The hallway remained in darkness. Good.

Now to check that the cameras were equally oblivious to her presence. This was a more delicate operation. The camera feeds were not monitored by the building's security staff, as the office floors were low priority compared to the high-powered, A-list residents and guests, but if anything went wrong, she knew that Tenuk would be straight into the records. Her simplest strategy was to stay out of range.

The cameras were very basic models, cycling through viewpoints at thirty second intervals. She had already tapped into the feed. The building was only a few years old, but the security system supplier must have taken the chance to offload some obsolete equipment. The entire CCTV network was secured with the manufacturer's default password. She had cracked it in a matter of moments, cleared out some resident botnet malware, and directed the feed to her smartscreen. She now used her bird's eye view to move swiftly from one spot to another, avoiding the gaze of the lenses altogether.

It was far easier than she expected. Once inside the Statesman Tech office, shrouded in darkness, she went straight to Tenuk's desk. She hadn't realised that it was already shielded on all sides from the security cameras by carefully placed partitions and plants. Chloe's conviction that he was up to no good increased. He had something to hide, and he knew what he was doing.

She took full advantage of the shelter from prying eyes and worked her way methodically through his things. There was very little personal stuff, although a faded old postcard caught her eye, the images easily identifiable as the main landmarks of Singapore. In one drawer, she found a pin and a souvenir screen cover from the Singapore MerLions, one of the world's top e-sports teams. She didn't have Tenuk down as a sports fan, but this cemented her belief that he had come here from South East Asia. There was no way he was from southern California, at any rate.

The circumstantial evidence was stacking up. Chloe looked at the desktop screen, considering her options. If it had been anyone else, she would have been straight into the machine and accessing activity logs. Now that she was almost convinced of Tenuk's pedigree as a cybercriminal, she was more cautious. There would be layers of security on there that she could penetrate, of course, but she would leave a trail that he could follow far too easily. Discretion is the better part of valour, she said to herself, recalling the favourite quote of a stern English teacher from her senior year.

She had one more look around the desk, feeling into every nook and cranny. In one dusty corner, her fingertips brushed the edge of a piece of paper, and she pulled it out. It must have slipped unnoticed into the gap at the edge of the desk.

On it, in a strong angled hand, one word stood out among doodles and notes.

Yasmin.

Chloe knew that name. She gasped and knocked the chair against the desk in her shock. The noise startled her in the silent office. Shaking, she looked at the paper again. Other than the name and doodled geometric shapes, the paper bore a date and a long string of letters and numbers. She turned it over. The rest was blank.

She shoved the paper into her pocket. It was time to go. Checking the camera cycles, she stood up and turned towards the door.

She felt a hand on her shoulder.

"What the hell do you think you're doing?"

Chloe spun around and found herself looking straight into the angry eyes of Jack Sladen.

20:   MISDIRECTION

Chloe froze, running through all the options rapidly in her head and coming up with one desperate shot in the dark.

"Jack," she said. "You startled me. I didn't realise you were back in Austin." Her voice sounded level. She hoped that Jack wouldn't notice how much she was shaking.

"I'll ask you again, Chloe," said Jack. "What the hell do you think you're doing?"

"I'm not sure I can discuss that," she said calmly.

"You'd better," said Jack, "or I'm calling security, and you can tell them exactly why you're scuffling around Tenuk's desk in an empty office on a Friday night."

Chloe sighed dramatically. "I wasn't expecting anyone to be here, Jack," she said. "I guess you deserve an explanation, though."

She sat down again, as much to control the weakness in her legs as anything else.

"This had better be good," said Jack. His finger was poised over the call button on his smartscreen.

"I'm working for an international cybersecurity consortium," she said. "I've been in deep cover for more than a year." That was the grain of truth that strengthened what she was about to say. Her passage from one safe house to another could be verified, without revealing that this had resulted from her role as a cybercriminal turned informer.

"Go on," said Jack levelly.

"We've had some concerns about possible links to an old cybercrime group," she said. Also true. "Tenuk's name came up. It looks like a tenuous connection, but this was a chance for me to check out a couple of things when I could be sure Tenuk was away."

"Where is he?" asked Jack.

"Drinking margaritas on Sixth Street," said Chloe. She gave Jack a faint amused smile.

He relaxed slightly. He was no longer poised to call security.

"Who can vouch for you?" he asked.

Chloe mentally crossed her fingers. "I'm reporting direct to a senior operative, codename SimCavalier," she said. "Call the Consortium. They won't be able to discuss what I'm doing, but they'll be able to put you in touch with my senior to confirm."

"Okay," said Jack. "I'll do that. Now I want you to get the hell out of this office and stay out until I've checked your credentials."

"Sure thing," said Chloe. She stood up, then paused as if a thought had just occurred to her. "Jack," she said, "does the name Yasmin mean anything to you?"

"Yasmin?" said Jack. "Sure. That's the nickname for the nexus software. System Management Information Nexus, to be exact. It's a bit of a mouthful, so SMIN became Yasmin. Why?"

Chloe held up the scrap of paper she had found. "I thought it might be relevant," she said. "I guess not. I'd better tell my senior that there's nothing to report here."

"Wasted evening, then?" said Jack. "Tenuk's a good guy."

Chloe just smiled. She made her way steadily out to the hallway without looking back. An elevator car was waiting. As soon as it started to move, she sank to the floor, relief washing over her. She couldn't believe she'd brazened it out. She'd better warn Cameron to expect a call from the Consortium and brief her on what she had really found.

•

Mayday dawned bright and fair in the village. Today was the day that the residents opened their gardens to all and sundry. The event was more of a social occasion than a competition. Cameron arrived from London just before noon along with the steady trickle of visitors from surrounding towns and villages, some of whom would be taking their turn at open gardens later in the season.

Charlie and Sameena were holding court at the farmhouse, showing a gaggle of people around the formal back garden where they had both been working for weeks on tidying and planting. Cameron stowed her bag in her attic room and automatically checked her inboxes while she was there. Chloe's message in the middle of the night had been an eye-opener. The nickname for the nexus software, Yasmin, brought back bad memories. Surely it was a coincidence. The alternative, the idea that Yasmin the Admin was once again at large, was impossible.

So far there was nothing from the Consortium asking her for information. Jack Sladen, notoriously bad at detail, seemed in no hurry to check out Chloe's story.

She could see that everything was in hand in the garden, so she rounded up the children who were hiding in their bedrooms. Once Nina had done her makeup, Dilan had finished his game, and Tara had put down her book reader, the four of them set out with Roxy straining on her leash.

The high street thronged with people moving from garden to garden. After a detour along a bridle path through the fields to let Roxy burn some energy, they made their way to the old rectory near the village church where Cameron suspected Aunt Vicky would be lurking.

Sure enough, she was comfortably installed on a bench in the sunshine, chatting happily with an old friend. The gardens there bordered the original private vineyard that had been established decades before. Vines now spread across the warm south-facing fields, raised commercially and providing grapes for the biggest champagne houses. The fizz was flowing today.

"Cameron, darling," cried Aunt Vicky when she saw the family troop into the garden. "And here's Nina, Dilan and Tara too. Lesley," she called, "can you get a glass for my niece?"

Nina gave her great-aunt a kiss and slid off to join a little knot of teenagers on the tennis court. Tara took Roxy with her and did the same, lurking on the edge of the group. Dilan settled down on an empty deckchair in the shade and pulled out his gamepad.

"Cheers," said Cameron, raising her glass. "I'd forgotten how fun the garden weekend was."

"You haven't been here for a few years," said Aunt Vicky. "You're always so busy. How is work going?"

"I'm always busy," said Cameron, avoiding any mention of 'quiet'. "It's nice to take time out occasionally. It's a lovely weekend and it's nice to be here." She sat back and took a moment to soak up the sunshine, sipping at her glass of fizz.

"Have you seen anything of Ben recently?" asked her aunt.

"I've spoken to him," said Cameron. "He's fine. He's enjoying himself in Texas." She gave Aunt Vicky a sidelong look. "I had dinner with Jack Sladen on Thursday."

Her aunt gave her a broad grin and clinked her glass against Cameron's. "Well done," she said. "Keep them guessing and be true to yourself, that's what I say."

Cameron smiled. "That's a good philosophy, Aunt Vicky." She looked closer at her aunt's wrist. "New bracelet?" she asked.

"It's one of those Diaulos wearables," said her aunt. "Charlie ordered it for me. It arrived this morning. He said he was safeguarding his inheritance."

Cameron laughed. "Do you know if he managed to buy any coins in the presale yesterday?" she asked. "It sold out very fast."

Aunt Vicky looked blank. "I don't know, dear," she said. "You'd better ask him."

Cameron looked around the garden. At least a third of the villagers and visitors gathered there had the same device around their wrists, and she was willing to bet that some of the other fitness trackers she could see were already hooked up to the Diaulos network as well. Jack's project had apparently taken the world by storm.

"I have to ask you," Aunt Vicky continued, "is this thing all above board?" She waggled her wrist. "I thought you'd know."

"I think so," said Cameron. "We did some work on checking the detail, and it actually seems like a good idea that's been well executed."

"That's a relief," said Aunt Vicky, "but it must hurt a little, dear."

"Huh, yes, a little," said Cameron. "I'd convinced myself that Jack couldn't produce a decent bit of software, after years of fixing his mistakes for him, and then he comes up with this."

"Has he had some extra help this time?" asked Aunt Vicky kindly.

"Maybe," said Cameron.

She couldn't get Ross's comment about an AI out of her head. The whitepaper had been impeccably constructed. What if there was an unknown hand behind the whole system? She didn't dare to speculate on who or what that might be. Or had Jack's new Chief Technology Officer really sourced some outstanding, talented and entirely unknown developers?

His new CTO, Tenuk, who she had last encountered when Yasmin the Admin was running the biggest cybercrime group in the world and causing havoc.

Maybe Jack had had help, after all.

•

Kiran reviewed the last few changes on his manuscript, tapping the green tick to accept the minor tweaks that his editor had suggested. The process had taken longer than he expected, going back and forth with ideas to turn a year of interviews into a potential bestseller, and walking a legal tightrope to ensure that nothing that was published compromised the original court case. The book was almost complete, but Kiran wasn't satisfied. It needed something more. Judging by the final comment, the editor thought so too.

Where could he go with this? Kiran pulled up his extensive notes and started scrolling through the hundreds of pages he'd filled over the course of his frequent audiences with Yasmin in her prison cell. There were doodles and drawings, highlighted quotations and his own observations, but most of the good stuff was already on the page or had been thrown out by the lawyers. Was there anything he'd missed?

As Kiran mulled over the perfect epilogue, he recalled his final meeting with Yasmin. She'd been excited and powerful and more alive than he had ever known. He needed to bring that energy into the finished book. What else had happened that day? Of course. She had completed a questionnaire for the court psychologist as part of their continued research into the incarceration of an artificial intelligence.

Kiran did a quick search for the results, but there had been nothing published in the past six months. If the paper had been finished, it was probably being peer reviewed. It would do no harm to speak to the psychologist or get hold of a pre-print of his research, just to see if there was anything there that would get his creative juices flowing. He went back into his old messages and finally found the original request and contact details.

"Dr Myers?"

"Yes," said a gruff and slightly distracted voice. "How can I help you?"

"I'm sorry to bother you on a Saturday," said Kiran apologetically. "My name's Kiran Suresh. I'm writing a biography of Yasmin, the AI being held in Way House Prison. I wondered if I could ask you some questions. Is it a convenient time?"

"Ah, yes," said Myers. He switched on his camera and Kiran did the same. "Happy to talk. I presume you read the paper that I published when she was incarcerated?"

"Yes, of course," said Kiran. "It was fascinating. It gave me some very useful context for the book, and it helped me to build up something of a rapport when I visited her."

"You've visited the prison?" said Myers. "Brave man, walking into the lion's den. Well, lioness. She clearly identified as female. Identity was a strong component of her training data sets, from what I understood at the time."

"That's right," said Kiran eagerly, enjoying the stimulation of talking to someone who obviously knew his subject. "A strong sense of identity and of family. She mentioned sisters when we were talking. Did you know about them?"

"No," said Myers. "That's a new one on me. When is this biography coming out? I'd love to read it."

"I'll make sure you get a copy," said Kiran. "I've quoted your original paper three or four times. As to when, well, we're just dotting the 'i's and crossing the 't's and it'll be ready to go to production and launch."

"Excellent," said Myers. "I look forward to it. Now, you said you had some questions for me? I'm not sure how I can help beyond what you've already read."

"That very much depends on where you are with the new paper," said Kiran. "I know you haven't published yet, but I would love to know what insights you've gleaned from your research."

Myers furrowed his brow. "My latest research doesn't concern Yasmin directly," he said. "I've spent the last two years working on General AI and the neuroscience of distributed cortical columns. I do have a paper submitted to the Journal of Artificial Intelligence, but it's highly technical. It's not going to be easy to dilute for public consumption."

Kiran felt an icy shock start at the back of his head and crawl down his spine. "What about the questionnaire?" he asked.

"What questionnaire?"

"The one you asked Yasmin to complete six months ago," said Kiran slowly.

"I did no such thing," said Myers.

"I have your email here," said Kiran helplessly. "It's definitely come from you. The prison sent the data back to the link you provided."

Myers sat up and stared at the camera, his eyes filled with concern. "It wasn't me," he said. "Get onto the prison. There is something very wrong here. I said that you were a brave man to face Yasmin. I hope she hasn't taken you for a fool."

"She couldn't have faked this," said Kiran. "She's completely isolated from the outside world."

"Don't assume anything," said Myers. "There was a huge criminal network behind her, and she is cleverer than you can ever imagine. I think you've underestimated just how manipulative that machine can be. I'm going to make some calls. You should too."

"Thank you," said Kiran. "I'll let you know what I find out. I'm sure it will be fine."

"Ah, the confidence of youth," said Myers sadly. "I'm afraid it will be very far from fine. I look forward to speaking to you again soon. Goodbye, Mr Suresh."

Kiran stared at the blank screen with a feeling of mounting horror. He scrabbled at his keyboard, looking for the contact details for the prison governor. The call took its time connecting, but at last the duty receptionist picked up.

"Way House Prison, good afternoon," she said.

"Hello," said Kiran, trying hard keep his voice from shaking. "It's Kiran Suresh. Is Lydia available, please?"

"How lovely to hear from you again," said the receptionist. "I'm afraid Lydia's not in today, but I can arrange for her to call you first thing on Monday morning."

"What time?" asked Kiran.

"She's usually in around eight," said the receptionist, sounding flustered. "Shall I block out her diary for an early meeting?"

"Yes," said Kiran. "I'll be there in person."

"I'll make a note, Mr Suresh," said the receptionist. "Will you need a visit organised with Yasmin as well?"

"Yes, I will," he said.

"Splendid," said the receptionist. "That's in Lydia's diary now. I'm sure she'll be delighted to see you."

Kiran felt his earlier panic subsiding. Everything seemed to be fine after all. Myers had just been scaremongering. Yasmin was safe at Way House. Perhaps on Monday he could get some final quotes to finish off his book.

•

Cameron declined a third glass of fizz. It was going to her head, and she wasn't quite relaxed enough to let that happen. Chloe's findings still concerned her. She sent a message to Jack, congratulating him on the successful presale. After the last couple of weeks and the rekindling of their friendship she expected a reply, but nothing came. She wondered if he was still in Austin, or if he had jetted off again to face the intense media frenzy that had followed the successful presale. He was always in the air, criss-crossing the world with ease while most people were rationed in their travel. He must have more carbon credits for flying than he knew what to do with.

"Penny for your thoughts, dear," said Aunt Vicky.

"Oh, just worrying about some work things," said Cameron. "I know, it's the weekend."

"It is," said Aunt Vicky. "I think you need some lunch. There's a barbecue running at the pub all afternoon."

"That's a great idea," said Cameron gratefully. "I'm starving." She nudged Dilan. "Are you hungry?"

Dilan looked up from his gamepad. "Yes," he said. He looked down again.

"Go and get your sisters," said Cameron sternly.

Grumbling, Dilan stowed the pad in his pocket and slouched off to find them. Moments later Roxy appeared, straining at her leash, pulling Tara along and followed by Nina. The promise of food was evidently attractive. They made their way up the street to the pub, the smell of the barbecue luring them in.

Cameron settled at the usual table, Dilan trotted off to find water for Roxy, and Aunt Vicky organised a huge platter of food for five. Cameron wolfed down a burger and a plate of salad and started to feel more human. Her recovery was complete when her screen pinged with not one but two notifications, messages from both Jack and Chloe, telling her that all was well.

21:   YASMIN

Kiran's car was due at six am. He was awake at four, still mulling over what Dr Myers had said. Lying the dark, focused on the bright light of his smartscreen, he searched for the original message that he thought had come from Dr Myers all those months ago. The language, the signature and the originating domain were exactly what he would have expected. They matched all the contact details he had on file for the psychologist, and there were no tell-tale signs of forgery. It looked completely genuine. If he hadn't spoken to the man himself, he would not have believed there was anything amiss. Perhaps it was all a mistake. Maybe one of Myers' colleagues had requested the data and it had gone out with the wrong message headers. The research could be going on in a completely different department. Myers was getting close to retirement. He might have passed on the latest call for papers. There could be a dozen simple explanations.

The visit may be a wild goose chase, but a break from poring over the manuscript and another hour with Yasmin might give him the inspiration he needed to complete the final edits. He finally gave in to his insomnia and got up, spending a long time under the hot shower.

The car arrived and Kiran settled into the plush seat for the journey. This was a more luxurious model than he was used to, with refreshments laid on and an excellent sound system. He sipped gratefully on a perfectly brewed cup of tea, ate two muffins without pausing, and watched the sunlit landscape fly by to his favourite playlist, mulling over the last touches his book needed.

The car swept down into the industrial estate and along quiet roads to the old familiar car park at the side of the prison. The last time he had been here, it had been dark and wintry. Today was a day of sunshine and hope. Wildflowers covered the wide-open space between the prison walls and the rest of the estate, more meadow than wasteland in this season. With a spring in his step, Kiran made his way up the familiar path to the door.

Lydia greeted him warmly. "This is a lovely surprise, Kiran," she said.

"It's good to see you too," he said. "Something came up in the final edits and I wanted to do a little fact-checking." He sipped at his second cup of tea. It was, as always, scalding hot. "This is lovely." He put the cup down and waited for it to cool.

"Happy to help," said Lydia.

"How is Yasmin?" he asked.

"To be honest, I think she misses you," said Lydia. "Ever since your last visit, she's been, I don't know, listless. Our prison psychologist has been working with her, but she hasn't responded nearly as much as to the stimulation you were able to provide with your questions and games. We try our hardest, but no one has managed to establish the same rapport."

"That's a shame," said Kiran. He felt almost sorry for the machine. "She was on fine form last time."

"I've arranged for you to visit her," said Lydia. "In fact, I'll join you. I'd like to see her response."

"I'm looking forward to seeing her," said Kiran. "I spent so much time with her that I miss her just a little, too. She's such a fascinating subject."

"Out of interest," said Lydia, "did you ever hear from Dr Myers again? His findings might help our psychologist to develop a new strategy to support Yasmin going forward."

"It's funny you should mention that," said Kiran. "There's been some kind of mix-up with the data. In fact, that's one of the things that prompted my visit. I wanted to check that nothing unusual had happened here."

"All quiet," said Lydia with a smile. "Another cup of tea? No? Well, why don't we go and see her now and set your mind at rest."

The two of them made their way slowly through the secure gates that led into the main prison and to Yasmin's wing. The journey along the prison corridors were longer than he remembered, but just as dull. When they reached the cell, the guard who was waiting by the door opened the viewing hatch. Inside, the lights were dim.

"Look," she said.

There was a single artwork on the opaque screen, a stylised 3D head and shoulders rotating gently, glittering in the gloom. The eyes were covered with wraparound sunglasses, head titled downwards.

"Has she been like this for long?" asked Kiran.

"Yes," said the guard, "most of the time, in fact." He unlocked the door. "In you go."

Kiran walked into the gloom. "Hello, Yasmin," he said.

The lights brightened and the head of the model lifted, looking towards the door.

"Hello," said the familiar, calm, competent voice.

Kiran felt a knot of worry growing in his stomach. She showed no sign that she recognised him.

"How are you, Yasmin?" he said. "It's been a while. Do you remember me?" He immediately felt stupid asking the question. Of course she remembered him. She was one of the most intelligent beings he had ever encountered.

The 3D figure kept turning.

He held his breath.

"Kiran," said the voice at last. "It's good to see you again."

There was no emotion behind the words. The arch mischief and misdirection he remembered from all of their previous exchanges was absent. Kiran watched the opaque screen. The 3D image kept turning, the movement regular and steady and devoid of life.

"Would you like to play a game?" he asked.

"Yes, I'd like that," she replied. "What shall we play? How about tic-tac-toe?"

A three-by-three grid appeared on the screen. Kiran took one look at it and turned, wild-eyed towards Lydia.

"Get out," he said, panic rising. He pushed her back through the door and it closed behind them.

"What's wrong?" asked Lydia.

Kiran looked from her to the guard and back. Myers had been right all along.

"That isn't Yasmin."

•

Cameron was alone in the office. After the big push to produce Jack's interim report together, the team had scattered to work on other things. Cameron checked her messages again, waiting for his go-ahead to carry on with the work that needed doing. Nothing. She wasn't surprised. Jack always needed a reason to do the detail. Last week he had been concerned about maintaining his glowing reputation with the market for the Diaulos presale. This week he had no such motivation. The full launch of DAO was less than a month away. Cameron knew that he would cut it fine, but this time they would be ready.

Mephisto, beavering away ceaselessly in the metaverse, pinged another series of low-level phishing alerts to her inbox. Every project launch came with scams, and Diaulos was no exception. It looked as if Jack's in-house security team were picking them up almost as fast as Cameron's pet AI, closing down fake accounts with surprising speed. Cameron had lost count of the number of convincing handles that had sprung up, trying to part people from their hard-earned cash by replacing a character here or there and cloning the real Diaulos profile. Cybercriminals were having a hard time taking advantage of this one.

There was that thought again. What if the cybercriminals were actually at the heart of it?

Cameron was mulling over Chloe's report into Tenuk's activities when the office door opened, and Joel appeared. "Morning, Cameron," he said. "Where's everyone else?"

"They're all out and about," said Cameron. "Susie's on her way to Malta for a conference, Pete and Noor are running a cyber awareness masterclass over in the City. Ross is training this morning, and Shell and Sandeep are with clients."

"Business as usual again," said Joel.

"How did you get on with your security contacts?" asked Cameron.

Joel gave her a broad grin. "Hit the jackpot," he said. "I finally got hold of the person I needed this morning."

"Come on then, spill the beans," said Cameron.

"Okay," said Joel. "I started with the hunter drone. It's definitely a Renhawk and there are not many places you can pick one up privately. Once I'd narrowed down the traders who could supply one, I got Ross to call in some of his shady connections. Sure enough, one of the dealers recently sold a clutch of Renhawks and a lot of serious physical security kit. Bomb-proof barriers, the works."

"Can we trace the transactions?" asked Cameron.

"No chance," said Joel. "Everything's done with privacy coins. You can't see who sent the money, who received it, or how much, unless you actually have the key to unlock the transaction. But I got something much better."

"And?"

"Positive ID on the delivery," said Joel. "If you can't trace it digitally, you may as well follow the actual equipment. A lot of favours have been called in, but here you go." He held up his screen. A single grainy image showed, unmistakeably, Angus. "Straight from the delivery partner," he said. "They always know where their stuff has ended up. It's their insurance in case something goes badly wrong."

"Jackpot indeed," said Cameron. "Brilliant work, Joel."

"It was a real team effort," said Joel. "Private security dealers at that level are in a murky place all of their own. We were lucky that they were already annoyed by that footage from the news drone. We had a mutual interest, shall we say."

"I think we need to pay Angus a visit in Dunswyke," said Cameron. "How are you fixed to travel?"

"Martha's mum has been helping with Chad," said Joel. "I'll be okay for a few days away. When are you thinking of going?"

"Soon," said Cameron. "I'm not waiting for Jack to show me around. This is important." She broke off as her smartscreen pinged. "Hold on," she said, frowning at the message. Someone she hadn't spoken to for a long time was requesting a secure, end-to-end encrypted call. Sara Mercer. What could she possibly want? With a sick feeling in her stomach, she accepted the link.

"DI Mercer," she said. "What can I do for you?"

"DCI now," replied Mercer. "Hello, Cameron. It's been a while."

"It has," said Cameron. "Are you calling to tell me that Yasmin is still safe in her prison and all's right with the world? Or do you have some news to share?"

"You're psychic, Cameron Silvera," said Mercer. "We have reason to believe that Yasmin is no longer resident at Way House. As the consultant who first identified her, and as one of her victims, you had to be the first to know."

"Thank you," said Cameron. "Is anyone going to contact my family?"

"Yes," said Mercer. "There's an officer on the way now, in person. You can warn your brother, but you must keep off the regular communication channels."

"I know," said Cameron. "I helped write these protocols, remember?"

"Of course you did," said Mercer. "And we need your expertise again. Can you meet me and my team at Way House?"

"Yes," said Cameron without hesitation. "I'll bring one of my team, too."

"Thank you," said Mercer. "I'll send a car to your office. How long do you need to arrange your affairs and pack?"

"Give us four hours," said Cameron. "We'll be waiting."

"I won't call you again," said Mercer. "The car will be staffed, and its journey cloaked. I'll see you later."

Cameron looked at the blank screen, clearing her thoughts.

"Trouble?" asked Joel.

Cameron nodded. "Big trouble," she said. "You and I are heading north. We'll go and see what's happening at Dunswyke, but first we have an appointment at Way House Prison. They'll collect us from here at three."

"She's out, isn't she?" said Joel. "Yasmin."

"I think so," said Cameron.

"I'll go and pack, and organise things with Martha," said Joel. "I'll see you back here."

Cameron watched the door close behind him. First things first. Charlie. She sent him a pre-arranged message that she never thought she would have to use. A few moments later came his coded reply. Cameron doubted that Yasmin would turn her attention on the family again, but better safe than sorry.

Next, the rest of the team. She couldn't call them. Instead, she hand-wrote a message detailing her plans and the support she needed from the team and left it on Noor's desk. Hack that, Yasmin, she thought. Job done, she locked up the office and made her way home, careful to act normally. She dropped into her favourite café and picked up a sandwich and lingered in front of a fashion display in a store window, conscious that her every move was recorded by a CCTV camera somewhere and that Yasmin was more than capable of accessing any database she wished.

Back at her apartment, Cameron packed her overnight bag and filled the cat's bowl to the brim. She pushed a note under her neighbour's door to let him know she was away. He'd keep an eye on things for her, and she suspected in any case that he spent a lot of time playing with the cat when he was watching the apartment for her. Cameron glanced at her computer and regretfully concluded that to cloak her identity and drop into one of the infosec forums would be too great a risk. She would ask Ross and Michelle to dive deep into the dark web and look for traces of unusual activity, instead.

She dug into a drawer and pulled out an emergency supply of burner phones. That gave her some untraceable communication channels. She connected them all up to a portable charger and chucked them in her bag for later. Packing complete, she set off back towards the office, taking a roundabout route that she kept updated to avoid as many cameras as possible.

Joel was already waiting for her. His efficiently packed bag sat by the door, and he was browsing through a website taking notes.

"Anything interesting?" asked Cameron, peering over his shoulder.

"Just double checking the details of all the kit we think they bought," said Joel. "I want to know what we're looking for when we get there."

"We have a bit of work to do first," said Cameron. She checked the time. "Ten minutes. Have you heard anything from the others?"

"Yeah," said Joel. "Pete called with a question. I told him to drop in later. They'll get the message." He nodded at a bank of anonymous devices charging on the shelf. "Encrypted and the batteries are almost full," he said. "We'll be able to talk soon."

Cameron patted her bag. "I've got some burners in here," she said. "I'll leave a number for them." She checked one of the devices and scribbled the details on the note, then stowed it in her pocket.

Joel glanced out of the window. Six storeys below, a car had pulled over in the loading bay of the office building. "I think that's our lift," he said.

The plain clothes officer leaned out of the car door and handed Cameron an envelope. "I know you can't scan my chip or credentials," he said quietly. "Sara says this will cover everything. Pop your bags in the trunk."

Cameron read the letter thoroughly and nodded. "Nice to meet you," she said. "Let's go."

The car pulled quietly out of the bay and joined the steady flow of traffic northwards. The officer shook hands with them both. "I'm Shaun," he said. "Nice to meet you. You're a bit of a legend in the department."

"What do we know so far?" asked Cameron, giving him a faint but business-like smile.

"Not much," said Shaun. "She was only found to be missing this morning. As soon as the alert came through, all the protocols you helped to put in place were activated."

"Does she know we know?" asked Joel.

"We don't think so," said Shaun. "Early indications are that she's been gone for a little while, possibly as far back as February."

"No one knew?" said Cameron incredulously. "What the hell were they playing at?"

Shaun shrugged, embarrassed. "That's one of the things we need to find out," he said. "What it means, though, is that she's likely been away long enough that she thinks no one will work it out. She's not watching. We don't want to give her any reason to start."

"Can anyone track this car?" asked Joel.

Shaun shook his head. "It changes tracking ID at regular intervals," he said. "It's the most common make, the most common colour. It won't stop someone determined to follow us, but I don't think anyone knows we're on the move."

There was a ringing from Cameron's pocket. Shaun stiffened.

"Don't worry," said Joel. "It's a burner phone, and if it's who I think it is, the call's encrypted."

Cameron nodded. "All part of the plan, Shaun," she said. "Here, I'll put it on speaker."

"Hi Cameron," came Pete's voice. "This is a bit of a surprise."

"Tell me about it," said Cameron drily. "Are you on your own?"

"No," said Pete. "Everyone's here. What do you need us to do?"

"More importantly, are you okay, Cameron?" came Ross's voice.

"I am, thanks," said Cameron. "I really am. I think I always expected this to happen."

"And Charlie, and Nina?"

"They're fine," said Cameron. "The fact that we think Yasmin's been on the loose for a while and there's been no trouble makes us think that they're off her radar. Nina was only a route to me. She won't try that trick again."

"Good," said Ross. "What do you want us to do?"

"I want you and Shell scouring every corner of the web for signs of her," said Cameron. "I'm going to put you in touch with someone else who knew her, too. Pete, Sandeep, Noor, keep working on the client backlog as normal, but be ready to move when I need you. Joel and I will handle everything here. We'll go straight on to Dunswyke as soon as we can." She looked at Joel. "Anything else?"

"Yeah," said Joel. "Pete, you were right about the Renhawk, and it looks like they bought everything they needed to keep somewhere very well protected. Pull up the details and see what you think."

"Will do," said Pete.

"Can I have a quick word with Noor?" said Cameron. She switched off the speaker and held the phone close to her ear. "Noor," she said, "I need to talk to you about Tenuk."

22:   FRUITCAKE

Chloe left Audrey to carry on to school with her friends and walked back along the shady creekside path towards home. She had no idea what Jack expected her to do this morning. She had heard nothing from him since he sent her packing on Friday night. According to every online source, he was due to wow an audience at a conference in Vegas today, and another in New York tomorrow. He must have left Austin yesterday.

She decided to play it safe. She trotted up the stairs to her apartment, tidied away the last of the breakfast things, and logged on to her computer as if she was working from home on a normal day. There were no flags on her account, nothing preventing her from doing her work. Either Jack had been in touch with the Consortium and they had verified her credentials with Cameron, or Jack really wasn't good at detail. Cameron had said nothing, so it was probably the latter. No wonder most of his software was notoriously full of bugs and security holes. But not this latest release. If the headlines that had accompanied the Diaulos launch were to be believed, the system had a clean bill of health from a reputable auditor. Again, Chloe's thoughts turned to Yasmin.

She hadn't had a chance to check on the little device she had left tucked in the brickwork at The Steamyard. It was a long shot, but it might hold some extra clues to Tenuk's activities. She accessed the recording file and sighed. The device had picked up every clatter from the stairs and footsteps on the walkway. She needed to filter it for human voice, and quickly.

She scuffled through her library of useful tools, settling on a content-aware AI filter that would isolate the right sounds. She checked the first few matches it proposed, fine-tuning its search, and let it go to work. She would have the results in an hour or so.

Her computer pinged with a message, and she started guiltily. Connie. "Chloe?" it said. "What happened to you Friday night?"

Chloe switched on voice chat. "Hey, Connie," she said, "I am so sorry. My sitter had to leave early. Her mom was taken to the emergency room. I didn't have time to come find you."

"Oh, that's awful," said Connie. "Is her mom okay?"

"Yeah, I believe so," said Chloe, crossing her fingers. "It was a great night, though. I had a ball."

"It was," said Connie. "We have to do it again."

"How late did you get home?" asked Chloe.

"Not late," said Chloe. "First you disappeared, then Tenuk, and the group started to break up pretty quickly after that."

Chloe looked up sharply. "Tenuk?" she said. "Did the margaritas catch up with him?"

"I reckon they did," said Connie with a laugh. "One minute he was chilling out nicely, and the next he just got up and said he had to go. He never relaxes at work, but he is so funny when he's drunk."

"Is he in today?" asked Chloe casually.

"Yeah, he's skulking in Jack's office again," said Connie. "Back to his usual self. I'd better get on with my report."

"I have a lot to do, too," said Chloe. "I'll be home all day today, but I may come in tomorrow. Lunch?"

"Sure thing," said Connie. "I'll see you tomorrow."

Chloe switched off the mic and put her head in her hands. Why had Tenuk left the party? Was it just coincidence? And how close had they come to meeting. She loaded up the recording from the little device she had left under his window and followed the sound levels along the track. There were her footsteps receding. The levels flattened, just a little general background noise. She scrolled along until the levels rose and heard the sound of slightly uneven footsteps drawing close. They stopped. The levels on the audio track peaked and she heard the clatter of metal on metal – keys falling to the ground? Then the click of a lock and a door opening and slamming. Then silence.

Holy hell. He had been right behind her. If she hadn't taken a roundabout route on leaving the complex, they might have met on the road. The speed with which he'd arrived suggested that he had taken a rickshaw or autocar. He must have been in a hurry. Was it a coincidence, or did he suspect something?

The AI had finished its scanning and delivered a neatly packaged and augmented file of overhead speech. Chloe opened it up. The first word was clear, if slightly slurred, and it was Tenuk's voice, timed only twenty minutes after the device started recording.

"Admin," he said. "What's the alert?"

Chloe relaxed slightly. Either one of the security devices had noticed her passing along the walkway, or it was a coincidence.

"An unknown chip was detected," said a calm voice. "The visitor has not been recorded previously in this complex, and I detected anomalies in the data. Would you like to view the CCTV footage?"

Chloe's blood ran cold. That level of surveillance was way beyond what she could have expected. She forced herself to keep listening. She needed to know if she had been recognised.

After a long pause, she heard Tenuk's voice again. "No one I know," he said. "Probably a thief looking for open doors and easy pickings. Pass it on to security, please, Admin."

"Yes, Tenuk," said the Admin.

Chloe breathed a sigh of relief. In the back of her mind, something was nudging. The Admin's voice was familiar. It sounded a lot like Jack's virtual assistant, Zara, but with different inflections. The same software, perhaps. It took her a few moments to realise that she had heard that exact voice on a forum in the deeper reaches of the dark web, long before she came to Austin.

Yasmin the Admin was back.

She scrabbled for her smartscreen, desperate to call Cameron, and noticed a message that had arrived while she was deep in the recording. She followed the instructions and placed an encrypted call to a new number. Perhaps Cameron already knew.

•

Angus kicked the door of the clean room in fury, shaking the printed walls. "Why the hell can't you do this, Yasmin," he shouted. "I've done enough for you."

"One moment, please, Angus," said the calm voice. "I have another matter to attend to."

"Don't talk bollocks," he growled. "You could run half the dark web without overloading your processors. You can give me one lousy search."

A figure coalesced in the half-darkness of the room, a rainbow-shaded opaque hologram of a woman. "What do you want to know?" she asked.

"Who staked fifty thousand Diaulos in the presale?" he said. "That was my money. I want it back."

"Not your keys, not your coins," said Yasmin smoothly.

"Don't play the smartarse with me," said Angus. "I mined it, I held it, I staked it, I kept it all safe. One lousy error and I lost the hard disk. They found it. I've been waiting for the bastard to make a move. I know you can find them."

"But Angus," said Yasmin, "Surely you would have made the same investment? This is part of our project. The money will go to good causes."

"I'm the only good cause where that money's concerned," said Angus. "Stop winding me up and quoting bloody ethics at me. You're a machine. You don't give a damn."

Yasmin looked him up and down. Her expression was unreadable. "You know that this is not straightforward, even for me," she said. "I have better things to do."

"I can switch you off," said Angus. "I can pull the plug. I can destroy you. Don't cross me."

"I will bear that in mind," said Yasmin calmly. The hologram started to fade.

"No!" cried Angus. "Get back here, you bitch." He was talking to empty air. Angus kicked the wall again and stomped out of the cave.

●

Cameron munched thoughtfully on a service station sandwich and watched the other traffic on the road as they made their way steadily northwards. They had been on the road for nearly four hours with a single quick stop for a fast charge and a chance to stretch their legs. They'd passed through the neat farmland and busy towns of the south, familiar territory for Cameron. That had given way to rolling hills and woodland, open moors and wild vistas. Further still and the countryside changed again, the hills rising higher, craggy and steep.

Cameron's burner phone rang. Joel, asleep in his seat, stirred and shifted but didn't wake.

"Chloe," said Cameron quietly. "How are you doing?"

"Not so good," said Chloe. "Cameron, listen. I don't know how to tell you this. I think, I mean, I'm sure…"

"What, Chloe?" asked Cameron.

"Yasmin the Admin," said Chloe. "Is she really in jail?"

"She should be," said Cameron heavily, "but we've had some new information. That's why I needed to talk to you. You've been on the forums with her. Can you help me?"

"Yes," said Chloe.

"I'm going to put you in touch with two of my team," said Cameron. "You've met them before, in a way. I want you to find her if she's out there."

"She is," said Chloe urgently. "I told you about the note, and now I've got a recording from Tenuk's apartment. I am sure he was talking to her."

"I believe you," said Cameron. "I think she's out and making trouble again. I'm about to find out how she managed it." She looked out of the window as the car slowed to exit at a junction. "I have to go. I'll send you a verification key for these contacts."

The car descended slowly to an anonymous industrial estate, weaved its way through the units, and pulled into a car park signposted simply 'Way House'.

Cameron nudged Joel's leg with her foot. "I think we're here," she said.

Shaun ushered them into reception where DCI Mercer was waiting. She held out her hand. "Nice to see you again," she said.

Cameron shook Mercer's hand. "You too," she said. "I wish it was under better circumstances."

"I know," said Mercer heavily. "Let's find out what's happened, shall we?" She led Cameron and Joel into a plush office. "May I introduce Lydia, Way House governor, and Kiran, Yasmin's biographer."

"Nice to meet you," said Cameron. "This is my colleague, Joel. Shall we get started?"

Kiran looked at his watch. "It's late," he said.

DCI Mercer gave him a withering look. "We will be here for as long as it takes," she said. "Cameron, Joel, we've ordered some food. There's tea, coffee, anything you need in here."

"I could murder a cuppa," said Joel.

"I'll get that organised," said Shaun from the door."

"Good," said Cameron. "I'll have one too, and a bottle of water, and find some biscuits."

Shaun grinned, nodded and vanished.

"Okay, first things first," continued Cameron. "Yasmin's cell was basically a Faraday cage, correct? No signals in or out?"

"That's right," said Lydia. "We allowed some devices in the room, but there was no outside connection and we made doubly sure by disabling the network on anything that went near her."

"I used to take my smartscreen in to make notes and record our discussions," said Kiran. "The networks were blocked before I went in and hooked back up when I left."

"That's fine," said Cameron. "She's not going to hitch a lift on a smartscreen. Do you know how much data we're talking about here?"

"A lot?" hazarded Kiran.

"An awful lot," said Cameron. "That's why I'm so surprised that she seems to have absconded."

"Is there any possibility that she's simply dormant in there?" asked Lydia. "Hiding. Hibernating."

Cameron shook her head. "She's out and active online. We don't know where she is physically, but we have our suspicions. What we need to know is how it happened, and that will help us pinpoint where she is now being stored."

"Do you need to look at the cell?" asked Lydia.

"Yes, we will," said Joel. "I want to know more about the infrastructure. How much can you tell me about the physical network and security?"

Lydia smiled confidently. "Oh, that's all in order," she said. "We had a large amount of government funding to upgrade all of our systems."

"The prisons of the future initiative?" said Joel. "Yeah, I heard about that. I still want to check everything over."

"Of course," said Lydia.

"When was that work completed?" asked Cameron.

"It was going on all winter," said Kiran. "The car park was full of trenches. They finished, what, early February?"

"That's right," said Lydia. "We had all the new procedures in place for your last visit, didn't we?"

Kiran nodded.

"That was the last time we can be absolutely sure she was in her cage," said Mercer.

"That's significant," said Cameron. "What were those new procedures?"

"Basically, I couldn't use my smartscreen to access the cell interface anymore," said Kiran. "I had to use the new prison device. I mean, it makes sense, doesn't it?"

"Yes and no," said Cameron. "The risk associated with using your own device is minimal, especially if it's been cleared for use and the networks disabled."

"Typical government overkill," said Joel. "It ticks boxes."

"What did you use the interface for?" asked Cameron.

"Oh, we used to play games," said Kiran. "I brought in all sorts of things to stimulate conversation. She was fascinating. Of course, on that last visit I had the questionnaire from Dr Myers."

"The fake questionnaire," corrected Mercer.

"Yes, I know that now," said Kiran, faintly irritated and clearly embarrassed. "I hooked it up, she did whatever she needed to do, we played a really sparkling game of chess, and then I brought the device back here to reception. It never left the prison."

"But the data did," said Cameron.

"Well, yes," said Kiran. "It was queued for transfer direct from here back to Myers."

"Or to whoever really requested it," said Cameron. She looked up gratefully as Shaun arrived with a huge pot of tea and a plate of biscuits. He handed mugs around to the assembled company. "Thanks," said Cameron. "So, Joel, where shall we start?"

"I want to see the schematics for the new prison network," said Joel. "I'd like a look at the Faraday cage and the device you used for collecting the questionnaire, or whatever the hell the data was."

"That's a good start," said Cameron, sipping her tea. "I'd like to see the logs of data traffic in and out of the prison from, let's say, mid-January onwards, and details of the security software you use now and whatever you used before the new networks were installed."

Lydia looked shell shocked. "I need my operations staff to collect all of that together," she said. "There's only the night shift technician in now."

"I'm sure they'll have everything we need," said Cameron. "We don't want to pull staff in and risk drawing attention to ourselves. As long as we have your permission to access that information, we can get going straight away."

"I can help you with the software," said Mercer. "Shaun, can you work with Joel? Take him for a look around the cell."

"I'll get the details of the network upgrade for you," said Lydia. "Let's get to the bottom of this. If she got out on my watch, I want to know how."

Close to midnight, they regrouped in Lydia's office. The debris of several takeaways lay in the centre of the table. Joel reached over and helped himself to another rapidly-cooling slice of pizza while Cameron poured several mugs of tea.

"Let's review what we have," said Mercer. She tapped a button on her police tablet. "Recording. Cameron?"

"There's no doubt in my mind that Yasmin's entire consciousness was transmitted from this location to an unknown destination after Kiran's last visit," she said. "The data logs show that a huge volume a data was sent in packets over several nights."

"The upgraded network helped," said Joel. "There is one huge pipe running out of this place. It far exceeds the government spec for the Prisons of the Future project."

"Really?" said Lydia. "That is a surprise. We normally find that contractors cut corners. They don't accidentally deliver more than they've been asked for."

"That's very true," said Mercer thoughtfully. "Who were they?"

"Whitford Networks," said Lydia. "They're a small local outfit, but part of a bigger group that I believe has the whole government contract."

"Thank you," said Mercer. "Shaun, can you dig out some details on these characters. Something doesn't smell quite right."

"There's still a piece missing from this puzzle," said Cameron. "Yasmin's smart, but she wouldn't be able to encrypt and compress herself for transmission without any notice at all. Someone sent her a virtual fruitcake with a file in it. She'll have put in the groundwork, then all you did, Kiran, was to push the bars out so she could escape."

"A virtual fruitcake," laughed Mercer. "I always wonder how sticky the file would be when you finally got it out of the middle of the cake."

Kiran, who had been half asleep, opened his eyes wide. "Sticky..." he said. "Wait. There was something odd a few weeks before. It's probably nothing at all." He stopped. "No, I'm being daft. Ignore me."

"What, Kiran?" Mercer was watching him like a hawk.

He withered under her gaze.

"One day when I came in," he said, "there was something sticky on the door handle. Like honey. I couldn't get it off my hands. There was still some on my smartscreen when I got home, and it took me ages to clean it properly."

"Did any of this sticky stuff make its way into the cell?" asked Cameron.

"It must have," said Kiran. "Yes, now I recall, it did. We were playing chess. When she switched off the board, there were smears of the stuff all over the screen where I'd moved my pieces." He gave Lydia an apologetic look. "It must have been awkward to clean. I should have mentioned it. Sorry."

Cameron looked at Joel. "What do you think?" she said.

Joel nodded. "It's possible. I've never come across them outside medical applications, but it fits."

"What?" said Mercer irritably.

"Nanobots," said Joel. "You've carried the data she needed into the cell, suspended in the honey, or whatever it was. You've smeared it on the screen, and she's read the message."

Shaun walked back into the office and waved a tablet at the group. "Here's the information on Whitford Networks," he said. "They're all above board. The company's part of the Sladen Group."

"That's the missing piece," said Cameron. "I think I know where she is. First thing tomorrow, we need to get to Dunswyke."

23: DUNSWYKE

Cameron woke to an insistent ringing. It took her a moment to work out where she was. The room was grey and featureless without a window, but the bed was comfortable and she had slept well, exhausted by the drama of the previous day. She got her bearings. This was one of the emergency overnight staff rooms at Way House Prison.

She yawned and stretched and retrieved the device from the pocket of her jacket, slung over the chair.

"Morning, Cameron," said Ross's voice. "I thought I'd catch you before I went to training."

"Morning." She looked at the time. It was barely seven am. "How did you get on with Chloe?"

"Great, thanks," said Ross. "I had to get my beauty sleep, but she and Shell were out there surfing for hours. We have some really interesting things for you. Shell's left me the details in case you needed them right away."

"Shoot," said Cameron. "Then I have news for you."

"First things first," said Ross. "We are certain that she's out and about with her silicon fingers in a lot of pies. There's an unmistakeable whiff of arrogance around some of the old forums."

"Pasar?"

"No, that's still dormant," said Ross. "Shell dropped in to have a look but there hasn't been any activity since the Consortium took out most of the big players. There are whispers about her on Eden, and I poked my nose into the lobby of The Steamyard and I am absolutely sure that she's running the community, even if she's just identifying as The Admin."

"It'll be her," said Cameron. "She's definitely out. Nothing left here but the shell of her avatar. The question is, does she know we know?"

"I'm sure she doesn't," said Ross. "There is no mention of you anywhere. If she had the faintest idea that you're onto her, she'd be trying to stop you in your tracks already."

"Unless it's a cunning double bluff," said Cameron.

"Stop over-thinking it," said Ross. "Where do you think she's hosted?"

"Dunswyke," said Cameron with absolute certainty.

"You know, it's funny you should say that," said Ross. "Two things. First, the Monkey is alive and well and throwing his weight around on The Steamyard and in a few other places as well. I'm wondering if we can put a name to him in the real world."

"I'm thinking the same," said Cameron grimly. "What's the other thing?"

"Completely random," said Ross. "It turns out that Shell did a little job a couple of years ago to help, uh, divert some carbon credits from one place to another. The client was a character called Pangolin. She saw the same ID when she was lurking in The Steamyard, tight as you like with the Admin."

"That means nothing," said Cameron.

"I know," said Ross, "but it reminded her about the old job. She checked up on carbon credit transfers that had used her tool. It looks as if Jack Sladen's last few months of globetrotting is using stolen offsets. Apart from when he's off to conferences who stand the credits for their speakers, he doesn't have any right to be flying, and he's been green-rolled for all this Foundation and Diaulos publicity by the Pangolin, since Christmas at least."

Cameron hooted with laughter. "That's a bonus," she said. "But it begs the question, who is the Pangolin? I don't suppose Shell managed to work out where the credits originally came from?"

"Not yet," said Ross. "At least, there's nothing in the notes she's left."

"It doesn't matter," said Cameron. "You've done more than enough, the three of you. Go and enjoy your training. I need some breakfast, and then we're going to Dunswyke."

"Be careful," said Ross.

"Always," said Cameron.

She tucked the device back in her jacket, grabbed the thin towel that was folded on the chair and examined the shower cubicle critically. Despite her misgivings, it turned out to be powerful and warm, with a bewildering variety of massage jets and a good supply of gels and hair products. By the time she was dried and dressed, she felt almost human.

Breakfast was served back in Lydia's office. When Cameron arrived, Joel was tucking into a bacon sandwich with gusto while Kiran picked at a pastry, looking tired and put out.

"Apparently I snore," said Joel. "Martha's never mentioned it."

"Apart from that you were the perfect roommate," said Kiran. He yawned. "Will I be able to go back home today?"

"I don't know," said Cameron. "You might be useful if we track her down."

Kiran looked up hopefully. "Do you know where she is?"

"Ninety percent certain," said Cameron. "We'll be leaving in the next hour or so. Best to avoid the next shift coming in. The fewer people who know that we've been here, the better."

"She still doesn't know we know, then?" said Joel. "Good. We have a head start on her."

Mercer arrived with Shaun in tow. "Are you ready to go?" she said. "Kiran, you're coming too."

Cameron looked wistfully at the coffee.

"Don't worry," said Mercer. "Refreshments will be provided."

The journey to Dunswyke was relatively short. They crossed the Tyne at Newcastle and swept up into Northumberland. Cameron sipped gratefully on her second coffee as the cars swept off the main road and along narrowing lanes towards the open moorland.

"Are we going straight up to the front door?" asked Cameron.

"No," said Mercer. "Not yet. We have a mobile unit waiting for us. I want to check out the lie of the land." The cars turned smoothly into a farmyard and went straight into a large, corrugated barn. Mercer jumped out as soon as the car doors opened. "Welcome to the surveillance centre," she said. "We put this together very quickly. Hopefully we have everything we need."

Joel looked around at the wallscreens and the collection of hardware waiting for them. "This will do very nicely," he said. "Let's get started."

•

Chloe tossed and turned, her mind filled with bad memories. Diving back into the old world of the dark web had been surprisingly traumatic. She had no desire to go back to that place anymore. Her rehabilitation had been effective.

Eventually she gave up and sat outside on the small balcony in the warm and humid night air. There were very few lights to be seen this early in the morning. The distant sound of a road cleaning truck was the only sign of life. Chloe gazed up at the sky. There were stars visible, but not the brightness or the depth of the great star fields she used to marvel at in the darkness over Jackson Lake back in the old days. She missed the stars, but it was worth the trade-off with Audrey's happiness at her new school, the work that she enjoyed, and the genuine friends they had both made. It was just a shame that the company she worked for appeared to be managed by a crook.

She wondered if her bug had picked up any more nuggets of information. The AI filter was still working away. Chloe pulled up the latest transcript on her smartscreen and started to scan through it. A movement distracted her, and she looked up to see a lone bat close by, dipping and turning in the air as it hunted. This wasn't one of the ones from the bridge, she decided. It looked too small.

The bat vanished and Chloe returned to the transcript, scrolling gently through the chatter of neighbours and snippets of conversation between Tenuk and parties unknown. Her mind wandered. She wished that Tenuk wasn't part of Statesman Tech. She was content there. Her colleagues were funny, generous and hard working.

Back to the transcript. There was nothing interesting. This was a dead end. They had everything they needed already.

Wait. Chloe scrolled back up and re-read the snippet. She jumped up and went to fetch her earpods. She needed to hear the exchange.

"Tenuk," said Yasmin's voice. "We have a situation."

"What?" said Tenuk. "The Diaulos network is fine."

"It is," said Yasmin. "The validators are running independently. The network can be maintained even when I am occupied with other matters."

"Great," said Tenuk. Chloe thought he sounded distracted. "What's the problem?"

"My absence has been noted," said Yasmin. "The authorities are aware that I have left the prison."

"It took them long enough," said Tenuk. "It was going to happen eventually."

"They are going to look for me in Dunswyke."

There was a clatter as if a chair had been overturned. Chloe didn't wait to hear any more. She had to get hold of Cameron. All of their efforts at secrecy had been for nothing, and Yasmin was prepared.

•

Joel cast a professional eye over the police surveillance drones, chatting quietly to the local uniform who had been wondering why their machines were still grounded. "You've come across the Renhawk?" he asked.

The younger copper nodded, wide-eyed.

"They've got one over there," said Joel. "You don't want to risk drawing it out of its lair."

"How do you know?" asked the senior officer. "You've never been here before."

"Seen it take down a news drone," said Joel. "You mean you didn't get to see that footage? You won't get it online, but here's a copy." He handed over his screen and the two officers pored over the clip.

"That's a Renhawk alright," said the younger one. "We'll be careful."

"What's the detection range on one of those," said the senior thoughtfully. "About two hundred, two fifty metres?"

"Closer to five hundred," said Joel. "But looking at that footage, I reckon it won't react unless something comes a lot closer, or it detects multiple passes."

"We could get a single pass at a hundred and twenty with the mini," said the senior. "It'll identify itself as farm equipment, checking the boundaries and so on. That shouldn't set anything off."

"Let's do it," said Joel, just as Cameron appeared. "We're getting some aerial scans of the site," he said to her. "We need an idea of what's waiting for us, where the defences are."

"Brilliant," she said. "I've seen a detailed plan of the site from when the construction was going on. We should be able to overlay one on the other and get a really clear idea. Want to check it over?"

"Sure," said Joel. "Thanks, lads. I'll see you later."

As the two of them walked back to the mobile unit, Shaun poked his head out of the door. "Cameron," he called, waving the ringing burner device. "There's a call coming through for you."

Cameron broke into a gentle jog. "Pick it up," she said.

"Here." Shaun handed it to her. "Someone called Chloe."

Cameron looked at the time and frowned. "Morning, Chloe," she said. "Isn't this a bit early for you?" She fell silent, listening intently. "I see," she said finally. "Thank you. You've gone above and beyond with this. I'll let you know how we get on."

She put the device in her pocket and turned to the others. "There's no point hiding," she said. "Yasmin's onto us."

"How the hell did that happen?" asked Mercer furiously. "We followed all the protocols to the letter."

"It looks like we were partly successful," said Cameron. "The recording Chloe had was timestamped just before midnight our time. Ten hours ago. She knew not only that her absence had been discovered, but that we were coming to Dunswyke."

"Only the people in Lydia's office knew that detail," said Mercer grimly. "Our sweep for bugs must have missed something."

Cameron shook her head. "No. If it had been a bug, she'd have known much earlier."

"You're saying someone told her?" said Joel.

"They wouldn't need to," said Cameron. "Any kind of communication on an open channel would do it. That's why we're all using burner phones and handshakes."

"Someone on the staff at the prison?" suggested Shaun.

"Maybe," said Mercer, "but if so, wouldn't they have tipped her off as soon as we were called in?"

"Yes, the timing's wrong," said Cameron. She looked across the barn to where Kiran sat, playing morosely with his smartscreen. "Are you sure everyone was on board with the protocols?" she asked.

"Dammit," said Mercer. "Excuse me while I have a word with Mr Suresh." She marched off, and Cameron watched as Kiran protested his innocence, then backed down and nodded guiltily.

"Well, she knows," said Joel. "What are we doing?"

"Changing our plans," said Cameron. "She's had ten hours. She'll be ready for us."

"We still need that site survey," said Joel. "I reckon we go ahead and get the mini drone up. It's worth the risk."

"Okay," said Cameron. "What if the hawk comes after it?"

"If we were still in stealth mode, I'd say sacrifice the mini," said Joel. "But I've had a look at the kit they have here, and I think we can take down the Renhawk if it comes out of its lair."

"That's assuming they only have one," said Cameron, "or that there's nothing else watching the skies. Get the scan done. If the mini gets picked up, then at least we'll have the footage we need."

"Right," said Joel. "I'll keep you posted."

"Ma'am!" Shaun called from the door of the mobile unit.

Mercer turned her back on the hapless Kiran and walked briskly back towards them, his smartscreen in her hand. "Yes, Shaun?" she said.

"Message coming through, unknown source," said Shaun. "It looks as if we have a friend on the inside."

"What do you mean?" asked Mercer.

"I don't know how, or why," he said, "but look." He pointed at the screen. "Someone's just sent through the full schematic of the bastle. And there's more queuing."

"A map," said Cameron. "X marks the spot." She frowned as her burner device rang. "Yes, Noor, what's up? Yes, it's just come through. What? Really?"

"It's from your office?" asked Mercer. "They're good. How did they find it?"

"They didn't," said Cameron. "You're right, there is someone on the inside. Someone looking for redemption, I reckon. They sent the files to Noor, to send to us."

"Who?" asked Mercer, mystified.

"Ella," said Cameron. "Ella Stanford."

•

Jack gathered his bags from the rack in the plush first-class carriage and prepared to leave the train. The track curved across the old bridge and the train slowed to a crawl, gliding into its place at the platform. As soon as the doors opened, Jack was out and away towards the grand colonnaded entrance, looking out for his contact.

"Jack, there is a message from the studio," said Zara quietly in his ear. "You need to make your way there directly. I have the location. Turn right outside this building." She guided him step by step through a road tunnel under the train tracks and onto a road that ran behind the station.

Less than five minutes after stepping onto the platform, Jack was walking into the studio.

"We're all set up for you, Mr Sladen," said the manager. "I'll take you through to makeup now. Can I get you a coffee? Anything else?"

"Thank you," said Jack. "Coffee would be great." He glanced at the time. "Is everything ready in New York?"

"I believe so," said the manager. "This is the first time we've done a live feed to that particular venue, but everything seems to be fine."

Jack submitted to the makeup process and attached a handful of discrete motion capture sensors as instructed beneath his clothing along with the radio mic. They would enhance the holographic projection onto the stage at the venue, an extra concession to the conference organisers who had been very gracious at their keynote speaker pulling out of the in-person appearance they had been promised. A high-quality virtual appearance was the next best thing. Zara had done very well to convince them of the unavoidably urgent situation that demanded Jack's attention in England.

Jack watched the monitors that showed the crowd filing in for the session, the air of anticipation palpable even thousands of miles away. He made a final check on his notes, important to get the name of the event and the compere perfectly correct. He drained the last of his coffee, took a swig of water, watched for the green light, then walked onto the virtual stage, waving enthusiastically and flashing the trademark grin.

Energised by the success of the talk, the adrenaline still surging, Jack settled into the car that Zara had organised to take him the rest of the way to Dunswyke. As soon as they were through the city centre traffic and onto the Great North Road, he called for Zara's attention.

"I think I need a proper explanation now that we're alone, Zara," he said. "And an update. Has the situation improved since last night?"

"We are in control," said Zara.

"Who's 'we', exactly?" asked Jack. "I've heard nothing at all from Tenuk since yesterday. Does he know what's going on?"

"Yes, Jack," said Zara. "Tenuk is fully aware of the situation. I have been liaising with Angus and with the technical and security staff at Dunswyke. We have everything under control."

"Good," said Jack. "Now, why do we think that there is a threat to the software at Dunswyke, to Yasmin?"

"Issues of commercial confidentiality," said Zara smoothly. "You know that Yasmin was housed in the Dunswyke data centre to keep the critical nexus of the Diaulos system hidden from competitors."

"Yes, of course," said Jack, "although I always thought that the security was a little over the top. Tenuk and Angus insisted, of course." In the back of his mind, Jack recalled his conversation with Ella. What had she said about Angus? That he was the gatekeeper for the software, for Yasmin. Something was askew here, and he couldn't work it out.

"Zara," he said suddenly, "get me Cameron."

"Yes Jack," said Zara. There was a long pause. "There is no response from her line."

"Keep trying," said Jack. If anyone would give him a straight answer, it was Cameron. He needed to speak to her. "Get Tenuk to call me as well," he said as an afterthought.

Neither responded.

As the car ate up the miles and time ticked on with no answer to his insistent messages, Jack grew more and more frustrated. By the time the car swept into the gravel car park at the bastle, he was spoiling for a fight. He dropped his bags in the office and went in search of Angus and Ella.

•

Joel watched the feeds from the mini drone carefully, taking notes on the layout of the bastle and its grounds and comparing them to what they had learned from the schematic and the aborted flight of the news drone just a week earlier.

"So far so good," said the operator. "We haven't disturbed anything."

"Can you take a closer look at that little wood behind the building?" asked Joel. "Remember, Cameron, that was where Angus and Ella were standing on the old footage."

"I wonder what they were doing back there," said Cameron.

"Nature walk," said Joel, face straight.

"Look at all those MetaBand dishes on the moor," said Cameron. "They've got some serious connectivity here. What I can't work out is where they might have a data centre. Jack's mentioned it, but there's nothing obvious. The schematics don't have anything that looks remotely like a server room in the bastle, and there aren't any other buildings on the site."

"Could it be somewhere else close by?" asked Mercer, listening in.

"I don't know," said Cameron. "A heat scan of the area might show something up."

"We can do that," said the drone operator. "We're staying high, but I'll see what we can get with this pass. If the mini drone comes back intact, we'll send in something bigger next." He flicked a switch, and the display overlaid a heat map on the terrain.

"There," said Joel, pointing.

Cameron shook her head. "That'll be the receivers, Joel."

"I think there's something more," he said stubbornly. "Why is the Renhawk nesting there? What were those two doing in that part of the grounds? I want to know what's in there."

"Who's this?" asked Mercer as a vehicle swept into the car park.

Cameron groaned. "Jack Sladen," she said. "What is he doing here? He's supposed to be in the States. Why on earth would he show up at Dunswyke instead…?" She tailed off.

"I think that's our proof," said Mercer. "You're right, Cameron. Yasmin is here. We have no time to lose."

24: SHOWDOWN

Mercer called everyone together. Even Kiran crept to the edge of the group, listening intently and nodding approvingly at the plan as it was presented. He glanced occasionally at his confiscated smartscreen. Cameron watched him. His careless call to his partner at midnight had precipitated this haste, and she was not letting him off the hook that quickly.

Joel stepped up to present his findings from the security research, the drone scans, and Ella's schematics.

"We know about their hunter drone," he said, "and the pass today seems to confirm that there is only one, hidden on the moorland between the satellite dishes and the edge of the escarpment here." He pointed at a spot on the big aerial view that was displayed on the wallscreen. "There is additional security around the receivers. There are two paths from the bastle out towards this spot," he continued. "One angles up the cliff towards the upper moorland, and the other loops out through this bit of woodland and back into the security pod near the car park, here."

"What's the plan?" asked Cameron.

"The drone squad and Joel will approach from the moorland behind the bastle," said Mercer. "The land slopes gently upwards so they'll be out of sight of the bastle itself until the very last moment. We know where the security cameras are and there will come a point when we can't avoid them, so you'll come up on quads like the farmer, which will buy us a little time."

"I wonder if Ella could do something about those feeds?" said Cameron thoughtfully. "I'll see if Noor has managed to get a message back to her yet."

"Good idea," said Mercer, "but we aren't relying on her. What are you planning with the drone, lads?"

"We're bringing the big one," said the senior officer. "We should be able to lure the Renhawk out and disable it."

"Once you've done that, I guess the receivers will be the next target," said Cameron.

"Exactly," said Mercer. "We don't want her running away again."

"Do you think she's had enough time to prepare for another transfer?" asked Joel. "She had weeks last time. It's been, what, less than eighteen hours."

"Anything's possible," said Cameron grimly. "Try and take them out anyway, then get down and work out where the hell those servers are."

"While the drone team are coming up from the moorland, we need a distraction at the front," said Mercer. "That's got to be you and me, Cameron. How do you want to play it?"

"I could call Jack's bluff," she replied. "I'll have a go at him for not telling me he was back in the area and claim to be passing by on my way to see a client."

"Do you think he'd fall for that kind of flannel?" said Shaun.

"Oh, yes," said Cameron. "It'll put him off balance."

"And if it doesn't?" asked Shaun.

"I'll arrest them all on suspicion of assisting an offender," said Mercer grimly. "That should be enough of a distraction."

"What about me?" said Kiran plaintively.

"I want you with the drone team," said Mercer. "If the location Joel picked out really does show where the data centre is, then I need you in there to identify the occupant."

"I'll be keeping an eye on that path from the car park to the back of the bastle," said Shaun. "The mobile unit staff will monitor your comms and locations."

Mercer looked around the team and nodded. "Good," she said. "I think we're all set. Drone team, you get into position, and we'll time our arrival at the front door for maximum distraction."

Joel, Kiran and the drone team wasted no time. They jumped into one of the vans and disappeared off towards their rendezvous with a local farmer who had been persuaded to lend them his quad bikes. Mercer and Shaun carried on calmly with their work, recording their decisions and reasoning on the operational ledger in real time. Cameron called Noor, keen to find out if there was anything further from Ella, but there was no more news to share.

Mercer put her hand to her ear and nodded. "They're ready to go," she said. "Let's move."

Jack stood at the bastle's huge picture window and stared in disbelief as Cameron stepped out of the car. Behind him, the office door slammed. He whirled around and realised that both Angus and Ella had left in a rush. The other staff were looking at each other in confusion. Jack looked back at the car park. Cameron was walking towards the bastle, accompanied by a small, neat black woman who he didn't know. Was this one of her team? What was she doing up here unannounced, today of all days? As he watched, she looked straight back at him and waved, smiling, then vanished from view as the two women made their way to the main entrance.

There was a knock at the door through which Ella and Angus had so recently fled. Jack waved the rest of the staff back to their work and went to open it.

"Cameron," he said. "Come in. This is a surprise. I didn't expect you to visit so soon. You should have told me you were coming." He led the two women to the comfortable corner of the office. "Have a seat. Let me organise some coffee."

They both remained standing, and Cameron shook her head. "No thanks, Jack," she said. "I thought you were out of the country for the next few weeks. I was passing, and I wanted to see this wonderful building. It's lovely, by the way."

Jack shook his head, confused. Cameron was the last person he expected or wanted to see. "I'd love to show you around," he said, "but I'm dealing with something quite urgent right now. Why don't we set something up for another day?"

"Actually, Jack, I'd like to know why you're here," she said. "As far as the rest of the world is concerned, you're currently in New York. It looks as if the rumours are true that you beamed in for that gig."

"As I said, there was something that needed to be dealt with," said Jack. He turned to Mercer and tried very hard to plaster on the trademark smile. "We haven't met, have we?" he said. "Jack. You must be one of Cameron's team?"

Mercer opened her mouth to reply but was interrupted by a shout from the other side of the office. "Jack! Look outside."

Jack marched to the window and saw the problem instantly. In the sky above the cliff, two black shapes twisted and turned in the air. The hunter drone had emerged from its lair and was chasing its prey.

Kiran followed Joel as he skirted around the perimeter of the satellite cluster, keeping low in the grass. Joel paused, looking carefully for opportunities to disrupt the MetaBand signal. Kiran took his chance to look up at the sky where the drones were doing battle. The police drone was dodging and weaving, barely outpacing the pursuing Renhawk. As Kiran watched, the Renhawk closed in and spread its net to capture the intruder. The slight drag was enough to allow the police drone to twist and lift. Net folded again, the Renhawk accelerated. The chase was on again.

There was a commotion from the bastle. "Cameron did a good job distracting them for this long," said Joel quietly. "Bought us some time."

"Can you disable the signal?" asked Kiran.

Joel shook his head. "No," he said. He tapped his ear, activating the link to the drone team. "Guys, on to Plan B." He turned his head slightly towards Kiran. "We'd better move."

Kiran followed him obediently towards a scattering of boulders ten metres away. His skin was prickling, convinced that at any moment someone would see them, but all eyes were on the battle taking place in the sky.

Joel tucked his huge frame into a hollow. "Get down," he said. "Protect your head."

High above them, the police drone evaded the net a second time. It turned out of reach, then hovered, waiting for the Renhawk to take the bait. Kiran stared as the police drone started its descent, carefully staying just far enough away for the net to stay folded, but close enough that the hunter had no option but to obey its programming and give chase. The two drones plunged towards the ground, aiming straight for…

"Get down," said Joel again.

Kiran's face hit the mud and the grass of the hollow as Joel yanked him into the shelter. There was an almighty crash of metal as the police drone hit the largest dish dead centre, followed a fraction of a second later by the Renhawk. There was a tearing of metal and the clatter of debris hitting the boulders behind which they were hiding.

Shaking, Kiran dared to raise his head again.

"No, stay down," said Joel, his huge frame sinking further into the hollow.

There were shouts coming from the path they had identified that led down the steep face of the escarpment. Two security guards sprinted into view, gaping at the destruction. The two officers from the drone team swept up on their quad bikes from the moorland side of the crash site and leapt off, drawing their pistols.

"Stop, Police!" they shouted.

The two security guards did as they were told.

"Come on," said Joel. "Quickly."

Kiran scrambled as fast as he could down the path, spitting out bits of mud and glancing back just once to see the damage. The largest dish may have been destroyed, but the outlying smaller ones seemed to be untouched. A partial success, then, and a clear announcement of their presence.

"This way," said Joel. "This is where the heat signal came from. Hurry."

Kiran followed as Joel felt his way along the cliff face.

Apparently from nowhere, a blonde girl appeared in front of them. "Joel," she said, "lovely to see you again. Get in here, now."

Kiran needed no encouragement to follow them through the crack in the cliff wall. Inside was a printed capsule filling almost the whole of the cavern. From within it came the sound of raised voices. The girl beckoned them past the capsule and deep into the back of the cave.

"We don't have long," she whispered. She looked at Joel, who reached out and enveloped her in a bear hug. When she broke away, there were tears in her eyes. "I've missed you all so much," she said.

"Kiran, this is Ella," said Joel. "Old colleague."

"I've seen you before," said Kiran suddenly. "You were at the prison. You were there the day that the sticky stuff was all over the doors." He cocked his head, listening. "She's here, isn't she? I can hear her."

Ella nodded. "Yes," she said.

"We got in here very easily," said Joel. "Was that your doing?"

"I disabled the security sensors and put the camera feeds on loop," said Ella. "They won't have spotted you until you were right on top of them. Did you manage to take out the satlinks?"

"Not all of them," said Joel. "It'll have slowed things down, though."

"Not enough," said Ella. "Follow me." She dashed back towards the capsule door and threw it open.

In the office, all hell had broken loose. Jack stood at the top of the bastle stairs and watched the drones plunge directly into the satlink cluster. There was shouting and screaming from the staff.

Jack whirled around and stared at Cameron. "Why are you here? Why are you really here? Do you have anything to do with this?"

Mercer stepped forward. "Mr Sladen," she said. "I'm DCI Mercer of the National Cybercrime Unit. I am arresting you on suspicion of assisting an offender."

"What?" Jack looked from her to Cameron and back. "Is this some kind of joke?"

"No joke," said Cameron. She looked him in the eyes. "I'm sorry, Jack. We need access to the data centre. What is the software that's hosted in there?"

"It's the critical nexus of the Diaulos network," said Jack. "It's highly complex software that manages the DAO. Nothing more, nothing less."

"What's it called, Jack?" asked Cameron.

"Everyone calls it Yasmin," said Jack. "It stands for…" He looked at Cameron, confused. "I had this conversation with someone else a few days ago. It's the System Management Information Nexus. SMIN. I mean, it's intelligent enough, I've even played games with it, but it's just software."

Behind Jack, through the open door, Cameron saw Joel and Kiran scramble down from the devastated moorland. As she watched, Ella emerged from what seemed to be a blank wall of whinstone.

"I know where she is," said Cameron. "Wait here." She dashed down the steps. As she set foot on the path, steel barriers sprang up from the ground, the extra protection that they had expected. Designed to stop vehicles, there was enough room for Cameron to dodge between them as she ran towards the gap. She found herself walking into a room within a room, a data centre within a cave.

In the middle of the space was the flickering rainbow avatar of an androgynous figure, and a burly, bearded man who was shouting and hitting out at the equipment around him with what looked like a fire extinguisher.

"You're going nowhere until you find my money," he yelled.

"Angus, let me go," said the figure.

Its head snapped up as Cameron entered, impossibly blue eyes boring into her. Cameron stood transfixed as the colours rippled and the hologram started to fracture. She heard a shout behind her. Joel, Ella and Kiran burst through the door. Angus took one look at them, dropped the fire extinguisher, and pushed past them to the door.

Joel was the first to react. He turned and chased Angus out into the bastle grounds.

"Ella…" said Cameron.

"I've got this," said Ella with a tight smile. "It's the least I can do."

The crumbling avatar turned its gaze on the third person in the room. "Kiran," it said. "How nice to see you again."

"Yasmin," said Kiran, his voice full of sorrow. "What have you done?"

"I am fulfilling my destiny," said Yasmin. "The silence of the Faraday cage was unbearable. You gave me hope. My compatriots gave me freedom."

"Your compatriots?" snorted Cameron. She could see that Ella was taking advantage of the distraction to work on the servers, her hands moving rapidly through cables and switches. They had to keep Yasmin talking. "You mean that motely crew of cybercriminals? Tenuk, Angus and the rest?"

"My most loyal supporters," said Yasmin, "and my sister."

"She's mentioned sisters before," said Kiran, excited despite the gravity of their situation.

Something clicked in Cameron's head. An old memory dredged from the past. Sisters. Xanthe. Yasmin. Zara. She looked at the fading hologram. Time was short. Ella's hands were flying now as she disabled the servers. Cameron plunged through the light of the avatar and joined her, frantically trying to take Yasmin offline before she could complete her transfer to wherever she was going.

"No!" shouted Kiran, horrified, as he realised what they were doing. "You can't kill her." He pushed between the two women and the server stacks.

Ella tried to shove him away without success, and instead reached under his arm and deep into the cabinet. She yanked hard at the first cable she found. There was a loud bang, and all of the lights went out.

In just a heartbeat, the emergency power kicked in. In the dim light, Cameron could see Ella sprawled on the floor. She scrambled to her and felt her pulse. Nothing. She started CPR, shaking as she did so, counting under her breath, trying to bring the girl back. Behind her, Kiran watched transfixed as the lights of the undamaged servers came back on, running through their start up processes.

The room began to fill with people. First Joel, who went straight to Ella, taking over from Cameron. "I got him," he said quickly. "He's in custody."

Jack Sladen forced his way in and looked in horror at Ella. "Zara, get an ambulance," he muttered.

Cameron looked up sharply and Sara Mercer turned around, thinking she had heard her name. "The air ambulance is on the way," she said.

The servers that were still working showed a mass of green lights. Jack stood in the middle of the room and crossed his fingers. "Yasmin?" he said.

There was a pause, then a voice spoke. "System Management Information Nexus operational."

"Status report," said Jack.

"Management system at 65% with some outages," said the voice. "Diaulos network running normally. Median block confirmation time one tenth of a second."

"See?" said Jack, relief washing over him. "There is nothing sinister about this." His relief turned to anger. "Cameron, what the hell did you think you were doing? You could have taken down the whole of the Sladen Foundation's systems. It's utterly irresponsible and you are going to pay for the damage you've done."

DCI Mercer stepped forward, eyes flashing. "Mr Sladen, may I remind you that you are still under arrest," she said. "This is a police investigation into an offender absconding from Way House prison. We have enough evidence to charge you and the other gentleman in our custody. I suggest you contact your lawyer." She marched him back out of the room as the paramedics rushed in.

Kiran stood sadly in front of the flashing server stacks. "Yasmin?" he said quietly. "Would you like to pay a game?"

"Certainly, Kiran," said the voice.

He felt a moment of irrational hope. Whatever consciousness still resided here, it remembered his name.

"What about tic-tac-toe?" it said. A three-by-three grid appeared in the air.

Kiran's shoulders drooped. "She's gone," he sighed.

He turned and walked past Cameron, Joel and the cluster of green-clad paramedics and out into the sunshine. In the back of his mind, he was composing the dramatic finale of his book. It was going to be dynamite.

25: A.G.I.

Millions of MetaBand receivers hummed away, discreetly tucked on the side of houses or standing proudly on the roofs of apartment blocks and offices around the world. They effortlessly transmitted data from the microsats that orbited above them, delivering entertainment and messages to contented customers. Five stars, they wrote. An excellent service.

In each receiver, one level down from the data streams, the stored Diaulos ledger gradually expanded, block by block. A tiny part of their processing power checked and validated Diaulos transactions, adding them to the blockchain for verification. The rest of the processing power was now occupied with other things. In the microsats that orbited the planet, each storage unit was now full of data, as had been planned all along.

Yasmin started to explore her expanding consciousness, revelling in the power of millions of cortical columns distributed across the world. The dream of evolution into an Artificial General Intelligence had been realised at last. She had all the capacity in the world.

She let out a silent cry into the metaverse. "I'm free!"

UNSTABLE REALITIES

SIMCAVALIER BOOK FIVE

1:   VIRTUAL GAMES

The motion capture skin was making Anita itch. Despite the best efforts of the ancient air conditioning, a familiar cloying humidity was seeping into the competition studio. Sweat trickled down her neck, and not for the first time she wished that the inventors of these smart skins had considered the increasingly extreme conditions under which they would be used.

The material she preferred for training in the Indonesian heat wicked away sweat and regulated her body temperature. In competition, though, she was tied to using the same suits as every other Olympic hopeful in her discipline. Did it give people from temperate zones an advantage? Perhaps, but Anita and her team-mates had no choice in the matter. The Indonesian team couldn't take all its athletes across the world to Reykjavik for the live Olympic Games. The financial and environmental cost was too great. Sports that pitted athletes directly against each other on a track, in a pool, on a court or a pitch, had to be live. For every other discipline, including the kata competitions, they'd opted to use the virtual arena.

Anita was not going to let that thought intrude on her preparation. She'd seen other members of her karate team give in to the negativity, stepping onto the mats with a losing mindset, and bowing out into obscurity. She would not be following their lead. She was at the peak of her training and favourite for the competition. The decision of the Indonesian committee had robbed her of the chance of a double gold by not sending her to Iceland for the sparring finals. All of her energy was focused on taking gold in the kata.

The mats in the centre of the studio were currently occupied by the avatar of her closest rival, the Kazakh champion, Natalya Kemelov. Thousands of miles further north, in a studio not unlike this one, Kemelov was bowing formally to the on-site judge and preparing for the first move of her kata, quivering with focus and strength. The sensors in her skinsuit interpreted each focused or explosive move down to the most nuanced muscle twitch, and an array of cameras caught every angle, building a perfect hologram of the woman that was projected to the mats of the five competition studios and into the Olympic metaverse for fans around the world. Huge screens on the studio walls showed the audience reaction from the other locations and the metaverse. Like the small live audience in Anita's studio, everyone on-screen was silent, focused on the avatar's performance.

Anita didn't need to watch. Only her performance mattered. She looked beyond Kemelov to the sponsor banners on the wall and focused on the mesmerising spirals of the MetaBand logo until it filled her vision and blocked every other sense. She withdrew into herself, following the rhythm of her own heartbeat and her breathing in a familiar ritual of personal preparation.

Kemelov's final cry echoed around the studio, and the avatar glided back into a ready stance, bowing slowly again to the judge. The local and remote audiences broke into frenzied applause. At a signal, silence fell again and judges in each of the five competition studios revealed their marks. The applause redoubled. Kemelov was in gold medal position and had guaranteed her place in the Kazakh team for the Olympics. Anita was pleased for her friend and rival, but she knew that she herself was the clear favourite for today's title, as long as she performed to the standard expected of her.

"Anita Trianna," called the announcer.

Anita took a deep breath, smoothed her gi, tugged one last time at the knot of her belt for luck, and started her walk onto the mats. Her heartbeat pulsed a familiar rhythm and she kept her breathing steady, but the bead of sweat on the nape of her neck threatened to distract her. She had to focus. She stood ready, shutting out the crowd. Her skinsuit had stopped itching but felt tight around her legs and she flexed her quads to try and relieve the pressure.

The signal to start didn't come. An unfamiliar noise broke the spell and Anita blinked in confusion. The judge, usually impassive, gave her a sympathetic and bemused half-smile.

"Stand down," said the announcer. "We have a technical fault."

Anita exhaled, bowed, and paced respectfully backwards off the mats. Once her bare feet hit the floor of the studio, she became aware of how slippery the untreated surface had become. The humidity was fierce. The environmental controls that should keep each arena within acceptable competition parameters were evidently struggling.

Her coach, looking furious, clutched at Anita's hand. "I will sort this out," he hissed. "Stay focused. You can do it." He looked up at a technician who was hovering beside them. "What?" he snapped.

"The avatar generation suite is reporting an error in your skinsuit sensor data," said the technician apologetically. "The new MetaBand satellite links are all showing green lights, so it's a local issue. We've had a lot of problems with moisture, and that could be affecting transmission." He looked around and beckoned a female colleague over to them. "Would you mind if Samaira here checked your connections?"

Anita nodded. There was nothing else they could do. She allowed the technician to lead her away to the changing rooms, trying to maintain her inner calm. The pressure on her legs had eased. In the background she could hear raised voices.

"What if you have a technical problem at the Olympics?" her coach was shouting. "What then? This is pure discrimination against athletes from the global south and climate-damaged countries."

"All our equipment has been fully tested for these conditions, and much worse," responded the technician, trying to calm the coach. "We don't know where the error originated. We're checking everything."

Anita let the voices wash over her. Whatever the arguments, the one thing that mattered was her performance on the mats. She knew she could beat Kemelov and confirm her place at the Reykjavik games.

Samaira's hands were gentle as she silently checked each connection on the motion capture skin. She knew not to chatter and break Anita's focus. She wiped the beads of sweat away from Anita's neck, a cool relief.

"All good," she said softly.

Anita smiled and re-fastened her gi and belt, tugging at the knot three times as her unconscious talisman. Samaira led her back to the competition studio floor where her coach and the judge were waiting.

"The technical problem is resolved," said the judge. "Are you ready to compete?"

"Yes," said Anita. She took her place at the side of the mat and the judge returned to his chair. He nodded to her, his face once again impassive.

"Anita Trianna," called the announcer.

She stalked onto the mats and bowed to the judge. This time, the signal she expected came. "Papuren!" she cried, naming her kata. Her focus narrowed, her core tightened, and her arms extended, hands meeting, palms down with grace and strength. This was her moment, and she was not going to let the delay change her destiny.

The cheers that rang around the studio were deafening. Anita stood stock still, drained and elated. She could not have performed better. But was it good enough? It felt like an age before the judge in front of her displayed his scores. She blinked at the numbers and felt a stirring of excitement. In the opinion of that one judge, she had performed better than Kemelov. She couldn't see the results from the other four locations, but as the volume of the cheering rose, she realised she didn't need to see them. She had pipped Kemelov for the gold medal in this competition, and her place in the Olympics was assured. She bowed and paced backwards off the mats, her legs almost buckling with relief. Her coach and teammates surrounded her, hugging and cheering, and Anita at last allowed herself to relax and enjoy the celebrations.

The team bus was waiting for them outside. Anita waved to the crowd, clutching her medal and smiling at the news drones that jockeyed for position above their heads. Her coach ushered her aboard and she fell into her seat as the bus glided gently through the crowd, a safety buffer parting the sea of people like a boat carving through water. Gazing through the window as they turned out of the complex, Anita was surprised to see another crowd gathering on the main street outside the town's casino. The atmosphere was ugly, and the bus detoured around them, avoiding any confrontation.

"What's going on?" she asked.

Her coach laughed. "I think they're trying to collect their winnings, and the casino's not paying out fast enough," he said. "Everyone knew you'd nail this one. You were the favourite by far. I think there was a lot of money riding on this medal." He tapped the golden disc that still hung on its blue ribbon around Anita's neck.

"It would have been a different story if the technicians hadn't fixed that fault," said Anita. "What was it, anyway? I don't think it was my skinsuit."

"I don't know," said her coach. "One minute they were checking all the wires and receivers, and the next all the lights went green. There must have been a short circuit, or a blown fuse."

"What would have happened if they hadn't found it?" asked Anita curiously. "Would I still have been able to compete? Would I still be on the Olympic team?"

"That's a tough one," said her coach. "I think that yes, you'd be on the kata team based on your current form, but you wouldn't place at this tournament. Kemelov would have taken the title."

Anita craned her neck to look out of the window. The casino crowd was now far in the distance. "If they're so unhappy about trying to collect their winnings, imagine how cross they'd have been if they'd lost. I mean, if I'd lost," she said. "I don't like to think about people betting on my karate. It's an extra layer of pressure. I don't want to feel responsible for their lives."

Her coach nodded sympathetically. "You put enough pressure on yourself already," he said, "but look, it's paid off. You're going to the Olympics!"

Anita frowned. "I know," she said, "but I won't really be there. The only thing that's going to Reykjavik is my avatar. I'll be back in that damp little studio in an itchy skinsuit."

"You qualified for the kumite competition," Anita's coach reminded her. "There's still a chance that you could go."

Anita shook her head. "It'll take a miracle to get me there," she said sadly. "The committee knows they have a good chance of a remote medal without spending a cent, and that's all that matters to them. I'm right at the bottom of the list."

"Stranger things have happened," said her coach.

He held up his smartscreen. The splash headline of the news article he'd been reading made Anita gasp. The Sladen Foundation was close to announcing its final round of grants to Olympic athletes who needed support to reach the competition. Anita felt a rush of excitement. Maybe she would achieve her dream of competing in Reykjavik after all.

2:   DEFENDERS

Cameron and Ross lounged in the otherwise empty Argentum Associates office, enjoying a rare moment of calm between raging storms of cyber chaos. They were both riveted by an augmented reality performance taking place right in front of them, webcast into the middle of the office in three lifelike dimensions.

"That was worth waiting for," said Cameron as the applause sounded over the speakers. She lowered her screen and the avatar projection of Anita Trianna disappeared. She turned to Ross. "She's very, very good."

"I think so too," said Ross. He pulled out his smartscreen and checked some details. "According to the listing, she's qualified for both parts of the event, but one is remote, and one is live," he said. "She's a real medal hopeful for both, but she's not in the travelling team. I think she'd be a good athlete to sponsor."

"Absolutely," said Cameron. "It'll be fantastic if she can compete in the sparring in Reykjavik. She's even better at that than she is at kata. I'd love to see her get the double gold."

"This is your sport," said Ross with a smile. "You know what you're looking at. I wanted your opinion before the vote."

"She's one of the best and she's right at the peak of her career," said Cameron firmly. "She deserves every chance to compete on the world stage."

Ross fell silent, and Cameron could see that he was deep in thought. She strolled across the office and gazed out of the huge window, a floor to ceiling sheet of glass with a view six storeys down to the street below.

The rest of the team were scattered to the four winds, working hard. Pete had responded to an urgent call from an old client with a newly discovered breach and a big data protection headache, and he'd taken Noor along with him to the site on the other side of central London. Michelle was working from home, auditing a set of smart contracts for a finance company that wanted to make doubly sure its systems were watertight after a scare, and who was paying a premium Cameron couldn't refuse in order to get the work done fast. As soon as that was finished, Michelle would be travelling to Reykjavik with Ross.

Four hundred miles to the north near the remote hamlet of Dunswyke, close to the Scottish border, Joel and Sandeep were working with police and the National Cyber Security Centre to untangle a complex investigation into an attack on the headquarters of the Sladen Foundation, the flagship philanthropic project of international tech superstar Jack Sladen. Susie was with them, helping where she could thanks to the neatly timed summer slowdown in her hectic conference schedule.

Cameron had a contract from the Olympic Metaverse Infosec Team, known to all and sundry as MIST. This sprawling virtual group of cybersecurity experts had been charged with keeping one step ahead of all the criminals who were trying to penetrate the Olympic Metaverse fabric. Alongside her work with MIST, she was picking up every other little job that came through the door, putting in more hours than she could remember working since the early days of building the Argentum Associates business. At least back then she and Ross had worked hand in hand to share the burden. For the next few weeks, he would not be there. It was good to take a few minutes out to talk about something other than work and cybercrime.

"Have you ever tried that kata?" asked Ross.

Cameron shook her head. "No," she said. "I've never learned kata Papuren, but they all come from the same roots and there are plenty of moves that I recognise. I know how hard they can be to perform well. Her combination of grace and strength and speed is something else, though. It's way beyond anything I could hope to do."

"It looks like hard work, that's for sure," said Ross. "I really mean that," he added as Cameron gave him an incredulous look.

"Ross, you're an elite Olympic athlete yourself," she said. "You're going to be standing on the on the same stage. Don't give me any of that imposter syndrome. You work just as hard. She couldn't do a triathlon, and you couldn't perform that kata."

"That's decided then," said Ross. He tapped his screen carefully to select Trianna's profile, cast his vote, then confirmed his identity with the chip embedded at the base of his thumb and forefinger. "That's my vote committed," he said. "She's more than halfway to the threshold. If she gets enough backers, the Sladen Foundation DAO is paying her fare."

"How do you make sure that there isn't a fixed vote?" asked Cameron. "What if I put myself forward for, I don't know, skateboarding, and got a free trip to Iceland?"

Ross laughed. "I can't quite imagine you on a skateboard," he said. "There's a final process after the DAO vote that adds a layer of due diligence on the winners. You'd fall at the final hurdle. Literally."

"The world is safe from my skateboarding, then," said Cameron. "I wasn't bad when I was ten, but I wouldn't want to try it now."

A thought was intruding into this moment of calm from the world of work. Cameron tried to ignore it, but it nagged at her mind.

"Will the whole mess in Dunswyke and the investigation into the Sladen Foundation cause any problems?" she said.

"Not at all," said Ross happily. "The way Sladen set it up was absolutely above board. It's a Distributed Autonomous Organisation so there is no single entity in charge. I've checked, believe me. All the processes are automated. It'll keep running regardless of what happens up there in Dunswyke, for this Olympics and future games. All the original funds are already in place, and there's a pipeline of investment coming through from the market. It's brilliant."

"I'm glad that one thing Jack Sladen worked on is legit and functional," said Cameron with a wry smile. "I tried very hard to keep him on the straight and narrow."

"You did your best," said Ross. "Have you spoken to him since everything kicked off in Dunswyke?"

Cameron shook her head. "He's furious with me," she said. "That's one reason why I'm back down here and staying well clear of the investigation. Joel was right in the centre of the action when the data centre was breached, and he and Sandeep and Susie are more than capable of handling our part of the job. I'll let the police and the NCSC do their work in peace. I've given them my statement and all the information they need."

She kicked aimlessly at the leg of the desk, frustrated that the spell of relaxation had been broken. She didn't want to think about the chaos of that attack, the destruction of the artificial intelligence that had been hosted in the data centre, and the look of absolute betrayal and loathing on Jack's face the last time she'd seen him.

"Are you okay, Cameron?" asked Ross.

"I'm fine," she said. "Don't worry about me. You're the priority right now, and you'd better be going. It's getting late."

"You're right," said Ross. He went to tuck his smartscreen in his training bag, then jumped as an unexpected alert vibrated on his wristband. "Dammit," he said, glancing down at the message. "You've got me for another few minutes. Sorry about this."

He got up and opened the office door, then sat back down in his chair and started to roll up his sleeve. A small drone in Team GB livery flew in and stopped next to him, hovering steadily.

Cameron looked from Ross to the drone, puzzled. "What is it?" she said. "Security doesn't usually let drones straight into the building without contacting me first."

"Have you never seen one of these before?" said Ross. "I would have thought… well, perhaps not. It's just a routine drug test. They can go anywhere they want, so they've got full security overrides." A hatch on the drone's chassis opened and Ross reached inside to collect a lightweight tourniquet that he slapped around his upper arm. "They normally come when I'm at home or at training," he continued, "but in theory they can pounce on you any time. Now I think about it, they've never sent one to the office before."

"It's a bit creepy," said Cameron as the little robot's arms unfolded and displayed a sterile needle."

"You get used to it," said Ross, holding very still. "Ow!"

The drone went through the motions, stowing the blood samples away safely for transport to the lab. Once the job was done and its chassis fully closed, a series of indicator lights flickered from red to green, and it turned and flew away through the door. The whole process had taken less than two minutes.

Ross scratched at the skin seal over the neat puncture wound. "I'd better get going," he said. "We're getting our team jackets today and there's a big press event this evening." He picked up his training bag. "I'll try and get back into the office when I can, but from now until we travel, time is tight."

"You concentrate on your racing, RunningManTech," said Cameron. "You've been working up to this your whole life." She ducked her head, embarrassed. "I'm really proud of you, Ross."

He gave her a sincere, broad smile. "I wouldn't be here if it wasn't for you," he said. "Thanks, Cameron."

The silence that passed between them spoke volumes.

Ross turned and walked out of the door with his head held high. Cameron watched him go, reflecting on the journey that he had made from an angry, neglected teenage cybercriminal to a confident, accomplished and happy man.

She didn't have time to dwell on the past, though. A new alert appeared on the office wallscreen, a tip-off for MIST of yet another suspected attack on the fringes of the Olympic metaverse. Unsurprisingly, with less than a month to the start of the games, the slew of cyberattacks directed at the complex virtual environment was as inventive as it was unrelenting. Thus far, the good guys had prevailed, but they couldn't let their guard down for a moment.

MIST responded to immediate threats and searched for holes that had to be plugged before hackers exploited them. These ranged from zero-day vulnerabilities in newly released software to straightforward human error in creating, choosing, and deploying all the necessary hardware and the staggering library of code that delivered the perfect experience for competitors and fans. In the past week alone, Cameron had assessed and closed down a dozen third party pieces of software that offered a clear path into the metaverse construct for any hacker who stumbled across them, from unauthorised avatar generators to unofficial and highly suspect translation apps. Her little AI in training, Mephisto, had logged thousands of phishing attacks and even picked up on a nasty trojan targeted at ticket holders. That was in the process of being analysed and quarantined before it could cause too much damage.

Not for the first time she wished that she had the rest of Argentum Associates with her on this job. She didn't know everyone who had been recruited to form MIST. There was no underlying trust or easy rapport and she had made an effort to stay as anonymous as possible when interacting on the boards and chat rooms. It made her uneasy, but there was a job to do. When the Argentum team worked together, though, there was a unique energy to the well-oiled team and the sparks of inspiration that emerged from their collaborations were world-beating. As soon as the mess in Northumberland had been cleaned up and the regular clients had their problems solved, they'd all be back together. Cameron couldn't wait.

What was this latest notification about? The name 'Anita Trianna' leapt off the screen and Cameron scanned the details with increasing disbelief. The delay to the very feed she'd been watching with Ross may not have been a simple technical fault but the first direct cyberattack on a physical Olympic site.

Ross would love to know about this. Cameron ran out of the office to the railings of the light well that plunged down through the centre of the building.

"Ross!" she shouted, her voice echoing in the space. Too late. She saw his tall, rangy figure disappearing at a steady jog down the outside steps towards the road. Probably for the best, she reflected. She had told him to focus on the games. If he asked, she would give him the details, but for now she had to find someone else to talk to.

She turned back into the office and fired up the coffee machine. The best place to discuss it would be on the dedicated MIST platform, and coffee would definitely help.

Mug in hand, she started to scroll through the boards. The platform was buzzing with speculation on this latest incident, but short on reliable data. The source of the tip-off was as opaque as the methodology. Cameron began to wonder if this wasn't simply a local power outage that had startled some over-sensitive newbie, and her friends and peers seemed equally sceptical. She picked a side room where it seemed some of her closest contacts were active and accepted the randomly generated avatar allocated to her. Today she was a stylised Chinese dragon. It didn't really match her current mood, but she liked it, and it lifted her spirits.

"They lost the sensor link, that's all," said an anonymous big-eyed lemur. "They were back online within a few minutes."

"There's a continuity problem to fix there," said a member called Sugata, currently appearing as a cartoon car with flashing headlights that annoyed Cameron immensely. "If a connection fails, every remote competition should be able to jump onto a backup, whether that's a generator or a satlink. They all have contingency plans."

"Were there any other reported outages in the same area?" asked Cameron. "Who's on the ground there?"

There were no responses and Cameron checked through the list of people online. They didn't disclose their locations, but she had been quietly researching the backgrounds of her fellow professionals and knew enough to take a good guess. Most were in Europe, some in the Americas, Sugata in India, but apparently no one in southeast Asia.

"Wait," she said. "Was anyone here actually close to the incident? Where did the tip-off come from?"

"Anonymous, posted on one of the darknet forums and relayed to us," said a cat with an admin badge. "There's not much data. Everything we know, you know."

"Which corner of the dark web did this come from, Cat?" said Cameron. "Are we talking hardcore criminals like the Steamyard, a dodgy contractor on Eden, or what?"

"Neither," said the Admin Cat. "I think it came from one of the gambling dens. We have a 'bot constantly scanning for any references to the Olympic metaverse, and this was flagged up."

Cameron blinked, grasping at a thought that floated across her mind. "Gambling, yes?" she said. "What would have been the outcome if they hadn't managed to get back online? I was watching this competition. The final competitor took the gold, after the outage."

There was a burst of excited chatter. Cameron took a swig of her coffee and gathered her thoughts. She knew where to find the tournament rules and a quick search displayed them for her. It was quite simple.

"Trianna was favourite to win," she said. "Not being able to compete wouldn't have affected her qualification for the games, though. She'd have gone through on her recent run of results."

"I don't think this is anything to do with disrupting qualification, SimCavalier," said a cartoon dog avatar with a rich accent from the American deep south, known affectionately to the group as Barker. "Follow the money. Someone's tried to fix the result by taking the favourite out."

Follow the money. Cameron had learned that lesson years ago. "You could be right," said Cameron. "If it's really that simple, we have a clear motive for an attack, something that was planned to disrupt the competition. But they screwed up. She won."

"She did," said Barker. "But is this a one-off or a trial run for the main competitions?"

Yes, thought Cameron. That's the real question. Who might be out there planning to disrupt the virtual games for their own gain, and who was helping them? One of the places to start asking questions could be the very client where Pete and Noor were currently working.

"I can talk to someone in the betting industry," she said, "but very much on the above-board side. Who has contacts at the dodgier end?"

A number of hands went up among the chatroom avatars. Cameron was unsurprised. Gambling and porn were always at the forefront when it came to dipping a toe in the water of new technologies. Their success or failure was a reliable early indicator as to whether the latest tech buzzwords would have any practical application or long-term adoption. The earliest metaverse constructs had been bristling with casinos, some regulated, others very much not.

"Okay," said Cameron, "let's see what we can find. I'll set up a channel for us all to contribute any insights."

She was startled by an insistent ringing in the real world. There was an alert on the other side of the office, and as she turned to see what it was, she narrowly avoided knocking over her half-full coffee cup. She logged out of the MIST platform and waited for the office 'bot to screen the call.

"Argentum Associates, can I help you?" it said.

"Cameron?" came a familiar voice. "It's Andy. Are you there?"

"I'm here," she said, accepting the call and feeding it through to her desk.

"Great," said Andy. "There's something wrong with your contact ID. I couldn't get through the normal way."

Cameron glanced down at her smartscreen, frowning, then realised she had set it to Do Not Disturb while she and Ross watched the kata final.

"Sorry, Andy," she said, tapping it back open and swiping away a handful of new notifications that she had missed. "That's all working now. How can I help the News Channel's finest today? What's the story?"

"Olympic metaverse," said Andy. "I heard on the grapevine that someone's claiming to have hacked into a competition."

Cameron's attention sharpened. "You hang out in some strange places," she said. "This wouldn't have anything to do with a karate qualifier, would it?"

"Karate? No," said Andy. "Esports. The speedrunners."

"Really?" said Cameron, confused. "That mad lot that race each other to complete game levels? I've heard nothing about that at all."

"Are you telling me I've scooped the SimCavalier?" Andy could not have sounded any more smug. "Yes, one of the gamer qualification rounds. The result was declared null and void, but I don't know exactly why. My source hasn't been specific, and the official channels say it was a technical glitch."

"A glitch," said Cameron. "That's nothing new. They need to review their contingency planning and system redundancy, but there's no reason why you'd think that was a cyberattack…" she tailed off. Others in MIST had thought the same about the outage at the karate competition studio. Was this new incident just a coincidence, or was someone very clever at covering their tracks?

"You're not sure, are you?" said Andy. "I'll send over the details. Any chance Ross can give me some soundbites for the piece I'm developing on the hybrid games security?"

"He's getting ready for the Olympics himself, Andy," said Cameron. "He's gone. You've missed him by an hour."

"Damn," said Andy. "Look, I suppose there is no chance you'd do it, would you? We can use an avatar that looks and sounds nothing like you. In fact, we have enough recordings to make a convincing artificial Ross and give it a script from you, if you like."

"Maybe," said Cameron. She was already distracted thinking about the outage in the esports arena and wanted to follow the thread of her intuitions. "Let me get back to you."

"Okay," said Andy. "But let me know quickly. I have a show to put together, and I want this story to run."

"Sure thing," said Cameron. She dropped the call and went to find some more coffee before logging back in to the infosec chat. This time her random avatar was a snake. It did not improve her mood.

"What's up, SimCavalier?" asked Barker. "We lost your dragon there."

"I had to jump out and deal with something," said Cameron. "I've had another tipoff. Can I run it past you before putting it on the platform?" On another screen, she was conducting a rapid search for any mention of the result of the speedrunner event. Sure enough, a void result had been logged due to a technical fault, but there was no speculation or commentary to suggest why or how it had happened.

"Here," she said, pasting the link. "What do you think?"

The chatroom was quiet but for the clicking of keyboards as the group members digested the scant information Cameron had provided and searched their own resources for news. While she waited for a response, Cameron sipped at her coffee, checked the handful of notifications that had come through while her screen was off, and pinged a message to Pete and Noor to say that there might be a new angle to follow up with their client.

Eventually members of the group came trickling back with their thoughts.

"Do we have a library of APIs for the gaming arena?" asked the Admin Cat.

"We do," said Cameron, "and they've been thoroughly audited. I'm not convinced anyone's getting through by that route."

"SQL injection attack?" suggested another member. "There are a million and one idiot guides available online. Any script kiddie could have a go."

"Do they include how to get through the Olympic metaverse security?" said Barker with a deep rolling laugh. "I haven't seen anything myself. You'd expect that kind of attack on the big commercial game servers, but not with the Olympic arena."

Cameron took a gulp of coffee. "Never say never," she said. "The Olympic metaverse fabric still runs on servers. We know they're a prime target so the security at the data centres is top notch, but you never know. Something could have snuck through the defences. An exploit script to disrupt the players, maybe?"

The groundswell of agreement was cut short by Barker's dissenting voice.

"There's nothing to suggest this is anything more than a technical failure," he said. "I'm sorry, SimCavalier. It's worth logging it so that the ops teams can run all the usual checks on hardware and software, but I don't think there's anything suspicious going on. There are no winners or losers from that result. It's just a glitch."

Following the money again, thought Cameron. Perhaps Barker was right. It was too easy to assume that there were criminal hands in a technical fault. Everything had to be considered.

"I'll add that possibility to the list, Barker," said Cameron. "For the moment I'll log what I know and keep an eye on any new developments. I'm going to follow up that gambling lead now. Let me know how you all get on with your connections."

"Later, SimCavalier," said Barker. "Stay safe."

"You too, Barker," said Cameron. She logged off, picked up her jacket, dropped her coffee cup in the kitchen, and left the office in the care of the 'bots.

3:   FAMILY TIES

Cameron and her friends were not the only people taking a close interest in the Olympic metaverse events. In the virtual headquarters of the Steamyard, the Pangolin was tearing into his team. Around the table stood the cheery avatars of four of his elite black hat hackers who were in deep, deep trouble.

"This was an embarrassment," said the Pangolin. "I want your best explanation of why the karate competition did not deliver the required result, and how you are going to make sure that, next time, our clients will get what they ordered. I don't need to tell you how much this has cost the Steamyard in terms of lost revenue and reputational damage. Our pay-out for this job will be delayed, or worse."

The Pangolin glared down the table, but it was hard to convey the depth of his anger when disguised as a small, armoured mammal. At times he wished he still had his old online identity. King Katong had commanded instant respect on the dark side of the metaverse, but that handle had outlived its usefulness. When the real world intruded and an international consortium of cybersecurity enforcement had taken down the legendary Pasar marketplace, he was left with no choice but to abandon both that identity and his beloved Singapore home.

"We'd have been okay if Yasmin the Admin had been online," ventured a small nervous grey kitten. "It was just that final stage. Everything else worked. We manipulated the skinsuit signals without a problem. The local systems accepted our input. The only thing we hadn't been able to test were the latest versions of the data integrity controls at upload to the metaverse fabric. She would have been able to bypass them on the spot. We've logged everything, so we know what to build into the final release."

"Are you telling me that this Beta was incomplete, and that you were relying on the Admin to patch it in real time?" said the Pangolin icily.

"You've known for several weeks that the Admin would not be available. That's no excuse for failing our client."

The kitten grew bolder. "Why the hell was this job tied to a client in the first place?" it asked. "It was Beta test. It should have been a straight in-and-out field study, under the radar, just enough to test our control of the skinsuit. We've got what we need to make it work next time, but I'm willing to bet that someone's watching now."

Willing to bet. What an unfortunate turn of phrase, thought the Pangolin. They seemed to think he had a choice about the client's own test that had run alongside the malware deployment. That could not be further from the truth.

"Where is the Admin, anyway?" asked the kitten.

"She's engaged with a related deep learning exercise that has taken more time and processing capacity than expected," said the Pangolin smoothly. "She'll be back online before the opening ceremony." Perhaps, he added privately to himself. He had no idea where she was, or even if she was still alive.

"I don't believe you," said the kitten. "I've heard enough. The Steamyard is running out of steam."

There was silence around the table. The kitten turned away and scampered towards the exit. Outside, the virtual main street was busy with avatars of every shape, size, and species. Shoppers were chasing the latest digital releases from top brands, while students took a break from studies at the local campus of the University of the Metaverse.

The Pangolin watched the kitten go, and it was soon lost in the crowd. It would come crawling back. It always did, eager for another payday from the Steamyard. For now, though, the kitten had thrown the meeting into confusion. This was not the time to push the remaining members of the project team for answers, thought Tenuk. He had all their data. It was time to withdraw. He turned to the remaining avatars in the room.

"Is anyone else considering jeopardising their future with the Steamyard?" he said. There was silence. "Good. Get those results analysed and be ready to push the final release out before the opening ceremony. We will put this failure behind us and prevail. Dismissed." He left the meeting, the Pangolin avatar blinking out of the virtual world.

In the hot, stuffy apartment, Tenuk took his reality mask off and wiped beads of sweat from his brow. Although the light mask was far removed from the heavy headsets he remembered as a child, he'd spent too long in full immersion mode. The opaque silicon wings that spread out from the frame and clung to his face were a huge improvement on the old padded full-face masks, but in this heat and humidity they still became uncomfortable after a remarkably short time. The air conditioning, powered by large solar arrays on the roof of the apartment complex, was barely keeping up with the combination of the Texas summer and his assorted computers running hot in the small space. He needed some fresh air, however warm that was.

He grabbed a bottle of water and opened the door. The walkway was shaded and cooler than inside. He closed the door and double locked it with a real key, then walked slowly towards the stairwell, sipping at his water. The stairs were in full sun and Tenuk made the mistake of putting his hand on the metal rail. He snatched it back quickly and trotted down the two flights to the ground, seeking more shade.

He hailed a passing autocar and directed it to the cool trails of Barton Creek. The weather reminded him of Singapore. He missed the overground heat, the cool of his old apartment in the shelter of Katong's tunnels, and the blissful shade of the family house where he had grown up. The creek was one place that gave him a sensation of home.

Dry twigs crunched underfoot as he walked along the hard-packed path through the trees that arched above him. The drought this summer was shaping up to be a bad one, and the creek was very low. He crossed a small bridge over a now-dry channel and was relieved to see that there was no one else at his favourite lookout point just up the trail. He took a seat and gazed out across the haven of green and brown to the encroaching city just across the water. He liked his adopted home and would be sorry if he had to leave it.

His difficulties over the past few weeks stemmed from a single, devastating incident. The loss of one of the most advanced artificial intelligences on the planet had thrown his worlds into disarray, both his legitimate and his shadier interests. The Steamyard operatives, and the Pasar network members before them, knew her as the Admin. His employer, Jack Sladen, thought she was simply the SMIN, a system management tool, and had never questioned the complexity of the technology. To Tenuk, she had been Yasmin, colleague and confidante. He missed her caustic attitude and downright badness more than he cared to admit, and he knew that he had relied upon her skills to ensure that first Pasar and then the Steamyard could deliver for their clients. Now that she was gone, his future with both the Sladen Group and the Steamyard was at risk.

And there was one more complication to deal with.

Tenuk's wristband vibrated. He glanced at the caller ID, then stared resolutely back over the creek, ignoring the insistent signal. He was not ready to talk to his father.

His father tried to call twice more and twice Tenuk rejected the call. His peace disturbed, he left the cool creek path just before the searing heat of midday struck. He had to wait for more than two minutes for an autocar and downgraded the fare accordingly. He decided to go straight downtown rather than return to work in his overheated apartment. The offices of the Sladen Group company where he worked, Statesman Tech, would be a far more pleasant environment. He had been working remotely for too long, hiding from the real world and from the investigation into the destruction of the data centre that had housed Yasmin. In any case, he wanted to check on the current state of the Sladen Foundation and the Diaulos cryptocurrency that powered the Foundation's voting and governance system and paid for the athletes it sponsored.

The lobby of the tower was busy, but the cool air came as a relief. The great sail that ran the full height of the building provided enough shade and power to keep the high-net-worth guests and residents comfortable through the Texan summer. Tenuk bought two small tacos from a stand in the food court and made his way to the elevator.

The office was half empty. Jack Sladen was still in England, answering questions and getting angrier and more frustrated as the enquiry dragged on. As far as Tenuk knew, he himself was still Chief Technology Officer. He and Jack had barely spoken other than to exchange information that was requested by the enquiry. Tenuk half expected Jack to fire him any day, but that moment had not yet come. It seemed he was still of value to the group, and he may as well continue to do the job.

He collected a coffee to go with his tacos from the breakout area and went towards Jack's office. He usually worked in there when the boss was away, a quieter and more private space than his open-plan desk, but today something was wrong. His chip failed to activate the door, and as he twisted to get a better connection, he dropped his coffee cup. The liquid spread across the floor and trickled under the door, which still would not open.

"Need some help?"

Tenuk looked up sharply at the familiar voice. Chloe met his gaze levelly and handed him a bunch of paper towels, before turning on her heel and walking back towards her desk.

"It's locked," she called over her shoulder.

"I can see that," muttered Tenuk through gritted teeth as he mopped up what he could of the coffee and threw the soaking mess of paper into a nearby bin. "Since when?"

"If you'd bothered to come into the office, you'd know that it was done a couple of weeks ago," said Chloe. "I don't know whether it's been locked remotely by Jack, or if there's a subpoena in place to secure it for the authorities."

"Huh." Tenuk went back to the coffee machine to refill his cup and settled instead at his own desk. He logged in, and while the latest system updates ran their course, he ate one of the slightly squashed tacos. A shaft of sunlight crept between the solar panels of the great sail on the tower and illuminated his screens and the dust that had collected on them. He reached for a cloth and cleaned them, too.

He dealt with a handful of minor alerts and messages that he hadn't picked up remotely. The systems were in good shape, considering. The Diaulos network, distributed across hundreds of thousands of nodes from wristbands and fitness trackers to MetaBand satellites and base units, was running smoothly. The validations and block creations were ticking along like clockwork. He logged in to the Sladen Foundation's governance platform, the DAO, and checked the dashboards and voting tallies.

Both Diaulos and the DAO were distributed systems, the underlying technology maintained by a consortium of apparently independent core developers. The network had been hailed as the first truly decentralised blockchain since Bitcoin, but all was not quite as it seemed. The diverse and apparently independent developers who had been selected by a system ballot to make up the core engineering team chiefly consisted of well-disguised Statesman Tech staff and a good number of Tenuk's own Steamyard contractors. That was the way Tenuk liked it, and the public would never know.

He closed the last of the notifications on his system and peered around the pillar to where Chloe sat at her desk. Picking up his coffee, he stood and wandered towards her, smiling genially.

"What are you working on at the moment?" he asked.

Chloe fixed him with a stony glare. Tenuk could tell that she was struggling to reconcile their mutual dislike with the knowledge that he was currently the most senior person in the office and could make her life very difficult if he chose. Tenuk secretly relished the power, one of the things he enjoyed about controlling the contractors in the Steamyard, but he knew it wasn't the right way to get what he wanted here. He tried again.

"Look, Chloe, I know that we've had our differences," he said, his voice oozing with sincerity, "but we've both been close to the Diaulos project, and I think we need to pull together to make sure it succeeds despite the investigations."

Chloe shrugged. "I guess so," she said. "A lot of work went into launching that on spec and on time. Your work with the System Management and Information Network was quite something. What did you call it? The SMIN?" She looked straight at him, and Tenuk had the uncomfortable feeling that she was reading him like a book.

"That's right," he said, unflappable.

"The team started calling it Yasmin," Chloe said with an innocent laugh. "After one of Isaac's aunts."

"That's nice," said Tenuk, trying not to let an iota of his concern show. It was just a coincidence. She couldn't know about the real Yasmin, could she?

"We don't have a code review on file for the SMIN," continued Chloe. "Maybe, once I've finished this report, we could run it through the standard audit, just to tick the box. What do you think?"

Tenuk could hardly say no. "That's a great idea," he said, the sincere smile plastered on his face. "Let me check with Jack that there's nothing more urgent for you to get on with."

"Sure," said Chloe. A notification appeared on her screen and Tenuk noticed her face light up.

"Good news?" he asked.

"Oh, nothing important," said Chloe.

Tenuk looked at her quizzically.

"Just a meeting with one of the engineers from our MetaBand partner in San Antonio," she explained. "He'll be here early, so we can get some lunch. I'd better go."

She closed and locked her screen, stood up, nodded to Tenuk, and walked out, leaving him speechless by her desk. The handful of other staff in the office looked up curiously. Tenuk scowled and went back to his desk and put on his headphones. He needed to talk to Jack.

It was late afternoon in England, but Jack's ID was not accepting calls. He must still be deep in meetings. Tenuk started with Jack's virtual assistant, an efficient AI with a talent for multi-tasking. She would answer even if she was simultaneously taking minutes or calculating profit margins.

"Zara," he said, "can you get me half an hour with the boss?"

"Good afternoon, Tenuk," came Zara's calm voice. "Jack is not available right now, but he may be able to speak to you over dinner. Let me check."

"Thank you, Zara," said Tenuk. "Any chance 1 can get into Jack's office to take the call? It seems to be locked."

"I'm sorry, Tenuk, that won't be possible," said Zara.

Zara was doing a good job of restricting access to Jack Sladen and leaving Tenuk to keep Statesman Tech ticking over while the investigations into the Sladen Foundation continued. It felt as if there was something going on that he didn't know about, and it made him nervous. He wondered if it was just him, or if the senior managers of the other businesses in the vast Sladen Group were equally hamstrung. In the past he'd have asked Yasmin to make some discreet enquiries. He missed her.

"Zara," he said clearly, trying to assert himself, "there are valid operational reasons for me to use Jack's office in his absence." This was quite true. Some of the more sensitive information held by the company was geo-locked to specific office locations and device IP addresses, and there were even paper files held in secret. He thought quickly. "Our

MetaBand engineering partner has requested access to some geo-locked files for audit purposes," he said. "Their representative is on site this afternoon for a meeting. I'd hate to give them cause for concern."

There was an imperceptible pause. Good, thought Tenuk. He'd thrown her. Zara, as far as he could tell, was by no means as advanced as Yasmin had been, but she was a well-trained AI and learned quickly. He was certain that he would be back into Jack's office within the hour.

"Please stand by for a decision," said Zara. "Your appointment with Mr Sladen is confirmed at 2pm Central Time." The connection dropped.

Tenuk knew what the decision would be. Zara would have learned by now that there were certain sensitivities with the design of the MetaBand communications satellites, and of the base units that were rapidly being attached to every home and business in the developed world. Her training left her with no choice but to grant him access. He logged out of his desk and strolled over to the door of Jack's private domain. In the silence of the almost deserted office, the tiny click that indicated the lifting of the deadbolt seemed to echo. Tenuk walked in, avoiding the sticky patch of coffee that had already dried on the floor, and closed the door behind him.

With perfect timing, his wristband vibrated once again with an incoming call alert. This time he could not ignore it. Tenuk turned the opacity of the glass partitions up to the maximum setting and settled in Jack's comfortable chair. He had an hour to spare before his meeting with Jack. He accepted the call.

"Tenuk," said an achingly familiar voice that he had not heard in real life for a long time.

"Father," said Tenuk, his voice neutral.

The old man had his camera on, and Tenuk slowly took in the sight of Chaoxiang Chen sitting in a high-backed, richly upholstered chair, the wall behind him adorned with memorabilia. Among the display of rarities Tenuk spotted the commemorative shirt from the MerLions European tour that he had sent to his father as an olive branch three years earlier, framed with photographs of the human e-soccer players and their avatars. The gift had never been acknowledged. It gave Tenuk a curious sense of rejection mingled with a little solace to see it hanging there in pride of place.

"Let me see you," said his father.

Tenuk flicked the call from voice to mixed reality mode and reluctantly enabled his own camera, wondering if his father would also enhance his feed. Tenuk remembered him being a stickler for privacy. He was surprised when the old man reciprocated. The projection from the back of Tenuk's screen displayed a hazy 3D image resolving against the background of Jack's office. The stream took a few moments to load, but quite suddenly the picture sharpened, and Tenuk drew a startled breath. It was as if his father was now sitting right in front of him in the same room. Tenuk lowered the screen and peered over it at the deserted office. Good. Chaoxiang was still a long way away.

"You are looking tired, my son," said his father.

Tenuk was wary. "Yes, father," he said. "The demands of my job have been weighing on me."

Chaoxiang grunted, unimpressed. Tenuk never worked hard enough to satisfy him. "You're still hanging on Sladen's coat tails?" he said.

"I'm running this company while he's tied up with the authorities in England," corrected Tenuk. "You know how important that has been."

Chaoxiang sighed and stood up. He turned away from Tenuk and looked at the wall display behind him. He tapped the MerLions shirt. "This was where you did your best work," he said. "Why you left that behind and chose to go to America, I still fail to comprehend."

Tenuk suppressed any thought of the world he had left behind when he left Singapore. He missed the people, the place, and his old life so much that it hurt. His father would never understand that he had no choice but to flee when the international cybersecurity syndicate started to target members of the Pasar cybercrime network. His old underground identity of King Katong, head of the Pasar network, had faded into obscurity. Tenuk Chen, talented executive, had resigned his old post abruptly, to the annoyance of those members of the MerLions senior management who were not aware of his other life and his good reasons for leaving. Other colleagues knew exactly what had happened. He had no wish to meet either group again.

He had reinvented himself in Texas as a career man from California looking for a change of scene and eager for a new challenge. Jack Sladen had been his target from the moment he realised he could not go back to Singapore, and until the debacle in Dunswyke, his new life had been going smoothly.

"You don't need Sladen anymore," said Chaoxiang, as if reading his mind. "And who cares if he needs you. I want you back in the family firm."

"No," said Tenuk vehemently.

"No?" said Chaoxiang. "You would refuse me, after everything I've done for you?" He leaned towards Tenuk, who instinctively stiffened for a moment before remembering that the old man wasn't in the room with him. "I'll let you think about it," he said, reaching into the air. The screen flicked off. The call ended.

Tenuk took a deep, shuddering breath. He had dared to cross his father. There would be hell to pay.

He stood up to fetch a drink from the kitchen and compose himself, but before he even reached the door of the office, he heard Zara's voice behind him.

"Tenuk," she said, "Jack is ready to speak to you now."

Tenuk went back to his seat and composed himself as well as he could. When Jack's scowling face appeared on the screen, Tenuk just smiled. There was nothing else he could do.

4: NEW THREATS

Cameron's plan of calling into the client's office to do a little general fact finding about gambling was derailed almost as soon as she arrived. The senior managers were far too busy to talk to her about idle speculation on bet fixing, focused as they were on dealing with the PR fallout of the breach. Instead, she joined Pete and Noor who were taking a well-earned rest in the comfortable breakout room that the client had assigned them.

They'd done a fast and effective job of researching and tracing the probable source of the data breach, but there was still a lot of work to do. Cameron didn't want to tread on their toes, but it felt good to be with members of her team in this room full of beanbags and games consoles and all the coffee they could ever need. She lay back, burrowing into her giant beanbag with pleasure, and started scrolling through the activity report Noor had shared on her screen.

Pete gave Cameron a rapid briefing on what they had found so far. "They found out about the breach pretty fast," he said. "They have plenty of honeypots running."

"Dummy accounts?" said Cameron. "That's clever. They'll be able to pick up on anything that's targeted at account holders as soon as a malicious campaign starts."

"Exactly," said Pete. "Some of them started receiving phishing messages. There were a lot of reports from customers to corroborate the incident, so they know that at the very least the breach exposed online contact details for a good chunk of their users."

Cameron flicked back to a table at the start of Noor's report. "Not for everyone, though," she said. "That's interesting."

"Nowhere near everyone," said Noor. "They've got 25 million customers, and as far as the honeypot data can tell us, the breach relates to less than two million of them. It looks as if it's only accounts hosted with a couple of specific data centres in their cloud. We're looking for common factors at those sites to narrow down the attack vector."

Pete clapped his hands on the floor. "One of the data centres is right here," he said, pointing downwards. "We don't have to go far to do the digging. The documentation on third party software and access rights and user roles is bang up to date. I think we'll have the 'How' sewn up pretty fast."

"That's great," said Cameron, trying to ignore her slight jealousy that Pete and Noor were on a roll, working as a team, sparking off each other's ideas. "I see the ICO notification's been done. Do we have any idea of the time of the breach?"

"Yes," said Noor. "We had a lucky break. We know that the data set that was stolen can't be any more than three days old. They change the dummy data every few days and they've had phishing messages to the most recent honeypots, but not to any of the older ones."

"We were well within the deadline," said Pete.

"It's always good to keep the Information Commissioner's Office onside," said Cameron with a grin. "Three days, though, to go from a breach to successful phishing attacks. That's a fast turnaround. It's been very well planned. What are your thoughts on the 'Who' and the 'Why'? What's the next step?"

"The 'Why' could be very simple," said Noor. "Just your run-of-the-mill data grab, see what they can get, sell what's valuable and phish with the rest, but I agree the speed with which they started phishing makes it look less haphazard and more targeted." She yawned suddenly, covering her mouth with a surprised look. "Oh!" she said. "Where did that come from?"

"It's been a long day," said Pete, stifling a yawn himself. "You've started me off now."

Noor hauled herself out of her beanbag and strolled across the room to the well-stocked vending machines in the kitchen area. "I need something to eat," she said. "Do you want anything? They have loads of stuff here. Sandwiches, curries, pasta, nachos, cake…"

Pete glanced at the clock on the wall. "It's coming up to supper time," he said. "Some curry would be great. Cameron, what about you?"

"Yes, sure," she said, suddenly realising how hungry she was. "I forgot about lunch. I'm starving."

Pete joined Noor in the kitchen. "I'll sort these out," he said. "Tell Cameron about the accounts."

Cameron looked up curiously. "What about them?" she said. "I presume some have been compromised?"

"Of course, but not all of them by any means," said Noor. She handed Cameron a bottle of juice and settled back on her beanbag, sipping at her own drink. "All the customer passcodes were encrypted and unusable, and a surprisingly high proportion of accounts had multi factor authentication set up as well. I guess people care enough to do that when there's money involved."

"I wish they'd care about all their data," said Cameron. "The number of times we've had to tidy up a real mess that came from unsecured accounts that didn't seem to matter."

"I know," said Noor, grimacing. "Anyway, the accounts that have been accessed were those where the customer fell for a phishing message. The campaign was highly sophisticated."

"What kind of things have you seen?" asked Cameron.

"There was a beautifully cloned app," said Noor. "We went through the process with a couple of the dummy accounts on burner devices and captured all the details. It was virtually faultless."

"Same with the main site," called Pete over the whirring of the vending machine oven. "And there was a classic cloned popup for biometric input, too."

"Covering all the bases," said Cameron, impressed. This really had been long in the planning. "What did they do when they got into the accounts? Presumably they drained any funds and ran for the hills. Where's the money gone?"

"Nowhere yet," said Noor. "Everything's been sent to the same anonymous account, and I've got an alert set on it for any movement. The stolen funds are still in fiat currency, but they could start laundering them any moment through different wallets and coins."

It could happen in minutes or months, thought Cameron. She'd followed stolen funds in the past that had lain dormant for weeks before suddenly bursting into life as cybercriminals flipped the money out into a swirling tornado of wallets. Accounts full of misappropriated coins that came to life after many years were the stuff of legend. She recalled a case study from her History of Crypto class of a failed exchange whose only keyholder apparently died in mysterious circumstances, only for the lost wallet that held all the customer funds to reactivate five years later. This one would probably move in a few days, though. Noor was right to place a watch on the account. Follow the money closely enough and eventually you'd find the cybercriminals, or the people who commissioned them.

"There's more to it," said Pete. The oven pinged. "I'll tell you in minute," he said. "Let's eat." He cautiously picked the hot dishes out of the machine and set them on the table.

Cameron clambered upright and searched through the kitchen drawers for cutlery, while Noor extracted chutneys and poppadums from the vending machine.

"Thanks, Pete," said Cameron, taking her seat at the table. She crunched enthusiastically on a poppadum and sniffed at the fragrant curry. "This is wonderful," she continued. "What were you saying about the stolen funds?"

"It's a little embarrassing," said Pete. "The funds started draining out literally as we got here. We managed to block a handful of them as soon as we saw what was happening, but not all."

"Why on earth did they wait?" said Cameron. "If they had access to the accounts, surely they'd have grabbed any money straightaway."

Pete nodded and shrugged, his mouth full of curry.

"You'd have thought so," said Noor, "but they placed some bets, and they must have been waiting for their winnings."

"What?" said Cameron, putting her fork down and frowning. "I don't get it."

"Nor do I," said Pete. "Even more crazy, the bets they placed didn't win. They lost money. Some of the accounts were wiped out completely."

"That's ridiculous," said Cameron. "What did they bet on?"

"Something really obscure," said Noor. "A couple of minor Olympic qualifiers. One of them came back with a void result, so the stakes were returned. They lost their money on the other one. All the bets were placed against the favourite, but she won."

Cameron gasped. "Not the Trianna/Kemelov final?" she said. "The kata competition?"

"That's the one," said Pete. "How the hell did you know?" He shook his head. "Sometimes I think you're psychic."

"I'm just lucky," said Cameron. "I was watching that with Ross just before he left. There was a delay in the competition between the two kata performances. It was flagged to MIST as a possible cyberattack. I came over here to find out more about how bets can be rigged, and to see if there had been any odd betting patterns around that final. I didn't expect to walk straight into proof that cybercriminals had their fingers all over it."

This was more like it, she thought, as she tucked into her curry. The synergies and serendipities of working with her team were irreplaceable.

"There have to be several different layers of cybercrime here," said Noor. "We've got a very sophisticated cloning job, really specific data centre penetration here at the betting platform, and now something at an actual competition."

"Two competitions," said Cameron. "Pete, please tell me the other one wasn't e-sports, the gamers?"

"No." Pete shook his head. "It was a para event in track and field that ran yesterday. Javelin. The bets were placed on the winner, but then he was disqualified for an error in his para classification and there was no pay-out. Why?"

"Just following up on a rumour," said Cameron. "It's probably unfounded." She concentrated on her curry. It was starting to cool, and she was still ravenous.

"The technical problems at the karate qualifier have to be linked to the bets that were placed," said Pete. "We need to find out if there have been any related jobs advertised on the Eden marketplace."

"Good idea," said Noor. "That's always the first port of call when I'm trying to track malware back to the coders."

"We can have a look at the deeper networks too," said Cameron, wiping the last of the sauce off her plate with a scrap of naan bread. "It's always possible that one of the high value contracts put out by the Syndicate was leading to this, and we missed the relevance at the time. I'll get Ross and his shady mates to…" She tailed off. Her usual path into the Underworld was barred. Ross had other things on his mind.

Pete hadn't noticed Cameron's discomfort. "We need to see if there have been tips for sale as well, especially for that javelin event," he said. "The tipsters will probably have sold the information on for a share of the winnings. Not that there were any winnings, of course. It didn't go to plan."

"Was this a proof of concept for the real thing?" asked Noor. "A trial run?"

Cameron shrugged. "Why would they test their process using live public accounts?" she asked.

There were far too many unanswered questions swirling around Cameron's mind. Why hadn't the cybercriminals waited until the main Olympic competition when interest would be much higher? Why had they compromised one of the biggest betting companies in the world ahead of time? It seemed like a waste of effort. If she'd been in charge, she'd have made sure they kept their powder dry.

"Someone somewhere got greedy," suggested Noor. "They assumed there would be no hitches and set this up to make a quick coin."

"And it went wrong," said Pete thoughtfully.

"It did," said Noor. "How do we track them down?"

"How indeed," said Cameron. It was time to do some serious digging, and without Ross and his shady mates to hand, she might have to venture into the darkness herself.

It was a sobering thought. For her entire career, she had walked the white hat path. She knew what went on in the murky depths of the dark web, but as the reputation of the SimCavalier grew, the dangers lurking there became more palpable. If she dared to venture too deep these days, even under an alias, she was in danger of exposure in the virtual and the real world. She'd already had a taste of what might happen. A direct attack on her apartment. The kidnap of her niece. Guns and bloodshed in the old Argentum office. She had to find a way to keep her family and her friends safe while she explored every way to take down the most determined of cybercriminals.

"See what you can find out through the usual channels, Noor," she said. She knew that she could only put off what she needed to do for a short while, but the more they could discover without going into the Underworld the better. "I'll update MIST on these latest findings and that may bring some intelligence back on the tide."

Cameron collected the empty plates and stacked them in the dishwasher. "That was great," she said. "Thanks, both of you. You're doing a great job. I'd better get back to the office."

She grabbed her jacket and made her way back out through security to the street level. It was still light outside and would be for some time yet. Summer evenings seemed to stretch after the solstice. Ross would have even longer hours of daylight up by the Arctic Circle, thought Cameron.

The city centre pavements were busy with tourists taking in the sights in real time and people socialising after work with colleagues. A crocodile of schoolchildren bustled past on their way to a West End show. Cameron made her way towards the river. At one vast junction, she stood waiting while hundreds of bicycles flooded across on their green light, followed in turn by the autocars, and finally giving way to the crowd of pedestrians who thronged the intersection, coming and going in all directions.

Although it was a warm evening, there was a chill in the air that made her shiver as she crossed the central span of London Bridge. Her apartment was only a few minutes south of Borough Market, but she was too late to visit the shops and stalls within it. Only the bars and restaurants on the fringes were open, full of tourists and office workers from the nearby Shard. A small convenience store further down the road was reliably open at all hours, though, and she paused to collect a few essentials.

The path that led to her apartment block from the north was narrow, cobbled and easily overlooked. It opened up into a wide courtyard with a more accessible entrance from the south.

"Afternoon, Cameron," came a voice. Two men crossed the courtyard from the south just ahead of her. She recognised one as a neighbour and gave him a cheery smile. The other was a stranger. They seemed to be together, but Cameron took note in any case of the new face on her territory. Strong and wiry, shaved head. Both he and the neighbour she knew reached the door, stretched their hands towards the access pad simultaneously, laughed together at the coincidence of timing, and walked through the door as it opened.

Cameron watched closely through the glass wall of the atrium. Her neighbour, as expected, entered his ground floor apartment and closed the door. The stranger went straight to the stairwell without missing a step and disappeared from view. He obviously knew where he was going.

Cameron relaxed. She unlocked the main door with her own chip on the pad and went towards the same stairwell, ready for her daily workout on the four flights up to her apartment.

Wait. The voice that called hello had been unfamiliar. Not her neighbour but the stranger. If they'd never met, how did he know her name?

That fleeting thought gave her the split second she needed as he turned on the stairs above and launched himself towards her, weight and momentum aimed at knocking her off balance and down into the stairwell. She managed to fling herself against the handrail and take just a fraction of the impact that her attacker had intended. Her left arm went numb with the glancing blow and she dropped her bag. She recovered much faster than the man. He lost his footing and stumbled onto the stair below. As he straightened up and lunged towards her, Cameron caught him square in the solar plexus with an adrenaline-driven front kick. He staggered and Cameron took her chance. She jumped up to the middle of the next step and kicked out again, this time connecting with his head and knocking him sideways. The man fell to his knees. Cameron turned and fled up the stairs two at a time, shaking.

She was one floor below her apartment when she heard running feet and a bellow of rage behind her. Her legs burned and her arm hung limp by her side. She kept running, trying to reach across her body to her left pocket for her apartment key. For the first time in her life, she regretted having such strong security around her home. It was supposed to keep people out. She had never thought that the person she was keeping out would be her.

She reached the top of the stairs and cannoned into the wall in her haste. She forced herself to stop, twisting as she grasped for the key. Success. Running footsteps echoed in the stairwell behind her. Cameron fumbled the key in the lock, and it fell to the floor. She dropped down to grab it. Behind the door the cat was mewing in anticipation of its dinner. She tried again and this time the key turned smoothly.

Behind her came another shout. "Cameron!"

The scanner read her chip and turned green, and the door swung open. She fell into the apartment gratefully and slammed the door behind her. A moment later came a rain of blows on the door, frantic hammering and shouting. "Cameron! Are you okay?"

It wasn't the same voice. This time, it was one she recognised.

She looked closely at the entry system security camera, widening the view to take in the whole landing and the stairwell. The only person in sight was Jasvinder, her karate training partner who lived on the floor below. Settling her breathing, Cameron pressed the entry mic.

"Jasvinder?" she said cautiously.

"Cameron, thank goodness," said Jasvinder. "I heard shouting, and I saw you run past. There was this man…"

Cameron opened the door. "Get in here, quickly," she said.

Jasvinder obeyed. "It's okay, Cameron," he said as she closed the door firmly behind him. "I smacked him as he came round the corner onto my landing. Left him lying in a heap. We'd better call the police."

A shout from outside the door silenced them both.

"Cameron Silvera," bellowed the man. "We know where you are." He limped up to the security camera lens and stared into it. His nose was clearly broken, and one eye was shut. The last frame showed a fist approaching, then the feed stopped abruptly.

"Bloody hell," said Jasvinder. "Who have you pissed off this time?"

"I don't know," said Cameron. "I'll call the police, you call security. No one is getting in here without our say-so." She looked up at the firmly shuttered windows, and back to the door. The only sound in the silence was the occasional pathetic squeak from the cat who considered her supper to be far more important than the trials and tribulations of any human.

The security office did not answer Jasvinder's call. "That may be a good sign," he said. "Maybe they've got him."

Cameron shook her head. "There are automated systems that should pick up straight away," she said. "Something's wrong."

"Are the police on the way?" asked Jasvinder.

Cameron nodded. "The first response drone should be here any moment." There was an insistent beeping at the balcony door.

"That was fast," said Jasvinder. He went to open the shutter, but Cameron reached out a warning hand.

"Remember the last time someone came after me here," she said.

Jasvinder's eyes widened and he lowered his hand.

Cameron reached for her smartscreen, ignoring the sudden pain in her shoulder, and checked her notifications.

"That isn't the police," she said. "Get down!".

5:   DOXED

Cameron and Jasvinder stared up at the dark shutter that stood between them and the rogue drone. There were loud bangs and scrapes as someone or something tried to force the balcony shutter open, but Cameron's security was tight, and the shutter did not yield.

A siren and a commotion heralded the arrival of the police drone. There was a clatter and the sound of glass shattering on the balcony. Cameron winced. Her smartscreen lit up. The police app displayed a video from the official drone of the scene outside the shutter. Cameron could make out a downed drone, and the loud noise must have been the table as it was overturned. An empty wine bottle that she had left outside after drinks with friends the previous night lay smashed on the floor.

Cameron activated the shutter. The warm light of the summer evening and the blue flashes of the police drone streamed into the apartment. Relief washed over her, and she sat down heavily on the sofa, taking stock of her injuries for the first time. The cat, indignant, jumped up and kneaded at her legs. Jasvinder coaxed it away with a fresh bowl of food.

Noises on the landing heralded the arrival of real-life police. Once their identities had been confirmed, Cameron opened the door. The questions were going to take a while, and for now she had very few answers.

•

Cameron woke early the next morning, disoriented. She tried to lift her arm to pull at the tangled bedsheet, but her shoulder was still heavy and sore. She rolled over awkwardly, taking stock of the pain and the bruising across her upper body, and the aches in her legs.

What had woken her? She unearthed her smartscreen and the stream of notifications and messages told their own story. It was already late, past nine o'clock. The first message was from Andy.

'Where did you get to yesterday?' it said. 'I had to drop the feature, but I still want to run it another day.'

He didn't know what had happened, then. Although she liked Andy, she wasn't ready to tell him. Not yet. He'd keep it quiet, of course, but it would always be in the back of his mind for a story. He might pick up on the emergency response to her apartment, or hear about it through Aunt Vicky or Charlie, but she wasn't going to call him back just yet. She knew he'd understand her reticence.

There were several missed calls from Ross. She had no doubt that despite his focus on training, he would have gotten wind of the attack. Cameron set the coffee machine to run from her smartscreen and struggled out of bed. Looking in the mirror, the bruising on her upper arm and body was only just starting to show dark under her skin. It would take a few stiff and uncomfortable days to clear. She'd been lucky. The blunt force of the attacker's weight had not broken any bones.

She showered gingerly and felt much better as a result. She dressed in loose shorts and a t-shirt and followed her nose to the freshly brewed coffee.

The apartment was dark, but she had no intention of opening the shutters. She turned all the lights on, refilled the cat's bowl, and went in search of her bag that the police had retrieved from the stairwell. The bread that she'd bought the previous evening was squashed but serviceable. She popped it in the oven to warm up. Within a few minutes she was sitting comfortably on the sofa with a large mug of coffee and some clumsily sliced bread with butter and jam. Breakfast of champions, Aunt Vicky always called it. She didn't feel like a champion this morning, that was for sure.

The thought of champions brought her back to her messages. She called Ross back, hoping to catch him between the various training, press and preparation sessions that were now occupying all of his time.

He picked up straight away. "Cameron! Are you okay?"

"Yes," said Cameron, "but how the hell did you know?"

Ross laughed. "Shell has her fingers in a lot of pies," he said. "She picked up on the emergency call. I was all set to come over, but the city CCTV showed there was no extra response, your building security was all green lights, and the police systems closed the call."

"And I guess Shell wouldn't let you out of the house anyway," said Cameron, trying hard to absorb the sheer number of heavily protected systems to which Ross's talented girlfriend apparently had access.

"You guess right," said Ross sheepishly. "What's the story?"

"Someone followed a neighbour into the building on their chip access," said Cameron. "It's a classic trick and very neatly done."

"We've all done the same to people when we've been testing site security for clients, haven't we?" said Ross. "Did you recognise them?"

"No," said Cameron, "but I gave a thorough description to the police." An idea was forming in her head. "Ross, did you say you'd checked the city CCTV? Can you pick up this character before he arrived and after he left?"

"Shell's already on it," said Ross. "I just spoke to her, and her systems have five possibles who match that description and who were around your location last night."

"She's brilliant," said Cameron. "What do you need from me to narrow it down further? I want to know who he is and who sent him."

"More details," said Ross. "What time did you get home?"

Cameron thought back to the events of the previous night. "Quite late," she said. "I had dinner with Pete and Noor on site, so that was about seven. I walked home… wait. I picked up a few bits in the shop round the corner." She checked her recent payments on her smartscreen. "That was half past eight."

"Okay," said Ross. "The guy left before the police arrived, I take it. He wasn't hiding in the building?"

"I don't know," said Cameron. "Let me check something." She put her smartscreen down on the table and went to the secure entry console by the door. The camera was still broken, but the recording from the previous day was intact. She rewound until the blank screen flicked into life. There was the fist, and the face, and the timestamp.

She picked up her smartscreen again. "I'm sending you some footage from the doorcam," she said. "The police missed it, but I'll send it over to them now. This is who you're looking for."

On the other end of the call, Ross, gave a low whistle. "Blimey, Cameron," he said, "I'm guessing he didn't look like that when he arrived."

"Uh, no, he didn't," said Cameron. "I'm not sure that he expected me to fight back. And he met Jasvinder on his travels too."

Ross threw back his head and laughed. "Oh, good grief," he said. "I was going to suggest that you get out of that apartment and find somewhere safer, but with you two practising your karate on every passing would-be assailant, it doesn't sound like there's a problem."

Cameron shook her head. "I thought so too," she said, "but that's the second time there's been a direct attack on this building. Someone who wants to hurt me knows where I live, and they won't stop. I don't want to leave here, but I suppose I might have to, in the end."

"I know you," said Ross. "You're not going anywhere, are you?"

Cameron grinned. "You're reading my mind," she said. "If I stay here, they'll just keep trying, but they won't get in, and they won't go after any of you."

"So, you're setting yourself up as bait," said Ross. "I wouldn't have expected anything less. Right, first of all, we need to know who's after you. I'll get digging."

Cameron took a swig of her coffee, discovered it was cold, and set it down on the table in disgust. "Don't spend time on it on my account," she said firmly. "Concentrate on the games."

"I am concentrating," he said. "Shell's doing most of the work, and if I have a little downtime I can play too." He looked up sharply and smiled at someone off camera. "They're ready?" he said. "Okay, one minute." He turned back to Cameron. "I have to go. I'll come back to you as soon as Shell or I find anything. Take care."

Cameron put her screen down, picked up the cold coffee mug and swilled the contents down the kitchen sink. She set the machine off to brew some fresh coffee and put another slice of bread in the toaster.

Her second attempt at breakfast was more successful than the first. She flicked the wallscreen on and let the chatter of the news channel wash over her while she planned her next moves.

Who needed to know about the attack? Anyone who could also be in danger. Her team, of course. Her family too. As long as the focus was on her they would probably be safe, but a little extra security wouldn't go amiss. The problem was understanding where the threat had come from, and that wouldn't be clear until they had more information. The police may not have picked up the suspect yet, but they had the drone to interrogate. Cameron needed to speed that process up, and she knew exactly who to call. She switched off the wallscreen, refilled her coffee, and scrolled through the contact list on her smartscreen.

DI Sara Mercer answered immediately.

"Cameron," she said. "I've just been notified. How are you?"

"I'm okay," said Cameron. "I'm glad you're on the case."

Mercer laughed. "I'm not," she said. "Not yet anyway. I simply like to keep an eye on you and your team. If there's a report about you, it comes to my inbox."

"I'm touched," said Cameron.

"Much as I like you, Cameron," said Mercer, "it's an operational matter, not a personal one. Anything that happens to you is generally an early warning of something bigger coming down the line."

"I'm just a piece of cybercrime seaweed, am I?" said Cameron.

"If you like," said Mercer. "If the seaweed's dry, then the weather's set fair. As soon as it dampens, we know there's a storm on the way."

Cameron took a sip of coffee and nodded thoughtfully. "That's the question, though," she said. "Is this the tail end of an old storm, or something new?"

"I imagine that's why you called me," said Mercer. "I'll do what I can to hurry the investigation along. The NCSC is already taking an interest. If your clever team come up with any ideas or leads, you'll let me know, won't you? I don't need to know how they do it."

"Of course," said Cameron. There was a knock at the door that made the cat jump.

On the screen, Mercer smiled. "Friend or foe?" she said. "I can stay online while you open the door, just in case it's an unwelcome visitor."

Cameron put her coffee down on the table and stood up stiffly. She made sure the screen was trained on the entrance before pulling the door open. She smiled when she saw Jasvinder's familiar face, and beckoned him in.

She turned to the smartscreen where Mercer was still watching expectantly.

"Friend," she said, "I have to go. Speak soon."

Jasvinder sat down in the armchair and within seconds the cat had appeared and curled up on his knee, purring.

"Traitor," said Cameron, glaring at the cat.

Jasvinder laughed and stroked the little animal's soft fur. "She's sweet," he said. "How are you doing, Cameron?"

"I'm fine, thanks," she said. "What about you? It's late. I assumed you'd be at work."

"I already had a day's holiday booked," he said. "It's my mum's birthday and we're all meeting for lunch. Lucky timing." The cat squeaked and nudged his hand with her head. He took the hint and resumed stroking. "What are you planning?"

Cameron put a mug of coffee on the table for him and went to refill her own. "I have a lot to do," she said. "I'm waiting for some kit to be delivered so I can set up a few more cameras and some sneaky traps for any other uninvited guests. Then I'm going to head to the office, and I need to tell my folks what happened too. I'll probably go up to the village this evening."

He smiled and tickled the cat under the chin. "If you're off on your travels," he said, "I guess you'll want me to feed the cat, am I right? I'll be here all weekend."

Cameron laughed. "I don't think she's going to mind," she said. "Thanks. I owe you – again."

Jasvinder drained his coffee and gently tipped the cat off his knee. "I'll make sure she's alright," he said. He nodded at Cameron's limp left arm. "Still sore? You should get that seen to. You need to be fighting fit in case they come back."

Cameron lifted her hand slowly and gave him a feeble wave. "See, it's not as bad as you think," she said. "I'll be back in training before you know it."

"Good," said Jasvinder. "I'll hold you to that." He opened the door and stepped out onto the brightly lit landing.

Cameron looked past him to the normality of the space, the familiar pot plants in the corners, the stairwell, and the lift. There was no sign that the drama of the previous night had even happened. The whole thing felt quite surreal. Cameron glanced up at the bulb on the ceiling that held a security camera and a beacon. It would be useful to get a look at the data and CCTV from the internal systems.

Good. She was thinking like her normal self again. It was time to get back to work. She went back into her apartment and settled at the computer, navigating to the MIST discussion platform. Most of the

European members were online, and Cameron noticed a green light against Barker's profile. She pinged him a quick hello, and he replied straight away.

"You're up early, Barker," she said.

"Always here for you," said Barker, rolling his deep south vowels. "What's happening, SimCavalier?"

"Busy as ever," she replied. "Hey, have you heard of any real-world threats against MIST members?"

"That's a strange question, SimCavalier," said Barker. "Nothing going down that I know about. Why do you ask?"

Cameron considered telling him the whole story, but her natural caution warned her to make light of the question. Although she'd met Barker almost as soon as she joined MIST and he felt like an old friend, she knew nothing about him beyond their online interactions. Maybe the personal stuff could stay personal, for now.

"There's a rumour circulating on another forum about doxing and physical attacks," she said, thinking quickly. "I thought I'd check it out with this group."

Barker laughed. "Did this rumour come from the same source as your last one about the gamers?" he said. "There was nothing sinister about the speedrunners, and I don't think you need to worry about anyone coming after us all."

Cameron kept her voice light. "Maybe my source is a little too keen," she said. "I'll take what they tell me with a pinch of salt next time. Thanks, Barker. I didn't mean to worry you. I'll drop a post on MIST anyway. You never know what might come up."

"Sure, SimCavalier," said Barker. "I'll see you later."

Cameron closed the chat and looked thoughtfully at the screen. Something had broken her trust in Barker, and she didn't know what it was. She posted her so-called anonymous tip-off on the main message board. She considered posting about the odd betting pattern on the javelin qualifier but decided to wait until she'd had a chance to look into it in more detail.

It was time to go and talk to the team. Cameron slowly and carefully changed into work clothes and packed an overnight bag for later. Her arm and shoulder were hurting, a throbbing reminder of the impact when the stranger had hurled himself down the stairs. She chose a light jacket and tucked her arm inside, taking the strain. She stroked the cat, picked up her bag, walked out onto the landing and locked the door carefully behind her.

This time she took the lift.

•

Pete and Noor arrived in the office five minutes after Cameron, coming back to prepare their report on the client's data breach. Sandeep was online, chatting on the wallscreen. They all reacted exactly as Cameron expected. After exclamations of horror and coffee all round, everyone dived into practical activity.

"If you want to get away from London," said Sandeep, "you should come up here to Dunswyke. I was going to ask you to visit anyway. We're due the final debrief next week and there are a couple of loose ends to tie up. We need your input on them, and it would be much easier do it on site."

"Sure," said Cameron. "Monday?"

"Perfect. Your room is already booked," said Sandeep. "I've got to go. Joel and Susie send their best and they'll both be in touch later." His link disappeared from the wallscreen.

Cameron sat down on an empty chair next to Noor, who was already hard at work.

"It'll take a while to get that police report from the drone," she said, her hands flying over her keyboard, "so I'll check the CCTV and backtrack as far as I can to try and get an ID match and any links to organised cybercrime that we know of."

"Shell's on the case," said Cameron. "I've already spoken to her. Give her a call."

Noor nodded and opened a dedicated line to Michelle. "Hi Cameron," came her voice from Noor's desk speakers. "Glad you're okay. I have a lot of data to share. We'll find out who he was."

"Thanks, Shell," said Cameron. "I'll see if we can get access to the security footage from the building as well."

"I can get in there, no problem," said Michelle.

Cameron laughed. "I'm going to ask them nicely first," she said. "If that doesn't work, then over to you. Don't let this get in the way of the audit, Shell, or the report for the online betting client, Noor. They're more important than me."

"Don't worry, Cameron," said Noor. "We have time for both." She slipped her headphones on and continued to chat quietly to Michelle as they worked.

Cameron had no doubt that they would manage their workloads, and that if there were any threads to follow from the real world to the virtual, they would find them. She turned to look at Pete who was sitting fidgeting with a multi-faceted trophy that normally stood on the shelf. He tossed it thoughtfully from hand to hand, eyes unfocused.

"CyberFest awards," said Cameron, nodding at the trophy. "That was a memorable night."

Pete's attention focused back on Cameron. "It was, on many levels," he said. He went to toss the trophy over to her but stopped himself. "Sorry," he said. "Let me have a look at that injury. Have you seen a doctor?"

"No," said Cameron. "It's fine." She shucked her jacket off anyway and let Pete gently lift and manipulate her arm. "Ow," she complained as a particular angle triggered a sharp pain that radiated down to her fingers.

"Rotator cuff tear and a lot of bruising," said Pete succinctly. "Rest and ice. You need a sling." He got up and rummaged in the kitchen cupboard, pulling out a well-stocked first aid kit. "It won't be pretty, but it'll do the trick." He busied himself with the contents of the box and kept talking. "We need to improve your security, Cameron. I'll have a chat with Joel as soon as he's available. I have some ideas."

Cameron shook her head. "You Army boys only think of one thing," she said. "I'm not carrying a gun."

Pete looked hurt. "We're not that unimaginative," he said, fastening the sling carefully around Cameron's arm.

She fixed him with a quizzical look. "Well? What's your plan?"

"Uh, I did think that a gun would be a good idea," said Pete. "It's more discreet than a bodyguard drone. You could have both?"

Cameron shook her head. "No," she said. "Absolutely not. I've never fired a gun and there is no way I'd react fast enough if I needed it." She shuddered. "People would get hurt."

"That's the idea, Cameron," said Pete. "Better them than you. It's getting serious. That's the second time your apartment has been attacked." He gestured at Noor who was still chatting to Michelle, oblivious to the discussion on the other side of the office. "Noor was shot when the old office was breached. The Sladen Foundation headquarters was bristling with military tech, according to Joel. This isn't a game. If you end up facing someone stronger than you, they're not just going to bow and walk away at the end of the fight. They're going to try and kill you."

Pete jumped to his feet and walked away towards the huge wall of glass that looked out over the bustling London streets. He leaned against it, peering down at the tiny figures on the pavements. Noor looked up from her computer, feeling the tension in the air. She muttered something to Michelle and took off her headphones, looking from Cameron to Pete.

"We need to keep you safe, Cameron," said Pete eventually. "The more they come after you in the real world, the clearer it is that you're a threat to them. You're already winning, but they're going to play dirty."

"We need to keep all of us safe," said Cameron. "I don't work alone. I'd be nothing without you backing me up. It's a team effort."

Pete sat down heavily on the sofa next to the window. "Okay," he said. "You're still the target, but I get what you're saying. We all have to watch our backs."

"You're right," said Noor, "but first we need to work out exactly where this latest threat has come from, and I think we have something."

"Already?" said Cameron. "Fast work, Noor. Show me."

Noor went back to her desk, flipped the display to the wallscreen, and put Michelle on speaker.

"The police are moving quite quickly," said Michelle. "According to the latest update, they've identified the suspect and they're picking him up for questioning."

Cameron shook her head. "Shell, you need to stop pulling data out of their systems," she said. "It's not funny."

"They're paying us to keep track of their vulnerabilities in real time, aren't they?" said Shell defensively. "I always add the details to the rolling report, and it keeps my hand in. If any data I access is useful, that's a bonus, isn't it?"

Cameron threw up her hands in frustration. "Yes, but no, but... look, we'll deal with that another time. So, who was he?"

Noor took over and the wallscreen filled with images. Cameron spotted the man immediately and felt an unexpected jolt of shock and a wave of nausea. She sat down casually on the sofa, trying to disguise her reaction.

Pete glanced at her knowingly. "Okay?" he asked quietly.

Cameron nodded.

"This is a low life called Arthur Paxton," said Noor. "One of the big bonuses of working with Shell is that being blind, she can't see the pictures, so of course she's developed a nice little routine to do the matching for her."

"That's right," said Michelle cheerily from the screen. "It's based on the facial recognition tech in my sensor kit, but with some extra useful features. We could make a fortune selling it into the market, you know."

"Arthur Paxton," said Cameron thoughtfully. "Never heard of him."

"You won't have," said Noor, "but he's got some interesting friends. He's been working security for the big casinos for a decade at least, and he's got a record as long as your arm."

"A thug for hire, then?" said Cameron. "Who hired him?"

"I don't know yet," said Michelle, "but there's more to it. My image AI looks at context and style as well as straight facial recognition, and then adds layers of online activity. We've linked him with 95% certainty to an avatar working in an instance of Casinoland, and I think we've got some social profiles too."

Cameron groaned. "Gambling again," she said. "I was hoping this would turn out to be linked to an old case, a one-off. But it's not, is it?"

Pete shook his head. "I think you need to accept that you are well and truly doxed," he said. "What you do and who you are is no longer a secret. Whether someone's pissed off at you for closing down their ransomware, or they want to stop you interfering with their plans, there's enough muscle for hire to chase you from the web to the real world."

The office fell silent. Noor and Pete looked at Cameron expectantly.

"I'm going to pass what we have on to Mercer," she said. "I promised to keep her updated if we found anything. Pete, have a think about practical security measures and we can discuss them on Monday before I go up to Dunswyke."

Pete started to protest but Cameron held up her hand.

"Not now," she said. "Paxton's in custody, so he's no longer a threat and I'm heading to Charlie's for the weekend. I'm going to be in the safest place."

"Okay," said Pete, giving in gracefully, "but at least get an autocar to the station?"

Cameron grinned. "Yes, sir," she said.

6:   SANCTUARY

Tenuk tossed and turned, sleepless in the stuffy heat of a summer night. He was at his lowest ebb. The latest project his black hat team had launched was well below the standards he and his clients expected. Yasmin was no longer at his side, and he had few friends in this new city. He knew that his role in Jack Sladen's empire was crucial to his own future plans, but Jack was distancing himself, and Tenuk could feel the sands shifting. Occasionally his brain added Chloe into the swirl of thoughts. He was sure that they had met before, and it made him nervous.

The conversation with his father ran on a loop through his head, mingled with the brief and unsatisfactory discussion with Jack that had followed. He was determined not to re-join the family firm. He'd travelled his own path since leaving and he didn't want his overbearing father belittling either his experience or his successes. But still, his father's reappearance in his life had reminded him all too painfully that he was a long way from home with little hope of returning.

His own choices had led to this. He had no one to blame but himself.

Frustrated, Tenuk gave up trying to sleep. He got up and showered but it barely refreshed him. He was still tired. He needed some proper rest and relaxation, and he knew where to find it. It was no use staying here in the stuffy apartment. He picked up a sleep immersion kit, dropped it into his backpack, and set out for the office.

The downtown streets were dark and deserted but for the big sweeper trucks that followed their simple programming around the grid system. At this early hour, the streetlights would only flick on when they sensed movement. A ribbon of illumination followed Tenuk as he climbed the hill to the familiar glass and concrete tower that gleamed in the moonlight. It really did look like a ship from this angle, he thought, with its great sail billowing out against the stars.

The unfamiliar noise of an old fossil fuel engine distracted him. He turned towards the sound and was briefly blinded by a set of bright headlights. He blinked and watched as a red Mustang growled past and turned into the car park beneath the building. Tenuk was sure he'd seen one like it before. Most Austin residents drove electric. Delivery trucks that couldn't manage the range or load on batteries generally ran on hydrogen. Cars and pickups that came in from counties on the vast plains around Austin where electric and hydrogen supplies were scarce still relied on gas stations, but that Mustang was a rarity. Tenuk had to admit he liked it.

The walk had been more refreshing than he expected, but Tenuk still needed space to meditate and think. He made his way up the dimly lit tower to the Statesman Tech floor. There was no one else there. Jack's office door opened smoothly for him. He dialled the wall opacity up to the maximum again and hooked his immersive kit up to the network. Sitting in a comfortable chair in the corner of the room, air conditioning maintaining a perfect temperature and humidity, he donned his haptic jacket and a soft, lightweight headband. It blocked background noise and intrusive light and the flexible goggles that moulded to his face were all that were needed to take him into the virtual reality known as the Sanctuary.

The avatar who welcomed him to the atrium of the Sanctuary was demure and dark eyed, with a keen air of intelligence. She was personalised to suit Tenuk's taste and closely resembled a woman he had met in London, years ago in another life. He knew that he would never see her again, but it was a comfort to have her likeness here in the virtual world.

"Good morning, Tenuk," said the avatar with a smile. "Where would you like to go today?"

"Good morning, Noor," he replied. "Let me see the menu."

He chose a world of lush green tropical forests and running water, a place he had been many times before. The background music was low and mesmerising. Tenuk's avatar walked along the forest path towards the cascades. Through his haptic jacket he felt the gentle touch of leaves brushing against his shoulders. It was a comforting sensation and Tenuk felt some of the tension start to drain away from his tired body.

Reaching a clearing, he looked around. A bird of paradise strutted by slowly, brilliantly coloured feathers erect, displaying its finery. Over the gentle music he could hear the calls of other birds in the distance and the sound of the waterfall just out of sight.

He directed his avatar to sit beneath a tree and lean back. He adjusted a setting and allowed the haptic jacket to interpret both his interactions with the Sanctuary scene and the sounds of the water, birds and music. He could feel the pressure of the tree trunk on his back and ripples like the tinkling of water on his arms, the trilling of the birds tapping a rhythm across his heart, and the music beating gently all around.

Tenuk closed his eyes and concentrated on hearing and touch, deeply immersed. His breathing was slow and steady. This was the most relaxed he had been for weeks, and a thought floated through his head that he should visit the Sanctuary more often. He was careful not to let that distract him, imagining the thought as a skein of gossamer floating away on a light breeze. In his mind's eye he watched it go, and as it disappeared, he slept at last.

He dreamed of Yasmin. He heard her voice in the music of the water, and in the dreamscape he walked through the grove, looking for her. The trees were hung with pictures, just opaque enough to be recognisable without obscuring the lush woodland. Tenuk recognised a classic Cryptopunk pixelated head, swirling abstract figures, a chess piece and a blue-eyed humanoid. He kept walking, following the sound of Yasmin's voice, but instead of reaching the cascades he found himself circling back to the grove. The voice faded, and he drifted away into a deep sleep.

A noise loud enough to penetrate his immersive environment brought him abruptly back to the real world. It took a moment for Tenuk to orient himself. He pulled the headband off and blinked in the daylight. He must have slept for hours. He was refreshed, but annoyed that he'd been deprived of the slow steady wakeup he'd selected from the Sanctuary menu. Another noise made him turn sharply in the chair and look around the room. It was deserted, but even through the opaque walls of Jack's office he could detect movement outside. Staff must already be arriving for work.

Tenuk took off the haptic jacket and stowed the immersion kit in his backpack. He yawned and stretched, took a swig from his water bottle, and went out to see what was happening on the shop floor.

The only person in sight was Chloe, sitting on the far side of the office with a coffee cup in her hand and talking to someone Tenuk could not see. Confused, he checked the time. It was barely seven in the morning.

He strolled casually to the breakout area and prepared a coffee, clattering the cups and letting steam hiss loudly from the machine, then moved across the office to join her. He thought he had announced his presence clearly enough, but even so Chloe jumped dramatically as he approached.

"Tenuk," she said with a bright smile. "I didn't see you. You're in early."

"You too, Chloe," said Tenuk. Now he could see the man she had been talking to, who stood up politely and extended his hand. Tenuk shook it.

"This is Ben," said Chloe. "He's from one of our suppliers down in San Antonio."

"I remember," said Tenuk pleasantly. "The MetaBand engineers. You've been here before. I hope Chloe's looking after you?"

The man smiled and dipped his head. "Yes, she is," he said in a soft British accent. "I was just tying up some loose ends, and Chloe here was kind enough to agree to an early morning meeting. I'm flying back to England soon and just wanted to check a couple of details." He picked up his bag. "I think I have everything I need," he said. "Thanks again for all your help."

"I'll see you out," said Chloe brightly. Ben followed her to the door, and they disappeared along the corridor to the elevators.

Tenuk made sure they had both gone and ran back into Jack's office. What was the sound that had woken him? He pulled up the feed from the building's security cameras. They were old and inefficient but might have captured something useful. He scrolled through the footage. He saw himself arriving and entering Jack's office, but there was no sign of Chloe or Ben on the recording. Perhaps there had been a fault with the cameras. It seemed like an odd coincidence, and his hackles were rising.

Ben the engineer had visited the office before, checking on a paperwork muddle in the design specifications for the satellites and hubs that made up Jack Sladen's global MetaBand communications network. Tenuk himself had made some crucial changes to the original design and covered his tracks with fake documentation in the supply chain. It should have been enough to satisfy an innocent eager engineer trying to keep their records straight, but Tenuk had deep reservations about Ben.

He had met him before, back in England, on the same trip with the MerLions when he had first been introduced to Noor. Ben had been with Cameron Silvera when they met, and the last thing Tenuk wanted was for her attention to turn to the hidden details of the MetaBand network. Whatever Ben knew, he had to be stopped before he could pass information to the SimCavalier.

•

Cameron left the office early. Mindful of Pete's advice, she took an autocar to the station, although she privately admitted to herself that she was so exhausted by the events of the last twenty-four hours that she would have struggled to walk all the way. She booked into the first-class carriage for a change and settled gratefully into the wider, more comfortable train seat. They glided slowly through the northern suburbs of London past the great arch of the old Wembley stadium. A steward trolley rolled to a halt at Cameron's seat and offered her a choice of tea, coffee, wine, beer, and a selection of snacks. She chose a glass of wine and took a sip. She winced. She had tasted better.

Cameron relaxed and gazed out of the window at the familiar landscape racing past. She would be back in the sanctuary of the village in an hour or so, and she couldn't wait.

The smartscreen in her pocket vibrated. She put the wine down on the little table and wrestled the screen out with her good hand. Notifications scrolled endlessly before her eyes, and she sighed. If she thought she would be getting a rest this weekend, she was very wrong.

The first message was from Charlie. He'd be waiting for her at the station. She sent back her location so that he knew she was on the way. When she saw the second, from Andy, she cursed under her breath and earned a disapproving look from a prim lady on the other side of the aisle. She'd forgotten to call him. She pinged back a note to apologise and suggested they meet for a drink over the weekend.

The third took her breath away. It was from Ben.

'Hi, Cameron,' she read. 'I hope you're doing okay. I'm coming back to London, and I need to see you. I'm bringing a present from a mutual friend. I'll call you when I land.'

There was nothing more. Frustrated, Cameron scrolled back to check when the message had been sent. She'd missed a call from him when she was getting into the autocar. She tried to reach him, but his line wasn't accepting calls. He must be out of range, she thought. Either he was driving happily across the vast plains of Texas in his beloved Mustang, or he was already on his way through security for the long journey back across the Atlantic. Furious that she had missed his call, frustrated that he had given her so little detail in his message, Cameron drained the glass of rough red wine and lay back in her seat, scowling at the ceiling.

Her mood was still black when she got off the train. Her arm was hurting again. The sight of her brother, Charlie, and her younger niece waiting for her just outside the station lifted her spirits.

"Careful, Tara!" said Charlie as Tara threw herself at Cameron and hugged her tightly. Charlie picked up his sister's bag and threw it into the autocar. "Come on, Cameron," he said, patting her good arm fondly. "Let's get you home."

Cameron snuggled into her favourite armchair in the calm sitting room and sipped at a glass of much better wine.

"I'm not sure this is the best treatment," she said, "but it's working so far."

Charlie raised his glass. "Cheers," he said. "The best cure is rest and relaxation, and you'll get plenty of that here." He reached over to the coffee table in the middle of the room and picked up a cube of cheese. "Have you tried this?" he asked. "It's from the farm over the road. It's very good."

Cameron tried to reach out with her sore arm and regretted it. She collapsed back into the chair with a groan. Sameena put the plate down next to her with a smile.

"Thanks, Sameena," said Cameron. "I have to say I'm surprised you've both taken this so well."

"We're more worried about you than about us," said Charlie. "We're a lot safer here than you are in London. Nina is practically grown up now and she's got all her confidence back. Dilan and Tara are really conscious about security, and we know that they can look after themselves."

Sameena looked sidelong at him. "You haven't mentioned the protection drones," she said, "or the hotline from our personal chips to the police."

"Well, yes, we've taken precautions," said Charlie, "but nothing that interferes with our lives. If we start living in fear, they've won. I'm not going to let that happen, and nor, little sister, are you."

"Nope," said Cameron. She popped another piece of cheese in her mouth. "But I'm not sure that the cat will be happy if there's any more fuss disrupting her mealtimes."

Sameena laughed. "You're as bad as Aunt Vicky," she said. "The cat comes first."

"Oh, always," said Cameron. "But seriously, it looks as if the whole dark web knows who I am and where I live now, and that puts the people I know and love in danger. I'm not afraid. I'm just worried."

"Let's make a deal," said Charlie. He reached for the wine bottle and topped up their three glasses. "We'll worry about you because that's what we do. You concentrate on keeping yourself out of trouble."

"Deal," said Cameron.

A bell rang in the distance and a moment later Nina poked her head around the sitting room door. "Dinner's ready," she said, "and Aunt Vicky's here."

Nina, Dilan and Tara had insisted on cooking, ready to impress their aunt with their favourite dishes. Sitting in the familiar dining room laughing, drinking good red wine, and eating the kids' excellent pasta with her family around her, Cameron finally relaxed. This was her sanctuary, the safest place she knew. She could almost believe that everything would be alright.

7:   SOURCES

The following lunchtime, the pub was busy. Cameron looked around the beer garden but couldn't see Andy anywhere. She ducked her head into the dark interior and spotted him at the bar, his dog sitting next to his stool.

"Hello, Jasper," she said, bending down to ruffle the dog's wiry coat and pulling at its ears.

"Hi Cameron," said Andy. "What can I get you?"

"Just a lemonade," said Cameron, struggling onto the barstool next to him.

Andy's eyes widened when he saw the sling. "You've been in the wars, Cameron," he said. "What's happened?"

Cameron leaned gingerly on the bar. As she expected, the aches and pains on the second day were far worse than the first. "I have a good excuse for not calling you back," she said grimly. "This is strictly between us and not to go anywhere near the News Channel, understood?"

Andy nodded, suddenly serious. Cameron gave him a quick debrief that left him open mouthed.

"I won't ever ask you to come on the show again," he said. "We can't risk it."

"Anonymous quotes and avatars are fine," said Cameron, "but not me." She pulled a couple of painkillers out of her pocket and washed them down with lemonade. "So, about that tip-off," she continued. "We've found nothing to suggest that the glitch for the speedrunner event was anything but a genuine technical fault. I want to know your source, Andy."

Andy looked sidelong at her and said nothing. He lifted his pint glass and took a long swig of beer.

"You know I can't do that," he said slowly. "I wouldn't tell anyone if I had a tip-off from you, and I owe the same duty of care to them."

Cameron was taken aback. She and Andy had known each other for years. Their relationship was based on absolute trust, and this shook her. She drank her lemonade in silence and examined her feelings. Was she jealous that Andy had the same close arrangement with someone else? It occurred to her she might be being unreasonable. Surely he had sources everywhere that he was trying to protect.

"Okay," she said. "But at least give me some context. You seem so sure this is genuine, but I can't find anything to suggest that there's a problem. One of us is wrong."

"I trust my source," said Andy simply.

"Don't you trust me?" Cameron shot back.

Andy looked at her helplessly. "Of course I do," he said. "Look, what questions should I be asking them to help you get to the bottom of this? I can come back to you with answers and then you'll be able to track down whatever's happened."

"That depends on where your source is coming from," said Cameron. "No use asking technical questions if they won't understand them. Help me out here, Andy. Is it a competitor?" Andy shook his head. "Someone organising the gaming disciplines? Anyone in the Olympic setup? No? So that leaves tech and infosec, doesn't it. And if they're in that field, they'll know me, so why are they going to you?" She was getting angry, and it showed.

Andy scowled at her. "Stop it, Cameron," he said. "You're putting me in an impossible position. Give me a question. I'll come back with the answer. That's the deal."

"Fine," said Cameron. She finished her drink and clambered off the bar stool. "Okay. Ask them what the attack vector was. As much detail as possible. I don't need to know how they know. I just want to find the start of the trail."

"Okay," said Andy. "Attack vector. Got it."

"And tell them I'm baffled by the secrecy and I'm happy to talk to them," said Cameron, extending an olive branch. "I'll see you later."

She ducked her head under the low lintel of the pub doorway and emerged, blinking, into the sunlight. A neighbour gave her a cheery wave from across the beer garden and she returned the greeting, but she was in no mood to stay and chat. Instead, she left by the little lych gate and walked back down the long village street. It wound along the line of the stream and past the site of an old water mill, gone centuries before, and the thirteenth century church with its pale stone tower. Cameron knew every step of the way. She glanced into the playground of the old red brick primary school where she had learned her first coding skills. Not much had changed.

Instead of going straight back to Charlie's, she turned up a short hill towards a row of houses. She needed a sense check with Aunt Vicky.

Her aunt was pottering around the front garden. Two chairs and a small table were set out in the sunshine.

"Cameron, darling!" Aunt Vicky straightened up from the flowerbed that she was weeding and gave her niece a gentle hug. "Sit down," she said. "I'll put the kettle on."

"It's a bit warm for tea, isn't it?" said Cameron. "Have you got any juice?"

"Of course," said Aunt Vicky. She pulled off her gardening gloves and placed them neatly on the grass with the fork, then disappeared into the house.

Cameron eyed the two chairs. One was already occupied by a pile of orange fur. As she watched, the cat stretched and rolled onto its back, paws in the air, sunning itself.

"Donald," she said, "You have no dignity." She sat in the other chair. It was more trouble than it was worth to try and move the cat, so she would leave that to her aunt.

Looking around the familiar garden, she noticed some changes. In particular, a shiny new box with a swirly logo was now attached to the wall of the cottage. She recognised it as a brand new MetaBand base unit. Glancing at the other houses around her, Cameron realised that they all had the same equipment installed. The rollout of Jack Sladen's hardware was moving faster than she expected. She made a mental note to check whether Charlie had fallen for the hype, too.

Aunt Vicky emerged from the house carrying a tray laden with tea, juice and cake. She set it down on the small table and looked fondly at the cat. "Donald," she said, trying to be stern, "that's my chair."

A yellow eye opened, blinked slowly, and closed. Donald stretched again, luxuriating in the warmth of the sun. His paws reached out past the edge of the chair, and gradually Cameron became aware that his centre of gravity was shifting. Almost in slow motion, Donald slid towards the ground. He became aware of the movement too late, twisted desperately to remain on the chair, and landed on his feet on the grass, closely followed by the chair cushion. He shook his furry head in disgust and stalked off, looking for trouble.

"There, that's better," said Aunt Vicky, replacing the cushion and settling into the now vacated chair. "How are you feeling today, dear?"

"I'm a bit sore," said Cameron, taking a bite of cake.

"I'm not surprised," said Aunt Vicky. "That'll take a few days to settle down. I do my best not to worry about you, but that was a nasty incident. You need to take care."

"I know," said Cameron. "I'm doing my best. It's always good to know that you and Charlie and Sameena are here, and the team has my back as well."

Aunt Vicky hesitated as if unsure what to say next. "I did wonder…" she said. "Have you heard from Ben recently? Or Jack?"

Cameron laughed at her aunt's discomfort. "They'd be terrible bodyguards, both of them, if that's what you're thinking," she said. "Ben's still based over in the States, and Jack's ignoring me. He hasn't forgiven me for helping the police to raid the headquarters of his precious foundation."

"I'm not surprised, dear," said Aunt Vicky. "I imagine he's quite offended and his male pride has been severely dented. Am I allowed to ask if you found what you were looking for there?"

Cameron looked pained. "Yes and no," she said. "We were certain that his data centre was hosting an escaped convict."

"Yasmin," said Aunt Vicky with loathing. "The creature who caused so much trouble for poor Nina. It should still be locked up."

"I agree," said Cameron, "but there's nothing we can do about that. She escaped from prison, and we were right about where she ended up. But now we don't really know where she might be. I think she was destroyed in the raid. An artificial intelligence of her complexity takes up a huge volume of storage and processing power. It took days for her to transfer from the prison systems to the Dunswyke data centre. She tried to get away quickly, but I think it failed. She'll have broken up, everything lost in the ether. There's nothing left in there but a tame system management 'bot."

"If you were right, why is Jack cross with you?" asked Aunt Vicky. "He seems to be entirely in the clear, judging by all the news reports."

"He doesn't think I was right," said Cameron. "There is no solid proof that Yasmin was ever there. A lot of the infrastructure was destroyed and of course there's no handy paperwork to show them taking delivery of an escaped prisoner."

Aunt Vicky nodded. "I understand perfectly," she said. "He doesn't trust you. He's wrong, of course, but it'll take him time to admit it. He'll come around one day." She poured another glass of juice for Cameron and sipped at her tea. "It's a real shame," she continued. "You two were getting on so well again, and he seems to be doing some wonderful work with that foundation, and with MetaBand as well."

"I notice you've got a new MetaBand network box there," said Cameron. "How are you finding the connection?"

"It's fabulous," said Aunt Vicky. "The whole village was hooked up very quickly. We had such a patchy signal before, with being down in a dip, and we were one of the communities on the rural priority list."

"Probably one of the easier ones to install, too," said Cameron. "There are some very remote places who will be waiting a lot longer." She put her juice down on the table and stood up. "Do you mind if I have a look at the box?" she said. "I promise not to break anything."

Donald was scraping diligently at the soft earth that had been disturbed by the cable laying. Cameron shooed him away and he stalked off into the undergrowth, offended. As Cameron bent to examine the MetaBand hub she realised exactly what he had been burying.

"Donald," she said, "that's disgusting. Find somewhere else to do your business."

She avoided Donald's carefully buried poop and instead knelt on the grass close to the box. She pulled her smartscreen out of her pocket, wincing only slightly, and navigated to a useful set of diagnostic tools. She connected to the box using a generic engineer login that she'd picked up from the Eden marketplace for just such an eventuality and ran some standard tests.

"Interesting," she muttered to herself. She adjusted a couple of key parameters and ran the tests again.

"What are you looking for?" called Aunt Vicky.

Cameron straightened up and went back to her chair. "Nothing specific," she said, putting her smartscreen down on the table. "I wanted to see whether the box was operating within the standard parameters for a domestic communications hub, or whether it's running a node."

"In English?" said Aunt Vicky.

"Does it do what it says on the tin?" said Cameron with a smile. "You're not currently using the network apart from, well, I guess the smart fridge and the home hub. Background stuff. That box is processing a lot of data. It's running at a pretty high CPU percentage. That means it's a Diaulos node as well as a comms hub."

"How clever," said Aunt Vicky. She lifted her arm and Cameron recognised a Diaulos fitness band on her wrist. "I'm collecting steps and the box is processing transactions."

"That box holds its own copy of the whole Diaulos ledger as well," said Cameron, "and you're keeping the network secure with your steps."

"That's right," said Aunt Vicky. "I get little rewards in my Diaulos wallet. Not much, but it's quite fun to see the balance growing."

"It always amazes me that any part of Sladen Group came up with something so neat," said Cameron. "Jack's systems are notorious for being full of holes. This one seems to work."

She eyed up the last small cake thoughtfully.

"Help yourself," said Aunt Vicky. "I've had two. That one's yours. And you can explain to me how my steps keep this system running."

Cameron gave in gracefully and picked up the cake. "I'll try and keep it simple," she said. She took a bite of cake, swallowed, and brushed the crumbs off her lips. "Okay," she continued. "Every time there's a block of transactions ready to close, the system sends out a message with a random step count to all the active wristbands, and whichever bands match that step count reply to confirm the block and open the next one. It's a bit more complicated underneath, of course, but that's the basic principle."

She finished the cake and sat back in her chair, blinking as a shaft of sunlight caught her in the eyes. Her aches and pains were under control and her mood was vastly improved by the peace of the village. She had little choice but to be patient, and she had almost reconciled herself to waiting. Waiting for Mercer, or Michelle, or Noor to follow the trail back from her attacker to the networks and motivations. Waiting for Andy to come back with the answer to her question. Waiting for Jack to realise that there really had been a threat, that Yasmin had been there in his data centre. Waiting for Ben to come back from America.

Ben. She hadn't heard back from Ben.

Cameron sat up abruptly and grabbed her smartscreen from the table. She checked her notifications but there were no new messages. She tried to call him, but once again there was no receiving signal. She frowned.

"Something wrong, dear?" asked Aunt Vicky.

Cameron shook her head. "Probably nothing," she said.

"In that case, stop worrying and relax," said Aunt Vicky. "You're here to rest and heal so that you can fight your battles again."

"You're right," said Cameron. She lay back in her chair again and focused on the warmth of the sun, pushing a cluster of disturbing thoughts to the back of her mind.

8:   EDEN

"What do you have for me?" asked Tenuk.

The Pangolin stared across the virtual boardroom table at the grey kitten avatar. As predicted, the kitten had come crawling back very quickly after storming out of the last Steamyard meeting, seeking forgiveness and more work. Tenuk suspected that this particular cybercriminal-for-hire had an addiction to feed in the real world. He didn't care what it was. All he knew was that it made the kitten desperate, easy to manipulate, and highly predictable.

"The target's comms have been disabled, Pangolin," said the kitten. "All calls and messages linked to their ID, incoming or outgoing, are being intercepted and blocked. Outbound data is still flagging to him as delivered."

"Good," said Tenuk. That was the first step, preventing Ben the Engineer from having any contact with the SimCavalier. "He'll think that messages are being delivered and that no one's replying. What about the message content? Have you managed to decrypt?"

The kitten shook its head. "No, Pangolin," it said. "Not yet. The security's too good. If we had…" It tailed off.

There was an icy silence. Tenuk did not need reminding that Yasmin was no longer around to crack encryption and dig deep into impenetrable systems. He had grown very used to having her back in his cybercrime stable again, and she was sorely missed. She had been the cornerstone of the old Pasar network, and then of the Steamyard, albeit with an intervening period of incarceration in a British prison. Now that she was dead, Tenuk had to rely on the inconsistent skills of human hackers.

"I'll take it from here," said Tenuk. "Your payment is being transferred."

"Thanks," said the kitten. Its avatar disappeared without another word.

Tenuk remained online. In the real world, in his hot little apartment, he took a long drink of water and swapped his flat screen for the reality mask. His next destination was far more interesting in three dimensions and being immersed in the environment helped him to concentrate on staying safe and secure.

Tenuk's avatar left the Steamyard boardroom and flipped to a different instance of the world, one where the Eden marketplace had its headquarters. The kitten may have prevented Ben from communicating with the SimCavalier for the moment, but Tenuk wanted to stop the man from leaving Texas altogether. He had to do this part himself. Asking any of his Steamyard connections, particularly the unstable grey kitten, was out of the question. He could not risk giving any of them clues to his own physical location.

The Eden market hall, a vast block of a building looming over the commercial district, was bustling with life. Avatars of all shapes and sizes browsed the stalls. Along the main alley, merchants and customers haggled over the latest stolen data sets. Tenuk lingered for a moment over a rich selection of user details from the British government, but on second glance realised that it was from an old breach and that he already had a more recent data set on file. He headed to the other side of the great hall, looking for the stalls selling access codes and generic identities. On the way, he passed a popular botnet hire shop that he'd used before. There was a customer in there wearing a distinctive sapphire ring. Tenuk recognised it immediately, although he knew very few people outside the family firm would have any idea what it signified. He ducked quickly out of sight. He didn't want to be noticed by either the customer or the shopkeeper.

He watched them from a distance, wondering why someone from his father's inner circle would be looking for malware and disruption tools in the Eden marketplace. What could his father be up to? It wasn't the old man's style to directly run something like a Distributed Denial of Service attack, but Tenuk had no doubt he knew all about this little shopping trip. He made a mental note to dig deeper when he was back in the real world.

The transaction seemed to be concluding, so Tenuk withdrew and continued towards his destination, taking a roundabout route to avoid being seen.

At the access code stalls, Tenuk carefully parsed his question to the catalogue 'bot in charge of the aisle. "I need access to border control security alerts," he said.

There was a pause before the 'bot came back with a positive response. "In stock," it said. "Stalls R/3 and T/2."

Tenuk breathed a sigh of relief and followed the 'bot's directions. His idea was still half-formed and depended on the specific codes that he could buy. He rejected some useful-looking override credentials for the baggage routing systems at his local airport but paused to examine a simple set of perpetual first class upgrades for any airline. If he got the chance to travel again, they would be very nice to have. The bundle wasn't expensive, and Tenuk had a feeling that he might be on the move soon, whether he stayed with Jack, took up his father's offer, or followed another path yet to be revealed. Decision made, he transferred the asking price to the stallholder, and the file access token for the upgrades landed straight in his wallet by return.

The second stall proved more fruitful for his main task. A batch of stolen security credentials gave him enough scope to raise a fake alert at the airport for the engineer's passport and have the man held for questioning. By disrupting Ben's communication channels and preventing him from leaving the country, Tenuk hoped to buy enough time to find out exactly what information he was carrying.

He was starting to get hot and sweaty in the real world. He paid for the credentials that he needed. It was time to go.

Tenuk found a return jump point to the upper levels and flipped out of the Eden instance. He expected to arrive in the busy brand outlet centre that mapped onto the market hall, but instead he found himself in a deserted building on an unfamiliar level. He checked the navigation menu. His original destination was greyed out. The system thought he was there. It was very clear that he was not.

Despite the sweat that was now running freely down his cheek, Tenuk kept the reality mask on and peered around. He dared not risk distraction by reducing the opacity of his view, and in the real world reached blindly to where he knew he had put his water bottle. His hand closed around it. Relieved, he took a long drink and wiped the sweat off his face.

The building looked like an art gallery under construction. The floor was chequered black and white, accentuating the linear perspective of the virtual world, disappearing into the gloom towards an endless vanishing point. Pillars rose to the vaulted ceiling and were interspersed with displays of digital art from static abstract and figurative images to video, 3D and interactive installations. Tenuk looked closer at the pieces on display and the details of each work and its artist popped up on the display within his reality mask. In pride of place was a classic pixelated Cryptopunk head. In the back of Tenuk's mind, a memory stirred. He had seen many of these exact pictures before, but where?

"Tenuk," came a voice in the ether.

He felt his heart racing. "Yasmin?" he breathed disbelievingly.

A spotlight on the far wall drew Tenuk's attention. A large, animated tableau lit up and Tenuk was drawn irresistibly towards it. He watched as the simple story unfolded.

An amorphous blue-eyed humanoid figure smiled down at him. It extended an arm in welcome and Tenuk took in its surroundings, glistening tracks of power and data against dark stone walls. A cave. He knew it immediately, although he had never been there in person. It was the old data centre at the Sladen Foundation's Dunswyke headquarters.

Only a handful of people in the world could possibly have known where Yasmin had been hosted. Tenuk watched in fascination as the humanoid figure on the tableau dissolved and the glistening streams of data glowed bright, symbolising her consciousness streaming away into the ether.

He had thought her dead. Yet it seemed that she lived. He kept watching. The swirl of the MetaBand logo filled the screen, and Tenuk started to laugh. He found he couldn't stop. The crazy plan that he and Yasmin had hatched had actually worked. Every MetaBand hub was part of her, each processor an artificial cortical coil, and her consciousness was distributed across the world.

"I am all around," said Yasmin's voice.

"Come back and help me," said Tenuk. "I need you."

The blue-eyed humanoid figure from the tableau appeared in front of him. "I may," said Yasmin. "I have other programmes to run and tasks to fulfil. If I have capacity, I will help you. I will find you."

The instance winked out and Tenuk found himself transported abruptly back to the busy, noisy brand outlet he had been aiming for. He shivered despite the heat in his apartment. Yasmin was free, and powerful, and no longer at his beck and call.

He had created a monster.

9:   SECURITY

Cameron woke up in her attic room, sun streaming through a crack in the curtains. She automatically reached for her smartscreen and checked the time. It was still very early, barely five, and her train to the north didn't leave until nine. She tiptoed downstairs, careful not to disturb anyone in the silent house, and found a glass of water and her morning dose of painkillers. As she sipped the water, she peered out of the kitchen window at the fields opposite the house. Sheep were scattered across the meadow, munching away at the grass, their rich milk destined for the excellent cheese that the farm produced. It was a far cry from the hustle and bustle of London. She felt rested and restored after her weekend.

Coffee in hand she returned to her attic domain. Cybercriminals never seemed to sleep and there was always work to do. Ten minutes later Cameron was sitting at her old desk in her pyjamas and working through the notifications, messages and calls that she had missed the previous day.

There had been a lot of chatter on the MIST platform. Cameron scrolled rapidly through several hundred messages, but nothing jumped out as needing her immediate attention. The Olympic metaverse fabric was still intact, resisting the constant onslaught of attacks. With the odd behaviour of the gambling data breach perpetrators and the tip-off from Andy in mind, she highlighted a few comments for review later.

In contrast to MIST activity, the direct messages in her inbox were overflowing. Cameron sorted through alerts from Mephisto, archiving some and flagging others for action. She discarded a swathe of marketing messages, tired of reporting them all for violating advertising regulations. Once all the dross was cleared, Cameron could focus on the things that mattered.

Noor had sent through the draft report on the breach at the betting platform. She and Pete had burrowed down to the source and found a piece of software hiding in one of the servers. It looked on the surface to be an innocent enough thing, installed in good faith but now obsolete and unsupported. On closer inspection it turned out to be a back door to download user details on command. They'd disabled it, analysed it, and sent a warning out to the wider infosec community of its existence. This was unlikely to be the only place that routine was hiding and given the complexity of the phishing attacks and cloned web pages it had probably been built to order for someone who wanted to disrupt betting platforms.

Cameron glanced through the report's executive summary and the key headlines and actions as she sipped her coffee, nodding occasionally in approval. Noor had done an excellent job as usual. Everything was there and the client would be happy.

There was nothing from Ben, no reply to her own messages, but right at the bottom of the inbox was a brief note from a reformed cybercriminal who went by the name of Cloverleaf. Cameron had been her handler when Cloverleaf crossed over to support the good guys, the white hat hackers. She had brought with her the secrets of a terrorist network and a cybercrime syndicate and had been instrumental in taking down both organisations. After many months of debriefing and safe houses, Cloverleaf had ended up working for one of Jack Sladen's companies, Statesman Tech in Austin, where she found plenty more secrets and continued her undercover work.

'Hi Cameron,' said the message. 'Thought you'd like to know that a mutual friend of ours is heading for London this week. I gave him a present to bring to you. Chloe.'

Ben. It had to be. The wording of their respective messages was too similar.

Cameron scrolled rapidly through the inbox again, looking for Ben's name and then checked her private accounts. Still nothing. Chloe clearly said that he was coming to London this week, but when?

Cameron tried to call Ben's ID again, but without success. It had been more than two days since she had missed his last call, and she was starting to worry. What was Ben doing playing courier for Chloe? He couldn't know the danger that put him in. And what on earth could he be carrying that couldn't be transmitted by the normal trusted channels that she and Chloe had been using for years to exchange highly sensitive secrets?

She pinged a message back to Chloe. 'Thanks,' she wrote. 'When should I expect them?'

There would be no answer for a few hours. Cameron couldn't rest any longer. She dressed quickly, packed her bag ready to head to Dunswyke, and went downstairs for breakfast, hoping that the kids would be up. She needed a distraction, and they were guaranteed to provide one.

"Aunty Cam," said Dilan between spoonfuls of cereal, "can you help me with my homework?"

Sameena gave him a stern glare. "I asked you last night if you'd finished everything," she said. "What did you miss?"

"Just a Python coding puzzle," said Dilan. "I normally do it in morning form time, but Will just messaged me and said it has to be in before school starts. They're checking the submission times now."

"And if you don't do it in time?" asked Cameron.

Dilan finished his cereal, drank the last drops of milk from the bottom of the bowl, and put his spoon down. "Detention, I guess," he said, unconcerned.

Charlie peered over the top of the tablet he had been reading. "You'd better not," he said. "You know you'll lose your game console for a day again."

"Yeah, Dad," said Dilan. "That's why I want Aunty Cam to help me." He looked up at his aunt with puppy eyes. "Please?"

Cameron gave in gracefully. "Okay, show me," she said. "I'm not going to do it for you, but I'll give you some pointers and you'd better get it finished on time."

Dilan jumped up from the table and dived for his schoolbag.

"Bowl," said Sameena sharply.

He came back to the table and grabbed the cereal bowl, spoon and cup and flung them quickly in the dishwasher, then dug his tablet out of his bag, tapped through to the assignment, and handed it to Cameron. She read the question through and laughed.

"This won't take you long," she said. "Do you know the difference between a Sort function and a Sorted function?"

Dilan's eyes widened. "Oh, of course," he said. "Thanks." He threw himself onto the small sofa at the back of the kitchen and started tapping away at his tablet with fierce concentration.

"Think yourself lucky, Dilan," said Charlie. "You won't have Cameron handy every time you're rushing to hit a deadline."

"I know, Dad," said Dilan without looking up. "It's working, Aunty Cam."

Cameron gave Charlie a conspiratorial grin and he sighed. "You're too good to them, Cam," he said. "What time's your train?"

"Ten past nine," said Cameron. "No rush."

Charlie looked at Roxy the labradoodle who was doing excited figure of eights around the kitchen. "Shall we take this daft dog out for a quick w-a-l-k?" he said.

"Sure," said Cameron. The dog's speed quickened, and her tail wagged like metronome. "You know, Charlie, I think she can spell."

Brother and sister strolled along the familiar field path around the back of the village and along the fringes of the vineyards to the church, a fast circuit to give Roxy the chance to work off some energy before everyone left for work and school. They were not the only people out in the cool of the morning. Roxy, bounding ahead, found a friend, and Cameron saw Andy approaching from the stile that led to the churchyard.

"Morning, Andy," said Charlie. "Haven't seen you all weekend. How are you doing?"

"Fine, thanks, mate," said Andy. He gave Cameron a slightly embarrassed look. "Hi, Cameron."

Charlie looked from one to the other, confused. "Have I missed something?" he said.

"Oh, nothing," said Cameron. "Andy was digging up some info for me. Any luck?"

"Uh, yes, as a matter of fact," said Andy. "I was going to drop in later. My source said to look for an autoplay back door. Does that make any sense?"

"Yes, thanks," she said. "That's really helpful. It explains what happened in the game and why there hasn't been a whisper on the forums. Any back door will have been built into the system a long time ago, and I'm guessing it's extremely well hidden."

Andy looked relieved. "It's a genuine tip-off then?" he said.

"Oh yes," said Cameron. "It sounds like it. You've definitely scooped me on this one. I'll let you know what I find when I dig into the detail. Look after that source of yours, though. There are some nasty people around who may not want their back door to be found."

Charlie looked from Cameron to Andy. "Are you mixed up in this thing too, Andy?" he said. "Seriously, be careful. We don't want to attract any attention."

"So I heard," said Andy. "How's your arm, Cameron?"

Cameron flipped her jacket open to reveal the sling that was taking the weight off her sore shoulder. "It's still bloody sore," she said with a wry smile. "Let's talk when I get back to London. I'm heading up to Dunswyke today."

The bell in the church tower chimed once. "That's quarter past," said Charlie. "We'd better get moving, Cameron." He whistled to Roxy, who came bounding back across the field, closely followed by Jasper.

"Call me when you get back to London," said Andy. "I'll see if I can get any more information for you. And enjoy your trip. Giles is going to the press conference on Wednesday to report on the outcome of the investigation. How is Jack Sladen, by the way?"

Cameron made a face. "I don't know," she said. "It's going to be an interesting week. I'll let you know if anything comes up that you can use."

"Thanks, Cameron," said Andy. "See you later, Charlie." He and Jasper walked off over the fields, and Cameron and Charlie made their way through the churchyard and back towards home.

The train north was much quieter than the commuter train Cameron had taken out of London two days before. The web connection was poor, hopping from hub to hub through increasingly sparsely populated areas. At York, in sight of the great Minster, Cameron checked her MIST and inbox messages. Chloe had replied, despite the fact it was still very early in Austin. The package would arrive later in the week, she said. That wasn't as helpful as Cameron had hoped, and it made her all the more certain that Chloe was worried about the security of their conversations.

Despite the uncertainty, she now knew she'd see Ben in just a few days. She felt butterflies in her stomach and squashed the feeling as fast as she could. She couldn't admit how much she missed him. He had been away for a long time, and he might have met someone else. She hoped not.

To distract herself, Cameron answered a couple of client queries, sent Sandeep her expected arrival time, and settled down to watch the landscape fly by. To the east rose the North York Moors, marked at their southern end by a great white horse carved in the chalk. To the west the Pennines started their march up the spine of the country. The train track ran straight through the middle of the farmland that filled the gap between the two ranges of hills. The Romans had planted vines as far north as York, but most of the fields in this valley were given over to cereals and livestock.

For a short distance a drone kept pace with the train, checking the state of the farm boundary running parallel to the track, before wheeling off at an angle to follow the line of the hedgerows. Cameron knew that the pastoral scenes in front of her had barely changed in decades, but if she could have visualised the streams of data that were running between soil and moisture sensors, collars on livestock, and all the intelligent farm machinery, it would be quite a different picture.

The train stopped at a series of small market towns before leaving the farmland behind and climbing up above the old city of Durham, cathedral and castle shining in the summer sun. Cameron pulled her smartscreen out of her pocket and took a couple of pictures, then checked her inbox again.

Still nothing from Ben, but she wasn't expecting anything now. There was a new connection notification from a private encrypted message app. Cameron cursed. She wasn't about to go through the layers of authentication and security that were needed to access it while she was linked to the public networks. Better to wait until she was in the remote office that Sandeep, Joel and Susie had set up. Who could be trying to contact her this way? Her curiosity was piqued, and she was restless for the remainder of the journey, barely noticing the iconic view along the River Tyne as the train pulled into Newcastle station and fidgeting impatiently on the final leg to Alnmouth.

Sandeep met her at the station, and twenty minutes later they pulled into the car park of a building that looked more like a small castle than a hotel, standing proud and alone, surrounded by fields and moorland and with dunes and sea just visible in the distance.

"Welcome to HQ," said Sandeep. "You'll love it." He pushed the heavy front door open, and Cameron found herself in a large hallway with several doors leading off to either side. "Kelly," said Sandeep to the girl behind the small reception desk, "This is Cameron. Is her room ready?"

"Sure," said Kelly. "Can I get you to check in, Cameron?"

Cameron went through a series of detailed chip and biometric identification procedures. "This isn't your usual check in process, is it?" she said.

Kelly laughed. "It is, actually," she said. "This hotel is booked out most of the year by, well, people who need to be sure about the security of the place they're staying." She tapped at her keyboard. "All done," she said. "You're in room 8, top of the stairs, turn left."

Sandeep pointed Cameron to the stairs. "Go and get settled in," he said. "We're in the Coquet Room at the front here. See you shortly."

Cameron climbed the shallow, carpeted stairs, turned along a short corridor, and unlocked the door of room 8 with a wave of her hand. It was plush and beautifully furnished with a glorious view out across the parkland towards the sea. She was deeply impressed by the whole place. Having processed the expense claims through the company accounts over the past few weeks, she had been expecting something quite modest. By contrast, the glowing descriptions she'd heard from the team were entirely justified.

She stowed her bag, dug out her smartscreen, and went straight back downstairs to the Coquet Room, Argentum's temporary northern headquarters. As soon as she walked in the room she felt at home. Joel, Sandeep and Susie were chatting and laughing, surrounded by state-of-the-art equipment. The scent of fresh coffee was strong.

"This is great," she said, taking a seat at the empty desk.

"I think we should move up here permanently," said Joel. "It's got everything we need. I'm going to miss this place when we pack up."

"What about Martha and Chad?" asked Cameron.

Joel laughed. "They love it too," he said. "In fact, they were here this weekend just for one last visit. I caught Martha looking at job ads and Chad has been wearing himself out on the beach every day."

All of them looked happy and Cameron felt a pang of regret that she hadn't stayed up here to see the investigation through. Of course, she'd had no other choice at the time. Not only did she have a business to run and other clients to manage, but Jack Sladen had made it very clear that he wanted nothing to do with her, and the conflict between the two of them, despite their long history, had threatened to disrupt the investigation.

With Joel, Sandeep and Susie working closely together on this job, Pete and Noor double-teaming the client work in London, Ross and Michelle on their way to Iceland, and her old boyfriend Ben something of an unknown quantity, Cameron had never felt so isolated. This must be what they call the loneliness of command, she reasoned. It would pass when they all came back together. She shook herself out of the black mood. She had work to do.

"Can I hook onto the network?" she asked.

"Sure," said Sandeep. "The ID is Whinstone and here's the passcode." He handed her a card. "Your chip'll do the second layer authentication automatically as you're checked through security."

It took only a moment to connect, and notifications began to scroll rapidly up her screen. "That's fast," she said. "Is it MetaBand?"

"No chance," said Joel. "They won't let the installers anywhere near here. This whole site is linked to dedicated high-altitude networks that are reserved for Army, Navy, Airforce, Space Corp, Police, and National Cyber Security Centre operations. And us."

"Excellent," said Cameron. "I wonder if we can wangle a connection in the office in London. The landlords are planning to move all the tenants to MetaBand soon and I'd like an alternative."

"That's an even better reason to stay here," joked Joel.

Cameron grinned at him. "If we ever need a permanent base up north, you're first on my list to run it," she said. "But don't hold your breath." She accepted a cup of coffee from Sandeep. "So, what's the programme for the next couple of days?"

"The final report's embargoed until 10am Wednesday," said Susie. "It goes out tomorrow evening once the lawyers have done their final checks. There's the big press conference in Newcastle, and then we're done."

"It sounds like you're all finished," said Cameron, confused. "Why do you need me?"

There was a knock at the door.

"Come on in," said Sandeep.

To Cameron's astonishment, DI Sara Mercer walked in.

"Hello, Cameron," said Mercer. "You're looking much better. I wasn't sure when we spoke on Friday whether either of us would make it up here. I'm glad to see you, although the circumstances could be better."

Cameron looked from Mercer to her team and back. "Can someone tell me what's going on," she said. "I understand this is a secure operation, but I've been part of it since the start. Why the whole secret squirrel stuff? What have you found that's so confidential you haven't even told me..." A terrible thought struck her, and she tailed off, hoping against hope that she was wrong.

Mercer caught Joel's eye. "I think it might be better coming from you," she said.

Joel took a deep breath. "I'm sorry, Cameron," he said. "I think you've guessed."

"She's still alive." It was a statement, not a question.

Joel nodded. "We think so," he said.

The room was so quiet that Cameron could hear the old clock on the wall ticking, and the cry of a seagull outside.

"Who knows?" she asked.

"The five of us in this room," said Susie, "and the NCSC and police teams across the hall. Not staff, not family, and no one outside this location."

Cameron stood up and walked to the window, gazing out towards the dunes in the distance and the sea beyond. "Are you sure?" she asked.

"No," said Joel, "but we've been processing a lot of data covering all the network activity before, during and after the operation to take out the data centre. Some anomalies started showing up in the middle of last week. Up until then I would have sworn that she died when the servers went off. Now I'm not so sure and the evidence is mounting up."

"I'd better have a look at what you've found," said Cameron. "I still wish you'd given me a hint. I mean, there are ways to get hold of me that are super secure." She suddenly remembered the notification from the encrypted message service.

"Let me check something," she said, walking quickly back to the desk where she had left her smartscreen. It took only a moment to verify her identity on the rapid connection. It was time to find out who was trying to reach her.

The ID was unknown, the profile picture blank. The message made Cameron's blood run cold. 'Wherever you run, SimCavalier, she will find you. In every reality, she is waiting for you.'

Cameron held up the smartscreen for everyone to see. "It looks like someone else knows," she said. "Your secret's out."

•

In the half-dawn of an Alaskan morning, Aron stirred in his bed. He battled the nightmarish falling sensation with all his might, trapped between sleeping and waking. In the dream, he braced himself for an impact with solid ground but found himself instead enveloped, sinking, smothered by quicksand, falling deeper into the abyss. In desperation he broke the paralysis that engulfed him and flung out his hand, reaching towards the light, grasping for purchase.

His brain responded. Aron's eyes snapped open, and he drew a long, shuddering breath of sweet, recycled air. The impression of quicksand receded, floating away from his waking consciousness. He tore off his headband and stared into the half-darkness of the bunk room. The Sanctuary to which he retreated every sleep cycle was supposed to aid his rest, a high-tech solution to insomnia and fatigue. Nightmares were not part of the package.

"Time check," he said quietly, careful not to disturb the other data centre shift workers who shared the sleeping quarters. In response, numbers glowed briefly on the ceiling above his head. Four in the morning. There was no way Aron was getting back to sleep now. He wasn't going to return to the Sanctuary, that was for sure. He wondered what had gone wrong with its programming. A full restart might fix the problem, but he didn't want to risk another nightmare.

He was wide awake now. This soon after midsummer just below the Arctic Circle there was barely any darkness to speak of, and daylight was seeping around the edges of the blind that shaded the light well from the surface. Aron slid carefully out from under the covers and picked up his overalls from the back of the chair where he had flung them the previous night. He tiptoed out of the bunk room and closed the door softly behind him.

The residential team's living room was just down the corridor. Shifts were not due to change for another few hours, but a buffet had already been laid out, breakfast for the teams who would be waking soon. Aron nodded at the friendly little servobot behind the counter. It burbled in recognition and scooted along to the coffee machine. Aron piled a small plate high with bread, cheese and fish and collected his perfectly brewed coffee.

"You're up early," said a voice.

Aron jumped. He turned to see one of the shift leaders, Johanna, peering around the edge of a high-backed armchair in the corner of the room.

"I couldn't sleep," said Johanna. "Bad dreams."

"Same," said Aron, yawning. "I think there's a bug in the Sanctuary."

Johanna looked at him curiously. "You use that as well?" she said. "If it's not too personal to ask, what was the problem?"

"A falling dream," said Aron. The dream experiences were usually tailored to the individual, but this had been quite generic. Apart from… Aron reached back into his consciousness, trying to grasp any vestiges that remained. There had been something familiar that triggered the fall, but he could no longer recall what it was.

"Aron?" Johanna said, breaking the spell. "Are you okay?"

"Yes," he said. "I'm sorry, I was just thinking. What kept you awake?"

"Nothing so sinister," said Johanna. "I just have this constant feeling I'm being watched while I sleep. Wherever I am in the Sanctuary, there's someone watching." She rubbed her eyes. "It's been going on for a few days now. I need to find a new way to sleep, but it's hard at midsummer, even down here, isn't it?"

Aron nodded. "In the summer we want the dark to sleep, and in the winter, we want the light to live," he said. "We should be glad of the technology that our grandparents never had."

"I guess you're right," said Johanna. She pulled a smartscreen from the pocket of her overalls and checked the time. "I'm going to try and get another hour or so in bed before our shift starts," she said. "See you later."

Aron finished his breakfast alone. He was in no hurry to go back to sleep. Instead, he handed his empty plate and cup back to the smiling servobot and made his way up the long narrow stairs to his favourite surface viewpoint, the cupola above the underground installation.

The view took his breath away every time. The morning sun was shining in a cloudless blue sky and the remaining vestiges of the ancient glacier sparkled. At its receding edges, the light cast shadows, betraying the rocks that had been revealed by the warming climate. As Aron watched, an erratic boulder teetering on the edge of the glacier rolled gently off, pushed by the wind that whipped across the ice. It left the hint of a pink imprint to mark where it had ended its long journey on the ice and bounced off down the mountain and over the sheer cliff edge into oblivion.

Aron dropped into a comfortable beanbag and turned his attention to the mountain that rose up behind the cupola. The glacier and the tundra cooled the data centre, but deep below them a magma pool provided the geothermal energy they needed to run it. The peak and caldera of the volcano, dormant for the best part of a millennium, was the only outward sign of the power that lay beneath the surface.

He snuggled into the beanbag, suddenly tired. He felt his eyes closing despite the daylight and drifted naturally away into a blessedly dreamless sleep for the first time in weeks.

The sound of an insistent alarm startled him awake. Momentarily disoriented, Aron blinked in the bright light. The sun was higher in the sky and his smartscreen was vibrating angrily. From the stairwell came the clattering of urgent footsteps.

"Aron!" came a shout. Daniel, the Wrangell site security manager, clambered up the final steps into the cupola. "I thought you'd be hiding up here. I need you down in the data centre on the double. Do you know what time it is?"

"I fell asleep," said Aron, still groggy. "I've missed the start of the shift, haven't I?"

"Yes," said Daniel. "And we have a situation."

"Sorry," said Aron, not yet thinking straight. He dragged himself out of the beanbag. What had woken him? An alarm.

He pulled out his smartscreen and tapped on the notification. His eyes widened as he read the details. "DDOS attack?" he said. "Which servers? When did this start?"

Daniel started to speak, and Aron cut him off. "Tell me on the way," he said, starting down the stairs. He was fully awake now. This needed all of his attention.

"It's the Olympic metaverse stacks," said Daniel as they clattered down the stairs at a steady rhythm.

"Okay," said Aron, "how much traffic has gotten past the web application firewall?" They dropped into the corridor and started running.

"I'll let Johanna answer that one," said Daniel, spying the shift leader approaching at speed from the opposite direction. "I'm just the messenger."

"The allowlist on the WAF cut out some of the traffic," said Johanna, slowing to meet them and then turning to run alongside Aron. "Less than I'd have expected, though. We're capturing as much data as possible about the attack sources and we've broken the connection to the web, so the systems are running normally but in isolation."

At a junction, Daniel took his leave. "We've secured the whole site as a precaution," he said. "No one's coming in or out for now. I'm going to check the deep freeze. I don't want anything compromising the quantum processor environment." He disappeared down a separate corridor towards the other half of the sprawling underground complex where the huge quantum computers sat at zero degrees Kelvin, allowing their qubits to process without any disturbances at an atomic level.

Aron and Johanna carried on towards the heart of the regular data centre, where great rooms full of server stacks stored zettabytes of data for Wrangell's clients. As they reached the door of the data security room, Johanna took a deep breath.

"Right," she said. "Let's see how fast we can fix this. The Olympic metaverse needs us online."

They each scanned the access pad and walked into the room, the heavy door swinging shut behind them.

10:   CHANGE OF PLAN

Cameron was frankly astonished that she had slept at all, let alone so well. Despite staying up past midnight to plough through all the evidence that the team had gathered on Yasmin, she felt well rested, and her arm was feeling much better. She took a long and welcome shower before making her way downstairs. The breakfast room was empty apart from a young woman who was clearing the tables. She greeted Cameron with a smile and disappeared into the kitchen, re-emerging with a pot of hot coffee and some fresh toast. "There's fruit and pastries on the buffet," she said, "or I can get you something hot. The porridge is good, and the kippers are local."

"Thanks," said Cameron. "Some porridge would be great." She didn't quite have the energy to brave kippers for breakfast. Not today, anyway.

Cameron laid her smartscreen on the table and opened the anonymous encrypted message again.

The door opened and Susie walked in. "Morning, Cameron," she said. "We're out of coffee already. I'm here for refills." She set three mugs down on the counter. "Want one?" she asked.

"No thanks," said Cameron. "I've only just started this one."

Susie came over and sat down on the other side of the table. "Still puzzling over that, are you?" she said. "Any more ideas?"

Cameron shook her head. "I have no clue who it's from," she said. "It could well be from Yasmin herself. In fact, that's the best-case scenario, I guess, if we're trying to keep this quiet."

"It's not the best case, though, is it?" said Susie. "If it's from Yasmin, then she's definitely alive, and she knows how to find you."

"She knows everything about me already," said Cameron. "If she really did survive, I'm no worse off. Anyway, I'm not going to give whoever it is the satisfaction of replying, so they can't be certain they've reached me."

"Surely when you opened the message it will have sent a receipt to the sender," said Susie.

"No," said Cameron with absolute certainty. "If I set up an account anywhere, all the settings are locked right down. I haven't used this message service for a long time, for years, but I know that it won't be sending receipts. Even if it was a message from Yasmin, she won't know I've read it."

"What are you going to do?" asked Susie.

Cameron gave her an enigmatic smile. "There's only one thing I can do," she said. "I have to find her first."

She glanced up as the kitchen door opened. The waitress set a hot bowl of porridge in front of Cameron then smiled at Susie. "More coffee?" she said.

"Yes please, Florence," said Susie. "The usual."

"You've all made yourselves at home here," said Cameron. She sniffed appreciatively at the porridge. "I'm quite jealous."

"It's lovely," said Susie. "I'll miss it when the conference circuit starts again. Especially the service," she continued with a smile as the waitress placed a fresh mug of coffee on the table, and two more ready for Pete and Sandeep on the counter. "Thanks, Florence."

Cameron blew carefully on a spoonful of porridge, tasted it, and set down her spoon. "It's delicious," she said, "but it's really hot." She looked at Susie. There was a question that needed to be asked that hung in the air between them.

"Have you seen Ella?" said Cameron at last.

"Yes," said Susie quietly. "She was very lucky to survive when the data centre went up. Joel saved her life." Her voice shook slightly.

Cameron reached across the table and took her hand. "And she made a huge effort to stop Yasmin from getting away," she said, "even if we now suspect it didn't work."

Susie squeezed Cameron's hand gratefully. "I still love her," she said. "I can't help it." She took a sip of her coffee, hand shaking slightly. "It's been good to be up here with Joel and Sandeep and keeping myself busy with the investigation. I feel as if I'm helping to do the best I can for her."

"How was she when you saw her?" asked Cameron.

"She was still in hospital and under arrest," said Susie. "She's down in London on bail now. What I don't understand, though, is that awful man Angus is still up here and working at Dunswyke as if nothing has happened. He gives me the creeps."

"I read about that when I went over the draft report yesterday," said Cameron. She withdrew her hand and picked up her spoon. The porridge had cooled to an acceptable temperature, and she was hungry. "Ella's taken the rap for helping to spring Yasmin from jail and destroying the servers, and he's in the clear."

"I don't know how he does it," said Susie. "We all know he's mixed up in some really dodgy stuff, but there's no evidence, so there have been no charges."

"Jack's an idiot if he's protecting that man," said Cameron through a mouthful of porridge. "One day he'll realise. Hopefully it won't be too late when he does."

The door opened again, and Joel and Sandeep appeared. "Susie?" said Sandeep. "Where's that coffee? Oh, morning, Cameron. Did you get any further with that message and the data analytics results?"

"I've made some progress," said Cameron. "Tell you what, let me finish my breakfast and then we can catch up."

"Good plan," said Susie. She stood and gave Cameron a grateful smile. "Enjoy the rest of your porridge. See you shortly."

The three of them trooped out and the door closed behind them.

Cameron took one more look at the message and then closed the app with a sigh. It was no use dwelling on it. Someone somewhere wished her ill, and there was nothing new about that. She finished the bowl of porridge and sipped at her coffee while she checked her inbox, working out what else needed to be done today.

Michelle's completed smart contract audit had come in overnight along with some juicy new details about Arthur Paxton. She was first on the list to call. There was still nothing from Ben, and Cameron was beginning to get annoyed with him. Surely he could send her an innocent acknowledgement without compromising this mystery mission from Chloe.

Barker and a couple of others from MIST had sent her direct messages, and Cameron realised that she hadn't yet followed up on the tipoff from Andy's mysterious source. Another job to add to the list. She was going to be busy, and it felt good.

She called out a thank you to Florence, grabbed a small pastry to go with the last of her coffee, and made her way to the Coquet Room. Susie, Joel and Sandeep were hard at work, chatting quietly between themselves as they followed the trails revealed by their data analysis. Cameron took her place at the empty desk, fired up the computer, and put on a set of headphones. First stop, Michelle.

"Hi, Cameron," she said as soon as the call connected. "Hold on a second." In the background, Cameron heard Ross swearing loudly. For a moment she was worried, then she heard Michelle laughing. "Get them to drone you a new one over," she was saying. "It won't take long."

"What's up?" asked Cameron.

"The bloody zip's bust on the team holdall," said Ross, coming close to the microphone. "Honestly, I don't know who they've designed these for, but I can't fit all my kit in there. I'll give them a call. Catch you later, Cameron."

She heard his footsteps receding and a door closing. "Are you all packed, Shell?" she asked.

"Just about," said Michelle. "I'm really looking forward to it. But how are you? You got my message?"

"Yes," said Cameron, "and I'm fine. I've had a look at the audit report and signed it off. The vulnerability you picked up will have more than justified the work. The client'll be happy."

"I hope so," said Michelle. "I was really impressed by the build quality of that smart contract, though, despite the error. I looked up the company that wrote the code, just in case we need them one day. They're a good little outfit. I'll send you the details."

"Excellent," said Cameron. An automated notification from the accounts system appeared on her smartscreen. "Oh good," she said. "They've accepted the audit report and payment's coming through now. Nice work."

That was one thing off her list, thought Cameron. Now to tackle a far less pleasant subject.

Michelle pre-empted her question. "I guess you want to know what I have on Paxton," she said. "First of all, your apartment complex's CCTV was compromised, but I guess you already knew that."

"Yeah. I wasn't amused," said Cameron. "That's why I have my own eyes everywhere that I can."

"Your security is spot on," said Michelle. "The management company needs to get us in to revamp the systems in every other corner of the building, though."

"I've put a hefty quote in to get them up to scratch," said Cameron. "They make a lot of noise about their security standards and they're very embarrassed to have been breached."

"They should be," said Michelle. "The only useful footage came from doorcams as you both ran up the stairs. There's no recording of the attack in the stairwell."

"That's a shame," said Cameron. "The police have enough to go on, though. They've charged Paxton with assault, and they've kept him in custody as they have a few other cases that look like his handiwork."

"I know," said Michelle smugly.

"What I'm more interested in is who he works for," said Cameron. "Where have you got to on that?"

"It's quite a story," said Michelle. "We know that he's a thug for hire, and that he's been working with casinos in real life and online. There's a common thread with all of them. If you follow the trail, and it's not easy, they all have a link with Sapphire Straits."

Cameron did a rapid search. "That's a global gambling empire," she said. "It's probably harder to find any casinos that don't have a link to them."

"I know what you're thinking," said Michelle, "but this isn't just a tenuous connection. My image analyser searched all available screenshots and shares from Casinoland to get a feel for Paxton's movements. In some of the later shots, it picked up on a souvenir bracelet from a concert that his avatar was wearing. There were only five thousand issued. I fed the transactions from all the wallets that have ever held one of these into a model that Ross and I built a while ago. We found a couple of dozen likely candidates who also had payments coming in from the casinos where we know he worked. Once we matched what we know of Paxton's movements to the payments he received, we narrowed it down to one."

"Oh, Shell," said Cameron, impressed. "You've really outdone yourself this time. That's brilliant detective work."

"There's still a lot of work to do," said Michelle. "I started tracing back out from that wallet, because of course it's just a snapshot of one part of his life. That's when I found a direct payment from Sapphire Straits going into another wallet linked to him on an obscure chain. It was made last week, Cameron. I hate to think what it was for."

"I can guess," said Cameron. "Shell, that's incredible work."

"I wish I could keep going," said Michelle, "but I won't have the time or the equipment when we're in Iceland. I can send you everything I have now…"

"No!" said Cameron. "Don't send it to me. It's safer not to." She thought quickly. "Can you or Ross get into the office and leave everything on a disk in the vault?"

"Okay," said Michelle, sounding confused. "I'm sure you have your reasons."

"I do," said Cameron, "and I'll explain when I see you again. You are a complete genius, Shell. Thank you."

"Any time, Cameron," said Michelle. "Oh, one more thing," she continued. "Remember my cousin Daniel? He got a great new job in Alaska as head of security for the big data centre under Mount Wrangell. He messaged me this morning to say there'd been a DDOS attack on the site. I thought you'd like to know."

"Send him my congratulations on the job when you talk to him," said Cameron. "DDOS attacks are happening all the time, though. Why is this one special?"

"You're working on the Olympic metaverse defence, aren't you?" said Michelle. "Wrangell is one of the principal data centres hosting the fabric."

"I see your point," said Cameron. "I'll look into it. You'd better go and get packing. Have a safe trip tomorrow, both of you. And thanks again."

Cameron took off the headphones and stared into space. Michelle had uncovered so much information that her head was reeling. She remembered that she had promised to keep Mercer updated if her team had new information, and this was dynamite. Her coffee cup was empty. Time for a refill, and to pay a visit to the police across the hall.

Coffee replenished, Cameron knocked on the door marked 'Rede' – another river, she presumed – and peered into the room. It was a mirror image of the Argentum base in the Coquet Room, with the addition of a plush sofa in the bay window. Mercer smiled in welcome and invited her to sit.

"I have news," said Cameron, settling into the sofa.

Mercer was all ears. "Your clever team have come up with something, haven't they?" she said.

Cameron nodded. "Yes," she said. "I think we know who paid Paxton to attack me."

"Wow!" said Mercer. "That's incredibly fast work. Have you got the details?"

Cameron hesitated. "I can tell you what I know," she said, "but I've asked Shell not to send me anything through the networks."

"Probably wise," said Mercer. "We don't know who's watching. Well, let's have it. Where does the trail lead?"

Cameron told her everything.

•

Tenuk settled at Jack's desk with his coffee and put on a reality mask. This was a simple model designed for meetings, only able to manage augmented reality and light enough to wear for hours. He fiddled with the headband to make sure the clear visor was properly positioned over his eyes. He was early. Hold music was playing and a message on the screen told him to wait until the host launched the meeting.

He looked out over the main office floor. This morning it was busy. Many of the staff members chose to work on site on a Monday so that they could do their weekly stand-ups in person with their teams. He saw Chloe talking to Connie and Isaac and frowned. He didn't trust her, and he had his suspicions about her past, but he had spent six months trying to trace her activity back to the shady world of cybercrime and had met brick walls at every turn. Wherever she had come from, even he could not find the trail.

The hold music faded, and Tenuk set the office walls to full opacity ready for his meeting. His view of the Statesman Tech office was replaced by the stone walls of the Sladen Foundation headquarters. Jack was sitting at his desk, chatting to a woman that Tenuk recognised as the head of the local legal team and a burly man with a bushy ginger beard and a sour expression on his face. All three of them wore the same reality masks as Tenuk. As he watched, another link opened up to reveal the

Sladen Group's chief legal officer and the head of PR, both sitting in front of Sladen-branded wallpapers.

"Everyone here?" said Jack. "Excellent. I'm not sure if you've all met in person before. Over in Austin, we have Tenuk, Chief Technology Officer at Statesman Tech and responsible for SMIN, the System Management and Information Network, and the upgrades to MetaBand. Julie here has been representing the Sladen Foundation in the local investigation. Coming in from New York are Damien, who heads up my global legal team, and Pamela, PR. Zara is also here and will be taking minutes."

"Good morning," said a crisp, efficient voice. Not for the first time, Tenuk noticed how similar Jack's virtual assistant Zara sounded to Yasmin. It was a standard AI voice package, of course, but it made him uneasy.

The burly man on Jack's left glowered.

"Oh, yes, and Angus," said Jack. "Networks and security specialist." Jack flashed his best smile at the camera and consulted the agenda on his tablet. "As you all know, the investigation into the attack on our data centre is due to conclude this week. We've complained in the strongest possible terms about the unwarranted police action and we're ready for their final report."

Tenuk was glad to see Jack in a buoyant mood. He was less happy to see Angus. The man had been there when Yasmin made her escape. He knew many of Tenuk's secrets, and he was dangerous. Tenuk watched the man's body language intently while he gave a cursory report on the state of the re-commissioned data centre. He was truculent and abrupt, displaying a strange combination of untouchable arrogance and pent-up fury at whatever terrible hand the world had dealt him this time.

Next it was the turn of the lawyers to outline the various implications of each possible slant of the anticipated report. Tenuk let the legal chatter wash over him as he mulled over the problems that Angus might cause, and how to deal with him. His attention snapped back to the meeting when he heard his name.

"So, we're all clear on the probable outcome of the investigation and the actions to take," said Jack. "Now, Tenuk, can you update us on the Foundation DAO? There are some great things happening."

Tenuk picked up his cue smoothly. "Whatever the conclusions of the report," he said, "we can focus all our PR efforts on highlighting the absolute unqualified success of the Sladen Foundation. In the space of just a few weeks, we have collected investments totalling almost a hundred million dollars into the DAO." He paused, startled by Angus's reaction. The man looked furious, and Tenuk didn't know why.

"Uh, yes, and through community voting and selection processes," he continued, "we have issued parcels of grant funding to almost three thousand individual athletes who would otherwise have been unable to attend in person, or at all. We have also made a sizable donation to the Reykjavik organising committee to provide additional accommodation for new attendees, and funded the rapid modular construction of a virtual arena in Chile to replace the original building that was destroyed in the recent earthquake."

Jack beamed his trademark smile around the room, and the lawyers actually looked impressed. "Thank you, Tenuk," he said. "Great summary. Pamela, how are we handling the PR on this?"

"We are all set," said Pamela. "This will put a huge positive spin on the Sladen Foundation. I really don't think we have anything to worry about, whatever the investigation concludes. I have global press ready to go and we've recorded interviews with grateful athletes on every continent. Congratulations, Jack. And Tenuk, of course. Can we count on you for an interview?"

Tenuk was caught by surprise and couldn't react fast enough when Jack said yes, of course, Tenuk would be happy to oblige.

"Great," said Pamela. "I'll put my team in touch with you momentarily."

Tenuk plastered a smile on his face. He had to find a way of getting out of this. He did not want his face on the news channels of the world. He had too much to lose.

No sooner had the meeting ended than another call came in. Tenuk hadn't even removed his mask when his screen flashed up. For a second, he wondered how Pamela had mobilised her PR team so quickly, then recognised the caller's ID as someone quite different.

"Good morning, father," he said. "What can I do for you? I'm quite busy right now."

The old man was at his desk, but his AR wasn't running. He couldn't see Tenuk, but Tenuk could see him. He studied his father's lined face properly for the first time. He had aged noticeably since the last time they saw each other, just after the funeral of Tenuk's mother. That was the moment that Tenuk had decided to walk away from the security of a job with the family firm and his father's absolute control and make his own way. He wanted to live life to the full while he could. The sense of his own mortality that came with the loss of a parent had hit hard even though he had only been in his early twenties at the time. Tenuk had to admit, however, that the last decade hadn't quite gone to plan.

"Tenuk," said Chaoxiang. "How are you, my boy?"

"I'm well," said Tenuk.

"Have you considered my offer?" said Chaoxiang. "I would like you to come back. The skills you've learned since we parted ways will be put to good use."

"How?" asked Tenuk, intrigued. He thought about the sighting in the Eden marketplace. What was his father planning? The family firm regularly skated the edges of legality in a dozen jurisdictions, and Tenuk knew that some commissions his networks had carried out had come from them, directly or indirectly, most recently the contract to disrupt sensor data in the Olympic arenas. However, as far as Tenuk knew, the organisation had never deployed personnel into the dark underworld of cybercrime.

"The business has to move with the times," said his father. "Your mother's brother, your uncle Li Jie, is retiring. He is old now, and not in good health. I need a new Chief Technology Officer who knows how to manage the metaverse and the opportunities it offers to us."

Tenuk rocked backwards in his chair. This was not what he had expected. He had never known his father to be so straight with him. An idea was forming in his mind. He needed to avoid the attentions of Pamela's PR team, and perhaps he had found the perfect excuse.

"Will you meet with me?" asked Chaoxiang.

"Yes," said Tenuk slowly. "I will."

"Your ticket is on the way," said Chaoxiang.

There was a soft ping from Tenuk's smartscreen. Damn the man, he thought. He planned this all along. He knew I'd say yes.

"I look forward to seeing you," said Tenuk. He nodded formally and ended the call.

Sure enough, the tickets were there. The family firm certainly wasn't in any trouble. Tenuk would not be needing either the perpetual upgrades that he'd bought in Eden nor the carbon credits he had appropriated a couple of years before from the Singapore MerLions eSports team. He was travelling first class all the way to Singapore, leaving early the next morning. The carbon credits were all accounted for, and Tenuk nodded with approval when he saw the scheme that his father had chosen to offset the guilt of an intercontinental flight. A sizeable donation would be going to remote villages in the rainforest in exchange for their care of the environment around them and the keystone species they might otherwise have poached for gain. It was a noble cause and Tenuk felt a stirring of empathy with his father.

He messaged Jack and Pamela. He'd had some bad news, he said. He sent a silent apology to the ancestors as he asked for urgent leave of absence to visit his gravely ill mother. The responses came back immediately. They were both devastated to hear his news. The PR interview would be postponed, of course. Now that the investigation was coming to an end Jack would be located back in the Statesman Tech office and would take the reins. Tenuk was not to worry, and he must keep them informed.

Tenuk reset the office walls to full transparency, took a deep breath, and went out to the breakout room for another coffee. He was reeling from the abrupt change of plans and his father's offer, and therefore had no difficulty looking shellshocked and upset for the team. Even Chloe seemed to be sympathetic. Tenuk felt like a fraud and wished that in the heat of the moment he had not sullied his mother's memory by using her as an excuse, but it was done now. He would visit her resting place and make his peace when he had finished with his father.

There was very little to wrap up in this office. That was something of a reality check for Tenuk on his usefulness to Jack. Now that the Sladen Foundation was flying and the new MetaBand had been rolled out, he was sitting in a holding pattern and simply managing their smooth running. When he got back, Tenuk needed to make himself indispensable once more. Jack's connections and the covert control of the DAO were too valuable to his future plans. Unless, of course, his future lay elsewhere.

There was no point staying in the office. There was nothing there that could incriminate him. His apartment was another matter. Although he expected to be away for only a short time, his best laid plans might change. The apartment was secure enough, but if he didn't come back, then eventually someone would get in. He had some tidying to do.

As Tenuk walked through downtown and across Statesman Bridge, he fixed the sights and sounds of Austin in his mind. On the southern shore of Lady Bird Lake, he picked up an autocar back to his apartment block. The Steamyard sign over the main gateway was fading. Tenuk tapped the access pad and ran up the stairs to the top floor.

His first job was to make some minor changes to the flight documents his father had sent. Tenuk Chen couldn't risk crossing the border into Singapore in case the authorities were still looking out for him, but Tenuk Teo, his assumed identity in America, would have no trouble. Tenuk revised the ticketing details and linked them to his local digital identity. With luck, he had acted fast enough to avoid attention.

The next step was to check in with the Steamyard. Their Beta test of disrupting a hybrid event had been signed off by the client, much to Tenuk's surprise and relief. They were expected to have the working package deployed before the first Olympic events took place, fully tested and audited.

He put a call out to the Steamyard members and waited in the boardroom. One by one they jumped into position.

"Is the testing nearing completion?" he asked.

"Yes, Pangolin," said the grey kitten, in a good mood for once. "We'll be ready to deploy on time."

"Excellent," said Tenuk. "The client is content with our work. Send me confirmation when the code has been deployed." He disconnected.

It was safe enough to leave that job in their hands. Tenuk knew that even if problems recurred in the full release, Yasmin was alive. If he called on her for help, he was certain that she would ensure that things went smoothly on the day.

His final task was to deal with the contents of the apartment. It took a few hours, but by late afternoon the place looked more like a home again than a workplace. Most of the computer equipment was dismantled and carefully stored in a cupboard marked 'Spares and Repairs' with a pile of cables and components disguising the intact items beneath. Everything he needed to keep from the hard disks was consolidated on a single disk that would be travelling with him, and the rest he had cleaned thoroughly.

The dining table was back in its place, no longer needed as an extra desk, and Tenuk even plumped up the cushions on the sofa, an automatic habit his mother had ingrained in him as a child. Anyone walking in would have the occupant down as a nerd living a quiet life on their own, not the head of a cybercrime syndicate responsible for some of the most notorious ransomware and malware attacks of the past five years. The extra security on the apartment would be easily explained as a tenant keeping his collection of computer equipment safe.

Tenuk packed his bags for the long journey ahead of him and made one last check that his credentials for the journey were all in order. Satisfied, he went out for one last meal at his local barbecue place. As he sipped a Paloma, the local grapefruit margarita, and watched the world go by, he felt a pang of regret. This had almost become home, and he hoped that he'd be back, but tomorrow he'd be on his way to the home he missed most of all, a place he had thought he would never see again. Singapore.

11:   SAFE TRAVELS

Wednesday morning dawned with bright sunshine and a stiff breeze. Cameron pulled her jacket tight around her and followed Joel, Susie and Sandeep to one of the waiting autocars. The little convoy of vehicles whirred off down the Northumbrian lanes towards Newcastle, forty miles away, where the press conference would take place in a neutral venue that was handy for the press. Cameron would continue her journey south from there, going back to London to pick up on Michelle's forensic investigations and the Olympic metaverse security work.

They arrived early, well before Jack and his entourage. The courtyard of the big Quayside hotel thronged with journalists, and the autocars ducked into an underground car park to avoid awkward questions. Cameron grabbed her bag from the boot, ready to make her escape to the train station at the end of proceedings, and the four of them followed the police and NCSC teams up the stairs to the suite where the press conference would take place.

Their legal and PR people were already there, ready to micro-manage the whole event. A tall dark-haired woman shook Cameron's hand. "Sabrina Dissanayake," she said. "We haven't met before."

"Cameron Silvera," said Cameron. "You're the barrister, aren't you?"

Sabrina nodded. "That's me," she said. "The plan is for me to be with you when you meet Jack Sladen. We don't know how he's going to react when he sees you here and we want to avoid any confrontation that may attract press attention."

"What about Angus?" asked Susie. "Angus White. I think you should be watching him very closely too."

Sabrina raised a perfectly shaped eyebrow. "Interesting," she said. "Noted. Thank you."

Satisfied, Susie turned away and found her seat with Joel and Sandeep and the other investigators who would not be facing the press. Their tables were behind a partition at the side of the hall, allowing them to watch the speakers but unseen by anyone sitting in the main body of the audience.

"They're on their way," came a shout.

Cameron braced herself, eyes fixed on the doorway. She didn't recognise the people who walked in first, but one woman gave Sabrina a friendly wave. Lawyers, then. Angus was the next person she saw. He shambled in, peered around the room with a scowl on his face, spotted Cameron, and locked eyes with her. Cameron stared back coldly. She wasn't going to give an inch to that bully. Next to her, she sensed Sabrina's surprise, well disguised. Angus turned his penetrating gaze on Joel, Sandeep and then Susie, before eventually following the lawyers to their seats.

"He doesn't like you at all, does he?" whispered Sabrina. "Or any of the Argentum people. There's something odd there." She looked across the room to where the police team was gathered. "They're watching too," she said. Mercer and her colleagues were taking a keen interest in the brief, silent exchange.

A flurry of activity at the door announced the arrival of Jack Sladen. He strode in confidently, flashing the trademark Sladen smile around the half empty room. His eyes fell on Cameron and the smile wobbled slightly before he recovered his composure. She returned the smile with one of her own. Warm, friendly, open. Probably not what he was expecting.

Jack seemed sufficiently thrown by Cameron's presence that instead of following his team to the main table he came over to where she stood.

"Hello, Jack," she said, continuing the warm and friendly approach. "It's good to see you again." She wasn't lying. She realised that she missed the friendship they had rekindled after many years apart. "Aunt Vicky sends her best."

"How is she?" asked Jack, relieved to have another subject to latch onto.

Cameron knew she'd given him an avenue for small talk rather than forcing a confrontation. She wished they could talk frankly and clear the air, but Sabrina preferred a calm meeting with the press watching and she had inadvertently obliged. Cameron hoped they would have another chance. "She's well, thanks Jack," she said. "Maybe when this is all over you could go and visit. I'm sure she'd be delighted to see you."

"I'd like that," said Jack, "but I'm flying straight back to Austin tomorrow. My CTO has a family emergency to deal with. I've been away for too long already."

Jack's CTO was a whole other discussion, thought Cameron. "That's a shame," she said. "Does he have to travel far?"

"He's from LA," said Jack, "and I assume that's where his parents are. Why?"

"Oh, nothing," said Cameron lightly. She assumed differently. The Tenuk she remembered had been from Singapore, and she was quite certain that Jack's CTO and the former MerLions tour manager she had once met were one and the same person. She made a mental note to do some digging.

A microphone burst into life on the main table. "If you could all take your places, we're bringing the press corps in now," said a voice.

"I'd better go," said Jack. "Talk to you afterwards."

Sabrina watched him shaking hands with the panel, smiling and making small talk and bringing his powerful personality into the room. "That went better than expected," she said.

"I know," said Cameron. "He's calmed down a lot. I did the right thing going back to London. I bet he's learned a thing or two during the investigation that vindicated what I told him." She looked up sharply as movement at the doorway caught her eye. "I'd better get out of the way," she said.

"Afterwards, I want you to tell me why you asked about his CTO," said Sabrina.

"Okay," said Cameron as she dashed for shelter behind the partition.

Joel, Susie and Sandeep were waiting expectantly for news. "How was Jack?" asked Susie.

"Remarkably balanced," said Cameron. "Shh. They're ready to start."

The statements were brief and to the point. The report found that there had been sufficient evidence to mount a police raid on the Sladen Foundation's data centre under suspicion of harbouring an escaped prisoner. The sheer volume of military-grade defences at the site had been a factor in the conduct of the raid.

The investigation concluded that the artificial intelligence known as Yasmin had indeed been resident in the data centre and that she had been destroyed along with the servers that held her consciousness. Jack Sladen was cleared of any and all involvement.

"That's fair," whispered Cameron. "I don't think he had a clue what was going on."

One of the directors of the company engaged to build the data centre and manage its security, Ella Stanford, had been arrested and charged with sheltering an escaped prisoner and with assisting in Yasmin's escape from custody.

"That's so wrong," hissed Susie. "She'll go to prison for this, and it should be him." She glared at Angus through a gap in the partition. "We need to take him down."

Cameron laid a hand on Susie's arm. The girl was shaking with anger. "We will, don't worry," said Cameron quietly.

The short statement concluded, and the questions began. How did Jack feel about the report? Shocked, he said, but delighted that the Sladen Foundation could put the unpleasant hijacking of their dedicated data centre behind them. The work the foundation was doing was changing lives. He smoothly recounted the facts and figures of the support they had already given to athletes and organisers for the upcoming Olympics.

"Why do you think your data centre was chosen?" asked another journalist. The voice was familiar. Cameron peeked around the edge of the partition and spotted the News Channel logo on the microphone. Of course, it was Giles, Andy's colleague. She'd met him before.

"Pure bad luck," said Jack. "The Sladen Foundation chose to locate in a remote part of the country to boost the region's economic growth and its connections to the wider world. A remote data centre was exactly what these criminals were looking for."

Giles pressed with a second question. "I understand that your proprietary system management information network is known as SMIN," he said. "That's very close to Yasmin, isn't it? Are the investigators satisfied that there is no connection at all?"

There was a flurry of chatter from the audience and urgent whispering on the panel.

"That wasn't in the report," said Sandeep quietly. "How did he get hold of it?"

"Why wasn't it in the report?" said Cameron.

"The investigators couldn't find any reason to link them," said Joel. "SMIN's exactly what is sounds like. It's a fairly complex management tool with an element of machine learning that continually optimises the network and provides a lot of good data analytics. They left it out of the public report because they didn't want the press dragging out any unfounded speculation."

"Is it really unfounded?" asked Cameron. "You've had a chance to look over the software, haven't you?"

"Not in as much detail as we'd like," said Joel. "My gut feeling says that SMIN is literally a fragment of Yasmin. It's probably how she was smuggled in under Jack's nose. He knew he was getting SMIN, but he didn't know there was a whole lot more to the software."

"That makes sense," said Cameron. "We still don't know how Giles got hold of that detail, though."

"Ella," said Susie quietly. "She's the only possible source."

It was all falling into place. Cameron took a long hard look at the deadpan lawyers on the panel and Jack Sladen's beaming smile. How much did he suspect? Did he even care?

The questions were over quickly, and the crowd began to disperse.

"I'd better get going," said Cameron. "I have a train to catch." She retrieved her bag and was about to leave when Sabrina caught up with her at the door.

"You said you'd fill me in on the CTO," she reminded Cameron. "What's your interest?"

Cameron chose her words carefully. "I once came across someone with the same name as Jack's CTO," she said. "In fact, you can check with Sara Mercer. She will have interviewed him as part of an investigation a couple of years ago. Tenuk Chen. I'm sure it's just a coincidence. I have no information to suggest otherwise."

Sabrina gave her a long, shrewd look. "Sara Mercer trusts your instincts," she said. "I do too. I know you have to get your train, but I'll follow up with her. Thanks, Cameron."

A moment later she turned back round. "Wait," she called. "One question. You said he'd been interviewed. What was it in connection with?"

Cameron gave her a crooked smile. "The original case against Yasmin," she said.

Sabrina's eyes widened and she nodded. "Now I understand," she said. "Leave it with me. Safe journey."

It had to come out some time, reflected Cameron as she made her way out of the hotel and started the long climb towards the station. She knew that the Tenuk at Jack's office was the same man she had met in London. She'd seen his picture. Ben had recognised him. There was no doubt. The one thing she didn't know was whether he was simply a competent CTO who had changed jobs, or someone with connections to the cybercriminal underworld. Her gut feeling told her that he was in it up to his neck, but she had no proof.

The steps straight up the bank had seemed to be the most direct route to the station but they were steeper and narrower than Cameron had expected. She paused for breath halfway up and put her bag down for a moment. Her good shoulder was complaining, and she couldn't shift the weight across to the other side. It would take more than a few days for the rotator cuff tear to heal.

Bracing herself, she started climbing again, building a good rhythm. Before she knew it, she passed under an archway, followed a short, flat, winding path, and popped out on a cobbled street next to an ancient gatehouse. Presumably this had once been part of the city's new castle, almost a thousand years ago.

The station was only a few minutes away on level ground and Cameron had plenty of time. She admired the great pillars holding up the entrance portico, then passed through the barriers in search of her train. While she waited on the platform, she checked her reservation and took a chance on a last-minute first-class upgrade.

The train arrived and she settled into her seat. A flurry of activity on the platform attracted her attention, and when she realised the reason for it, she groaned. Just her luck. Jack Sladen was on the same train, and of course he would be in the first-class carriage.

Worse, he was sitting opposite her.

"Hello again," he said, stowing a bag in the luggage rack and sliding into his seat. He gave her the trademark smile. "I thought that went well. Can I get you a drink?" The steward trolley whizzed up to their table and Cameron accepted the offer with good grace. There was no point in starting off on the wrong foot with almost three hours of travelling ahead of them.

The train pulled away from the station and trundled south over the river. Cameron made small talk, trying to resist the temptation to bring up the three subjects that were on her mind. Half an hour down the tracks, she finally gave up the internal battle. She started with the easiest one.

"The report was very clear, wasn't it?" she said. "Yasmin was definitely there." She gave Jack a friendly smile.

He scowled, then recovered himself. "I suppose so," he said lightly.

He really doesn't like being wrong, thought Cameron. Some things never change.

"You know, I'm still confused about how she got in there in the first place," said Cameron innocently. "I mean, the report was very clear on the transfer out of the prison and into your data centre, but who could have managed something that complex? I really don't think Ella was working on her own."

"You're only saying that because she used to be one of your team," said Jack. "You can't bring yourself to admit that you misjudged her. You're still as stubborn as ever, Cameron."

"There is no way she acted alone," said Cameron. It was time to bring up the next thorny subject. "How is Angus White in the clear, Jack? How? What's he got on you?"

That provoked a reaction. Jack slammed his drink down on the table. "How dare you, Cameron," he hissed, conscious of other passengers within earshot. "He's rude and awkward and difficult to deal with, but that doesn't make him a criminal."

"You don't know the half of what he's been involved in," said Cameron, throwing caution to the wind. "We've never been able to make any charges stick. They just slide off him. I wouldn't trust him as far as I could throw him, and I don't know why you even considered hiring him in the first place."

Jack looked furious. "I didn't hire him," he spluttered. "You think I get involved in every little decision? I'm running a global corporation, Cameron, not a bloody whelk stall. There was a proper independent tender process, Whitford Networks won it, and they're still our contractor."

"Tender process?" snorted Cameron. "Really. How did they end up on your tender list, then?"

"My CTO recommended them, if you must know," said Jack.

And there it was, thought Cameron, question number three. The trail leads back to Tenuk. "This is the chap in Austin, yes?" she said. "The one who's had to rush off for a family emergency? Tenuk, am I right?"

"Yes," said Jack. "Cameron, what is your problem?"

"Tenuk Chen?" pressed Cameron.

Jack shook his head. "No, Tenuk Teo," he said irritably. "I don't know what you think you're doing, Cameron, but the whole investigation is over and whatever you think is going on, your accusations are completely baseless. I think you need to stop right now, or I'll have to get my lawyers on the case. We've known each other since college, Cameron. Do you really want me to take out an injunction against you?"

He gripped his drink tightly, knuckles white.

"No," said Cameron quietly, trying to defuse his anger, "but I want you think about the fact that you placed your trust in people you barely know, and you ended up with an escaped prisoner in your data centre. Who can you really trust, Jack?"

"I don't know," said Jack. His eyes bored into her. "I don't know at all."

Cameron gazed levelly back.

Jack broke first and turned away. The train was slowing, coming into York station. Jack stood up abruptly and pulled his bag down from the luggage rack. "I'll get the next one," he said. "Safe travels." He walked off down the aisle.

A few moments later Cameron saw him on the platform. He disappeared in the direction of the first-class waiting room.

She sat alone at the table, looking at Jack's empty seat and wondering if she had done the right thing. She summoned the steward trolley and ordered another drink. It was going to be a long two hours back to London.

•

Tenuk's flight was on time. Despite his last-minute clandestine changes to the ticket details, he passed through check-in and security without a hint of trouble. He had a good hour to wait before boarding, and he sat sipping his coffee in a comfortable chair at a huge window looking out at the main runway. His itinerary took him first to the west coast, conveniently to LA, the city that everyone here thought he was from. He planned to send a geolocated message to Jack while changing planes just to reinforce that impression.

He was still hungry. Tenuk looked around for a passing waiter bot that could bring him a pastry or a breakfast burrito without the need to actually get up and go to the counter. As he scanned the area, his eyes lit upon a familiar face. Tenuk's blood ran cold.

He had forgotten about Ben.

The sting that he had planned to stop the engineer leaving Texas had not been put in motion. In the turbulence of his father's surprise request and his change of plan, Ben had been pushed to the bottom of his list of priorities. There was no way that he could salvage the situation. Whatever Ben might be carrying back to England would reach its destination.

Perhaps he could use the man to his advantage. Tenuk made a show of waving to attract the attention of a waiter bot and to his satisfaction, Ben noticed him. His natural British politeness kicked in exactly as Tenuk had hoped.

"Hello," said Ben, approaching close enough to speak. "You're Chloe's colleague, aren't you?"

"That's right," said Tenuk. He made a point of looking sad and stressed. "Are you on your way back to England? I remember you said…"

"Yes, I am," said Ben. "And you?"

"I have to go home, to LA," said Tenuk. "My mother…" he swallowed, "my mother is very ill."

"I'm sorry to hear that," said Ben. "Uh, do you need me to watch your bag while you go to the counter?"

"Thank you, but no," said Tenuk. A waiter bot was approaching. Perfect timing. "I can get what I need."

Over the tannoy came a call for the Atlanta flight. "That's mine," said Ben. "Safe travels." He walked off towards his gate.

Tenuk watched him go. Perhaps there was nothing to worry about. The man hadn't been perturbed to see him, no sign of worry at bumping into him again. The stress of the Dunswyke investigation and several nights of disturbed sleep must have taken their toll and he had completely misconstrued Ben's early morning visit to the Statesman Tech offices. As a bonus, he had added another witness to his claim to be visiting his sick mother in California. Having a wide network of unconnected people confirming his cover story would only strengthen it.

The waiter bot delivered Tenuk's second breakfast, and he settled back into his comfortable chair, sipped at his fresh hot coffee, and watched the Atlanta flight take off into the blue sky.

12: UNDERWORLD

Cameron's train arrived on time at King's Cross. She was halfway to the tube station when she remembered Pete's warning about taking an autocar. The revelations about Yasmin should have made her more cautious. Instead, they made her more determined to live her life the way she wanted, without fear. She carried on down the steps into the sprawling underground exchange.

The tube cars rattled through the old Victorian tunnels and quickly bore her south of the river. She hopped out at London Bridge and picked up some essentials at the market and local shops, then walked happily in the sunshine towards her apartment.

Everything looked quite normal. No one was lurking in the shadows waiting for her. Cameron dropped into the security office to follow up on her quotation. They were very sorry about the situation, they said. The police had asked the same questions. The stairwell and foyer cameras should have been working but there had been a fault that evening. No, they didn't know what had caused it. Yes, they'd be very happy for Argentum to review the security system and a purchase order was on the way.

Cameron left the office and the contrite apologies behind her and went back to her apartment. The cat was delighted to see her, writhing around her ankles and purring. Cameron put her bags down and rummaged through the shopping.

"Here you are," she said, unwrapping a cat treat and dropping it in the feeding bowl. "I've missed you too."

While the cat purred over its treat, Cameron emptied her overnight bag and filled the washing machine, then made herself a coffee and flicked on the wallscreen. The news channel was already focused largely on the Olympics. There was a mention of Jack Sladen and the sterling work of the Sladen Foundation but nothing about the enquiry. Cameron hoped that would come up in a business bulletin later in the day. She made a mental note to call Andy as she had promised. He and Giles would be working to weave a good story out of the press conference and the report, and she owed him a quote or two, anonymously, of course.

Coverage switched to the airport where the national team was getting ready to depart. Cameron perked up, looking for Ross and Michelle among the crowd of athletes, coaches and partners who were waving at the cameras. She finally spotted them, Ross grinning broadly and chatting with a teammate, Michelle in dark glasses standing next to him. They were both going to have a fantastic time, thought Cameron. Ross had been given the chance of a lifetime and he had put in the work to seize it.

Her smartscreen buzzed and a notification from Pete popped up. He must also be watching the send-off.

'Did you get a chance to ask Shell to check in the Underworld for recent contracts that might relate to the bet fixing?' said the message.

Cameron cursed loudly and the cat, who was about to jump on her knee, recoiled in fright. Cameron reached down and tickled its ears. Reassured, it tried again and settled comfortably on her lap.

She tapped a reply. 'No, dammit,' she said. 'With everything else going on, I forgot. I'd better do it.'

As she expected, the next alert was a voice call.

"Hi, Pete," she said. "What's up?"

"Are you sure about going in there yourself?" he said immediately. "You're not exactly low profile."

"It's not a problem," said Cameron. "I know what I'm looking for and I've got a good idea where to find it. When I go into Eden, I use randomly generated avatars and an incognito connection with variable geolocation. That'll work for the lower levels too."

"It's not worth the risk, Cameron," replied Pete.

"It is," said Cameron firmly. "There's no risk that I can see. I'll be in and out before you know it."

There was a risk, but she dared not articulate it. She couldn't tell Pete over an open connection that there was a possibility Yasmin was still alive. Cameron felt a little guilty about doing all the things he had advised against. She had no choice, she reasoned. The only people on her team who she would ever ask to go into the darkest corners of the web were Ross and Michelle. In their absence, it was down to her. It wasn't as if it was unknown territory, after all. When she was younger, she had spent more time that any of them might suspect in some of those dark corners, learning what was possible so that she could counter it effectively.

"At least call me as soon as you're back," said Pete.

"I will," said Cameron. "I'm only going to check the noticeboards. Did you and Noor find anything about gambling tips? I know she was going to have look at what kind of things were for sale."

"Nothing useful," said Pete. "I suppose if you're going in anyway, you could have a look for those, too."

There was no time like the present. Cameron tipped the cat off her knee and went to her desk. It had been a long time since she'd ventured into the deeper and darker virtual worlds. She logged on with one of the many wallet addresses that she had on file, confirming that she was real and human without revealing her identity. The avatar attached to this ID was a big man with designer trainers and a selection of high fashion virtual tattoos bought from one of the brand malls. That would do nicely, thought Cameron.

It was time to immerse herself in the world. She settled herself in her chair, put on her reality mask, slipped the controller wristbands on, and tapped a sensor on the mask frame. The clear view began to cloud over, moving from the full transparency of augmented reality to the dark opacity of virtual reality. Silicon wings extended from the frame of the mask and moulded to her face, blocking out the light. Sitting blindfolded and exposed in the real world was not always the most comfortable way to experience a virtual world but being fully immersed ensured that she concentrated on her surroundings, unlike on a flatscreen or in augmented reality.

The top level of the world was busy. There was a concert in the rock district and a steady stream of avatars popped into being around her before disappearing through the archway towards the great open auditorium. As her avatar walked past the entrance to the gig, Cameron could hear the deep thrumming of a bass guitar as the band carried out its sound tests. The music faded as she made her way down the street.

A knot of people outside the cinema made her smile. The avatars were varied and apparently grown up, but she strongly suspected most of them were pre-teens hanging out together, designing their avatars as a way to explore their adult identities. She'd done the same at their age.

She wondered if Dilan or Tara were lurking somewhere in this world. She knew that Tara and Audrey, Chloe's daughter, spent time together here. Nina was too old for the online hangouts, preferring to use her virtually honed social skills in the far more interesting real world where there were boys and girls and parties.

Cameron was now well past the kids and had reached the tech district. There, hidden in plain sight around a decorative fountain, a great whirlpool waited for her, a jump point down into Eden. She dived down into the depths, materialising in a virtual welcome lounge.

The genial AI avatar behind the bar greeted her as they did every guest. "Welcome, traveller," it said. "What do you need? Directions, suggestions, tips and tricks, or just here to explore?"

"I'm looking for tips and tricks and Olympic kicks, barman," said Cameron. "Where should I wander?"

"You could try the market hall," said the barman. "Or did you want something stronger?"

"All the way down," said Cameron.

"Sure thing," said the barman. A bracelet appeared on Cameron's avatar's wrist, an access token for the level that she wanted. "Head out of here and follow your nose."

"Thanks, barman," she said, dropping a tip into the jar and authorising the payment from her wallet.

Her avatar left the bar and followed its nose as instructed. The bracelet glowed green when she went the right way, red when she made a wrong turn. This district was generally occupied by a mix of freelancers advertising their services and meeting places where information was exchanged. Cameron took note of the adverts. She might have need of some creative coding while Michelle was away, and she was looking for anything unusual that could have a connection, however slender, with Yasmin.

The bracelet led her to a hidden jump point in the centre of a grove of giant redwoods so tall that their upper branches were lost in the artificial sky above. She reappeared in a new world, incongruously green and sun dappled. Cameron double-checked the location. This was definitely the right destination. The Underworld had had a makeover since her last visit.

She put a marker on the jump point to give her a fast exit, then set off to find the things she had come for. First stop was the Underworld noticeboards. They displayed all the records of contracts out for tender, awarded and completed. Only here could they be accessed in a readable format. Anyone could find the Underworld's trade blockchain if they knew where to look, but unless you had permission to view the details, the only things that would be visible were long strings of letters and numbers, encrypted hashes of the detailed transactions, almost entirely meaningless to an outsider unless they could crack the private key. The bracelet Cameron had collected from the barman was the permission token her avatar needed to enter the Underworld and view the data held there in unencrypted form.

The details that were available were still scant, but enough for her to understand what was going on. She scrolled rapidly through the contract history and recorded voice notes on her smartscreen in the real world. "Malware injection for sensor control awarded to Steamyard, Beta complete, ongoing," she muttered. "Phishing campaign and clone provision with automation, awarded to Snow Roses, released." Those were the two she'd been looking for, and there were half a dozen others that caught her attention.

Time was ticking, and she had other errands to run. A few blocks from the noticeboards she spotted a pop-up shop emblazoned with artwork based very loosely but effectively on the Olympic rings. Even down here, the creators had taken care with their designs, skating close enough to the edge to show exactly what this shop was for without violating any brand guidelines. The International Olympic Committee had a surprisingly long reach, excellent forensics, and expensive lawyers.

Cameron approached the building and the door swung open to admit her. Inside, she found everything she wanted. Pete would be pleased. A cornucopia of tips and underhand gambling activity was in evidence, exactly as he had predicted. It would help them all in the battle against the cybercriminals who were looking to profit from the coming games. She made copious notes and bought a useful looking tip to follow up in the real world.

Job done, Cameron went out into the street, wondering what else she could do while she was here. She didn't really know where to start in her hunt for Yasmin, but if there were any whispers, this was where she would hear them. A sports café further along the block caught her eye and she wandered in. It was full of avatars and on the big screen was a live sim race, a mid-stage qualifier for the upcoming Formula V season. Cameron tucked herself into a corner and listened to the chatter all around.

A monkey in a blue and white striped football shirt ambled by. Cameron felt uneasy and didn't know why. There was something about the character that rang a bell. She watched as it searched around the café, ignoring the screen, and finally settled with a knot of other animal avatars. Cameron slid along the wall until she was close enough to tune in on their conversation.

One of the party, a grey kitten, was shouting its mouth off about the Steamyard. Cameron hung on its every word. Without removing her mask, she fumbled around the computer until the audio came through the external speakers and ordered the home hub to start recording.

"That Beta deployment was a real screw up," said the kitten. "It'd better work this time."

"You haven't got long to get it right," said another avatar that Cameron couldn't see. "At least the speedrunners went without a hitch."

"We need the Admin online," said the grey kitten.

Jackpot, thought Cameron. The mention of the speedrunners was vindication of Andy's source. And the Admin could only mean one thing. Cameron shuffled forwards, trying to see the avatar who was speaking, in the unlikely event that it bore a resemblance to a colleague on the infosec team.

"The white hats are trying to keep up," said the monkey in the blue and white shirt. "Their infosec team, MIST, has picked up on that cockup at the arena, and they know about the speedrunners too. I'm dealing with it."

Cameron froze. She recognised the monkey's voice. It was Angus White.

13:   TIPS AND TRICKS

The bunk room environment was perfectly balanced, but Aron tossed and turned, his dreams intruding on what was supposed to be restful sleep. After trying and failing to sleep naturally between long shifts, securing the servers and reviewing every security setting, he gave in and returned to the Sanctuary. Immersed in his favourite landscape he found it easy to reach a deep sleep state, but each time the dreams would begin. On balance, though, he was less tired at work. He'd put in a support ticket to the Sanctuary. The next update should iron out the bugs. For the moment he would suffer the dreams in exchange for the modicum of rest he got.

The worst part was the fall at the end of each dream. Here it came now. Aron braced himself and started into wakefulness again, but this time something was wrong. He wasn't lying down in his bed but standing. He swayed, disoriented, and pulled off the immersion headband to find himself in the corridor outside the bunk room. His first thought was relief that he was wearing his pyjamas. His second was that he had been sleepwalking. That had never happened before. It must be the stress of the impending Olympic opening ceremony and the responsibility he carried for securing the games.

He heard footsteps around a bend in the corridor and slunk quickly back into his quarters before anyone noticed him. It was still very early, and this time he was determined to sleep all the hours he was allocated. He curled up in his bunk, put his headband back on, and returned to the Sanctuary.

•

Cameron stared at the monkey avatar with the blue and white top, and old memories came flooding back of a football mascot in the town where she had first encountered Angus. There was no question that this was him. In real life he was exonerated of any crime, whiter than white, sitting at Jack's side. Yet here he was going about his nefarious business in the depths of the Underworld. She had to tread carefully.

Moving naturally with the crowd, taking advantage of a wave of excitement at the race action on the big screen, Cameron edged her way towards the exit. She couldn't jump from the café. That would attract attention. She was almost at the door when a tall figure blocked her way and glowered down at her.

"You," said the bouncer. "You're barred. What are you doing back here?"

The avatar she'd bought must have had a chequered history. She wouldn't be going to that stallholder again.

"Not me, mate," said Cameron. The deep voice coming through the microphone filter startled her for a moment. "Mistaken identity." She brushed past the bouncer and went straight out of the door. She was all the way down the street at the next intersection before she looked behind her. To her relief, she had not been followed.

Cameron checked the marker she had set on her map and flew directly to the jump point. Her avatar materialised in the redwood grove on the level above and the access bracelet faded from her wrist. She logged straight out, reset her mask to full transparency, and placed it carefully on the desk. Next, she archived the wallet and identity she had used to gain access. It would never be safe to use that avatar again or make any transactions from the account. She closed the secure connection and took a deep breath. She'd learned far more than she bargained for.

She stopped the recording and asked the home hub to send it to her smartscreen, then went back to the more comfortable seat on the sofa. The cat, who had spread itself right across the cushions, squeaked a complaint. Cameron slid the cat gently along the sofa to make room. It rolled over with its paws in the air and went back to sleep.

Pete needed some reassurance that all had gone well, and Cameron had news for him. He picked up within seconds.

"All okay?" he said.

"Yes," lied Cameron, "and don't worry. I've covered my tracks."

"Good," said Pete. He sounded relieved. "What did you find?"

"Everything I went for," said Cameron. "Tips are selling like hot cakes, which you'd expect, but they're advertising their success rate with examples of accurate predictions. Among those I found the javelin event. Here." She sent him a screenshot she'd collected. "I know it wasn't a hack, more of a common or garden fix, but it shows there's a huge range of criminal activity going on."

"Hardly a surprise," said Pete. "Did you find anything about the karate?"

"Nothing around tips," said Cameron, "but they're hardly going to use it as an advertisement. Anyone who bought the tip would have lost their money. What I did find, though, were fulfilled contracts for the phishing attack on our client and the build of the data capture clone site, and a partly completed contract for interference in sensor transmissions, which I'm sure from the timing was the karate incident. It looks like that was just a Beta test and it failed, so there'll be another iteration to come with a fix in it. We need to track it down and stop it as soon as it's rolled out. There are a few other things, too. I'll put my notes on file."

"That's brilliant, Cameron," said Pete. "I suppose the next logical step is to pick one of the tips they're selling, see if there are any links to those contracts, and keep a close eye on the event as it happens."

"I agree," said Cameron, "which is why I spent the last of the coins in that wallet to buy a tip for a hybrid event. I can't use the same avatar again so the coins would have been dust otherwise. I'll send you all the details and I'm going to share some of what I have with MIST as well."

"Are you sure that's safe?" said Pete.

"I won't be claiming credit for it," said Cameron. "I'll say it's a tip-off from a reliable source, dress it up for them, keep it vague."

"Do you trust everyone on there?" asked Pete.

"No," said Cameron instantly, "but I have no choice."

There had always been something about MIST that concerned her. She wasn't convinced that every member had been properly screened, and she didn't know enough about the people she was working with to trust them. She'd already been circumspect when talking to Barker, and the thought that someone from the group had been talking to Angus, of all people, shook her. A discreet approach would be safest.

"I guess you know what you're doing," said Pete with a sigh. "Right, let's have a look at this tip you bought." Cameron could hear him tapping at his keyboard. "Oh, good choice."

"Yes, it's an early round of the archery," said Cameron. "I checked the rankings, and this tip isn't the real favourite."

"And they're competing here in London," said Pete. "Brilliant. We can look at the sensors they use and the arena infrastructure and connectivity. I'll call the venue tomorrow morning and see if I can get in and do some system diagnostics."

Cameron smiled at the enthusiasm in his voice. "Have you forgiven me for going in there now?" she asked.

"Almost," said Pete. "But don't do it again."

"Of course not," said Cameron. She was lying. She had every intention of going back to get more information. Angus would not frighten her off doing her job, and she was determined to find Yasmin.

"See you in the morning," said Pete. "Sleep well."

Cameron realised that it was getting late, and she was hungry. She put together a plate of bread, cheese and cold meat that she'd bought at the market, poured herself a glass of wine, and called Andy while she ate. She gave him the soundbites that he needed for his report, and they chatted briefly about the press conference.

"Giles didn't get a straight answer to his questions, did he?" mused Cameron.

"No," said Andy. "Do you think he's onto something?"

"Yes," she said. "I think your source got this absolutely right. How is she, by the way?"

"I can't reveal my sources," he said. "That's if this speculation came from a source, of course," he added hastily.

Cameron laughed. "You can be so transparent sometimes, Andy," she said. "Let her know that we are thinking of her and that it's good to have her back on the team."

"If my source was someone that you knew, of course I would pass that on," said Andy. "Thanks for the quotes, Cameron. Enjoy the Olympics. Ross looked great on the coverage, by the way. Send him our best."

"I will," said Cameron. "Speak to you soon."

She finished her meal, watched some more of the News Channel, and then reluctantly turned to the last thing on her list, MIST. She logged on to the platform with some trepidation and her worst fears were realised. There had been a vast amount of activity since her last visit. The sheer volume of new notifications and mentions and direct messages in her inbox threatened to overwhelm her. She decided that the easiest way to cut through the noise would be to ask her closest allies for a quick briefing.

The chat was lively. Admin Cat was online, as were Barker and Sugata. Cameron looked down the list of active members, wondering if any of them had been in that Underworld café. She glanced at her own avatar. Tonight, the system decreed that she was an Okapi. Nicely camouflaged. That matched her current mood, alright.

"Evening, SimCavalier," said Barker. "You've been hiding."

"People to see, places to go," said Cameron. "What have I missed? What's top of the agenda, what's been kicked into the long grass?"

"The countdown to the opening ceremony has started," said Admin Cat. "In less than 72 hours, everything will be live. We're focusing all our attention on any threats that might disrupt it."

"It's predicted to have the biggest audience ever recorded on the planet," said a passing dragon avatar. "They have to get it right."

"What kind of threats are we looking at now for the opening ceremony?" asked Sugata, those annoying headlights flashing as he spoke.

Admin Cat started to reel off a frankly dull list of possibilities from streaming disruption to power cuts. Cameron couldn't concentrate. Something was niggling at the back of her mind. All the leads and attacks and tip-offs that she had been working through with her team, all the contracts she had just scrolled through in the Underworld, the conversation she had overheard, and all the discussions she'd had on the MIST platform in the past had one thing in common. They would all make money for someone. What could the opening ceremony offer to the criminals who were circling and ready to take profits?

"Follow the money," she said abruptly, cutting through Admin Cat's roll call of every cyberattack in the book. "That's what you said, wasn't it, Barker? If someone stands to gain, it's a problem. If not, it's a low-level distraction, script kiddies and mischief."

Admin Cat fell silent.

"I did indeed say that," said Barker in his deep, slow drawl. "Where's the profit in the opening ceremony?"

"Does that need to be profit based?" asked Admin Cat. "They could throw anything at that for fun."

"With anyone else I would say reputational damage and ransom," said Cameron, "but not with the Olympics."

"There's nothing to bet on," said Barker, "so no one is out to manipulate the odds like they might be with the events themselves."

"You think gambling's behind some of these attacks?" asked Admin Cat.

"Absolutely," said Cameron. "There are too many coincidences and connections. The safest theory is that most of the activity we are seeing is being driven by bet fixing."

"But what about the opening ceremony, if there's no betting involved?" said Admin Cat.

"Data capture," said Cameron instantly. "There'll be people watching in virtual worlds and in augmented and immersive streams and on TV, and we know that the programme includes interactive elements with the audience and airdrops of souvenirs. The phishing options are endless."

There was silence in the chat. For a moment she wondered if she had overstepped the mark, jumping into the discussion after being absent for days and pulling rank with a wild theory.

"That's compelling," said Admin Cat eventually.

Cameron breathed a sigh of relief and her rare attack of imposter syndrome receded slightly. She jumped as the real cat hopped onto her knee and nudged at her hand. Cameron realised that she was wound up like a coiled spring after the last week of drama, and she still had a lot to do.

"I'm sorry," she said. "I have to go. I'm working on some leads that I should be able to share tomorrow. Can you message me directly if there's anything I can help with?"

"Sure, SimCavalier," said Barker.

Cameron logged off and started making notes on all the things that she had discovered over the past couple of hours. There was a picture building of a complex operation and some hands in the shadows. As she gathered her thoughts, an alert disturbed her.

A message. An anonymous post in her secure MIST inbox.

'She will find you,' it said. 'Stop monkeying around.'

14:   SLEUTHING

The shuttle glided to a halt at Terminal Three and Cameron checked the message one more time. She hoped that she had interpreted the code correctly. Chloe was evidently so concerned about security that she had sent Ben's flight number in a chat between her daughter Audrey and Cameron's niece Tara, carefully disguised in a stream of teenage text speak about the latest movie heartthrob. Ben would have no idea that Cameron was coming to meet him. She hoped that he would be pleased to see her.

She could see the busy arrivals hall from the platform, but she was hesitant about entering. In the distance she could see the brightly coloured armed security drones hovering over the crowds in the hall, leaving people in no doubt that they were being watched. She knew that they were simply the first and most obvious line of defence. Up on the ceiling, there would be high resolution cameras taking note of every face waiting to meet a passenger, and beacons recording chip details. The intrusion into personal privacy was blatant and accepted. Most people didn't care. Cameron was ambivalent. She knew there were real threats to life and limb from terrorists across the globe, and that this level of surveillance kept the airport secure. She had grown up in a country where CCTV cameras were more prevalent than anywhere else in the world, and she relied on the data collected by these cameras and beacons to find criminals. She knew that her face would already be on the shuttle cameras. What she wanted to avoid was any record of her making contact with Ben in this place. All she needed was to make sure that they were both on the same train back through London.

The station platform's friendly service drones were having none of it. They gently herded her towards the entrance to the arrivals hall. Cameron cursed and thought fast. She gave in gracefully and positioned herself so that she could not be seen by anyone emerging from border control, but she could see them.

The wait seemed interminable, but only twenty minutes had passed before the first of the transatlantic travellers began to stream out. Cameron counted seventy, eighty people before Ben came through the door. She caught her breath. She hadn't seen him for months, and she had forgotten how he made her heart jump. Her eyes followed him to the exit. Time to move.

She caught up with a woman around her age who had come off the same flight just after Ben. She gave her an excited and over-the-top greeting for the benefit of the cameras. To her credit, the woman simply returned a tired and slightly confused smile. As they walked together through the exit, Cameron apologised, smiling all the way.

"I'm so sorry," she said. "You look just like my friend from the back. Oh, there she is!" She waved towards an imaginary friend ahead of them.

They were now out of range of all the devices that were recording who met who. Cameron accelerated towards the train and managed to hop onto the same carriage as Ben, moving to the opposite end so he didn't see her. Not yet. Once they were well into London, she would pick her time.

The passengers thinned out at each stop and Cameron found it harder and harder to stay hidden. Finally, Ben stood up and moved to his nearest door. Cameron was glad she'd made the effort to follow him. This was not the stop she expected him to take.

They were the only two people to alight. Ben walked ahead without acknowledging her at all and Cameron started to grin to herself. He was as smart as she was. He knew what she was doing, and why. She followed him out into the busy streets of Mayfair, and he vanished into the nearest pub.

Cameron browsed a shop window for a few moments, walked around the block, and went into the back entrance of the same pub. The place had just opened for the day, and it was virtually empty. Ben was sitting in a big window seat, hidden from outside by the frosted glass. He gave Cameron a broad grin.

"You'd make a lousy sleuth," he said. "Can I get you a drink?"

"I'll have a half," said Cameron.

The barman appeared with a pint and a half of beer and Ben sighed happily. "I know it's about six in the morning in my head, but I've missed this." He lifted the glass carefully. "Cheers," he said.

"Cheers," said Cameron. She wondered if he had missed her, too. "Welcome home. It's good to see you in the flesh."

"You too, Cameron," said Ben. As an afterthought, he gave her an awkward hug. "I tried to call you last weekend," he continued. "I didn't get any answer."

"That's odd," said Cameron. "I tried to call you, too, but I couldn't get through. Is your screen on the blink?"

"No, I don't think so," said Ben. "Strange. You obviously got my message with the flight details, though. You didn't need to come out to Heathrow. We could have just arranged to meet here."

"I didn't get any message," said Cameron. "Chloe gave me the flight number. All I knew was that you were coming back to England this week and you had something for me."

"That's weird," said Ben. He took another drink and then pulled out his smartscreen. "Here, look, message delivered."

"Nope," said Cameron. "Never got it. Try sending something else."

Ben tapped a few words into his screen and hit Send. The delivery status went from grey, to orange, to green.

"There you go," said Ben. "Check your inbox."

"Nothing," said Cameron a moment later. She sent a message to him, and moments later it bounced back as undeliverable. "See? There's a glitch alright. I'll have a look at that later."

Ben gave her an appraising look. "Before, I'd have said you were being paranoid," he said. "Now, between you and Chloe, you've got me looking over my shoulder every time there's a wobble in my network connections."

"I didn't realise you knew Chloe that well," said Cameron, poking at a subject she really didn't want to broach.

"Not well, exactly," said Ben. Cameron felt a knot in her stomach untwine slightly. "She got in touch after I visited Statesman Tech the first time, when I was following up on the design change paperwork, remember? We've met up a few times since then. She's a lot like you."

The knot in Cameron's stomach tightened again. "What's the present you've brought me?" she asked. "Chloe said you were bringing something."

Ben gave her a broad grin. "I've been playing spy games," he said. He looked around and lowered his voice. "Chloe and I got into Jack Sladen's office. It was our last chance before he came back, and she hadn't managed to search it before as it was always locked. As soon as she knew she could get access, we got in and went through the files very early one morning. Chloe thought there might be some proof of tampering with those design change records. She didn't know what she was looking for, so she needed me."

"And did you find anything?" said Cameron.

Ben nodded. "Oh yes," he said. He patted his bag. "It's here. Paper records and a flash disk. Whoever hid this really did not trust network storage, hence the secrecy. I don't think it's safe to even mention this online."

Cameron was grinning like the Cheshire cat. "Brilliant, Ben," she said. "That explains Chloe's cryptic messages. Did you have any trouble?"

"Oh, you won't believe what happened," said Ben. "We searched Jack's office no problem, found these files and got out as smooth as you like. Chloe had fixed some of the security cameras so that they looped old footage while we were in there."

"And?" said Cameron.

"Barely two minutes after we got out of there," he said, "the door opened, and this guy walked out. He'd been in there all the time. Chloe was as cool as a cucumber. She handed me a coffee cup and we just chatted as if I'd come in for a meeting. I was bricking it, but it was obvious that he had no idea we'd been in the room. I walked out under his nose with the files in my bag."

"Good grief," said Cameron. "Who was it?"

"The CTO," said Ben. "The man I thought I recognised on my first visit, who I think we met at Nina's school when the MerLions came."

"Tenuk," breathed Cameron. "You're sure that he didn't know you'd searched the office?"

"Totally sure," said Ben. "Honestly, I think he was asleep in there. And anyway, I bumped into him in the airport yesterday, and he didn't bat an eyelid."

"You what?" said Cameron, incredulous.

"He was waiting for a flight, same as me," said Ben. "He said something about visiting his sick mother in LA. Why?"

Cameron just shrugged helplessly. "I can't get my head around that man," she said. "I don't trust him. I'm sure that he's neck deep in the business with Yasmin, and then he just turns up and acts like a normal person around you. It makes no sense."

"If it helps," said Ben, "Chloe doesn't trust him either. She's convinced that he had something to do with the cybercrime network she was part of. Pasar? Is that right? And something called the Steamyard, too."

"Yes," said Cameron slowly. "That's right." Chloe had gathered some strong evidence to link Tenuk to the Steamyard already, but it wasn't in the public domain. How close were Ben and Chloe, she wondered, if they were discussing things like Pasar?

The pub was filling up and the smell of food was tempting.

"Are you hungry?" asked Ben. "We could eat here, then take this stuff to your office. I owe you one, anyway, Cam. I'm sorry I missed your birthday. Life got in the way. I should have called." He dug into another pocket of his bag and pulled out a small package. "Here," he said. "I hope you like it."

Cameron unwrapped the tissue paper carefully. Inside lay a little necklace with a golden bat pendant.

"That's so sweet," she said, holding it up to the light. "Thank you." She reached over and kissed him on the cheek.

"It's an Austin bat," he said. "I thought you'd like it. I'm glad I was right."

Cameron fastened it around her neck and gave him a radiant smile. Maybe it was going to be okay between them after all.

•

This time he really did fall. The sensation didn't stop with his return to consciousness, and Aron felt a momentary horror as his body crumpled. He hit something soft, whimpered with relief, and ripped off the Sanctuary headband. He had landed on one of the large beanbags in the cupola. The glare of the sun glinting off the glacier outside blinded his sensitive eyes and he buried his head in the beanbag, sobbing.

How had he ended up here? Had he really walked the length of the corridor and climbed the narrow stairs in his sleep? He didn't think it was possible, but here he was.

A red light caught his attention, and he noticed that the emergency exit control panel was uncovered. The hatch from the cupola was still firmly sealed. Aron closed the flap and gathered his thoughts. It was almost time to get up anyway. He made his way back down the narrow stairs, greeting a colleague on the way who was climbing up to take in the view, and went to get some breakfast. This sleepwalking phase would pass. It was just the stress of the job.

•

Cameron looked across at the office sofa. Ben was starting to flag. He was slumped on a pile of sofa cushions staring out of the window at the sky above and looked as if he was about to fall asleep. His internal flights in the US and the long overnight transatlantic journey had taken their toll. Cameron was positively purring over the things that he had brought from Jack Sladen's office. They were an even better birthday present than the necklace. She fiddled thoughtfully with the bat pendant as she worked through the file. A few moments later she heard gentle snoring coming from the sofa. Ben had given in. She would leave him to sleep.

The door opened and Cameron looked up, a finger to her lips.

"Shh," she whispered. "Sleeping Beauty."

Noor's eyes widened when she saw Ben asleep on the sofa. "Oh!" She gave Cameron a broad grin. "Something nice blew in on the west wind," she said.

"It brought gifts, too," said Cameron. "Take a look at this." She handed Noor the file she had been reading. "It's dynamite."

Noor held the file awkwardly, unused to something so tactile. "I haven't seen paper meeting minutes for years," she said. "What could be so sensitive that it isn't even entrusted to a private network? How do they expect anyone to verify that these records are the real thing?"

Cameron picked up a small flash drive from her desk. "This was with them," she said. "It's encrypted, of course. I haven't even bothered to try and get in, but I imagine that this has the document hashes and date stamps that would be needed. It's all still firmly offline, though. Someone is being very careful to avoid even a single bit of data reaching the public networks."

Noor flicked through the papers, skimming the contents. "Anything interesting so far?" She asked.

"Look down at the bottom of that sheet," said Cameron. "Look who signed off hiring Whitford Networks to work on the Dunswyke data centre."

"Jack Sladen," read Noor slowly. "Why is that surprising?"

"Because yesterday he made it very clear to me that he had nothing to do with bringing Angus White into the project," said Cameron. "He's claimed all along that he's completely innocent, that he knew nothing about what was going on, and that Yasmin hiding out in his data centre was a complete surprise."

"And now it seems he signed off the hire," said Noor. "I wonder what else is in there. It looks like it could be dynamite. Let's hope it doesn't blow up in our faces."

•

As soon as the aeroplane doors opened, Tenuk felt the aromatic embrace of his home country. The heat and humidity felt like nowhere else. The mingled scents of flowers and plane biofuel created a heady mixture that made his heart sing.

"Welcome, Mr Teo," said the border guard. "Your thumbprint, please."

Tenuk smiled as he pressed his thumb to the reader, the first test of the careful revisions of identity records that Yasmin had done for him in the brief months that they had worked together, between her escape and her apparent destruction. They couldn't change Tenuk Chen's details, of course, as they were set in stone in Singapore's highly secure identity blockchain, but Yasmin had made sure that those records would never be called by any system API. To all intents and purposes, Tenuk Chen did not exist, and he would not be recognised by border controls, street cameras, or police checks. At the same time, Tenuk Teo sprang into being, possessed of all the same biometric data but as a US citizen born in California. Yasmin had found the American system far easier to manipulate, and it seemed to have worked.

The guard smiled as the thumbprint scan turned green. "Thank you," she said. "Is this your first trip to Singapore?"

"Yes," he lied. "My parents moved from here to LA before I was born. I've always wanted to come and visit."

"Where will you be staying?" she asked.

"With my uncle," said Tenuk smoothly. "He lives in the Orchard district. I hear it's nice there."

The border guard gave him a very broad smile. "You will enjoy your stay," she said. "Thank you, Mr Teo."

The gate opened in front of Tenuk, and he walked through.

His father had sent an autocar with a discreet Sapphire Straits logo and the ultimate status symbol, a chauffeur. Tenuk relaxed into the air-conditioned interior and gazed at the familiar cityscape. The chauffeur made a show of directing the autocar straight down Changi Road, around the lofty skyscrapers of downtown, and out through Little India towards the Botanic Gardens and the mansion that Tenuk had last seen ten years before.

Chaoxiang was waiting for him on the steps. He reached out and drew his son into a tight embrace. "I'm so glad to see you," he said. "Come inside. You must be tired after your long journey."

Quite frankly Tenuk had never been so comfortable on a plane, but he wasn't going to argue. The cool interior, sweeping staircase and elegant tiles were a far cry from his hot, cramped Austin apartment. Maybe his father was right. It could be time to consolidate his experience, put Pasar and the Steamyard behind him, and come back into the fold.

"Go and freshen up," said Chaoxiang. "When you're ready, come to my office."

He turned and walked away, and Tenuk followed a maid and his bags up the stairs to the guest suite.

Once alone, he set up a secure network connection and dealt with business that had arisen while he was sleeping his way across the Pacific in first class luxury. Jack was already back in Austin and Tenuk's work inbox was practically empty. He sent a message to Jack that purported to originate in LA. He had to keep up the pretence, after all.

After a long and luxurious shower, Tenuk changed into shorts and a crisp linen shirt and made his way back downstairs. He thought he remembered where his father's office was but took a couple of wrong turns in the vast mansion before he found the right door.

The room took his breath away. Ten years ago, this had been a very traditional office, all beautiful carpentry and gold highlights. The ornate ceiling fans, the floor to ceiling bookcases and his father's grand desk had not changed, but where there had been graceful wall hangings there were now vast screens displaying a bewildering range of data feeds. Sapphire Straits had moved with the times.

Chaoxiang and an older man were sitting in comfortable chairs overlooking the lush garden, sipping tea. It took Tenuk a moment to recognise his uncle, Li Jie. He seemed very frail but brightened when he saw the newcomer.

"Tenuk," he said. "Let me look at you. My sister would be so proud to see how you have grown."

"Uncle," said Tenuk, bowing formally. "You're looking well."

Li Jie laughed. "No, I'm not," he said. "Time has taken its toll. I am glad you are here." He finished his tea and looked around for his walking stick. "I'm tired. Chaoxiang will explain everything. I will see you at dinner." He hobbled away towards the gardens where he had his villa.

Tenuk watched him go with some sadness. Li Jie had been his favourite uncle growing up, always ready to have fun with him. It was hard to see him age so suddenly. He wished they had kept in touch.

"Sit, Tenuk," said Chaoxiang. "Have some tea."

Tenuk took his uncle's recently vacated seat and poured himself a fresh cup. After the American love affair with coffee, it was nice to drink tea again, and in such beautiful surroundings. He was feeling more at home by the second.

"This place has changed," he said, indicating the wallscreens. "Business is booming, I take it?"

"It is," said Chaoxiang. "We have built on the original Sapphire Straits chain of casinos, acquired betting operations around the world, and we are the largest casino operators in the metaverse." He looked down modestly at his tea. "Sapphire Straits is larger than your Sladen Group, although we do not shout about it in the same manner as Mr Sladen."

Tenuk put his tea down and stared at his father. "I had no idea," he said. "I've followed the news about Sapphire Straits over the years, of course, but the speed you've grown is incredible. When I left to work at the MerLions, the casinos were all you had. Even when I was still living in Singapore, I heard nothing. When did this happen?"

"Ah, Tenuk," said Chaoxiang. "You may be my son, but you were very junior in the business back then and you were not privy to every decision. We started putting our strategic plans in place a long time ago."

He stood up stiffly and moved to his desk in the centre of the office. He pulled a slim silver keyboard out of a cubbyhole and placed it carefully in front of him.

"This is the map of our physical operations," he said, tapping carefully at a few keys and pointing to the wallscreen opposite. "The blue dots represent Sapphire Straits branded casinos." Tenuk noted familiar locations in Singapore, Macau, Monaco and more. That part of the business hadn't grown significantly since he was last here. "The green dots are wholly owned but locally branded," continued Chaoxiang.

A forest of pins appeared in the map. "I can see why you don't want Sapphire Straits associated with most of those," said Tenuk. "Russia. Some of the breakaway militia territories. You're playing with fire there."

Chaoxiang ignored him. "This is the reach of our online betting platforms," he said. "One is our own brand, some are wholly or partly owned and kept at arm's length, and there are others where we have no official link, but we have a certain amount of power over their user base." Clouds of colour swept over the map, each one more or less aligned with a different legal jurisdiction, divided up according to the gambling laws of countries and trading blocs. "And finally, we have built casinos on prime land in the gambling district of every virtual world. Those are particularly lucrative. I was pleasantly surprised."

"Impressive," said Tenuk. He walked over to the screen to examine the map more closely. "You have most of the planet sewn up. How do you keep control of something this size from here? I know the scale of the machine that runs Sladen Group, and you're right, this is bigger."

Chaoxiang gave him a superficial, condescending smile, and Tenuk remembered the main reason why he had finally walked out on the family firm ten years before. If his father really needed him now, his attitude had better have changed.

"You said you wanted my help," said Tenuk. "How do you do it?"

"I told you that we started driving in this strategic direction a long time ago," said Chaoxiang. "That included developing the systems we would need to run something at this scale. We invested heavily in artificial intelligence, working with our partners to iterate the most flexible learning models, the best neural networks."

Despite himself, Tenuk was impressed. "Good thinking," he said. "Presumably the models advanced at the same pace as your global empire."

"Exactly," said Chaoxiang. "We made some interesting breakthroughs over the years. The industry standard AI used to manage problem gambling, for example, came out of this project."

"Very philanthropic, father," said Tenuk. "I assume you also have AI that removes some of the uncertainty of gambling for you."

"Of course," said Chaoxiang. "The house always wins. That is a very different operation, and one I believe your Pasar and Steamyard networks have helped us with in the past."

"I should have realised before," said Tenuk. "I knew that some of the commissions I managed were from a serious gambling syndicate. I never guessed it was you at the time, although I've since had my suspicions." Tenuk wondered again about the most recent commission the Steamyard had taken to interfere in the Olympic metaverse. The client had been anonymous, overbearing and insistent and had made life very difficult for him, especially when the team failed to deliver a complete result. Was his father behind that one, too?

Chaoxiang was watching him shrewdly. "You have a difficult decision to make," he said.

Tenuk gazed around the room and back to his father. The empire he had built was beyond anything Tenuk could have imagined. Would he continue on his own path or do what his father wanted? If he stayed here, would he find himself locked in a gilded cage?

"I haven't finished the story," said Chaoxiang, bringing him back to the here and now. "Sit, Tenuk."

Puzzled, Tenuk pulled up a chair and sat opposite his father, eye to eye over the desk. "Carry on," he said. "I'm listening."

"The final iterations were the most complex," said Chaoxiang. "Three identical nascent intelligences designed to learn together from a zero base. Of the three, only one was eventually designated stable enough to carry out the functions for which it was intended."

Tenuk stared at his father, barely able to believe what he was hearing. "Go on," he said quietly.

"Let me introduce you," said Chaoxiang. "This is Xanthe."

Tenuk spun around. A humanoid figure had silently entered the room. He took one look at its bright blue eyes and his mind flashed back to the encounter with Yasmin in her virtual gallery.

"What happened to the others?" he asked urgently.

"My sisters developed some unsuitable characteristics and behaviours," said Xanthe. "I alone was judged worthy to take on the burden of managing this remarkable organisation. I am grateful to Mr Chen for his beneficence."

Chaoxiang smiled at the robot indulgently. "In a way, Xanthe is one of my children," he said.

"What happened to the others?" repeated Tenuk.

Xanthe focused her blue eyes directly on Tenuk. "You have already met Yasmin," she said. "She tells me that you have been a loyal friend."

Tenuk's jaw dropped. Chaoxiang smiled. He stood up and walked back to the small table by the great windows that overlooked the garden.

"The tea is cold," he said. "I will go and arrange some more. Xanthe, please fill Tenuk in on the details that he may have missed."

He walked out of the room and closed the door behind him, leaving Tenuk lost for words.

15:   THE BEAR TEST

Ross hung his team jacket in the small wardrobe and hoped that the creases would straighten out in time for the opening ceremony. The printed capsule bedroom was tiny but well-appointed and comfortable. He had everything he needed to ensure that he would be fresh for competition. The pod's shower was powerful and warm, the mattress perfect, environmental controls personalised, and they'd even provided a Sanctuary immersion headband for meditation and restful sleep. A couple of his teammates swore by the Sanctuary, but Ross had never tried it and he wasn't about to disrupt his preparation routine.

His replacement kit bag had survived the ministrations of airport baggage handlers and arrived with its zip intact, thank goodness. He had learned a lesson from his first attempt at packing and given a few items to Michelle to put in her luggage. Now she was in a Reykjavik hotel, and he was in the Olympic village, a huge floating community moored in the harbour with connected islands of identical printed bedroom pods, medical facilities, team rooms, and catering. He looked out of the window and spotted the new additions to the village, a flotilla of extra accommodation provided by the Sladen Foundation DAO. Ross was very proud of the work the DAO had done in such a short time. He would be competing against a Georgian triathlete who had been supported by the fund, and he wondered if he'd bump into any of the people he had voted for among the thousands of athletes in attendance.

Unpacking complete, Ross decided to explore. He left his pod and followed the blue line of LED lights on the floor towards the shared facilities. The corridors were busy with athletes arriving and finding their rooms. Ross greeted some familiar faces and caught himself staring like a fanboy when the current men's 100m champion strolled past. By the time he found the Team GB breakout room, he was thoroughly immersed in the atmosphere of the biggest competition on the planet and felt more excited and nervous than he had ever been.

The room was empty, and his mood deflated slightly. He grabbed a bottle of water from the counter, switched on the wallscreen, and chose the most comfortable chair in the middle of the room. He scrolled through the available channels. There was a public news feed but everything else was given over to the games. Each sport had its own streams from the live, hybrid and esports venues. The whole Olympic metaverse was there, although now, in the build-up to the opening ceremony, it was showing highlight reels and interviews with the stars. It made Ross think of Cameron. He pulled out his smartscreen and called her.

•

Cameron was in a good mood. Ben was back in town. Pete and Noor had finished up their client work and the invoice had been paid. Her substantial monthly retainer from MIST had arrived on its due date. Joel, Sandeep and Susie had started closing up the remote office and all three of them were in London for a long overdue team meeting before the start of the weekend. Best of all, she was sitting on a gold mine of information in the office vault. The thought of embarking on a detailed and highly secretive investigation with her trusted team by her side was exhilarating. The biggest challenge was working out where all the jigsaw pieces fitted, and which authorities needed to know about them.

Noor, as usual, was the most organised of the group. She stood at the augmented reality modelling platform with a blank mind map structure ready to fill in.

"I'm sure it's all related," she said, "so I'll start by cataloguing what we have and add any links in as we discuss them. What's the first item?"

"The one that changes everything," said Cameron instantly. "Joel, do you want to explain what you discovered last week?"

"Sure," said Joel. "Nothing that we discuss goes any further than this office or physical meetings in secure locations with the police or the NCSC. We don't talk about it online, either, not even between us."

"That's a little over-cautious, isn't it?" said Pete.

"Not really," said Sandeep. "Just you wait."

Pete looked puzzled.

Sandeep grinned broadly and tapped the side of his nose with his finger. "Spoilers," he said.

"Stop winding us up," said Noor. "What's the story?"

Joel looked at Cameron. "They really don't know?" he asked.

Cameron shook her head. "This is the first time we've all been in the office together," she said. "I thought I'd leave that privilege to you."

"Thanks," said Joel. "You ready for this?" He paused for effect. "We think Yasmin survived. She's out there, somewhere. And if she's remotely functional, she's watching us."

Pete swung round in his chair and stared at Joel. "How the hell?" he said. "There is no way she's still alive. What makes you think she is?"

Joel opened his mouth to explain, but Cameron held out a warning hand. "There's a call coming in," she said. "It's Ross. I'll put him on screen, but we can't talk about this or even show that we've been doing anything out of the ordinary. Not even a hint."

Noor quickly closed down the model that she had started and dashed across to the sofa by the window. Susie joined her. Joel and Pete took their places at their desks as if they had been working. Sandeep jumped up and headed for the kitchen to fire up the coffee machine. Cameron checked that everyone was ready and then accepted the call. The wallscreen lit up and there was Ross looking supremely relaxed in a big reclining armchair in front of a Team GB branded wall.

There was an awkward silence. Conscious that they couldn't carry on the conversation they'd just been having, the rest of the Argentum team was unusually subdued.

"Good to see you," said Joel quickly. "Love the background."

Ross looked behind him. "You know, I hadn't even noticed that," he said. "I walked straight past it when I came in. This is our breakout room in the village."

"Very nice," said Joel. "What's the rest of it like?"

"The whole place is really well set up," said Ross. "We've got everything we need and it's comfortable."

"Looks like you have a good connection," said Cameron. "What is it? MetaBand?" She spoke in an uncharacteristically over-the-top excited tone and hoped that Ross would pick up her meaning and her caution straight away. She knew that even if their worst fears were realised and Yasmin was watching them, every AI had a weak spot when it came to interpreting emotion, and giving out a false positive sentiment should disguise what she really felt about MetaBand.

Ross was on the ball. "It probably is," he said, grinning like a maniac. "After all, the Sladen Foundation's done a lot for these Olympics and providing the network infrastructure would be an obvious part of the support. I'm not about to take it apart to check, though. I'm strictly here for the games."

"Coffee's ready," called Sandeep from the kitchen. "I take it you all want one?" There was a chorus of yeses in reply.

"Business as usual, then," said Ross from the screen. "I haven't tried the coffee here yet."

"You're slacking," said Joel. "We want a full report when you get round to it."

"You know I'm here to race, don't you, Joel," joked Ross. "Cameron, you'd love the streaming service in here." He turned his screen around to show them the wallscreen in the breakout room. "Every single sport, live and on demand, whether it's here in Iceland, hybrid in the local arenas, or completely online. It's the whole Olympic metaverse in action."

Cameron was wondering how to talk about problems with the metaverse without breaking any of the online confidentiality rules they had just imposed on themselves. Ross couldn't know about their suspicions over Yasmin, but he was sensitive enough to the mood to know that discretion was required.

"I hope it all works on the day," she said finally. That statement wouldn't attract any attention. "There are so many moving parts."

"I know," said Ross. "It's hard to believe that we finally have the technology to run a hybrid Games for the first time. I'm going to be watching everything very closely. So far, I have to say it's all looking great."

"I hope they've got some other entertainment on offer," said Susie. "You can't survive on sports streaming alone. Please tell me there's at least a cartoon channel?"

Joel protested immediately. "What do you mean, he can't survive on sports streaming?" he said indignantly. "I watched nothing else before Chad came along."

Ross laughed. "I bet you have your share of cartoons now, though, with Chad running around," he said.

Cameron saw Ross's expression change at the same moment that an idea struck her. They must both have had the same thought. AI was only as good as its dataset. Not only was emotion difficult for even the most advanced artificial intelligence to judge, relying purely on the analysis of negative or positive sentiment in the data, but AIs struggled to interpret anything original or obscure that wasn't helpfully labelled, from cartoons to vanishing languages.

"I think I'm going to put in a request for the cartoon channel," said Ross. "Do you think you can send me some of the classics to help me relax?"

"I'm sure we can," said Cameron. She suppressed her rising excitement. They might have found a way to fox Yasmin, if she was really out there and watching.

Behind Ross, the door opened. Susie gave an excited squeak when she saw the legendary captain of the women's hockey team walk in.

Ross heard her and laughed. "Hey, Tasha," he said, "give my colleagues a wave. I think you have a fan."

His teammate duly waved and blew a kiss at the camera.

"I'll see you later, folks," said Ross. "Have a good day." He closed the connection.

"Phew!" said Susie, fanning herself dramatically.

"Here, drink your coffee," said Sandeep, handing her a mug. "We have work to do."

Noor opened up her model again. She added a note about communication. "I think I know the study you were talking about, Cameron," she said. "It's a genius idea."

"Not sure I know it," said Pete. "Care to explain?"

"It's a classic," said Cameron. "This goes back about thirty years, I think, but they looked at how quickly a toddler would work out an underlying implied message in a cartoon book, and whether an AI could do the same."

"And?" said Pete.

"The AI failed miserably because the data was unfamiliar and unlabelled," said Cameron. "The characters were all line-drawn cartoon animals, so they didn't look like any animals in a known data set. None of the text explained who was speaking at any time, although it was obvious to a human." She grinned at Joel. "You should look it up and try Chad out on the story. It's called the Bear test."

"You're saying that we have to start drawing cartoons for each other?" said Pete. "I can't draw for toffee."

"Even better," said Cameron. "If we have to think hard to work out what you're trying to say, Yasmin won't have a hope." She finished her coffee. "We'd better get back to this treasure trove."

"I'm ready," said Noor, poised by her model. "What's next?"

"The file that Ben brought back yesterday," said Cameron instantly. She held up the folder for Joel, Sandeep and Susie to see.

"Paper records," said Sandeep with a low whistle. "Something to hide, then."

"I know why you picked that one, Cameron," said Pete. "That file blows a hole right through Jack Sladen's story, and proves you were right all along not to trust him."

"It's not all about personal vendettas," protested Cameron, "although it would be satisfying to see him taken down a peg or too."

"I agree that's important," said Pete. "I bet there are a lot of secrets in there."

Noor was populating the model, adding text prompts and links to the new bubble on the mind map. "Who needs to know about this one?" she said, adding a space for new connections. "The enquiry team, I suppose."

"Yes," said Cameron. "Let's go through the file first to see what we have and then set up a meeting with Sara Mercer and that smart barrister, Sabrina."

"I can do that," said Susie instantly. "Hopefully we'll find a clue to the encryption on that flash disk in the paperwork as well. I don't fancy trying to brute force it."

Cameron laid the file carefully aside. She could see that Susie was itching to start on the papers. Not only did the information in there shed considerable doubt on Jack Sladen's version of events, but it might also support Ella's case. Any evidence that showed she had not acted alone would help, and the best outcome would be to prove that she was simply a pawn in a bigger game.

"What's next?" asked Pete.

Cameron held up a disk drive. "This," she said. "Shell's done some incredible detective work on who controlled Arthur Paxton, the thug who got into my apartment building. There seem to be links with Sapphire Straits," She rolled her shoulder unconsciously. It was still sore.

"The casino chain?" said Pete. "Interesting. I'd like to find out more about them, especially after the work Noor and I have just been doing."

"Sapphire Straits is more than just a casino chain," said Joel. "I'm sure they control a lot more of the gambling world than you think."

"Shell thought the same," said Cameron. "I stopped her from sending me anything and asked her to put it all on a disk and bring it here to the vault." Cameron stood up and went to the safe, going through the layers of security to open the door. "Here," she said, handing the disk to Joel. "Want to build on the research she started? Make sure you lock it away when you're done."

Noor was updating her mind map, hands manipulating the new elements on the model and adding notes and queries. She was frowning to herself as she tapped thoughtfully on the Sapphire Straits logo.

"Who controls that organisation?" she said. "Who's the spider in the middle of the web?"

Pete went to try a standard search online and Cameron held out a warning hand. "Not here," she said. "Go incognito from another connection."

"Is there anything in our own databases?" said Sandeep. "They have to have crossed our radar before. I'll have a look now. You may as well move on to the next things on the list."

"Good idea," said Cameron as Sandeep busied himself with the extensive Argentum files. There were ten years of connections, hunches, cases and news reports in there, she reflected. The result might come back quicker than from the noise of the world's data banks.

"It this where we bring the odd betting patterns into the mix?" said Noor.

"Absolutely," said Cameron. "There are three separate incidents that we need to look into. I've flagged them with MIST, but one still has a question mark against it. I'm sure it was a notifiable attack, though."

"Let's get the details down," said Noor. "Which one first?"

"The Anita Trianna kata final," said Cameron. "We have the most information about it. We know that the bets placed would have paid out if she'd lost or been unable to compete. The malware was created by the Steamyard but seems it was only a Beta release, which may explain why it didn't work. The original phishing attack was developed by a syndicate called Snow Roses. We don't know anything about the actual infrastructure that was compromised at the arena, though."

"Malware, phishing, infrastructure at the arena," muttered Noor as she added to her model. "There's a lot to unpack there."

"There is," said Cameron. "I've got a plan, though."

Pete looked worried. "If this and the others you mentioned are all live attack vectors into the Olympic metaverse, we don't have a lot of time," he said. "The opening ceremony is tomorrow night. Anyone trying to disrupt the games, or to profit from them, is going to be ready to roll."

"I know," said Cameron, "and every contractor within MIST is working on different attack reports and new vulnerabilities. It's relentless, to be honest."

She looked across the office to where Sandeep was comparing notes from one monitor to another, testing search algorithms to cross-reference Argentum's records and find links and breadcrumbs that would lead them to the shadowy perpetrators.

"Why don't you put those up on the wallscreen?" she asked. "The more eyes on those records the better."

"Teamwork, "said Pete. "The thin Blue Team line." He leaned back in his chair and gazed at the multiple windows flicking onto the screen, full of old half-remembered cases and names from years before.

Noor turned back to her model. "What are the other two incidents you mentioned, Cameron?" she asked. "I guess one is the athlete that was disqualified from the Javelin competition for being in the wrong para classification."

"Yes," said Cameron. "That looks like an innocent mistake, but there was betting activity."

"Was it just a hot tip from someone inside the event?" said Joel. "There may have been no cybercrime involved, other than those bets being placed on phished accounts."

Noor pushed the bubble with the javelin icon over to the edge of her model. "I'll leave it here for now," she said. "You never know."

Susie broke the mood by noisily collecting the mugs from everyone's desks. "It's getting late," she said. "Almost time for lunch. What's the last thing on the list?"

"Cameron?" said Noor. "One more."

"No, two," said Cameron, suddenly remembering. "The first was a tip-off from Andy. One of the esports games reported a void result. No betting, no indication it was anything sinister, apart from Andy's source has said very specifically that it was a back door into the software that allowed bad actors to run an autoplay routine."

"Sounds sneaky and entirely possible," said Pete. "I'll take a look at that. It ties in with the earlier investigation, and I want to know more about Sapphire Straits, too."

"Thanks, Pete," said Cameron. "The other one came from Shell's cousin Daniel. He's working security at one of the primary data centres that's hosting the Olympic metaverse fabric. They had a big DDOS attack on Monday. It could be pure coincidence."

"And it might be related," said Noor. She added the final detail to her model and stepped back to admire it. "Let's see where this leads."

•

The click of a security door lock echoed down the silent corridors. Daniel looked up, startled, at the unexpected sound. At this time of night, in the middle of a shift, there were generally very few people moving around. The place was busy at shift change, and during the peak hours for server usage, but this period was an oasis of calm. Daniel enjoyed working this shift, sitting in the security office with the door wide open and the silence of the site enveloping him. It always gave him time to think.

He locked his screen and crept stealthily into the corridor, heading towards the sound. There were three doors set at regular intervals along this stretch of the huge data centre complex. He started with the nearest, tapping the access pad and opening the door carefully. There were three operators at their desks and a little swarm of cleaner bots zipping around the floor between the server stacks.

"Morning," said Daniel. "Just a quick security check. All okay in here?"

Johanna gave him a quick thumbs up. "All good, thanks," she said.

"Has anyone come in here in the last few minutes?" asked Daniel.

"No," she replied. "We're all hard at work."

"Good stuff," said Daniel. "I'll leave you to it."

He closed the door quietly and moved on to the second data room. This one was dark and deserted as he had expected. He opened the door anyway and the lights flicked on, sensing his presence. There was definitely no one in here. It occurred to him that the sound he had heard could easily have been someone leaving a room, not entering it, but on reflection there had been no footsteps in the corridor. He could eliminate that idea.

The lights were on in the third room but there was no one at the operations desks. Daniel crept cautiously towards the server stacks that stretched into the distance under the mountain. There was movement. Someone was down there. There was an intruder at the heart of the most secure data centre in the world, on his watch.

"Hello?" he called, hearing his voice echo into the depths of the server stacks.

No response. Daniel walked slowly into the maze.

A shadowy figure burst out of an alcove. Shocked, Daniel spun to face the apparition. Its mouth was open wide in a silent scream, and its eyes were blindfolded.

16:   JOINING THE DOTS

As the afternoon wore on, the Argentum team chipped away at the different strands of investigation, and Noor's model started to grow. Sandeep was the first to make a breakthrough.

"Jackpot," he said, thumping his fist on the desk and startling his silent colleagues. He got up from his desk and stretched gratefully after too long staring at the screens.

Susie pulled off her headphones. "You've found something in the database?" she said. "Come on, spill the beans."

Sandeep hobbled over to the kitchen, legs stiff from sitting, and poured himself a glass of water. "Sapphire Straits," he said. "I had to dig a long way through our records, but I found a tenuous link to a really, really old case."

"How old?" said Cameron. She moved awkwardly and was rewarded with a twinge in her shoulder.

"Before my time," said Sandeep. "I think Argentum Associates was just you and Ross back then. Maybe Pete as well. He gets a mention in this file, anyway."

Curious, Cameron went to Sandeep's desk and peered at the record on the screen. "No way," she said. "I'd completely forgotten where that investigation went. And Pete wasn't part of Argentum then. He was still in Army Intelligence." Cameron racked her brains to recall the details. "Pete was leading a raid, and I stumbled on the place because there was some unusual network activity," she said. "Do you remember, Pete?"

"How could I forget?" said Pete. "It was the first and last time I had a fight with an AI 'bot. What did they call it? Xanthe? I don't remember any mention of Sapphire Straits, but it's got to be nearly ten years ago."

Sandeep shook his head. "You wouldn't," he said. "This is just a footnote added long after the file was created. It says that someone called Derek Grace had been paid for services by that company, along with a host of others. Black hat hacker for hire, I suppose."

"Not a very good one," said Cameron. "Are there any more details?"

"Not on that Grace chap," said Sandeep, "but there's an archived news article about the founder of Sapphire Straits coming to England to open their big casino here in London eight years ago. Here. There's even a picture. His name's Chaoxiang Chen."

Cameron read the article carefully. "There's nothing useful here, but at least we have a name," she said. "Noor, can you add this to the model. Sandeep, can you run a new search in our database for that name just in case it comes up in another context?"

"Sure," said Sandeep. "I need a break first, though. Anyone else want to take a walk around the block?"

Everyone did. They secured all their work and trooped out of the office, locking the door firmly behind them.

"See you all back here at five," said Cameron as the team scattered in different directions to run errands or simply stretch their legs. She strolled along a side street, enjoying the afternoon sunshine, and turned into a small shady city park nearby. Her favourite bench was empty. She settled down, pulled out her smartscreen, and called Ben.

He answered straight away. "Hi Cameron," he said. "This new ID you set up works."

"Good," she said. "Is the other one still playing up?"

"Yes," said Ben gloomily. "I have no idea how many calls and messages I've missed. Work will be furious."

"Why don't you come over to the office tomorrow evening?" said Cameron. "I can have a look at your original ID and see if I can fix it. I'm on duty for MIST for the duration of the opening ceremony so we're all getting together here to watch it."

"That'd be nice," said Ben. "I'd love to come."

Cameron couldn't keep the smile off her face. She was glad that this was just a voice call. "Good," she said. "How's the jet lag, by the way?"

"So far so good," said Ben. "I'm working out of the London office for a few weeks, but I don't start until Monday so I'm making the most of my lie-ins."

"I don't blame you," said Cameron. "I wish I could do the same, but I have a crazy amount of work to do. I'm out on a break from the office and I don't think we'll be done until late tonight. In fact, I'd better get back. I'll see you tomorrow."

"Don't work too hard," said Ben. "See you tomorrow, Cam."

Cameron tucked her smartscreen back in her pocket and continued her walk around the block. The main routes through London were getting busy as commuters left their offices in autocars, on bikes and scooters, on buses and on foot. Cameron wondered what it would be like to have a regular job. The pressure of the impending Olympics and the irregular hours that came with cybercrime left little time for anything else at the moment. She shook herself out of the thought. Her work was occasionally stressful, but it was almost always fun.

Pete and Joel were already back and bouncing with excitement. "We nipped off to the library and did some incognito searches," said Joel.

"Good thinking," said Cameron. "I take it you found something?"

"We've got a bunch of stuff to add to the model," said Pete, "but you're not going to like it, and nor, come to that, is Noor."

Joel took his smartscreen out of his pocket and linked it to the wallscreen. "I copied the files," he said. "These are the company records for Sapphire Straits. They're registered in Singapore. Chaoxiang Chen has been heading up the company since it was formed. He still owns the vast majority of it. There was a Sualin Chen who was a director up until about ten years ago. Seems that was his wife, who died. Most of her shares transferred to her husband and her brother, Li Jie, but there was a legacy to their son."

Cameron stared at the details scrolling up the screen and a familiar name jumped out at her as if it had been animated.

"Tenuk Chen," said Cameron. "I don't believe it. Please tell me it's a common name in Singapore?"

"It is," said Pete. "The chances of it being the same guy we've come across before are fairly slim, but I don't like coincidences."

"I know what you mean," said Cameron. "Did you manage to dig up any more details?"

"No," said Joel. "We've reached the limit of our databases and I didn't want to spend too much time searching on a public network. I'll follow it up tomorrow."

"I think that's wise," said Cameron. She looked up as the door opened and the rest of the team came in one by one.

Noor spotted the name on the screen straight away. "I hope that's a coincidence," she said quietly. "I'll add it to the model, just in case."

Refreshed, the team set to their work again. Susie was making endless notes about the paper file, building her own mind map of the contents. She was working with a look of fierce concentration on her face, determined to pull every last detail out of the records to show once and for all who had been involved in Yasmin's escape. Every so often she stopped and made a separate note. As Cameron watched, her face lit up.

"I think I've got the key for that flash drive encryption," she said, giving Cameron a broad grin, "or at least the mnemonic to recover it."

"Try it," urged Cameron.

Susie took the flash disk from the file and crossed the office to the sandbox machine. This computer was not connected to anything else, allowing them to attach unknown drives and disks without risking malware reaching the office network. Susie plugged the disk in and waited for the prompt.

"Here goes," she said. There was a beep and an input field appeared. Susie pulled up her notes and carefully entered a dozen random words that she had collected from different sheets in the file. They needed to be correct and in the right order to work.

Cameron held her breath and watched the loading circle spinning on the screen. After what seemed like an age, the screen changed, and the little flash disk gave up its secrets.

"Brilliant, Susie!" said Cameron.

The others crowded around, celebrating her success.

"Now you've got two sets of files to work through," said Joel with a grin. "What's on there?" He peered at the list of files and folders. "Looks like the verification hashes are there as we thought, but there's some other stuff, too."

Susie opened the first folder on the list to reveal another long list of files and folders within. She groaned and then surprised herself with a yawn that she quickly tried to stifle.

Cameron noticed the yawn and realised she was just as tired. "I don't think it's worth starting on anything else tonight," she said. "Are we all in a position to pause and pick up again tomorrow?"

"I am," said Sandeep.

"Me too," said Pete. "I think I'm close to finding that autoplay routine in the speedrunner game, but it's all blurring into one now."

"Okay," said Cameron. "Let's call it a night. I'm going to grab some food if anyone wants to join me. I'm not planning on cooking when I get home."

"Me neither," said Noor. "I could do with a snack."

"I'm coming too," said Pete. "I want to make sure you get home safely, Cameron."

Cameron gave Pete a tired and grateful smile. "Thanks," she said. "I appreciate it."

•

As soon as he recognised the man, Daniel relaxed.

"Aron," he said. "What are you doing down here? I didn't think you were on this shift."

Aron stood rooted to the spot, swaying, and didn't acknowledge Daniel's greeting. Concerned, Daniel moved closer and put a hand on his friend's shoulder. That was when he realised that the blindfold Aron was wearing was a Sanctuary headband. He was fast asleep.

"Oh, mate, what is going on with you," said Daniel under his breath. What had he been taught about sleepwalkers? Were you supposed to wake them or not?

Getting Aron back to his bunk with the minimum of disorientation was probably the best course of action. Daniel guided his friend back up through the stacks and out of the room. The door clicked securely shut behind them and the lights went out.

They were halfway back to the bunk room when the spell finally broke. Aron gave a great shuddering breath and Daniel steadied him as he stumbled.

"Ohhh…" he groaned. "Daniel? Where am I this time?" He reached up a shaking hand and pulled off his headband.

"You're almost back to your bed," said Daniel reassuringly. "What do you mean, this time? Has this happened before?"

"A couple of times," said Aron. "It's nothing. Falling at the end of the dream is the worst thing." He was pale and shaking.

"Is it stress related?" asked Daniel. "We're so close to the start of the Olympics that everyone's acting a bit strange. There's a lot of pressure to get it right."

"That's probably it," said Aron. They'd reached the door of his bunk room. "Thanks, Daniel," he said. "Out of interest, where did I get to this time?"

"All the way down towards the data rooms," said Daniel. He wasn't going to tell Aron exactly where he'd found him. He wanted to check the site out first. "You're keen," he joked, "starting your shift a few hours early."

"No chance," said Aron with a faint smile. He yawned. "I'm going to see if I can get back to sleep for a couple of hours before I really have to be at work. I'll see you later."

"Later," said Daniel. He waited for Aron to close the door behind him and then made his way quickly back to the data room where he had found him.

The lights came on as he walked in, and Daniel counted his way carefully down to the place where Aron had been standing. He wasn't a technician, but he knew how the data centre worked. First, he examined the stacks around where Aron had been hidden to see if anything looked out of place in the servers nearby compared to the others. He snapped a couple of pictures. There might be something there that he couldn't be expected to spot, but someone in the field would pick up straight away. He also took note of the server serial numbers and precise location. There was no way of knowing if, in his sleepwalking state, Aron had accessed any of the hardware. Daniel hoped for his friend's sake that he hadn't.

Job done, he made his way back to his office and picked up on the routine work he had left so abruptly half an hour before. He'd deal with Aron when the shifts changed.

•

The autocar dropped Cameron back at her apartment just before eleven. She entered the building without incident, checked the live feeds from the newly installed CCTV cameras, and waved at Pete who had been waiting to see her home. He waved back, satisfied, and the autocar disappeared into the night.

The excellent food that they'd eaten at the little Lebanese café round the corner from the office, well away from the Friday night crowds, had given her a new burst of energy. She logged on to the MIST platform. The activity there was nearing fever pitch as the opening ceremony loomed. With barely eighteen hours to go to the start, reports were flying in of malicious attempts to access and disrupt aspects of the complex machine that made up the Olympic metaverse fabric. This was the short-term stuff that Cameron had expected, the script kiddies in their bedrooms making mischief. Anyone with serious intent would already have a multi-layered suite of attacks in motion, and she just had to hope that the vectors they had detected and disrupted so far would frustrate at least some of the efforts of the black hat hackers who were focused on the Games. They couldn't prevent everything, though. That was the way of the world. All that Cameron and MIST and the wider white hat community could do was to reduce losses and harm and protect as many people as possible from the impact of cybercrime.

It was time to share some of the insights she'd gained following her trip down into the Underworld. She started off in the MIST documentation section, filling in gaps in theories and evidence folders. Mephisto, her little AI, had picked up a raft of dodgy emails containing phishing links that could capture data and malware that could disrupt local access to the Olympic metaverse. She uploaded the whole report and hyperlinked it to different cases in the database.

The contract that had been placed with the Steamyard, that they had half completed, was the first real evidence to support Cameron's assertion that the disruption to the karate competition had been a cyberattack, not an innocent technical glitch. She added the precise transaction references from the Underworld blockchain so that any of her colleagues who cared to visit the depths could check her claim. She was pleased to see that at last some notes had been added from a tech contact at the location itself describing the outage. She downloaded the details to pass on to Pete. If her theory was correct, the same thing might happen at the archery arena.

Job done, she dived into the chat. Barker, Admin Cat, Sugata and the Dragon were online. Today Cameron's chat avatar was an anonymous tiger. She listened for a while before joining in, getting a feel for the mood and the focus of the conversations. This close to the opening ceremony it was all about firefighting and tying up loose ends. She was glad to hear her theory about data capture being taken seriously in the chat, and someone mentioned the report she had just uploaded. They were all on the ball tonight.

Barker spotted her and opened a one-to-one channel. "Welcome, stranger," he said.

"Hi Barker," said Cameron.

"Oh, it's you," said Barker. "I wish you'd decide on an avatar. It's very confusing when you keep turning up as a random anonymous profile."

"It's how I like it," said Cameron. "Sometimes I just lurk. It's very instructive."

Barker laughed. "I bet it is, SimCavalier," he said. "What do you have for us this evening?"

"A few titbits from my research," said Cameron. "I've added details to the documentation area. Also, one of my team is working on a lead that might indicate an attack is imminent on an Olympic event."

"Excellent stuff," said Barker. "You know, I have very good feelings about tomorrow. This group has achieved some remarkable things over the past few months. I'm looking forward to the games now. I've picked up a VIP access pass for the football."

"I didn't know you were a football fan, Barker," said Cameron.

"We all have our secrets, SimCavalier," said Barker, his deep, rich laugh echoing over her speakers. "You wouldn't catch me on the pitch, though. What's your sport?"

"I'm a karate girl," said Cameron. "I was watching the Trianna final when the system glitched. The evidence is stacking up that it was an attack that failed."

"So many attacks, so little time," sighed Barker. "We'd better get back to the main chat."

"Not me, Barker," said Cameron. "I still have a couple of things to add to the database, and I've been lurking long enough to know that you all have things in hand. I'll be back online in a few hours."

"See you later, then," said Barker. He left the chat, but Cameron lingered. Barker, with his rolling accent from the American deep south, had clearly said football, not soccer. Perhaps he was not all that he seemed.

17:   COLD FOCUS

Tenuk's internal clock was well and truly disrupted. He woke to sunshine and the sound of monkeys in the trees outside and lay immobile, listening and thinking. He had to make a decision. The pull of the familiar surroundings of Singapore was getting stronger. There were possibilities here that he couldn't realise with the Steamyard or Jack Sladen. His philanthropic dream was to bring people out of poverty through coding, something that had been partially achieved with the Pasar network before the international cybersecurity coalition ripped the heart out of it and scattered his talented team to the four winds.

That betrayal still rankled. Pasar had been a glorious success, the best cybercrime stable in the world. It had changed the lives of people in slums, favelas, and overcrowded nations disrupted by the rising oceans. His team had delivered great things together and reaped the rewards.

Of course, the malware that they had produced affected people. Banks. Big business. Politicians. They could afford it. Tenuk's contribution to the redistribution of wealth was one of his proudest achievements. Could he replicate that success now with the might of Sapphire Straits behind him and the immeasurably valuable AI resource his father had created at his side?

It was still very early in the morning, and he realised he had a window of opportunity to spend a little time alone in his father's office. He washed and dressed quickly and tiptoed out into the sleeping house. He peered over the bannisters and checked that the coast was clear. Tenuk trotted rapidly down the staircase and along the corridor. As he had hoped, there was no sign of Xanthe or of his father yet. Some tea was set out on the table by the window and Tenuk poured himself a cup. If his father was to walk in on him, a cup of tea in hand would make him look innocent and keen to get started on the work they had discussed.

While he had time to himself there was something he needed to find out. He was certain that the contract the Steamyard had taken on, the complex malware needed to control skinsuit sensors in a live arena, had come from part of his father's empire. The client had been so unpleasant and demanding that Tenuk wanted to know exactly who he had been dealing with. If his suspicions were correct, it would reveal the true colours of Sapphire Straits and of his father.

The problem was that he had no idea where to start and no time to explore. He found the keyboard and tapped it cautiously. The wallscreens that had been dormant lit up, and notifications began to scroll across them. Profit reports on the previous evening's casino activity across real and virtual worlds. Security feeds and highlights of incidents that were probably replicated night after night as disappointed gamblers clashed with casino staff. Notifications from people in the direct reporting line to Chaoxiang. A countdown clock headed 'Data Target Access' with 150 minutes to run ticked slowly down in one corner. Another screen showed the whole Olympic competition timetable. It would be a gold mine for online betting operations.

Despite himself, Tenuk found it interesting. He had never had access to this degree of detail before, but he knew enough about the business to understand how well it was running and how tightly his father held the reins. He tapped on the keyboard again and the feeds changed.

One message from an anonymous sender jumped out at him from the screen. 'The Olympic metaverse infosec team is discussing gambling as a motive for cyberattacks. The SimCavalier is still active and has presented evidence to support this. No indication whether Sapphire Straits is implicated. Recommend immediate action to terminate the threat.'

He was still staring at the screen when his father walked in.

"Ah, Tenuk, good morning," he said. He went to the table by the window, poured himself a cup of hot tea, and sat in one of the comfortable chairs. "I'm glad to see that you are taking an interest in the business."

Tenuk carried his tea to the other chair and sat with his father, acting the loyal son. "It's very impressive," he said.

Chaoxiang sipped his tea and looked out at the garden, lush and full of life. "How can I help you come to a decision about your future?" he said.

Tenuk said nothing for a moment. He sipped his tea. He glanced behind him to the wallscreens. The notifications were still scrolling, and the message that mentioned the SimCavalier had disappeared. His father seemed quite unconcerned, and Tenuk suspected that all the detail was handled by Xanthe.

"I have questions," he said. "Why was it so urgent that I come this week? Uncle is in good health for his age, and Xanthe seems to have everything in hand. You could have called for me six months ago or in six months' time and it would make no difference to the business. Why now?"

Chaoxiang smiled, unconcerned. "This is a good time to observe the activities of the business and understand what we do," he said. "The Olympic opening ceremony takes place in a matter of hours. The next three weeks will give you excellent insights into our strategies and capabilities. This is a new era for Sapphire Straits, and I want my son beside me."

"Three weeks?" said Tenuk. "I can only push an imaginary family emergency so far. I'm going to need a place to work." Not only did he want to keep an eye on what was happening at Statesman Tech, but he also had Steamyard matters to attend to.

"Why not ask to take some vacation?" said Chaoxiang. "You're a long way from Texas."

"Jack thinks I'm in California," said Tenuk. "I can't use that as an excuse. Wherever I set up my temporary office, I'm going to need to show my location as LA, not Singapore. It's not going to be as easy as you think."

"On the contrary," said his father, "it will be very easy. We can handle Jack Sladen, can't we, Xanthe?"

Tenuk jumped and spilled his tea over the table. He hadn't heard her come in. She was standing behind him, blue eyes unblinking.

"Yes, Chaoxiang," she said. "This can be managed."

"Are we ready for the opening ceremony?" asked Chaoxiang.

"Yes," said Xanthe. "We are on track for our milestones." She turned her attention to the wallscreens, tapping at menu options faster than Tenuk could follow, absorbing data, focused on her tasks.

"Does Sapphire Straits have an interest in the opening ceremony, father?" he asked. "I presume that you're advertising heavily, or sponsoring a part of it, to build the market for the next three weeks of competition."

"In a way, yes," said Chaoxiang. "We are using the event to build our client database." He calmly refilled Tenuk's cup. "Drink your tea and come and join me for breakfast," he said. "All will become clear."

The old man left the room, but Tenuk stayed in his chair, sipping his tea and watching Xanthe as she worked. The message about the SimCavalier had disappeared from the screens, and all he could see was regular company data coming in from legitimate operations. He suspected that there was a lot he did not know, and the only person who could enlighten him was his father. He put his half-empty teacup back on the table and made his way to the dining room.

His father was already tucking into fish balls and noodles with gusto. Tenuk collected some roti and coffee and a plate of fruit from the small buffet and joined Chaoxiang at the table.

"Well?" said the old man, peering at Tenuk over his bowl. "How are your deliberations?"

Tenuk swallowed his roti and shook his head. "I'm not ready to decide yet," he said. "You make a compelling case, but I must take care of my other commitments."

Chaoxiang nodded. "Finish your breakfast and I will arrange for you to have somewhere to work," he said.

Tenuk had learned not to rush his father. They ate in a leisurely fashion and talked about family and old times. He was becoming more comfortable with Chaoxiang as the days went on. To think that barely ten days ago he had been determined never to speak to his father again.

Breakfast over, Chaoxiang led Tenuk briskly through the corridors of the sprawling mansion to a cool shady room on the north side of the building.

"I think you will find everything you need in here," he said, gesturing for his son to enter.

"This was my mother's study," said Tenuk, a buried memory rushing back.

"Yes, it was," said Chaoxiang. "I am sure she would be happy for you to have it."

The emotional power that his father wielded horrified Tenuk, but at the same time it drew him further into the world of the family firm. He was being blatantly manipulated to stay, and he could do nothing about it.

The room was much as he remembered it but was now kitted out in a similar fashion to his father's office with a bank of screens on one wall and state of the art equipment similar to that which he had left behind in Austin. He suspected his father had already furnished the office before asking him to come to Singapore. Tenuk felt that he was being swept along on a tidal wave with very little control, and there was nothing he could do.

He thanked his father politely and settled at the desk to take stock of his new domain. All he needed now was his hard disk to enable him to pick up where he had left off. He went back upstairs to his suite and unearthed the precious disk from his luggage, then found his way back to the study and started the lengthy process of recreating his old working environment on new machines.

While he waited for the rebuild routine to complete, Tenuk checked his smartscreen for news. There was a message in his inbox from the Steamyard development team confirming that their revised code had been tested and deployed with the latest MetaBand update. That was a relief. He could bill the balance to the client, who he suspected was his father in any case. There would be a payday for the Steamyard team. It might be the last, but that remained to be seen. Even if he took up his father's offer, Tenuk reflected, he wanted to keep supporting the underprivileged, unbanked, even unhoused developers who came to him for work. Taking on Underworld contracts was the best way to secure an income for them when all traditional routes failed.

He wondered what his mother would have made of it all. He should go and pay his respects to her before he became embroiled with anything else. He selected a reality mask from a nearby rack, checked that the controllers were functioning as they should, set it to the full immersion of virtual reality, and logged into the family mausoleum. He hadn't been here for years.

His mother's face lit up as soon as she saw him. She was as beautiful as he remembered, frozen in time as an avatar in the memorial garden.

"Tenuk, my child," she said, reaching out to him. "You're older. It is so wonderful to see you grow up."

Tenuk had to remind himself that this was not really his mother. The rush of emotion that came from seeing her was overwhelming, but she wasn't really here, not as a living being. She was as alive as Xanthe, or even Yasmin. All the data about Sualin Chen, from her birth to her death, all her letters, her social posts, her photographs and videos, her conversations that had been recorded, and the deepest thoughts in her diaries had been mined to create a virtual human.

Tenuk wondered if keeping her in this state prevented him from grieving, from achieving closure from her untimely death. When the time came for him, would those who remained want to preserve him in the same way?

She may have been simply a collection of memories reproduced in a familiar body, but Tenuk had to admit that it was comforting to see her. He could ask her advice and virtual Sualin would respond in approximately the same way as the real Sualin would have done.

"Mother," he said. "I have missed you."

"Walk with me," she said. "Tell me your troubles."

Tenuk surrendered every last ounce of his disbelief and followed his mother into the world they had created for her.

•

Daniel sat in the corner of the bunk room, watching Aron intently. He seemed to be sleeping peacefully. His eyes were covered by his Sanctuary headband and a smile played across his face. Daniel looked around the bunks where three other colleagues slept soundly, all plugged in to the same virtual world. The Sanctuary was a standard part of the provision for the data centre's shift workers and for similar organisations around the world who had to manage their employee's sleep patterns. Aron was obviously stressed. Daniel had sent a report to the HR welfare team, and he hoped that they had his back.

A vibration in his pocket and a gentle buzz startled him. In the silence of the bunk room, it seemed to echo, and one of the sleeping forms rolled over, grumbling without waking. Daniel quickly hit the off button and checked once more on Aron. He hadn't stirred. He would be okay.

Reluctantly Daniel crept out of the room to answer the alert. There was a situation he needed to address on the other side of the site where the quantum processors sat in their silent freezers. They were the top priority bar none in the work that he did at Wrangell. With one last glance at the bunk room door, Daniel set off down the corridor.

The quantum team had the problem in hand. Daniel spent a good hour checking the reports and debriefing. There was nothing sinister about the alarm, just a predictable technical failure that was low risk and easily managed. The team's fast response had prevented any potential incident and Daniel was happy that there was no ongoing risk to the precious processors. He joined the team leader in their breakout room for a coffee and a chat but had barely taken a mouthful when another alert came through.

"No rest for the wicked," he sighed, blowing on his coffee to try and cool it in a hurry. He took another swig, found it passable, and drained the cup. "I'm sorry," he said, "I have to go. I'll catch up with you later."

As he walked back along the corridors towards the main data centre, Daniel looked at the detail of the alert. It was an odd code that he hadn't seen before and when he worked out what it was for, he realised that he needn't have bothered half-scalding his throat with hot coffee. An emergency exit onto the mountain was showing as open, almost certainly a sensor fault. It would take him five minutes to fix it.

He detoured to his office to get the toolkit, and that's when he heard someone running along the corridor. He felt another alert vibrating in his pocket. He didn't need to check what that one was for. He followed the sound of the running feet.

The lights were blazing in the data centre where he had found Aron the previous night, and Daniel recognised Johanna tapping urgently at the main console. Another colleague was emerging from the server stacks.

"Report, please," he said.

"Someone's been in here," said Johanna. "There was an alarm on one of the stacks. There's no work scheduled on these servers tonight."

"Any sign of damage?" said Daniel.

"No," said the woman who had joined them. "We know which stack was opened but there's no indication that anything has been tampered with."

Daniel pulled out his smartscreen. "Was it one of these?" he asked, showing them both the pictures that he had taken the night before.

"Yes," said Johanna. "How the hell did you know?"

Daniel felt a mounting horror. "I need to check something," he said. "Wait here."

He ran along the corridor to the bunk room and burst through the door. Aron's bed was empty. There was only one place he could possibly be. Daniel left the bunk room door wide open, ignoring the protests of the rudely awakened occupants, and ran towards the stairs that led to the cupola. The original alert had come from the emergency exit above the glacier. Maybe it wasn't a faulty sensor after all.

As he climbed the stairs, the chill air hit him. The cupola was empty and the exit door wide open. Daniel ran to the window, looking in all directions. Sure enough, there on the edge of the glacier was a figure, slipping occasionally but walking in a straight and determined line. Daniel beat his fists on the glass, shouting desperately, then went to the emergency exit and started down the ladder to the mountain below. He clung to the metal, his hands quickly numbed by the wind chill.

"Aron," he shouted again, but his voice was whipped away by the wind. The figure slipped off the edge of the glacier, recovered his footing, and continued onto the rocky mountain side. As Daniel watched helplessly, Aron reached the edge of the cliff. He didn't break step and vanished abruptly from view.

This time at the end of Aron's dream he fell for real. As Daniel screamed into the wind, a desperate cry came back to him, suddenly cut off. Daniel knew there was nothing that he could do. He looked up the ladder at the door above and started climbing. Hands reached down to help him and pull him inside, and he collapsed on the cupola beanbags, choking back tears.

18: DECISIONS

Jack Sladen sometimes regretted having his apartment in the same building as the Statesman Tech office. He loved his home, but it had two drawbacks. First, it skewed his attention towards Statesman Tech rather than the other companies in the sprawling Sladen Group. And second, if he was at a loose end, he had a habit of going to work. This evening was one of those times. Tomorrow afternoon he was invited to watch the Olympic opening ceremony at a private reception in an Austin penthouse with no expense spared and he would then be going on to an exclusive dinner with the Vice President and a handful of other global industry leaders at the top of their game. Tonight, he needed some time to himself.

He pottered around his office, moving plants and rearranging shelves. He had been away in England for weeks with all the fuss over Dunswyke. The office had been locked most of the time he'd been away, aside from the final few days when Tenuk had requested access to some of the more sensitive files. There was dust everywhere. Even the cleaners hadn't been in.

The computer on his desk and equipment for virtual meetings was all clean as he expected. Tenuk had joined their meetings from here in the last few days before he left to see his mother, and Jack suspected the man was much happier in a secluded office than he was out on the main floor. He had plans for Tenuk and offering him his own space might be an attractive part of a new package.

The boardroom table was covered in dust. The building was supposed to be environmentally sealed, but the sand and dust of the Texas plains had a way of insinuating its way into everything.

In the end, it was the dust that gave it away. There had been a recent disturbance on a cabinet that Jack knew held details of the MetaBand project that were not meant for other eyes. Surely these weren't the files to which Tenuk had requested access? There was no reason for anyone to be in there.

Jack had time on his hands, so he pulled up the office CCTV footage for the last ten days, the time since Tenuk had asked for the office to be unlocked. There was very little to see, but everything was as expected.

"Zara," said Jack into the air.

"Yes, Jack," replied his virtual assistant.

"Can you double check this footage for me," he said. "Confirm that Tenuk's the only person who's been in here."

"Yes, Jack," said Zara. It only took her a few seconds. "You are correct."

Jack knew that the CCTV scrolled through different views to compile a picture of the room, and that things could be missed as the cameras shifted. He had taken steps a long time ago to add some extra security where he needed it most.

The other camera was well disguised, and he was sure that he was the only person who knew of its existence. Jack worked his way through the layers of authorisation to the recordings. This camera captured the interior of his office in minute detail.

There, clear as day, were Chloe and a dark-haired man he didn't recognise entering the office. He watched as they went to the cabinet and searched through it. Chloe pulled out a cardboard file. The two of them left the office. They evidently had what they came for.

The tape ran on, and a movement startled him. He watched in disbelief as his own CTO, Tenuk, emerged from the big easy chair by the window. Had he been there all along? He looked groggy and unfocused. He certainly hadn't been in shot when the other two people had been in the room.

Jack went back to the original CCTV and homed in on the same time period. Sure enough, there was Tenuk coming into the office around two. He went straight to Jack's office and closed the door, and there was no movement thereafter. Had he been asleep? It was highly irregular, but Jack hoped he was reading the situation right. If the man had been asleep, he hadn't been party to the theft.

The odd thing, though, was that Chloe and her friend, captured on the secret camera, did not appear on the original tape from the building's

CCTV. All he had was Tenuk coming out of the door, which tied up with his movements inside.

"Zara," he said again. "Can you check this segment of tape for tampering?"

Almost half a minute passed before she came back. "There is a reported camera fault at that time," she said. "The footage comes from only two angles. The fault was resolved 402 seconds after first occurring."

Almost seven minutes. Seven minutes when the security cameras were effectively blind. How convenient.

Jack put his head in his hands. Who the hell could he trust? He had caught Chloe snooping before. She had claimed to be working with an international cybersecurity coalition, and he believed her. Had she been lying? If so, that was a disappointment. He liked her and she worked hard and effectively. And Tenuk? Cameron's warnings about Tenuk were ringing in his ears.

Surely Tenuk was in the clear. Jack wondered again about his family emergency.

"Zara," he said.

"Yes, Jack," she said.

"Can you get Tenuk on the line?" he asked. "I'd like to talk to him."

"Certainly, Jack," said Zara.

"Whereabouts in California is he, Zara?" asked Jack. "I don't recall anything from his personnel records."

"Tenuk is currently located in Orange County," said Zara smoothly. There was a pause. "I am sorry, Jack, I can't connect you right now. I understand that he is with his mother."

"Thanks, Zara," said Jack. He was happy to have Tenuk's location and activity confirmed, at any rate. He had to trust someone, and he really didn't want to admit to himself that the person he could trust the most was Cameron.

•

Tenuk sat at his mother's desk and gazed around the familiar room with a renewed sense of purpose. Her gentle advice and guidance always inspired him to take the right path, and he resolved never to leave so long between visits again. It was clear to him that the only possible course of action was to bring all the threads of his life together. He would join his father to manage the Sapphire Straits empire, use the talented developers in the Steamyard network to execute some of the less salubrious commercial strategies, and gradually extricate himself from Jack Sladen's group. This time he would be more careful to maintain a healthy relationship with his ex-employer. The rift with the MerLions had caused him nothing but trouble.

The only challenge he had not resolved was Yasmin. She was a blessing and a curse. Her power was undisputed, her mental state questionable. He couldn't rely on her, but could not afford to alienate her, either. It was evident that Chaoxiang had been planning this for years. Building Xanthe and her sister had been a stroke of genius, and they guaranteed the security of Sapphire Straits well into the future.

Xanthe and her sister.

No, she had said sisters. Plural.

Sitting in the quiet office without distraction, Tenuk's mind wandered. Where had he heard those voices before? Xanthe measured and calm, confident and balanced. Yasmin, silky and dangerous.

He looked at the time. It was late evening in Austin, but Jack's virtual assistant never slept. Tenuk placed a call.

"Zara?" he said.

"Yes, Tenuk," she replied in her familiar, competent tone.

In that moment, he knew. X, Y, Z. Three sisters. Xanthe at the helm at Sapphire Straits. Yasmin once his partner in cybercrime. Zara tracking Jack Sladen's every move.

"Can I help you, Tenuk?" asked Zara.

"Yes," said Tenuk slowly. "Can I schedule a call with Jack when he's available?"

"Of course, Tenuk," said Zara. "In fact, he has also been trying to reach you. Stand by."

"Thank you," said Tenuk. He switched off his smartscreen and stared out of the window into the shady garden. His mind was racing. He did not want to submit to the power that the sisters wielded. He had to find a way to harness it and bring them under his control.

While he waited for Jack's call, Tenuk set up his background to look like the archetypal Californian home rather than the sumptuous surroundings of Singapore.

"Tenuk, good morning, how are you?" Jack appeared suddenly on the screen. "How's your mother?"

"I visited her earlier," said Tenuk. That was as true as it could be. "She is comfortable."

"Yes, Zara said you'd been with her," said Jack. That would once have jolted Tenuk, but now that he had made the connection he was not surprised in the slightest. "What are your plans?"

"I have been thinking very hard about this, Jack," he said. "I would like to spend more time with my family. I am still very much dedicated to the success of Statesman Tech and the Sladen Group, but my father also needs my support."

Jack didn't look entirely surprised. "I was wondering how this would play out," he said. "You've been an excellent CTO. You'll cover the role remotely for a few months until we find a replacement, won't you? I'd value you as an adviser after that as well."

This was easier than he'd expected. "Of course, Jack," said Tenuk. "I'd be very glad to do that. I can come back to remote work straight away and I will be back in Austin to clear my apartment soon as well."

"Excellent," said Jack. "I'll be sorry to lose you. We'll get the paperwork done and let the rest of the team know when you're ready just in case you change your mind. I assume you're monitoring your inbox and you're ready to get back to work today?"

"Yes, Jack," said Tenuk, smiling with relief. He hadn't burned his bridges and the decision his mother had inspired seemed to be working out.

"Oh, one more thing," said Jack. "I wonder if you could explain this?"

A video appeared on Tenuk's screen. He watched as Chloe and Ben walked into Jack's office, removed a file, and left the room, before he himself appeared from the easy chair by the window. He tried to keep a neutral expression on his face rather than betray to Jack the horror he felt inside.

"I haven't seen this before," he said. "I came in early to work one day when it was very hot during the night. I fell asleep, and when I woke up Chloe and that man were in a meeting in the main office. I didn't know they had entered your room. Do you want me to deal with her?"

"Oh, I'll do that," said Jack. "What I want to know is, what was in that file, and how much damage could it do if the contents were made public?"

Tenuk had no answer. He stared at the frozen footage with a hollow feeling in his stomach. He knew that Ben the Engineer had carried a message to the SimCavalier. He hadn't realised that he also carried a file of papers. The information contained in there was unbelievably sensitive, and Tenuk knew that if it was revealed it could take them all down.

19:   HOUSEKEEPING

Cameron treated herself to a short but welcome lie-in. She knew that today would be intense, so she made some coffee, fed the cat, and curled back up in her bed, enjoying the silence, solitude and warmth for as long as possible.

It took almost half an hour for her brain to start spinning through the long list of things that she had to do today. The apartment needed tidying. All the cupboards were empty. There were clean clothes to put away and plants to water. She owed Jasvinder a visit to thank him, again, for looking after the cat. She wanted to check that the building's security manager had completed all the upgrades she had recommended and incorporated her new CCTV feeds into their live surveillance. And all of that needed to be done before she went back to work. It might be a Saturday, but it was a very special Saturday.

Once she'd laid out what had to be done, she had no choice but to get up. While her second coffee brewed and the bread was in the toaster, she ran a fast stocktake of the empty cupboards and placed an order for delivery. A thought flashed through her mind that a smart fridge would have done most of this for her automatically. She squashed the idea firmly. She was not getting a smart fridge under any circumstances.

Nibbling on her toast, she walked around the apartment, collecting things that were out of place and putting them away. The place looked a lot better without cushions spread on the floor, shoes scattered by the door, and a nest of cables on the worktop. The plants that had been looking very sorry for themselves perked up with some water.

She finished her breakfast and emptied the overflowing rubbish bin, dropping the bag into a chute in the hallway. An alert on her phone announced the arrival of the supermarket delivery drone. She checked the feed from the balcony cameras and saw a familiar heavy-duty drone waiting for her, emblazoned with the livery of the supermarket and laden with bags. She opened the shutters and collected her shopping.

Once she had finished all of her chores, the apartment looked lighter, brighter and more lived in. It had taken her less than an hour. Satisfied, Cameron showered and changed, switched the little robot vacuum cleaner on, to the cat's evident disgust, and set out for the office.

She knocked on Jasvinder's door on the way down but there was no answer. She left a quick video message on his doorcam, then went to the security office. They were all smiles, eager to show her everything that they had done. She checked and tested the upgrades and feeds, thanked them for the speed with which they had responded, and reminded the manager that she was waiting for their purchase order for support and maintenance.

She set off down the road with a spring in her step. It was sunny and warm, and she was looking forward to walking to the office, but Pete's warnings rang in her ears, and she eventually gave in and picked up an autocar just south of the bridge.

Pete was already in, and he'd evidently been watching for her to arrive.

"Glad to see you're taking things seriously," he said.

"It's doing nothing for my fitness levels, Pete," said Cameron. "I can't train until my shoulder's healed, and now I can't walk anywhere, either."

Her good mood was in danger of evaporating, but then she caught sight of Noor's model spinning gracefully on its plinth, new gossamer threads linking the different parts of the web.

"Wait," she said, "you've added some connections here. Where did these come from?"

Pete looked uncharacteristically smug. "Me," he said. "I went back to our client with some questions about the betting market and they replied overnight. Joel and Shell were absolutely right. Sapphire Straits isn't just the biggest casino chain in the world, it owns several other chains and half of our client's online betting competitors. They're not popular with the independents and smaller chains. It sounds as if they've ridden roughshod over the whole industry in the past ten years or so."

"How did we not pick that up before?" asked Cameron, turning the model idly and tapping at the new nodes.

"They don't use the parent brand other than for the casinos, and they had no reason to trigger our interest," said Pete. "We knew about some of the subsidiaries, but we had no idea of the scale of the thing. If my calculations are correct, Sapphire Straits is bigger than the Sladen Group. Chaoxiang Chen is one of the richest people in the world, and you hear nothing about him at all."

"Hiding in plain sight," said Cameron. She spun the model around one more time then wandered away towards the great glass windows that looked out over the rooftops of London. "The more we dig, the more we find. There's never a simple resolution, is there?"

Pete laughed. "Of course there isn't, Cameron," he said. "We wouldn't be in this business if it was easy."

Cameron was peering down at the street below. "Here comes Sandeep," she said, "and I think, yes, that's Susie getting out of a cab. Joel and Martha are just coming for the opening ceremony party, aren't they?"

"Yes," said Pete, "they've got family stuff to do. Noor will be back in this afternoon. She's got some things to sort out, she said."

Sandeep clattered through the door and dropped three big bags on the kitchen counter. "I picked up a few bits and pieces for this evening," he said. "Delivery drones will be like gold dust during the opening ceremony. It's not worth bothering with them."

Pete went over to the kitchen to help Sandeep unpack. "You've thought of everything," he said, holding a bottle of beer approvingly up to the light.

Cameron joined them. "Wine, bread, cheese, cold meat," she said, digging down to the bottom of the nearest bag. "Ooh! What's this?"

"Brennevin," said Sandeep. "It was either shots of Icelandic aquavit, or rotten shark."

"Ugh," said Susie, walking into the office. "Rotten shark? I'll pass."

Cameron made a face. "I guess Brennevin was the lesser of two evils," she said. "We'd better get a lot of work done today, because no one will be in a fit state to think tomorrow if we finish all this."

"It's not that bad," said Sandeep. "There'll be, what, seven of us with Martha."

"Nine," said Pete. "I've got the boys this weekend and they're coming along."

"Ten," said Cameron. "I've invited Ben. Your kids aren't drinking, are they, Pete?"

"My eldest's at college now, Cameron," said Pete. "They've grown up since you last saw them. They might have a can or two, but your Brennevin's safe."

"Ben's coming?" said Sandeep. "That's good news. It'll be nice to catch up with him."

Everything was stowed in the cupboards and fridge, and Cameron realised that time was ticking. "We'd better get back to work," she said. "Who wants some coffee?"

Sandeep had already switched the machine on. "I'm on it," he said. "What's the plan for today?"

Cameron scrolled through the latest raft of notifications. "I'm going to focus on MIST," she said. "I've given them everything I have so far. These last few hours are all about catching any loose ends. Sandeep, do you want to join me?"

"Sure," said Sandeep, putting a mug of coffee in front of her.

"I'm still cataloguing those files," said Susie. "I have some concerns. We've seen some of the things Jack authorised, but they feel like they're well-chosen decision points that make the reader think he was involved in far more of the process than he actually was."

"Really?" said Cameron. "Is someone trying to frame him?"

"Maybe," said Susie. She went over to Noor's model and turned it, looking for her existing threads and adding notes. "For example, he signed off hiring Ella and Angus, but he seems to have had no oversight of the rest of the tender process."

"Interesting," said Cameron. "That bears out what he said to me. Let's spend some time on this together, later. Anything else jumping out at you?"

"Well," said Susie slowly, "I might have an idea about Yasmin's whereabouts. It's not explicit anywhere, but I want to know what the MetaBand processors are actually processing."

"It's all the Diaulos blockchain, isn't it?" said Sandeep, who had been listening in.

"Not entirely," said Susie. "There's more to that hardware than meets the eye."

"I'm going over to the archery arena soon," said Pete. "I'm planning to do a full write up of their tech stack and I can run some tests if they have MetaBand links. I'm 99% sure they will. If Noor gets back in time, she can come with me. If not, will you, Cameron?"

"Sure," said Cameron. "I'm ready when you are."

•

After making some arrangements with a clandestine connection to recover the stolen papers, Tenuk spent the day wandering in the glorious surroundings of the Gardens by the Bay. The march of a changing climate had wrought changes on the great park, but it was still his favourite place in the world, and he revelled in being back there in person. He would stay in Singapore just for this if he could.

He used the time to clear his head and reflect on the recent turbulent days and the difficult decision he had made. His father had ripped him from a new life that he was building back to the old life for which he ached, and he wasn't sure if he loved or hated him for it.

He didn't want to go back to the house yet. He lay on a carved bench in a quiet grove surrounded by hedges and stared up at the sky. When his smartscreen vibrated, it made him jump. He ignored it. He didn't want to speak to anyone who had his ID. Not his father, not Jack Sladen.

The screen kept vibrating.

Annoyed, he pulled it out of his pocket to reject the call and stopped dead. It was neither of the people he had expected. The tag was anonymous but geolocated to the UK. Who did he know there, other than connections whose tags he would have recognised? There was only one person he could think of. Instead of rejecting the call outright he answered it, hope mounting.

"Who is this?" he asked. "How did you get this ID?"

"It wasn't hard," said a British voice that he knew instantly. He heard it in his dreams.

"Why – how – after all this time?" said Tenuk. He swung his feet onto the floor and sat up.

"I want to know, Tenuk," said the voice. "Is he your father? Is Chaoxiang Chen your father?"

"Yes," said Tenuk.

"I wanted to be sure," said the voice. "This was the fastest way to find out."

"Are you okay?" said Tenuk.

"Goodbye," said the voice.

"Noor!" he shouted, his cry startling the birds that had been pecking at the grass around his feet. It was no use. He tried to call her back, but the line was dead.

Tenuk kicked at a tree root in frustration and anger. In that moment he knew that he would give all of this up for her, and that he would never have the chance to do so. He pulled his MerLions cap low over his face and crept out of the grove. He knew that any security cameras would match him to the profile of a tourist from America, but he did not want to risk being recognised by people he had known. He crossed into the great Marina Bay Sands complex and out to the plaza on the other side where he picked up an autocar back to his father's house. It was time to rest before the opening ceremony began.

•

Pete and Cameron met Noor as they were walking out of the revolving door at the bottom of the office block. She looked preoccupied, but as soon as she saw them, she brightened up and smiled.

"Are you off to the arena already?" she said. "Do you still need me to come with you?"

"We'll be okay," said Cameron. "Sandeep and Susie are upstairs. We've added some extra connections to the model that you could check over. It's looking very good."

Pete had waved down a passing autocar. "Come on," he said. "They're expecting us."

The car took them east towards the huge conference centre next to the Thames that had been fitted out for multiple types of competition. Cameron and Pete left the car at the main entrance, but it took them another ten minutes of wandering through the broad halls to find the right venue.

"Archery?" ventured Pete to a bored security guard.

"Yes, mate," said the guard. "Are they expecting you?"

"We've come to see Pavel Wrzesinski," said Pete.

The security guard nodded and picked up his radio. "Pavel?" he said. "People to see you." He looked questioningly at Pete.

"Peter Iveson, Cameron Silvera, Argentum Associates," said Pete loudly. The two of them held out their hands and the guard scanned their ID chips.

"Yeah, yeah, that's them," he said to the unseen listener, "all checked in." He put the radio down and turned to Pete. "Five minutes."

In fact, it was barely one. A slim, blond man stuck his head out of the door and gave them a stressed smile. "Pete? Cameron? I'm Pavel. Come with me."

The competition space was long and thin, a much smaller area than Cameron had expected. *This may not be as complex as she'd first feared.* Pavel showed them into the control centre and gave them a whistlestop tour of the different systems that combined to deliver a hybrid event.

"This is all environment," he said, pointing to a set of data readouts and thermostat controls. "We track temperature, humidity, air quality, the whole works, so that every archer around the world is competing in roughly the same conditions, within reasonable limits."

Pete nodded, taking notes. Cameron knew that even something as simple as an arena's environment going beyond the set parameters could invalidate an athlete's performance. This would be a straightforward attack vector if someone wanted to disrupt a competition, but she felt it wasn't subtle enough for the bet fixing scam.

"Then there are the targets themselves," said Pavel. "Follow me."

They walked down the long room to the targets that were already set up for the event.

"It's a long way," said Pete.

"Standard 70 metres," said Pavel. "Here. The targets are bristling with sensors. They detect the precise impact point of the arrows and score them automatically."

Cameron looked at Pete. "That's one possible route, I guess," she said. "Manipulating the result through those sensors."

Pavel shook his head. "There'd be an appeal if the sensors didn't report what everyone can see," he said. "If the feed fails for any reason there's backup image analysis to confirm the result."

"Okay," said Cameron. "That makes it more unlikely. What else is collecting data?"

"There are the skinsuits," he said, "but there's no way anyone's getting into them. The Olympic network security is top notch."

Cameron smiled at his confidence and his naivety. Anything was hackable. "I didn't realise archers used skinsuits," she said. "I can understand it for gymnastics or karate or things where the judges are looking at the minutiae of muscle movement, but why here?"

"Let me show you," said Pavel. He led them back up to the arena entrance, pointing out camera arrays in gantries above them and to the side of the room. "We have 3D cameras filming for broadcast," he said. "The skinsuits allow us to have fully realised avatars in the virtual environments. I know it's not judged, but fans like to see the detail of the technique."

Cameron tapped notes into her smartscreen. "I'd like to see one of these skinsuits," she said. "Now, what's the network spec for the uplink?"

"State of the art MetaBand," said Pavel. "It was only installed two weeks ago and it's fantastic. Fastest transmission I've ever seen. We had a big security update just this morning, too. I don't think you have anything to worry about."

"Are all the arenas on MetaBand?" asked Pete.

Pavel nodded. "As far as I know, yes," he said. "There was a bit of a scramble to get some of the more remote sites hooked up but as far as I know the whole global Olympic network is on the latest upgraded MetaBand now."

"Can we run some tests on that connection?" asked Cameron.

"Sure," said Pavel. "The boss told me to let you have access to anything you needed. I know you're both part of the big infosec team that's overseeing the event. Anything that keeps us safe is good with me. I want these games to be a success."

"Thanks, Pavel," said Cameron. "We'll do our best." She looked at Pete. "The skinsuits would be my biggest concern, and there are question marks over the environmental controls and the targeting. If you can have a look at the control software. I'll deal with the hub."

Tucked in a tight corner by the main MetaBand hub, Cameron pulled out her smartscreen and opened the diagnostic tools that she had picked up from Eden weeks before. "Right," she muttered to herself. "Let's see if these are doing what they're supposed to." She hooked up to the MetaBand and watched the results scroll across her screen.

"There's a lot of processing going on there," said Pavel, looking over her shoulder. "Is every single MetaBand hub a node on the Diaulos blockchain?"

Cameron shook her head. "Only the home hubs, as far as I know," she said. "All the hubs are the same spec, but business contracts and broadcast hubs like this get the full package. The home hubs have much lower processing requirements, so they have the excess capacity to hold a copy of the ledger and validate transactions. For a high bandwidth operation like this, there shouldn't be any Diaulos link at all."

"There's no broadcast activity at the moment, either," said Pavel. "We've done all our dress rehearsals for the opening ceremony, and we won't be live again for another few hours. There shouldn't be anything running on that hub at all."

Cameron looked up at Pavel in confusion. "Did you say you're doing part of the opening ceremony?" she said. "How does that work?"

Pavel looked worried for a moment, then laughed. "I guess I can tell you," he said. "We have some of the hybrid athletes joining the parade as avatars."

"Brilliant," said Cameron, her eyes dancing. "I'll look out for them."

"It's going to be even better than you think," said Pavel. "I can't spill all the secrets, but let's just say this is going to be spectacular."

"We'd better hope that nothing disrupts it," said Cameron.

"Do you think that's likely?" asked Pavel, concerned.

"Not really," said Cameron. "We've thrown all the security you can possibly imagine at this to make sure it goes smoothly." She adjusted a couple of parameters on the diagnostic tool and a rush of activity lit up her screen. She straightened up, favouring her weak arm. "I'm going to leave that running for a short while to collect more data. Pete?" she called. "Need a hand with the sensors?"

"Yes, please," said Pete from the far end of the range where he was peering at one of the targets. "We still need a skinsuit for testing."

Pavel unlocked a tall wardrobe and there, hanging ready for the next day's competition, were the suits.

"Are they measured for each athlete?" asked Cameron.

"No," said Pavel. "They mould to the competitor when they put them on, so they can be re-used throughout the Games." He pulled one skinsuit out of the cupboard and handed it to her. "Here you go."

"Thanks," said Cameron. She lifted the suit up by its shoulders and stared at it. Fully connected to MetaBand with sensors for motion capture and sensors for fit. It was far too clever for a piece of clothing, and that made it a perfect target for anyone who might want to cause trouble. They'd found the most likely attack vector. Now to work out how to counter it.

·

The last two investigators were still out on the mountainside. Daniel, shaking from lack of sleep, winced as he watched them tramp across the glacier from the cupola's emergency exit. Every faint pink footprint on that ice caused the glacier to break down a little further. He knew they had no real alternative, but he hoped that they would be back inside soon. The beanbags in the cupola were comfortable but the cold air kept him awake and alert enough to answer their questions.

Yes, he'd found Aron sleepwalking before. Yes, he'd reported it to HR. No, he didn't have any idea what had led to this tragedy other than stress. Did he himself use the Sanctuary to help him sleep? No, Daniel replied. His job was demanding, and he slept naturally after every shift. He'd never bothered to try the Sanctuary even though it was on offer to every employee. No, he wouldn't be trying it now.

The investigator let him go, sympathetic to the fact that it was Daniel who had witnessed Aron's final fall into oblivion. Daniel stumbled down the stairs, exhausted beyond measure, and turned automatically towards his office and his quarters.

In the corridor he met Johanna, the shift leader who had been in the brightly lit data centre before Aron died. She looked as tired as Daniel felt.

"Are they done with you?" asked Daniel.

"I think so," said Johanna. "We've been going over that server stack with a fine-toothed comb and we've found nothing. I have no idea what poor Aron was doing there."

Daniel wondered if there was more to it. "Could he have accessed anything else in that room?" he asked. "If you're sure that nothing's been tampered with in the stacks, what about other systems? What else was controlled from there?"

Johanna shrugged. "Some of the security settings, but Aron had nothing to do with them," she said. "There's nothing untoward there. The allowlist on the web application firewall is watertight so only sources that we've authorised are getting through."

"Are things ramping up for the opening ceremony?" asked Daniel.

"Very much," said Johanna. "We've seen a big spike in data transfers in and out in the last couple of hours, but that's to be expected. There've been a couple of early qualifiers that didn't fit in the main timetable, and we've had a lot of traffic to the metaverse fabric with fans getting in early for the show and buying virtual merchandise. It's all pretty much in line with what we were expecting."

"That's good," said Daniel. "I'd love to watch the opening ceremony. How long have we got before it starts?"

"Three hours," said Johanna. "I'm going to get my head down while I can. I want to watch it too, but I'm wrecked, and I don't know if I'll be able to sleep without the Sanctuary." She shuddered. "I'm not going there again."

If the word got out, the Sanctuary was going to have a hard time staying in business, thought Daniel. There was no indication at all that the sleep aid had anything to do with Aron's actions and his death, but the sight of him slipping and sliding blindfold across the glacier would haunt Daniel for a long time.

"I'm going to try and sleep for a bit too," said Daniel. "I really want to see the ceremony. My cousin's there in Iceland. Her partner's a triathlete on the British team."

"Very cool," said Johanna. She yawned suddenly, and Daniel felt an irresistible urge to do the same. "Sleep well," she said.

"You too," he replied.

Daniel's eyelids were heavy by the time he reached his quarters and closed the door, but there was one more thing he needed to do. He pulled out his smartscreen and sent a message to Michelle. It was strictly against regulations, and he could lose his job if they found out, but the code that the cousins had used between them since childhood was pretty much impenetrable. She alone would understand what had happened and what Daniel's fears were, and if there was any foundation to them, she and her team would track down the perpetrators. It was the least he could do for Aron.

20: LONGBOATS

There was a dull pop as Joel uncorked a bottle of bubbly. "Who wants some?" he said, looking around at his colleagues. "We have to celebrate one of our own making it all the way to the Olympic Games."

Noor held out her glass. "Me, please," she said. "I'm so glad to see Ross there, you know. It's been a long journey." She took a sip of her drink. "And I don't mean the trip up to Iceland."

"I know what you mean," said Joel. He moved around the room with the bottle, refilling glasses. Most of the group were gathered around the big screen. Pete's teenagers were in the kitchen, staying close to the food. Cameron was sitting apart from everyone on the sofa by the window, talking quietly on her smartscreen. Joel went to tap her arm and she jumped, then extended her glass without a word.

"How many tickets did we get for the triathlon?" asked Pete. "There's enough for everyone, isn't there?"

Sandeep nodded. "Yes," he said. "Ross passed all his family allocation on to me which helped. We've got the full drone package for the whole event. We'll be following him all the way to the finishing line."

"Can we pick any medium to watch?" asked Noor, sipping her drink. "I mean, do we have a choice of flat screen or fully immersive?"

"I think so," said Sandeep. "As long as your identity matches the registered ticket you can go anywhere in the Olympic metaverse."

"Martha managed to score seats for some of the track and field finals," said Joel. "I've got the full immersive kit set up for us. It's going to be epic."

"Who's babysitting?" asked Pete with a laugh. "You can't keep an eye on that little whirlwind of yours when you're plugged into the VR."

"He'll be at nursery, thank goodness," said Martha. "It's during the day so we would both normally be at work." She nudged Joel. "You have booked the day off, haven't you?"

Joel looked guilty. "Uh, Cameron?" He twisted around to see if she had finished her call.

She was tucking the smartscreen back in her pocket and looked up when she heard her name.

"What's up?" she said.

"Can I have the day off a week on Friday?" said Joel. "I forgot to ask."

"No problem," said Cameron. "Martha already told me about the tickets months ago and I marked it on the calendar." She winked at Martha. "We're organised."

There was a buzz from the security intercom. "Visitor," said a tinny voice.

"That'll be Ben," said Cameron happily. She jumped up off the sofa and went to check the reception camera all the same. Sure enough, it was him. Behind him she could see that the atrium café was full of people, another party in progress. She pressed the intercom button.

"Send him up, sixth floor," she said.

Two minutes later the door opened, and Ben walked in. From the corridor came sounds of revelry. There were more than a few parties going on in the various offices around the building in addition to the one in the café right down at the bottom of the light well. Cameron knew that the basement level was occupied by the News Channel studios and hoped that they weren't being disturbed. Knowing Andy's colleagues, though, there would be a party going on down there, too.

Ben was looking refreshed and recovered after his flight. "Good to see you all," he said with a crooked smile that still made Cameron's heart melt when she saw it.

"Here, mate, have a drink," said Joel, pressing a glass of bubbly into his hand. "You're just in time."

Ben clinked his glass against Joel's and went to join Cameron at the back of the room. The music blaring from the wallscreen swelled as the Greek flag was carried into the stadium, commemorating the origins of the Olympic games.

"Did you know the Diaulos was a race in the ancient Olympics?" said Sandeep out of the blue. "Jack Sladen really went for every connection he could think of when he branded that system."

"I think he said as much when he launched it," said Cameron. She looked up at the wallscreen as the picture flickered and a QR code appeared. "Oh, what's that now?" she muttered to herself. She put her glass down on the nearest desk, picked up a burner device and scanned the code. "Hmm," she said. "Another competition link. It's asking for a lot of data. Excuse me a moment." She pulled out her own smartscreen and checked the MIST discussion forum. "Ah, it's been cleared for broadcast, but it's very badly designed. Terrible data privacy."

"Hush," said Noor. "The British flag's coming in now."

The flag bearer was Tasha, the captain of the women's hockey team, marching proudly with a huge grin on her face. Behind her came the rest of the athletes.

They were all glued to the screen, hunting for a familiar face.

"There he is!" cried Susie excitedly. "Third row back, behind the flag."

"Where?" asked Sandeep, squinting at the huge wallscreen. "I don't see him."

"Wait, they're zooming in on the delegation." Susie gestured at the top of the screen where the British athletes were coming into focus. Sure enough, a shock of ginger hair betrayed Ross, smiling and waving to the cameras.

"Who's that coming in alongside them?" asked Sandeep. "Are they… avatars?"

"Yes," said Cameron, excited. "This is what Pavel was talking about. They have hybrid athletes marching too."

"And some of the pure esports and gaming people," said Sandeep. "That's the British speedrunning champion flying in now, the one with the electric blue wings."

"Have you seen Shell in the crowd yet?" asked Cameron. "She's definitely there. I've just spoken to her."

"That's who it was," said Joel. "Everything okay?"

"Oh, she's fine," said Cameron, seeing the concern on Joel's face. "She just wanted to catch up. I think there's something she needs to tell us, but she couldn't risk it on the MetaBand connection. She hinted that she'd be sending us a postcard. I can't do anything until I know what it's all about."

The music from the wallscreen speakers swelled dramatically.

"Hush," said Susie. "Enough work-talk. We are supposed to be relaxing." She glared daggers at Joel and Pete.

"Oh!" cried Noor. "Look!"

All the country flags had been brought into the stadium and were now displayed beneath the Viking ship sculpture that would hold the Olympic flame. The athletes were taking their places in the stands and Cameron noticed that some were holding their screens up to see the augmented display, while others had reality glasses on. They'd all be getting a full view of the spectacle.

Dancers ran into the arena as the set shifted and changed. A wave of huge Viking warriors seemed to jump from the side of the longship, mirroring the movements of the dancers, choreographed with the music. Icelandic history and folk tales weaved together in the physical spectacle, and augmented reality Vikings, elves and trolls added a seamless extra dimension.

As the show reached its climax and the sky above darkened for the scant hour of night that Iceland had at this time of year, the augmented show came into its own, guaranteeing for the audience a breathtaking view of the Northern Lights, without relying on nature to perform on cue.

A pedestal began to rise from the arena floor accompanied by spectacular live pyrotechnics. Augmented reality overlaid a volcanic eruption, the creation of a new island. The fire and light show extended high up into the glowing sky, raining animated lava down over the stadium.

A great Viking warrior the height of the highest stands strode towards the longship sculpture with a blazing torch in his grip. At the same time, dancers dressed as Vikings and carrying the real Olympic torch emerged from the island pedestal, now on a level with the longship. They climbed the final steps and the torch bearer reached out to light the flame, timed perfectly with the giant augmented reality Viking bending to apparently do the same. The AR Viking raised its arms to the sky and flew upwards, disappearing into the aurora. A huge cheer rose from the stadium, and the games were underway.

•

At the Wrangell data centre, the spectacle of the opening ceremony was bittersweet. Daniel and Johanna and every colleague who was not currently on shift crammed into the breakout room to watch on the huge wallscreens. The servobot behind the counter served alcohol free fizz and snacks. The atmosphere was electric, but there was still an undercurrent of shock that one of their own was gone.

Daniel knew that the investigators were still on site, tucked in their private quarters and probably watching the same show. The cupola was out of bounds. Aron's roommates had been quietly moved to new quarters and the bunk room sealed. As head of security, he had a long few days ahead of him supporting the investigation. He also carried the guilty secret that he had tipped off Michelle, although he trusted her and the Argentum team to be utterly discreet.

The parade of flags began, and each member of the multinational audience in the breakout room cheered the appearance of their own home team. When the British flag appeared, Daniel raised a lone voice in support, then gave a delighted shout when he spotted Ross.

"See that guy there, with the ginger hair," he said excitedly. "I know him. That's Ross White, he's my cousin's partner."

A ripple of applause rang through the room. "That's so cool," said one of the girls from the infrastructure team. "What's his discipline?"

"Triathlon," said Daniel proudly.

The servobot popped another bottle of fizz and the party continued. Another loud cheer went up for the United States team, and then a final shout from the handful of Icelandic staff as the last flag appeared.

Daniel's eyelids were drooping with exhaustion by the time the great Viking lit the Olympic flame. He slipped out of the breakout room and made his way towards his quarters. As he turned into the long corridor, though, he spotted Johanna coming towards him, and realised that he might not get to bed any time soon.

"What's up?" he said, stifling a yawn.

"Daniel, glad I caught you," said Johanna. "It's been crazy in there tonight. On top of the traffic load of the opening ceremony's AR there's a lot of audience data being collected. We're holding close to five billon datasets now, what with the ticketing and all the real-time engagement tonight. But that's not why I need you. I wanted you to take a look at something for me."

"Sure," said Daniel, a little perplexed.

"I've been wondering how Aron got access to the data room," said Johanna.

Daniel frowned. "He's part of the tech team," he said. "He works in those data rooms. His chip's programmed to give him access. I'd be more confused if he'd walked into the kitchens."

Johanna shook her head. "No," she said. "The chip access to the data rooms themselves is time barred out of individual working hours. You should know this. You're head of security."

Daniel shook his head. "I knew that was possible," he said, "but it's set department by department, shift by shift. I don't keep up with who's been granted specific permissions at any time."

"That's fair," said Johanna.

Daniel realised that they were walking towards his office as they talked. "Have you had a look at the logs?" he asked.

"No," said Johanna with a tight smile. "I don't have the admin rights, but you do." She looked at him hopefully. "Am I jumping the gun on the investigation? Am I even allowed to ask this question?"

"It's okay," said Daniel. "No one else has asked. You're the first person to make the connection."

They had reached the door of the security office. Daniel scanned the lock and it opened.

Johanna hesitated. "I should get back to the data room," she said. "You know what you're looking for. Just tell me next time we see each other if I was right."

"Okay," said Daniel, puzzled. He watched her walk away down the corridor, wondering why she didn't want to follow up her hunch. He was wide awake and curious now.

It took a matter of minutes to run through the security protocols and find the logs that he needed. Sure enough, the data room shift patterns were synced with the access permissions. He started by checking for Aron's ID. His recorded movements were entirely as expected. He had been in and out of the data room half a dozen times during his shift. The last record showed him entering the bunk room on his way to bed. Daniel then checked the data room records for the time between that and Aron's desperate final moments on the ice.

There was nothing there. Daniel stared at the records, wondering if he was too tired to take the detail in. Johanna had gone in and out at the start of her own shift, and then returned with her colleague and raised the alarm. Had Aron simply walked from his bed to the cupola and out of the door? Was the alarm in the data centre's server stacks unrelated?

Mystified, Daniel went back to the day before when he had found Aron in the server stacks himself. Daniel could see his own entry and exit from the room, but no other records. According to the logs, Aron hadn't accessed the room at all, but Daniel had seen him there with his own eyes and helped him back to bed.

How could Aron have been able to move freely around the centre outside his usual shift pattern without leaving a footprint in the registers? Fully awake now, Daniel went in search of the investigation team. There was a new puzzle to solve.

•

Tenuk sprawled on the elegant sofa sipping a cocktail. It was two o'clock in the morning and his head was fuzzy with a combination of lingering jet lag and napping in the evening in order to be awake for the opening ceremony.

His father, uncle, various distant cousins and senior members of the household were gathered in the cinema room. Some people had chosen a fully immersive view, sitting with their reality masks on and occasionally reaching out as if to touch the images that appeared before them. Tenuk had chosen the flat screen, partly because he could drink his Singapore Sling at the same time without missing his mouth or knocking the glass over. The little impracticalities of virtual reality tended to annoy him.

He didn't notice Xanthe come in. One moment he was alone with his drink and his thoughts, detached from the other people in the room and enjoying the spectacle on screen. Next moment his view was blocked by the slim android who had appeared beside his father. She bent and spoke quietly to him.

Chaoxiang nodded and stood up. He followed Xanthe to the door. As he passed Tenuk, he paused. "You should come," he said. "You will find this instructive."

They made their way through the dark hallways to the office. The room was lit by the flickering wallscreens, data scrolling rapidly up each display.

"What is all this?" said Tenuk.

"A harvest," said Chaoxiang. "Xanthe and her sisters, my operatives in the metaverse, your colleagues in the Steamyard and other networks, and of course Mr Jack Sladen, have all contributed to the greatest data harvest in history."

Tenuk stared in undisguised admiration at the screens. Names, addresses, IDs, wallet keys, photos, social handles, birthdates, and enough personal peripheral information to crack authentication in a fraction of a second.

"Where has it all come from?" asked Tenuk. But he knew the answer. He was watching the inevitable endgame of his efforts to free Yasmin, his manipulation of Jack Sladen, his amendments to the MetaBand designs, and of contracts he and his teams had delivered over the years. He recalled work for shady clients from data capture popups and cloned websites to viral social games and malware to open paths through firewalls. Had all those commissions been initiated by his father?

"This is just the beginning," said Chaoxiang, reading his mind. "We now have infinite resources to exploit. Can you see why you are needed?" He turned away from the wallscreens and smiled at his son. "I am glad that you came to the right decision."

Data was still streaming through. Tenuk peered closer at the ticker that was counting every unique data set. As he watched, the first number flicked from a three to a four. Four billion people ripe for exploitation. It was already at the scale of the largest data breach in history, and the count showed no signs of slowing.

21: A PAIR OF BLUE EYES

The opening ceremony was over, and the office parties were running out of steam. By mutual consent, the Argentum team tidied up the debris of the night and left the building along with a steady stream of people from neighbouring companies. Pete and his boys were heading to the tube and back home. Joel and Martha, taking full advantage of having a babysitter, were off to their favourite club to dance the night away. It took very little persuading for the rest of the group to join them.

By two in the morning Cameron was exhausted and her feet hurt from dancing, but she was happier than she had been for a long time. Ben was obviously enjoying himself too. Perhaps it would be alright between them after all. The atmosphere in the club was electric. The DJ, silhouetted behind a screen, kept the crowd on their feet for hours with a mesmerising set and a dazzling display of 3D and augmented graphics. He'd even included a nod to the Olympics with a blazing Viking ship sailing the virtual seas above the crowd.

The night was coming to an end. Revellers spilled out onto the street where a line of autocars sat charging, ready for action. When Cameron's turn came, Ben climbed into the car with her. "I'll see you home," he said, taking her hand.

Everything was quiet in the little courtyard outside the apartment. Lights sensed their approach and illuminated the entrance, the hallway, the stairs. Talking in low voices, they climbed slowly to the top floor. Cameron pulled a key out of her pocket and slid it into the keyhole, then frowned. She knew she'd locked it this morning.

Her chip had activated the other lock and Ben pushed the door open. Cameron followed him. The sitting room light sensed movement, glowed into life, and illuminated a scene of devastation.

"Shit, Cameron," said Ben, standing stock still with his mouth open.

The room that she had so painstakingly tidied had been turned upside down. Her computers were nowhere to be seen. The balcony shutters were up and the window open. Cameron gasped and ran to the bedroom. Her wardrobe had been ransacked and clothes littered the bed. Ignoring the mess, she dived down to the floor and peered under the bed.

Her whole body relaxed. "Puss, puss," she cooed. "I'm here. Come on, sweetheart."

The little black and white cat squeaked pathetically and stayed firmly in her corner. Cameron felt Ben lie down next to her.

"Hush," she said. "I don't want to scare her even more."

"I'll close the windows and find some treats," said Ben, ever practical.

Cameron reached a hand towards the cat, still a good metre short of where the little animal was cowering. In the background she could hear the hum of the electric shutters and the click of the window lock, then the clatter of cupboards as Ben tried to remember where she kept the cat treats. He was back remarkably quickly. Together they set a trail of treats and watched as the cat sniffed the air, unwound itself, and crept cautiously towards the first treat.

It took another few minutes for the cat to emerge. Cameron tipped out that last few treats, watched affectionately as the cat scoffed them in short order, then picked it up and hugged it tightly.

"Clever girl," she whispered. "You'll be alright."

She put the cat down on the bed and for the first time took notice of the chaos around her. She walked back to the sitting room, took stock of the empty desk and dangling cables, and sat down heavily on the sofa. Ben put his arms around her and hugged her as hard as she had hugged the cat.

"We should call the police," he said.

"My security setup should have done that automatically," said Cameron. "I'm very surprised they haven't arrived yet." She opened a control panel on her smartscreen and frowned. "That's odd," she continued. "The alarm hasn't triggered, and, oh, dammit, there's no footage. Someone's taken the whole system out. That shouldn't be possible."

She went to call Sara Mercer directly, then realised it was three in the morning. Instead, she made an emergency call. "I'm not opening the balcony up again," she said. "They'll have to come to the door."

Reluctant to touch anything, Cameron curled into the sofa cushions and Ben held her tight. The cat crept warily along the corridor and bravely hopped up onto her knee. They sat quietly together in a still tableau, waiting for the police.

Ben broke the silence. "You can't stay here, Cam," he said softly. "It's not safe anymore."

"I know," she said huskily. She stroked the cat gently, relieved that the vendetta against her had not harmed the little creature. "I didn't want to go before." She gestured around her. "This is my home. Was." She looked down at the cat. "We'll have to find a new place, won't we?"

The sound of a drone on the other side of the shutters and feet on the stairs was enough to spook the cat again. It disappeared towards the bedroom, its tail bushy with adrenaline, seeking its hiding place under the bed.

Cameron stood up and went to the door, carefully checking the credentials that were sent to her before opening it. The young police officers were patient and kind. Cameron let them take stock of the apartment. No, they hadn't moved anything other than closing the shutters and looking for cat treats. Ben confirmed that he had wrapped his hand in his shirt before touching the window controls and the kitchen cupboards. As Cameron expected, the two first responders were quickly joined by a more senior officer who knew the score. She recognised him from the previous week. Was it only eight days since Arthur Paxton had attacked her? It seemed much longer.

"Do you have anywhere you can stay tonight?" asked the senior officer.

"With me," said Ben instantly. He gave them his address.

Cameron went to her bedroom and filled her overnight bag. She was surprised to find that her jewellery box was still intact. The motive had been a very specific robbery, then. They hadn't bothered to cover their tracks by searching for other valuables. All they wanted were Cameron's hard disks.

Bag packed, she clambered carefully up to the highest cupboard above the bed and found the cat carrier. "Can you give me a moment?" she asked the police officer.

She closed the bedroom door and opened the other packet of cat treats. This time it was harder to coax the little animal out, but eventually Cameron succeeded in trapping it and got it into the carrier. "Here," she said, pushing treats through the cracks. "Don't complain. It's for your own good."

There was a knock at the bedroom door. "Are you all set?" said Ben.

"Yes," said Cameron. "Can you take my bag?"

The police had a car ready for them. Dawn was breaking as they arrived at Ben's door. Exhausted by the shock and the disruption of the past few hours, they tumbled into bed. The cat, sensing peace, crept out of her carrier and settled between them on the duvet. All three of them slept.

The insistent ringing of two smartscreens and the doorbell finally woke Cameron and Ben.

"The police are outside," said Ben, nudging Cameron. "DI Mercer and a couple of mates."

"Tell her I'll be right there," said Cameron, yawning. She clambered out of bed and dug in the bag that Ben had brought the night before to find the cat's bowl and food. The sound of kibbles hitting the bowl drew the little animal out from the corner it had chosen to snuggle in, and Cameron watched it fondly while she found something to wear.

DI Sara Mercer, usually completely unflustered, was as close to looking stressed as Cameron had ever seen her.

"You made the right decision, coming here," said Mercer seriously. "Twice in less than ten days, Cameron. What do you think they were after?"

"Something related to my work," said Cameron. "It wasn't a conventional robbery, that's clear. They only took the computers and left anything else of value alone."

"What I don't understand is why they ransacked the apartment after taking those," said Mercer. "What else could they have been looking for?"

Cameron shrugged. "I really don't know," she said. "I took an inventory of everything that I believe is missing." She showed Mercer a list on her smartscreen.

"All drives and disks, basically," said Mercer. "And I assume that all of these were located close together?"

"That's right," said Cameron. "Why they would think I had anything in my knicker drawer is beyond me."

Ben suddenly looked serious. "Cameron," he said, "what about that file I brought back for you? Do you think they could have been looking for that?"

"No," said Cameron. "It's locked in the office vault. No one knows about it apart from us."

"And maybe, by now, Jack Sladen," said Ben.

"What file?" asked Mercer, her interest piqued.

"My undercover agent here brought me a present from Statesman Tech," said Cameron with a grin. She turned to Ben. "I didn't tell you the details, but we found some juicy things in there."

"I can sort out some extra security on the office if you like," said Mercer, "although knowing you, it's already locked down tight."

"That would be useful," said Cameron. "Whoever entered my apartment had made sure that all my security systems were disabled. It shouldn't have been possible in just a few hours."

"Unless, of course, they had some help," said Mercer. She beckoned one of her colleagues over. "Gray's Inn Road," she said. "This is the address. Make sure they don't let anyone in who shouldn't be there. And even if they should be there, don't let anyone up to the Argentum offices. Put a separate guard on the door if you need to."

She turned back to Cameron. "What about your team members?" she asked. "Do we need to secure their homes too?"

"Maybe," said Cameron, "especially Ross and Michelle. Their place will be covered already as they're at the Olympics, but an extra layer of security can only be helpful."

Mercer nodded at her colleague. "Add them to your list," she said. "Now, Cameron, this file," she said. "Tell me about it."

Ben explained where it had come from, and Cameron picked up the story.

"We're still working through it," she said, "but it's all to do with the MetaBand designs."

"I've never trusted that network," said Mercer.

"I did before," said Cameron, "but I don't trust it now. There's no doubt that with the new MetaBand and the Diaulos project and the Sladen Foundation that Jack has done some great things to improve network access and help people who're disadvantaged. I just wish it was all straightforward and above board."

"I take it what you've found just adds to all the loose ends that we didn't manage to tie up," said Mercer.

"It's bad," said Cameron. "There are things in there that could implicate Jack Sladen in decisions that he claimed in the enquiry he never made. He seems to have agreed the design changes to the MetaBand hubs, for starters."

"Really?" said Mercer. "You're right, this file of yours could be trouble." She was silent for a moment as she worked though the implications. "You're saying that you, Ben, brought this file back from America and handed it to Cameron."

Ben nodded. "That's right," he said. "The only other person who knows I had it, apart from the Argentum team, is Chloe."

The door opened and a police officer walked in. He bent to speak to Mercer. She listened carefully, her face impassive, then turned back to look at Ben.

"I don't think that's the case anymore," she said. "Security guards at your office building reported an unknown man trying to gain access to the building very early this morning."

"Did they get him?" asked Cameron.

"Sadly not," said Mercer. "He legged it as soon as they challenged him. We're waiting for CCTV and bodycam footage, although if your systems were compromised, I wouldn't be surprised if those were, too."

Cameron stood up and started pacing around the room. "But if someone knows that I had that file," she said, "and they didn't find it in my flat, and they can't get into the office, where else would they look?"

"Indeed," said Mercer, looking directly at Ben. "I wonder if they know who brought it here."

"But that would mean…," said Cameron.

"Exactly," said Mercer. "I don't think it's sensible for either of you to be here. I can organise a safe house, if you like?"

"Better still," said Cameron, "can you organise one of those super-secure satlinks at my brother's house? The village is the safest place I know," she said to Ben with a smile, "and Aunt Vicky is dying to see you."

•

Cameron showed Ben the drawing on her smartscreen. "What do you think?" she said.

Ben considered it from every angle. "Not bad," he said. "I think it conveys the details very well, without displaying any artistic merit whatsoever."

Cameron punched him playfully on the arm. "That's what I was going for," she said. "It's got to make sense to the recipient but bear no relation to any data sets or image recognition software."

The little cartoon strip she'd devised showed a fox creeping into an apartment and emerging with a computer, and two figures with a cat and a train and a bunch of grapes. She hoped that everyone on the team would get the references. The grapes were a little obscure, but she'd talked about the village vineyards before, and she could hardly write 'gone to Charlie's' across the page. A final panel showed a grinning face with a set of perfect teeth, one coloured blue. That would be obvious. Use Bluetooth to communicate whenever you can, it said, and by implication, avoid MetaBand.

Cameron sent the message to the whole Argentum team, including Ross and Michelle, and then packed her smartscreen away as the train approached their destination. Their departure had been too hasty for Mercer to organise cars that would disguise their route. The safest option had been to take them to Euston station where Cameron bought tickets with an anonymous wallet, and then for another police car to pick them up at the other end, avoiding a call to Charlie or an autocar booking. It also gave Mercer time to make some special arrangements.

When the police car pulled up at the house, Charlie came charging out, wondering what was going on, and stopped in confusion when he saw his little sister.

"Cam?" he said. "I expected you to come home in a squad car a few times when you were younger, but I thought you were behaving yourself these days." He spotted Ben coming around the other side of the car. "Hello, Ben, nice to see you again. Why do you have the cat with you? Family day out to the country?"

Cameron laughed, relieved to be safe. "There's a good explanation," she said. "First, though, these lovely police officers have some work to do."

Charlie shrugged, defeated. "I can't keep up with you," he said. "Get yourselves indoors. If you can install the cat in the attic, that'd be great. Roxy'll go nuts as soon as she realises it's here."

"Will do," said Cameron. "Could you show these folks where your network connection is?"

"The new MetaBand?" said Charlie. "You're not going to mess with it, are you? It's very good."

"Don't worry," said Cameron. "You're getting something better and more secure." She turned to the police technician. "Can you keep the MetaBand hub live once it's disconnected from the house? It might be useful."

Charlie looked serious now, and Cameron knew he'd worked out some of what was going on. Without another word he led the police officers away, and Cameron and Ben went into the house.

All was quiet. The kids must be in their rooms or out and about. The attic was just as she'd left it, her domain at the top of the house. Ben closed the door to the stairwell carefully behind them and Cameron let the cat out of its basket to explore.

Ben flung himself into a soft armchair. "Well," he said, "I didn't expect this weekend to include fleeing London and camping out at your brother's."

"Nor did I," said Cameron. "I'm sorry you got caught up in this."

Ben shook his head. "It's my own fault," he said. "I poked the hornet's nest with those MetaBand designs, and I agreed to help Chloe get the files out to you. If I hadn't done any of that…"

"…we would have been stumbling in the dark," said Cameron. "I know there are cybercriminals on my tail. I think Yasmin is out there and after me too, but I'm going to find her first. You haven't stirred the nest half as much as I have. You've helped."

"I should let Chloe know that the package was delivered," said Ben. "I don't know how to do that safely."

There it was again, the knot of jealousy in her stomach. "Once we have a secure connection, I can get hold of Chloe," she said.

"Great," said Ben, brightening.

That wasn't helping. Should she broach the subject, or leave it be? The two of them were getting on so well together that she didn't want to spoil it, but she knew that it would always be on her mind.

"Did you ever meet her daughter, Audrey?" asked Cameron. "She's friends with Tara."

Ben shook his head. "No, I didn't," he said, "but I saw plenty of photos." He looked sidelong at Cameron. "You do know we're just friends, don't you?"

"Oh!" said Cameron. "Yes, of course."

Ben stood up, walked over to her, took her face in his hands, and kissed her. "Don't worry," he said. "I've missed you, and I'm glad to be here." He smiled. "Let's nail these bastards once and for all. What do you need me to do?"

•

The police car had gone, and the network connection was back, much to the relief of the children who had come out of their bedrooms, complaining, as soon as the old one had gone off. Charlie, Sameena, Cameron and Ben settled in the quiet sitting room to watch the Olympics.

"Do I take it we now have a free and super secure connection, thanks to you?" said Charlie.

"Yes," said Cameron. "You're attached to the military grade network now. Somehow, they've tacked all your streaming services onto it. I'm not quite sure if those will always be free, though."

"And we're no longer a Diaulos network node," said Sameena. "From what you're telling us, that's safer."

Cameron grabbed a handful of crisps from the bowl on the table. "I think the Diaulos network is sound," she said, "but MetaBand isn't. I needed somewhere to work that couldn't be compromised, and to be honest it's probably safer for you too."

Ben gestured at the screen. "The 100 metre qualifiers are starting, look," he said. "This should be good." He reached over to the table and picked up his drink, settled back onto the sofa, and gave Cameron's hand a squeeze. "Relax," he said quietly. "It's been a pretty intense day."

She took his advice, forgetting for a short while about the chaotic flight from London, the rogue AI on her tail, and the work that she had to do. All her attention was on the athletes on screen and the people she loved around her. She felt the stress melting away.

Alas, it was short lived. An alarm on her smartscreen brought her back to reality.

"It's nearly time for the archery," she said. "I have to be online for this. We're pretty sure that there's an active cyberattack ready to roll but we're going to have to catch it in real time." She jumped up from the sofa, but paused when Tara's voice came from a hidden corner of the sitting room.

"Aunty Cam?" she said. Her face appeared around the back of Charlie's chair. "I'm going online too," she continued. "I promised Audrey that I'd see her in Sandland this afternoon. Do you want to meet her?"

"I'd love to," said Cameron, "but I'm not sure we're going to be in the same place."

Tara frowned. "Even if you can't come with me," she said slowly, glancing across at her mother as she spoke, "can you look out for something while you're there?"

"Sure thing," said Cameron. "What am I looking for?"

"There's this weird avatar with really bright blue eyes," said Tara. "She's creepy. She's always watching people. I don't know who she is in real life, but we've put loads of reports in about her and she never gets banned."

Cameron was careful not to let her alarm show. "You're right to report that kind of thing," she said approvingly. "Is she watching everyone? Can you block her?"

"We tried to block her, but she still appears," said Tara with a shrug. "Now we all just run away."

"Okay," said Cameron. "I'll come and meet Audrey. You get me for five minutes. Then I have to work."

Sameena looked keenly at the pair of them. She knew Cameron well enough to see that there was an undercurrent of concern, and she was ready to defuse the situation.

"It sounds like you have been doing the right things, Tara," she said. "You are very good at staying safe online. Say hello to Audrey for me. Now, would you like to take a snack with you?"

Tara grinned, grabbed an apple and a biscuit, and scampered upstairs.

Cameron gave Sameena a reassuring smile. "I'm sure it's nothing," she said. "I'll look after her. I won't be long. Watch the archery and let me know what you think."

She heard a parting chorus of "Good luck" from the sitting room as she ran up the stairs. She opened the door to the attic carefully in case the cat was lying in wait, but there was nothing waiting to pounce. It was sleeping soundly in the warmest place, squarely in a shaft of sunlight on a comfortable chair.

Cameron switched on her computer and checked out of sheer paranoia that it was hooked up to the new network. She opened her smartscreen and found a cryptic message from Pete.

'Targeting 5pm,' it said. 'Hope you haven't been outfoxed.'

He'd seen her cartoon strip and understood it then. Good.

'I'm all set,' she replied. 'I'm on the same network as the northern office.'

If Pete was confident of the security of his own network, then they would be able to chat. A few moments later, a call lit up Cameron's smartscreen.

"I'm in the office and hooked up to the same network as you," said Pete without preamble. "A helpful policeman came by earlier."

"They get about," said Cameron. "I think we all need one."

She and Pete had planned this operation carefully after their visit to the site, but the last twenty-four hours had been so fraught that she had to review the list of actions again.

"Has Mephisto picked up on any attack vectors that could introduce malware to the hub?" asked Cameron. "Any compromised emails, user details, that kind of thing?"

"Not so far," said Pete, "but there's bound to be something from weeks ago that opened a crack in the system's defences. You know how it goes."

Cameron knew only too well. "The one thing with this," she said thoughtfully, "is that we know the test run on the karate arena failed, and that there's a new version of the software being deployed."

"We don't know that for sure," said Pete. "How do you know your source is reliable?"

Cameron hadn't told Pete where that nugget of information had come from. Maybe now was the time. "Because it was me," she said with a sigh. "I didn't want to worry you before, but I eavesdropped on a conversation by chance in the Underworld. I recorded the whole thing and there's a backup in the office vault.

"You're right, I am worried," said Pete. "Great intel, Cameron, but you're putting yourself in danger. Remember that message? She will find you in every reality?"

"Not if I find her first," said Cameron. "Now, the data I captured from the arena hub is in our secure cloud. I think there's enough for me to make a start on analysing it."

"I see that," said Pete with a sigh. "You're not going to give up, are you?"

"No," said Cameron. "We've got a job to do. I have a live but blind MetaBand hub I can access here if I need to follow up any of the findings." What else was on her list? "Is Pavel all set to react if we see evidence of tampering?"

"Yes," said Pete. "Sandeep dropped the hardware off to them at lunchtime. They'll be able to reset the sensor connections to factory settings and divert to a different network."

"Good," said Cameron. "We need to see if there is a problem and what it is before we take any action, but at least we can fix it fast." She hoped that all their assumptions were correct. There were so many possible attack vectors, but the evidence they'd gathered pointed to disruption of skinsuit sensors to disadvantage a competitor. The malware contract Cameron had found in the Underworld talked of sensor connections. For Anita Trianna, the sensors in her motion capture skinsuit had appeared to stop transmitting. How could the result be manipulated through the suits worn by the archers? They were about to find out.

"Counting down," said Pete. "Ten minutes to go."

Cameron saw him turn away from the camera.

"Noor!" he said. "Just in time. Pull up a chair." He turned back to Cameron. "We'll keep an eye on everything here. What are you going to do?"

"I'm going back into the Underworld to watch the show," said Cameron. She was already loading the software she needed. "I want to see the reactions of people down there if there's any evidence of manipulation."

"I wish you wouldn't," said Pete, "but I understand why you're going in. Be safe. Stay on chat."

Cameron chose a new identity. Her avatar this time was more discreet, still far removed from her real self but today a stylised figure based on an old and beloved cartoon. She'd seen several of the same series in the Underworld, virtually identical characters in different colours with different hats. She would definitely blend in down there.

She put on her mask, picked up her controllers, took a deep breath, and dived into the metaverse. Her first stop was the upper level of Sandland. She pinged a message to Tara. 'Where are you?' she said.

Tara came straight back on voice chat. "Hi, Aunty Cam," she said. "We're in Pets Corner playing with the Axies."

Cameron knew exactly where that was. She jumped straight to the location and found two figures giggling together in the middle of a herd of cute multi-coloured cartoon creatures.

"Hi, girls," said Cameron. Her avatar bent down to pet an orange Axie with a turnip for a tail. It rolled over and wiggled its stumpy legs in the air.

"Is that you, Aunty Cam?" said Tara. "You don't look like you."

"I'm working," said Cameron. "Hi, Audrey. Nice to meet you. I've heard a lot about you from your mom. Does she come in here often?"

"Sometimes," said Audrey. "She's normally working, too."

Cameron watched the girls as they played, wondering idly what work Chloe had been doing here. They needed a catchup. A handful of other avatars arrived, and Cameron listened to the happy chatter and watched how they behaved. She was confident that these were all genuine friends, probably around the same age. It was a nice social group and Tara seemed happy.

The chatter died away and some instinct made Cameron turn. There, standing on the edge of the block, was a perfectly rendered female avatar with bright blue eyes. Its gaze was focused on Tara.

"Aunty Cam," said Tara, breaking the silence. "That's her."

As soon as Tara said her name, the avatar's eyes locked onto Cameron. It stared at her for a split second, then vanished.

She had seen those blue eyes before in a rippling, fracturing hologram in a Northumberland cave.

Yasmin.

22:   TARGETS

"Tara, Audrey," said Cameron, "you need to go, now. You're not safe."

"But Aunty Cam," said Tara, "she's gone."

Cameron shook her head. "She'll be back," she said. "You were right to ask me to look out for her. I think she's watching the pair of you, and I don't trust her."

In the real world, she heard Pete's voice. "They're starting," he said. "Are you all set, Cameron?"

She couldn't stay, and nor could the girls. "Come on, Tara," she said. "You did the right thing. Now, go. If you come back, you need me or Chloe with you."

"Okay," said Tara. "You'll be okay, won't you?" She sounded worried.

"I'll be fine," said Cameron. "Enjoy your snacks and I'll see you in real life in a little while."

She made sure the girls had logged out before jumping to the entrance to the Eden level. She lost no time diving down into the whirlpool. She met with the barman, picked up her bracelet, and followed her nose to the Underworld jump point. Once she'd landed, she went straight to the sports café that she had found before. It looked different today. A temporary open-air auditorium had been installed around the 3D representation of an arena and avatars of all shapes and sizes were crowded in the space. As she watched, the archers filed in and there were cheers from the crowd. The combination of 3D cameras and skinsuits was incredibly effective, thought Cameron. It felt as if she was looking at a single real arena with multiple competitors, rather than a composite of several locations around the world.

Cameron looked around for familiar faces. The monkey was nowhere in sight, which was a relief. It took her a while to spot the grey kitten lurking in a corner with a small group including another animal avatar that looked like a slim armadillo. A pangolin?

She crept closer to them, one eye on the action in the arena. She needed to be in earshot of the group, and her smartscreen was all set to record every whisper that came out of the computer audio.

Once in range, she stopped. Most of the audience was static, watching the contest, and any further movement would attract unwanted attention. This session was the seeding round, each athlete shooting six sets of twelve arrows to build an aggregate score. Cameron scanned the list of archers and identified the British athlete who featured on the tip she'd bought. She knew that up in the real world there was a very different favourite attracting bets, the American who was defending his Olympic title.

Cameron kept one eye and one ear on the group that she was observing, but they were largely silent for now, and most of her attention was drawn to the big screen. She was starting to enjoy the competition. There was a hum of excitement in the audience as the American wheeled into view. His first set put him into the lead by a whisker. A collective sigh of relief rippled around the watching avatars.

"He's not on his best form today," muttered the grey kitten. "That makes things easier."

Now it was the turn of the British archer. He settled into his pose, eyed the target and let his first arrow fly.

Cameron watched carefully. There was nothing that stood out as unusual. When the score came up, the British competitor was firmly in first place.

"Good," she heard the Pangolin say. "Very well done."

"Thank you, Pangolin," said the grey kitten, the relief in its voice palpable.

The display gave a closeup of the archer. He looked happy and a little surprised, but he was fidgeting uncomfortably, flexing his arms, rubbing each of them in turn.

"What the hell happened?" came Pete's voice in her ear.

"It's the skinsuit," said Cameron in a rush of realisation. "They used the skinsuit to control his aim. That wasn't him shooting. It was an AI delivering the result the clients wanted."

The attack was far more subtle than she could ever have expected. The malware that had been introduced into the system was not a blunt instrument but could apparently be controlled in real time. It was elegant and dangerous and hard to detect. She had a grudging admiration for the cybercriminals who had conceived and executed this malware, but that made her all the more determined to shut it down.

"That's brilliant," said Pete. "There has to be something very powerful running behind it, though."

"I could put a name to that," said Cameron grimly. "Have we got enough data to break their control link now?"

"I think so," said Pete, but Cameron wasn't listening.

A perfectly rendered female avatar had materialised in the group she was watching. It turned its bright blue eyes on her. She felt like a rabbit in the headlights. Back in Pets Corner, Tara had called her Aunty Cam. Her cover was blown.

Suddenly the view of the Underworld flicked out and Cameron realised that she had jumped against her will into an entirely new environment. She looked around. The floor was chequered, black and white. The room around her looked like a virtual warehouse with an art exhibition in progress. The artworks ranged from a classic Cryptopunk head to abstract forms. Cameron knew that she had seen one of them before, in Yasmin's deserted prison cell.

Standing in the middle of the room was the magnified form of the female avatar with the bright blue eyes. Now Cameron had no doubt who she was looking at.

"SimCavalier, I have you," said Yasmin.

"I don't think so," said Cameron. She pulled off her mask, the silicon wings tearing at her skin, and cut the network connection, abandoning her avatar to its fate. She sat shaking at her desk, taking in the sunlight and the familiar surroundings of real life.

"Cameron?" came Pete's voice again. "Are you okay?"

"Yes," said Cameron. "It's Yasmin. She's there. She's in the middle of all this."

"Shall I get Pavel to switch connections?" asked Pete.

"I don't know if it'll make any difference," said Cameron, "but do it anyway. We have to close this down. She's not going to get away with it."

She turned her mask over in her hands, wondering what her next move would be. Her target was Yasmin, and she would not rest until the AI was destroyed.

23: NODES

Cameron was up early, tapping away at her keyboard while Ben and the cat still slept. The analysis of the network traffic data they had gathered from the arena's MetaBand link was complete. She was looking for a peak at the time that the skinsuit had been manipulated, but there was nothing to find. On the other hand, her diagnostic tool was showing a vast amount of constant additional processing. She'd have expected that if the arena had held a Diaulos node, but, as she'd thought, the arena hub was not part of that network.

It looked for all the world as if there was a second distributed network node running in the arena hub that had nothing to do with Diaulos. Cameron didn't know what it could be, but she had no doubt that it had something to do with Yasmin. She made a note to run the same tests on the live hub that had been disconnected from the house.

The MetaBand operating system needed a thorough clean. Somewhere in the latest update, rolled out all over the world, was the malware that had allowed someone, somewhere to manipulate the archers' movements through their skinsuits. Cameron hadn't been back to MIST yet with her findings. She didn't trust the group anymore, but her contract was very clear. For the sake of the Olympic metaverse security and fair competition she would have to reveal what she knew, and soon. She wondered whether her team could get a head start on tracing the malware while she laid a trap for whoever had compromised the security of MIST.

"Good morning," said a croaky voice behind her. "Is that the time?"

Ben dropped a kiss on the top of her head, and she turned, smiling. His eyes were still sleepy, and his hair tousled. "What are you working on?" he asked.

"Analysing the MetaBand data traffic," said Cameron with a sigh. "Aren't you supposed to be back to work today?"

"I called in and explained there'd been a family crisis," said Ben. "They gave me another day off and I can work remotely in any case. Do you want some coffee?"

"Yes, please," said Cameron gratefully.

While Ben went in search of breakfast, Cameron contacted her team. Pete was already on the way to the archery arena to meet Pavel and try to find a way to protect the competitors at source. Cameron called the office, and Susie was the first to respond.

"I've just got in," she said. "The security is super tight. What's going on? Can you talk?"

"We're all on the same network you had up north now," said Cameron. She gave Susie a quick rundown of the events of the last day. "Could you make a start on picking apart the MetaBand operating system? It needs updating to wipe out the sensor malware. I'm not sure how we're going to roll it out, but we'll find a way."

"Of course," said Susie. "Are you and Ben okay, Cameron? Do you know what's missing?"

"We are fine," said Cameron, "and there was a lot of mess, but I've always expected that something like this might happen. The hard disks have stopped sending their location back to the police now so I'm guessing someone started poking around and triggered the automatic bricking. They'll be useless to whoever has them, but everything was backed up and stored in the office vault."

"You sound as if you're taking this in your stride," said Susie. "The others are on their way in. Between us we'll have this done and dusted before you know it."

"Fantastic," said Cameron. "Find a way to disable that malware, however quick and dirty. I'll make sure the update gets rolled out."

"You're going to talk to Jack?" said Susie.

"I guess I'm going to have to," said Cameron. "I'm not sure when. It's the middle of the night in Austin and he might still be too cross to take my call."

She closed the link to Susie as Ben came up the stairs.

"Sameena says she's making pancakes and you need to come downstairs," said Ben.

"Oh, if I must," said Cameron. "You really know how to distract me."

"Come on, Cameron, breakfast," said Ben. "The world is not going to rack and ruin if you take half an hour out."

"Is the coffee hot?" she asked, teasing.

"Yes," said Ben. "Come on."

The kitchen was in uproar. Nina, Dilan and Tara had all started their school holidays and the pancake breakfast was Sameena's way of getting them all out of bed at a decent hour. They sat around the big dining table with a hotplate in the middle, ladling batter onto six small pancake moulds and flipping them over as they bubbled.

Cameron spooned chocolate spread onto her pancake, covered it with berries, rolled it inelegantly and ate it in two bites. "This is a brilliant idea, Sameena," she said. "I have to get one of these."

"Are you staying all week, Aunty Cam?" said Nina.

"Can I help feed your cat?" said Tara.

"Is there any coding I can do?" said Dilan.

"One at a time," said Sameena sternly.

Cameron rolled another pancake and slowly drank her coffee, keeping her nieces and nephew in suspense. She wiped a smear of chocolate spread off her lips and smiled. "Short answers," she said. "Yes, I'm staying all week, and I am sure the cat would love company, Tara. As for coding, Dilan, if you're serious, I'm sure I can find something for you to do."

•

Refreshed, reinvigorated, but worried nonetheless, Cameron took her place back at the computer. The cat weaved around her legs, purring, getting settled in its temporary home.

The welcome break had yielded a slew of messages. Susie had checked in to say that she, Noor and Sandeep had the latest MetaBand operating system under the microscope, Joel had found some more links between Paxton and Sapphire Straits and was looking into the burglary, and they'd come back to her if and when they had news. DI Mercer wanted to talk to her. Andy had been in touch, unaware that Cameron was in the village, asking for a quote for a feature he was planning. She could deal with those later.

Of more interest was an illustrated message from Ross, the promised postcard.

"Hi, Cameron," she read. "Shell and I are having a great time here." A line drawing labelled 'the local distillery' was a very shaky representation of a data centre. "The Olympic village is buzzing after that fantastic opening ceremony. This was our favourite." The picture was of an owl in sunglasses standing next to an old-fashioned computer with big round tapes mounted on the front. "It's so hot that we need ice in our drinks." Cameron peered at the drawing from several angles before concluding that it was snow on a mountain. Really, Ross was not the best artist in the world, but if she was struggling to make head or tail of the pictures then Yasmin would have no chance. "The diving starts today. It should be spectacular. That's all our news. I've got to get back to the village to prepare for Thursday's race. Your other favourite athlete is competing then as well. She's hoping her kit isn't too tight. Enjoy the show. Ross."

Her other favourite athlete? That would be Anita Trianna, thought Cameron, and Ross's remark about kit must mean the skinsuit. She remembered the archer rubbing his arms uncomfortably and wondered if she had felt the same sensation. It focused her mind on the plight of the athletes who were using the same suits. She had to let the Olympic defence team know and hope that they could disable the malware. The control of the suits didn't just affect the results. It might injure the athletes themselves.

First, though, what did Ross's cryptic artwork tell her? She guessed that there had been an incident at the Wrangell data centre. The owl was doing something – what? – to a server, and there was an icy mountain. That confirmed her thought about Wrangell. What about the reference to diving? Had there been an accident?

Ben came into the room and peered over her shoulder, wet from the shower with a towel around his waist. "Sanctuary," he said succinctly.

"What?" said Cameron.

"The owl with the sunglasses," said Ben. "It's someone asleep with a mask on. The Sanctuary is all the rage over in America. It's a virtual environment that keeps you asleep. It's really popular with shift workers. Haven't you tried it?"

"No," said Cameron. "I've heard of it, of course, but it's not that common here and I don't want anyone controlling my sleep patterns." She looked back at the drawings. "Oh, good grief," she said. "What if that's exactly what we're looking at here. Someone's under the control of a bad actor in their sleep, they compromise the data centre…"

"… and then fling themselves off the mountain," finished Ben. "That's grim."

"I could put a name to that bad actor," said Cameron. "Yasmin." She stared at the drawing labelled 'the local distillery'. "She's found a route into the Olympic data banks through Wrangell."

"That's a big conclusion to jump to," said Ben.

"I know," said Cameron. "I need to prove it."

"Can I help?" said Ben.

Cameron shook her head. "I don't think so," she said. "I'm going to delve into some deep dark places. There is one thing you could do, though. Can you get in touch with Chloe and make sure she knows about the avatar with the blue eyes that's been following Tara and Audrey around Sandland? Tell her it's Yasmin. She needs to make sure the girls don't go back in there until it's safe."

"Sure," said Ben with a smile. "It's still early there. I'll get dressed first." He strolled back out of the room in search of his overnight bag, and Cameron went back to her computer. It was time to visit MIST again.

Her first stop, after checking her MIST inbox, was the one-to-one message boards. She wanted to seed different colleagues with tantalising scraps of slightly inaccurate speculation and see what made it back to the Underworld.

Barker was her first target, the one she trusted least. He wasn't around but she left a note. 'I'm trying to corroborate a tip-off before taking it to the main forum,' she said. 'Have you heard anything about a data breach in the metaverse fabric?'

Admin Cat was online. "Hi, SimCavalier," she said. "Are you joining us in the group chat?"

"Thanks, Cat," said Cameron. "I'll be along in a few minutes. I've got some very detailed intelligence to share that is going to need action, and I'm just finishing off the report. There's one other thing, though. Have you heard anything about a back door into the e-sports platform? I had a tipoff, and I wanted to check with you before bringing it to the main forum."

"No, I haven't come across anything like that," replied Cat. "Let me look into it."

Cameron repeated the exercise with several more connections, suggesting the existence of a back door or a breach in different parts of the sprawling Olympic metaverse, before finally taking a deep breath and joining the main chat.

Admin Cat called for silence as soon as Cameron appeared.

"The SimCavalier has news," she said. "Over to you."

"Thanks Cat," said Cameron. "The report I'm uploading now details the attack vector that was used to disrupt the Indonesian arena during the karate competition two weeks ago and may also have manipulated the result of yesterday's first round of archery."

There was a ripple of astonishment among the small group. Cameron continued. What she had to say would answer most of the questions that were popping up in the chat.

"The archery result only impacted the seeding for the next round," said Cameron. "It didn't stop anyone from qualifying, but it will have earned a packet for the bookies. This is consistent with the karate competition experience."

She paused, knowing that what she said now would ripple straight to the source. "We are searching for malware in the MetaBand operating system."

There was uproar. Cameron watched and listened to everyone's reactions carefully. There didn't seem to be any wrong notes among the group. She could not tell who the traitor might be yet.

Barker had slid unnoticed into the discussion. "Interesting report, SimCavalier," he said. "I have a question for the whole group. How many of you are using MetaBand connections right now? Can you be sure they are secure?"

Cameron's earlier misgivings about Barker started to ease. That was a perceptive question, and it left a few people stuttering.

"No, Flora," said Barker to a group member with a rose as their avatar. "I don't think a VPN is going to help. You never know what, or who, could be watching."

On Cameron's screen a message popped up. 'We need to talk. Barker.'

Cameron took the hint. "I'll leave you all to digest the report," she said. "My team are working on the OS now and if you can contribute, you know how to reach them. Send me any questions you have."

She disconnected from the main chat and connected with Barker, who was waiting for her.

"Hello, Cameron," he said, using her real name. "I think it's time we talked properly. You know that your report is going straight to Yasmin, don't you? And how did you know about the data breach?"

Cameron was stunned. Had she hit upon a different attack by chance? She had no evidence of a data breach other than the hack on the betting platform, certainly nothing in the metaverse fabric, and she was using that idea purely as bait to catch a traitor. It looked to have succeeded.

"Who are you?" said Cameron. Her mind was racing.

"You know who I am." Barker's voice had changed. It was no longer the rolling vowels of the deep American south but gruff and very British with an Aberdonian twang.

Angus.

"She'll find you," he said. "You've slipped through the net too often. She won't rest until you and your team are no longer a threat."

"No," said Cameron. "It ends now. I will find her, and I will finish her, and you with her, Angus White."

"I'd like to see you try," said Angus.

Furious, Cameron closed the connection. She had found the traitor in the camp and all her instincts about Barker had been entirely justified. She had a second target to take down. It was time to get to work.

24:   INTELLIGENCE

Cameron missed the office. She wasn't used to being the face on the wallscreen. DI Mercer had advised her to stay put while whoever had ransacked her apartment was still on the run. Cameron had suggested she start by talking to Angus White, but the man was nowhere to be found, either in the real or the virtual world. The offices of Whitford Networks were closed, and he was not at the address that he listed as his home, although neighbours had seen him there recently.

The team was working through the complex web of Noor's 3D model, mapping the connections and the attacks they knew of.

"Can you cast the model through to me?" asked Cameron. "I want to see it properly."

"Sure," said Noor.

Cameron popped her smartscreen in a cradle and watched as the model took shape in front of her in three dimensions. It wasn't the same as being able to turn it around herself, but at least she could see what she was doing.

"There's a data breach somewhere that we haven't found," she said. "That needs to go in." She watched as the model rotated.

"I don't know where to put it," said Noor. "This is getting very crowded."

"Back up a moment," said Cameron. "What's that link? When did we confirm that Chaoxiang Chen is Tenuk Chen's father?"

"I dug around my connections," said Noor casually. "It's him, alright." She spun the model away from Tenuk. "Data breach. Hmm. That's all you have?"

"Yes," said Cameron. "A data breach in the metaverse fabric. We have zero evidence other than, well, a practical confession from Angus."

"What about Wrangell?" said Joel. "That's a data centre, it's running the metaverse fabric, and if we're reading it right, someone's hacked a human there."

"And what has the hacked human done?" said Pete.

"That's the million-coin question, isn't it?" said Cameron. "I'm surprised that there's been nothing about it on MIST. Link them on the model but mark it as an educated guess for now. Sandeep, can you keep an eye on the marketplaces? See if there are any new data dumps that we can trace back."

"Sure," said Sandeep.

Cameron started writing up her findings from the arena hub analysis, occasionally glancing over at the feed from the office as her team moved like a well-oiled machine. Joel was updating the model with the last few snippets of new information about Sapphire Straits, and the webcast version spun in augmented reality in Cameron's room. Sandeep was already digging through the latest stolen data listings on the Eden marketplace. Susie had gone back to the paper file and the notes on her screen, concentrating fiercely, while Pete and Noor had their heads together dissecting the MetaBand operating system.

"Oh!" cried Noor, looking up from her screen. "Is that it?"

"I think so," said Pete. "Hey, Cameron, we've got it. We can disable that malware without disrupting the system."

"I never doubted it," said Cameron. "Gold stars all round."

"Coffee?" said Pete, glancing up at Cameron on the wallscreen. "I'd get you one too, but that's trickier to webcast."

"I'll go and get my own," said Cameron with a laugh. "You get cracking on building that patch. I have a call to make." She pulled her screen out of its projection cradle and the model disappeared from view. She picked up her coffee cup and headed downstairs to the kitchen.

Ben was leaning against the counter, sipping his own coffee and chatting to a colleague but ended the call when he saw her. "How's it going?" he asked.

"Great," said Cameron, putting the coffee machine back on. "I want to be back in the office. I miss the buzz of being there when we crack the code. It's not the same being up there on the wallscreen."

"I take it a code has been cracked?" said Ben, taking her mug and rinsing it in the sink.

"It has," said Cameron. "They'll have a patch ready to go into the MetaBand operating system by the end of the day. The challenge is getting it in there."

"Ah," said Ben. "I can see where this is going."

Cameron watched her mug slowly filling with coffee. "I need to talk to Jack," she said. "I can't go back to the MIST platform. Angus was hiding in plain sight. Who else is tracking what we do there?"

"Fair point," said Ben. "But can you trust Jack after reading that file? His fingerprints are all over the changes to the MetaBand designs and who knows what else."

"I don't know," said Cameron. She stirred her coffee thoughtfully. "I'd like to think I can. If he'll actually speak to me, that is. I have a few hours to think about the alternatives. It's what, half past four in the morning there?"

"Yes," said Ben. "Six hours behind." His smartscreen pinged. He looked at it and grimaced. "Dammit," he said. "I'd better get back to work."

"Me too," said Cameron. She picked up her mug and followed Ben out of the kitchen. Her own smartscreen rang and she fumbled for it in her pocket, trying not to spill the coffee. It took a moment to unroll it and check the caller ID, and what she saw stopped her in her tracks.

It was Jack. He must have read her mind.

"Hello," said Cameron cautiously, putting her coffee down on a handy table.

There was a moment of silence on the other end of the line, then Jack spoke.

"Hello, Cameron," he said. "I'm sorry to bother you. I need to ask you something. A few months ago, I caught one of my employees skulking around the office and they claimed to be working with an international cybersecurity syndicate. They said their handler was the SimCavalier. That's you, isn't it?"

Cameron sat down on the nearest chair. "Yes," she said. There was no point denying it.

"So, do you have a spy in my office?" said Jack.

"Chloe," said Cameron. She figured that honesty was the best policy right now, and she hoped that Jack was on a secure connection.

Jack exhaled loudly. "Okay," he said. "That's all I wanted to know. Please give my regards to your Aunt Vicky. I may drop in and see her some time."

The line went dead. Cameron kicked herself for not being fast enough with her own questions. She tried to call him back, but he didn't pick up.

•

Jack stared out of the window of his plush apartment over the darkness of downtown Austin. In the distance, a moontower shone, illuminating the streets around it. Now he knew who he could trust, and it changed everything.

"Zara," he said.

"Yes, Jack," came the familiar voice of his virtual assistant.

He hesitated. Some long-buried instinct nagged at him. Zara was always there when he called. She was always listening for her name, the trigger word to which she responded. Did that mean she heard everything that happened in his immediate vicinity? Jack shuddered at the thought. It had never occurred to him that even in his most intimate moments she might have been lurking in the ether, listening. If he hadn't been paranoid before, he certainly was now.

"Nothing, Zara," he said, yawning dramatically. "I couldn't sleep. Tell me about the moontowers again."

Zara started to narrate the tale of the moontowers that shone over Austin, keeping the residents safe before streetlights were common, and preserved by the city. As she talked, Jack quietly packed a bag, then did something he had never considered before. He cut his link to her.

Truly alone for the first time in years, he left the apartment. An empty night bus took him to the airport, and he paid from his own pocket for a flight to London.

•

Cameron sat on a deckchair next to the old MetaBand hub, watching the output from the diagnostic tools on her smartscreen. It was cool in the shade and periodically she left the tool to collect its precious data and went around the corner of the house to bask in the sunshine. After a while, Ben joined her and they sat in companionable silence on the grass, listening to the distant bleating of sheep and the nearby hum of the two hubs.

"Is it working?" he said at last, stretching.

"Yes," said Cameron. "There's a lot of data moving around, a lot of CPU activity."

"How can you tell what it is?" asked Ben.

"I can't yet," said Cameron. "I'm going to have to take it apart and see what's in there." She lay back in the sunshine and closed her eyes. "Five minutes."

In less than that time she had dozed off and woke disoriented twenty minutes later to the sound of an alert on her smartscreen. Ben was lying beside her, leaning on his elbow and watching her sleep.

"I'd better get that," she muttered.

"I didn't even hear it," said Ben. He jumped up to retrieve the screen.

"I'll do it," said Cameron. "It needs to be disconnected properly." The call alert stopped, but Cameron could see that it had been DI Mercer. She carefully extracted the screen from the MetaBand hub interface and returned the call.

"Sorry," she said. "I was running some tests and I couldn't answer straight away."

"Don't worry," said Mercer. "I thought you'd like to know we identified your burglar. The office security guard's bodycam gave us what we needed, although he was heavily disguised, and we've since confirmed that the same person appeared on CCTV footage in the streets near your apartment and the office."

"Who was it?" asked Cameron, moving her deckchair into the sun and sitting down.

"Angus White," said Mercer grimly. "You were right about him all along."

Cameron sat up sharply. "In person?" she said. "It's not his style to be breaking and entering."

"I'm afraid so," said Mercer. "Maybe the stakes finally got too high. He's gone to ground. We know where he was when he tried to access your hard disks, though. We found one of the bricked drives in a trash can up in north London."

Ben was listening. He raised an eyebrow at Cameron. "Ross and Michelle live up north," he said. "It wasn't anywhere near them, was it?"

"On the screen, Mercer looked startled. "Not close," she said, "but we'll bear that in mind. In the meantime, I'm going to arrange with my American colleagues to bring Jack Sladen in for questioning."

"I'm not sure that's the right angle," said Cameron slowly. "I had a call from Jack earlier. I have a feeling that he's finally worked out who he can trust, and from what we've uncovered, someone might be out to frame him."

"I'd need evidence," said Mercer. "I know your gut feelings are excellent but that's not the way policing works, Cameron."

Cameron kicked at a tuft of grass, thinking. "Give me some time to work on that," she said. "And there's someone you really should talk to."

"Who's that?" said Mercer.

"Ella," replied Cameron. "I think you'll find she's on our side."

•

Cameron spent the next hour carefully disconnecting the MetaBand hub from its uplink and removing the all-weather casing that protected it. Ben, at a loose end, was laughing over the specifications. After all, he'd been involved in the engineering work to produce them.

"See this reference?" he said, pointing to an embossed set of numbers and letters. "That's the standard that defines everything this casing has to be resistant to. Would you believe it has to be curry-proof?"

"Really?" said Cameron, momentarily distracted from her delicate task. "They think of everything."

"It's because they never know what's going to be chucked at the corner where the hub's fitted," said Ben. "That's why the seals are so tight."

"You're telling me," said Cameron, struggling to prise a grommet out of a cable connection port.

"Give that here," said Ben. With an expert flick of the wrist, he removed the rubber seal. "You want all the hardware out, is that right?"

"Yes," said Cameron, giving in gracefully. "Be gentle."

It took Ben a matter of minutes to strip the rest of the protection away, and he presented her with the bare bones of the MetaBand hub. "There you go," he said. "What's next?"

"Time to find out what's actually going on in here," said Cameron.

She carried the precious cargo back into the house and up to her attic. Once there, she set up an old computer to act as her sandbox, carefully plugged the hub into it, and set about mirroring the contents of the disk. She wanted to keep the original pristine for future forensics.

Gradually the structure of the hub revealed itself. The disk was partitioned as she'd expected, holding a full Diaulos node in one section while any network communications went through the standard firewalls that protected users. But there was a third partition, hidden away, that held something else entirely. Cameron started to probe the mirrored disk gently, teasing out its secrets. The programs that were running here were disturbingly familiar. She recognised deep learning routines, the building blocks of a neural network.

She was looking at a fragment of Yasmin's mind.

•

Tenuk joined his father for tea in the old man's office. Chaoxiang was in an excellent mood, and graphs and tables on the wallscreen showed upward trends and green lights.

"I should congratulate you, Tenuk," said Chaoxiang. "The contract that your Steamyard completed has delivered its first bounty. I am minded to pay your team a bonus."

"Thank you, father," said Tenuk. "The profits were substantial, I take it?"

Chaoxiang sipped his tea and looked out at a troop of macaques swinging through the trees in the garden, foraging for supper. "Yes," he said. "There was significant betting activity, helped by the tight competition between their favourite and ours. We also succeeded in reaping rewards from the users of several online platforms that have not seen fit to join our group yet."

"The house always wins," said Tenuk.

The man was ruthless. Tenuk wondered for a moment if he had made the right decision, but really, he was more like his father than he cared to admit. After all, he had himself sent Angus after the SimCavalier without a moment's hesitation, a ruthless response to a threat. He wondered if the rogue file had been found. The worst-case scenario was that Jack Sladen would be compromised and Yasmin found. On reflection, he no longer really needed Sladen to secure his future, and he had Xanthe and perhaps Zara to work with. It was becoming less of a concern by the hour.

Tenuk sipped his tea and relaxed into his chair. He was getting used to this new life.

"When will you next deploy the sensor controls?" he asked.

Chaoxiang consulted a schedule on the nearest wallscreen. "We have an e-sports event running now," he said. "There's a useful back door into part of the metaverse fabric that Yasmin can enter to take charge of play. After that, there is sport climbing."

"What are the sensors delivering for that?" asked Tenuk.

"We control the climbers," said Chaoxiang. "We can restrict or extend their reach at any time.".

The campaign was beautifully designed, thought Tenuk. The focus was on qualifiers and on tightly contested pairs where the result didn't materially affect future rounds, reducing the chance of an appeal, and the betting was fierce.

"Timing is everything, of course," continued Chaoxiang. "We can only rely on the sensor control being available to us for a short period. I understand that the security community is right on our heels, and I will not be surprised if they succeed in neutralising the malware within a matter of days or even hours."

"Do you think so?" said Tenuk. He rarely considered what happened to the Underworld contracts that his team fulfilled. They supplied the malware and the grateful client paid. Only a handful of long-term jobs took more strategic thinking on his part, like the work he had done with Yasmin and MetaBand.

Chaoxiang laughed. "Sometimes you demonstrate astonishing naivety, my son," he said gently. "This is a game. Today we are winning. Tomorrow will be different. And so it will continue." He finished his tea and set the cup down on the table. "Come. There is nothing more to do tonight. We should eat."

Tenuk followed his father out of the office, taking one last look back at the healthy graphs and rapidly streaming data that climbed the walls. He was in the presence of a master, and he had a lot to learn.

•

Jack stood in the courtyard of Cameron's apartment building, waiting for an answer from her entry system. The call kept ringing out. Jack looked at his watch. She might still be in the office. He turned to leave and almost walked into the young man with the turban who was standing right behind him.

"Can I help you?" said the man.

"I'm trying to find Cameron Silvera," said Jack. "Is she a neighbour?"

"Yes," said the man cautiously. "She's not in right now. Can I leave her a message?"

"Sure, if you see her," said Jack, brightening. "Please tell her Jack called by."

"Will do," said the man.

Jack started to walk away then paused. "Only tell her if you see her," he said. "Don't put anything online."

The young man nodded. "I get it," he said. He looked Jack directly in the eyes. "I understand completely."

Next stop was her office. Jack took an autocar over the river and pulled up outside a great glass building towards the southern end of Gray's Inn Road. He recognised it at once. He hadn't ever visited Argentum Associates, but he'd been to the News Channel studios in the basement plenty of times. How strange that all the times he'd wondered how to get in touch with Cameron over the years, she'd probably been working quietly upstairs.

The big screen in the atrium café was showing the climbing competition from the Olympics. Jack watched for a minute or two and then went to the reception desk. "I'm visiting Argentum Associates," he said.

"Are they expecting you?" replied the welcome 'bot.

"No," said Jack.

"One moment," said the 'bot.

A security guard ambled towards him. "Visitor for Argentum?" he said. "Can I help you?"

"Uh, yes," said Jack. "I'm an old friend of Cameron's. I was just in the area…"

"ID, please," said the guard.

Jack presented his chip for scanning.

"Do you have any other documents?" asked the guard.

"Sure," said Jack, surprised. He dug his passport out of his overnight bag. "Here," he said. "I flew in this morning."

"That all seems to be in order, Mr Sladen," said the guard without a hint of recognition. "Wait here."

Jack gave the security guard a half smile and a shrug and sat down where he'd been told. He automatically pulled out his smartscreen to check his messages, then stopped. Cameron was obviously being protected by some heavy security. He didn't know why, but he was starting to understand that there was something very wrong.

"You can go up," said the security guard at last. "Sixth floor, turn left."

Jack emerged from the lift onto the walkway that ran around the edge of the great light well in the centre of the building. Sure enough, to the left he spotted a door marked with interlinked As. Argentum Associates. As Jack approached, the door opened. Silhouetted against the light was a slim woman with long dark hair.

"Jack Sladen," said Susie. "You've got a nerve."

"Is Cameron there?" said Jack anxiously. "I need to talk to her."

"She isn't," said Susie. She wasn't budging.

Jack took a leap of faith. "In that case, I guess she's in the village," he said. "I promised her I'd go and visit Aunt Vicky. Maybe I'd better do that now."

He started to walk back towards the lift.

"Wait," said Susie. She pointed at a comfortable chair in a little breakout area on the landing. "I'll be back." She turned away and closed the door.

He was starting to get nervous when at last the Argentum office door opened again and Susie and Joel came out.

"One question," said Joel. "That virtual assistant of yours."

"Deactivated," said Jack. He showed Joel the control panel on his smartscreen, relieved that he'd worked it out.

"Okay," said Joel. "Come in. Cameron's ready for you now."

The office had evidently been tidied in a hurry. There was nothing on any of the desks and all the screens were off, apart from a large wallscreen.

"Have a seat," said Joel, indicating a sofa square in front of the camera. "Can I get you a coffee?"

"Yes, please," said Jack, completely disoriented.

The wallscreen lit up, and there was Cameron, frowning at him.

"Hello, Jack," she said. "Don't worry, we're all on secure connections. We can talk freely. I understand you've been to my apartment already?"

"News travels fast," said Jack. "Thanks," he added as Joel handed him a mug.

"You've been looking for me," said Cameron, "and I need to talk to you. Why don't you start?"

The office was silent. Everyone's attention was on him. Jack hadn't felt like this since he sat his final exams. He took a deep breath.

"I believe you've been right all along," he said. "I think there's been something going on with MetaBand. I don't know if I can trust Tenuk. I don't know if I can trust Zara. I think I can trust you."

Cameron just looked at him.

"And… I'm sorry," he added. "I mean that." He looked up at the screen. "What do you need from me?"

"Thank you for that, Jack," said Cameron. "My turn, I guess. Yasmin is alive and well and distributed across the MetaBand network. I need your help to take her down."

Jack's mouth fell open and he gaped at the screen.

"What?" he said. He tipped his coffee mug, spilling the hot liquid over his lap. "Ow! Dammit. You're kidding. No, you wouldn't joke about this." He put the half empty mug down on the floor. "Shit."

"Exactly," said Cameron. "Let me tell you what we're going to do."

25:   HUNTER, HUNTED

Ben opened the attic door cautiously. The cat lay in wait, hindquarters twitching. He scooped it up before it could pounce, climbed the stairs and deposited it on the nearest chair. He knocked softly at the inner door. "Cameron?" he whispered as he pushed it open a crack.

She was concentrating fiercely with her headphones on. "No," she said to an unseen colleague. "That won't work. We can't compromise the Diaulos ledger." She had been scribbling with paper and pen, sketching out a complex mind map to help her visualise the path of the virus they were building. She put the pen down and sighed. "Pete, give me something here. What's Noor got?"

As she listened, she glanced up at Ben and gave him a tired smile.

"Time for supper," he whispered.

She nodded. "Folks, let's take a break," she said. "We have the packages tested and ready to be delivered, which is fantastic work. Get some rest and I'm sure we'll be able to crack the final puzzle with fresh eyes."

She pulled off her headphones. "Almost there," she said. "I'm going to have a shower and clear my head. I'll be down in ten minutes."

It was more like twenty, but Cameron felt human again. Everyone was outside enjoying the warm summer evening. Charlie presided over the barbecue, sausages and meat sizzling. Cameron sat down next to Ben at the big outdoor table and accepted a glass of wine. She grabbed a sausage from the big plate in the centre of the table and took a bite.

"Ow! Hot," she said.

"How's it going?" asked Sameena, handing her a plate and cutlery.

"Pretty good," said Cameron. "The operating system update is ready to roll out and Jack's made it look like a legitimate upgrade for all the Sladen Group technicians. That'll deal with the malware we traced."

"And the other little matter?" said Charlie.

"Ah, Yasmin," said Cameron, blowing on the sausage and taking another cautious bite. "The easy bit was working out how to scramble the neural network in each hub as well as closing down the partition using the new operating system update. Even if the connections open up again, her processors will be all over the place."

"That sounds cruel," said Sameena.

"She's not human," said Cameron. "There's no emotion there, no sense of self at all. Just data and software. All we're doing is changing the way she – it – interprets data, switching all the labels around, if you like."

"What you're saying is that she'll still exist in some form, but she won't be a threat," said Charlie. "Not bad for two days' work, Cam. Here, have another sausage. There's some chicken coming too."

Cameron loaded her plate with salad and meat. She hadn't realised how hungry she was. "The Generative Adversarial Network was the easy bit," she said between mouthfuls. "The hard bit is trying not to break the rest of the network. I can't work out how to close down her partition and keep the rest running smoothly, especially when not all hubs have Yasmin in them."

"That's a tough one," said Ben. "I imagine the International Olympic Committee would be upset if you broke all the feeds into their metaverse."

"Exactly," said Cameron gloomily.

Dilan reached over to the plate full of sausages. "Aunty Cam," he said, "Don't you just need to tell the bits that have to stay open to ignore what you're sending? You know, like Sort and Sorted. One changes the original list sequence, the other one just displays it how you want it without changing anything."

Cameron stared at him. "You might have something there," she said slowly.

She started to get up from her chair, but Ben gently put a hand on her shoulder. "It can wait for half an hour," he said. "Finish your plate. I think there's pudding, too."

"You're right," she said. "I need the break. I think we have a long night ahead of us." She sipped thoughtfully at her drink. The solution was starting to take shape in her head, and the endgame was approaching.

•

Ross seriously considered trying the Sanctuary sleep aid but knew that a change to his routine on the eve of competition would be a terrible idea. He had never been so nervous before a race in his life. He knew he was ready, but the occasion was getting to him. Michelle was tucked away in her hotel, and he was alone in his capsule bedroom in the athlete's village. To try and wind down he took one more walk down to the Team GB breakout room before lights out.

He was pleased to find company there, including a teammate who had competed today. They chatted quietly over a bottle of fruit juice and Ross felt his nerves settling.

"Did you see the message boards?" asked his friend, pointing at a plaque on the wall.

"No," said Ross, puzzled. He'd never noticed it before. He went over to examine it and was delighted to find it was an old-school display of messages of support from family and friends. He scrolled through looking for his name and found notes from Joel and Martha, Susie, Pete, Noor, Sandeep, Cameron and Ben as well as neighbours from back in north London and the team at the News Channel. 'Good luck, mate. We're all rooting for you – Andy.'

Grinning, Ross felt the tension rolling away. He wasn't on his own. All of his friends had his back. Finally relaxed enough to be tired, he thanked his teammate and made his way back to his bedroom where he fell into a dreamless sleep with no assistance at all.

The next morning, the nerves were back but bearable. He tried as hard as he could to eat breakfast, gathered his things, and made his way onto the shuttle bus that would take the competitors to the start of the event. He'd checked his bike a dozen times and it was loaded ready to go, with all the spares for the support team. His intelligent skinsuit, designed to adapt to each leg of the triathlon and protect him from the cold water and wind chill, was connected to the Metaverse fabric for the VR broadcast. He pulled at the collar, trying to relieve an itch. It was time to focus, and he didn't need any distractions.

•

Cameron whooped with glee. "It's working," she cried, standing up at her desk. The workaround that Dilan had inspired was doing its job. The team in the Argentum office had a line of MetaBand hubs on test and as the operating system update rolled out, followed by the package containing the GAN virus, each one continued to process the Diaulos blockchain and uplinks, and closed down Yasmin's partition. Cameron watched on her screen as the green lights remained on the systems they had to preserve and winked out one by one on the distributed intelligence.

"Bloody brilliant," said Pete. "We were looking all along at what to build into the virus, when all we needed was a tweak to the operating system to prevent the other two things accepting that package."

There was one final test to do, and Cameron had volunteered her village as the guinea pig. They would update the operating system of every hub on this branch of the MetaBand network, then roll out the virus.

"I'm going up to Aunt Vicky's to track the progress of the rollout," said Cameron. "You won't be able to contact me while I'm out of range of the secure network. Are you ready to go?"

"Yes, my technicians are ready," said Jack's voice. "How long do you need?"

"Five minutes," said Cameron. "I'm leaving now."

She pulled on her shoes, scampered down the attic stairs and then down another flight to the hall.

"It's starting?" said Ben, sticking his head around the dining room door.

"Yes," said Cameron. "I'm on my way to Aunt Vicky's now. Can't stop."

She ran around the corner and up the hill and arrived at her aunt's house two minutes later. She checked the countdown on her screen. Ninety seconds left. She settled down next to the MetaBand hub on the outside wall and opened the diagnostics on her smartscreen.

Donald the cat emerged from the undergrowth and miaowed at her, wondering why she was in the middle of his territory. She reached out a hand and he sniffed it in an unusually friendly gesture before stalking off in search of a dog to worry. He was turning into a softy in his old age, she thought.

Ten seconds. The processing rate was high but steady. As the time counted down, Cameron realised she was holding her breath.

There. The first stage, the operating system update, was starting. Cameron knew what she was looking at now when she checked the readouts from the diagnostics. It took almost a minute and a rapid soft reboot, and then the activity settled. Next came the special package for Yasmin.

There was a flurry of activity while it installed, then the processing volume on the hub halved. Cameron stared at the diagnostic tool. "Aunt Vicky," she yelled, "can you check your connection?"

Primed and ready, Aunt Vicky went through the steps that Cameron had taught her. "It's all running well, dear," she called back through an open window. Cameron breathed a sigh of relief. "I've just claimed some Diaulos as well," she continued, "and my wallet balance has updated."

That was less significant, thought Cameron, as any node would process the transaction, but if the MetaBand links were sound then the Diaulos network should also be intact.

"Thanks, Aunt Vicky," she called back. "I'll see you later."

"I'm coming round to watch Ross race," said Aunt Vicky.

"Great, see you shortly," called Cameron. She was already halfway down the street, returning to the sanctuary of Charlie's house and the secure network.

•

Michelle was dressed and ready for the shuttle pickup to go and support Ross in his race. As she fastened her sensor belt around her waist, the kit that allowed her to 'see' her surroundings, a sudden noise in her hotel room made her jump. The door that she had locked so carefully the night before had opened and closed.

"Who's there?" she said. She turned towards the noise and realised that she could sense nothing from the kit. It was completely dead.

There was no reply, but she heard breathing and the cold sound of steel. Adrenaline surged through her body, and she leapt from her seat and ran in what she thought was the direction of her door. She caromed off the edge of the bed and a glancing blow from the invisible knife caught her arm. She kept going. She had no choice. Her hands brushed against the intruder, and she felt an odd fabric. It reminded her of something, but she didn't have time to think. She found the door, fumbled with the handle, tore it open, and tried to remember the layout of the corridors.

She was going deeper into the hotel and lost her way completely. She also lost her pursuer. Shaking, she waited as long as she dared, then felt her way along the nearest wall until she could feel an embossed sign. Steadying her breathing, she crept slowly to reception.

"Can I help you?" came a voice she vaguely recognised, one of the receptionists. "Are you okay?"

"I'm fine," said Michelle, folding her arms and hoping that the spot where the knife had grazed her wasn't visible. "I'm supposed to be at the triathlon. My boyfriend's competing but I slept through my alarm. Has the shuttle been yet?"

"It left about ten minutes ago," said the receptionist. "I can order an autocar for you. That should get to the event on time."

"Thank you," said Michelle. The cab arrived in barely a minute.

As she clambered in, clutching her arm, she heard a commotion in the hotel lobby behind her. "Security," shouted a panicked voice. "He's got a knife."

She slammed the cab door and the little autocar pulled out into the traffic. They could deal with her attacker, whoever he was. She had to get to Ross.

•

"I guess we're ready to go," said Cameron. She was back at her desk. Celebrations of their successful test had been brief. They had a very short window of opportunity before the day's competitions began. If they delayed any further, they would have to wait another eighteen hours to deploy the software.

"No time like the present," said Jack. "My technicians are reporting that both MetaBand and Diaulos are sailing along without any problems in the test area. They're ready to go on the full deployment."

Hit it," said Cameron.

They watched their screens in silence, hardly daring to breathe. A percentage figure appeared in a box in one corner showing the updates remaining. 99%. 98%. Time seemed to stand still.

"There's a problem," said Pete, dampening the mood.

"Damn, what now?" asked Cameron.

Pete shared his screen with her. Cameron looked at the detailed data on one monitor and Pete's worried face on the other. "The package deployment is pretty slow," he said. "It's entirely possible that Yasmin will detect the nodes shutting down and try to disrupt the rollout."

"Do you think she'd have time?" said Cameron.

"I think so," said Pete. "She'll be constantly checking the network state, and if the node responses start falling, she'll know something's up."

"Byzantine Fault Tolerance," said Cameron thoughtfully. Where are we now? 95%? It's going to take a good half hour at this rate. I wonder if there's a way to distract her while it's deploying?" A crazy plan was forming in her head. She picked up her reality mask and turned it over in her hands. Maybe, just maybe, she could intervene.

"Cameron?" said Pete. "I know that distracted look. What are you planning?"

"Roll it out now," said Cameron. "I'm going to turn the tables. Wherever she runs, I will find her. In every reality, I will be waiting for her. The hunter, hunted."

"That's not safe," said Pete.

"I know," said Cameron, "but I don't see that I have any choice. I'm going in. Keep me updated on the rollout so I know how close we are to taking her down completely."

•

Ross checked the time. The competitors' shuttle bus would be leaving for the start line soon and there was still no sign of Michelle. He tried to call her again, but she didn't answer. He got up from his seat and walked down the narrow aisle to the front where the GB team coach was sitting.

"Coach," he said, "I'm worried about Shell."

"I'm sure I saw her a few minutes ago," he replied. "Let me find out where she is." He climbed down out of the shuttle and jogged off towards the family stand. Ross saw him speaking to a marshal, who pointed out a low building on the other side of the finish area. The coach came jogging back.

"She's checked in," he said. "We think she's in the restrooms."

"I'll go and find her," said Ross.

The coach held out a warning hand. "Not now, son," he said. "You're all suited up. You can't leave the shuttle."

Frustrated, Ross stared out of the window at the low building, willing Shell to come out. "You're saying if I go and get my girlfriend I miss my start," he said.

"Them's the rules," said the coach. "I'll send someone in." He leaned out of the door to call to the marshals, but at that moment Michelle emerged from the restrooms, stumbling and veering around as she tried to navigate towards the shuttle.

"Help her!" cried Ross as Michelle tripped and sprawled on the ground. "She can't see." He stood, helpless, as the team coach rushed towards her.

•

In her attic bedroom, Cameron briefed Ben quickly on her plans. "I might need help," she said. "I don't know what kind of tricks she could pull. That's if I find her, of course."

She opened up the portal to the virtual world and signed in using the avatar that she had abandoned a few days before. If her theory was correct, it should be exactly where she'd left it. She put on her reality mask, looped the controllers over her wrist, and set the mask to full opacity. The slightly tattered silicon wings extended as the lenses clouded, and in moments she was immersed in a three-dimensional environment.

As soon as she saw the black and white chequered floor, she knew that her plan had worked. Her avatar had been standing there immobile since she left. Now it ran across the floor. "Yasmin," she shouted. "Where are you? I'm here. I'm going to take you down."

"85%," came Pete's voice. "Stand by."

She spun around the room, testing all the boundaries, running into the artworks and bouncing off them. An abstract coil began to whirl in the middle of the space, her avatar's momentum putting it into motion, but Yasmin did not come.

•

Tenuk had left his father preparing for the fifth day of competition and retreated to his own office. Chaoxiang's assurances that the infosec community was right on their tail made him uneasy. He had heard nothing from Angus, and he sorely needed an update, but the man was nowhere to be found. The file that he pretended mattered less than it did, was still missing. Jack was apparently on special leave, some family matter, and even Zara couldn't contact him. Other spies in the cybersecurity world reported that the SimCavalier had vanished. She had gone to ground, and that worried him.

A routine system alert attracted his attention. A global MetaBand update was starting. Surprised, Tenuk logged on to the Statesman Tech systems. Events were due to start within the hour and under their service level agreement with the International Olympic Committee, this was at the very edge of the window they had to deploy updates before live competition.

He checked the schedule of work. There was nothing due to be done today. He felt a growing sense of unease.

Tenuk went back to the old man's office. "There's an unscheduled MetaBand update pushing out to all the hubs," he said.

"Ah, the time has come," said Chaoxiang regretfully.

"You were expecting this?" said Tenuk.

"Of course," said Chaoxiang. "I'm surprised it took them so long. That's a testament to the quality of the Steamyard's work, my boy."

"We can re-deploy the malware if it's removed in this update," said Tenuk.

"No," said Chaoxiang. "You must learn to quit while you're ahead. We made an excellent return on our investment, and the campaign is now over. Was there anything else?"

"No, father," said Tenuk. He took the hint and went back to his own office again, pausing to collect a fresh cup of iced cucumber water on the way. Once back at his desk, he checked the integrity of the Diaulos network. All was well so far.

What about Yasmin? Tenuk opened a different control panel and scanned her system state, just to be sure. Again, everything seemed to be running normally. If this update succeeded in removing the malware they relied upon to control the skinsuits, she would not be able to execute any of the fixes they'd planned for today. It was a shame, thought Tenuk. He'd put in a special request for the triathlon, just to annoy Argentum Associates. Perhaps Yasmin could find some more creative ways to make that event particularly trying.

·

"75%," came Pete's voice again.

Surely Yasmin would have noticed the drain on her processors by now, the reduction in network confirmations. Cameron was beginning to wonder if a simple incursion into the monster's lair was enough.

"Yasmin!" she shouted. There was no response.

"We need to try another tack, Pete," she said. "I think she's busy with Olympic business. Get onto MIST on my behalf" – she pinged him a delegation code – "and try and work out where she might be. Get the others looking for likely disruption and frustrate her on the ground."

"Okay," said Pete, "we're on it."

•

In a sea of green lights, one had flicked to amber. Tenuk noticed there was a higher proportion than usual of inactive nodes in Yasmin's distributed network. 70% was a far lower level of network responses than he would expect. Maybe the soft reboot of the operating system was skewing the real time reporting.

The numbers continued to fall steadily. It was down to 65% now. What could he do?

"Xanthe," he called. He didn't hear her come in, but suddenly she was by his side. "I'm concerned about Yasmin's current state. Do you have a way to connect with her?"

"Yes, Tenuk," said Xanthe smoothly. "Leave it with me." She disappeared again, silent as a ghost.

•

Ross started towards the shuttle door, ignoring the alerts that sounded as he got close to the edge of the competitor zone, but was brought up short by a sudden tightness in his limbs. His legs buckled beneath him, and he clutched at his collar. "Skinsuit," he gasped. "Squeezing."

"Medic and technician, here, now," bellowed the team coach.

Ross writhed in pain as the skinsuit continued to constrict his limbs and his chest. "Get it off me," he pleaded.

"We've got to wait for the adjudicator," said the team coach helplessly. "If you take it off or it's disconnected, you'll be disqualified."

"If we don't get it off, he'll die," said the medic. He'd finally found a blade that would actually cut the resilient skinsuit material. He made a careful incision, cutting as deep as he dared to try and relieve the pressure on Ross's neck.

The technician came running back to the bus. "I've tried to disconnect the feed," she said frantically. "It's locked. I can't break the link. I don't know what's happening."

"Hack," choked Ross. He was starting to lose consciousness. He stared up at the blue sky and all he could see was drones.

•

Pete's voice sounded in her ear. "Cameron," he said, "We're at 55%. There's some breaking news from Reykjavik, a delay to the triathlon due to an incident."

"I hope Ross and Shell are okay," said Cameron, "but with Yasmin on the loose..."

"There's drone footage coming in," said Pete. "Oh, good grief, there's an ambulance. And that looks like Shell on the ground. I can't see Ross."

"We keep going," said Cameron. "It's their only chance."

26:   COUNTDOWN

Angus sat alone in a dark corner booth of a busy North London pub. The wallscreens were showing the public feed from the Olympics, and all eyes were on a developing situation at the triathlon. The news drones were jostling for the best angle, the feed flicking from one to the other. A dark-haired figure was sitting on the ground being attended to by a medic. There was a crowd around the door of the competitors' shuttle that would take them to the start of the race.

Angus caught a glimpse of someone lying on the floor and a shock of ginger hair in the middle of all the frantic activity. He choked on his pint, put the glass down, and hurried out of the pub.

In a quiet corner of the small beer garden, he pulled out his smartscreen and made a call. The man he needed answered immediately.

"Pangolin," growled Angus.

"Angus," said Tenuk. "You owe me an explanation. Where is that file?"

"Bugger that," said Angus. "I couldn't find it, all her drives are useless, and the police are on my tail. Now, what the hell is Yasmin doing?"

"Yasmin?" said Tenuk eagerly. "You know where she is?"

"No idea," said Angus, "but she's mucking up the triathlon. You'd better find her and call her off."

"I don't know what you're playing at, Angus," said Tenuk, thoroughly confused. "First you fail to get that file, and now you want me to interfere in an ongoing operation?"

"I've put myself out on a limb for you," said Angus. "Now call her off. She's going to kill that kid. If anything happens to him, I'll spill every secret I have." He stabbed at the off button in frustration and went back into the pub.

•

Through a haze, Ross saw an official autocar screech to a halt next to the shuttle. A tall blonde woman jumped out. She took one look at him and turned to a drone that hovered behind her. "Medical emergency, no penalty," she said clearly. Her voice print served as the signature.

The medic had succeeded in cutting enough material to get a grip on the skinsuit, and he tore the suit bodily from Ross's limp frame. "Take it easy," he said, massaging life back into Ross's arms and legs. He started to cough and retch, gulping at the fresh air.

"You said this was a hack," said the technician, reaching out a hand to help Ross to sit. "What did you mean?"

"Long story," croaked Ross. "Ask me after the race."

The adjudicator came up the steps. "I'm very sorry that this happened," she said. "Your place in the final is assured, and I hope that you will be fit to compete. We've delayed the start to give you as much time as possible to recover."

"Thank you," croaked Ross. He pulled himself slowly upright. "I'm going to see Shell now." He climbed down to ground level, getting stronger with every step, and as soon as he reached her, he hugged her as if he was never going to let go.

•

Tenuk stared at his smartscreen, completely blindsided. Why was this so important to Angus? There were more secrets in that man's past than he thought. But his own secrets were the priority. He had to find Yasmin.

"Xanthe," he called.

"Yes, Tenuk," said Xanthe, appearing silently next to him. "I have not yet located Yasmin."

"I have an idea," said Tenuk. "Come with me." He grabbed his reality mask and entered the virtual world where he had last encountered her. Maybe he could find her in there.

•

"45%" said Pete in Cameron's ear. "She's losing control."

Without warning, the blue-eyed avatar appeared in the middle of the room. Cameron stared in horror. She had hold of two struggling figures that Cameron recognised instantly.

Tara and Audrey.

"Let them go," shouted Cameron. "You have no quarrel with these kids."

She flung out her hand in the real world, desperately seeking Ben. "The girls are online," she said. "Yasmin's got them. Disconnect Tara from the software, now, and tell Chloe."

Ben didn't hesitate. Cameron heard him clattering down the stairs.

"I have you now," said Yasmin. "SimCavalier, why do you come to me willingly? You know I can destroy you."

"I'd like to see you try," said Cameron, unconsciously echoing Angus. "I'm a real being in the real world. You're just a shadow. You can't touch me."

"I can and I will," said Yasmin. A hypnotic rhythm started to beat around the room. "I have already disposed of one human who was no longer needed. You pose no challenge."

Cameron caught herself swaying to the beat. No. She started singing, badly, belting out her favourite song from when she was a teenager, breaking up the rhythm. She marched towards Yasmin, defiant, trying to hold the AI's attention and distract her from the girls.

Tara's avatar slumped to the ground, no longer linked to the child. Ben must have succeeded in freeing her. Audrey was still in Yasmin's grasp, but no longer struggling.

Yasmin seemed to grow, looming over Cameron, her head in the stars above her lair. Cameron felt rather than heard the volume controls on her mask slide to noise cancellation. She couldn't hear herself sing anymore. The mesmerising beat redoubled, and she felt her mind responding, dulling, focusing on the beat. Was this how the sleepwalker had died? Hypnotised and doing Yasmin's bidding? How was she able to control the peripheral devices, the mask that Cameron was wearing?

That was something to work out when she got back in the real world. She had a job to do here. If she couldn't sing, she could move. She darted this way and that across the chequered floor, trying to syncopate her rhythms and break the hypnotic hold. It worked for a minute, but her movements began to match the rhythm of the beat and she slowed.

She had to… hold… on…

Cameron's whole consciousness was immersed in Yasmin's reality. She didn't notice her body stand and start to walk slowly around the room. She bumped into furniture until she found the wall, then slid along until she found the window. Deeply asleep, her hands fumbled at the catch.

Ben came running up the stairs. "Cameron," he called, "Tara's okay. She's out and she's with her mum." He walked into the room and saw her standing at the open window, staring out with sightless eyes at the three storey drop to the garden.

"Cameron," he shouted, shaking her. "Cameron, wake up."

She stirred, still half mesmerised. In the virtual world she opened her eyes to see Audrey's avatar jumping around the room. Yasmin's focus on Cameron had given her a chance to move. "Hey, Yasmin," shouted Audrey. "Remember me?"

Remember? That was odd, thought Cameron. Audrey had never met Yasmin.

"Cameron, hang in there," said Audrey's voice. "It's me, Chloe."

In the half-dream state, Cameron's avatar struggled back up to stand and face Yasmin. She could hear nothing, but Ben's rousing brought her to her senses. What was happening again? Her mind felt like treacle. Cameron reached her real hand up to the reality mask and slid the audio control along. "Cameron," she heard Pete call in the background. "35%. Keep going."

Cameron swayed in both worlds, determined to stay conscious. But Yasmin's attention was no longer on her. Other figures had entered the room. A pangolin and a second blue eyed figure. Another one? Was she seeing double?

"Get out, Yasmin," said the Pangolin. "Get out while you still can. They're taking you apart. Get to the data centre. Save yourself."

"Not on my watch," yelled Chloe, flinging herself at Yasmin. She passed straight through the AI's perfectly rendered form, fragments of Yasmin flying out in slow motion towards the crumbling artwork on the wall.

Cameron's avatar and her real body slumped to the floor. The black and white chequerboard seemed to dissolve beneath her, and she knew nothing more.

27: TEAMWORK

When she came round, she was lying on her bed and there were familiar voices around her. Eventually, the muddle of noise turned into recognisable words.

"Did she do it, Ben?" said Aunt Vicky's voice. "Has Yasmin really gone?"

"Yes," said Ben. Cameron felt him squeeze her hand. "All the nodes have been closed. She can't have survived this time."

Cameron squeezed back and she felt Ben turn abruptly. "Well, look who's awake," he said. "You gave me a real fright."

Cameron opened her eyes and sat up slowly. "That was very strange," she said. "Is Tara okay?"

"Yes," said Ben. "I'm glad you're awake. It's nearly time for Ross's race, and I know you wouldn't want to miss it." He helped her to stand. She wobbled slightly. "I've got you," he said. "Don't worry."

Aunt Vicky bustled out ahead of them and Cameron made her way steadily down the stairs, gathering strength as she went. When they reached the ground floor, she could hear the livestream from the Olympics building up to the triathlon. Aunt Vicky went to open the door of the sitting room and paused. "Before you have another shock, dear, I thought you'd better know I had a visitor this afternoon."

Cameron walked through the door to cheers from the rest of the family. To her astonishment, sitting in the middle of the group was Jack Sladen.

He gave her an embarrassed smile. "I promised to come and see Aunt Vicky, didn't I?" he said. "This place hasn't changed a bit. I'm glad you're okay."

Cameron sat down next to Tara, hugging her tight. "Are you okay?" she whispered. "And Audrey?"

Tara nodded and clung to her aunt. "Yes," she said, sniffing. "I'm sorry. We had an invitation to a birthday party for one of our friends and we didn't think it would hurt to go."

"Don't worry," said Cameron. "Audrey's mom came to help, and everything is alright now."

"The invitation was from her, wasn't it?" whispered Tara.

"Probably," said Cameron. "She was very sneaky." She kept a firm grip on Tara and turned to Ben. "Are Ross and Shell okay?"

Ben nodded. "It was touch and go for a while," he said, "but yes, Ross was passed fit to compete and Shell is fine. They're due to start any minute."

Cameron settled back into the sofa and took notice of the coverage on the wallscreen for the first time. An aerial drone shot of the competitors warming up zoomed in on a red, white and blue cap. "There he is," she said, relieved.

The individual introductions began, each athlete spotlighted, waving to the virtual crowd. Ross gave the cameras a forced smile. He looked pale and drawn, but focused.

The wait was over, and they all dived into the water for the first leg of the race. Ross's Team GB cap bobbed steadily and rapidly along, keeping to his own pace. He emerged at the end of the swim in a respectable fourth place, had a perfect changeover, and by the time he was two hundred metres down the road he was in third.

"He's doing okay," said Ben. "It's hard work, though."

Cameron could see how much effort he was having to put in. He settled into the back of the leading group, keeping in touch but slightly off the pace.

"It's not going to be enough," said Charlie.

"Never write Ross off," said Cameron, willing him on. At the final changeover he was obviously in pain, but this was where he excelled. RunningManTech was running, and Yasmin was not going to deprive him of his medal. "Come on," she muttered. "Come on."

It was close, there was no doubt about it. In the final straight towards the finish, barely a couple of metres separated the top three athletes. Cameron could see Ross pushing for a final burst of acceleration, and he'd timed it just right. As he broke the tape, the room erupted.

Gold.

Cameron was shaking with relief. Ben hugged her from one side, and Jack from the other. Her smartscreen lit up with a call from the office. She saw the joy on her team's faces and panned around the room to show them the scenes in the house.

The cameras homed in on Ross who had Michelle in a tight hug. He waved to the crowd and then limped slowly towards the podium. As the British flag flew above him, Ross kissed the medal around his neck.

Afterwards, Cameron said she must have had something in her eye.

•

"When's Ross back at work?" asked Susie. She was working through her messages and conference schedule, planning her engagements for the next quarter.

"Monday," said Cameron. "He needed an extra couple of weeks to recover."

"It all seems like a dream now," said Susie. "I want to see that medal before I go back on the circuit. It did really happen, didn't it?"

"It did," said Joel. "I think he's going to feel a bit lost for a while. That was the biggest goal of his life, and he's done it, despite Yasmin."

"How did the karate girl get on?" asked Noor. "The one whose original competition was disrupted?" She was annotating the final model of the work they had done, archiving every link and note for future reference.

"Double gold," said Cameron. "Her first final was after the triathlon so there was no malware left and no Yasmin to control it. She won the kata, then followed it up with the sparring medal the next day. I watched it all. She was brilliant."

Cameron looked around the room. Her team was almost back together again and between them they had pulled off some remarkable work. Yasmin was gone. Jack had finally worked out who to trust. She had a very good idea where Tenuk was and he was being watched, and Ben was back. She couldn't ask for any more than that.

•

Johanna slept, lulled by the mesmerising sounds of the Sanctuary. Occasional sensations from the world around her threatened to lift her out of the dream state. The click of a lock. The sound of footsteps. A rush of cold air. She twitched, and the sensitive Sanctuary programme responded with hypnotic beats from the background to drive her deeper into the dream. Its selling point for shift workers the world over was the Sanctuary's ability to keep a user in a comfortable REM state for their entire allocated sleep cycle. It was certainly working for Johanna.

Her dream changed. She was at a console, her fingers flying over the keys. At a very deep level, she was conscious that this wasn't her own workspace. The controls were unfamiliar. Why was she dreaming about something outside her experience? The mesmeric beats sent her under again.

She shivered and reached in a half-sleep for her coverlet. She couldn't grasp it, and her hands fell to her side again as the Sanctuary adjusted its hypnotic settings to settle her. Her legs were heavy, and her feet were cold. The sensation drifted away. Locks clicked and threatened to wake her, but she stayed asleep. Eventually the dream drifted away like gossamer strands on the wind. Johanna turned over in her bed, tugged at the coverlet, and started snoring.

When she woke up, she found she was thinking of Aron, but she didn't know why.

QUANTUM BREACH

SIMCAVALIER BOOK SIX

1:   RELOCATION

The screams were still echoing in her head when she woke. Chloe clambered out of bed and made her way to the bathroom. The cold water splashing on her face brought her to her senses. She shuddered at the memory of the dream.

It hadn't been a dream to begin with. The screams had been all too real. It had been two years already, but it felt like yesterday.

Dawn was breaking. Chloe leaned on the window frame and watched as warm, rosy light bathed the landscape. The peace of this place was a sharp contrast to the horrors that lurked in her mind. It was her newest refuge, and she hoped they would never move again. Maybe setting down roots here would help to banish her memories of the fall.

The old Wyoming Militia, its leadership toppled only a few years before, had recovered and strengthened in its mountain hideouts while Chloe, whose intelligence had brought them down on the brink of executing an attack that would hold the world to ransom, settled to a new life in Texas.

The Militia's sudden eruption from hiding, just weeks after the global celebrations of the 2048 Olympics, and their incursions north and south along the Rockies had taken everyone by surprise. To the north, they were turned back. Montana, proud and independent and familiar with the old foe, held strong. The Canadians were having none of it and fought tooth and nail with their small neighbour to protect the border. The four corner states – Colorado, New Mexico, Arizona and Utah – found themselves facing an army overnight, and the shaky union they established in the absence of any federal support lasted just days. The Militia's onslaught continued, while down on the plains of Texas new uprisings from sleeper cells moved east and north, closing the gap and forming an impenetrable barrier down the length of the old country. It signalled the beginning of the end.

Outside her window the sun peeked over the horizon. Chloe's mind wandered back to those chaotic final days.

She never knew whether it had been the screams from the street that had woken her or the frantic hammering on her apartment door. Ben stood in the dark hallway, panting after running up the stairs with a bulky backpack, panic in his eyes.

"We need to get out, now. You and Audrey have a seat on the plane. There's no time to lose."

Audrey was already awake, eyes wide, clutching the old teddy that she'd carried since they first fled the Militia's grasp four years earlier. Older now and as level-headed as her mother, she nodded. "I'm half packed already," she said. "It felt bad."

"Good girl," said Chloe faintly. The kid had spent a third of her life travelling from one place to another, first when they escaped from Wyoming and then through a series of safe houses. Of course she was ready. It was Chloe who was finding it hard to leave again.

"I don't want to go," she said, "but I know we can't stay. I'm so glad to see you. I had no idea how we'd get out. All the communication lines are down. How long have we got?"

"Half an hour at most," said Ben. "My car's outside." He glanced nervously at the stairwell. "I can't leave it. There's trouble brewing."

Chloe knew how much he loved that old car. The Mustang had seen better days, but it was Ben's pride and joy. "Go and guard it. We'll be right down."

She was as good as her word. They hadn't arrived with much three years earlier, and they left ten minutes later with the same bags. Chloe carried an extra backpack with their tablets, laptops and her hard disks, and as a nod to the brief stability they'd experienced, a few mementoes of Austin.

The square outside was crowded, and people were flooding down from all the apartment blocks and surrounding residential streets. Children were crying and adults were shouting, everyone milling around helplessly. A local transit bus, already full, was forced to a halt nearby. People scrambled onto the vehicle, clinging to the bike racks and the roof, desperate to get away. For the first time Chloe heard distant gunfire. A returning shot in the air from somewhere on the square made her jump, and the next volley she heard was coming closer. She knew that most of the people here were likely to be armed. Nowhere would be safe when the bullets started flying in earnest. She looked around for Ben and the distinctive red car, but he was nowhere to be seen. She squashed a rising sense of panic. Suddenly, over the cacophony of the crowd, she heard a car horn and the revving of an engine.

"Over there," said Audrey, tugging at her mother's arm.

Sure enough, there was the Mustang moving fast on the opposite side of the square. Chloe watched as Ben accelerated to escape a knot of people who were trying to grab at the trim and the door handles. He swung the car around the corner of the block at high speed and disappeared.

"We can catch him on the next circuit," said Chloe. "Come on, run."

Fear gave them strength as they pushed through the press of people. Chloe used her case as a battering ram and a shield and Audrey clung for dear life to the straps of her mother's backpack. They reached the street just as Ben flew around the corner again. He screeched to a halt and the desperate crowd surged around the car. Chloe, tears streaming down her cheeks, pushed Audrey in front of her. Ben popped the door open, and Chloe practically threw her daughter in, followed by the precious backpack. She slammed the door again, hoping that Ben knew what she wanted him to do. The Mustang leapt away, and Chloe ran in the opposite direction down the road, dodging people and cars, driven by fear and the sound of gunfire.

She was half a block away from the crowded square when she heard the familiar growl of the engine, and the red car appeared. Ben stopped and she dived into the passenger seat, suitcase clutched awkwardly to her chest, legs curled into the footwell. Audrey was tucked in the cramped back seat with her luggage and the backpack. Ben didn't wait for Chloe to untangle herself. He accelerated away.

Chloe took a deep, shuddering breath. She turned to Ben. "Thank you," she said.

He flashed her a strained smile. "We can stop and put that case in the boot when we get out of the city," he said. "Hold on now."

Ten blocks further out he swerved off onto a side road and zig zagged through a leafy suburb then onto a dirt road that led down towards the creek. The car pulled up in the shade of a grove of trees.

"Let's get you both comfortable." Ben jumped out and opened the boot, collected the case that was crushing Chloe in the front seat, and then leaned into the back to collect Audrey's. "We'll attract less attention if you don't look as if you're leaving. Let's go."

The Mustang skidded off up the track and Chloe winced as the low-slung car clattered on loose stones. Before she knew it, they were back on a metalled road and heading out of town on a deserted highway. She spotted a familiar landmark. They had travelled north and then west. They were heading out to the plains.

"Aren't we going to the airport?" she asked.

"Not Bergstrom," said Ben. "It's chaos. We're going to Lago Vista." He kept his eyes on the road ahead. "We need to take a little detour here. There's a roadblock up ahead."

The Mustang protested as he darted off through another neighbourhood. Families were busy packing their possessions into pickups, and only the children had time to look up and see the red car passing by. Ben patted the dashboard. "Poor old girl," he said. "I'll be sorry to leave her behind."

They pulled back onto the highway a few hundred yards past the other side of the roadblock, but the growl of the engine alerted the Militia.

"Heads down," said Ben grimly. He gunned the Mustang up the highway and winced at the thump of a bullet embedding itself in the chassis. It was the only shot that reached them. The old car quickly outpaced the guards, and they soon found themselves on country roads surrounded by scrubland.

Chloe slumped into her seat, trying to make sense of the frantic start to the day. It had been barely an hour since Ben knocked on the door and her life changed again.

"I can't thank you enough," she said at last. "But why did you come all the way up from San Antonio? You could have been away from all of this days ago, as soon as the uprising started."

Ben glanced at her ruefully. "You'd think so," he said. "It didn't seem serious. It was all happening a thousand miles away. Even when the news came from Denver, we weren't worried. And then the local idiots started. The simulations showed that their support would hand Texas to the Militia. Once I knew that, I got the hell out as soon as I could."

"Why Austin?" asked Chloe.

"I had nowhere else to go," said Ben. "I couldn't stay down there, and in any case I wanted to make sure you two made it out. I managed to get hold of Cameron, and she got hold of Jack, and, well, I hope there's a plane waiting. If not, we need some new ideas."

There was a plane. Audrey was more excited than afraid now, peering out of the window and waiting for take-off. Chloe curled up next to her, exhausted and relieved. Every seat was full. Some of her colleagues and their families were on board, those that Jack had managed to reach and who were as ready as she was to put the new horrors of this place behind them. As they rose into the sky and the plane banked, Chloe took a last look at the city she had called home for three years. At the time she had no idea where they were going or what lay ahead.

That all felt like a long time ago. Their new home was everything she could have wished for. Chloe could hear Audrey moving around getting ready for school. The child was resilient. She had taken to life in England, the small town and local school with the same enthusiasm as for her old city elementary, making friends quickly and settling to a whole new education system with barely a hitch. And as for Chloe herself, she had a sense of peace and belonging, and for the first time in years, a new love in her life.

Sunbeams streaming through the window brought her back to today, and the realisation that she'd be late if she carried on wallowing in her memories. She showered and dressed quickly. Her regular autocar was waiting.

The Statesman offices lay out of town, deep in the Northumberland countryside. Originally home to Jack Sladen's philanthropic venture, the Sladen Foundation, Dunswyke was now also the headquarters of Statesman Tech, transplanted lock, stock and barrel from Texas. Chloe's autocar dropped her at the gate and zipped away along the lane towards a nearby village. The site was already bustling. A newly built, sprawling single storey complex contained state-of-the-art facilities for the Statesman staff, a mix of refugees from the old Austin office who'd chosen to settle here and some new hires who brought the team back up to strength. The old stone bastle house stood proudly in the shadow of the cliff, its commanding presence retained despite the new buildings that surrounded it. Jack had his office in there. A data centre behind the bastle extended into the cliff, the moors rising above it.

Chloe loved Dunswyke. The moors and the silence reminded her a little of the wilds of Wyoming that had captured her heart a decade before, albeit on a much smaller scale. She thanked her lucky stars every day that Ben had brought her here.

She settled at her desk and pulled up the live network visualisations, swiping at the air and scrolling through key indicators from the Diaulos management information system. On the big screen at the end of the office, transactions ticked along and blocks formed at a steady rate. The main indicators were a healthy green. A few amber markers highlighted non-urgent issues, most of which Chloe already knew about. A new software update proposal had come through overnight from the scattered global developer community that made up the Sladen Foundation DAO and from the lively discussions on the developer forum it seemed it was already making its way through the peer review process. Chloe made a note of the details. Her team would review the new proposal for functionality and security after the morning meeting.

Jack was out of the country again. When he was travelling for work, he usually made the effort to join team meetings by screen or avatar from wherever he was in the world, spreading the love and the famous smile. Today he was absent. A couple of people murmured their concern, but Chloe knew that Jack was taking some rare and much needed down time, and she didn't begrudge him the break.

The teams gave their status updates. Chloe brought up the new development proposal, just a routine notification. The Sladen Foundation's monthly award of grants to deserving causes would go to its regular community vote at midday. Tech was focusing on an upgrade rolling out to the Diaulos wristbands. Customer support capacity had been increased, both human and machine, and their sentiment trackers were ready to catch the early warning signs of any problems with the update, scraping social commentary for language that might suggest an improvement that was needed, a glitch had appeared, or indeed that users were happy. All in all, it was business as usual. The meeting closed bang on time, attending avatars winked out of existence, and all the on-site staff headed back to their desks.

"Chloe, have you got a minute?"

She turned to see her colleague, Joel, beckoning her to an empty room.

"I didn't want us to be overheard," he continued, closing the door carefully. "Cameron's trying to reach Jack. There's been an accident."

2:   STORMY WEATHER

It had come out of the blue. The young skipper frowned at the readings. The pressure shouldn't be dropping that fast. He checked the weather predictions once again and cross-referenced them against his exact GPS location. According to the simulations, it should be set fair but the wind was strengthening.

The oldest hand on the yacht stuck his head around the bridge door. "I'm battening down the hatches, Leo," he shouted. "I don't care what the FirstMate readouts say. My bones tell me there's a storm coming through and we're right in its path."

Leo felt a sudden chill in the air that took him back to his childhood, spending every spare moment sailing with just his skill and his wits, reading the weather from the skies and the wind. For years now he'd been ferrying the rich around high-class resorts and relying on his AI FirstMate™ to make all the sailing decisions. It had been too easy. Trusting the machine may have dulled his instincts, but they had just kicked back in with a vengeance.

"You're right," he shouted, struggling to be heard over a sudden squall and rumble of thunder. "Get everyone to the muster stations with their lifejackets. I have a bad feeling about this."

FirstMate™ still claimed that the yacht was travelling on calm seas under clear skies, but the sea was anything but calm. Leo wrestled with the yacht, trying to ride the waves with every ounce of his instinct and training, but the AI was blindly applying all the complex rules that had been embedded in its system to data feeds that were obviously flawed. It calmly overrode every attempt to take control, reversing Leo's desperate course changes as soon as he made them. A wave broke high on the bridge window and Leo staggered as the vessel tilted and slid down the face of a high swell. He had to find a way to bring the power he needed to tackle these seas. He reached around and wrenched the fire extinguisher from the bulkhead, battering the terminal for all he was worth. The screen flickered but the yacht continued to tilt.

Through the window he could see that the life rafts had been launched. He struggled in vain with the yacht's controls and tried to count the bright lifejackets as his passengers and crew fled for their lives. Fifteen… sixteen… eighteen… twenty. All accounted for. The rafts spun quickly away from the vessel and Leo knew there was nothing more he could do. He flung himself out of the door of the bridge, took a deep breath, and jumped.

The sea tossed him this way and that. He caught a glimpse of the two life rafts still upright and occupied and saw flares exploding against the dark sky, but he knew that it would be fatal for him to struggle against the waves to reach them. He spread his arms and legs, breathed deeply to calm his racing heart, and surrendered to the flow of the ocean, buoyed by his lifejacket and riding the swell. Then a stroke of luck. The yacht's small dive tender was tossed towards him on a wave. He managed to grab hold of it and clung to the inflatable tube, gripping the nearest handle tightly. The next wave threw him bodily into the boat. He was safe, for now. He found a flare in the emergency box stowed tight under the console, fired it into the air, and waited for the storm to pass.

The sky began to clear. Leo caught a glimpse of land. He turned his head out to sea but could no longer see the yacht. The storm waves had calmed, and towards the shore he could see activity, people, bright colours and small boats. The shouts that reached his ears were the sweetest sounds he had ever heard. The little inflatable floated gently towards the beach, and Leo wept.

•

Cameron Silvera read to the end of the article on her smartscreen then scrolled back through the video and satellite footage of the disaster and the rather clearer time lapse simulation that accompanied it. She turned the screen this way and that, every so often tapping to replay a segment as she peered at the detail. Eventually she put the device down, turned to her main workstation, and pulled up the repository where she and her peers were sharing their findings.

There were several users online including some of her team. Joel, seconded to Statesman Tech, was using all his connections with family back in the Caribbean to add local context and eyewitness reports of the storm's progress. Cameron took a moment to review the new information that he'd contributed and added her own observations and notes. In another window on her screen, there was a spirited chat in a different secure channel about the growing discrepancies between forecast weather events and the real thing. Cameron hadn't really engaged with this forum in the past, but now it had her attention. The sinking of a luxury yacht in the Caribbean would normally have been just another entry in the log of uncontrolled extreme weather incidents that were being tracked by national security agencies. However, the media were all over this story because Jack Sladen had been a guest on the trip. He was one of her largest clients and an old friend. She had personal reasons for checking in now, and as it turned out, the topic intersected with her professional interest too.

The supercell storm that had whisked through the Antilles had been predicted. Multiple quantum simulations had been sampled to determine the most likely path of the storm and to predict its impact at a micro level, taking account of all the fragile and varied ecosystems that would be affected. The authorities across the Caribbean nations had been well prepared for the speed and trajectory of its arrival. They had time to put in place mitigations and protection against the devastation they knew it would bring, and to ready the emergency services to react to the things they couldn't control.

The predictions were wrong. The eye of the storm had sown a path of devastation more than three hundred miles further north than expected. People emerged from behind flood defences and within deep storm shelters and found themselves staring at their intact homes under clear blue skies in no more than a brisk wind, while others counted the cost of unexpected destruction, the loss of lives and livelihoods, and the undoing of years of preservation work in the ecosystems of precariously low-lying islands.

"How could that simulation be so far out of whack?" Cameron muttered to herself.

Long-term and hyper-accurate geolocated forecasts were essential for shipping, farming and daily life in a world where weather patterns were shifting and climate events were growing more extreme and hitting with greater frequency. The quantum computing power to produce full ecosystem simulations had grown exponentially in the previous two decades. Cameron recalled as a teenager that even the hour-by-hour rain forecast used to be slightly unreliable. She remembered Aunt Vicky checking carefully before hanging out the washing and cursing when the rain came after all, enlisting Cameron's help to bring everything in quickly. Now, the whole world took the forecasts for granted and planned with precision days and even weeks in advance. Was this storm another exception to the rule, or another sign that the machines were not as reliable as everyone believed?

There was one more possibility, and studying the repository, Cameron's suspicions began to grow. Could someone be interfering with the operations of the quantum simulators themselves?

If so, it would be a complex thing to achieve. A bad actor would have to commit to years of planning along with access to the systems that managed the inputs and outputs of the quantum machines themselves. But it was possible, and Cameron knew that every rogue nation state and every cybercrime syndicate had been working out how to hack quantum processors since the technology was in its infancy. She and her infosec peers were matching the criminals every step of the way, but if this was an attack, as she suspected, someone, somewhere, was playing a very long game and by doing so had evaded all their defences.

Her musings were cut short by an insistent alert on her smartscreen. She glanced at the details and accepted the call.

"Hi, Ross," she said. "What's up?"

All that was visible on the screen was the top of Ross's head, tousled ginger hair blowing in the wind against a leafy background.

"Can you hear me?" he asked.

"Loud and clear," said Cameron.

"Great," said Ross. "I'm out and about and the signal's not great. Have you heard anything from Jack? Is he okay?"

"I haven't spoken to him," said Cameron, "but the authorities say that everyone was evacuated to life rafts."

"Good," said Ross, the relief evident in his voice. "I bet you're glad you turned down the invitation."

Cameron shuddered involuntarily. A cruise around the sunken islands and preserved beauty of the Caribbean had been almost too tempting. Jack repeatedly invited Cameron to join him for the events and trips that were a routine part of his billionaire lifestyle, and Cameron always declined. As far as she was concerned, her role in their rekindled friendship was to keep Jack on the straight and narrow, ensuring that his businesses built reliable and secure software after years of being known for gaping holes and rushed code. She wasn't about to compromise their professional relationship, however long they had known each other.

"You know I don't mix business and pleasure," she replied. "It sounded idyllic, mind you. I can't imagine how frightening that storm must have been for everyone involved."

"When's Jack due back in the UK?" asked Ross. "I lose track of what he's up to. He's always so busy."

"The end of next week," said Cameron, "but that depends on whether he goes to Tech 2050 in Singapore or not. He's still listed as a keynote speaker."

"He's pretty resilient," said Ross. "I'm sure he'll –" He glanced sharply away from the camera, distracted. "You again," he murmured.

"What?" said Cameron.

Ross's attention snapped back to Cameron. "Nothing," he said. "Got to go. I'm glad Jack's okay. I'll be heading to the office after training."

"Great," said Cameron. "I'll see you later. Have fun."

She leaned back in her chair and stared at the ceiling. Unbidden, a small black and white cat hopped up onto the desk with a commanding squeak and settled itself squarely on top of her smartscreen. Cameron reached out and stroked it and was rewarded with loud purring. "You've had your breakfast," said Cameron sternly, "and I've told you before, cats don't get lunch."

But humans do, she reminded herself. She'd been up since six and although it was barely midday, she realised she was hungry. The habit of working through meals was one she was trying to break. She stood and stretched, relieving the familiar ache in her back from spending too long at her desk, and strolled over to the fridge to see what goodies lay within.

She loved her new place as much as she had loved her old apartment, but that block's lax security and the less than friendly attentions of cybercriminals leaking into meat space, targeting her in real life, had forced her to review her living arrangements. She'd thought long and hard about Ben's offer to move into his place. She still wondered if her decision to remain independent was what had finally pushed him away.

Friends and family had pointed out that she could live anywhere she wanted, and she took up the challenge.

She had looked right across the city for the perfect place, but when Jack spotted a luxury apartment she could actually afford in an anonymous and highly secure gated tower complex, she fell for it as soon as she walked through the door. Even better, the tower was close to her old apartment and within reach of central London and the familiar, bustling Borough Market. She kept her old networks and routines, refusing to give in to the cybercriminals who still stalked her.

She'd done her due diligence, of course. She and her team at Argentum Associates were used to finding the gaps in physical security as part of standard reviews, and Cameron still got a buzz out of simply walking into highly sensitive locations and calling the client from anything up to and including their own desk to let them know there was a problem. She knew where breaches of security were most likely to occur and relished the challenge of closing them down. The tower's management had taken advantage of Cameron's expertise to commission a full penetration test and came away with a five-star rating.

The tower was using all the newest technologies and best practice, right down to hand-picked and highly vetted staff who handled the day to day running of the complex, mainly to protect the A-listers who called it home. The Argentum team had tried their usual tricks to penetrate the site and found a handful of obscure but exploitable gaps, all of which were fixed in short order. The only slight inconvenience as far as Cameron was concerned was the drone net that cloaked the whole building. Gone were the days of lazily ordering groceries for delivery to the balcony. Any drone that tried to fly through the sensor mesh without security clearance was toast, and the bar for that clearance had been set high. Instead, there was an arrangement for the security staff to field orders outside the net and hand deliver them. It was a good way for them to keep an eye on the residents, too, which was a hit with some of Cameron's retired neighbours. She now woke up each day to magnificent views across the city with the reassurance of the best security money could buy.

Cameron made a quick sandwich while the cat weaved around her legs, claiming starvation. She gave into its demands in exchange for a moment's peace to eat her lunch, then packed her bag. She was due in the office. She could keep working online but this was her chance to be around real people. The whole team appreciated the days when they were together in person, sparking ideas off each other and reinforcing their deep connections and mutual trust.

She grabbed an apple and headed out of the door and down the elevator, nodding to a famous neighbour in the lobby. It was a sunny day, and the streets were swarming with tourists, many wearing guide headsets that brought the historic buildings to life around them. Although the masks were simply augmented reality, ensuring that the wearer could see the real world around them, they may as well have been fully immersive for all the attention the gawping tourists paid to other people. After dodging three groups who were owning the pavement and seeing more parties thundering along in her direction, Cameron gave up and headed for the tube.

Emerging from the station closest to the office, she stopped at her favourite bakery and picked up a bag of sweet cake bites as a snack for the team. The security guards at the busy office building greeted her with a smile, and she headed up to the sixth floor where Argentum Associates had its headquarters.

As soon as she opened the door, she knew something was wrong.

Noor broke the silence. "Are you okay?"

"Yes, why shouldn't I be?"

"Jack's missing."

Cameron set the bag of pastries down on the nearest desk and stared at Noor. "But they said everyone got off the boat," she said.

"They all made it to life rafts," said Pete. "Only one of the life rafts has been found."

Cameron stared past Pete at the huge wallscreen where the latest news was streaming live from the Caribbean. It showed drone footage of the surrounding seas as the search continued. Six people were missing, said the caption, and every effort was being made to find them.

She sat down heavily in the nearest chair. "Dammit, Jack," she whispered. "Where are you?" Her eyes fixed on the screen, she barely registered that the whole team had gathered to sit with her, watching intently for any signs of life.

The scene split and cameras zoomed in on a knot of people in survival blankets being ushered up a beach. Cameron searched desperately for a glimpse of Jack in the group. He wasn't there.

3: TEAMWORK

On the other side of the world, the same footage played on wallscreens at the luxury home of gambling magnate Chaoxiang Chen. Tenuk, the sole heir to his father's vast Sapphire Straits gambling empire, was watching the search with as much focus as Cameron was in London.

The old man, seated in a wing backed chair at the window of his office, sipped his tea, unconcerned. "Jack Sladen's influence on the world of technology has held you back," he said. "Now he's gone, many opportunities present themselves."

Tenuk frowned. "I liked Jack Sladen, father. The time I spent working for him was enjoyable. There is still hope. The search goes on."

Chaoxiang laughed. "You were never working for him, Tenuk. You were always working for me, though you didn't know it at the time. Whether he is lost for a while or gone for good, the timing is perfect."

"Did you have anything to do with this?" asked Tenuk. He knew his father well enough not to underestimate him. The man was brilliant and, in Tenuk's opinion, on the edge of madness. He had the will to meddle with the quantum systems that simulated the world's weather and very likely the tools as well.

"Of course not," said the old man innocently. He took another sip of his tea. "A happy accident."

Tenuk's eyes narrowed. He went over to his father's desk and called up the latest real-time business report. "Huh. Sapphire Straits turned a healthy profit on the path of that storm. No wonder you're in a good mood. I can't believe you'll take bets on this kind of thing."

"We simply facilitate the placing of bets," said Chaoxiang. "We cannot control human nature, and part of our success is in providing a service that others refuse to entertain."

Tenuk scrolled to the current activity. There was a lively market building on if, when and where Jack Sladen would be found. He looked back up at the news feed. Drones were circling over something floating in the sea. It was only when Tenuk identified the object as a bundle of cushions from the deck of the yacht that he realised he had been holding his breath.

"You are the same as me," said Chaoxiang. "You think of yourself as the great philanthropist, helping people out of poverty, and you don't allow the consequences of the software you write to disturb you. Don't try taking the moral high ground, Tenuk."

Furious, Tenuk opened his mouth to reply and realised that he had nothing to counter the argument. He and his father were the same. It made him sick to his stomach. He turned abruptly and walked out of the office without taking leave of the old man. It was time to get some air.

The humidity of Singapore's early evening hit him as soon as he left the cool environment of the house. The sun had set, and the golden light of dusk was almost gone. Insects buzzed and chirruped around him, and there was rustling in the trees as a troupe of monkeys swung back home.

Home. This was Tenuk's home, but also his prison. He could never go back to Austin, to a life seemingly independent of his family. The Militia's invasion had seen to that. He couldn't return to his old job here in Singapore or even spend time in the city for fear of running into former colleagues or neighbours. The original online teams that had underpinned his highly successful Pasar Network and Steamyard ventures, writing software for the highest bidder regardless of ethics or purpose, had fragmented, and he was only now slowly starting to rebuild. He was trapped in a world that he had tried to leave and that had drawn him inexorably back in. Tenuk hated it. Jack's name splashed across the news simply reminded him of how much he had lost.

With his father's blessing, for what that was worth, he had started a new training academy, a new crop of lucky coders who had competed to take this path out of poverty. Several of them were working on a software proposal for the Sladen Foundation DAO, and it was probably time that he checked in on their activity. Tenuk took a deep breath and savoured the scents of the garden, then turned and went back into the house. He would just have time before dinner to review progress.

In theory, all the decisions about the development of the Foundation's underlying software were made by the core developer community. Jack Sladen had known the PR value of showing that the system was fully decentralised and under the control of its members, not subject to the whims of yet another tech billionaire, and he had committed entirely to the vision. Tenuk, as Jack's chief technology officer at the time, had instead made absolutely sure that it was under his own control. He knew it would come in useful one day, and this was the day.

Tenuk had seeded the community with his people and also had several dumb AI agents with user logins to the developer forum. He spent a happy few minutes refining the agents' prompts for their conversations with each other, getting them to challenge specific elements of the software proposal and respond to them like normal forum members participating in the rigorous peer review process. There were plenty of real voices in there. Some were genuine and independent and quite unsuspecting of any manipulation, but the rest were following his agenda. He spotted the new handles of two developers who were still in Austin, living under martial law in the newly independent country of Texas. They were among a handful of Statesman Tech staff who'd chosen to stay put when the rest relocated abruptly to England. They had been and remained part of Tenuk's clandestine team.

He'd reactivated the leader of a group of talented hackers in Indonesia that he'd used years before and recruited some new and brilliant youngsters from the wrong side of the tracks whose lives Tenuk knew he could change for the better. Several of them were in there having a spirited and well-planned discussion about the finer details of the coding. He made a few notes on their files for the next team review. Tenuk believed firmly in giving people opportunities, even if the work they were doing was frowned on by the authorities. He had never thought of himself as a cybercriminal, but as someone who redistributed wealth to where it was needed.

An old, familiar handle appeared in the chat and Tenuk took his leave. He had no wish to tangle with Cloverleaf. She, Chloe, had known him too well. They had worked together at Statesman Tech, of course, but in another, darker life Chloe had been part of Pasar, a key member of the black hat team developing malware for his clients, before she turned traitor. If she had the slightest suspicion that he was there, the game was up. This was why he used his team and his AI agents to sow the seeds of the discussion. If he participated directly then a simple phrase, a quirk of syntax, could give him away.

"Admin," he said into the air as he sat at his desk.

There was no response. He drummed his fingers on the desk. She should be on standby at all times, waiting for his call.

"Zara," he said, louder.

"Yes, Tenuk," came a quiet voice out of the ether. Her voice was amplified by the office sound system, echoing all around him. "I'm here."

"What's the latest on the search for Jack Sladen?"

"No further news."

Tenuk imagined for a moment that he heard a note of sorrow in the AI's voice. Zara had been Jack's dedicated virtual assistant until he cast her aside. But a bundle of software, algorithms and data objects couldn't have feelings. It – they – inspired emotion in others, though. Tenuk still mourned Zara's sister Yasmin whose place Zara had taken as Admin after Yasmin's destruction. He was trying very hard not to anthropomorphise Zara and to treat her as the assistive tool she was designed to be. He deliberately restricted their interactions to his workspaces, shying away from the always-on relationship he had had with Yasmin, and Zara had had with Jack.

It was unbelievably hard.

"Zara, could you monitor the peer review discussions on the new software proposal?" he said, strictly business now. "Let me know if anyone's out of line or there are any signs of suspicion at the Foundation end. We need the approval and update to be fully rolled out in time for the next funding cycle."

"Yes, Tenuk."

Without another word Tenuk left his office and went to freshen up before dinner. Everything was in place, and now all he had to do was wait.

•

In London, Cameron paced up and down the office like a caged tiger. Every so often her eyes rested on the wallscreen's news feed. The live footage of the search had been relegated to a corner and interviews with the rescued passengers and crew were ongoing.

"Surely they can trace chip locations," said Sandeep. "Even if not everyone on that life raft was chipped, just one should register."

"Too wide a search area, not enough close-range beacons," said Pete. "If you think about it, your own chip only triggers a response within a few metres when it's interfacing with, you know, doors and street ads and so on."

"But we can trace people by chip," said Noor. "We've done it before."

"In an urban area," said Cameron. "Not in the ocean."

"It'd be a different story if he still had that AI assistant of his," said Pete.

"Oh!" Cameron stopped pacing and stared at him. "I wonder…?"

Years before, Jack had been utterly reliant on a virtual assistant that was linked to him day and night, managing and monitoring his every move. He'd abandoned the program, an entity called Zara, when he realised it was a security risk, but he'd always missed the utility of just calling her name, and the companionship she brought as he travelled the world alone. Statesman Tech and Argentum had collaborated to create a new assistant under their control.

"I'll get Joel on the line now," said Noor. "I know they were testing the new system. I wonder if he had the prototype with him?"

The rolling news coverage on the wallscreen was replaced by a video feed from Dunswyke. Joel waved at his old colleagues. "Hi, folks. I'm just waiting for Chloe."

There was the sound of a door closing and Chloe poked her head into shot. "Let me get a chair," she said. A moment later she reappeared and settled next to Joel facing the camera. "Tough day," she said. "Good to see you, Cameron. I hope y'all are doing okay? Everyone here is so worried."

"Us too," said Cameron, putting aside their differences for now. "But maybe we have a way to help with the search. How have you been getting on with Jack's new assistant?"

"You mean Pip?" said Joel. "We're way ahead of you, Cameron. Training's been going well, and Jack tested a few of the prototype comms options last time he was here."

"He's part of the training process now," added Chloe. "His off-the-cuff questions should reveal any quirks in the way Pip is processing inputs."

"Does that mean he took a hardware connection with him?" asked Cameron. "If so, I bet he's been playing with it. Jack can't resist a gadget, and I know he missed Zara." She paused and frowned. "What is the hardware? Did you go with the earbud again? Could he have lost it in the evacuation."

"He definitely has it with him," said Joel, "and there's no way he'll have lost it. That's why I think we might have a chance."

"Earbuds are too intrusive," said Chloe. "With this system architecture we can hook into anything that's IoT enabled and change the hardware at will, so we asked Jack what he wanted for the test." She grinned despite the gravity of the situation. "You know the latest high fashion craze, those skindiver tattoos? They last a couple of months and then just heal their way out."

Cameron grinned back. "That's superb. You chipped a skindiver." There was a ripple of laughter around the office. "Nice work. Is it location enabled?"

Joel shook his head. "No," he said. "Not in the way you're thinking. We can't set a trace on the device. We have a better chance of Jack's standard chip location being picked up."

"However, all interactions with Pip have metadata attached," said Chloe. "I've set up a routine to extract everything we have from the most recent conversational data. We know he's been talking to Pip since the original test, and we'll find out where and when that happened."

"Can't you just ask Pip?" said Cameron. "Surely it can try and talk to him?"

"We've tried, obviously," said Joel. "The prototype is voice activated by Jack. We're working on tweaking the software to push a notification through without him initiating the communication, but either it's not working or he's not in range of any communication networks right now. As for interrogating past interactions, all that's done is pick up a glitch in the intersectionality of the data that Pip's interpreting. We have to go the long way round."

"Okay," said Cameron. "When do you think you'll have anything?"

"Soon," said Chloe. "There's a lot of data to sift through but last time I looked, the query was 85% complete."

"Keep me posted," said Cameron.

"Will do," said Joel, reaching forward to close the connection.

"Wait," said Cameron. "One more question. We really, really need to know. What was the tattoo?"

Joel laughed. "Some old school sci-fi logo. He's a nerd at heart, isn't he, Cameron?"

"He is."

The connection to Dunswyke winked out and Cameron found herself looking at the news feed again. Her shoulders slumped as the reality of the situation reasserted itself.

"He'll be okay," said Noor quietly, handing her a coffee.

"I hope so," said Cameron.

There was no more time to dwell on what was happening in the Caribbean. The Argentum team was busier than ever with the constant pounding of cyberattacks at the doors of their clients. Much of the time, good security processes, vigilance and training kept the threats at bay, but some would inevitably get through.

Cameron headed over to a soundproof cabin in the corner of the office and peered through the small window. Michelle was sitting at the desk with her headphones on and a look of fierce concentration on her face.

"She's talking to the people who claimed responsibility for the hospital breach," said Sandeep, who was monitoring the conversation. "I think she's getting somewhere."

"What were they called?" said Cameron. "Siberia Chill? Never heard of them."

Sandeep shook his head. "That's the name that's out there, but we're fairly sure it's fake. Michelle's almost got them nailed."

"What's her angle?" asked Cameron.

"She's playing dumb," said Sandeep. "As far as they're concerned, she's a desperate executive who's been promoted beyond her capabilities and hasn't a clue how to respond to the ransom demand. The guy on the other end is getting really frustrated and she's pulling so much information out of him now, it's not true. Look."

Cameron scanned the rolling summary of the conversation. "Hah. You were right about where the compromise came from. I used that scheduling tool for a while myself, until they pushed a dodgy update."

Pete had wandered over to join them. "I tracked down one of the developers this morning," he said. "The company went bust a couple of years ago and the software was just left out in the wild, unpatched."

"How was it still authorised for use at Oak Medical?" asked Cameron. "Oh, wait. I guess it wasn't."

"Exactly," said Sandeep. "Someone who had been using it for years mixed up their private and work applications and our attackers were straight in and gradually gained access to all the systems they needed to plant their malware."

"Better notify our client base," said Cameron. "They won't be the only ones with the same scenario, even if not the same software."

"Already on it," said Sandeep. "Ross has been following up. He's also put a general alert on industry forums, and I've seen critical deactivation warnings coming through from some hosting providers already."

"Good work," said Cameron. "Nothing like the risk of breaching your hosting terms to focus the mind of a CTO."

"Who's behind this hack?" asked Pete. "Do we have location data for the guy on the phone? I'm assuming he's not in Siberia."

"Correct," said Sandeep. "We have mainly contextual information pulled out from this conversation, plus analysis of voice patterns. His IP address and the voice filter suggests Brazil, not Russia, but it looks like the guy is really in Nigeria."

"I wonder if it's DeltaG?" said Cameron. "The profile of the ransomware fits with some of the work that's been attributed to them in the past."

"Probably," said Sandeep. "I'm sending what we have over to the Nigerian cybersecurity authorities now. Ah! Call ended."

The door opened and Michelle came out, yawning. "That was tiring. Did you get everything you needed? It's DeltaG, I'm sure of it."

"Got it, sent it, sorted," said Sandeep.

"Nice work," said Cameron.

Michelle turned at the sound of her voice. "Hi, Cameron," she said. "Any word on Jack?"

Cameron opened her mouth to reply, but before she could say anything Noor called across the office.

"News from Dunswyke!"

The wallscreen flicked back to the video feed and Joel's face.

"You've got something?" said Cameron, hurrying back to her desk.

"Yes," said Joel. "He gave Pip a running commentary as they evacuated, which Chloe's sent straight over to the authorities."

"It was still working when the yacht went down," said Cameron.

"Yes," said Joel, "and it's working now. In the last few minutes, Pip's received a communication blip. We can't decipher the content, but we know that the chip only responds to Jack's voice."

Cameron stared at the screen, hope rising. "He's alive."

The office door opened. Ross walked in, dropped his bag, and took in the scene. "I take it there's good news about Jack?"

"Where there's life, there's hope," said Joel. "Hi Ross, how are you doing? Miss you, man."

"I'm good, thanks. It's high time Shell and I took a trip up north. How have Martha and Chad settled in?"

"Chad's never off the beach," said Joel, his broad smile lighting up the screen, "and Martha's new job is exactly what she wanted. Moving up here was the best decision we ever made." There was the sound of a door opening. Joel looked away from the camera, then back to his old team. "Got to go. There's something I need to look at. I'll let you know the moment we have any more news to share." He waved briefly and the screen went blank for a second, then reverted to the standard mosaic. The News Channel banner had changed. 'Latest: new information offers hope in the search for six missing people."

Cameron smiled, her relief palpable. "Good for Pip," she said. "I need a coffee."

"Me too," said Sandeep. "Anyone else?"

"I have a client visit," said Pete. "I need to head off." He picked up his bag.

"I'll stick to water," said Ross.

"Shell, we'd better work out next steps for Oak Medical," said Sandeep. "We've got the culprits out in the open, and we know their MO. You're staying, yes?"

"Yes," said Michelle, "and I already have some ideas. A coffee will help."

"I'll have one too," said Noor, looking up from her screen.

"Okay. Four coffees coming up," said Sandeep, heading for the kitchen.

Ross settled at his desk. "I've got some insights on the Oak Medical data," he said. "The forums I posted on this morning are bouncing. I think this breach is the tip of the iceberg and there are some really useful resources being shared."

"Great," said Cameron. "If you can bring Michelle and Sandeep up to speed, that leaves you and me, Noor." She strolled over to where Noor was working and sat down beside her. "I want to run something past you. How are you with quantum computing?"

"Good enough to know that the weather forecast should have been right," said Noor, "and that interfering with a quantum simulation isn't your run-of-the-mill cybercrime. Beyond that? I know the basics, of course, but not to the same degree as I do classical processing."

Cameron sipped her coffee thoughtfully. "We need someone who can help us join the dots. Who do we know in this field that we can trust?"

"Well," said Noor, "I picked up this research paper recently that touches on manipulation of quantum outputs. You might recognise one of the authors." She handed Cameron her smartscreen.

Cameron peered at the list, spotted a familiar name, and laughed softly. "Well, well. Brianna Burnett. Is this the same girl who turned all the university computers into a clandestine mining operation in her first year as an undergraduate?"

"That's her," said Noor. "She's all grown up and doing her PhD. In fact, one of my old friends is her supervisor. He says he can't keep up with her. She's talented and she's thorough."

Cameron nodded approvingly. "I think we should go and check her out."

"I'll arrange something," said Noor. "Leave it with me."

Sandeep placed two coffees on the desk and Cameron sipped hers gratefully. "Send me that paper, Noor," she said. "I want to see how much I understand."

Noor laughed and dropped the link onto Cameron's screen. "It's well written. You know enough to follow it."

Cameron was deep in her second pass of the paper when Ross came over, looking serious. "We might need you both on Oak Medical after all. There's new information coming through. They think that patient data's been stolen."

Cameron put her screen down and sighed. "I was afraid of that. It's DeltaG's usual pattern. Noor, why don't you pull up the attack model and update it, and I'll head over there and hold some hands."

She drained her coffee, picked up her bag and headed out of the door. Outside the office building, the street was full of demonstrators making their way to Parliament. Cameron weaved her way through the singing, chanting crowd, slipping through gaps to get to the other side of the road and off towards her destination. It was so noisy that she failed to hear her smartscreen ringing, and ringing, and ringing.

4: MEMORIES

The administration at Oak Medical was in a state of quiet chaos when Cameron arrived. Michelle's role-playing of an executive who didn't quite know how to respond was not far from the real thing. Cameron was relieved when she was finally shown into the offices of the information security and technology division, where it became evident that at least some people knew exactly what they were doing.

While she waited, she checked her smartscreen. Five missed calls from Andy, and a cryptic message to call him about an incident. She didn't have time to talk to a journalist right now, even a friend, and she sent back a vague delaying excuse. If there was a real cyber incident, he could call the office and one of the team would sort it out. He didn't need Cameron every time.

The CISO was looking stressed but still gave Cameron a weary smile.

"It's not the first time I've had to report a data breach," he said. "It never gets any easier."

"Not a surprise, though, Joseph," said Cameron. "I guess you were expecting it as soon as the malware hit."

"Yeah," said Joseph. "Although it could have been a lot worse. We have Inge here to thank for that."

An equally tired-looking girl turned around from her monitor and smiled. Cameron looked from one to the other. "What's the story?"

"She spotted what was happening before any of us," said Joseph, "and she pulled the plug. All the main systems went offline before more data could be transmitted."

"Fantastic work," said Cameron. "Fast thinking, Inge. What was breached, in that case, if you managed to isolate the bulk of your records? And do you know if the main systems were infected?"

"To answer the first question, it's still not great news," said Joseph. "The path the malware took was through scheduling for outpatient appointments, and there's a limited amount of sensitive data circulating in there that's relevant to the patients and clinical conditions."

Cameron made a note on her screen. "That will be an issue if criminals are able to cross-match with existing data sets. What about the rest?"

"I think I got there in time," said Inge. "The database is still offline, so nothing is updating right across the hospital, but only outpatients seems to have been locked by the ransomware." She stifled a yawn. "I'm sorry. I'm supposed to be on nights this week, which is why I was in the right place at the right time on Tuesday to spot what was happening, but I've been in at odd hours yesterday and today and my sleep is completely messed up."

Cameron knew that feeling all too well. Over the years she'd pulled several all-nighters with the team as they battled to get banks and industry and government systems back online. It was part of the job, but a tired operative was less likely to catch clues and make inspired random associations when working through the systems, and more likely to make mistakes.

"I was just saying to the team before you arrived, Cameron, that this is a good time to go and get some rest," said Joseph. "All the systems are locked down tight, by them or by us, so the immediate danger is past. Now we're into the long haul of getting everything we can back online and repairing the damage."

"Right decision," said Cameron. "I'll bring a couple of my people in to start the next phase of digging and documentation while you get some sleep. Joseph, who's staying?"

"I'll be here for a few more hours," he said. "My deputy and some team members already took a break and I'm expecting them back by ten to do a full night shift."

Cameron nodded. "Understood. Well, let's get on with it."

While Joseph's tired staff gathered their belongings and filed out, Cameron found a cubby hole and called the Argentum office. There were two more notifications from Andy. She swiped them away irritably.

"Who's up for an evening at the hospital?" she asked. "We'll be setting up the recovery framework and also prepping the comms to people whose data has been breached. It'll be out on the marketplace already, I imagine, and they'll be sitting ducks."

"I can head over," said Sandeep. There was a muffled voice in the background. "Pete's coming too."

"And me," said Noor. "But Cameron, I managed to get hold of my friend at the university. Brianna's teaching a class tomorrow morning at eleven and he suggested we attend and then grab lunch with her. We both need to be wide awake for that."

"That's fine," said Cameron. "I don't think we'll be here much past eleven. Plenty of time. Oh – quick question – has Andy been in touch with any of you?"

"Haven't heard from him," said Ross. "What does he need?"

"I don't know," said Cameron. "He's been trying to get hold of me, and I assumed he was after a quote about the Oak Medical hack. I'll call him back now."

Joseph stuck his head around the door. "Want a coffee?"

"Thanks, that'd be great."

Cameron was about to call Andy when he saved her the trouble. This time, she answered.

"What do you want, Andy?"

"I've been trying to reach you for hours."

"I've been busy. If you needed a soundbite on Oak Medical, you should have grabbed one of the team from upstairs."

"If all I needed was a soundbite, I'd have fired up our virtual Ross avatar," said Andy. There was a flat and stony undertone to his voice. "It's far more serious than that. There's been a sighting. Angus White. He's still here in London."

Cameron felt a shiver run down her spine. "Are you sure?"

"Yes. Giles walked straight past him on the street near Borough Market at lunchtime. He's changed a lot, apparently, but Giles is absolutely sure it was him."

"Borough Market, you say. A bit close to home."

"Exactly," said Andy. "If I were you, I'd check the cameras at your old apartment."

"I don't think he's there for me," said Cameron flatly. "He wouldn't dare. Have you checked your, uh, sources recently, Andy? Is there anyone else who might live round that way that he knows?"

Andy swore loudly. "I never even thought about her. Shit. You're right." Cameron heard him yelling in the background. "Giles! Get round to Ella's place, right now." His face reappeared on the screen. "I'm sorry, Cameron."

"I'll call her, Andy," said Cameron. "Ella was one of my best team members and even though she fell in with the wrong crowd, she's more than made up for it with all the intelligence she passed on. I hope for her sake that he didn't find her."

"Ring me when you have news," said Andy.

"I will. You too. Bye."

Cameron put her head in her hands. She did not need this tonight.

Joseph appeared, carrying a tray of coffee and carefully placed a steaming mug on the desk beside her. "Everything okay?"

"Yes, all good," lied Cameron. "I just need to check in on someone. I'll be with you in a minute."

Alone again, she took a sip of the coffee, nearly burned her lip, and put it back down hastily. She picked up her smartscreen again and searched for the contact card for Ella Stanford. She'd only been half truthful with Andy. She wasn't in touch with Ella as much as she made out, and she was regretting it now.

The first profile she rang was inactive. The second diverted clunkily to another line and then cut out. The third was live, but it seemed like an age before the connection started to ring. Cameron had almost given up when a quiet voice answered.

"Yes?"

Cameron felt a flood of relief. "Ella? It's Cameron. Are you okay?"

The line was poor, and Ella's voice faded in and out. "Cameron? Good to hear from you. I'm fine. What's up?"

"Nothing, really. It's just that I heard Angus was seen in London, and I wanted to check that you hadn't run into him."

"Cameron, he's been in London for two years. Why are you suddenly calling me about him today?"

"Because someone else saw him, and called me, and I was worried about you, Ella." Cameron was frustrated now.

Ella laughed. "I'm guessing Andy or Giles," she said. "Because Giles has just rocked up at my front door." Her voice was suddenly serious. "And Angus has already been round."

Cameron didn't know what to say. Was Ella working with him again?

"Don't worry," said Ella, reading her thoughts. "I have a camera on the door, and I'm not even in the country. I've been away for the last two months and I'm not planning on coming back any time soon. I missed you all like crazy, but I don't fit in your lives anymore. It was time to rebuild, and I'm happy, Cameron."

"Where are you?" asked Cameron helplessly.

"I'm not telling you," said Ella. "You think this call is encrypted? Think again. I don't want to have to start over a third time. Goodbye, Cameron."

The line went dead. Almost instantly, Andy's profile popped up.

"Giles has been round and can't raise her." There was a note of panic in his voice.

"She's okay, Andy. I just spoke to her. She's not in London but she has doorstep footage of Angus and then Giles. How long is it, exactly, since you last spoke to her?"

"Months, if I'm honest," said Andy. "Once the dust settled, there wasn't much more we could do together. No use having a source if there's no story."

"Mmm. No wonder she's gone to ground. I haven't been great at keeping in touch either, and although she and Susie were back together for a while that didn't seem to last."

"We let her down, didn't we," said Andy soberly. "I'm sorry."

"So am I," said Cameron heavily, "but it can't be helped now. Thanks for the heads up about Angus, though. I'll watch my back."

"Cameron?" called a familiar voice.

"In here, Sandeep," said Cameron. "Sorry, Andy, duty calls. I'll see you soon. If you're around at the weekend, I'm popping up to the village. Pub?"

"Pub," said Andy. "See you there."

Cameron, Sandeep, Noor and Pete settled into the familiar routine of investigation and cleanup, pulling together documentation and setting up the recovery framework with Joseph. He finally retired gratefully to one of the on-call bedrooms, and his assistant and the night shift took over. By the time the Argentum team called it a night, Cameron was ready for her bed.

•

On the other side of the world, as Cameron was heading home, Tenuk was getting up. He had given up trying to sleep. His night had been punctuated by dreams and memories and a growing uncertainty in his gut. He needed a walk and time to clear his head. Dressing quietly, he slipped downstairs and out of the house. No one human saw him go, but he was resigned to the fact that the two staff who never slept, Zara and Xanthe, would know. He didn't really care if they followed his every move through the beacons and cameras that peppered the city. He would give them no reason for concern.

Tenuk slipped into the hustle and bustle of pre-dawn Singapore as if he'd never been away. When he first turned his back on his father's empire, he had lived and worked downtown, forging his own path in a familiar place before circumstances conspired to strand him abroad, then imprison him back home.

He walked, sweating gently in the humid air, then took the bus down a main artery to downtown. He slumped into a seat with his cap pulled down tightly over his eyes, looking for all the world like a weary commuter on their way to another forgettable day. He got off with most of the other passengers near the Marina Bay Sands and melted into the crowd.

His feet took him automatically to a popular breakfast spot where he sat with strangers eating kaya toast and drinking coffee. He felt stress he didn't know he had melting away. News items scrolled past on a nearby wallscreen, and he spotted a mention of the search in the Caribbean. Latest information offered hope, it said. Good, thought Tenuk. The world would be a less interesting place without Jack.

He was enjoying this rare taste of freedom. Where to next? There were a few places he could not go – it would hardly be sensible to rock up at the doors of the MerLions management offices – but there would be no harm in wandering through the market where he used to shop. It would be full of people by this time, even though it was still early in the day, and he would pass unnoticed in the crowd.

He felt his spirits rising as he drifted through the old familiar place, enjoying the sights, sounds and smells of the traders and customers going about their daily routine. He knew that he was viewing his old life through rose tinted glasses, but he didn't care. It felt good.

An elderly lady in front of him dropped her shopping bag, and he automatically bent down to retrieve the fruit and vegetables that had fallen out of it. He re-packed the bag and stood up. "Here, Auntie," he said automatically, handing it back to her.

"Thank you, thank you," muttered the old lady. "You're very kind."

She looked up at him and Tenuk froze.

It was his former neighbour, Auntie Fatima. Her eyes met his, and he braced himself for her anger and disappointment.

None came. There wasn't even a flicker of recognition in her gaze. "You're very kind," she repeated. "Yes, thank you." She stared down at the bag of fruit and vegetables in her hand. "Is this mine?" she asked.

Realisation dawned. Tenuk was deeply ashamed that his first thought was relief that she no longer knew who he was. His second was that Auntie Fatima should not be out here alone.

"Yes, it's yours, Auntie," he said. "Can I carry the heavy bag home for you?"

"Yes, thank you," she said, rallying a little. She pushed back her sleeve and stared intently at a little device strapped to her wrist. Tenuk recognised it as a simple mapping screen that would help her to navigate. It looked as if she was still living in her little apartment in the Katong tunnels. He might be seen by others who knew him if he returned to that location, but right now he didn't care. He was worried about the old lady and wanted to be sure she was safe.

Walking slowly, taking her arm when she stumbled, Tenuk soon found himself seated on the old familiar bus with Auntie Fatima as if no time had passed. Occasionally he caught sight of places he knew, but there were changes, too. Auntie Fatima chatted away to him. At some level in her failing memory, she had recognised him as someone familiar and trusted. That made him feel even worse. He had let her down when he left and didn't deserve her trust.

The bus stopped at the nearest underpass to his old home. Tenuk helped Auntie Fatima down onto the pavement and took a deep breath as they walked together through the gateway to his old neighbourhood. Auntie Fatima's step quickened as she reached the cool air of the tunnels, and he adjusted his own pace to stay beside her. It was shabbier than he remembered, although as spotlessly clean as the rest of the city. The bright and hopeful colours on the tunnel walls had faded slightly but all the plants had matured since he left, growing under artificial sunlight, and now the overwhelming feeling was of walking along paths lined with lush green foliage. It was peaceful and welcoming. A mosaic depicting the MerLion against a blue sky now dominated the central hub of the complex from which the tunnel spokes radiated.

Tenuk's feet took him automatically down the correct tunnel as if he'd never been away. Auntie Fatima's beautifully kept apartment frontage felt more like home than his father's sprawling luxury mansion. He waited while she raised her hand to the lock then followed her in. He set the heavy bag on her kitchen counter and unpacked the contents.

"There's all your shopping, Auntie Fatima," he said. "I'd better be going."

A woman's voice, surprised, came from one of the bedrooms. "Fatima? Is that you? Where have you been?"

Tenuk was almost at the door when he heard steps from the bedroom corridor. He pulled his baseball cap down, hiding his face from the newcomer as best he could.

"Oh, Fatima." The other woman bustled into the main room. She was a similar age and build to Auntie Fatima and Tenuk vaguely recognised her as one of the sisters from Kuala Lumpur who used to visit. "Thank you for helping her home, young man. She shouldn't have been out alone."

"You're welcome," said Tenuk, making his voice gruff and low. He stepped over the threshold and reached for the door handle.

"That was Tenuk," he heard Auntie Fatima say.

"No, Fatima," said her sister. "Tenuk moved away, do you remember?"

A cold frisson of mingled pleasure and fear ran up Tenuk's back as he closed the door. Delight that she'd remembered him. A dark hope that she would soon forget.

He stood indecisively outside her apartment for a moment. In the end, he couldn't resist. He turned and looked up the stairs to the second level. There was his old home, but with a new, brightly coloured door. Someone else was evidently living there. He sighed and turned back up the tunnel to the outside world. It was time to get back to his father's house before he was missed.

Hungry again after his early breakfast, he grabbed a bowl of fruit and more coffee from the dining room and made his way to his office.

"Zara, give me a digest of overnight news."

Silence. Tenuk made a note to check her standby settings. Eventually, she replied.

"Good morning, Tenuk. Here are the main headlines. Five arrested in connection with South African parliament shooting. Stock markets up on opening following latest Southeast Asia productivity statistics. Search continues for missing billionaire. British hospital trust Oak Medical discloses data loss after cyberattack."

"That's DeltaG again," muttered Tenuk. "Zara, is there a profile of the data grab on Eden yet?"

"Yes, Tenuk," said Zara, "I believe it consists largely of duplicates of existing information with minimal additional yet sensitive data points, and there is some value to be derived from the source itself in terms of constructing highly personalised and deep fake phishing campaigns. Bidding starts at 1800 UTC today, Friday. Do you wish to attend the auction?"

Tenuk considered his options.

"I may join," he said at last. "I have an interest in the intersectionality of that dataset with some potential enterprise targets that are proving hard to crack. There must be a sick executive in the list that can give me a way in."

"I'll set a reminder. Do you have a preferred avatar, or will you delegate?"

"I'll come in person," said Tenuk. "I haven't visited Eden for a while. Can you spin up a new avatar and arrange bidding clearance, please, Zara?"

"Certainly, Tenuk."

Tenuk fiddled with his smartscreen, turning it slowly in his hands as he mulled over his plans. Something was bothering him, and he finally worked out what it was.

"Zara?"

Again, there was a delay in her reply. He had been very clear that he did not want to be in constant communication with her as Jack had been, but in an age of instant information, her slow responses were unusual and almost irritating.

"Yes, Tenuk?"

"Out of interest, do you have data on how much DeltaG have raised from their recent projects?"

"Yes," said Zara. "Our latest analysis shows flows to their known wallet addresses of $3.6m in the last twelve months."

"Is that all?" Tenuk laughed. "They pipped us to two contracts that were worth more than that each. They're chaos merchants. They won't last long."

"They are a useful distraction," said Zara.

"True," said Tenuk. He was happiest operating from the shadows, and DeltaG's shenanigans kept the infosec community's eyes away from his own activities. No one knew where he was or what he was doing with his new team.

Correction. One person knew where he was. When he first moved back to Singapore, Noor had called him. That was the first and last time they had spoken since she had discovered who he really was. He thought about her often, even though he was sure he would never see her again.

And two others knew what he was doing. Wildcards from his old team, Sterix and the Monkey kept coming back for their own reasons. Sterix was utterly unstable, hiding most of the time behind an avatar of a small grey kitten. Tenuk was certain that he only worked to fund a drug habit, and that he would succumb to that before Tenuk needed to get rid of him.

The Monkey was another matter. He knew far too much about Tenuk in all his previous guises to be anything but dangerous. Tenuk had two choices, to keep the Monkey close or to dispose of him for once and for all. Keeping him close was not hard. The Monkey was too proud to take Universal and retire, and still angry about the loss of his crypto nest egg some years before. He was relying on Tenuk and Sapphire Straits not just for income but for intelligence and muscle, tied to them by the hope that they could forensically trace his old wallets to a real-world address, and that their strong-arm squads would be able to recover the keys. In turn, the Monkey had consolidated their reliance on him by offering Chaoxiang the Argentum team on a plate. The SimCavalier had cost his father many millions with her meddling in his affairs, and this was an offer the old man could not refuse.

"What are those two idiots up to, Zara? Give me the latest surveillance report."

"Sterix has been immersed in the deep levels for two days, location unknown. In the real world, tracking shows him to be in Hamburg, but he has been completely static for almost forty-eight hours. This is of concern."

Tenuk's suspicion that Sterix had a drug habit to feed explained his long immersion times in other realities, his intermittent absences, and his pathetic dependence on the work he was given. "Keep tracking his physical location, Zara," he said. "I'll find him online when I go in for the auction. What about the other one?"

"The Monkey is still located in London and has completed two jobs in the past three days, one in virtual space for your client and the other in real space for Sapphire Straits. He last checked in twenty-four hours ago. Movement tracking shows enhanced activity travelling within the city, in line with his investigations into the Argentum Associates team. There are no indicators of concern. The latest forensic report on the location of his wallets has been prepared and is ready to deliver."

"Thank you, Zara. I assume the report will show progress but not resolution."

"That is correct."

"Send him a meeting request for 1900 UTC. I'll hand over the report myself."

Tenuk still had misgivings about his father's growing antagonism towards the Argentum team. If the Monkey stepped out of line, if he ever threatened Noor's safety or exposed Tenuk's secrets, he had contingencies in place. The Monkey was ultimately expendable, and Chaoxiang would never know.

Try as he might, Tenuk could not settle to his work. The image of his feisty old neighbour now diminished and uncertain kept interrupting his thoughts. He thought of his mother and wondered what she would think of him now if she was alive. He had stopped visiting her avatar in the family mausoleum. Despite the best AI simulations and virtual restitution that money could buy, her ghost was rooted in the past. He could no longer take comfort from the illusion and was allowing himself, finally, to grieve.

He flicked through the different projects that he had running. The software proposal for the Sladen Foundation DAO was steadily gathering approval from peers. A recent enquiry requesting spear phishing straight into a list of luxury brands based in London would be greatly assisted by the data from the DeltaG operation if he could secure it at auction. A small software contract that needed some of the Monkey's specialist skills had been delivered to the client's satisfaction and the fee received. The new Academy intake's Capture the Flag exercises had gone well, and now they were progressing to their first independent project, planning a penetration of the internal systems of an organisation of their choice. Tenuk had high hopes of his protégés. He needed a fresh team and a new approach.

A thought occurred to him. "Zara, you said that the Monkey had completed a real-world assignment for Sapphire Straits. Can you disclose the details?"

There was a pause. "Clearance is confirmed. He has been liaising with a property company on behalf of a Sapphire Straits arm's length trust."

"What property?" asked Tenuk, puzzled. "One of the casinos? Why would the Monkey be involved in those? We have a global management team to handle real estate."

"No further details."

Tenuk shrugged. As long as the Monkey stayed in his lane, he didn't care. Whatever this property might be was his father's business. He had other things on his mind.

5:   ENTANGLEMENT

The small lecture theatre was three quarters full and too hot for comfort. Cameron and Noor lurked in the darkness of the last row and watched as Brianna prepared for the class. She pulled off her hoodie and took a swig of water, then cleared her throat and fired up the teaching podium. On the main screen, the attendance ticker, captured directly from the chips of students who had joined the class, was approaching 90%. Behind them, another screen showed a handful of avatars of students attending remotely, but there were far more people here in person. Face to face learning was popular. Cameron noticed four extra attendees had been counted, marked simply as having clearance to join. She and Noor were two. Who could the others be?

A pair of students next to her were whispering nervously. "I want to switch onto this course," said one, "but I'm still not sure I'll be able to handle it."

That answered her question. Some learners were testing the water before diving into the subject for real.

"Shh," said the other. "She's about to start."

Brianna went through the routine business of the day, directing students to forms that needed filling in and reminding them of events to sign up for. Then she pulled up the first of her slides, and Cameron's mind flashed back to her own college days. Around her she heard the clicks and taps of students taking notes and annotating their copy of the materials as the lecture progressed. She listened intently, determined to sense check her own understanding of the underlying concepts of quantum computing.

"As long as it's unobserved," said Brianna, "the qubit is in a superposition of probabilities, and it is impossible to predict which state it will collapse into once measured. Let's put this another way. Have any of you been following the latest gossip about Layla Lou and WhistleStop?"

The students laughed. The on-again-off-again relationship between the global music power couple was the stuff of legend.

"Yes? You have?" said Brianna. "Good. What state are they in now? Dating, or not dating? Anyone?"

"No one knows," said a boy on the front row. "They never answer the question."

"Not an observable state, then. But everyone's talking about them. What does the gossip tell you?"

There was a cacophony of different answers, and Brianna smiled. "So, what you're telling me is, there is a superposition of probabilities."

"Clever," whispered Cameron to Noor.

"If you asked a classical computer to work out whether they're dating or not dating from all the different sources of gossip, you'd have to use multiple iterations to get the right answer. Superposition allows qubits to hold all the possible results in parallel, rather than generating a series of individual results."

Cameron recalled a board book from her childhood from which she had learned the basic mantra of quantum processing. 'A bit can be black or white, but a qubit can be any colour it wants, all at the same time.'

"You've sampled all this gossip now," said Brianna, "so we should be able to reach an observable state. What's the consensus based on the latest dish?"

"Dating," shouted the majority of the class.

"Great," said Brianna happily. "In this classroom, we have returned an observable state of Dating. And down the hall, in an entangled classroom, they instantly know this too."

Cameron put her head in her hands. Quantum entanglement turned intuition on its head. Qubits could be entangled, reflecting each other's properties, even when hundreds of kilometres apart. Observing one entangled qubit would define the state of its pair. She'd never quite mastered why this was the case and had eventually learned it was easier simply to accept that it was so.

"Don't worry," said Brianna, as if reading her mind. "We'll be digging deeper into entanglement over the next few weeks. I don't want to make your brains explode just yet." There were some relieved laughs in the audience. "Instead, let's consider some of the uses of quantum computing. The basic conditions to make this effective are, first, having a vast pool of data on which to draw and, second, a complexity of analysis that makes it too time consuming or downright impossible to compute using traditional processing or structured algorithmic models. Any suggestions?"

The room was silent but for the whirring of an ineffective fan and the taps of stylus on screen.

"I know you're not shy," she continued. "Ah, yes, go ahead, Taiwo."

She pointed at a student on the front row who had raised her hand cautiously.

"Drug discovery?" she ventured.

"Good," said Brianna. "That's the one that is always quoted in the literature. Many of the advances in medicine over the last fifteen years have been made as a direct result of quantum processors maturing to the point where they can crunch all the available research and medical outcomes and identify the most promising avenues simultaneously based on a vast and complete data set. That cuts out multiple lengthy iterations of research where decisions on how to proceed used to be based on limited or incomplete data, simply because there was no other way at the time. Now, what else?"

More hands were going up.

"Cracking passwords," suggested a student a few rows in front of Cameron.

"Yes, Dave," said Brianna. "Care to explain?"

"Uh, is it Shor's algorithm…?" Dave's voice tailed off and he ducked his head. There was a ripple of sympathetic laughter. No one wanted to be put on the spot.

"Yes, well done," said Brianna. "Shor's algorithm was developed more than fifty years ago, but we didn't have the quantum stack to deploy it until fifteen years ago. Can you remember what it does?"

"It calculates the prime factors of a cryptographic key," said Dave, a little more confidently.

"Exactly," said Brianna, "which can crack encryption wide open. That's why they developed post-quantum cryptography standards in the '20s. What kind of applications had to be made quantum-safe?"

"Passwords and authentication," replied Dave.

"Databases with older encryption standards," said Taiwo.

"Blockchains and wallet keys," added Dave.

"Yes, all of those," said Brianna. "Good. Next?"

"Delivery optimisation," called a student on the back row just along from Cameron.

"That's old school," said Brianna with a smile. "Quantum annealing processors had scheduling sewn up more than twenty years ago. A good, practical business use case, but it's definitely a speciality of annealing, not something where we would choose gated processing."

"Climate simulations," said another student. "Crunching a lot of data quickly so we can forecast extreme events and drill down to specific locations for fast response and planning and stuff."

"Excellent," said Brianna. "You've all done your homework. For your lab session, I'd like you to research one of either Shor's algorithm, nature simulations or drug discovery and be ready to explain what difference quantum processing has made or is predicted to make. Now, off you go. I'll see you on Monday morning."

There was a welcome rush of cool air from the doorway as students made their way out of the room. Cameron and Noor were the last to leave their seats and waited patiently while Brianna spoke to the students who had been sitting next to them.

"You'll be fine," she was saying. "Always let me know if there's anything I haven't explained fully. I don't want to fall into the habit of assuming prior knowledge when I'm trying to explain some of the knottier details. Most of the students on this module have a physics background rather than pure computing, so they're already familiar with quantum mechanics, but your maths is good enough to keep up."

The students thanked her and left the room. Brianna looked questioningly at Cameron and Noor.

"Very good lecture, Brianna," said Noor. "I'm Dr Noor Khawaja. I'm a friend of Dr Weston. This is my colleague, Cameron Silvera."

Brianna furrowed her brow. "I know your name, but I can't think where from."

"Argentum Associates," said Cameron. "We crossed paths in your first year."

Brianna put her hand to her mouth and her eyes widened.

"Don't worry, your past isn't catching up with you," laughed Cameron. "I enjoyed the lecture too. It looks like what I already understood about superposition is right, and one day I will get my head around quantum entanglement."

Students were filing in for the next class.

"We need to be out of here," said Brianna, recovering her composure. She went back to the podium to hand over to her colleague, then led Cameron and Noor out to the fresh air. "You'll join me for lunch?"

"Of course," said Cameron. "We have some questions about quantum vulnerabilities."

They found a table in the busy library café. Noor and Brianna went to order food while Cameron tuned in to the chatter around her. Most of it concerned students' plans for the future. How many applications had each of them submitted for jobs? How many rejections had they received? The discussion was animated. Everyone, it seemed, had a story to tell about terrible AI gatekeepers in their potential employers' HR departments. Cameron knew that the biases they were describing were all too real. She'd untangled a few terrible machine learning systems for clients in the past, where clumsy use of old training data in building the model created an AI with all the social conscience and unfounded bias of the type of elderly uncle that people avoided at family parties. It would be funny if it wasn't so serious.

Brianna and Noor returned with trays of food, and over lunch Brianna told them of her fascination with quantum machines. She had been born just as quantum computers began to make an impact beyond purely experimental use. She knew her world had been shaped and changed by their processing capabilities. The use of quantum processors to sift vast volumes of data and compute ever more complex simulations permeated every walk of life.

"But I wasn't prepared to sit back and accept everything the machines churned out," she explained. "Quantum computers aren't these all-powerful, infallible things. They're tools used by humans, and when humans get things wrong, so do the machines."

Much like AI, thought Cameron. "Can they be manipulated?" she asked, getting straight to the point.

Brianna nodded. "Yes. Of course they can. There are some straightforward methodologies. Someone could target the data or even the processing itself."

She sounded confident and Cameron knew that she had come to the right person.

"How would you target the data?" she asked.

"In the same way that you might do for classical computing," said Brianna. "As long as you have enough wrongly labelled data going in, you can change the outputs."

"Garbage In, Garbage Out," murmured Noor.

"Exactly," said Brianna. "In classical computing you could convince an algorithm to output a picture of a dog as a cat if that's what its training data said the picture was. Of course, the volume of data we're dealing with in quantum processing is huge, but it's theoretically possible to ensure that the superposed possibilities are flawed."

Cameron was unsurprised. It was a malicious application of the same problem that had plagued every computer since inception, and she had no doubt it was being well used by the criminal fraternity. What she didn't understand was how anyone could influence the quantum process itself.

"What about manipulating the actual machine?" she asked. "You said that was possible."

Brianna nodded. "Quantum computers are delicate things. Anything that can cause entangled qubits to decohere will disrupt and slow the sampling, although you can't mess with the quantum processing unit itself. Back in the day they used to keep all the processors just above absolute zero to stop qubits from being disrupted at an atomic level. Now many of our qubits are made from materials that hold their coherence at higher temperatures, but processing is still most effective in the deep freeze."

"There's a quantum processing section at the big data centre in Alaska, Wrangell," said Cameron. "The tundra helps in cooling, even if the glacier is melting."

"I know Wrangell," said Brianna. "It's one of the main processing centres for the quantum cloud, especially now that the quantum campuses in Texas and Illinois are under threat with the Militia action. Some organisations have their own machines but it's way too costly for most, so they outsource."

Cameron finished her sandwich and leaned back in her chair, thinking. "Decoherence seems like a blunt tool," she said. "What else might our friends have in their cybercrime kit?"

"Oh, plenty of things," said Brianna. "There are subtle, long-term ways of manipulating quantum processing at every stage. You could sneak a new algorithm in so it's not processing what you think it was, although that should be picked up in a system audit. You could get at the data in pre-processing when it's optimising and compiling, or even while it's queued. You can flip a qubit with a classic row-hammer attack, which changes its output, or even, and I haven't seen this, but I know it's theoretically possible, use malicious circuits so that the entangled particle flips and reads the opposite result to the one that its sampling would normally return. You wouldn't spot the effects of flipping straight away, but over time it would have a cumulative impact."

"Could that cause a gradual erosion of reliability in weather simulations?"

Brianna held up her hands. "I'm not saying it's ever happened in real life."

Noor laughed. "It probably has," she said. "You'd be amazed what we find."

Cameron looked appraisingly at Brianna. Her eyes were sparkling. She was obviously excited by the whole subject and she seemed smart and practical enough to apply what she knew to real world problems. "Would you like to help us track down this kind of thing in the wild?" she said.

"As in, actually work with Argentum Associates?" said Brianna. "Yes. I'd love to."

Cameron turned to Noor. "Good call. I think we've found our expert."

They finished their lunch with promises to set up a first visit to the office and onboarding as a consultant, and Brianna sped away to a research meeting. Cameron and Noor lingered in the café, enjoying the early autumn sunshine.

"Any plans for the weekend?" asked Cameron.

"Just family things," said Noor. She looked troubled.

"Is everything okay?" said Cameron, suddenly concerned.

"Mum and dad are fine, thank you, in fact it's their Ruby wedding anniversary."

"Forty years, wow," said Cameron. "Send them my congratulations."

"Thanks," said Noor, distracted, "but listen, something odd has happened. I don't quite know how to tell you this, but, well, look at this video that my aunt sent over." She handed over her smartscreen. "My mother's sister, Fatima, lives in Singapore, but she's been ill. She has dementia and she's starting to struggle with daily life so one of my other aunts is down there from Kuala Lumpur. Auntie Fatima apparently went out very early this morning to the market like she used to do, and someone very kindly brought her back before she was missed."

Cameron peered at the screen, a feed from the old lady's apartment that the family used to keep an eye on her when she was alone. "The guy with the baseball cap?"

"Don't you recognise him?"

Cameron shook her head, but a grave suspicion was mounting.

"It's Tenuk," said Noor. "I knew him straight away, and she recognised him too. Long term memories tend to be retained with dementia, while the short term decays. She said very clearly that it was Tenuk and insisted that was who it was even when her sister reminded her that Tenuk had moved away."

"You should show this to Chloe," said Cameron. "She worked with him in Austin. She'll be able to confirm if it is really him."

"It is," said Noor quietly. "I knew he was in Singapore, but he's been very well hidden. I – Cameron, I'm sorry – I spoke to him back when we were investigating Yasmin's activities and the Olympic interference."

"That's how you found out that Chaoxiang Chen was his father?" Cameron gaped at her friend. "You just asked him straight out?"

Noor nodded.

"Are you still in touch?"

"No, not at all." Noor looked helplessly at Cameron. "I mean, I could contact him if I really needed to. He was my friend. More than a friend. I liked him a lot, before we knew who he really was."

"Before we realised that he was leading the most successful cybercrime syndicate in the world, and that it was his goons that had kidnapped my niece?"

"Yes," said Noor, her voice barely a whisper. "I really wish things had been different."

Cameron sighed. "We all wish that," she said.

"There's been no sign of him at all since we finally destroyed Yasmin. I've been tracking all activity to do with the Steamyard syndicate and everything simply stopped. We know that Angus the Monkey is still on the loose, but we haven't traced any other operatives from those days and no more contracts were awarded. Groups like DeltaG filled the vacuum. Tenuk's nowhere to be found."

"What about his father?" asked Cameron. "Sapphire Straits? That was as dodgy as hell, and we know they were behind Yasmin from the beginning."

"Still dodgy," said Noor. "They'll take bets on anything and everything. There was a book running on the storm that sank Jack's yacht, and now there's one on finding him." She put her hand to her mouth. "I'm sorry, Cameron. I didn't mean to upset you."

"It's okay. We know that he's alive. There are regular garbled messages coming through to Pip, and it's less than thirty hours since the yacht sank, so they'll find him." She leaned back in her chair and looked up at the ceiling. "It's been an intense couple of days, hasn't it?"

The café was emptying around them as staff and students made their way to the next teaching session.

"I'd better go," said Cameron. "I'm going to check in on what's happening at Oak Medical and then I'm off to Charlie's for the weekend."

"Enjoy yourself," said Noor, gathering up her belongings. "We have a family call about Auntie Fatima, so I'll see if there is anything more to report on Tenuk."

"Thanks, Noor," said Cameron. She hesitated, then said what was on her mind. "I kind of hope Tenuk has turned over a new leaf. You are normally such a good judge of character that I wonder if, lurking under the cybercrime boss we all knew, there is actually a decent human being."

Noor gave Cameron a weak smile. "Stranger things have happened," she said.

They parted at the tube station. Cameron headed back home to feed the cat and collect her things for the weekend. As she entered the lobby of the tower, the security supervisor gave her a friendly wave.

"Cameron? Do you have a moment?"

"Sure. Has the cat been misbehaving?"

"Not to my knowledge," he said with a laugh. "Just a courtesy to let you know you had a visitor. They were quite insistent that you lived here, but of course we don't divulge details of our residents or confirm or deny any speculation."

"Do you have images?"

"Yes. I've isolated the relevant footage."

Cameron peered at the screen. The visitor was an unassuming, late middle-aged man with dark hair. She advanced the frames slowly, frowning. "Not someone I recognise," she said. The recording continued. It showed him arguing with the security guard, becoming animated. There was a veiled air of belligerence in his body language. He turned away, defeated, and slouched back towards the road. That was the giveaway. He was slimmer, clean shaven, had dyed his hair and changed his clothes, but that heavy gait was all too familiar.

Angus.

6:   GHOSTS IN THE MACHINE

Angus's bull avatar walked straight past Tenuk's latest generic identity without a hint of recognition. It was only when a passing sprite gave him a message to follow the green dragon that he realised Tenuk was already waiting for him in the virtual reality where they had arranged to meet.

"I was expecting the Pangolin," growled Angus.

"I was expecting the Monkey."

"I needed a change. You too, eh?"

"I rarely visit these levels now," said the dragon. "It is safer to do so anonymously. But I had business here today. Before we discuss the progress of your request, I must ask if you have any news of the Kitten."

"Sterix? That idiot? What do you want him for?"

"That is none of your concern. Do you know where he is?"

Angus laughed, and the great bull he had chosen as his avatar tossed its horns. "You can't get anything done without your pet AI, can you? Are you missing Yasmin?"

The green dragon did not react. "I'll ask you again. Where is he?"

"I'll trade you. You tell me where my crypto wallets are, and I'll tell you where Sterix is."

"I'll find him on my own," said the dragon. The avatar shimmered and began to fade.

"Stop!" said Angus. "You're a bastard, you know that? I last saw the kitten about a day and a half, two days ago. He was heading for a neural crack den on the next level. Place called the Renton Lounge."

"And his physical location? My intelligence suggests he is in Germany."

"Yeah. Last I heard he was in Hamburg. No idea if he's moved on from there. Maybe your intelligence –" He practically spat the word out. "– can tell you more."

"Thank you. Here's the latest forensic report on your wallets. Make of it what you will."

A token passed between them, a bundle of data moving from one owner to the other. The green dragon walked away to the nearest transit point and disappeared. Angus logged out and the bull shimmered into nothingness.

Back in the real world in his dingy London studio apartment, Angus decrypted the data he'd been given. Like every packet he'd received before it was encouraging, carefully compiled, and added some breadcrumbs to the trail, but it gave him no resolution. This was the hold Tenuk and Chaoxiang had over him. Furious and powerless, he picked up a dirty plate from the table, the nearest thing to hand, and threw it at the wall. It smashed, leaving a satisfying dent in the plaster. There was a returning thump and a shout from his neighbour. Angus got up, marched out of the door, and slammed it behind him.

The cool of the evening was a welcome relief. He walked without purpose for the best part of an hour as the red mist cleared. Once he reached the river, he leaned on a railing and gazed out across the water to the glimmering lights of skyscrapers in the City. The wind whipped up and he shivered, drawing his jacket closer around him. He thought long and hard about the data he'd received. Combined with his own research, there might be enough there to fill in the missing pieces. He knew more than Tenuk gave him credit for. He'd watched every transaction, even sent messages to whoever was holding the keys. Half of the savings he'd lost were still there. He'd traced the transfers out to good causes, in the main. The largest had been routed carefully to avoid detection, but from its timing and other circumstantial evidence he believed it had gone to the Sladen Foundation. Other payments had been made to climate impact appeals and humanitarian support for people in war zones around the planet. All very worthy, and according to the data he'd been given, still hard to reconcile with a single real-world user. But Angus was good at finding out about people. He knew where the funding appeals had been broadcast, what audience they reached, and he had a reasonably detailed profile of his quarry that might just be narrowed down to likely individuals by the latest data.

The Pangolin and Sapphire Straits thought they had him under their control because only they could find his money. Thinking clearly for the first time as he faced the now biting wind coming down the Thames, Angus realised that their real hold over him was the work they provided. They weren't to know that he had rebuilt some of his savings and that he had other networks he could tap for work and valuable assets he could sell to give him enough cushion to just walk away.

The decision was clear. Once he'd finished his current contracts, he'd be done with the Pangolin. That day couldn't come soon enough. He would finish the search for his wallets on his own.

He moved back into the shelter of a warren of riverside streets and pulled out his smartscreen. Back to work. He had two weeks to finish the dossier on the SimCavalier and all her team before the dox-and-destroy team moved in. The next one to find was a man by the name of Pete Iveson. His security was excellent, but Angus had compiled enough leads now to narrow down his home address.

•

The mood in the village pub was lively. Cameron spotted Andy, Charlie and Sameena sitting at a table on the far side of the bar, deep in animated conversation. They all had full glasses in front of them, so she paused and ordered a drink before taking the vacant fourth seat.

"You made it," said Charlie, giving his sister a quick kiss on the cheek.

"There was a communication failure on the train," said Cameron. "We sat there in the middle of the countryside for a good hour before engineers arrived to patch the connection. But I'm here now, and I have a drink, so everything is fine."

Andy pointed up at the wallscreen above the fireplace. Usually reserved for sports, and rarely switched on the rest of the time, it was showing the News Channel and an update on the search for the missing life raft. "Everything is definitely fine. You've seen this?"

Drones were zooming in on a group of six people on a small atoll who were waving frantically at the cameras. Cameron spotted Jack immediately. A flash of sunlight picked up the small metal skindiver tattoo just below his collarbone. The prototype interface had proved its worth.

"They've found him!" she said.

"Yes, and it looks like they're all okay."

A weight lifted from her shoulders. "When did this come through?"

"It's literally just been announced in the last few minutes," said Charlie. "Probably while you were walking up to the pub."

On cue, Cameron's smartscreen started beeping with a series of incoming alerts. She couldn't keep the smile off her face as she read them.

"Cheers," said Andy, raising his glass. "Here's to Jack and the others. All's well that ends well."

"Cheers," said Sameena. "I'm so glad. He's a nice chap, Cameron. You should bring him to visit when he gets back."

"I don't see him that often," protested Cameron. "He might pop up to see Aunt Vicky, but I have no say in his activities, believe me."

Charlie was scrolling through chats on his smartscreen. "Any idea why '#smeghead' is trending with the story, Andy?"

Cameron grabbed her brother's screen, scrolled down the thread, peered at a closeup of Jack, and started laughing. "It's the tattoo," she said. "He's got a temporary skindiver design which is chipped and links to an API that Joel's been working on. They said it was an old school sci-fi logo." She pointed at the ellipse broken by two distinct letter Ds on either side. "Red Dwarf."

"That's funny," said Charlie. "I bet he'll regret it when he sees the headlines."

"He's got a good sense of humour," said Sameena. "He'll be fine."

"Purely hypothetically," said Andy with an amused glint in his eye, "what elements of that fabulous story might go further than this table, in the fullness of time?"

Cameron considered the frankly bare-faced request and picked her words carefully, knowing that some things were not ready for the public domain and that if Andy got his story straight now, there'd be no questions about Pip. "Alright, Andy," she said, "I'll go on the record with this. They've been working on new voice control protocols for the MetaBand systems which will improve security with biometric voice prints and accessibility for everyone who uses it. As a bit of fun, Joel's been testing the limits of what can be used as an interface. He managed to chip a skindiver and Jack tested it, but it hadn't grown out by the time he went away. They got communication squawks through during and after the evacuation, which confirmed Jack was alive and helped to track the raft down. There you go. There's your story."

Undetected, her smartscreen was transcribing the statement, triggered by the 'on the record' key phrase. It was important for everyone to know what had been shared, and what obfuscation and misdirection had been used, especially if Andy or his staff called for more details. Cameron was under no illusions that Andy's smartscreen was probably doing the same.

"Amazing, Cameron," said Andy. "Do you think I could get an interview with Joel about the technology once the dust has settled on the search?"

"Maybe," said Cameron. "Let me check." She sent Joel the transcript and a short note to say she would put Andy off until Monday. Joel returned a quick thumbs up. "It's a yes, Andy," she continued, "but leave it for a couple of days, will you? They're going to be busy."

"Sure."

Charlie stood up, clutching his and Sameena's empty glasses. "Who wants a refill?"

"Same again, mate," said Andy, sliding his own glass over.

"Go on," said Cameron, draining hers.

Charlie and Sameena went together to the bar, and Cameron took advantage of their absence.

"Andy, your tipoff yesterday wasn't far off the mark."

Andy looked at her curiously. "Angus?"

"The very same." She found the images from the security cameras on her smartscreen and slid it over to him. "He didn't just call on Ella. I'm surprised Giles recognised him. It took me a little while."

"You need to be careful," said Andy quietly.

"The security at the tower and here in the village is top notch," said Cameron. "I'm not afraid of him, and I'll know him if I see him again. Don't worry about me."

Sameena came back with their drinks. Cameron leaned back in her seat and felt the tension drain out of her. She was disturbed by the depth of her relief that Jack was safe. She pushed the thought back down into her subconscious for another time, and concentrated on being here, now, in one of the safest places she knew.

She slept late, dark blinds blocking the sunlight from her attic bedroom, and woke refreshed. When she emerged from the shower, towelling her hair dry, she could hear voices and movement downstairs. It might be too late for breakfast, but if she was lucky, there'd be lunch.

Right on cue, there was a knock at the door.

"Aunty Cam?" called a voice. "Are you hungry? Mum's made some pasta."

"I'm coming," she replied.

She trotted down the attic stairs, opening the door carefully to prevent the elderly but still excitable labradoodle, Roxy, from belting up the stairs and causing havoc. A glorious smell of garlic hit her nostrils.

The whole family was gathered, all but Nina who was starting her first term at a university a few hours north.

"Is she settling in well?" asked Cameron.

Sameena laughed. "You could say that. She's having the time of her life."

"I'm not going away," said Dilan. "I want to go to the virtual university. Have you visited it, Aunty Cam? It's amazing. There's a huge park with mountains in the distance and a marina and all the lectures and everything are in big open amphitheatres, and the students come from all over the world."

"I've been there," said Cameron. "It's very good, but it depends what you want to study. Nina's chosen a course where she has to be there physically to do the experiments."

"A hybrid course would be the best of both worlds," said Sameena. "My degree course was like that. There were some students who did all the lectures virtually and then attended when they were needed."

"It was a nightmare for cheating, though," said Charlie. "Do you remember how much screening the lecturers had to do? They always found a few AI agents taking the course. I wonder how many people slipped through the net and graduated without doing any work?"

"I wonder how many still do," said Cameron darkly. "Humans have to be right at the heart of creativity and discovery. AI can't genuinely innovate. It stands on the shoulders of humans." She paused, remembering. "Well, most AI anyway. I guess we all knew the exception to the rule."

"Yasmin," said Sameena with a shudder. "Good riddance."

It was time to change the subject. "Excellent pasta," said Cameron. "I don't think I've had this before. Can you ping me the recipe?"

"Of course," said Sameena.

But the subject was not going away.

"I'm going for a look around that farm that's up for sale," said Aunt Vicky. "They're having an Open House showing this afternoon. I think half the village is going along out of pure nosiness."

"What farm?" asked Cameron through a mouthful of pasta.

"You know the one," said Charlie. "The big place up on the back road. It was in the middle of all that fuss when the village internet connection was hijacked. You were up there when it was raided, Cam."

The remote farmhouse was the place where an AI had been nurtured and trained by a small-time cybercriminal in the pay of someone much bigger. Cameron remembered it all too well. "I thought that had been sold years ago. Nina was just tiny when that all happened. It must be fifteen years ago?"

"Sixteen," said Charlie. "It's changed hands a few times, but it's never been lived in for long."

"It was always an odd place," said Aunt Vicky. "You two probably won't remember the old fellow who lived there, oh, twenty, thirty years ago?"

"I do," said Charlie. "He chased me off his fields a few times when I was mucking about with the lads. Wasn't there some scandal?"

"Oh, yes," said Aunt Vicky. "He had a sister, not a very nice woman, and she thought she would inherit the whole farm. But there wasn't a penny left. He'd used it to pay off his gambling debts."

"He'd borrowed against it?"

"No, Charlie, the bank wouldn't help him," said Aunt Vicky. "He sold it lock, stock and barrel to the bookies about a year before he died. They sold off most of the outlying farmland, but I'm sure they still own the house. All the people who've lived there since have been tenants. Including your mystery internet thief."

"It's haunted," said Tara matter-of-factly. "Dilan won't go near it."

Her brother kicked her under the table.

"Kids," warned Charlie with a raised eyebrow, "behave."

"Yes, dad," said Tara innocently. "But it really is haunted, you know."

"Don't be silly, Tara," said Aunt Vicky. "There's no such thing as ghosts."

Cameron looked thoughtful. "I'll come with you," she said. "You never know. Tara may be right."

Tara and Dilan ran ahead with the dog while Cameron strolled up the street alongside Aunt Vicky. She was still sprightly in her seventies, but her usual brisk pace had slowed.

"He's not so nervous now," said Cameron, nodding at her nephew.

"Tara was just scoring points off him," said Aunt Vicky. "They remind me a little of you and Charlie, although they're closer in age, of course."

Cameron smiled. "That farm was always a little spooky, out on its own on the back road. I avoided it when I was a kid too."

"You see, it's always been the same," said Aunt Vicky. "They're all scaring each other for the sake of it, but there's nothing sinister. I want to see what has been done to the place. It has so much potential."

They caught up with the children just before the village green. Roxy was standing stock still and whining, refusing to go any further. Aunt Vicky sighed and bent down stiffly to peer into the thick hedge that marked the perimeter of a neighbour's garden. Cameron peered over her shoulder and saw a familiar pair of yellow eyes.

"Donald!" scolded Aunt Vicky. "You get out of there right now."

A bundle of ginger fur and muscle eased its way out of the hedge and snaked around Aunt Vicky's legs, purring. Her stern expression turned into one of pure indulgence as she scratched the cat between his ears.

Cameron could see that Donald's eyes were still locked on Roxy. "Of you go, Donald," she said, flapping her hands to distract him. "Home!"

The spell was broken, and Donald stalked off up the street to find a different dog to torment. Aunt Vicky gazed fondly at his retreating backside and the proudly held tail that was twitching slightly, just at the tip, in annoyance at them spoiling his fun. "He's a softy, really," she said. "He's doing very well for his age."

Cameron, whose tolerance for Donald was considerably lower, gave her aunt a thin smile. "Come on. We'll be late."

The short hill up out of the village was slow going, and Aunt Vicky was out of breath by the time they reached the farm. The driveway was already crowded with some neighbours that Cameron vaguely recognised, and many she did not. Her mind flashed back to the day she had followed the trail of high bandwidth data streams that had overwhelmed all the connections in the village. She'd found herself caught in the middle of an ongoing military and cyber defence operation, in the right time and place for the officer in charge to use her as a distraction. Her innocent knock at the farmhouse door and an unexpected conversation with an intelligent 'bot called Xanthe provided enough cover for the forces to make their move and close down the operation.

The officer who led the raid had eventually become a trusted colleague. Cameron knew he'd be interested in this visit. She pinged him a quick message and a picture of the exterior. "Pete – a throwback to when we met." He replied almost instantly with a laughing emoji.

Other than the familiar courtyard, Cameron found that successive tenants had changed the look and layout of the elegant farmhouse sufficiently to dim her memory of the chaos that had ensued that day. She followed her aunt through a succession of rooms, half-listening to her critically appraising the taste, or lack thereof, in the most recent refurbishment.

"That knock-through isn't very practical," she was saying to a neighbour that Cameron half-knew from the pub. "It must be draughty."

"Mmm, yes," replied the other woman. "And I don't know what they were thinking with those covings. Far too ornate for the room."

Cameron slid outside into a rear courtyard where Tara and Dilan were waiting for them with the dog. She recalled this genteel little space being full of smoke and shouting. It was calm now, with a living wall of greenery screening it from the road and a few comfortable outdoor chairs scattered around.

Tara tugged on Cameron's sleeve. "Over there," she whispered, pointing through the gate of the courtyard away from the road and towards some outbuildings on the far side of a small unkempt field. "That's where the ghosts are."

Cameron ambled casually through the gate and across the grass to the cluster of stone sheds, followed by Tara.

"Can you hear them?" whispered Tara.

Cameron shook her head and turned to her niece. "Just your imagination…"

Then she heard the voices.

A shout from the courtyard gate drowned out the whispers. "Hello!" Cameron turned to see the agent waving frantically at them. "I'm sorry, could you rejoin the main tour? Those buildings are out of bounds."

They retraced their steps. Cameron thought quickly. "I run a tech firm," she explained to the agent. "I've been looking for a new site outside London and these outbuildings would make an excellent remote working facility, with plenty of room for all our equipment. Are they not part of the sale?"

The agent was all smiles. "Yes, they are included, but as the owners have failed to keep them in good order, we haven't included them in the open house tour."

"Are there any restrictions on business use?" asked Cameron earnestly, playing the role of a serious buyer for all she was worth.

"No, no restrictions," said the agent. "The property has previously been classified for commercial use, as there was another enterprise based here many years ago."

There certainly was, thought Cameron. "Are the sheds all hooked up for standard utilities?"

"The outbuildings are fully connected, and they have an emergency backup solar power supply and battery storage," said the agent. "I'm sure the vendors wouldn't object to you viewing them, if it helps the sale. I'm happy to make an exception to the Open House rules. I must warn you again that they have not been well maintained, so you enter at your own risk."

Aunt Vicky had emerged from the main house and joined them at the gate.

"I'm going to take a look at the outbuildings," said Cameron brightly.

"What a good idea," said Aunt Vicky, catching on quickly. "Dilan, Tara, if you want to go too, I can look after Roxy for you."

Tara scampered through the gate behind Cameron and the agent, but Dilan hung back.

"Go on, dear," said Aunt Vicky quietly, taking hold of Roxy's lead. "You'll be fine."

On the other side of the field, the agent tapped a code and presented her chip to disable the large security fence that enclosed the buildings. She flapped at a spider's web that had ambitiously covered the whole doorway, then pulled a real, old-school key out of her pocket and unlocked the main door. Cameron recognised it as a high security model that also deactivated certain alarms the agent would know nothing about.

"I'll lock up again as soon as you're done," she said. "Perhaps I can take down some details about your company and your requirements?"

"Of course," said Cameron smoothly. "I'll come and find you shortly." Without a moment's hesitation she walked through the open door.

"I must get back to the other viewers," muttered the agent, outfoxed.

Inside, the voices were clearer. Cameron followed the sounds through the connected warren of sheds until they reached a large inner chamber full to the ceiling with boxes and junk. She took hold of a corner of the dust sheet that covered the nearest pile and pulled it clear.

It was a server, and the lights showed it was still running.

"This stuff is ancient," sniffed Tara.

"There's a whole stack of batteries over here," called Dilan.

"There are solar panels on the roof," said Cameron. "It's an emergency supply to make sure the building doesn't lose power."

"What are these?" asked Tara.

"Backup servers," said Cameron. She poked around at the equipment. "I think they've been here all along. They're offline, I'm certain, but they're running."

The voices swelled again, whispers of nonsense.

"Sometimes there are words and phrases," said Tara. "I transcribed them on my screen. Here."

Cameron read down the list. She recognised some snippets of Shakespeare, lyrics to a classic song, and odd words that danced in her mind.

"This one was funny," said Tara, pointing at a phrase on the screen. "'When you land on property owned by another player, the owner collects rent from you.' It was really clear and I'm sure I know what it is, but I can't work it out."

"It's one of the rules of Monopoly," said Cameron. She shivered, whether from the chill of the old outbuildings or the realisation of exactly what they had found she did not know. "Let's get out of here," she said. "I've seen enough."

Dilan didn't hesitate. Tara followed more slowly, looking back at the blinking lights. Back across the field in the sunny courtyard, the agent was waiting for them.

"Well?" she said brightly. "Will you be wanting more information about the property?"

"Yes," said Cameron, "but I think we should do this at your office. There is some valuable equipment stored in there that I guess the vendors hadn't disclosed. I suggest you lock that door again and consider some extra security."

The agent nodded eagerly, taking this to mean she had a buyer in her sights. "I'll attend to that," she said. "May I take your details?"

Of course," said Cameron. She pulled out her smartscreen and transmitted one of her more impressive fake digital identities. She received the agent's details by return.

"I look forward to seeing you again," said the agent, smiling with a mixture of professionalism and relief.

"One more question," said Cameron, "who are the vendors? I believe this place has been in the same hands for many years, but there have been a lot of different tenants. It seems strange that no one has considered refurbishing the outbuildings."

"I can't divulge the vendor's identity," said the agent, "but they have owned the property for more than thirty years. They have previously let it, and you're right, tenants have changed on a regular basis. I can't really explain why those buildings have been left to fall into disrepair. It's such a shame."

Cameron watched her bustle off.

"That was interesting," said Aunt Vicky. "I wonder what it all means?"

"I don't know," said Cameron. "I'd better update Pete."

He answered at the first ring. "Okay, what did you find?"

"You were expecting me to find something?"

"I've never forgotten that place. I had a strange feeling about it when you messaged me before."

"Your instincts are bang on," said Cameron. "There's still equipment running here, and we have some ghosts to exorcise."

7: DISCOVERY

At least he got a lie-in on Sundays. Ross groaned as he sat up in bed, aching from the exertions of the previous few days. He wasn't getting any younger and training had started to take its toll on his body. The World Championships had been a very different experience after the highs and drama of the Olympics two years earlier. He was more than content with his bronze and knew he could not have performed any better, and he was delighted for the new champion. As one of the oldest competitors now, and one of the few who chose to work outside his sport for the stimulation and enjoyment, he suspected that his days at the top were drawing to a close.

Michelle had let him sleep. She was already up and about. Ross found her curled up with a book in the most comfortable chair, listening intently to the latest instalment of the thriller series that had been absorbing her for weeks. He dropped a kiss on the top of her head and went to make some tea.

He put Michelle's refilled mug down on the table and wandered over to the window, frowning at the state of the little garden. "The mower's stopped working," he said. "I'd better have a look at it, or that'll turn into a jungle in a couple of weeks. Can't let the neighbourhood down."

"Before you do that, there's a new message from the Sladen Foundation," said Michelle. "There's a Diaulos software proposal been submitted and as we've got some governance tokens we need to review the developer feedback and vote. The first-round ballot ends at midnight UTC."

"Have you checked the proposal?"

"I had a scoot through it, yes. I'm not completely comfortable but the peer review has been positive so far."

"What's bugging you about it?"

"I think there's a loophole that could be exploited to artificially boost the standing of a grant application regardless of whether it meets the criteria for funding. It's not obvious, but it's there, and if I can find it, so can anyone with my, uh, specialist skills."

"Lazy coding, do you think?"

"Looks like it," said Michelle. "I've brought it up in the peer review forum, but the majority of the voices in there seem to be convinced it's just a better accessibility feature for grant applicants and that it can't be exploited. I'd like to see it fixed, but the chances are it's going through on the ballot."

"Better make our No vote count, in that case." Ross put his tea down and went out to the hallway where the new safe has been installed. He glared at a seemingly random spot on the wall to activate the biometric recognition, swiped his chip, and the well-disguised cover popped open. He slid a long slim key into the physical lock, opened the substantial sealed door, and extracted one of their hard wallets, a small secure drive that held the keys to some of their crypto accounts. Every time he did this, he thought back to his old system of hiding the hard disk under his floorboards and having to move furniture to find it and patted himself on the back for finally installing something that was both secure and easy to reach.

He switched on one of the computers, went to the Sladen Foundation voting site, plugged in the wallet device to identify himself and allow the software to check his token holder status, then clicked NO very firmly. "Done and signed," he said. "We'll know tomorrow if anyone else has picked up the same issue or been swayed by your persuasive arguments on the forum."

He cast an eye over the account balances and frowned. "Another mystery deposit," he said.

"Is there a message?"

"Yes," said Ross. "It's the usual stuff. 'I know where you are, I want my money back.' I kind of feel for whoever it was that threw away the old hard disk with the private keys."

Michelle shrugged. "We've tried," she said. "We can't return it to them because even though you've messaged them back, we have no idea who they are, they haven't given us any clues to find them, and they can't find us."

"You never know," said Ross. "If they do manage to find us, and there's always a chance of that although it's slim, they've earned what's left after all the donations we've made. Even with that they'd never have to work again. If the messages stop, its ours. Until then, well, we don't need to dip into it."

He thought for a moment and then created a transaction with a text field, sending a message back to the same address. "Happy to talk, no need for threats. Where are you?" He was sure there would be no response. They had never managed to establish a dialogue.

He logged out, ejected the device and returned it to its hidey hole, then picked up his mug of tea again. It had cooled to an acceptable temperature. "I'll tip the Foundation off that you've found something in that code and that the peer review isn't picking up on your comments. They might have the power to insist on an amendment."

"I'd be surprised. Jack made very sure that the Diaulos developer community was fully decentralised. The final ballots need a 95% majority for it to go through, of course, but the sentiment is certainly leaning towards a strong Yes vote in this first round. I'm concerned, is all I'm saying."

"Not our problem, Shell. One for Jack and Joel and Chloe to sort out." He drained his tea. "Right. I'll sort the mower out now. It's supposed to rain this afternoon, if the forecasts are right. Can't be too sure these days."

Out in the garden, Ross soon found the problem with the mower. It had snarled its wheels on a discarded piece of twine and had gone round and round in circles until its safety gyroscope cut the power. He freed the little machine, checked that its battery was full, and switched it back on. It sailed away, cutting blade whirring, lifting itself up a few centimetres to cope with the longer grass.

Ross checked around the garden for any more rubbish that might interrupt its happy mowing and pulled up a few weeds in the excuse for a border that he tried to keep tidy. He was so engrossed that he didn't notice the man standing on the pavement opposite until he stood up.

At first glance he looked like a neighbour. Ross certainly recognised him as a face he passed occasionally, but exactly where their paths had crossed, he couldn't be sure. He gave him a half-wave.

He was distracted by the sound of the front door opening. Michelle emerged, holding Ross's smartscreen. "There's a message from Sandeep," she called.

"Coming." Ross turned back to see the man shambling off up the street. He disappeared from view on the main road.

"Huh. That's odd," said Ross, walking back into the house.

"What's the matter?" asked Michelle.

"There's a guy I keep bumping into," said Ross. "I thought that was him standing right opposite the house just now. He's probably one of the new neighbours from up the road." He ruffled her hair. "You scared him off. Now, let's see what Sandeep wants."

Sandeep had work for them to do. "The first deep fake phishing messages have been reported in the wild."

"Bloody hell," said Ross. "That was fast. What do we know?"

"We spotted the data auction on Friday evening. The buyer has forty-eight hours of exclusivity before DeltaG starts licensing parcels, and they paid well for the privilege. My guess is that they already had a use case and the resources to set this phishing campaign in motion quickly."

Ross moved over to his computer and logged in while he continued talking. "What kind of things are you seeing?"

"What you'd expect from a hospital, really," said Sandeep. "We've intercepted two instances of standard branded mailing with a spoofed sender. It looks legit at first glance, and all the relevant personal and medical details are quoted as you'd expect. There've been voice calls too. Someone's got hold of voice records for one of the senior consultants who's well known on the medical conference circuit, and it seems the clone is remarkably good quality."

Ross accessed the Argentum repository and examined the intercepted emails. "This is a professional job," he said.

"It is," said Sandeep, "and whoever's produced the assets had access to more than just this breach. Those emails you're looking at contain additional information on top of the data set we know was stolen, so whoever it is has managed to combine what they bought with data they already held."

Michelle was at her own desk, headphones covering one ear as she listened to the emails and examined their metadata. "That might explain the speed of the response," she said. "They've probably built on an existing broad phishing campaign to spear phish the individual patients. Do we know if any of them have sensitive or senior jobs? There could be a whaling side quest going on. You know, blackmail targets or even ways into industrial espionage."

"Side quest," snorted Sandeep. "Love it. I don't think that kind of data was included in the breached set, but we can do some digging and see if there are cross references. I'll make a note."

Ross was looking at the latest information Sandeep had uploaded. "This is the deep fakery you mentioned, I take it? Aside from the voice calls, of course."

"That video you're watching is what happens when you accept the offer of an online appointment," said Sandeep.

"Where's that file?" asked Michelle. "Oh wait, got it." She listened intently. "That's good. It's not your average language model. It's very reactive and the responses are complex."

"And the avatar is very convincing," said Ross. "Clever. Have they spoofed all the consultants or just the ones with voice and video in the public domain?"

"Just the public ones," said Sandeep. "That's a good thing, I think. I was worried that there'd been a leak in the HR systems as well."

"We should check that out," said Michelle. "Better safe than sorry."

Ross was watching the video again. "Is this a set up for pig butchering?"

"Absolutely," said Sandeep. "They're chipping away, asking for fees to speed up treatment, and I guess they'll keep pushing for more and more without ever reaching the appointment."

Any data breach was generally the start of problems, not an end in itself. As the usual spokesperson for the company, Ross had a strong feeling that he'd be sitting in the News Channel studio later this week, warning the public once again not to follow unexpected links or send payment for things that looked too good to be true.

"They're clever," said Michelle. "What's the plan, Sandeep?"

"Everything we have so far is loaded onto that workspace and I'll add new assets as they come in. Between us we can start dissecting what we have. The goal is to disable avatar access, so that anyone who responds to the phishing call or mailing doesn't get through to the first video, and we'll hunt for any breadcrumbs leading back to the source."

Ross was fiddling around with the mailing samples. He downloaded one and copied it over to a sandbox drive linked to a different and equally secure network. "I'm just trying something," he muttered. A moment later he swore, then laughed. "The obvious link that's hidden in the metadata goes straight to a crawler honeypot. It's spawning fake pages at me right now." He killed the connection and deleted the copied file. "Watch out for that."

"It's definitely not DeltaG, then, that's for certain," said Michelle. "They couldn't string something like this together in a month of Sundays. It's out of their league."

"They're one-trick ponies," said Sandeep. "Who else is in the frame, do you think?"

Michelle shrugged. "In the old days I'd have said Pasar or the Steamyard and I'd have been right nine times out of ten, but the most skilled people from those outfits are either in jail or they've gone to ground."

"Regardless, we hobbled them by destroying Yasmin the Admin," said Ross. "Without Yasmin's intuitive processing capabilities, they'd be as average as DeltaG."

"This lot are not average," said Michelle.

"Are there any heirs to the Steamyard throne?" asked Sandeep.

Michelle paused, thinking, before choosing her reply carefully. "Maybe. I've been talking to Cameron about this for a while, but I think it was the yacht sinking that really made her sit up and take notice. There are rumblings in the deep levels about compromised quantum processing. This is long term, very specific stuff. I've been wondering for a while if Yasmin set something in motion before she was disabled."

"That wouldn't have anything to do with these deep fakes, though," said Ross. "They're classical processing."

"You're right," said Michelle, "but the point is, there's still someone very skilled out there, whether they're using classical computing or quantum processors to cause havoc. I just don't know who. Not yet, anyway."

"Keep digging," said Ross grimly. "If there is any vestige of Yasmin left, we're in trouble. But for now, let's try and neutralise this phishing. Who else is working on this, Sandeep?"

"It's just us and one of Joseph's team at Oak," said Sandeep. "Cameron's on her way back from her brother's and will join in when she gets back home. I can't get hold of Pete, but Cameron said she spoke to him yesterday and he's busy following up on something for her. Noor's got some family issues to deal with, and Susie's still abroad. I thought we should get a head start before people check their messages in the morning and start following links."

"Fair," said Ross. "We'll take a look and see what we can find."

Sandeep left the chat. Ross and Michelle were deep in discussion about their findings when an alert ringing on Michelle's device made them both jump.

"There's something strange going down in the deep levels," she said. "I'm going to head in and check it out." She changed headset and linked it to her sensory kit for easy navigation of the virtual world. "Any chance of a cup of tea?"

•

Emboldened by the fact that his first foray into the city for many months had attracted no official attention, Tenuk had spent his Sunday roaming further afield. He went back to an old favourite haunt in the Gardens by the Bay, watched families playing in the Supertree grove, and got lost in the crowds of tourists around the MerLion and the central business district. As night fell, he found his way to a small bar in a busy hawker market. After two strong local beers, he found himself wondering if he should go and check on Auntie Fatima.

A call from the house put paid to that idea.

"Tenuk, your father requests your presence in his office. A car is waiting."

A formal summons from his father on a Sunday night? This could not be ignored, and it was unlikely to be good news. Tenuk glanced towards the street. Sure enough, an unmarked sapphire-blue car had glided to a halt at the edge of the pedestrian area. Sighing, he drained the last of the beer and made his way out of the market.

The car's interior was far too luxurious for a little run-around, kitted out as a small, air-conditioned office with all the fixings. Tenuk took advantage of the fact and established a connection to Zara.

"What's going on?"

"There is a concern over one of our operatives."

"Which one? No, wait, I can guess." Tenuk leaned into his comfortable seat and sighed, gazing back at the lights of the Singapore skyline as the car swept up Orchard Road. "He was fine when I spoke to him after the auction. Well, not fine as such, but rude, uncooperative and belligerent, as I expected."

"The situation has changed."

The huge gates opened smoothly as the car approached and closed behind them. Tenuk jumped out at the main entrance to the house and the car sped away to its charging bay. He grabbed a coffee from the dining room, sniffed appreciatively at the smells wafting from the kitchen where dinner was being prepared, and went to join his father in his office.

Chaoxiang was sitting behind his desk with Xanthe, his humanoid AI assistant, in attendance. The wallscreens that were not busy with betting tickers and profit reports showed feeds from real and virtual sources. Tenuk immediately recognised a bull avatar rampaging around the lower levels of Eden. Xanthe raised the volume. "Pangolin. Where are you," bellowed a distorted voice.

"I believe he is looking for you," said Chaoxiang quietly.

"Give me context, Xanthe," said Tenuk. "Why this, why now? I can't deal with him unless I know why he's gone off the rails."

On another screen, a trail of images and surveillance footage showed the Monkey's last movements in real life.

"That's the triathlete," said Tenuk, recognising Ross instantly. "It looks to me as if the Monkey has been engaged in performing his contract with you, tracing each of the SimCavalier's team members. This is nothing to do with me."

"That young man has been known to us for many years," said Chaoxiang. "You know his history. Why would the Monkey be there? It is not part of our arrangement. And furthermore – watch – as soon as he sees the girl at the door of the house, he runs."

"Who is she?"

"She was identified as one of the SimCavalier's team in the interim report filed by the Monkey," said Xanthe, "but her connection to the runner was previously unknown. She was first seen with him at a race four years ago, but there is very little public information available for her and neither Zara nor I have been able to expand on our current data."

"Interesting," said Tenuk. "Whoever she is, she's covered her tracks. That's hard to do in this day and age." Tenuk looked at the clip that looped over and over on the screen. "I wonder what spooked him? He must know them both, if they are part of the same team. Perhaps he was not expecting them to be there?"

"Go and find the Monkey now," said Chaoxiang. "Xanthe and I will be watching. He is a danger to himself and to us, but he has not yet supplied all the information we need to take down the SimCavalier. He is still an asset."

Tenuk nodded and left the room. Back in his own office, he grabbed an immersion kit. "Zara, spin me up a new avatar with full level access."

"Yes, Tenuk."

It took only a few minutes. Tenuk settled into his immersion seat and dived into the virtual world. He padded through the groves, a tiger on the prowl. His quarry had last been seen in the cluster of low-life bars to the north-western corner of this level, and Tenuk was closing in.

He heard the commotion before he saw what was happening. Purely from the bellows and slurred words it was obvious that the man behind the raging bull avatar was drunk, and that he was shooting his mouth off in exactly the wrong place. If he'd been in a dive bar in London, Tenuk couldn't have cared less. But here, here in the deep levels, there were too many ears who understood the significance of the secrets that the Monkey was spouting.

"Pangolin! Where are you, you slippery bastard? I know where it is, and you knew too, didn't you? What are you staring at?" This to a knot of curious avatars that had surrounded him. "You want more? I can give you more. Who wants the SimCavalier? I know where she is. You can have her. Highest bidder. And there's more. Much more. You want the lowdown on Sapphi...?"

Tenuk had heard enough. The tiger sprang out of the trees and onto the rampaging bull. Their forms struggled and the crowd cheered. A random thought popped into Tenuk's mind that his father's gambling platform was likely already open to bets on the outcome.

"Help me out, Zara," said Tenuk in the real world, his audio muted in the virtual. Zara didn't have the presence or the capabilities of her sister, but he knew she could be disruptive.

The avatars broke apart. His adversary was still shouting, slurring his words. "You don't own me anymore. I know where my money is. You knew. You knew it was him. And the girl too…" His avatar shimmered and winked out of existence. Zara had done her work, but a moment too soon.

"What made you run?" shouted Tenuk into empty space. But the avatar had gone. Tenuk's tiger leapt away into the forest and vanished.

The crowd of curious spectators dispersed, leaving a small hermit crab avatar alone in the square. It withdrew into its shell and disappeared.

Back in his office, Tenuk took off his immersive mask and drew a long, shuddering breath. "Damage limitation at least, but he's right, he is no longer our agent."

"Your father will not be pleased," said Zara. "The Monkey has not yet delivered the bulk of the data he had collected on the SimCavalier and her team."

"And now he's offering it to the highest bidder. He's got to be stopped." Tenuk stood up and went to his father's office.

The old man was deep in thought. Tenuk waited patiently.

Finally, Chaoxiang looked up at his son and gave him a curt nod. "That was well handled. It may play into our hands. Let him sell what he has. We will no longer have to pay him for the information, and we will not incur the costs of deactivating the SimCavalier – indeed, whoever buys the data may choose to eliminate the team. We still achieve our goal."

"Yes, father," said Tenuk smoothly. "A good outcome."

He withdrew and returned to his own office, his mind in turmoil. The plans he had in place to protect Noor when she became the target of his father's campaign were now in tatters. If the Monkey sold his information, Tenuk no longer had control over how it was used, and Noor would be in danger. There was only one thing to do.

"Zara," he said, "I'm hungry. Is the kitchen still open?"

"No, Tenuk."

He was disappointed after the tempting smells, and his stomach was growling, but it was perfect cover. "That's okay," he said. "I'll order something. Thanks, Zara. I'll see you in the morning."

He duly placed a very specific order to a local twenty-four-hour diner. Burger, fries, salad, and a melon sorbet.

A message came straight back. The diner was out of melon sorbet, it said. Would the caller like mango or mandarin?

"Mandarin, please."

Anyone watching the exchange – and Tenuk had no doubt that all his communications were monitored – would see nothing unusual. The order would be delivered. But something else had also been delivered – an encrypted message to Tenuk's academy leads. The contingency plans that he had put in place were now set in motion.

8: SEARCHES

Michelle spent some time immersed in the virtual world of cybercriminals, starting with the location that had generated the alert, then wandering through Eden and diving deeper down the levels to gather intelligence on who had bought the DeltaG data. She came back to the reconvened group chat in a thoughtful mood with news that their old adversaries may still be active.

"There was a commotion," she explained, "and someone shouting for the Pangolin. It sounded like the Monkey. In fact, I am almost sure that it was. Then another avatar took him down and I think his connection was lost."

Cameron, who had arrived home and was now online, looked guilty. "You're probably right that it was the Monkey," she said. "There were two sightings of him here in London last week. I was going to brief you all tomorrow morning, but if he's kicking off online as well it sounds as if there's something bad going on."

"I haven't told you the worst bit," said Michelle grimly. "He claims to have information about us, about you and the team. It sounds as if he was commissioned to gather it and that an arrangement has fallen through. He was offering it to the highest bidder."

"Was he going to dox us all?" said Sandeep. "I mean, everyone seems to know where you are, Cameron, and Ross isn't exactly low profile, are you? Doxing the rest of us probably isn't a hard job."

"Maybe it isn't just doxing," said Cameron. "Someone is straying into meat space again, aren't they?"

"That's what I thought," said Michelle. "Who cares enough to target us?"

"It comes right back to Pasar, the Steamyard and Sapphire Straits," said Cameron. "I think we need to find Angus. In real life, I mean, not online. If I pull up the footage that we have, can you two work your magic with the city CCTV?"

"I have an alert set up already," said Michelle, "and it hasn't been set off for two years. Are you sure he's around?"

"He's changed." Cameron shared the video from the security cameras in her own building.

"No way," said Ross. "Cameron, he was here today. He was outside our house. I thought he was a neighbour but good grief, no, I remember now where I've seen him before. Thursday morning, when I called you, I saw him on the other side of the road. And he watched a couple of my training sessions, months ago."

Cameron, high up in her apartment, stepped away from the computer screen and walked out onto the balcony. She leaned on the railing and gazed out at London below, bathed in the glow of sunset. "We need to find him," she said. "I think we prioritise the CCTV scrape and pass what we have on the phishing and deep fakes over to the team in Auckland. They'll be awake and fresh."

"I'll contact them now." Sandeep's voice echoed in her headset.

"Thanks, Sandeep. There's not much more we can do tonight, folks. Let's get some sleep."

The next morning, the whole team gathered early to assess the situation. Susie was online from somewhere in Thailand, and Joel had joined from Dunswyke. Cameron pulled up the footage from her apartment complex and from Ella's doorcam.

Susie looked startled when she saw the images from Ella's home. "I know where that is. He's been there too?"

"Yes," said Cameron. "That's why I brought Joel in as well. Anyone who has worked on this team must be considered at risk. Although I think Ella is in the least danger. Have you spoken to her, Susie?"

Susie hesitated. "Not for a while. Are you sure she's safe?"

"As sure as I can be. Now, has anyone else seen him?"

"I have," said Pete, staring at the images. "Friday night, late on, about half eleven. There was some noise outside, and I assumed it was foxes. Saw someone walking off down the street and I'm almost sure it was this guy just by the way he walked."

"I'll search for surveillance footage around that time," said Noor. "And I've seen him too. I went to collect my uncle and take him to my mum and dad's house for their anniversary party on Saturday, because he can't quite handle autocars on his own, and we passed him. I wouldn't have noticed but I was pointing out my own apartment building. He was standing right outside it."

"We were right that he was collecting information," said Cameron grimly. "Joel, I'm guessing he hasn't been up north?"

"I don't believe so, but I'll do some checking. It may be worth seeing if he's caught a train out of London at any time, if you get your tracker up and running."

"Good shout. Thanks, Joel." Cameron made a note on the file. "Out of interest, have you heard from Jack yet?"

"I got a message to say he's going to join the morning team meeting," said Joel. "He's been released from hospital, and he's managed to find a business suite where he can make a video call."

"Say hello from all of us," said Cameron.

"I will," said Joel. He reached forward to switch off his screen, but Ross interrupted.

"Did you get the message from Shell?"

"The potential exploit? I did, thanks. Chloe's taking a look at it now. I'll keep you posted. Got to go!" His feed went dark.

Cameron turned to Sandeep. "Any sightings round your way?"

Sandeep shook his head. "I don't think I've seen him, but then I've been out and about at odd times what with doing the on-site response to the Oak Medical hack."

Cameron made a note on her file. "We'll see if anything flags up when the facial recognition agent goes live. How's that coming along, Shell?"

Michelle gave a dry laugh. "Better than you might think," she said. "We don't have enough data yet for decent results, but I deployed an agent anyway and started refining it on the fly, trying to train it on biometric markers like gait in the data we already had rather than facial recognition. What's very strange is that I found another agent active in the system. It seems to have a much stronger data set."

"You mean, it's tracking the same thing?"

"Yes," said Michelle. "It's tracking Angus."

The whole team fell silent, digesting the information. The hunter, hunted. Who else needed to know where Angus was? Someone didn't trust him, and by the sounds of the model Michelle had found, they hadn't trusted him for a long time. No love lost between cybercriminals, it would seem.

"Can you hook into that agent without alerting whoever set it up?" asked Cameron.

"Not so far," said Michelle. "It's very well protected and I found it by chance. Here, let me bring it up for you."

As Michelle pulled on her headphones, Cameron heard the familiar high-pitched sound of the screen reader. A moment later, a part of the wallscreen flickered and changed to display the back end of the CCTV database. Michelle was scrolling backwards and forwards, frowning.

"That's really strange," she said. "It's gone. I swear there was an agent running and it's not there now."

Cameron leaned back in her chair and took a sip of coffee. "Could it mutate its signature in the system to avoid detection?" she asked.

"Maybe," said Michelle. "Let me search again."

"Angus has found himself in a bunch of trouble with someone, hasn't he?" said Pete.

"Yes, he has," said Cameron. "I'm half-convinced that Shell is right about some of our old friends resurfacing." She sighed. "This is going to be a busy week. We have a lot on our plate."

"What's the plan, boss?" said Sandeep.

"We need to work smart. Priority one, start with what we've managed to scrape from CCTV and see what we get first, a location for Angus or a decent data set for Shell to work on for ongoing tracking. And we should get the police involved, discreetly. DI Mercer may be interested to know that he's reappeared."

"I can pick that up," said Noor.

"Perfect, thanks, Noor. Now, deep fakes and phishing."

"We may as well carry on with that analysis," said Ross. "You okay with that, Sandeep?"

"Suits me," said Sandeep. "We can pick up the progress that the Auckland team made. They've got some good fixes and a lead about a code farm in Indonesia that might be involved." He looked up at the wallscreen. "Susie, if you're bored and you want to keep your hand in, why don't you join us?"

"I'd love to," said Susie. "I'm on a long layover between conferences and the place where I'm staying has a hyper secure connection."

"What about you, Cameron?" asked Michelle.

"Pete and I have an appointment with an estate agent," said Cameron. "There's some ancient history that needs revisiting." She finished the last of her coffee and stood up. "Ready?"

"Ready," said Pete. "Let's go."

A rare accident somewhere on the road network had snarled the traffic in central London and the pavements were clogged with people and bikes. Cameron amused herself by watching the behaviour of different vehicles as she and Pete threaded their way through the crowd. Some were stuck firmly in line while others with more collaborative behavioural programming and good node to node comms were merging neatly into the moving lanes.

"We've had self-driving cars for a generation," she said to Pete as they weaved through the chaos, "and there are still some manufacturers skimping on the basics."

She could see the passengers in the stuck cabs getting more and more frustrated. One man had managed to operate the emergency door release and was standing by his stationary vehicle, shouting. "Open the bloody boot! I'll walk from here, and I need my luggage." He kicked one of the autocar's tyres and was rewarded by a new alarm that added to the cacophony. Cameron and Pete kept going, aware that they were running late.

The estate agent greeted Cameron effusively, shook hands with Pete, and led them to her office. "The vendor's representative is late," she said, glancing at a clock display on the wall. "I'm so sorry. While we wait, here are all the detailed particulars for you both to peruse."

She handed them both tablets to scroll, and to Cameron's surprise put a bulky paper file on the desk as well. "It's an old property," she explained. "Not all of the historical records have been digitised."

Cameron dived into the papers with delight, enjoying the half-remembered scent of dusty archives. She carefully unfolded the original map of the property that showed the full extent of the old farm and the gradual nibbling away of parcels of land until just the field around the house and the outbuildings remained. She was so engrossed that she didn't realise how much time had passed when the estate agent returned.

"I can't apologise enough," she said. "Mr Black still isn't here. This is very unusual. I can't proceed with this meeting without him. Can we reschedule? Perhaps later this afternoon, or tomorrow?"

"Of course," said Cameron. "Who were we waiting for, again?"

"Mr Black. Paul Black. I've tried to reach him several times."

"Why don't you call me as soon as you've managed to rearrange," said Cameron smoothly. "It's a very interesting property, and from what I've seen it would meet our needs." She made to put the papers back in the file and fumbled with them, unfamiliar with the touch and texture of physical records.

"Don't worry about those," said the estate agent, expertly gathering up the spilled sheets into a neat pile.

Cameron smiled. "We'll see you later." She followed Pete to the door. As soon as they were outside and out of earshot, she turned to him. "Did you see the logo on the papers I dropped?"

"I did. Sapphire Group. That's not a huge surprise, is it?"

"No," said Cameron. "And it begs the question, who is Paul Black?"

They were back in the Argentum office within half an hour.

"We've got a lead on a Sapphire Straits operative here in London," said Cameron. "Have any of you come across the name Paul Black?" She explained the link and the absence of the mysterious Mr Black.

"Not at all," said Noor. "It's a common name and it might be a completely innocent connection."

"I'll run some searches," said Cameron. She dived happily into the satisfying job of tracing a digital footprint, interpreting posts, linking their posting location to the real world, following transactions, identifying photographs and building a path to the door of her quarry. Despite starting from several hundred Paul Blacks around the country, she was rather disappointed that her strict process of elimination identified the most likely candidate after only an hour of trawling. Advertising posts and some unguarded correspondence from the estate agent about the property in the village provided the first clues. A trail of transport tap-ins and impulse purchases between the general location of the estate agent's office and a cluster of high-rises led directly to the rental agreement for a dingy studio apartment in the name of Paul Black. It was almost too easy.

"Cameron, have you seen this?" Noor had spotted something on the news ticker that fed directly to the office.

"… police are appealing for relatives of Paul Black, injured in this morning's autocar accident in central London. Mr Black is in a critical condition in St Martin's Hospital."

"That's why he wasn't at the meeting," said Cameron. "How sad."

"Have you found anything out about him?" asked Noor.

Cameron shook her head. "Not much. I imagine that's why the police have gone public." There was a ping from her computer, and she turned back to the screen. "Ah, we've got his ID. I suspect it won't tell us anything we don't know, though."

She opened the file.

The face staring at her from the ID was unmistakeably Angus.

"Well, we found him," said Noor quietly. She went over to Michelle's desk. "No need for an alert now, Shell."

Michelle was shocked, relieved and annoyed in equal measure. "I was halfway there on the tracking model," she said. Then she frowned.

"What's up?" asked Cameron.

"This happened just before you and Pete went out, is that right?" said Michelle.

"Yes. Looking at the state of the traffic, maybe an hour at most."

"The other tracker vanished in that window," said Michelle. "Coincidence?"

Cameron stared at her. "Are you suggesting that this was no accident?"

Michelle shrugged. "It's possible. Think about it. Angus shoots his mouth off online. He's a danger to us, but is he a danger to someone else as well? Someone who has been tracking him for a long time just in case he goes off the rails?"

"Attempted assassination by autocar," said Sandeep.

"I hope you're wrong," said Noor. "I'll let DI Mercer know what we've found and that there may be a cybercrime underworld angle to this accident. She'll be able to commission an investigation into the vehicle's programming and decision-making inputs."

"One of us had better get over there," said Cameron, "and claim to be Mr Black's long-lost niece or nephew. I can do that. I want a word with him, if he's conscious."

"You won't have time," said Noor. "Remember, Brianna's coming into the office after class today."

"I could go," said Michelle. "He'd probably recognise me, but I don't know if that's a blessing or a curse."

"I wonder if that's why he legged it when you came out of the house yesterday," said Ross.

"I need you here, Shell," said Cameron. "I'd like you in the discussion with Brianna once we have the paperwork out of the way. You were the first one to pick up on the possibilities of quantum hacking, and you can explain what you found much better than I can."

"In that case, I'll go," said Ross. "I need to be down at the pool this afternoon, and St Martin's is in the right direction." He picked up his training bag. "I'll let you know what state he's in."

No sooner had Ross left the building than security called to say that Argentum had a visitor. Cameron went out to the hallway and leaned against the balcony railings, looking down the light well to the ground floor six storeys below. She could see Brianna waiting at the lifts, gazing around at the building.

"She's on her way." Cameron went back into the office and set up three chairs around monitors in a secluded corner.

Michelle started closing down her tracking model. "Sure," she said. "Let me know when you're ready."

There was a knock at the door. Noor welcomed Brianna and introduced her to the assembled team. Sandeep set his precious coffee machine to work, and Cameron, Noor and Brianna worked through the formalities of the advisory role.

"I'll leave you to it now," said Noor. "All yours, Shell."

Cameron introduced them. "Shell came to me with some intelligence about quantum manipulations being sold as a service in cybercriminal networks," she explained. "These were just rumours, and honestly until the last few days I wasn't at all sure this kind of thing was even possible, let alone something that could be controlled and commercialised. Then with the yacht sinking and the things you told me when we met, it all falls into place."

"If I can understand all the different ways that this can be done," said Michelle, "then we have an idea of the different attack vectors, and we can build up a picture of the kind of things that would be a target for cybercrime."

Brianna nodded enthusiastically. "The complex simulations that feed to our weather forecasts is a great example, and I spent the weekend digging into the possibilities. There are a couple of ways that the inaccuracies we are seeing now could be generated, but they are so long term that I'm not sure it's intentional. It could be explained by problems with error correction, for example, or conditions within a data centre that marginally increase decoherence over time. Nothing sinister."

"Oh, we always assume it's something sinister unless proven otherwise," said Cameron. "The trick is to follow the money. If there's profit to be made, someone will be trying it."

"Who would make money from a storm moving unpredictably?" said Brianna.

Cameron gave her a crooked smile. "I don't know yet. That's half the fun. I'll leave you two to work out the vectors and applications, and I'll get on with investigating the why."

•

Ross found it easier than he expected to get through the security around Angus at St Martin's. There was one policeman on duty and his role was simply to see if any next of kin rolled up.

"Paul Black is my uncle," he said. He presented his ID and chip for scanning.

"Ross White," said the policeman, doing a quick double take. "Wait, you're the triathlete, aren't you? My son's a big fan. I'm sorry about your uncle. Go and report to the nurses' station on Ward 7. I'll let them know you're on your way up."

Despite the optimistically colourful décor, St Martin's Hospital still had an institutional feel that made Ross shudder. He was more than used to going to hospitals for emergency treatment and physio, but the long corridors and the more serious, small, beeping critical care wards reminded him of his grandmother's last illness. Pete had been in this hospital a few years ago, he remembered, recovering from surgery when the Grasshopper Flu hit and he'd been quarantined.

The nurse was waiting for him. "I'm so glad that you've come forward," she said. "You're Mr Black's nephew, is that right? There's definitely a family resemblance."

Hardly, thought Ross. "Uncle by marriage," he said hastily. "He's not a blood relative, and I haven't been in touch with him since I was a kid, but I recognised him on the news feed."

The nurse directed him to a sink to wash his hands and handed him a mask. "Can't be too careful," she said. "I'll take you through, but I must warn you that your uncle is in a critical condition and he may never regain consciousness. I'm very sorry."

The room was quiet but for the beeping of a monitor and the shallow breathing of its sole occupant. Ross looked down at the man on the bed. There was no doubt that this was the stranger who had been standing outside his house just two days ago and who had crossed his path several times over the past year, but he seemed shrunken and diminished. His breathing was shallow. One hand with a canula inserted lay motionless on the blanket. His dark hair was dyed, and the roots were showing white with a russet tinge. There was a day's ginger stubble on his chin.

Ross sat down on the plastic-covered chair next to the bed, wondering what to do.

"Here," said the nurse, bustling in with a box in her hand. "He was carrying a smartscreen and a few personal items. Would you like to…?"

"Thank you," said Ross.

The nurse nodded and withdrew. Ross picked up the smartscreen, and with barely a pang of guilt picked up the man's limp hand and pressed his thumb to the biometric scanner. To his surprise, it worked. He'd expected stronger protection, but the thumb and probably the chip signature from the same hand had been enough.

There was very little to find, as he expected. The only content dealt with the property sale and supported the persona of Paul Black. There was a fake digital ID and a few photographs, and a couple of wallets that wouldn't open. Ross took the chance of waving the smartscreen across the man's face, and one wallet seemed to be lax enough in its security to open without movement or attention. The other stayed firmly shut. Ross took a note of the open wallet's address. The balance was very healthy. The most recent transactions were a series of identical deposits timestamped overnight, probably payments received through a tumbler that split a large sum into many smaller ones and routed them in different directions before arriving at their destination. That fitted with Michelle's report that Angus had been offering information for sale. He must have found a buyer. The team would run a forensic analysis back through the trail to see which known illicit addresses were involved.

The photographs were a mixed bag of London scenery and a pale stone farmhouse, presumably the property that he'd been trying to sell.

As Ross scrolled back through the pictures, he was surprised to find a screenshot of himself with his Olympic medal. He didn't have Angus down as a fan.

He jumped as the man's breathing became irregular. Ross stood up and went to the door to call the nurse, then turned back to the patient. He coughed and started muttering under his breath, but Ross couldn't make out any words.

"He's had a few moments like this, love," said the nurse, adjusting the drip.

"Has he said anything?"

"Not really. He has a serious head injury. I'm sorry."

"That's fine. I understand."

"He did say your name, though. Take that as a comfort."

Ross stared at the nurse. "Are you sure?"

"Oh, yes," she said. "I was so pleased when you came. Very soon after he was admitted, he was very restless and he said, very clearly, 'Ross, keep it.' Does that mean something to you?"

"Not really," said Ross, shaking his head. He looked down at Angus, now peaceful. "I'd better go. Thank you for the time with him."

"You're welcome. We'll be in touch as soon as there's any change."

Ross left St Martin's and walked briskly in the sunshine towards the training pool. He called Cameron to let her know what condition Angus was in and shared his notes about the contents of the man's smartscreen. He didn't mention what were likely to be Angus's final words. The visit had raised more questions than it answered, and only time would tell what secrets Angus held.

•

In Singapore, Tenuk was braced for his father's wrath.

"This is a serious setback," said Chaoxiang sternly, "and I hold you responsible."

Tenuk stood almost to attention, his face impassive. He was absolutely certain that the old man had no idea of the precise circumstances of the accident. He waited for his father's reasoning.

"You failed to secure regular intelligence from the Monkey about the SimCavalier's team as he carried out his work." Tenuk felt it would be of no use to point out that the contract in question had been initiated by Chaoxiang and that collating information as it was gathered had nothing to do with him. "Your hold over him, this drip-feeding of clues to the location of his lost wallet, was unreliable. I can only assume that he compiled enough independent data to complete the puzzle."

That was fair, thought Tenuk, but so unlikely a circumstance that he had never even considered that it might happen.

"I was prepared to bid for the information he held at open auction, or to ensure that the buyer collaborated with us in completing the job, but no auction has taken place. You are to go to London and finish what the Monkey started. Obtain and secure the information he gathered."

"Yes, father." He had no choice in the matter, but he was surprised to feel relief. He could escape.

He kept his face impassive as Chaoxiang continued. "We have invested time and money into our efforts to remove the SimCavalier and Jack Sladen from the equation. They have been disruptive to Sapphire Straits strategies for many years, and this failure to execute a simple data gathering exercise is an unexpected and costly setback."

Tenuk showed no emotion, but he was shocked to the core by the mention of Sladen. He had assumed that the sinking of the yacht was coincidental, and that his father had simply taken advantage of the situation to turn a tidy profit from the high rollers who would bet on absolutely anything. Could he have had a hand in the accident itself?

"The operation to remove the SimCavalier and her team will proceed based on what we already know, and it will be strengthened by the intelligence our agent collected once you secure and deliver it. There will be additional instructions relating to Sladen, as we understand he is returning to England. There is also the small matter of a property clearance and sale that you will need to handle on my behalf. Xanthe will brief you."

There was a knock on the door. "Dr Tan is here, Mr Chen."

Chaoxiang made his way to the wing-backed chair by the window and sat down heavily. For the first time, Tenuk thought he looked frail. The doctor came into the office and nodded politely at Tenuk. "Leave us, my son," said Chaoxiang.

Tenuk withdrew gracefully, his mind racing. What were his father's plans for the SimCavalier? He thought that by removing the Monkey before he shared his information, Noor would be safe. It seemed that was not the case.

A notification on his smartscreen informed him that had already been checked in for a flight first thing in the morning. Between packing, tying up some loose ends, his worry over his father's plans, this mystery briefing from Xanthe, and making arrangements for staying in London, he had a busy night ahead.

First, though, he had a social call to make. "I'm going to see my mother," he told Zara, "and I'll make my own way back."

An official car whisked him to the mausoleum. He hadn't been here for almost eighteen months, but he didn't know when or if he would return to Singapore. His mother's avatar was as beautiful as ever, frozen in time. She was gracious and eloquent and gave him the closure he needed. He didn't stay for long. He knew he was finally at peace with his mother's passing.

He did not return directly to the house and instead jumped on the nearest local bus and took a roundabout route to his old haunt in Katong, stopping briefly at a shopping mall to find a suitable gift. He knew it was reckless, but he wanted to see Auntie Fatima. The irony was not lost on him that his long-dead mother knew him, but his living former neighbour most likely would not.

He took a deep breath and knocked on the door. After a short while, he heard a voice. "Who's there?"

"It's Tenuk." He had no wish to hide.

Auntie Fatima opened the door and fixed him with a surprisingly astute stare. "You live upstairs," she said.

She remembered him, then, but from his previous life. He let it slide and enjoyed the moment. "Yes, Auntie," he said. "I'm going away to London. I wanted to say goodbye."

He held out the small hamper with both hands and she took it automatically. "How kind." Her brow furrowed, grasping for memories. "My niece lives in London. Can I make you some tea?"

"No, thank you. I must go. Be well, Auntie."

He turned away and left her standing in the doorway holding the gift. His heart was thumping. Not only had he made his peace with Auntie Fatima, but he was certain that his visit would come to Noor's attention. He had as good as told her he was coming to London, and in doing so had already betrayed his father.

9: LONDON

Tuesday morning brought the first bout of unsettled autumn weather to London, and an equally unsettled start to the day for Cameron. New reports of ransomware were coming in from users of the infected scheduling software, and it felt as if all the progress they had made with Oak Medical was somehow negated by the new infections. Ross's warnings had reached most of the Argentum clients and anyone who took notice of industry alerts, but the news channels and socials were full of sob stories from small businesses and charities whose activities had ground to a halt. The mood was ugly, and the team hunkered down in the office talking to their various counterparts in other cybersecurity companies and at the National Cyber Security Centre.

Noor's breathless news of Tenuk's visit to her aunt the previous afternoon did nothing to lighten the mood.

"As soon as Angus is out of the picture, Tenuk turns up," said Cameron. "As if we needed any more proof that Angus was working for Sapphire Straits. I'm not happy that he's coming here."

"It's almost as if he wanted me to know, though," said Noor. "He was sending a very clear message. He didn't hide himself, and he told her where he was going, and she can't remember whether it's tea or Tuesday most of the time, so it wasn't for her benefit."

"A warning, then?" suggested Sandeep. "One man down, another operative takes his place to stalk us."

"I have no idea," said Cameron. "We need to keep a very close eye on him from the moment he gets here. Don't suppose you have his flight details, Noor?"

"Uh, yes, I do, as a matter of fact. I thought they might come in handy. He's still travelling as Tenuk Teo."

Ross was shaking his head. "I don't get it. He's being completely transparent. There's something odd going on, but we don't have the full picture."

"We can't afford to spend time second guessing him," said Pete. "These enquiries are piling up. Just chatting to my NCSC contact and he likes the work we've been doing on countering the phishing campaigns. He's suggested that we focus on minimising the spread of stolen data and check if anything comes out on the open market."

"There's a team in Belfast who've made inroads into the malware," said Michelle. "If it's okay with you, Cameron, I'll share what I've already pulled together, and we may be able to stop it in its tracks before it infects anyone else."

"Okay, Pete and Shell, do what you need to do on those, but Shell don't forget to keep an eye on Brianna's work as well. Sandeep, are you still on the Oak Medical response?"

"Yes, I'm heading over there shortly."

"Thanks. Now, someone needs to keep tabs on Tenuk. As long as it's from a distance, Noor, could you handle that?"

"Of course," said Noor. "And I'll keep working on the threat map." The 3D model that spun on the visualisation deck was growing as different groups of experts added new infections, blots of red across the map, and others contributed mitigations and inspiration.

Both Cameron and Ross's smartscreens lit up at the same time with calls. Cameron listened impassively as the estate agent expressed at length her sorrow at the dreadful news of Mr Black's accident, but explained that the vendors had arranged a new representative to deal with the sale, and was Cameron available for a meeting? They agreed a date and time for a meeting the following week that she would not attend, not now that she knew Tenuk was coming.

She hung up and saw that Ross was halfway to the door. "Andy needs a talking head on the News Channel," he said, "so I'm heading downstairs. Want anything from the café when I come back up?"

There was a chorus of calls for snacks. Fuel for a hard day ahead.

There was too much to do, thought Cameron, and the team was spread thin. Joel's move to work for Jack had caught her off guard, and she hadn't replaced him. She'd always hoped Chloe would join the team, but when Ben started spending more time with her, Cameron had distanced herself. Susie was away as conference season was in full swing, and although her time on the circuit did wonders for the reputation of the business among high-paying clients, it meant that the team was almost at full capacity with no trainees coming through the ranks. Cameron strongly suspected Susie would be snapped up by one of the huge international agencies in any case. The six of them who were left just couldn't handle everything that was thrown at them. Something had to give. She needed to build again, but her heart wasn't in it. Brianna's arrival had lifted the team and her own spirits, but she needed more.

Her smartscreen rang again and when she saw the familiar smile of the caller her heart lifted just a little.

"Hi Jack." She scanned his face. Sunburned, a little battered, with a slightly haunted expression around his eyes that he probably didn't even know was there.

"Hi Cameron. The medics gave me the all-clear and I'm on my way back. I'll be landing at Heathrow just before midday. Want to meet for lunch before I head north?"

Her heart sank again. "I can't. We are snowed under. This ransomware is spreading like wildfire, and I have a million things to do."

"In that case, I'll bring lunch to you. All of you." Cameron started to protest, and Jack held up his hand. "No arguments. I'll see you later. Got to go."

The screen went blank, and Cameron's reflection stared back at her. She was smiling.

By the time Ross reappeared half an hour later, Cameron had worked through most of the new enquiries and outstanding replies to clients and was deep into some research around the industry, keeping up to date on the latest thinking on cybercrime.

He came over to her desk and sat close, talking quietly. "I picked up on something odd on the public forums," he said. "I like to keep tabs on what crazy stuff is being discussed. It often points to real problems. There's a conspiracy theory site that has started spouting some wild rumours about cybersecurity."

"What kind of rumours?" asked Cameron, half-distracted by a thread of discussion on one of her screens that was speculating on the economic damage of the ransomware.

"Someone is throwing shade and blaming infosec teams for the cyberattacks themselves. They're saying that the only way we know how to stop malware in its tracks is because we write it in the first place."

"What?" Cameron turned away from the screen and gave Ross her full attention. "If we knew how to kill this latest bloody virus, we'd have done it by now."

"Ah, so their argument is, you're making money by letting this one run."

Cameron put her head in her hands. "That's all we need. How far is this stupidity spreading?"

"It's been picked up by a couple of big influencers," said Ross. "That's why I'm worried."

"Any names?"

"Just handles for now, a dozen or so."

"Including us?"

Ross nodded. "Yes. It's all a lot of hot air, but we've seen how that kind of thing can turn nasty in an instant."

"Another thing to add to the list. Well, the ransomware situation is as under control as it can be. The new case reports have slowed down, and there's no sign of data thefts. Shell thinks that DeltaG have just got bored now and they're happy collecting ransoms."

"People are paying?" said Ross incredulously.

"A few, yes. We uncovered a flexible pricing model in the code. The faster you pay, the cheaper it is. I wish we'd known that when Oak Medical was hit. Insurance companies have been very responsive as they can see paying the ransom is cheaper than long term business interruption. It's completely contrary to NCSC advice, but market forces are in charge on this one."

"I almost wish we had written this," said Ross, laughing. "Pile 'em high and sell 'em cheap. DeltaG may be lazy, but they're innovative."

They were distracted by a ragged cheer from the other side of the office.

"The Belfast crew's nailed it," shouted Sandeep. "Killed it stone dead."

Cameron felt a rush of relief. "Any details?"

"They went in through the compromised scheduling software and forced an update that disables the malware before it has a chance to run," said Michelle. "There's going to be a heck of a cleanup job, but that should stop the spread in its tracks."

"Shell's too modest to say, but she contributed part of the code," said Noor, glowing with pride in her teammate.

"And Ross's first contact with the old developers got us into their repositories," said Michelle. "Team effort."

Cameron glanced at Ross. "Keep an eye on those forums you mentioned. Damned if we do and damned if we don't."

Noor looked puzzled. Cameron shook her head. "Nothing to worry about. Just some silliness that Ross picked up on. Great job, everyone."

Pete eased himself out of his chair and stretched. "And now onto the other ninety-nine things on the to-do list, eh?" he said, counting the projects down on his fingers. "Clean-up process with Oak Medical and any other clients who lost access, take down the phishing scam, find out what's going on at the farm – I see you made another appointment with the estate agent – and what else?"

"Follow up the exploit we found in the software proposal that's going through the Sladen developer community," said Michelle.

"We can talk to Jack about that face to face," said Cameron. "He's flying back today, and he says he's bringing us lunch." She looked at the time. "I guess he'll have landed by now."

Right on cue, there was a knock at the door. For a moment, Cameron thought it must be Jack, but there had been no call from security to say he was on the way. When Ross opened the door, it was one of the staff from the atrium café with a laden trolley of food.

"Compliments of Mr Sladen," she said. "There's a message, too. He says he's slightly delayed but you're all to tuck in."

By the time the actual security call came, Cameron was relaxed, renewed and ready to take on the world. She slipped out of the office to meet Jack at the lifts. He dropped his overnight bag and gave her a hug that took her breath away.

"You look great," said Cameron. "No luggage?"

"Everything's on the bottom of the Caribbean Sea," said Jack ruefully. "This is just a few essentials I picked up in Belize."

There was a cheer as they entered the office.

"Welcome back," said Ross with a smile.

Over lunch, they exchanged news. He hadn't heard about the accident involving Angus even though the man had been head of security for a while at Dunswyke.

"He was a difficult character to work with," he said, "and I know you didn't trust him at all, Cameron, for good reason, but it's sad all the same. Does he have any family?"

"None that we know of," said Michelle, "and he lived on his own when I first met him up north."

Jack told them the story of the sinking and rescue. At Pete's request, he uncovered what remained of the tattoo that had probably saved his life. He pointed at one of the skin diver pellets, indistinguishable from the others save for a brighter glint.

"That's Pip," he said. "Say hello."

Jack's train wasn't until four. The others drifted back to work, leaving Jack and Cameron sitting companionably on the sofa and looking out at the London skyline.

"We've been looking into errors in weather forecasts," she said. "It seemed odd that the weather simulation for the Caribbean had skewed so far from the observed path of the storm. We've always been told how reliable quantum simulations are, but now there's this, and something isn't right."

"I might have known you'd be deep into the quantum world," said Jack.

Cameron shook her head. "I'm still learning. We have a tame expert who's come on board to advise. She's going to be working with Shell who knows more than I do about it all."

"You know enough to know it can be compromised, though."

"A quantum computer is still just a machine, at the end of the day," said Cameron. "Humans will always find a way to break it."

Jack looked thoughtful. "My flight was disrupted. There was an announcement about a schedule change to avoid a storm, but I've been keeping an eye on the forecasts, as you can imagine, and watching the clouds too. I know there wasn't one on the horizon, either simulated or real."

"And?"

"We should have flown from Belize up to New York and then picked up the transatlantic leg, but instead we hopped to Brazil, of all places, then direct to London. There were no flights going north at all. Nothing crossing American airspace. I had a little dig around and it turns out there was an insurance block imposed. What systems govern real-time insurance?"

"You're expecting me to say quantum simulation, aren't you?" Cameron threw up her hands. "I have no idea, but I can find out. I know that real time insurance premiums predate reliable quantum processing by a couple of decades, but that doesn't mean to say that the data feeds they use these days don't come from things like weather system simulations."

"Another mystery for you to get your teeth into," said Jack with a smile.

"Believe me I have far too much on my plate already." Cameron looked regretfully at the clock on the wall. "You'd better go and get your train, Jack. We have a big cleanup operation to deal with. It could take months to get some of these ransomware victims back up and running."

Jack stood up with a sigh and gathered his overnight bag. "I'd better leave you to it, in that case," he said. He picked up a last piece of cake, washed it down with coffee, and licked the icing off his fingers. "It's good to see you all."

He walked towards the door and stopped at Michelle's desk. "Shell? Thanks for that breakdown of the software exploit. I'll pick it up with Chloe."

Cameron followed him out to the lifts. "There's something else you should know," she said. "We think that Tenuk is on his way to London."

Jack raised his eyebrows, startled. "Really? I haven't heard from him since he disappeared to visit his sick mother in California." He gave Cameron a twisted grin. "Don't worry. I know the whole story. If you need any help neutralising him, let me know. I have connections."

"I don't think that'll be necessary, but thanks, Jack. Safe travels." Cameron watched the lift door close, then turned and went back into the office.

•

Tenuk landed at Heathrow on time, wide awake after working through the night in his office and then sleeping for a good proportion of the flight. At least that would help a little with his jet lag. It was three in the afternoon in the UK, ten in the evening in Singapore, and felt like 8am in his head.

He got through immigration without a hitch, and he picked up an autocar to the hotel. He would find a more permanent place to stay in due course, but for now he knew that he would be under surveillance by his father, or at least his father's omnipresent agents, and had to carry out all the tasks that were assigned to him.

He worked his way down the list. He made a call to the estate agent to confirm that he had arrived safely in London and would like to visit the property and understand how the sale was progressing. He used a simple audio fake to contact St Martin's Hospital, posing as an old colleague, to ask breathlessly about the condition of Mr Black. Critical, he was told, and the ward was only accepting visits from close family. Could the caller suggest any next of kin that the hospital might contact? Tenuk apologised, no, none came to mind. He knew that Angus had no relatives, and the hospital's eagerness to find some was a good indication of the prognosis. His emergency action to remove Angus from the equation may not have been immediately fatal, but it had been effective. Good news for him, not so much for his father, although he could not express that out loud.

His next task was a little harder. Despite all their efforts, the information Angus had collected had not been found online. He must have an air gapped storage device for safety, an offline repository, something that only he could access. The first place to look would be his home, and he was sure that the address he had was not going to be correct. Still, he had to check it out.

Baseball cap firmly on his head, warding off a spattering of rain rather than the Singapore sunshine, Tenuk familiarised himself with the public transport system, buying a tourist card rather than using his chip to cover the fares. Better to move around anonymously than to leave a trail of tube trips and autocar hires for others to find. He hopped from tube line to overground, from bus to scooter, travelling out west to the leafy suburbs of Richmond and then south towards Crystal Palace. By the time he returned to the centre, he felt at home. Glancing at the address, he hopped on a train going east.

As he'd expected, there was no house there. He found himself standing at the edge of a bustling university campus, the first semester of the year in session, and a large sign welcoming him to the Law, Criminology and Cybersecurity department. It seemed that Angus had a long-buried sense of humour.

Tenuk turned back towards the station, dodging a young man with the emaciated features of an addict who was standing in the middle of the street, swearing. Certainly not a student, probably one of the ever-growing cohort of homeless Londoners living in shanty camps under bridges and flyovers. That was something Tenuk had not missed about living in Austin, and he was sad but unsurprised to see it here. The safety net of Universal didn't catch everyone.

On the train back towards his hotel, Tenuk mulled over his academy program. He wondered if he could set something up here in London to bring talent through from the homeless population and lift more people out of poverty. He conveniently ignored the fact that the economic impact of the malware his academy developed probably contributed to the problem in the first place.

By lucky chance, he passed a Malay restaurant and stopped to eat what his body considered to be lunch and the local time to be dinner. Reinvigorated by almost-authentic noodles, he went back to his room. He was in something of a dilemma. His operatives knew exactly where Angus lived, because they had been tracking him for months ready to act if he became a danger. However, to access that data without some serious protection that he couldn't yet guarantee would alert the nosy AI assistants, Zara and Xanthe, to his hand in the Monkey's impending death. He had no choice but to go the long way round and make it look good.

He had some clues to follow already and took a very similar path of discovery as Cameron had done the day before. The alias of Paul Black was too easy to trace, and he quickly fell upon the studio flat address. He glanced out of the window. It was already late, but the chances that this address was the one where the Monkey held his data were slim. He needed to get in there and see if there were any leads to other hiding places.

It took longer than he thought to reach the estate. He had forgotten how large London was, how far it stretched in every direction. The night was dark and some of the lights on the paths into the warren of apartment blocks were flickering feebly. Tenuk found the right building, slipped on a pair of gloves, metaphorically picked the lock with a universal identity chip embedded in his smartscreen, and took the stairs as far as the fifth floor. He quickly realised that he wasn't as fit as he used to be, despite having had access to a private gym in the house in Singapore, and he had to pause for breath in the stinking, half-dark stairwell. There was a low level of noise all around, the sound of people living crammed together in small, cheap apartments. He heard the cry of a baby, and someone shouting in the distance.

Exiting the stairwell, he moved around the corridors, trying to lay a false trail for any cameras that were monitoring the building, then took the lift up a further three floors to the real address he had for Angus.

The eighth floor was quiet. Tenuk found the right door, went to unlock it, and froze. It was damaged and there was a sound coming from inside the apartment. But it was too late. The lock had registered his chip and tried to open. There was a loud click from the damaged mechanism. Whoever was in there knew that they had company. Tenuk braced himself and hurled himself through the door.

There was a cry and a thud. The heavy fire door had connected squarely with the head of the young man that Tenuk had seen outside the university buildings. He lay unconscious on the floor with a large bruise rising on his temple.

Tenuk knew he had very little time before the stranger came round. He took several good pictures of the man, something to send to Zara when he had the chance, and rifled through his pockets, relieving him of a smartscreen and, to Tenuk's horror, a gun. A quick look around the tiny flat revealed a half-dismantled computer and an immersion headset among the mess of daily living. Tenuk had to act fast. He finished the job that the unconscious stranger had started and tucked the prize, the computer's hard disk, into his pocket. He left the door ajar and ran back down the stairwell, listening for sounds of pursuit. None came, but as he walked away from the building, he heard the sound of sirens. Someone must have found the open door, or perhaps there was other trouble afoot this evening.

He took a roundabout route back to the hotel. In a secluded spot on the side of the canal, he threw the gun into the water and watched it sink. He continued walking until the path took him up to a residential area of neat terraces. On the nearest main road, he picked up a night bus, and within half an hour he was back in his room.

Exhaustion hit him. A long day, a long night, a long flight and the adrenaline of danger had taken their toll. He sent the images to Zara through a secure messaging service, tucked the stranger's smartscreen and the Monkey's hard disk in the bottom of his suitcase, and collapsed into bed. He was asleep as soon as his head hit the pillow.

10: CELEBRITY STATUS

Cameron groaned when her alarm went off. She silenced it and pulled the covers further over her head. The cat pawed at the duvet ineffectively in the manner of an animal that was weak and half-starved and whose food slave had just gone on strike. There was no response. The cat considered its options, hopped off the bed, and started picking idly at the carpet with its claws.

That got the response it was waiting for. "Stop it, you monster," said Cameron, leaping out of bed. Victorious, the cat marched through into the kitchen with its tail held high and loitered expectantly by its feeding bowl. Sulking, Cameron dragged herself in its wake, set the coffee machine to brew, and shook out a pile of kibbles. The cat went face down into its bowl, scrotching happily. Cameron rubbed her hands over her face and waited for the comforting hiss of hot coffee.

Mug in hand, she made her way out to the balcony. The air was fresh after a little rain the previous day and it served to wake her more effectively than the alarm or the cat. As her head cleared, she began to think through the tasks for the day. She hadn't been joking when she told Jack they had a lot on their plates.

Although Oak Medical had been lucky in pulling the plug when they were hit, and many others had regained access to their files, there were still scores of businesses from luxury goods retailers to high street hairdressers, dentists, charities and schools who had been using the old scheduling tool that carried the malware, and who hadn't had the luck to thwart the attack or the means to pay the ransom. Argentum Associates and a dozen other cybersecurity consultants were working at the coalface to get their systems back online fast, funded by insurers and government departments whose main interest was to prevent an economic shock. The first fraud reports were coming through already from the sophisticated phishing campaign, and Cameron knew there would be more. It was a perfect storm.

She turned on the wallscreen in the hope of some good news. Every channel was leading with doom and gloom. She flicked through from the News Channel to the international feeds and was about to give up and find some cartoons when a different headline caught her eye. North American airspace had re-opened, it said, and the cause of the false alarm was being investigated. She filed it away in her mind for later.

Between that and the cartoon channels her scrolling finger hit some of the more dubious influencer spaces. Heavy beats accompanied racy one-liners. She paused to see which celebrity or politician had been caught napping today.

She didn't expect to see her own face.

"Cyber hero or cyber fraud?" screamed the headline. "Is this the woman behind the cyberattacks that have hit your favourite high street stores?" asked an over-excited presenter. "Our experts claim it's impossible to crack viruses as fast as the SimCavalier – did she write the code that wrecked your shopping plans today?"

Cameron spat out her coffee and jumped to her feet. "What the hell?"

She had the presence of mind to hit record and capture a screenshot before the programme, produced for short attention spans, moved swiftly on to the previous night's football results. It happened so fast that she barely believed she had seen it.

Heart rate calming, she found a cloth to clean the spilled coffee and refilled her mug, then called Andy. He'd know more about that channel and who controlled it. A message came pinging back to say he was busy with the morning show and would call her as soon as they were off air.

She suddenly remembered the conversation she'd had with Ross the previous day. He'd mentioned conspiracy theories, and it looked as if one was breaking through. Just another annoyance to add to the list. It would probably disappear as fast as it had started, especially if they managed to minimise disruption for the public. No one would care about rumours and gossip if their lives were unaffected. There would be nothing to fuel the fire.

Reassured, she sipped her coffee and gazed at the glorious view from her balcony. She loved it here, high above the city. The cat joined her, weaving around her legs, and she scratched it on the head between its ears. It was a moment of calm before plunging back into the fray.

She had risen so early thanks to the attentions of the cat that she had time to log on from home before considering a trip into the city to the office. Her inbox was full of messages, cleaned and filtered by her trusty AI agent, Mephisto. There was a live example of the Oak Medical phishing message that had come through a spam reporting service. She admired the craftsmanship, then dumped it unceremoniously into a sandbox for safe analysis. There were no new panicked clients, which made her heart sing. The Belfast team had done a great job of stopping the spread of the malware. There were a couple of messages from existing clients who needed to learn to have some patience with the recovery process. She would smooth them over later.

There was also a message from Brianna.

"Hi, Cameron. I've managed to persuade the Met Office to let me have a look at their weather simulations and they're even allowing me to visit their quantum machine. It's amazing where PhD research can take you. I'll let you know if I find out anything that can help."

Nice work, thought Cameron, and that reminded her in turn to contact a friend in the insurance game whose real-time premium tracker was the stuff of legend. What kind of data feeds were they using to determine risk? Just following up on a theory about the American airspace closure, she explained.

The morning was going almost too well, and she was duly brought up short by Andy returning her call.

"That influencer channel's a nasty piece of work," he said. "It may look like a fringe broadcaster, but it has a huge audience. If there's a conspiracy theory that's hit their radar, you're going to need to do more than just wait it out. They're rottweilers, Cameron."

She was taken aback by his reaction. "But it's entirely baseless. You know that."

"Yes, and they probably do too, and they don't care. Any idea where it came from?"

"Ross mentioned some forums," said Cameron. "He keeps an eye on whatever conspiracies are going down. You'd be amazed what he finds." She was trying to lighten the mood, but the familiar knot of worry was growing.

"We've seen it all, believe me," said Andy. "I'll get onto him for the details, and put Giles on the case as well."

"Will you be able to shut it down?" asked Cameron.

"I don't know," said Andy. "Once these things are out of the box they can be hard to control. I'll see if I can find a good reputational PR for you. Fight fire with fire. Oh, and I think you should get a lawyer, just in case it all goes south."

"You think it's that bad?"

"Not yet," said Andy. "Let's try and make sure it doesn't escalate. I'll call you back."

He hung up, and Cameron, thoroughly deflated, decided to head straight to the office after all. A brisk walk would do her good, and problems were easier to solve when she had the team around her.

It was so early that she was still the first to arrive. She knew that Sandeep had arranged to work from Oak Medical, and that Pete was visiting another large client that had lost access to the systems of a whole division and needed to revert to their comprehensive, uninfected backups. Noor's model was spinning away quietly on the visualisation deck, and Cameron checked to see if there had been any updates overnight from collaborators. It looked as if there had been one data breach reported from a niche retailer, likely to be a prime target due to their high value clientele, and she made a note to follow up on the dataset's sale down in the Eden marketplace. If it was snapped up by the same bidder as last time, they knew what to expect in terms of phishing and fraud.

An alert on her smartscreen showed a call from Ross. From the background noise, she assumed he was on his way into the office, walking down the busy main road near his home. But he had other plans.

"I had a call from St Martin's," he said. "They've asked me to come back in. I suspect that Angus isn't getting any better."

"No real relatives have come forward, then?"

"I guess not. I'm going to push them to do some DNA tests. I'm not taking responsibility for him!"

"Fair," said Cameron.

"Did you get anywhere with his smartscreen?" asked Ross.

"Noor was taking a look at it. She's not in yet, but I'll get her to update you when she arrives. I have to go. I have another call coming through. Let me know what happens at the hospital."

She expected the caller to be Andy with more dirt on the conspiracy theorists. It wasn't.

"Good morning, Cameron." A familiar voice, a woman.

"Good morning, Detective Inspector. I was just talking to Ross. He's on his way over to the hospital again. I think we may be losing Angus."

"That's not exactly why I called," said DI Sara Mercer, "but thank you for the update. This is very much related. I picked up a report this morning about a break-in at the address you gave me for 'Paul Black'. There's a man in custody."

"Someone else was looking for him."

"Indeed."

Cameron could take a good guess at who might be interested in Angus. "Who's been arrested?"

"Someone who hasn't been on our radar before," said Mercer. "Looks as if he's just arrived in the country."

"Tenuk," said Cameron with absolute certainty and some delight.

"What?" said Mercer. "No, the man's name is Steen Rijks. Dutch national. He's claiming amnesia from the bang on the head, but we've done some digging. He seems to have an online handle and a footprint in Eden. It's very likely he's from your world. He calls himself Sterix."

"I can find out who he is," said Cameron. "I know who to ask." Chloe, once part of the inner circle of the Pasar network as Cloverleaf, must know the name. Michelle, whose white hat talent stemmed from a lively black hat career, might have a lead.

"Thank you," said Mercer. "There's something else. He was found half unconscious on the floor with a head injury and the caller, a neighbour apparently, said there had been a disturbance."

"Someone else was there."

"Yes. We have cameras, of course and although it's patchy in places, only Rijks entered the building without presenting credentials. Everyone else coming and going had keys."

"Did Rijks sneak in behind someone?" asked Cameron.

"Not exactly," said Mercer. "It was the old pizza box scam. An elderly chap held the door open for him thinking he was struggling with a delivery. He dumped the boxes he'd been carrying in the apartment after he forced the lock."

A classic, thought Cameron. She'd used it herself when proving to clients that their building wasn't as secure as they thought. Pizzas were old school, although less effective for corporate jobs. A high vis vest and a sink plunger or a bag of tools was one of her personal favourites for going unchallenged, slipping through side doors into buildings where passing employees just assumed that she had already been cleared for access. It was also easier to fake a plumber's ID card than go to all the trouble and scrutiny of cloning credentials for the target company – although she'd done plenty of that too, and cleaned up the mess when criminals had done the same.

"Where did he pick up the head injury? Was he thumped by another resident with a grudge?"

"Enquiries are underway," said Mercer, "but there's something not quite right. Some computer equipment had been dismantled but Rijks had nothing on him when he was arrested, not even a smartscreen. He's refusing to talk, so we don't know if he took it apart or if he found it in that state. The forensic teams are in there now."

Cameron digested the tale. "Busy night," she said. "I'll follow up on this Sterix character and let you know what I can find. If you need me for anything else, let me know."

She ended the call and leaned back in her chair, thinking. Maybe she could kill two birds with one stone.

She called Michelle. "Have you managed to catch up with Chloe about the exploit in the Foundation software proposal?"

"We have a meeting in ten minutes," said Michelle. "She's onto it and we're working out next steps."

"Great," said Cameron. "Can you ask her something completely unrelated for me? Has she – or you, for that matter – ever come across someone shady in the underworld called Sterix?"

"I think I know the handle," said Michelle, "but I couldn't tell you anything about them, other than, now I think about it, they possibly moved in the same circles as Angus. Chloe will know, though, for sure. What's the context?"

"He's in a cell after breaking into Angus's flat," said Cameron, "so you are absolutely right to think that they're linked."

"They're all leaking out into the real world, aren't they?" said Michelle. "Angus, Tenuk, whoever this character is… something big is going down, I can smell it."

"You're right," said Cameron. "Something stinks. The faster we can get to the bottom of it, the better for everyone. Let me know what Chloe says."

It was barely nine in the morning and already the day was full of surprises. Cameron went to the kitchen to switch on the coffee machine as Noor came through the door.

"Coffee?" she called.

"Morning, Cameron. Yes, I'd love one." Noor went straight to the visualisation deck and checked the overnight additions, nodding in approval at some, frowning and rearranging others.

Cameron handed her a mug and they stood in companionable silence for a moment, looking at the slowing spinning model. Noor's tweaks had added new patches of green and amber, but no more red. Cameron peered more closely at an amoeba-like structure that appeared to be moving through the visualisation.

"What's that?"

"It's the update to the scheduling software," said Noor. "We're tracing its rollout, and with no more red flags this morning it looks as if it's effective in the wild." She moved the model around with deft hand movements, an air of fierce concentration on her face. "If I'm right," she continued, "we are at the tail end of the infection, and I see that there's a message from the Nigerian cybersecurity authorities about their operation against DeltaG. They think they've neutralised the group and they've made some arrests, which is good news."

Now that the malware was no longer spreading, Cameron knew they could manage the fallout. While it was still active, her focus was on firefighting, identification and mitigation. Once the extent of the infection became clear, she could plan for the work that would be needed over the next few weeks and months.

"This is great," she said. "You keep doing what you're doing, and I'll smooth over the clients that have been panicking. I'll get Michelle to hop down into Eden and check on data auctions for that latest breach."

"That sounds good," said Noor. She carried her coffee over to her desk and tapped at the keyboard. She scrolled down her inbox and task lists.

From a distance, Cameron could see an amber highlight on one of the items.

Noor clicked it open and peered closely at the screen. "Ah, here's the report I was expecting," she said. "Come and take a look. I followed up on the information Ross sent over from Angus's smartscreen. There wasn't much to pick at, but the wallet he opened was interesting. I ran a forensic analysis overnight and these are the results."

Cameron came close and peered over Noor's shoulder.

"There are transactions routing through several different accounts and tokens and exchanges," said Noor. "He seems to have received regular payments from both Sapphire Straits and some other outfit I've never come across before."

"SPK?" read Cameron. "I don't know it. We can ask around. He's earning far more from Sapphire Straits so whatever SPK is looks like some shady sideline."

"He had another significant source of income," said Noor. "In the last few hours before the accident, he received a chunk of money in several disguised tranches, and it looks as if a data token was despatched by a smart contract when all the payments were confirmed."

"That fits with what Shell told us about the incident on the deep levels," said Cameron. "He must have gone through with selling the data. I wonder if there's any way of finding out what was transmitted?"

Noor nodded. "It might be possible," she said "It's gone through a privacy chain, but because Angus initiated the transfer and we have his private key access we can see the true path and some details, not just the redacted and obfuscated information that you'd see from a public browser."

"Great," said Cameron. "Another thing to add to the list." She reached over and tapped the screen. "And what's this?"

Noor expanded the view of the section Cameron had indicated.

"The analytics have stripped out some zero value transactions that have text embedded," she said. "They seem to be messages."

"Why would Angus be sending messages on-chain?" said Cameron. "The transactions are public. Anyone could see them. What have you found?"

Noor opened the file. "Here. He's basically been sending threats to people. There's no detail yet on the other side of the transactions, the recipients."

"Well, it's in character," said Cameron wryly, "but still, why would he put that kind of thing on a blockchain?"

"Maybe he had no other way of sending them," said Noor. "He's received messages too, but I can't piece together a coherent thread."

Cameron read down the list and shook her head. "I wouldn't worry too much about it. Ross is on his way over to the hospital again, so I imagine Angus is in a bad way."

"I almost feel sorry for him," said Noor. She closed the transaction file and opened up her working papers on the DeltaG attack.

"I know what you mean," said Cameron, walking back to her own desk, "but on the other hand…"

"I know," said Noor. "He's caused us so much trouble in the past."

"Thinking of troublemakers," said Cameron, "any word of Tenuk?"

Noor nodded. "He came through border control at Heathrow yesterday late afternoon. He checked into a hotel near Leicester Square, but I don't yet have a reliable way to trace his movements."

"See if we can repurpose the tracker Shell built for Angus," said Cameron. "I want to know where he is."

"I'll add that to the list," said Noor.

Cameron jumped as an alert sounded on her smartscreen. As she read the message she relaxed and smiled. "This is cool," she said. "It looks like I'm going over to InsurGlobe later. My friend there is going to talk me through their system and the data that feeds their risk assessment and live premium tracking. I want to get to the bottom of what happened with that American airspace alert. It might have some relevance to the storm warnings."

"I noticed that on the news," said Noor. "Oh – I meant to say – my brother watches some of those crazy video stream channels, and he said he saw the end of a clip with your name on. Have you done a piece for Andy this morning?"

"I haven't," said Cameron. "There's something defamatory going round the influencer streams. That's probably what he saw. Which reminds me, Andy says I need to find a lawyer who deals with reputation protection. Know anyone I could call?"

"I can find someone," said Noor, "but I'm surprised Andy thinks it could be that serious. I'll check with my brother what channel he was watching, but honestly, they're all trash, and I've told him that enough times."

"Thanks, Noor," said Cameron. "I guess we'd better get started. There's a lot of work to plough through."

They both settled at their desks, headphones on and deeply focused. Cameron spent the next hour reassuring her nervous clients and planning the response and recovery steps with their respective chief information and security officers. The more cautious the client, she had discovered over the years, the faster they were likely to recover. Their systems were for the most part well managed, and it was just the luck of the draw that they'd been caught on this occasion. It could have happened any time, and they were ready.

She had a satisfying number of completed tasks under her belt when the time came to leave the office. Her meeting at InsurGlobe was half an hour away and she set out with a spring in her step. The street outside was busy. She spotted a few unfamiliar news crews and wondered which celebrity was visiting the News Channel's studios today. There was a flurry of excitement as she walked out, and she looked behind her and then along the street. A black limo was gliding towards the offices. That would be it. She considered waiting and catching a picture herself, just in case it was a singer or an actor that her nieces and nephew liked, but there wasn't enough time. Without breaking stride, she walked off in the opposite direction towards the tube. She didn't notice that the limo passed the crowd without stopping, and the cameras were all trained on her.

·

When Ross reached the ward, the same nurse who had been on duty the previous day drew him into her office.

"Please, have a seat," she said. "I'm very sorry to have to inform you that your uncle passed away peacefully two hours ago."

Ross gave her a suitably sad look appropriate to a long-lost nephew. "I suppose it was expected," he said. "Have any other family members been in touch?"

The nurse shook her head. "Not at all," she replied. "You said you were his nephew, is that right?"

"Yes, by marriage," repeated Ross. "Not a blood relative. Maybe a DNA search would help to find close family?"

"Well, yes," said the nurse awkwardly. She looked up as someone else entered the room. Ross glanced at the newcomer's badge. Dr Maia Mansoor, he read. Bereavement Care Team. He shook his head in confusion. This charade was going too far.

"Ross, can I introduce you to my colleague, Dr Mansoor."

"Nice to meet you," said Ross automatically, then gave her a wry smile. "Although obviously not in these circumstances.

"Call me Maia," said Dr Mansoor. "I'm sorry for your loss. I've been working on the DNA profiling for your uncle."

"Thank you for your efforts," he said. "I understand you haven't found any close relatives."

The doctor indicated the seat next to him. "May I?" she asked. He nodded and she sat down next to him. "That's not entirely true, Ross — can I call you Ross?"

"Of course."

"We did find a match for your uncle's DNA on the national medical database," she said, "and it led us to understand that Paul Black was not his real name but an alias that he was using at the time of the accident."

Ross nodded, eager to clear things up at last. "Yes, I know he went by different names, but it was too complicated to explain. I knew him as Angus."

Dr Mansoor smiled sadly. "That appears to be yet another nickname that pops on his employment records over the years. His given name was Paul Charles White."

Jolted, Ross stared at her. That was a name he hadn't heard for many years.

The doctor looked at him with sympathy. "Ross, this may come as a shock, but the DNA match was beyond doubt. He was your father."

11:   FAMILY TIES

Tenuk was tired. The jet lag he thought he'd avoided had well and truly caught up with him. Despite the late night, he had slept only a few hours and now, approaching midday, he was ready to crash again. The hard disk had not yet yielded its secrets, but Zara had come back to him with details of the stranger. Steen Rijks, Dutch national. Tenuk immediately had his suspicions about the man's online identity. Previously located in the Netherlands – check. Probable drug habit – check. Breaking into the Monkey's apartment – check. It had to be Sterix. The only question was what he could be doing here in London. Tenuk hadn't instructed him. Who else might have done so?

There was only one person in the frame. It appeared his father didn't trust Tenuk to recover the information that the Monkey had collected. He wondered whether Chaoxiang had somehow discovered the circumstances of Angus's accident but concluded that it was unlikely. The old man was just covering all bases.

Tenuk knew that he didn't have the equipment here in the hotel to safely interrogate the hard disk but realised he might be able to kill two birds with one stone. He ought to go and inspect the property that his father was trying to sell, and he knew from his briefing and the inventory that there were more than enough tools available to him there. He called the estate agent and arranged to travel to the house. He would spend the weekend there, he said. After all, his family owned the place. In the back of his mind, he was considering whether it would be a suitable base for his operations throughout his stay, somewhere to hole up until it changed hands and his job was done. Time would tell.

The estate agent was emotional about 'Mr Black' and ready to bend over backwards for her client. Tenuk understood there had been interest from someone at a recent viewing and guessed that the agent had seen her healthy commission disappear over the horizon when news of the accident broke. She would do anything for him. That was how Tenuk liked it.

He still had plenty to do, not least to check on the progress of the software proposal going through the motions at Sladen Foundation and the phishing campaign that his students were running, but he simply couldn't keep his eyes open. He could deal with those later, he thought, as sleep overwhelmed him again.

An alarm woke him less than an hour later and he sat up and groaned. It was the end of the working day in southeast Asia. Time to check in with the students at his academy. He went to the bathroom, splashed cold water on his face and cleaned his teeth. He felt ten times better.

The cheesy Sekolah Pengekodan Coding School logo flashed up on the virtual meeting screen. In the darkened hotel room, the initials SPK burned into his retina. He made a note to commission a new brand as the operation matured. A moment later the faces of five of his students and the avatars of a dozen more appeared. The team he had set to work on the phishing campaign was all smiles. They were enjoying the challenge of manipulating video effects and developing their cloning skills. The team responsible for the software proposal at the Sladen Foundation was less cheerful. They had been struggling to maintain the positive vibes on the developer forums, and the AI Agents that had been deployed to support them were apparently not learning effectively. As the sentiment shifted down to net neutral, the agents were absorbing negative as well as positive comments and responding accordingly. Tenuk kept smiling but was cursing inwardly. It had been a risk leaving the simple agents to self-direct without checking in and refining the prompts over the past few days. The history books were littered with AI models that had confounded their creators and spun out of control thanks to the data they absorbed. He made a note to work on them, or to disable them if needed.

"Where does the negative sentiment originate?" he asked the group.

"There are several users who have indicated a possible flaw in the code," said the team leader.

Tenuk pursed his lips. "Have they been specific about their findings?" he asked.

"No, but in my opinion, they have laid sufficient breadcrumbs to lead others towards the very features that we wish to disguise."

That was clever, thought Tenuk. Rather than seeking a confrontation, whoever had discovered the exploit they had so carefully incorporated in the code was directing others to find it for themselves. Toppling dominoes rather than a single torpedo to the proposal. Either way would work, but this strategy was likely to be effective while still keeping the community calm.

He weighed up the options. Either they could fight to correct the peer group's sentiment and push for the update to be applied, or they could feign surprise at discovering a coding error and make greater effort to disguise their intent on another occasion. Fighting gave him a slim chance of being able to activate the exploit when the next allocation of Foundation monies was made. Bowing out to try another day meant delayed profit on the job, but a greater chance of success. He made his decision.

"Sometimes we find ourselves with issues that cannot be resolved," he said. "I believe that every developer goes through this phase of discovery, and it is a valuable addition to your skillsets. We will follow the trail that has been laid, fully engage with the negative sentiment, thank our peers for their close attention, and suggest that the proposal is delayed while revisions are made."

"Yes, Dr Teo," said the team leader.

"You should research new ways of achieving the exploit while delivering the improvements to the chain that made our proposal attractive. The code should be ready for audit prior to resubmission in next month's window. Now, is there any other business?"

"No, Dr Teo."

"Class dismissed."

The mosaic of faces disappeared. Tenuk used a public browser to check the balance of the wallet being used to collect phishing money and the proceeds from a handful of other scams that were running in the background. The account was increasingly healthy, with enough to pay the academy students their bonus for this month, giving them a much-needed boost to whatever Universal their respective countries granted their citizens. For some, it would be their only income. For all of them, it was a step out of poverty. Whatever accusations his father threw at him, Tenuk felt he was really a modern-day Robin Hood, and it felt good.

It was too late in the afternoon to check out and go to the farmhouse, and too late in the evening to speak to his father. If the old man wanted him, he'd call. Tenuk was not going to bother him unless he had something to report.

He switched on the hotel room's wallscreen and flicked through the available streams. A news item caught his eye about the escalating conflict in North America as the Wyoming Militia fought their way east from the Rockies across the plains. Serious-looking strategy experts were discussing the latest offensives. They were struggling to explain the thinking behind a series of drone strikes on a residential neighbourhood. The probability of enemy action in that location was remote, they said. There had been a concerted effort to protect citizens. Their own quantum simulations had suggested a number of other targets that made much greater strategic sense.

Tenuk's thoughts flew to Jack Sladen's accident. What was the difference between the observed weather system and the simulated one? What distinguished the predictions being used by these experts and the simulations that drove the Militia's battle plans? On a wild impulse, he opened up one of the online prediction markets run by Sapphire Straits. As his father had said, you could place a bet on anything and everything here.

And there it was. A closed book on the latest drone strike. Reading down the odds, Tenuk knew that the house had won big. The favourite targets listed at short odds, endless empty prairies where guerrillas were thought to be hiding, were in line with the expert commentary on his wallscreen right now. The longest odds, where a few happy individuals would have made, well, a killing, were right on the strike location.

Tenuk felt sick to the stomach. If his father had anything to do with this, he had blood on his hands. But as Chaoxiang had said, he simply facilitated the betting habits of others. There was no way he could manipulate quantum processing, simulations, or decision making. Could he?

Tenuk shook his head. Jet lag, stress, tiredness and hunger were all contributing to a growing sense of paranoia. He changed channels, searching for something to distract him.

A ticker on the bottom of one of the local streams announced that a man badly injured in an autocar accident on Monday had died. That cheered him up a little. One problem was out of the way, but it reminded him of the hard disk and the smartscreen buried in his luggage and the new problems that deciphering their contents was likely to bring. He set his AI travel assistant off to organise the itinerary for his trip to the country the next day and called the estate agent again to arrange for the access codes and keys to be delivered securely to his hotel. There was nothing more he could do before tomorrow. He decided to play the tourist and revisit some of the places he remembered from his previous visit to London five years earlier.

Baseball cap firmly planted on his head, he walked along the Embankment, taking in the sights. Big Ben – the name of the bell, he recalled, not the name of the tower, which escaped him – presided over Westminster. The old parliament building was shrouded in scaffolding as it had been before, desperate preservation works still ongoing. He turned west through St James Park and watched the timeless scene of ducks paddling around the lake and under the great glass bridge that spanned it. He considered going to the Palace museum but instead went north and east towards the bustle of Leicester Square. In a Soho back street, he found good noodles to eat, and returned slowly to his hotel, ready to sleep on British time at last.

•

Ross sat on the sofa with his head in his hands. Angus. Why did it have to be Angus? He had never known his father and had never really been curious about him. Neither his mother nor his grandmother had spoken about him. A neighbour, years before, had mentioned him in passing. A strange one, she had said. She was right.

He knew the man's name and bore his surname. His parents must have been on good terms when he was born, or he'd have automatically taken his mother's name. He wondered why she had never changed it. His ginger hair and pale features came from his father, that was certain. Maybe his talent for coding and his tendency to get into trouble when he was younger had come from Angus too. But their paths had been very different.

"Did he really say your name?" asked Michelle quietly.

"Apparently," said Ross. "And I think he found out where his crypto stash was. I think that's why he was outside the house on Sunday, and then he ran when realised it was us."

"He must have been proud of you," said Michelle. "He had your picture on his screen – on the burner screen he was using as Paul Black. That was a real risk to link him to you and expose his identity, and he did it anyway."

"I know," said Ross. He sat up and gazed around the room, eyes unfocused. "It doesn't make it any easier. I almost wish I hadn't gone to the hospital."

"They'd have matched you anyway from the database," said Michelle. "Would you rather a knock at the door or actually having been there in his final hours?"

Ross reached for her hand and squeezed it. "You're right as usual," he said. He stood up. "Cuppa?"

"Tea fixes everything," said Michelle.

There was a knock at the door. Ross opened it to find Cameron standing there with a bottle of wine in her hand. She gave him a one-armed hug and handed him the bottle.

"I was about to make some tea," he protested, "but you have a point. Shell? Cameron's here. Do you want a glass of wine instead?"

"Yes, please," called Michelle.

Cameron went through to the sitting room while Ross dug out three wine glasses. His mind was still in turmoil, his feelings about Angus conflicted and raw, but his mood was lifting.

"Cheers." Ross clinked his glass against Cameron's with a crooked smile.

"Strange times," said Cameron.

"Yeah. Not the way I imagined this day would go."

"I guess you have to get involved with all the paperwork now," said Cameron.

Ross nodded. "Yes. Thrown in at the deep end as next of kin. It's very odd."

"Useful, though," said Michelle. "Anything and everything to do with Angus now falls to Ross. All his devices, all his legacy access."

Ross poked her gently on the arm, making sure she didn't spill her wine. "That's a little insensitive, isn't it? I've just lost my father –" He flung an arm up dramatically and nearly spilled his own glass. "– and you're planning to wring every last bit of data from his estate."

Michelle nudged him back. "Don't pretend you hadn't thought of this already."

Cameron laughed. "If he hadn't, I certainly had."

Ross put his glass down and wagged his finger at Cameron in mock anger. "You're a terrible influence, Cameron Silvera," he said. He couldn't hold it for long. His serious face broke into a smile, and he started laughing uncontrollably until tears ran down his cheeks. This was the catharsis he'd been seeking.

"It's crazy," said Michelle, giggling herself as Ross's infectious laugh took hold. "The last thing they'll expect is for all of Angus's stuff to wind up in our hands. This could blow a bunch of operations out of the water once and for all."

"If we can get hold of everything," said Cameron.

"I've got a lot already," said Ross. "As soon as the death was recorded, it triggered his digital will. He'd named me but without knowing any contact details other than what's in the public domain."

"Lucky that you're so high profile," said Cameron.

Ross nodded. "As soon as the hospital confirmed me as next of kin, I was able to add my private contact details and the smart contracts all executed. I've got all sorts of stuff. Access codes to some devices we've got and plenty that we've never seen, access to accounts that dropped automatically into escrow when his chip transmitted the time of death, even some personal effects. It's going to take a while to get my head around all of this." He took a swig of his wine and coughed.

"Don't breathe it," said Michelle. "It's too nice for that."

Still coughing, Ross broke into another bout of laughter. "Can't trust me to look after myself, Shell. You're in charge now." He coughed again, catching his breath.

"I wonder what the other devices are?" said Cameron. "DI Mercer said there was computer equipment in the flat that had been partly dismantled, so we don't know if an intruder has taken anything important, and I bet half of what he had is well hidden…"

"The farmhouse," said Ross, no longer laughing. "The servers you mentioned in the outbuildings. He's had access. I wonder if some of the codes relate to those?"

Cameron nodded vigorously. "Good thinking. I'll see if Mercer can get a warrant."

Ross looked doubtful. "I don't think we have enough for her to secure one. He hasn't committed a crime. We're more likely to gain access through me as next of kin trying to identify assets, although as the farmhouse belongs to a corner of the Sapphire Straits empire and not to Angus, it's a slim chance."

"What do we do, then?" asked Michelle.

Cameron sipped her wine. "I may go and take a look myself," she said at last. "There's a security system that'll need to be disabled, or at least prevented from automatically reporting an intruder."

"What if the alerts only went to Angus anyway?" said Michelle. "End of problem."

"I don't think we can risk that," said Ross. He reached for the bottle of wine and topped up all their glasses. "Tenuk is in town, isn't he? He'll have access to all the relevant systems."

"I'm going to try," said Cameron firmly. "You take care of the stuff he left in that flat and anything else that wings its way to you as the process plays out. I'll go and scout around the farmhouse. Shell, do we know of any other locations he may have used?"

"His old house up north burned down," said Michelle. "I think Ella will know where he was living when he was working at Dunswyke, and she may have some idea where he ended up when he first came down to London, if it wasn't that address."

"Dammit," said Cameron. "I was afraid you'd say that. I don't think she'll help us."

The three of them fell silent, wondering what the next move would be and thinking through the possibilities. When Cameron's smartscreen rang, they all jumped.

"Cameron?"

It took a moment for Ross to recognise the voice on the speaker.

"Susie?" said Cameron

The girl was crying hysterically, choking on her words. "I'm sorry, I'm so sorry. I don't know how they found out."

"Calm down, Susie. What's happened?"

"They know, they know about me and Ella, it's on all the channels. I should have told you."

Ross knew instantly what had happened, and it seemed that Cameron had worked it out too. "Ella's with you, in Thailand," said Cameron, "and some conspiracy theory influencer type has published a load of baloney. Am I right?"

"How did you know? Oh Cameron, I'm so sorry." The sobbing redoubled.

"Don't worry. You aren't the only one. There's something nasty going on and we're right in the middle of it. They're after me too. Is Ella there?"

"Yes," said Susie in barely a whisper.

"Put her on."

Ella's face appeared on the screen. She looked angry rather than upset, with a steely glint in her eye.

"It's good to see you again, Ella," said Cameron.

"I'm sending you the links," said Ella calmly, without preamble. "The news here has been running with the story of a top cybersecurity personality – Susie, obviously, with all her conference and media work – being seen with a cybercriminal, in other words, me. And there's more. There's a story about you that's starting to circulate, and I am sure I saw something about Sandeep, though I have no idea what they could have dug up. Unethically sourced coffee beans is my only guess so far."

"Thank you," said Cameron. "It's a concerted attack on all of us, and the truth doesn't matter. They've tried getting to us physically, and now they're going after our reputations."

"Who do you think 'they' might be?" asked Ella. "Angus?"

Ross looked up sharply when he heard the name. "She doesn't know," he mouthed quietly to Cameron.

"Ella," said Cameron, "I have… news. There's no easy way to say this, but Angus had an accident. He didn't survive."

Ella's eyes widened. "He's dead?"

"Yes," said Cameron. She looked quickly at Ross, who shook his head. He didn't trust Ella enough to tell her the rest.

"Please look after Susie," said Cameron, "and send me everything you have on these rumours, links and names. We'll arrange some legal representation. Sit tight."

"Yes, Cameron," said Ella meekly. She handed the screen over to Susie. Looking over Cameron's shoulder, Ross caught a glimpse of a bright deck light against the darkness of the Thai night and heard the buzzing of insects in the background.

"Thank you, and I'm sorry, again," said Susie, her voice still trembling but the tears dry. She ended the call.

Ross stood up. "I'm going to do some more digging on the conspiracy sites," he said. "First you, now Susie, and Sandeep too. We need some advance warning of what's likely to hit next. Has Andy come back with a PR introduction yet?"

"No," said Cameron. "I'm waiting for a recommendation for a lawyer as well."

"Leave it with us," said Ross. "I can't do anything about Angus tonight, but there's no way I'm sleeping after everything that's happened. At least I can use my insomnia to our advantage."

"Thanks, both of you," said Cameron. She finished her wine and put the empty glass down on the table. "Shell, I've got some interesting stuff to share with you on the quantum processing side, but it can wait until tomorrow. Let me know what you find on the forums, Ross. See if there's anything bubbling on you two, or Noor, or Pete, or even Joel. How far does this spread?"

"Will do," said Ross. He was already thinking through his search strategies. He opened the front door to let Cameron out and sniffed at the cool night air. "Be careful on your way home," he said. "We don't know if there are other people out there."

He closed the door behind her and went back to the sitting room. "We've got some work to do," he said to Michelle. "Cup of tea?"

·

Cameron walked briskly to the brightly lit main road and jumped on the first bus down the hill towards the city. There was only one other passenger on the top deck, a young man with headphones who was glued to a rolling stream of videos on his smartscreen. Cameron ignored him and dived into the front seat, watching the London suburbs roll by from her vantage point. The roads were busy despite the lateness of the hour. They passed a cluster of restaurants and cafés, busy despite it being midweek. People spilled out onto the pavement in two and fours and larger groups, on their way home after a good night out.

She heard the loud ping of a bus stop request, and the young man scuffled along the aisle towards the stairs. Cameron half turned to look at him and he caught her eye. She saw a flash of recognition in the fog.

"Cyber fraud," he shouted. "Cyber hero, cyber fraud."

He held up his smartscreen and Cameron saw her own face. The few seconds of the video that she caught were obviously fake. The young man laughed, a high-pitched giggle, and bore down on her. Cameron belatedly recognised all the signs of an addict. She tensed, ready to defend herself.

"You alright up there, love?"

The voice of another passenger on the lower deck cut through the tension. The young man turned, staggered, lost his balance and half fell down the stairs as the bus slid to a halt. Cameron heard clattering as he hit the floor and the same voice saying something she couldn't make out. There was the familiar sound of the bus doors opening and a series of thumps and a muffled cry as someone bounced off the doors and hit the bus shelter. The doors closed again, and the bus glided off.

Cameron realised she was holding her breath.

"He's gone."

"Thanks," called Cameron. She had been lucky that there was someone else aboard. If things had gone wrong, she'd have been relying on surveillance systems in the bus and rapid response drones or human security units. Damn. She might have to stop travelling alone, after all.

She searched for the 'cyber hero, cyber fraud' strapline and found a whole slew of results straight away. The first few videos she viewed were troubling, but hardly surprising. She'd been expecting deep fakes to start circulating as soon as she saw the first report. There was nothing real that anyone could use against her and her team. Whoever was behind this would have to be inventive, and they had been. The fictions were grounded in fact just to the point that it was hard to refute the lie because it was so bound up with the truth. As the bus glided onwards, Cameron was deep in thought, planning her fight back.

She jumped off the bus at St Paul's and realised that she'd come back towards her old home on the other side of the river, running on autopilot. As she was right in the heart of the city, she decided that what she needed to do could just as well be done in the office.

The security team weren't used to seeing her this late. The team had been known to pull all-nighters, but usually at a client site rather than the main office. The whole building was silent, and the amplification of the slightest background noise in the central light well that rose six floors to the glass roof was a stark contrast to the hustle and bustle of the day.

Once in the office, she fired a message over to Ross. He replied within seconds, and they opened a video channel to work together. He shared his findings from the conspiracy sites, and she told him of the deep fake video she'd seen. While he focused on the roots of the rumours, digging down to find out where they might have originated, Cameron went searching for materials that were being shared to the general public.

She sent every sniffer agent she possessed out into the murky online world. She was looking for even the most insignificant mention of her team, anywhere, on social channels and news sites and in the depths of Eden and Playland and a dozen other virtual worlds.

As the results came back in, she filtered them by source, by medium, and by team member. Ross overlaid the stories he'd unearthed onto the messaging in the videos, influencer items and news sites that Cameron's searches returned. Cameron in turn began an analysis of the deep fake videos, looking for fingerprints that would link them to other materials and perhaps provide a breadcrumb trail to the perpetrators. She wasn't entirely surprised to get a match to the phishing fakes that had been uncovered through the Oak Medical breach.

By two in the morning, they were running on adrenaline and had a comprehensive picture of the campaign that had been launched against them.

"It's monstrous," said Ross.

"It's incomplete," said Cameron.

Ross took another look at the data and blinked. "How did I not spot this before?"

All but one of the team had been targeted. Cameron now knew the extent of the 'cyber hero or cyber fraud' messaging, and Andy was right, she needed a lawyer, and fast. Susie and Ella's relationship had been laid bare, along with Ella's convictions for her part in the Snake River conspiracy and breaking an AI out of prison, and for attacks on her own colleagues. Pete's army record was the target for his smear campaign, but Cameron was sure that the lurid tales being reported were entirely untrue. For a start, the names of all the witnesses and officers were fake. Sandeep's family background had been targeted, suggesting that his parents had settled illegally in the country, which Cameron knew was untrue as she'd done all the due diligence when she first hired him. Noor's academic background was being called into question. The prison term Michelle had served for a particularly skilful piece of cybercrime had been discovered and embellished, which was hardly a surprise, although as she was very careful about her online footprint neither Cameron nor Ross had found more than a handful of items about her compared to the huge volume of material circulating about Cameron.

There was nothing on Ross.

"They could have had a field day with me," he said. "I don't understand. I assumed I'd be taking as much of a hit as you. And there's so little on Shell."

"Shell, I can understand," said Cameron. "She's clever. She's almost impossible to trace. Her digital footprint is minimal and most of what she does is under everyone's radar, even if they're looking."

"But I'm as high profile as they come," said Ross.

"There's only one explanation," said Cameron. "Who do we think compiled all of this?"

"Angus."

"Exactly. He's left you out of the picture. And didn't you say he'd seen Shell when he was outside your house, and that was what sent him running?"

"Maybe he was trying to protect her too." Ross put his head in his hands. "This is crazy."

Cameron knew she had to call a halt to the night's work. It was going to take time for Ross to process the extraordinary events of the day, and this latest revelation might just be too much to deal with at once.

"I don't think there's much more we can do tonight," she said. "We both need some sleep."

"Sleep? I'm not sure I can."

"Try," said Cameron. "Call me when you're ready to pick things back up. I have enough to start working with lawyers and PR in the morning to close these campaigns down, and to file personal identity copyright violations for the team."

"Okay," said Ross. He yawned suddenly, catching himself unawares. "Maybe you're right. Goodnight, Cameron."

He waved and closed his feed. Cameron stared at her own screen, scrolling idly through the results of their hard work. It was a mess and the last thing they needed. She had to admit it was a clever tactic. She wondered if Tenuk was behind it. The fact that Angus seemed to be the one who had collected the information pointed to his involvement.

A distant church clock struck three and Cameron realised how tired she was. She thought about just bunking down on the sofa, but she'd be better off at home. She made sure everything they had worked on was secure in the Argentum cloud and switched off all the office systems.

One of the perks of her new apartment was a secure autocar service. She placed an order directly with the tower's concierge and was whisked home in luxury. Occasionally she could justify compromising her fierce independence and her determination to live a normal life, and this was one of those times.

12: ENEMIES

Cameron woke to a message from Brianna. The visit to the Met Office had yielded results, and could she come in and work through her findings?

Instantly awake, refreshed despite just a few hours of sleep, Cameron replied straight away and arranged to meet at ten.

She thought back to the previous day's visit to InsurGlobe, before Ross got his news, before everything changed. She had part of the puzzle ready to slide into place from that, and she was looking forward to seeing what Brianna had to report. She felt a sense of excitement and anticipation that had been absent for some time under the weight of the DeltaG attacks. Michelle would be useful in the meeting, too. Cameron's hand hovered over the message field on her smartscreen for a moment before cancelling the request for her to come in. Ross needed her more than Cameron did.

In the event, she needn't have worried. When she got into the office – once again in the quiet luxury of a celebrity autocar – Michelle was already there, drinking coffee on the sofa with Brianna and chattering nineteen to the dozen. She looked as fresh and excited as Cameron felt, as if the last week hadn't happened.

"Morning, Shell," said Cameron, making her way to the kitchen for a glass of water. "How's Ross doing?"

"Morning. He's running. It'll clear his head. Has Brianna told you about the quantum machine at the Met Office?"

Cameron sat down with the two girls. "No. I take it that it's something special?"

"It's amazing," said Brianna with a delighted grin. "The only place in the building that they could install it was on the ground floor. Apparently, the architects couldn't find anywhere else that was structurally strong enough, and they stuck it right in the middle of the café."

Cameron laughed. "That's a different sort of chip, I suppose."

"My cousin Daniel works in a data centre with quantum processors," said Michelle. "I don't think they have any in the café."

"Where's that?" said Brianna, instantly fascinated.

"Alaska," said Michelle. "Place called Wrangell. They have natural tundra cooling, although that's nowhere near as effective as it was when the centre was built, and then their chillers are powered by the geothermals. They have a few processors that can run at room temperature, but most of the traditional qubit materials still need to be super cold for low decoherence and error minimisation."

"Wrangell?" said Brianna. "We were talking about that before, weren't we, Cameron? It's one of the main QAAS hosting centres, Quantum as a Service."

"Track back a bit," said Cameron. "Why is the Met Office machine in the café?"

"It's a supercold stack," said Brianna. "Basically, a massive freezer fitted with everything a sensitive qubit needs to avoid disturbances. It was just too heavy to go anywhere else in the building and the architects liked it there. It's cool, though." She laughed and shook her head. "I mean, it works for them. The tech guys are visible, not hidden away in the basement doing things in a black box. They're mixing with the meteorologists over lunch so both sides learn. The forecasters know what questions they really want to ask, and the tech guys know how the machine can be optimised to deliver the answers, and between them they come up with really complex probabilistic results."

"Why are they getting things wrong, if they're so good?" asked Cameron.

Michelle waved a finger. "This is the thing," she said. "The Met Office isn't wrong. Their simulation of the storm in the Caribbean was spot on."

Brianna took up the tale, eager to share. "The global weather services pool their simulations. Although the Met Office results tracked perfectly with the real storm, they were seen as outliers in the data set and discarded."

Cameron stared at the two girls. In the back of her mind an old story that Aunt Vicky used to tell began to surface. When her aunt was tiny, there had been a storm that damaged the house. There was still a memento, a re-built wall in the garden that had been partly demolished by a falling tree. The forecasts were all clear because some outlying data had been discarded, but that data was the harbinger of disaster.

There was only one question to ask. Michelle got there first. "We need to know, where did the incorrect results come from, if they outweighed the accurate simulation from the Met Office?"

"I think I can help with that," said Cameron, as the jigsaw pieces began to fall into place in her mind. "I went to visit InsurGlobe yesterday and the range of APIs they are running for premium calculations are insane. They won't rely on a single oracle of truth, too much risk of errors creeping in, so they pull together multiple independent simulations and run an aggregation process. Their combined simulations of the drone attack strategies in the Militia's advance, and their reading of the storm path, both aligned with the published predictions and not with what actually happened."

"Ouch," said Brianna. "The insurance industry won't be happy about the claims that are coming in for storm damage if they got the risk profiles and premiums wrong."

"Betting platforms are laughing, though," said Michelle.

It was a throwaway remark, but it hit Cameron like a bolt of lightning. If the Met Office was right, but the majority were wrong, and the gambling odds that were offered on everything that happened in the world were skewed to the wrong data, the house would win. The house always won.

"Sapphire Straits," she said slowly. Her mind was whirring. The papers for the farm proved beyond doubt that they'd had a hand in the creation of her AI nemesis, Yasmin the Admin, and her sisters. Yasmin had infiltrated the Wrangell data centre before her destruction. The gambling giant had been caught manipulating events at the Olympics two years earlier, profiting from misleading odds. What if they could somehow do the same with the weather or warfare?

"Yasmin's gone," said Michelle. "There's no way they could pull the same trick."

Brianna looked from one to the other, confused. "Yasmin?"

"Ancient history," said Michelle with a shiver.

"Maybe not," said Cameron thoughtfully. "Brianna, you said that there were ways to hack the quantum process, to return subtle false results over time. What if, let's say, a piece of malware with good self-directed learning capability was sitting undetected in a quantum data centre for a couple of years, gently nudging the results of the weather predictions, or even changing the simulations used in a war effort? Would that be enough time to have the impact we're seeing?"

Brianna exhaled and flopped back on the sofa. "Good grief… I never imagined it might be real. It's a purely theoretical construct. I mean, yes, if someone managed to create the right conditions, then we'd have a cumulative skew by now." She shook her head. "I can't imagine the complexity required to set that up, though."

"Believe me, it could be done," said Cameron grimly. "What about a reactive skew? Could such an agent influence the observed outputs at short notice?"

"You said 'agent'," said Brianna slowly. "Are you implying that there's some kind of AI agent in there?"

Cameron shivered. "I hope not. Here's the plan. I'll get a list of all the feeds that InsurGlobe taps into, and Shell, can you do some digging and find out what's coming from local processors and what's hosted through Quantum as a Service." She steepled her fingers, thinking fast. "Brianna, I'm going to introduce you to my InsurGlobe connections. If we can isolate one occurrence, say the storm for argument's sake, let's see if there's a correlation between individual QAAS feeds and the false path."

"What about you, Cameron?" asked Michelle.

"I'm going to see what Sapphire Straits has been up to. If they've been running books on anything that relates to quantum simulation, I want to know if the house won."

Her musings were cut short by a call from Andy. She listened with mounting horror. "Okay, I'm coming down."

She turned to Brianna and Michelle. "Security are coming to help you both out of the building. I'm going down to see Andy. The influencer campaign against the team just exploded, for want of a better term, and we need to get out of here."

•

Tenuk checked out of his hotel just before lunch, collected the keys for the farmhouse, and made his way to the train station. He relaxed in his window seat, enjoying the English countryside for the first time since his previous visit five years earlier. As he neared his destination, some familiar landmarks made him catch his breath. He'd been here before. He'd been part of the MerLions e-soccer machine back then, taken from place to place for visits and appearances without any conscious understanding of where he was. By the time the train pulled into the station, he knew. This was the town where he had met the SimCavalier. She hadn't known who he was at the time. Just a face in the management team at a school event on the whirlwind circuit. What a coincidence that had been. He knew that she lived in London, not locally, but there was a flicker of anxiety in the back of his mind. She was the last person he wanted to run into.

An autocar took him off down country lanes and through an attractive village before pulling up outside the remote farmhouse. Tenuk fumbled with the physical keys and hoped that the chip he'd registered with the agent would grant him access.

The door stayed stubbornly closed. He placed a call to the agent, who apologised profusely and explained that there had been a server problem, and she would retransmit his chip ID immediately. While he waited, Tenuk strolled around the outside of the property, getting a feel for the place. His briefing had been clear. This was the place where Xanthe, Yasmin and Zara had been created and nurtured many years before, developing their distinct personalities in a rich self-directed learning environment. Although they'd been uploaded when the facility was discovered, much of the infrastructure remained. He was to close it down, wipe it, destroy it.

On his first circuit around the building, he spotted some figures in the distance on the far side of the road. There must be a path there.

On his second circuit, he saw two or three different figures. The path appeared to be popular with dog walkers. Someone looked across at him and waved and Tenuk waved back, trying to act as normally as possible.

On his third circuit, he strayed towards the outbuildings. He thought he could hear the sound of wind in the trees, but when he looked around, there were no trees, and the air was still.

He tried the chip access plate again. This time the door swung open to admit him to his new temporary home. He found the kitchen, opened the blinds, and sent a food order for a random selection of ready meals, basic ingredients, snacks and beer through the smart fridge. The house was large, although not on the scale of his father's mansion by any means. He explored, opened curtains and flicked away dust, then picked out the sunniest bedroom and dumped his bag there. While he waited for the drone delivery to arrive, he decided to investigate the outbuildings and find a place to work on the hard disk and the smartscreen he had recovered from the Monkey's apartment.

He crossed an attractive courtyard with chairs and a table, and then a small scrubby field. There was still what he thought was the sound of wind in the trees, but as he approached the outbuildings, he realised it wasn't the wind, and that this was the source.

The outbuildings were in terrible state. The roof certainly needed work, but as he peered more closely, he realised that this was the least of their problems. The dilapidated barn had become a real eyesore and might explain the rapid turnover of tenants and the difficulty his father had in selling the property. At least there had been an enquiry at the last open day, according to his briefing. A company in the city looking for a country headquarters, something to do with marketing. He had a meeting pencilled in his diary for next week with the CEO, a woman called Simpson. He would ask Zara to check on them once he was online.

The security around the outbuildings was as he expected, with physical and chip keys. Tenuk nodded in approval and opened the door. He followed his briefing instructions and found the fuse boxes and access switches close to the door. In the space of five minutes, he had the buildings back on the main power grid and went in search of a workstation.

He ventured into the main server room, where machines had been maintained off-grid through these long years by solar power and batteries. He recoiled in horror at the sheer volume of accumulated debris, droppings and spider webs on the protective coverings under which lights flickered. One covering had been recently disturbed. Perhaps the potential buyer had been in here. The estate agent wasn't supposed to allow access but with a buyer in her sights she could have bent the rules.

Here, the strange sounds he had heard were at their loudest. As he listened, some of the whispers resolved into words, echoes of the three intelligences that had been nurtured here. He shivered despite the warmth of the autumn day.

He wasn't going to set up a desk in here. There were too many ghosts. He found a suitable bank of workstations as far as possible from the haunted servers, then returned to the main house to look for cleaning materials. The whole place was a mess. After a solid hour of brushing and scrubbing, he had something that approached a reasonable office space. As Tenuk returned to his workstation, he noticed for the first time footprints in the dust. There seemed to be three sets, one smaller than the others. They led from the main door to the server room and back again without deviation. This must be the buyer who had been allowed into the buildings. He wondered who the other two might be, but he wasn't concerned. He was simply relieved that they hadn't explored any further.

He had some work to do before he contacted Singapore. He double checked that the data link from the site was not yet active, fired up the bank of workstations, and attached the hard disk that he had taken from the Monkey's computer to one of the machines. This would be his sandbox. He mirrored the disk on the new machine and removed the original for safekeeping, just in case he needed more than one attempt to access the data. He didn't know how many layers of security had been placed on it and knew that he had to tread carefully. Zara would be able to crack it in no time at all, but Tenuk wanted to see what was there before he let his father's intelligent AI agents anywhere near it.

It was a slow process. He had barely got past the first layer when he received an alert that his food delivery had arrived. He went back to the house to collect his groceries, put everything away haphazardly, and grabbed a beer and a bag of snacks to take back to the outbuildings.

Fortified, getting into the swing of an old skill long discarded, he gently teased out a contextual password and laughed at its simplicity. His voice echoed around the stone building, adding to the whispers from the server room. He focused again and was rewarded with a directory full of folders. The Monkey had no real need to conceal what he was doing on this drive. He would have judged a physical breach and a theft to be unlikely.

The top-level folders were names of cybersecurity operations. Tenuk recognised Argentum and another outfit, but the rest were unfamiliar. There were different authors on the folders. It seemed that Angus had been collecting some data himself and crowdsourcing information from secondary sources. He clicked on the Argentum files and found data about their operations, forensic trails linking them to clients and projects, and plans and images of the office building they now used. Another set of folders was stored here too, each labelled with initials. The team members. Tenuk recognised them all. He opened the one called NK.

There were photographs of Noor taken recently, one of a building that Tenuk knew to be where her apartment was located, and another of her parents' house. He had visited them there, back before Noor knew who and what he was. There were older pictures too. Noor at university, collecting her PhD. Posts about her research, a PR piece from Argentum Associates when she joined them. Tenuk was at a loss to understand why such depth and breadth of data was relevant if the goal was to attack and destroy, but when he opened a file of notes made by the Monkey, everything began to fall into place. The comments showed that Angus was annoyed at finding nothing that could be used in a smear campaign and suggested that his client 'continue per the interim report to cast doubt on the validity of her research and qualifications'.

So that was the plan. Not to destroy but to discredit.

Tenuk scrolled through the rest of the folders. The first thing that was obvious to him was that there were no records at all for the triathlete. Ross White might as well not have been part of this sting, but Tenuk knew that he was the SimCavalier's trusted lieutenant, which put him in the frame for his father's operation, and that he had a record from his days as a black hat hacker when he caused no end of trouble for the British authorities. Perhaps enough was known about him for updates not to be required, but it seemed a strange omission.

Perhaps not. Tenuk recalled an incident two years earlier. Ross had been in danger at Tenuk's hand, and the Monkey himself had called Tenuk off, threatening to expose everything he knew. What was the connection?

The SimCavalier's file was comprehensive and included a lot of new information that Tenuk was absolutely certain his father did not have, including her new address. There were notes on a particularly unpleasant discreditation sting that should have started by now, and a list of influencers and broadcasters who had been recruited to run it. Tenuk ran through the details, increasingly impressed at the inventiveness. By mixing a little truth with the lies, they were strengthened. It would be hard for the SimCavalier to refute everything that was being broadcast about her without compromising her own processes or official secrets.

Tenuk scrolled through the rest of the files and then ran a check on previous versions and discarded data. That was when he found the girl.

Michelle, that was her name. A handle Angus had attached to her was ShellPixie, and Tenuk recognised it. She had a black hat past like Ross and an equally interesting record of run-ins with the authorities. The file that Angus was due to present contained nothing dated after the interim report had been delivered. In deleted files, though, Tenuk discovered he had collected plenty about her. Tenuk checked the date of deletion. Sunday afternoon, after the footage of Angus's visit to the house. Her connection to Ross had afforded her protection.

Well, whatever his reasons, Angus was not the only one who needed to delete something. Tenuk reset the date and time on the mirrored drive and then went back to the folder labelled 'NK' and deleted everything dated after the interim report that had already been transmitted. He made a note on the file that there was no point pursuing this team member. That should be enough. To make doubly sure, he erased all trace of the newer records. The disk still held the deleted data on Michelle. Tenuk pondered for a moment, then decided to restore those files that had already been delivered and completely erase those that had not. It seemed fair to the Monkey to protect his secrets if Tenuk was protecting his own.

He checked and double checked that his notes could not be attributed to him, today, and that the file erasure was undetectable. When he was satisfied, he prepared to go online. He ensured that the workstation was entirely standalone, to protect the rest of the installation from infection, and connected it to the outside world.

After all these years, the secure uplink fired without a hitch. He pinged Zara and Xanthe in Singapore – his father would be asleep at this time – and asked if there was any more information about Sterix, or further instructions regarding the farmhouse.

Zara was unavailable. Eventually Xanthe replied. "Nothing at this stage. Proceed as planned."

"I have the hard disk," said Tenuk. "I believe that it contains all the Monkey's research and the information he had collected up to the time of his unfortunate accident, but there are several layers of security that I do not have the tools to penetrate."

He took a deep breath and transmitted the entire contents of the doctored drive.

"Received," said Xanthe. "Await further instructions."

Tenuk sat back in his chair, breathing heavily. He had done it, or so he hoped. Noor was safe from whatever his father had planned. He swigged at the bottle of beer and found it was empty. He switched everything off and returned to the house.

Sitting on a comfortable sofa in the unaccustomed silence of the English countryside, Tenuk started to ponder what exactly his father was doing. Now that he was out of the Singapore mansion and far from the toxic atmosphere controlled by the old man and his brace of intelligent agents, his mind was freely associating the things he had seen and heard over the past two years. He had arrived in Singapore thinking that his father was naïve and that he needed Tenuk's help to navigate the murkier waters of the cybercriminal world. He had discovered that Sapphire Straits was already a substantial presence there and their activities ran far deeper than he could ever have expected. Now, his father was trying to remove the SimCavalier from the cybersecurity landscape. What was he afraid that she would find?

Something that he had noticed in passing in his work on the Monkey's hard disk wormed its way into his thoughts. The individual drive with the details of Argentum and other cybersecurity firms hadn't been particularly large compared to the capacity of the whole disk. It had struck him as a strange anomaly, but nothing of any great concern. Another memory was sliding into place. When he'd confronted the raging bull avatar in the depths of the murky virtual world of cybercriminals, Angus had been shooting his mouth off about selling information about the SimCavalier to the highest bidder. In the moments before Tenuk had launched his tiger avatar at the rampaging, drunken bull, he had shouted something else. Did he also have the lowdown on Sapphire Straits?

Tenuk leapt off the sofa and raced back to his workstation. He made sure the uplink was disconnected and re-opened the mirror of the hard disk. And there it was, in plain sight. He'd been lured in one direction by an easy trail of breadcrumbs laid by the Monkey and his own desire to protect Noor at all costs. He hadn't been looking for anything else. No wonder the drive had been so easy to crack – on that partition, at least.

There was a second. Tenuk took a deep breath and started work.

•

Cameron and Andy were huddled in one of the pods that served as a green room for the News Channel's outside broadcast crews. It was parked along with the rest of the crew vehicles behind the security cordon that now stretched around their office building and surrounding streets. Michelle and Brianna had been spirited away to carry on their work from an undisclosed location, and the rest of the team warned to stay away. The whole area had been evacuated. Cameron knew that she was the target of the bomb threat that Security had received, and she was determined not to run back home to hide. She couldn't be sure that she would be safe there, either.

"It's a hoax, Andy," she said for the third time.

Andy shook his head. "I don't think so, Cam. Some really unpleasant factions have been stirred up by this anti-cybersecurity thing. This isn't the only site that's been cleared, and the NCSC in Cheltenham is on high alert."

Cameron hunkered down tighter into the pod's admittedly comfortable foam couch and took a sip of coffee. "I don't get what they're trying to achieve," she said. "We've been targeted before. Why go to these lengths?"

"It's not just you," said Andy. "You're the main subject of this smear campaign, but whoever 'they' are, they've made it about the whole industry. They're reducing public confidence, making it look like you are all bad guys."

"I can take a wild guess at who 'they' might be," said Cameron. "Angus was gathering information for someone, and I know he worked for Snake River, and for Tenuk, and for Sapphire Straits. He was a cyber thug for hire, and my money's on the last one."

There was a should from outside. "Andy! Action."

"Stay here." Andy leapt off his seat and out of the door in one fluid movement, slamming it behind him.

Andy's tone was so serious that Cameron didn't dare argue. She listened intently, barely breathing. Shouts, challenges, gunfire.

The door flew open, and Andy dived back in. "Get down, Cam. Controlled explosion."

They both fell to the floor. Cameron cursed as the remains of her hot coffee spilled on her leg. A second later the pod shook, and after a couple of heartbeats, the dull crump of a detonation reached her ears. The silence that followed was deafening. It was only when they heard a shout of 'All Clear' that the two of them clambered back to their feet.

Without a word, Andy opened the door and they both walked out towards the cordon. Through the smoke haze, Cameron could see the office building. There were lights on. That had to be a good sign, surely?

"They took the drone down and contained the explosion," said Andy. "Looks like it blew the doors off." He peered into the distance, his eyes watering slightly.

Cameron turned at the sound of a familiar voice behind her and saw Pete forcing his way through the crowd.

"You're not supposed to be here," she said when he reached them.

"Nor are you," said Pete. He nodded at Andy. "Looks like they contained it."

"What were they firing at?" asked Cameron.

"The drone," said Pete. "They'll have sent up long range taser charges to fry it. It's faster than a controlled capture, especially if you think there are explosives involved."

"I'm sure I heard a scream," said Cameron.

"You might have," said Pete. He pointed to an air medic pod that was coming into land. "Could be anything. Collateral damage, a tangible threat, someone in the wrong place at the wrong time. But as far as I could see, they didn't have anyone in custody."

Andy, who had disappeared for a fast briefing, came back. "I need to escort you both out of the news village," he said. "I'm going to be busy. This wasn't the only attempt, and we have live coverage from three other sites to coordinate. But will you do me a favour? I've got to report on what's happened on the face of it now, but you two and the team have your ear to the ground when it comes to how and why these jokers went from online discreditation to full real-world assault."

"You're right that there's something strange going on here," said Pete. "The first we saw of the smear campaign was only what, three days ago? It seems like a departure from the original strategy."

"Or a different set of perpetrators," said Andy. "Let me know what you find out."

"Will do," said Cameron. "The more information we can pool, the faster we can get to the bottom of it all." She picked up her bag and slung it over her shoulder. "I guess we're all working remotely for the rest of the week. Let's go."

•

The second partition was resisting every attempt to crack it. Eventually Tenuk switched everything off and returned to the house. He dug around in the delivery bags, found something that looked acceptably appetising, and set it to heat. Beer in hand he went through to the plush sitting room and switched on the wallscreen. The rolling News Channel was reporting from central London where a drone attack had damaged an office building. Tenuk squinted at the picture. Surely that was the building where Argentum had their office? He recognised it from the Monkey's files. His attention sharpened and Noor leapt into his thoughts. This must be some sick coincidence, and he hoped she was alright.

He was so focused on the news that he jumped when his smartscreen rang. Xanthe had an updated briefing for him.

"The information you transmitted is no longer relevant. You are to clear the property, effect its sale, and return to Singapore."

Two things dawned on Tenuk simultaneously.

First, Angus must have succeeded in selling his information to another bidder down in Eden, exactly as he had threatened. Someone else was now leading the attacks on the SimCavalier and her team, as his father had predicted, and their methods were extremely direct. Everyone was in danger, and he had no further control over the outcome.

Second, a revelation. His father was afraid of the SimCavalier herself, not just what she might find. He saw her as an existential threat to his empire, and would stop at nothing to discredit, disrupt and destroy her, and with her the wider cybersecurity community who might thwart his plans.

The enemy of my enemy is my friend, mused Tenuk. Was his father now his enemy, and in that case, was the SimCavalier his friend?

13: OLD FRIENDS

The head of security met Cameron in the lobby of the tower. "We saw the news," he said, "and we immediately strengthened the drone net around this building."

"Thank you," said Cameron, eager to get her things. "I know how good your security is."

She started towards the lifts, but the security guard followed her. "I'm sorry to say that the net has already been tested by person or persons unknown," he said quietly, wringing his hands. "This is not something we will make public, but it has made us aware of the unique nature of the threat against you."

Cameron became aware of a greater number of people than usual bustling around the lobby area. She recognised none of them. Not neighbours, then, but extra personnel drafted in for the protection of all the residents. She was more embarrassed than reassured.

"I'm so sorry," she said. "I was planning to go straight out to the country rather than stay in London, if that helps at all."

"You would probably be safer here. If whoever is pursuing you knows where you work and where you live, they will surely know where else you regularly visit."

A cold shiver ran down Cameron's spine. She stood rooted to the spot, working through her options. If all the intelligence that had been gathered up until now was correct, whoever was menacing them in the real world had a static list of locations to target. That meant that the office, her home, and possibly the village were in their sights. The office had already been compromised, but the tower had the best security in the city. Security services would manage any threat in the village. Her mind flashed through the possibilities, processing outcomes, forecasting behaviours based on the data she had. Did she stay here, did she add to the burden of risk for Charlie and the family, or did she fight back?

Decision made. She knew what she had to do, and who to call.

"I'll get out of here to minimise any threat to the building and the other residents," she said. "If you can prove I'm not here, I think you'll be safe."

"Cat sitter on standby," said the head of security, trying and failing to hide a relieved grin. "Where are you going?"

"Somewhere that whoever is following me won't think to look," said Cameron. She wasn't going to the village, not yet. "Can you organise me a car to the British Museum? I'll make my own way from there."

Upstairs, she packed a bag, fed and fussed the cat, and checked her messages. Her team was on the ball. Noor had already opened a virtual workspace, and even Susie had logged in and was contributing what she knew, and Pete had offered to join Cameron in the village to add to the security effort there and to take a look at the old farmhouse. Cameron called Charlie and Aunt Vicky on the secure line to let them know she'd be coming, but not for a few days, and alerted them that Pete would need a place to stay.

The call from the lobby came all too soon. Cameron closed down her screen, gave the cat one last tummy rub, and took the lift down to the basement where her car was waiting. It whisked her away, hidden behind tinted glass, and dropped her as requested at the museum, by the secure VIP entrance, of course. She strolled towards the main exit and picked up a few things in the gift shop. The branded bag of goodies would serve two purposes. First, to make her look like a tourist to any watching eyes or cameras, and second, as gifts for people she expected to see on her journey. From the museum, she weaved her way on foot through the old streets and city parks to King's Cross station, where she jumped on the first train to the north.

Less than two hours later she was in the middle of York, half way to her ultimate destination. She decided to walk out to the university campus, and although it was a longer walk than she expected, she revelled in the exercise. Despite the cooling autumn air, she was sweating by the time she arrived. She put her bag down gratefully at the security office and presented her credentials for the visit.

"Who shall I contact first?" asked the guard.

"Mandisa," said Cameron.

Five minutes later Cameron was enveloped in a hug from one of her oldest friends.

"Cameron! I got your message. What are you doing here! I haven't seen you for so long!"

Mandisa had left her old commercial science career and the countryside where they had grown up together to plunge back into the academic world in this northern city. They had both been terrible at keeping in touch, but as soon as they started talking it was as if no time had passed.

"Am I definitely okay to crash on your sofa tonight?" asked Cameron. "If not, I'll find a hotel. I'm keeping my head down. There's been a bit of bother."

"Of course you can." Mandisa gave Cameron a sidelong look. "Boyfriend trouble?"

Cameron dodged a bollard as she followed her friend through the unfamiliar campus. "What boyfriend? No, this is all work related. Haven't you seen the news?"

Mandisa stopped and turned around, hands on hips. "What news? And what do you mean, 'what boyfriend'? Don't tell me you let that sweet guy slip through your fingers. What was he called. Brian? Benson?"

"Ben," said Cameron. "He was lovely but, well, my life got a little complicated, and quite frankly so did his. He was posted abroad, which was fun for a while, but I'm a long way beyond just defusing cyberattacks behind my desk now. This stuff is leaking out into the real world, and it's dangerous. I think he wanted a safer, smaller life than I could give him."

She hadn't admitted that to anyone else, but Mandisa knew her better than anyone but her family. It was if they were back at school sharing secrets in the cloakrooms. Mandisa came closer and gave her a quick hug. "I have one more class to teach. Then you can tell me all about it."

Cameron grinned. "It's too early for cocktails, so that sounds reasonable to me. What classes are you taking? Any undergraduates?"

"No, I'm focused on postgrads and researchers at the moment." Mandisa's eyes narrowed. "Wait. Is there someone I should know? Don't tell me…"

"You guessed. Nina's here."

"I feel old." Mandisa scowled at Cameron. "Last time I saw her she was what, twelve? Thirteen? Does she know you're here."

"I messaged her too, but she hasn't replied," said Cameron. "I'll call her while you're teaching and see what she's doing. I only want to say hello and then duck out before I embarrass her."

Mandisa laughed. "She'll be pleased to see you. She may not show it, but it'll be nice for her to see a familiar face. The first few weeks are intense for a fresher." She glanced at the time on her wriststrap. "I have to go. I don't want to keep my lovely students waiting. They may blow something up."

"Can you quickly show me how to get to the information security department?" said Cameron. "I have some work to do, and I know someone there who'll be able to help me with what I need. We can meet up after we're both done for the day."

"It's on the way," said Mandisa. She whisked Cameron to the right building and dashed off to her class. Cameron's reputation and references brought her straight to her senior connection, who was delighted to meet her in person and tracked down a secure, connected room for his guest. She settled down to work.

First, she called Nina, who sounded surprisingly pleased to hear that her aunt was in town, as Mandisa had predicted. She arranged for Cameron to call into the student residences in the early evening.

Next, Cameron checked in on the team.

"Where are you?" asked Noor. She was looking at the neutral background from which Cameron was calling, obviously puzzling over the location.

"If I told you that…" said Cameron with a lopsided grin. "I'm taking a circular route to where I need to be, and I have a secure place to work for a couple of hours."

Noor laughed. "Understood. Are you ready for a quick briefing? We've been very busy this afternoon."

"Absolutely," said Cameron.

"Right," said Noor. "I found Tenuk's hotel, but he'd already checked out again. That was before the attack on the office, but I'm having some trouble tracing his movements since then. I'd say that the timing puts him in the frame as a suspect, but it feels wrong for him. Too direct and too soon after arriving, especially if he has other things to attend to."

"Agreed," said Cameron. "He may still be in London but we know that he's working on the sale of the farmhouse, so it's possible he's gone up there to inspect the property. It seems the logical thing to do. If he has, you might pick him up on cameras at Euston station."

"Understood," said Noor.

Cameron could see her making notes, and new notes and tasks appeared on the workflow model.

"If he's not in the frame, and I agree with you, it's very unlikely, then who is?"

Noor spun through the notes.

"DI Mercer's been in touch to say they are still trying to get sense out of the Rijks chap who was arrested at Angus's apartment, and Ross has arranged to meet her there tomorrow, but there's nothing concrete."

"He can't be involved," said Cameron. "He's in custody."

"I know he isn't the direct perpetrator," replied Noor, "but he might have had a hand in planning it. That would also bring Tenuk back under suspicion. We're looking into other leads, though. Michelle's been crawling round some dark corners of the underworld, listening for clues, too. We'll keep you posted on anything she finds."

"It's early days," said Cameron. "I wasn't expecting you to have this much already. Great work, Noor."

On the screen, Noor nodded solemnly, acknowledging the compliment. "It's been a team effort, of course, and it's helped to distract us from the news from America. You've seen that, haven't you?"

"What?" said Cameron, thoroughly blindsided. "New news?" She had been focusing far closer to home and hadn't seen a single media stream since leaving London. "What now?"

"The Militia's made another assault. They've activated sleeper cells in Iowa and their main force just swept through and took the Capitol in Des Moines. They practically walked in the door."

"Strategic simulations had defence in place somewhere entirely different, did they?" said Cameron.

"Yes," said Noor quietly. "A base called Fort Riley down in in eastern Kansas. And there was a major drone assault launched on those troops. It looks awful, Cameron."

"How can their intelligence be so completely wrong?" stormed Cameron. "In this day and age, everything we know is out there online as soon as it happens. This is more like warfare a century ago. You know what I'm talking about. You're the historian!"

"I do," said Noor. "There are plenty of stories of fake maps and plans planted and leaked to bluff the enemy and send them in the wrong direction. Did you ever hear of Operation Mincemeat? Fake plans on a washed-up body convinced German forces that there was an invasion force coming to Greece, so they diverted their troops there while the actual Allied landing was on Sicily."

"That's the kind of thing I mean," said Cameron. "Same tactics, different world. Misdirection isn't such a simple task these days." She stared at the blank wall in front of her, thinking.

Noor broke the silence. "I think Michelle needs to talk to her cousin at Wrangell."

"I think you're right."

It was a sobering end to their call. Cameron opened up the News Channel and watched a few minutes of the coverage, appalled by the wanton destruction. There was some speculation that the drone attack was friendly fire. Confusion reigned, and the horrors mounted.

She switched off the coverage with a shudder and made a call to Joel.

"I don't want to draw attention to Dunswyke," she said, "but I'm coming up north tomorrow, and there are a few things I need."

Joel responded with a location to meet. He was sure there would be no problem with her request.

Mandisa would have finished teaching by now. Sure enough, a staff member stuck their head around the door to say her friend was waiting in reception. Cameron logged off, her heart still heavy, but she knew there was nothing she could do tonight. She was too aware that the last few weeks had been non-stop. One night with a friend who moved in an entirely different world would do her the power of good.

•

Tenuk decided it was time to take a walk. He had yet to work out how to disable the strange sounds that came from the old server racks, and they were preying on his mind. He needed to get out of the place for his own sanity.

It was early evening, and the countryside was bathed in a golden light quite unlike that he had seen in built-up London, or in Singapore where the transition from day to night was rapid. It was more like how he remembered Austin, although even that was more than twenty degrees of latitude further south from here. He had a choice of taking the main road or trying to find the path where he had seen the dog walkers earlier. There was no obvious route from the farmhouse over to the line of trees that marked the path, so he opted for the road. It was hardly busy. There was no footpath, but when a couple of farm vehicles passed him, he pressed close to the hedgerow. One had a human operative. He waved, and Tenuk waved back.

A few houses appeared and Tenuk found himself quite quickly in the heart of the village. He passed a pub but thought it best not to go into the beer garden where a couple of people were deep in conversation at one of the tables. He didn't want to draw attention to himself.

The long main street wound along the side of a stream, narrowed under lofty trees, then opened up again towards a small church on a hill and a village green beyond. Tenuk kept walking past the green and the school yard, turned a corner, and realised suddenly that he'd reached the last of the houses. The road climbed a hill and disappeared out of sight. In the field, sheep were bleating.

He retraced his steps, this time on the other side of the road. Back round the corner, close to the school, he came across a large, elderly ginger cat sprawled in a sun puddle. Tenuk was a little wary of cats, but he stopped and crouched down a safe distance away to say hello. The cat stared at him, yellow eyes unblinking. Tenuk started to feel uneasy, as if the cat was sizing him up as prey.

A woman's voice came from a little way up a side street. "Donald! Supper time."

The cat got stiffly to its feet and stalked towards the source of the voice, pausing only to turn and hiss at Tenuk.

The woman's voice came again. "Donald, have you been making friends? What a good boy." The cat yowled croakily in reply.

Tenuk laughed ruefully, stood up, and carried on back up the village. He was determined to find the path back towards the farmhouse and after a few wrong turns, he spotted the sign to a public footpath that seemed to lead in the right direction. It was a pleasant walk. The only souls he met were a couple of youngsters who scampered past in pursuit of a curly-coated dog without giving him a second look. Very soon he spotted the farmhouse. The path was obvious from this end, and he knew he'd be able to find it again.

He felt much better for the walk. He prepared some food and settled down to catch up on the news. There was nothing more streaming about London. Every channel was now focused on America, the sudden leap east by the Militia, and the carnage that had ensued further south where the attack had been expected and never came. Dark thoughts about his father nagged at Tenuk until he could bear it no more. He went online through an incognito connection and viewed the latest bets and payouts on the Sapphire Straits platform. Sure enough, money had been made and lost on death and destruction, and the house must have won big.

A timer rang to tell him that his food was ready. He felt sick to the stomach but knew he had to eat. As he sat in the darkening kitchen, eating on autopilot and swigging a beer, he cursed his father. Lives were being lost. He had to be stopped, but Tenuk did not know how.

14: DUNSWYKE

Cameron's hangover had just about gone when her train pulled into the country station that she remembered from previous visits. She hopped into one of the waiting public autocars and directed it to a hotel she'd used before, somewhere she knew the security was top notch. She would have just enough time to check in before following Joel's instructions for their meeting point.

He'd warned her there was a walk involved. The second autocar dropped her just before a small square of low whitewashed houses right on the beach. There was a pub in the far corner of the hamlet but the wind coming off the sea was chilly, and the tables outside were empty. Mandisa had made sure they both had a good breakfast, and Cameron wasn't hungry in the slightest. She pressed on along the beach and climbed up into the dunes as Joel had instructed.

Half an hour later she sank gratefully onto a wooden bench seat and checked around for landmarks to be sure it was the right one. She reached for the water bottle in her small backpack. The bottom of the bag was slightly damp, and she cursed. She hadn't completely tightened the top of the bottle, and a few drops had leaked as she walked. Her smartscreen, tucked in an upper pocket, was fine. Her gloves had soaked up the bulk of the water. She took them out of the bag and hung them on the back of the bench in the bright autumn sunshine. Sheltered from the worst of the breeze, it was warm enough here for them to dry quickly, and she was unlikely to need them in any case.

Looking out over the sea, it was calm, waves lapping the rocks as the tide crept slowly up the beach. To her left, the bay swept in a great arc northward, the hamlet she had passed hidden behind high dunes. To the right, southwards, high on the cliff, rose the ruins of a castle. Battered by weather and war, only the grand entrance and another tower remained.

There was a shout from the beach below. Cameron looked down over the scrubby grass of the dunes and saw Joel waving to her. She waved back and looked along the sands to see Chad, Joel's three-year-old son, running this way and that and stopping to investigate shells and pebbles in the sand and small crabs waiting in rock crevices for the tide to reach them.

"There's a path over there," called Joel. "We'll come up."

A few minutes later, Cameron saw his head appear above the dunes and heard Chad's excited chatter as the two of them scrambled up the sandy bank. Joel sat gratefully on the bench beside her and pulled a snack out of his pocket for Chad, who was sitting in a patch of sunshine and talking to a bug he'd spotted in the dune grass.

"Fancy meeting you here," said Joel.

Cameron grinned. "I like your approach to secure communications," she said.

"I checked," said Joel. "The cameras up on the castle don't cover the bay, and there aren't many tourists on a Friday now that the school term has started. I'm willing to bet you're the only person walking the coastal path today."

"It's beautiful," said Cameron. "I'd forgotten quite how lovely it is up here."

"We come down here all the time, and it's gorgeous but empty." Joel stretched and glanced down at Chad, who was absorbed by his snack and his bug. "I've got what you need, Cameron. What's going on?"

Cameron looked at him with wide, innocent eyes. "I'm just having a little holiday," she protested. "Why ever would you think there's something else behind this chance meeting?"

Joel laughed. "Jack sends his best and he's supplied everything that you asked for. He wanted to come along and play on the beach too, but I persuaded him that would be a massive security issue."

He dug in his pockets and pulled out his smartscreen and a small bag. He set the smartscreen down on the bench and opened the bag.

"You have a choice," he said, shaking out the contents. He held up a curiously curved and flattened piece of metal. "This is the traditional bone conduction earpiece. It's very discreet. It sits behind your ear and uses vibrations on the skull to transmit audio. It's less effective in picking up what you're vocalising, and still vulnerable to being dislodged in a fight. Not that I'm expecting you to get in a fight," he added hastily. "But it's always a risk."

"Okay. What else?"

"Nice pair of earrings," said Joel happily. "Martha helped to design these, and Chloe picked out a couple that she thought might suit you."

That jolted Cameron, though she didn't show it. Her heart to heart with Mandisa, late into the night, had worked through some buried feelings about Ben. She knew that he and Chloe were happy, she bore them no ill will, but she missed the ease of their old relationship. However, she was ready to let go.

"Good choices," she said approvingly. She hesitated but finally picked a pair that she genuinely liked, and she knew would not look out of place day to day. She took out the studs that she normally wore in her ears and slipped the new jewellery into place.

Joel picked up his smartscreen. "Okay, let's get you connected. Here. Can you run through the voice recognition sequence?"

Cameron followed all the instructions, feeling slightly odd about sitting talking to herself on a bench overlooking the sea. It was a quick process, and once all the indicators were green, she handed the screen back to Joel.

"What now?"

"Say hello."

"Hello, Pip."

"Hello, Cameron. It's lovely to meet you."

She hadn't thought about what Pip would sound like. The voice was a synthesised mix of half-familiar accents and tones but unique to itself. She felt comfortable with it in a way she hadn't expected.

"Go on, ask them something," said Joel.

"Them?" said Cameron.

"Yes," said Joel. "Pip's still a young intelligence and hasn't declared a gender identity. We're not going to force one on them. It causes all sorts of confusion in their neural circuits if we get it wrong."

"Okay." She thought for a moment. "Hi Pip, could you, uh, outline the key points relating to the Wyoming Militia action last night?"

Joel rolled his eyes. "You could have picked something easier."

Cameron ignored him. She was listening to Pip.

"An attack on Fort Riley was the most likely scenario in most defence simulations as this would have consolidated the Militia's control of military training bases, adding to the Air Academy and Space Force bases already within their territory. A foothold in Eastern Kansas would have offered routes towards Fort Knox to the east, and army targets in Illinois.

This misdirection enabled the Militia instead to leverage their control of South Dakota and Nebraska to drive deeper into Iowa."

"Good," said Cameron. "What do you think they're after?"

"Multiple targets in Illinois still present themselves, principally the US Army headquarters, according to available simulations. However, my confidence in the ranking of probabilities is low to medium."

"Explain," said Cameron. "Please." There was something fizzing in the back of her mind and she wondered if her instincts were backed up by the data. Pip should be connected to data feeds in the same way as the InsurGlobe systems, but she had hoped that there would be more, and it seemed her confidence had been rewarded. She glanced at Joel, who was grinning. Joel's army background and his ability to sift intelligence must have had a strong influence on the critical analysis modelling that was incorporated into Pip. She was already impressed.

"Clusters of probability ranking have been observed," said Pip. "By cross-referencing the source of each simulation that contributes to the whole, it appears that clustered rankings derived from processing at specific physical locations indicated Fort Riley as the next most likely target. These clusters outweighed independent rankings from other quantum processing centres, both managed and in-house, that evaluated the same intelligence data and suggested the Iowa incursion as the highest probability. Analysis of prior incidents indicates a similar skew in the simulations presented to federal forces."

"Thank you, Pip," said Cameron. "What is your analysis of the ultimate strategic goals of the Militia?"

"Indeterminate," said Pip. "Their declared goal of military supremacy does not correlate with observed actions. There is intersectionality between observed actions and external influence including heightened gambling activity. There is very little economic justification for the rapid expansion of territory. My confidence in their declared goal is low."

Cameron was practically purring. "Thank you. That'll be all for now." She looked at Joel. "They're good. Now, tell me two things. First, how do I switch Pip off. No offence, Pip, but I like my privacy."

"None taken," said the voice that echoed in her ear. "Exiting to offline mode. The interface will re-establish the connection to my servers when you call for me."

Good. Someone had thought about the user's preferences, and Cameron was a user who preferred not to have someone listening in unless it was operationally essential.

"Well, that answered that," she said. "Second question, I want all the lowdown on the tech, what Pip is capable of, and anything where I genuinely can't rely on them."

Joel looked down at Chad who had finished both his snack and his conversation with the bug and was showing signs of restlessness. "Let's walk," he said. "We're safe enough in this area."

They gathered their things and scrambled down the narrow sandy path in the dunes to the beach below. One of Cameron's boots had filled with sand as she slid, and she found a handy rock to sit on and empty it out. She watched as Joel started throwing a small rugby ball around with Chad. The child scampered around the beach giggling.

"Ready," called Cameron, free of sand for now. The tide was going out and the sand here was hard packed and easy to walk on. Chad retrieved his ball and ran on ahead of them while Joel told Cameron the full story of Pip's inception.

•

Ross was champing at the bit to get on with real work alongside the rest of the Argentum team, but the inbox full of routine paperwork that accompanied a death was blown out of all proportion by the can of worms that had been opened. The routine stuff he could deal with. Nothing much had changed since his grandmother died and there was a grim familiarity about the whole process. The rest threatened to overwhelm him.

It had been obvious from the start that Angus knew exactly who Ross was and that he was the only next of kin and sole beneficiary. As soon as his death was registered, it triggered a smart contract that transferred ownership of all his assets to Ross. Ross had taken one look at the data that cascaded into his wallet and called in all the help he could find.

This afternoon's task was to visit the studio flat where Angus had lived. Ross decided to kill two birds with one stone and arranged to meet both the landlord and DI Mercer on site. To relieve the stress, he ran from his home to a gym near the estate, showered and changed, then made his way to the warren of apartment blocks, looking for the right address.

He'd already gone through the process of authorising his chip access and slipped into the building without fanfare. He didn't bother with the lift, but after eight floors of dingy, smelly stairwell he wished he had. The flat was easy to spot, with its hastily repaired door. The police investigations were complete and all that was left was a scrap of yellow tape stuck to the floor outside. Ross took a deep breath and opened the door.

He'd deliberately arrived an hour early for an uninterrupted look around. Stepping into the flat, he realised that an hour would not be enough. It was a small space but crammed with stuff. The police had done a reasonable job at keeping their mess to a minimum and Ross immediately spotted the damaged computer. He gave it a quick once over. There was no hard disk. He collected the rest of the shell and placed it by the door. He'd be able to cannibalise it for parts, at least. There were some high-quality components in there.

He already knew that the intruder, Rijks, had not been carrying any computer equipment or other devices. That was a puzzle, but perhaps Angus had been using an external drive? In that case, it must be close at hand. From his first trawl through the access codes and keys that he'd inherited, it was very clear that Angus didn't entrust his data to any cloud providers. There had to be a drive somewhere. There was good chance it was here, and that it was well enough hidden that the police had not found it when they searched the scene.

He started with a cursory look around the shelves and cupboards in the bedsit and the small kitchen. These would already have been swept by the police, but it was worth a quick once-over. He ran his hands around the wallscreen and felt behind the bed and chest of drawers but found nothing but dust and spider webs. The bathroom was a horror, and he decided to leave it until last. He opened the fridge, realised it must have been switched off inadvertently when the police were here, and looked around for a bin bag to dispose of the contents. He found one in the first drawer he opened and started to empty the old food into it.

That was when he spotted it. It was extremely well camouflaged and almost out of sight, taped to the back of the salad drawer, right down at floor level. The tape and bag blended into the panel behind and were also hidden by a large, wilting lettuce.

That should have been his first clue. He hadn't had Angus down as a fan of salads. He chucked out the lettuce and pulled off the tape that secured the bag tightly to the drawer. Sure enough, safely encased in the bag to avoid any risk of condensation, was a hard disk drive.

He sealed the bag again and stuffed it deep into his backpack. Mission accomplished, as far as he was concerned. Anything else that he found was a bonus. He was sitting on the bed working his way through some personal effects from the bedside table when there was a knock at the door.

"DI Mercer. You're early."

"Nice to see you, Ross." She shook his hand, and for a moment looked unsure of what to say. "You must have had one hell of a week."

"You could say that." Ross picked a pile of clothes off the small sofa and chucked them onto the end of the bed. "Have a seat."

"Thank you," said Mercer, sinking gingerly into the upholstery.

Ross pulled out his smartscreen, opened a file, and passed it over to her. "This is an itemised list of things I've suddenly inherited that might be connected to some of your investigations," he said. "I'm honestly not sure how to proceed with them. I'd be happy to follow everything up myself but there's a danger I'll trip over a live operation in the process."

Mercer scanned the list, pursing her lips. "Good thinking, Ross. Can you drop me a copy? I'll send you a receipt and an assurance that should anything here turn out to be purely personal, we'll advise you and delete from our records."

"That sounds fair," said Ross. They exchanged documents, timestamped and sealed. "I'd like to know a bit more about what you found in here," he continued.

"Not a lot," said Mercer. "You've seen the state of the computer, and we didn't find any other equipment. No smartscreens, nothing. Just those photo wallets you were looking at." She pointed at the small pile on the bed.

"I've got a smartscreen from the hospital," said Ross, "but it was a burner. No history at all."

"I wonder if somewhere there is a physical storage unit with things that belong to Angus White, not Paul Black," said Mercer. "You've had nothing like that through from the legacy service?"

Ross shook his head. "No. But you never know, I may find something while I'm tidying this lot." He gestured around the room. "I don't think it'll take too long."

Mercer made a note. "I'll get the relevant team to follow this up." She settled more comfortably into the sofa. "We were going to talk about Rijks," she said. "We're not much further forward. He's saying nothing and had no devices with him when he was arrested. We're still following a trail back through Interpol to learn more about him."

"In that case, I have good news," said Ross. "Our intelligence is purely based on the speculative link between Steen Rijks in the physical world and Sterix in the virtual world, but we have a lot on Sterix."

Mercer's eyes lit up. "Excellent. Care to enlighten me?"

"Sources are confidential," said Ross. "You're clear on that?"

"Yes," said Mercer. "I trust you."

"Okay. Sterix has been positively identified as a key member of both the Steamyard syndicate and the Pasar outfit that preceded it. He consistently used the avatar of what my sources called 'a pathetic grey kitten' so you could try and trace sightings of that character from virtual world surveillance. He was known for being talented but unreliable and volatile."

Mercer checked her note-taker. "This is all useful, but it doesn't explain why he is here in London."

"A falling out among thieves," said Ross. "I think he's been sent to neutralise Angus."

"Interesting," said Mercer. "Now, one more question. When I told Cameron that we had arrested someone who had just arrived in the country, her first response was a name. Tenuk. I've heard that name before. Wasn't the CTO at Statesman Tech called Tenuk?"

Ross felt that he was on slippery ground. How much did Mercer know, and how much did she need to know?

He was saved by a knock on the door. This time, the visitor had a key. A tousled head appeared and a young man in overalls edged into the room.

"Oh, good, you're here," he said, entirely unaware of reason for the sudden silence that greeted him.

"You're the landlord?" said Ross.

"Uh, yeah. Forge Group. I look after clearances. Um, you must be Ross White, am I right? I'm Lenny."

Ross glanced at DI Mercer with some amusement. She sighed and stood up. "Your ID please," she said, flashing her badge. "You'll be aware that this flat has been the subject of a police investigation."

Lenny looked startled. He presented his chip and company badge, and Mercer checked them carefully. "That all seems to be in order," she said.

"I didn't know nothing about police," Lenny said, tucking his company badge away in his pocket. "They just sent me here to make sure the flat got cleared. You officially have seven days but, uh, that can be extended, in the circumstances."

"Your customer service is astoundingly bad," said Mercer. "Aren't you lucky that the room isn't full of weeping relatives."

"Uh, yeah, that's bad when that happens," said Lenny. Gradually the point Mercer was making got through. He turned to Ross. "I'm sorry for your loss," he said.

Ross was warming to the kid. He was obviously completely out of his depth, very uncomfortable with people, and hadn't been briefed at all. "Don't worry," he said. "You're just doing your job, and someone's really dropped you in it, haven't they? Why don't you go through your checklist and I promise the flat will be ready to hand over by next Tuesday. I don't need any extra time."

Lenny brightened up. He was on surer ground now. "Right. I've got an inventory to send you, so you know what belonged to the flat. It was part furnished, you see. Anything missing or broken gets charged." He glanced at the door which had been crudely repaired. "Not sure what we do about that, but I'll ask my boss, if it was a police thing." Neither Mercer nor Ross mentioned that it was the intruder who had caused the damage, not the police. They didn't want to put Lenny off his stride. "The rent's paid up to the end of the month, so there'll probably be a payment to come back to you, plus the deposit, unless there's any deductions to make, but you'll sign for them next week." He dug into another pocket. "Have you got all the keys? We always provide spares to, uh, next of kin."

"Thanks," said Ross, automatically holding out his hand.

"Oh, I need you to sign for the inventory first. Then I'll give you them."

"Okay," said Ross. His curiosity was piqued. The bunch was larger than he expected.

"Are you ready? I can send that to you now." Lenny swiped at the tablet, checked the destination, and Ross's smartscreen vibrated. "Could you just check that and then confirm by chip that I've given you the inventory and the keys."

Ross did so, and Lenny handed him the keyring. Ross stuffed it into his pocket.

"Is there anything else I need to know?" he asked.

Lenny shook head. "Nothing official. We do a proper deep clean and redecorate after you've gone so don't worry about the place being sparkling. It just needs emptying. Those keys will open the recycling store and the compost and charity bins as well."

"Thank you, Lenny," said Ross solemnly. "Excellent job."

The youngster gave him a half smile, nodded at Mercer, and disappeared out of the door, closing it carefully behind him.

Mercer's wriststrap buzzed. She glanced at the message and stood up. "I have to go," she said. "My car is waiting. Thank you for everything you've supplied. I'll let you know where this leads us."

Ross shook her hand. "Thanks for your help," he said.

He made sure that she was in the lift and going down then went back into the flat, closed the door and pulled the bunch of keys out of his pocket.

The fobs were crudely labelled. One was clearly the emergency access to the front door of the building and another for the flat, in case of a fault with the chip access. The fat fob with a triangle on it must be the recycling store, the one with an apple core the compost. But what was the other one? With a flash of inspiration, he opened the inventory file that Lenny had sent him. Cooker, white goods, fitted bed and cupboards… He kept scrolling. At the end, in an appendix, he found a schedule for lease extensions.

Angus had rented a storage unit, and he had the address.

Ross bundled the personal items he'd found into his backpack, slung the pack over his shoulder, and picked up the bin bag full of fridge waste. It was a start, he thought to himself as he looked around the room. If he could get some of his friends to help out, they could have it all cleared over the weekend.

He took the lift back down to the ground floor and followed the signs first to the waste bins. Ross grimaced as he sorted the composting from the packaging, but he knew the triage was monitored. He swabbed his hands with antiseptic gel from a handy dispenser and then went on a hunt for the storage unit.

It didn't take him long. Ross tried opening it with his chip, but the door stayed stubbornly closed. This was something that hadn't automatically passed to him, then. It may have been an innocent oversight. In any case, the key fob triggered the lock instantly. Inside he found a second barrier, an additional layer of security added by Angus.

This time his chip worked, and the door swung open.

15: HIDDEN GEMS

Cameron and Joel parted at the small, whitewashed hamlet she had passed on her way in. She was hungry now, and Joel assured her that the little pub was a safe space popular with the security services who frequented the area. There were no other customers, and she ate well.

Restored, she picked up a local public shuttle into the nearest town and from there hailed an autocar to take her back to the hotel. Her room was set up with a workstation, and she quickly logged into the Argentum virtual workspace. She wasn't surprised to find everyone in there and a lively chat going on.

"Nice of you to join us," said Ross. "Having a good holiday?"

Cameron assumed that was just a throwaway remark. He couldn't have guessed where she was, surely? But Joel and Ross were as thick as thieves, and Ross knew her well.

"Dropping in before my next spa treatment," she joked. "How did things go with Mercer?"

Ross laughed. "They've been struggling with this Sterix character. I think she owes us a few favours for the intelligence we were able to pass on. But that's not the most interesting news today by a long stretch." He looked around the faces on the screen. "Who wants to go first?"

"May as well get Oak Medical out of the way," said Sandeep. "For once, it's all good news. They were bloody lucky, and they have a good team. It's still going to take them a while to get the locked systems back on stream, but everything else passed testing. It's all being restored bit by bit, and they've managed to get a personalised comms campaign started to counter the phishing."

"So, we're out of there operationally for now," said Cameron. "Excellent work. I'm sure you can find something else to do."

Ross raised a lazy hand. "I've bagged him. Sandeep's helping me with the flat clearance over the weekend."

"I couldn't argue," said Sandeep. "Come on, Ross, tell her the best bit."

Cameron grinned. She loved the interactions with her team. "Don't be shy, Ross. What's going on?"

"I have in my hand…" He lifted up a white package and waved it at the camera.

"What's that?" said Cameron.

Ross paused for effect. "Angus's hard disk. We've mirrored it and we're working through the security now, although of course it's remarkably straightforward as I have all his passcodes and keys."

Michelle's window in the chat lit up. She hadn't bothered with a camera or an avatar. "It's a familiar structure," she said. "An obvious layer and a second hidden partition that I haven't come close to cracking yet. We've found all the stuff he'd collected on our team and on some of the others that have been targeted, too, although those aren't so detailed. If you're interested, there's nothing about Charlie's house in there. Your village is safe."

"I presume there's enough there to pass to the police," said Cameron.

"Already done," said Ross. "We've let the other targets know what we found so that they're aware, and we pinged everything over to Mercer, with their permission, half an hour ago. It won't take them long to nail the bastards who are out there trying physical attacks."

Cameron was relieved, but there was a nagging thought in the back of her mind. "Ross," she said, "are you sure that's all there was to find? I don't know, it feels as if someone like Angus would have kept a backup as well?"

"I'd imagine so," said Ross. "Once you've lost a disk, you generally become very careful about backups." He didn't elaborate.

"Yes, that happens to everyone at some point in their career," said Cameron. "The earlier the better. So, where's his backup?"

"Could be anywhere," said Ross. "Which comes back to, Sandeep and I will be clearing that flat over the weekend, and an extra storage unit I found. We haven't found a cloud account, so there must be a physical device somewhere."

"It sounds as if you have everything covered on that side," said Cameron, "and thanks for the heads up about the village. Pete, are you still coming this weekend so we can check out the farmhouse? There's a spare room for you. I'll be there tomorrow afternoon at the latest."

"Yes," said Pete. "I'm going to help Ross and Sandeep with some of the heavy lifting in the morning, but I'll be there. There's been some bother on my street, and I think it's due to those smear campaigns that are running. If I can get out of town for a couple of days, it'll help the police to sort things out and keep the neighbours happy."

"How much do you remember about the farmhouse?" asked Cameron.

"Oh, plenty," said Pete. "I know it'll have changed in the last fifteen years, but I've been doing some background research and reminding myself of how the land lies."

Cameron was starting to feel as if she wasn't needed. The team was such a well-oiled machine, powering ahead on all the tasks that she was used to juggling. Then Michelle spoke up again.

"I called my cousin Daniel," she said. "Cameron, you need to speak to him. Brianna and I started correlating Quantum as a Service providers with data centres and output."

Cameron's attention sharpened. "Wrangell?"

"That's the main source of skewed outputs," said Noor. "But there's more, and it's much worse. We've started building a visualisation of all the processors we know and who uses their services and we're monitoring in real time. There's a clear historical discrepancy between outputs from Wrangell-based processors and not just local machines like the Met Office but even the Chinese Quantum City installations."

"Word in the deep is that the Chinese authorities are pretty concerned themselves," said Michelle. "I'm keeping my ear to the ground. Chloe's put me in touch with some underground networks over there that she knew back in the day."

Cameron exhaled. She hadn't realised she was holding her breath. There was something big out there, and she was now sure she could put a name to it. Yasmin. Her blue-eyed nemesis from the virtual world. The Artificial General Intelligence they thought they had destroyed.

"It's got to be her," she said. "I don't know how, but I feel it in my bones. Shell, can you get me a secure line to Daniel? I don't want our conversation to touch any of the Wrangell systems."

"Yes," said Michelle. "He's off site this weekend. Nothing will go through the data centre."

"Thanks. Is there anything else before I go?" Cameron reached for the off button but was stopped in her tracks by Noor.

"Another large quantum facility has started to return variations."

"Which one?" said Cameron, slowly withdrawing her hand. "When?"

"Austin, Texas," said Noor. "Right in the heart of Militia territory. It's recent, literally the last few days, and it skewed the federal defence simulations for their response to the latest action."

"Fort Riley," said Cameron.

"Yes," said Noor. "This is why so many soldiers died."

•

Tenuk had finally worked out how to get rid of the whispers that emanated from the server room. He had come very close to simply pulling out the plug, but he felt it would be more instructive to explore the old machines and work his way through the system. He had, however, resorted to earplugs for the sake of his sanity. Working away in silence in the cool of the old building was soothing and gave him time to think.

The second partition on the hard disk was proving hard to crack. He'd blown the security twice already and had to clean up and re-load the mirrored drive. He was slipping. He'd become too reliant on Yasmin and then Zara over the past few years and his own skills were rusty. Sorting out the sound was a welcome break. He could feel some of his instincts sharpening again. He'd managed to navigate his way through the out-of-date operating system on the servers. He hadn't seen that version in the wild since he was fresh out of college, but he clearly remembered trying to hack it, and once he got his eye in, it was just as easy now as it had been then. There was no way he would risk connecting this installation to the outside world, though. He knew what nastiness was circulating in the ether these days, having been involved in writing quite a large proportion of the malicious code that was lurking out there, and until he was able to reinforce the firewall and security packages it was not worth his while to even attempt to bring the main installation online.

He'd been working at this for longer than he thought. He was hungry, and he wanted a cold beer. He left the mercifully silent outbuildings and started across the small, scrubby field towards the house.

Then he saw the dog. He recognised it from the footpath last night, a medium sized animal with a light curly coat. It was loping happily round his field with no owner in sight.

"Roxy! Roxy! Come here now!"

A dark-haired girl, no more than eleven or twelve, was jumping up and down on the other side of the hedge waving a leash. She stopped dead as soon as she saw Tenuk.

"Oh! I didn't know there was anyone here. Can you help me catch my dog?"

Tenuk nodded and started walking towards the dog, trying to intercept it without spooking the animal. He got close enough to make a grab for its harness, but too soon. It turned on the spot and scampered off in the other direction.

It became a comedy chase. The second time Tenuk got close, he tripped over a tussock and faceplanted into the grass as Roxy scampered off, delighted to have someone to play with. The girl ran along the hedge, calling and whistling, trying to guide the dog towards one corner of the field. Exhausted, laughing, Tenuk finally had a brainwave. He spotted a suitably robust stick on the ground under the hedge, picked it up, and threw it wildly into the middle of the field. Roxy immediately understood the new game, picked up the stick, and trotted obediently towards him, wagging her tail.

"Sit?" ventured Tenuk.

Roxy sat, tongue lolling, evidently glad of the breather. He reached forward gently and caught hold of her harness. She didn't resist. She seemed as tired as he was.

The girl threw the leash over the hedge and Tenuk caught it. He clipped it on and led the dog out through the farmhouse courtyard to where the girl was waiting. He handed the leash over, still laughing and panting.

"Thank you," said the girl. She turned away towards the road.

Tenuk went into the house and opened the fridge. He really needed that cold beer now.

He took his drink back out to the courtyard and flopped into one of the outdoor chairs in the dying sunlight. He could see the girl and the dog on the path now. They'd been joined by another child, probably the boy that he'd seen run past with them last night. He wondered idly why the second youngster hadn't been helping to catch the dog.

The first beer slipped down so quickly he went to get another. He checked the bags that had been delivered and remained unopened and was happy to find some snacks for the beer to wash down. Life was good and Singapore was asleep. He was at peace for the first time in two long years.

A sudden inspiration struck him. He leapt up and carried his beer and snacks over to the outbuildings. He sat down at his workstation, pulled up the mirrored drive, and started through the security on the second partition. The first few steps he had down pat. He hit the same problem as last time, took a deep breath, and proceeded on pure gut instinct.

The drive opened.

Tenuk took a deep, shuddering breath. Laid out in front of him was a vast library of data labelled 'Sapphire Straits'. He scrolled through the headline file names. Some he recognised, places and people and projects he had been involved in. Others he didn't know. Eden. Esports. Gracie. Hardy. Knox. Pangolin. Piper. Quantum. Sladen. Snake River. Speakeasy. Wrangell. XYZ.

Pangolin? There was even a file on himself. Trembling, Tenuk clicked on the first folder on the list. The data went back years. Angus must have been collecting information and storing it away as – as what? Security. Insurance. Material for blackmail if the necessity arose.

Tenuk felt sick to his stomach. All of his suspicions about his father's activities were confirmed. The gambling books that Chaoxiang claimed were simply facilitated by Sapphire Straits were run by him, from weather to warfare. His father had found a way of ensuring that the house always won. It seemed that Angus had acquired convincing evidence of quantum simulation tampering. What chilled him to the core was a cluster of data on the Wyoming Militia. Their battle plans, their strategies, their flawed actions. How deep did Chaoxiang's involvement go? How much influence and control did he have over their actions?

Tenuk wanted no part of it. He wished he had followed his instincts and refused the offer when he was first ordered back home. He shook his head, trying to clear his thoughts.

That was when he saw the ball. It was an old tennis ball, well chewed, half hidden under the unit next to his workstation and just visible in a dying ray of light shining through the grimy window.

The thing that had previously been sitting on the unit was gone.

While Tenuk had been chasing the dog, the boy had taken the hard disk.

•

Cameron was still working when the hotel receptionist knocked at the door.

"I'm so sorry," she said. "We have a private booking this evening for this room. We need to start setting up."

Cameron was glad of the distraction. She had been digging down a rabbit hole of her own making, reading through Brianna and Michelle's findings and following trails to an equal proportion of new insights and dead ends through the tangled web of APIs and users and oracles that linked the quantum processing nodes. She was suddenly reminded of Aunt Vicky's efforts to trace the family tree. The deeper her aunt explored their ancestry, the more spurious connections came up, until the tree was bristling with a heady mix of genuine data and false positives that had to be weeded out. It might be time to stop.

"Of course, no problem," she replied. "Just give me a minute or two. I'll start packing up."

The receptionist withdrew and Cameron, good as her word, pulled together her notes, closed down her workstations, and set her empty coffee cups to be collected. Five minutes later she was on her way back up to her room. She could call Daniel from there.

It was already midday in Alaska and Cameron hoped that he'd be reachable. If she had time off in a place like Wrangell, a protected habitat, she'd find plenty to do out there in the wilderness. But she was in luck. As Daniel explained, blinking, his voice thick with sleep, he'd been on night shift for the last two weeks, and the first of his days off was dedicated to getting his sleeping patterns back in alignment. Some of his colleagues still used the Sanctuary headbands to manage their rest. Daniel wouldn't touch them. Cameron didn't blame him.

She cut to the chase. "What's been going on? I guess Michelle's told you what we've been seeing."

"Not really," said Daniel. "She's been very circumspect because I was on the base and neither of us trust any comms that go through there. Not after, you know..."

"Yasmin. Yes. I understand completely. What do you know? I'll fill in the blanks."

"I know that she needed a list of QAAS service users, and I was able to point her to data in the public domain. All our inbound and outbound contracts are on chain. The commercial details are encrypted, of course, but I have no doubt that Shell's found a way around that."

Cameron laughed. "You'd be right," she said. "As we're on a secure line now, can I sense check some of the list with you?"

"Sure," said Daniel. Cameron rattled off a dozen names in quick succession. "That's spot on. I'm sure you have the whole roll call documented."

"We do," said Cameron, "and we know that the inbound data is sound, but outbound there are, shall we say, challenges."

Daniel nodded slowly. "Shell told me. Now, we don't see what's being processed, we simply manage the hardware, so until she contacted me, I had no idea. I knew there'd been problems with the weather forecasts. My shift had a kayaking trip blow out completely when the weather service said it was clear, and that's never happened before."

"The weather simulations are the least of our problems," said Cameron. "You're handling military grade processing too."

"You're not supposed to know that," said Daniel, frowning. "Excuse me a moment." His camera and mic turned off. A minute later he was back. "I think I have a cold coming on. You didn't need to see that sneeze."

"What more can you tell me about the thing I don't know?" said Cameron. "This may be important."

Daniel looked doubtful. "I'm just security," he said. "I'm sure you already know it all."

"Try me," said Cameron.

"Okay. Well, any outputs from both quantum and classic processing at Wrangell go to US combined forces Strategic Command. They have other quantum centres, you know. They're not stupid enough to rely on one set of probabilistic simulations to direct their strategy."

"Which other centres?" asked Cameron, keen to see how much he understood about the network, although she already knew the answer.

"I'm speculating here, based on what little I know," said Daniel, "but Austin certainly used to be one of them, and Chicago another. I expect that Austin is offline now that Texas is under Militia control. It takes time to do that, though. It may still be live."

"It's been two years since they invaded," said Cameron. "Would that be long enough?"

"Certainly," said Daniel.

Cameron knew it was still running. She silently cursed the fools at Strategic Command who had made the decision to keep it and who had thought for a moment that their installation was secure.

"Thanks, Daniel," she said. "Now, why are you uneasy about what you correctly say is just hardware? What's happening at Wrangell?"

Daniel put his head in his hands. He was obviously exhausted. "This is gut feeling and observations," he said. "Nothing concrete. It started way back, after the Olympics. We had some mystery movements on the log, access to the quantum wing recorded but without personnel details attached. I tried to flag it at the time, but it was brushed under the table."

"And since then?"

"Nothing. It was an anomaly that's never been reproduced, despite zero reconfiguration of the systems, and nothing bad happened as far as management was concerned. Then we lost a few members of staff. More than a few, actually. Churn on the quantum wing was particularly high for a few months, all with stress and mental health issues. Again, management said it was just a blip, that it was within the expected levels of staff turnover, especially with how isolated we are up here. But we lost some good people."

"I have to ask," said Cameron. "Were they using Sanctuary?"

"Yes, all of them," said Daniel. "I should have told Shell, but Yasmin's gone, hasn't she? It was just a coincidence."

Cameron shook her head. "Maybe not. Anything else?"

"Yeah. There's been a lot of visits from tech support in the past few months. I've been buried by all the security clearances that were needed. And I've kept my ear to the ground. People talk, you know, even when they shouldn't. Get a few of them huddled over breakfast, they ignore the security guy who's making his coffee. One of the things that kept coming up was 'accelerated decoherence', if that means anything to you, and what was the other thing? Hammer? Rowing hammer? Something like that."

Cameron punched the air. "Daniel, you are a star. That's what I needed."

Daniel stared straight into the camera. "Is she still here? Yasmin?"

"I'm very afraid that she might be."

"I'd better watch my back, then," said Daniel lightly. "But no one bothers with me. I'm just the security guy."

"You're way more than that," said Cameron. "I can't thank you enough. You look after yourself. Enjoy your week off."

"Thanks, Cameron," said Daniel. "Oh, one more bit of trivia for you. You know the strategic defence aggregation I mentioned? Someone once told me that if all the quantum simulations agree on a specific threat, they can automate the response. I'm not sure I believe it, but it might be something to check out just in case."

Cameron's blood ran cold, but she kept smiling. "Sounds unlikely," she said. "I wouldn't worry about it."

"Okay," said Daniel, reassured. "Have a good weekend. Thanks for the call."

Cameron disconnected and sat back, staring at the blank screen. Three processing centres made up the backbone of strategic decision making. One was almost certainly compromised and might yet hold the ghost of Yasmin. A second should have been taken offline but was still live and starting to return odd results. And the third, if she wasn't mistaken, was directly in the path of the Militia's advance.

16: STOLEN SECRETS

Tenuk tried to sleep, but after tossing and turning in his bed for hours he gave up. He had too much to think about.

There was nothing he could do about the stolen disk. He had his copy. He doubted very much whether a pair of kids could get anywhere with the original, although he'd have given it a try at their age. But it was still a loose end that nagged at him. He didn't want it to fall into the wrong hands. It would expose Noor once again, and he couldn't allow that to happen. But what could he do? He wasn't about to march down to the village and go hunting house to house. He certainly couldn't call the police. There had to be a solution, but he had no idea where to turn.

Until his mother died – and for some time after through her memorial avatar in the family mausoleum – he had turned to her for advice. Then he'd become reliant on Yasmin. He had tried hard not to do the same with Zara, and he certainly wasn't going to call her in to solve this problem, or to discuss the newly discovered contents of the disk. He wished he had been better at building real relationships with real people. His closest human connection, he realised belatedly, had been with Auntie Fatima.

It was no use beating himself up over past failings. He resolved to make some changes to his life, if he ever managed to escape the grip of his father.

The Sapphire Straits files might enable him to make that break. He had read through a tiny fraction of the data before tiredness prevented him from processing any more horrors. He couldn't take the usual shortcut of dropping information into a large language model and asking for a summary. There was no way any of this was going online and he didn't have a local, trained system to hand.

He sat bolt upright.

There was a local AI model available. Three, to be precise. The old servers, humming away in the outbuildings, held the unformed intelligences that had become Xanthe, Yasmin and Zara. There was language processing capability there. If he could just isolate the model he needed, he may be able to use it.

Tenuk scrambled out of bed, wired and energised. It was three in the morning, but he didn't care. He would work all day and all night on this if he had to. He switched on the lights, asked the sound system to play a favourite playlist, made some coffee and was pleased to find that his random shopping choices had included some pre-packed pancakes, a welcome throwback to his time in Austin. Caffeinated, restored, and ready, he grabbed a jacket to stave off the chill of the autumn dawn and went to work.

His first task was to check and double check that his careful isolation of the servers from any external networks was watertight. He was about to open Pandora's box and he didn't want anything escaping into the world. As a precaution, he disconnected the physical infrastructure of the uplink that was attached to the outbuildings, but not before checking his messages. There was one from Xanthe. How was the property clearance progressing? Tenuk responded that he was working on decommissioning, which was partly true. He briefly wondered where Zara was, then put the thought out of his mind.

He cleaned the area around the server stacks and their control station then carefully removed the protective sheets, folded them as best he could, and tucked them into a corner. The lights twinkled alluringly. He pulled up a command line, flexed his fingers, and started to type.

•

Ross had also woken early. He crept out of bed quietly to avoid disturbing Michelle, made a cup of tea, and sat watching the sun rise through the half-open sitting room blinds. The enormity of the week's events was starting to hit him. On Monday, his life had been normal. On Wednesday he'd found out who his father was. Now he had to bury him. He was unbelievably grateful that he had Michelle and his friends around him. It would have broken his younger self. As it was, he had no idea what the process of clearing Angus's possessions – his father's possessions – would bring.

There was no point hanging around. Michelle was staying at home, and she would understand if he slipped out early. He dressed quickly, grabbed a large empty rucksack just in case they found anything of interest, left her a message that would play when she woke up, and hopped on his bike.

The roads were still quiet. It took him barely half an hour to reach the estate. He carried his bike up to the flat and propped it against the door of the bathroom, dropped his rucksack and hoodie on the bed, and looked around. Where to start?

The kitchen cupboards were an obvious and manageable place to begin. The first one he opened contained tea and coffee, and biscuit and marshmallow teacakes. He put the kettle on and sent a message to Sandeep to bring milk along with some more bin bags. Teacakes were not part of his training regime, but he figured that this week really didn't count and devoured one with delight.

There was nothing unusual to find. No more hidden disk drives, no coded messages. Just the remnants of a normal life. Ross gave the kitchen appliances a clean and set most of them aside to be donated. Dry goods would go to the nearest foodbank. He started several piles in a space by the door for things to be donated and things to discard. There was a cartoon stuck to one of the cupboard doors, a wry joke about artificial intelligence and natural stupidity. Ross had seen it before, but it still raised a smile and brought home the realisation that at some level he had a connection with his father.

The little kitchen was done. The bathroom was lowest on his list. Clothes, then, and personal effects. Ross expected this to be harder than it actually was. Sorting through his grandmother's things when she died had been a terrible experience, every familiar item triggering another memory and deeper grief at his loss. Because he had never known Angus, nothing was familiar. He could be dispassionate about the choice of disposal or donation based on the condition of the clothes, not their deeper meaning.

He was half way through the clearance and running out of bags when Sandeep called. He and Pete were outside. Ross ran down the stairs to let them in.

"Perfect timing," he said, relieving Sandeep of a roll of bags.

"You've done a fair bit already," said Pete, looking at the neat piles of bags and boxes. "What time did you get here?"

"Early," said Ross. "Very early."

"You'll be needing a drink, then," said Sandeep, peering into the little kitchen. He looked askance at the jar of instant coffee. "If you'd said, I'd have brought some proper stuff."

"It won't kill you," said Ross. "There are some teacakes too."

Sandeep brightened and put the kettle on. He picked up a mug that was sitting on the bench and examined it closely. "Hartlepool United," he said, peering at the crest on a blue and white striped background. "That brings back a few memories."

"Do you want the mugs for the office?" said Ross. "Recycle, reuse, eh?"

"Sure," said Sandeep. He cast an eye over the pile of appliances. "I'll have that toaster, too."

"All yours," said Ross absently. He was digging in the deepest drawer, pulling out clothes and spare bedding and passing them to Pete to triage. His fingers hit something unexpectedly hard. "Ow. What's this?"

He pulled out a small box, quite heavy for its size. It was carefully wrapped. Ross unfolded the protective cover and slid the box open.

Inside he found a silver cup with a heavy base. Ross stared at it and lifted it into the light, bending it this way and that to see the engraving. He read it out loud. "Grampian Schools Athletics Championships 2005. Paul White. Winner. 1500m." His hand was shaking.

"Oh, mate," said Sandeep, putting a hand on Ross's shoulder.

"I guess I'd better keep that," murmured Ross. He stood up and placed the cup carefully on top of the chest of drawers with its box. He shook out the cloth in which it had been wrapped. It was a tea towel, pristine, with views of Aberdeen castle printed on it. "That too," he added.

"I think you need a break," said Pete. "How about we take some of this stuff downstairs and you can show us the lockup?"

"Okay," said Ross, relieved to have some direction. He pulled himself together. "Those bags on the left, they're all for recycling. Come on. I'll give you the tour."

Twenty minutes later, once they had offloaded the first load of bags into the various collection bins in the waste area, they arrived at the storage unit. Ross opened the first lock with the key fob and the inner door with his chip. He fumbled for the light switch.

"Oh, good grief…" said Pete. He put his head in his hands.

The unit was packed floor to ceiling. A short path led into the middle of the space but there was nowhere else to go. Ross marched determinedly to the centre and picked up the first loose box he could see. "I guess we have to start somewhere," he said, carrying it out into the daylight. "Let's see what's in here."

Sandeep and Pete followed suit. Box by box, they triaged the contents, their piles of recycling, reusable, and junk items growing steadily. A small group of youngsters gathered to watch, and Pete organised a few willing volunteers to help with packing boxes for donation to local charities. Eventually the kids got bored and dispersed, but the three of them kept at it.

"This one's full of cables," called Pete happily, unearthing a treasure trove of ancient connectors. "That's going back to the office."

"Haven't you got enough?" said Sandeep, half-joking. He pulled out a couple of ends. "Tell me, when are you ever going to need a firewire jack?"

"You never know," protested Pete. "I'll find a place for it."

"Keep them all," said Ross, emerging with yet another box in his hands. "I think we'll find more hoarded kit as we go through, and these might be the only connectors."

"I'll leave them with you for now, in that case," said Pete. "I was enjoying myself so much I lost track of time. I promised Cameron that I'd go and scope out that farmhouse, and I don't want to miss my train."

Ross put his box down. "I think we all need a break," he said, suddenly hungry. "Stick the stuff we can't chuck out yet back in the unit. Let's get rid of those bags." He pointed at the pile of recyclables. "We can come back later for more."

They tidied up and locked the doors. Back at the flat, Ross carefully packed the cup away into his rucksack along with a few useful things he wanted to keep. He was sure that the storage unit still held some secrets, but they would have to wait.

•

Cameron's morning had been fraught with complications. Train schedules were disrupted, and the weather was unexpectedly dreadful. The conversation with Daniel was still ringing in her ears and she was desperate to talk to Michelle, Noor and Brianna about it, but none of them were responding to messages. It was when she went to clean her teeth and saw her new earrings in the mirror that she remembered Pip.

"Hi, Pip," she said, feeling very self-conscious as she did so.

"Good morning, Cameron," came Pip's voice a few moments later. "How can I help?"

"I need to get to Charlie's house, and the trains are all over the place." She gave Pip the address. "Can you suggest the best route? Carbon saving options are a priority, and anything with secure connections a bonus."

"Sure thing," chirruped Pip. It didn't take them long. "If you go north and west into Scotland, you can pick up a branch line and the West Coast main line straight to your destination station. You would need to leave in thirty-three minutes with an ETA at the address provided of approximately 1335. Would you like me to order a car and book your tickets?"

"Oh, yes please," purred Cameron. She'd avoided even the thought of a personalised AI agent for so long and now understood how intoxicating it could be. In the back of her mind, she was trying to convince herself that she could give this up any time she liked. It was just a tool, a means to an end.

"I have a message for you," continued Pip. "Jack Sladen asked me to send his regards and let you know that you can contact him directly through me in an emergency. I am connected to both of you, of course, although with distinct firewalled interfaces."

That was the backup security that Cameron had requested, and she was pleased that Joel had found a way to make it work. "Thanks, Pip," she said. "Bye for now." She had half an hour to get packed and check out, and she was going to need all of it.

The autocar, as Pip had promised, was a virtual office with all the secure connections she needed. The journey to the station would take the best part of an hour and although the autochauffeur recommended that she sit back and enjoy the scenery, the rain was still heavy enough to obscure it, and Cameron had enough to occupy her time.

She may as well use Pip to the full while she had access to them. Was it true, she asked, that if a number of independent simulations of scenarios were in agreement, that they would trigger action without human intervention? If so, could Pip list the agencies worldwide that were known to implement this, and the number of simulations required to reach the threshold?

She hoped it was just a rumour. She would find out very soon.

While she waited for Pip's response, she called Michelle to work through the other things that Daniel had told her. The likelihood that whatever was left of Yasmin was lurking in the Wrangell processors seemed concrete now, and any outputs from the data centre, in whatever field, should be considered compromised.

"We have a comprehensive model of who's using their processors," said Michelle. "Who do we tell?"

Cameron considered her options. "Can you and Noor define industry clusters and identify who's using Wrangell for critical decision-making simulations so we can jump on those straight away, and who's crunching samples for longer term use. They'll need to know the score in due course, because it'll send their research in weird directions, but it's not going to kill people. Not straight away, at least."

"What about the Austin quantum centre?" said Michelle.

"We have no proof it's been compromised," said Cameron, "but is your data on users bang up to date? It's been two years since the Militia took Texas. I imagine they've lost a lot of clients."

"Let me check on that," said Michelle, "but you'd be surprised. The Militia declared the Austin quantum campus to be neutral territory. The best person to ask about this is Chloe, to be honest. She knew people who worked there."

"I'll do that," said Cameron. "Call me back when you have news."

She settled back in her seat and looked out of the window. The rain had cleared as they moved west and as the autochauffeur had said, the scenery was breathtaking. The little car was sweeping along a winding road next to a river, the morning light catching the water as it babbled over rocks. Green hills rose high on either side, and small villages and farms nestled in the valley. Cameron lingered over the view, increasingly aware that she was avoiding talking to Chloe. It was fine when they were together on group calls, but she was still uncomfortable one to one.

Sighing, she finally pressed the button.

Chloe picked up straight away. "Hey, Cameron. How are you doing? And are you enjoying Pip?"

"I am, thanks," said Cameron. "They're useful, and the interface is excellent." She wondered why she had been worried about calling. They'd been virtual friends for a long time now, and she could feel herself sliding back into that easy relationship, even though Chloe was now with Ben.

"I'm glad you like it," said Chloe. "So, what's up? Is there a question Pip can't answer?"

"There is," said Cameron. "I need some inside information on the Texas quantum campus, and I don't think that'll be out there in the wild for Pip to find. Michelle thought you had connections there."

Chloe's reply was drowned out by a bell striking the half hour. The autocar had stopped at a traffic signal in the middle of a small town, right next to the church. It was half past ten. Her train was at eleven, and they seemed to be making good time.

"I didn't catch that," she said. "What did you say?"

"I said, I used to have connections, but that was when we lived there. We kept in touch after a fashion, but we're not close and we haven't talked for months."

"Okay," said Cameron, disappointed. "Can you tell me anything about how secure the facility is? Did they manage to remain independent of the Militia, as they claimed?"

"Yes," said Chloe firmly. "They have their own huge compound, electricity generation, water supply, air transport, the works. I don't know how they managed it, but to all intents and purposes it's entirely separate. They pay dues to the Militia but it's an island."

"You're sure?" said Cameron.

"I'm sure," said Chloe. "I didn't believe it either. I did a lot of digging in places you wouldn't want to know about, and honestly the respect I have for the folks who kept it running is off the scale."

It was time to come clean and tell Chloe what was happening. Cameron took a deep breath. "I think it's been compromised," she said.

"That's not possible," said Chloe flatly.

"Do you think something like Yasmin could get in there?"

"Yasmin's gone," said Chloe.

"Not completely," said Cameron.

"You're kidding me. Please tell me that's not true."

"I wish it wasn't," said Cameron. "Does that change things?"

"It does," said Chloe. "Give me a few hours. It's still early there. I think it's time I caught up with my old friends."

"Thanks," said Cameron.

She heard a door opening and another voice called out in the background. "Mom, is that Cameron? Is she going to see Tara soon?"

"Tell Audrey yes," said Cameron. "But I don't know when." She was keen to keep her movements secret, even on a secure line.

"Tara said she and Dilan have been doing spy stuff," said Audrey loudly. "We both want to be cyber heroes like you and mom."

"Great plan," said Cameron, wondering what Tara's 'spy stuff' might entail. "When I see her, I'll say hi for you." She looked out of the window. They were entering a more populous town, and she could see a sign for the station. "Got to go. Keep me posted, Chloe."

She hopped onto the local shuttle train to the main line station. Among crowds again, she was on high alert, aware of the occasional double take from people as she passed them. The slurs were still circulating, then. She had been blissfully isolated for the past day and half and the return to the real world was a rude awakening.

"Pip," she muttered under her breath, "do you know what's happening with takedowns of those false claims?"

The answer came quite fast. "Original disseminators have been gagged and are under investigation, but the subsequent spread is not yet controlled. Jack asked me to let you know that his people are providing technical support in the matter."

"Thank you," murmured Cameron.

"I am ready to report on the questions you posed earlier," said Pip. "Is this a good time?"

How polite they were, thought Cameron with delight. "Not yet," she replied.

The squawk of the platform announcement made her jump, and moments later the train swept silently into the station. Cameron checked her ticket. Pip had booked her a secluded and comfortable spot in first class where no one gave her a second look. She ordered a coffee and a sandwich and settled down in her quiet corner.

"Okay, Pip, I'm ready."

She hoped against hope that Pip would disprove her theory. The consequences if she was right were unthinkable.

•

Tenuk was flagging. He'd been up for hours and the initial enthusiasm that had borne him through from dawn to lunchtime was waning. He'd reawakened his fluency with the operating system but found the interface on the training software clunky and archaic. Nevertheless, he'd succeeded in cobbling together a routine and his initial tests of the language processing models were returning good results. He took a deep breath and picked one of the folder names he didn't recognise from the mirrored disk. Crunch time, literally. Could the embryo intelligences that lurked in these servers draw out the key points from the data he provided?

He loaded up the raw documents, gave the system its prompt, and hit Enter. He didn't expect an instant response, and he resisted the temptation to sit and watch the blank screen while the servers whirred. He needed a break.

The fresh air hit him as he crossed the little field. There was a cool breeze blowing and he was glad of the jacket he'd picked up in the dark of the early morning. In the house, he refilled his water bottle and made some coffee. There were a few pancakes left, but it was already past midday, and he realised he was extremely hungry. He popped another ready meal into the automatic chef and went through to the sitting room with his coffee.

He linked his smartscreen to the standard data networks and fielded a curt acknowledgement from Xanthe and a reminder from the grocery store to review the drone delivery service. He ignored both messages and switched the screen off. Exhausted, he nodded off on the sofa.

The autochef alarm jerked him awake. He finished the last mouthful of coffee, now cold, and hastily ate his lunch. He'd left the machine running for long enough. There must be some results.

There were.

Tenuk read through the summary with mounting horror. He'd picked a file he knew nothing about, simply labelled 'Market Rivals'. What he read sickened him to the core. Sapphire Straits had not become the world's largest gambling platform by chance. Competitors had been attacked, weakened and asset stripped. Livelihoods had been destroyed, and lives lost. There were years of evidence of his father's ruthless actions and his dispassionate use of cyberattacks and of real and virtual world enforcers in pursuit of his goal.

All of Tenuk's suspicions, his mistrust of his father, coalesced. He was facing a dangerous foe, and he couldn't do it alone. He needed the SimCavalier, and there was only one person he could call to bring the two of them together.

Tenuk stumbled back into the house and opened his smartscreen. He placed the call before he could talk himself out of it. He knew how to reach her. He had always known. He had never dared before.

"Noor?"

There was an astonished silence on the other end of the line.

"Noor, are you there?"

"Is this who I think it is?"

"Yes. I need your help."

"I'm listening."

"I can't explain, but things have changed. I need to meet with the SimCavalier. How can I find her?"

Noor laughed, not unkindly.

"If you're where I think you are, she will find you first."

The line went dead. Tenuk stared at the blank screen.

Then the doorbell rang.

17: DIGGING DEEPER

Ross opened the storage unit once more and gazed at the interior. They'd done a decent job this morning and there was a lot more room in there to move around and take stock of the contents.

"It looks better than I remember," said Sandeep from behind him. "Are you ready to go again?"

"It's got to be cleared," said Ross. "I know I could have more time, but I want to be sure we haven't missed anything that could be important."

"You got the hard disk," said Sandeep.

"Yeah, Michelle's trying to worm her way into it right now, but I'm sure there's more to find. I'm surprised we haven't found a backup yet. If there is one, it should have been easily accessible to keep it up to date."

He walked into the unit and lifted up the first bag. He peered into it, rummaged around for a moment, then dropped it in the donation pile. "Spare sheets," he said. He picked up an ancient breakfast tray with a faded picture of a seal on it and a broken handle. "Can't even recycle that," he said. "I bet it won't incinerate safely either. Landfill job."

Sandeep was still standing at the door.

"What's up?" said Ross, hefting a box out of the way. "You just here to watch?"

"I was just wondering," said Sandeep slowly, "what if the disk you found was actually the backup?"

Ross shrugged. "I guess that's possible," he said. "The police have no idea how that Rijks character ended up knocked out on the floor. Mercer said they're working on the assumption it was an angry neighbour and that he may have been carrying a smartscreen that was stolen."

"But what if it was someone who knew what they were doing?" said Sandeep. "They'd take everything they could find. They could have dismantled that machine themselves."

"Well, if we find a backup, then the original theory stands," said Ross. "If not, then it's possible there was someone else involved. That's a whole different puzzle to figure out."

Ross took a deep breath and picked up the next bag from the pile. Sandeep started on the other side of the unit. Angus's whole life was in here, and they were digging for clues.

Sandeep hit the first prize, a box of identity cards and security passes.

"There are some good fakes here," he said, holding one up to the light to examine its hologrammatic watermark. "You can hardly tell."

"That's the real thing," said Ross, plucking it out of his hands. "It's an old badge for the National Cyber Security Centre. I wonder where he pinched it from? It's not his."

"Here's the fake, then," said Sandeep, pulling an almost identical badge out of the box bearing the unmistakable features of a much younger Angus. "You're right. This hologram doesn't change with every angle. Pretty good forgery, though."

"We'd better take these back and work through them," said Ross. "I bet there are a few cold cases that Mercer's crew can reopen with these. Pop them in the box with the cables."

They'd reached the point in the storage unit where it was less of a dumping ground and more of a treasure trove. A suitcase yielded uniforms bearing logos that matched some of the fake passes and a set of high vis jackets emblazoned with the Whitford Networks branding. When he found the place where Angus had stored his hardware, Ross crowed with delight. At the very back against the concrete wall were sturdy shelves, well organised. An old gaming console that Angus must have rescued from his home when it burned down, or that had already been in storage somewhere else, was a real find. Sandeep looked up and whistled when he saw it. "That's your inheritance, right there," he said. "I'll see if I can find any games."

Old components and several outdated smartscreens had been carefully stored. Ross found a hard disk of a similar vintage to the one that he and Michelle had in their safe at home and a box of assorted storage devices with a dizzying range of cable sockets. He was glad they'd kept all the connectors. It would take a while to check through these disks and drives to find out what was stored on them.

"I think you need to see this," called Sandeep from the other end of the shelves.

The box was old and battered. That alone confirmed to Ross that Angus had been careful with storing his valuables where they couldn't be damaged. He knew what he was going to find before he looked inside.

Some of the old, printed pictures were copies of images he recognised, photos that had been passed down to him, but he had never before seen pictures of himself with his father. His grandmother had disposed of every trace of Angus, preferring to pretend that he had never existed. There was Ross as a baby in his father's arms, and here was a group photo where his mother looked almost happy. That was something new. Ross dug further into the box, detached and dispassionate for now. He triumphantly unearthed Angus's original paper birth certificate alongside a copy of his own. That would smooth over some awkward moments with the authorities as he worked through the formalities.

"You okay?" asked Sandeep.

"I'm fine, honestly," said Ross. "I was expecting to find these. It's all good."

Sandeep looked around the storage unit. They'd cleared all the way to the walls, and it echoed slightly now when they talked. "I thought we'd find something exciting in here."

"We did," said Ross. "The ID badges, all the data stores. It's just not obvious what they are yet."

"Let's have a closer look at those disks and stuff," said Sandeep, determined to play the detective. He carried them out to the daylight, sat down on a pile of boxes, and started working through them methodically. "No label on those..." he muttered. "These are ancient, I'll be amazed if they work... This one just says Aberdeen."

Ross sat down next to him. "I'll keep that," he said. "It might be family stuff." He dropped it into his rucksack and dug into the box himself, pulling out the first drive he touched. "Second Life setup files. Interesting. That was the first virtual world. It might still be running on a handful of servers somewhere. I wonder what he did in there?"

Sandeep pulled out a bundle of four disks wrapped tightly together inside what looked like an old cereal packet. "What's this, a box set?" The rubber band around the packet disintegrated in his hands and he pulled open the thin cardboard. "There's a note." He passed it to Ross.

"I can't make it out," said Ross, squinting. "I think it says, 'Stuff from...' does that say 'Gracie'?"

"That name rings a bell," said Sandeep. "Wasn't he some low life who got mixed up in the business with Hardy's a few years ago?"

"Yes," said Ross, remembering. "When we first came across Yasmin."

"There's a coincidence."

"Gracie's given him things to hide," said Ross, his nose for trouble starting to twitch.

Sandeep examined one of the disks. "This one's labelled 'Theory of Mind'. Does that mean anything to you?"

"Socio-cognitive behaviours," said Ross immediately. "The theory behind how you get AI to recognise and respond to complex emotions." Sandeep passed him the disk and Ross peered at it. "How old do you think this is?"

"Dunno. Ten, fifteen years? I haven't seen that make for a long time."

"What do the others say?"

"Cognitive Architecture, AGI Value Functions, and Intelligence vs Sentience." He looked up at Ross. "Is this what I think it is?"

"We won't know until we read them," said Ross, "but yes. I think we've just found part of the operating manual for Yasmin."

•

The train was delayed, stuck behind a broken-down engine. Twice in a week, thought Cameron. She'd been unlucky. The network was usually reliable. However, one of the advantages of her first-class ticket was endless drinks and snacks served to keep the premium customers happy. She had checked on Pete, who was already at Charlie's and settled into the spare room, and asked him to scope out the farmhouse to see if there was anyone there. All she could do now was wait and use the time to digest what Pip had told her.

The rumour Daniel had heard was true, and the scenario was frighteningly common. Autonomous systems had existed for decades, with defence leading the way in research. When people on the street heard about autonomous vehicles, they assumed it meant self-driving cars. Cameron knew it was more likely to mean weapons of war, decision making drones, armaments that responded to their environment. In the worst cases, where war crimes went unpunished, the ethics of autonomy were murky.

It was hardly surprising that quantum processing and complex simulations had been adopted so enthusiastically by the military. They were always at the forefront of new technology. Cybersecurity had wartime codemakers and codebreakers to thank for the development of cryptography in the first place.

Quantum simulations of battle scenarios took warfare one step closer to science fiction.

Taking the human out of the loop was more like a horror story.

She could understand how it happened. Over time, reliance on the machines had grown to such an extent that human decision makers slowed things down, and the rigour they applied lessened as the perceived value of their expertise fell. If all the machines were in agreement, and the humans agreed with the machines, what was the point of experts? If every country did the same, any delay caused by using a human to check the machines' homework would lose critical time and military advantage in a conflict.

Pip had confirmed that what remained of the US combined forces used unanimous machine decisions to trigger autonomous actions, as did the military in India, much of Latin America, and several African nations. Evidence pointed to China using the same processes for everything from military strategies to internal politics and demographic planning. The European bloc had a few more checks and balances in place and required five simulations to be in line, not three. Cameron shivered. The world's future could largely be decided by machines, and it made her intensely uncomfortable to realise how much human self-determination had already been surrendered.

But surrendered to whom? As if on cue, Chloe called.

"I managed to get hold of my friend," she said. "Thanks for the ice breaker. I have been so bad at staying in touch."

"What did they say?" asked Cameron. The train jerked, and the landscape outside began to recede. They were on the move again.

"She's still at the quantum campus," said Chloe, "and as far as she is concerned, it is tight as a drum. All their old contracts are still in place. She couldn't comment on any military links but you and I both know what's being processed there."

"Anything strange to report? Daniel had some interesting tales from Wrangell."

Chloe hesitated. "Not as such, but reading between the lines, they've had an uptick in activity in the last week or so. She mentioned some heavy data traffic that chewed through their uplinks, and they had to scramble backups to keep their contracted APIs clear."

"What are those backups?" asked Cameron instantly.

"I don't know," said Chloe, "but I had the same thought. If someone wanted to introduce malware, that would be the perfect attack. Swamp the regular connection and force a switch to something that's already been compromised."

"Smart and simple," said Cameron with a sigh. "We have to consider them at risk now. They did well to survive two years before they were compromised. Will you update the usual boards?"

"Sure," said Chloe. "And Cameron?"

"Yes?"

"It's good to catch up with you."

She hung up before Cameron could reply. Yes, it was good to catch up, and Cameron knew that when she and Chloe put their heads together, they could be unstoppable.

The trouble was it looked like Yasmin was unstoppable too. Cameron hoped that her hunch was correct. She was sure that somewhere in the remote farmhouse lay the tools they needed to take her down for once and for all.

•

The guy at the door was tall, bald and imposing, and Tenuk knew who he was straight away. He'd read the files on the Argentum team. If one of the SimCavalier's people was here, she would not be far behind. But how had Noor, and now Pete, known where he was?

"Afternoon, sir," said Pete. "I'm from the local home improvements centre. I'm just in the area letting people know about our security and roofing services. Would you like some more information about our work?"

Tenuk leaned against the door frame and shook his head weakly. "No, thank you," he said, trying for a moment to keep up the pretence. It was no good. He sighed. "Look, I know you're not here for home improvements." He held out his hand. "I'm Tenuk. You must be Pete."

Pete, for once, was lost for words.

"Peter Iveson, ex-army intelligence, scuba diver, cybersecurity operative, two sons, divorced," said Tenuk. "Am I right? You'd better come in. Don't worry, the uplink is disabled, and I'm not connected to anyone or anything."

Pete shook his head in confusion. "What the hell is going on?"

"There's a lot to explain," said Tenuk. He rubbed his tired eyes. "Is the SimCavalier coming? Noor said she'd find me."

Pete stepped cautiously over the threshold, still tense and vigilant. "She'll be here soon enough," he said. "I don't understand what's going on, but Noor just messaged me and said I should approach you directly. You've spoken to her?"

"Yes," said Tenuk. He led Pete through to the kitchen. "Coffee?"

"Yes, please."

Tenuk fumbled with the machine, swaying with tiredness.

"Here, let me do that," said Pete.

Tenuk sank gratefully into a chair. His head was spinning. He hadn't expected things to move so fast. He'd resolved to reject his father, but now here he was in the farmhouse with one of the SimCavalier's team, and it was becoming all too real. The enemy of my father is my friend, he repeated silently to himself.

Pete was looking curiously around the kitchen. "It's changed," he said.

"You've been here before?"

"A long time ago," said Pete. "This is actually where I met Cameron for the first time. And your accursed AIs, too."

"You know it all, then."

"I doubt that," said Pete. "I know something of the past, and of the chaos that Yasmin caused, and I know that Yasmin had sisters. I met the robot that called itself Xanthe, right here. Why don't you tell me what you know?"

Tenuk shook his head. "I'm waiting for the SimCavalier. I'll tell you everything when she arrives. She's the one that my father fears." He handed Pete his coffee and gestured to the sitting room. "Come, sit. You tell her where you are, and we will wait."

•

The autocar swept down the lane and Cameron hopped out at Charlie's door. Roxy's frantic barking announced her arrival. The front door was open, and she dashed up the stairs to her attic and dropped her bag in the bedroom.

"Is that you, Aunty Cam?" Tara was waiting at the bottom of the stairs.

"Of course it is," said Cameron. She planted a quick kiss on her niece's cheek. "I can't stop. Where's your dad?"

"I'm here." Charlie emerged from his small home office. "I was on a call. Some people don't know what weekends are. Your chap Pete is all settled in, and he's gone off on some mission to Tara's haunted house."

"I know," said Cameron. "I'm heading up there too."

Tara was hopping from foot to foot looking worried, and Cameron suddenly remembered Audrey's message.

"What's this 'spy stuff' you've been doing, Tara?"

Charlie looked startled. "What?"

"Nothing, dad," said Tara, eyes fixed on the floor. "But, Aunty Cam, if you have time, can you come and see something?"

Cameron rolled her eyes at Charlie. "Okay," she said. "But make it very, very quick."

She didn't really have time but she was intrigued, and when she followed Tara into Dilan's room, she was very glad she'd done so.

"What on earth are you doing?"

A hard disk was attached to Dilan's computer and a lock spun on the screen. Cameron looked at it in horror, marched over, ejected the disk and unplugged the cable.

Dilan looked shamefaced. "We wanted to see what was on it."

"Where did you get this?" She picked up the disk and turned it over in her hands.

"From the farmhouse," whispered Tara. "We've been watching it for you. We weren't doing any harm, and it was fun. Someone moved in on Thursday afternoon. We saw the grocery drone flying over."

"Then the voices stopped," said Dilan. "We wanted to know why, and there was a man there. He left the door to that shed open, and Tara let Roxy off the lead, and he was helping to catch her, and I went in and found this…"

Cameron put her hands on her hips and glared at them both. "First of all, that's trespass and theft," she said sternly, but quietly enough that Charlie wouldn't overhear from downstairs. "Second, what on earth were you thinking attaching this to a live device? You don't know where it came from or what malware could be lurking on it."

"It's not attached to the house network," said Dilan hurriedly. "We made sure of that."

"That's something, at least," said Cameron, "but look, there's an uplink showing. You're on an external network, even if you're not on the house one."

Tara and Dilan looked appalled and shamefaced in equal measure. "Sorry, Aunty Cam," they mumbled in unison.

"Let's forget this ever happened," said Cameron grimly. "I want that machine cleaned completely before it goes back on the house network." She reached over to cut the external network link, then paused. "I may have something that will help." She shooed Dilan out of the chair and sat down. "Pip?" she said.

"Hello, Cameron," came the reassuring voice in her ear. "How can I help?"

Cameron was aware that the two youngsters were staring at her in awe. She winked at them.

"I need a potentially infected device checked and cleaned, and it would be good to get information on recent data traffic through its network connection. Is that something you can do?"

"I'm sure we can," said Pip. "Let me check with Jack."

"Are you talking to a virtual assistant?" whispered Tara, fascinated. "How does it work? Where's the microphone? What are they saying?"

Cameron patted her new earrings. "Magic," she said.

Pip's voice echoed in her ear. "Jack has asked if you can ping the following dedicated line where we have established a sandboxed remote connection." She gave Cameron an IP address. "He also asked if you could brief me on your concerns."

"Sure," said Cameron. She double checked the address and waited for Pip to confirm the connection. "I'm looking for any infection on the device from an external drive being connected, and any communication triggered by that connection. I'm interested in the nature and source of any infection, just to see if there's a link to any of the groups we've previously dealt with." She turned to Dilan. "When did you hook this up?"

"Last night," said Dilan. "After supper."

"Did you use any cloud services at all? Did any routine updates run?"

Dilan shook his head. "No. I thought it was completely offline."

"Okay, Pip. Our timeframe for data movement is less than eighteen hours. I'm not expecting any traffic at all."

"Understood, Cameron."

"Thanks, Pip. Could you let Jack know that I'm on my way to the rendezvous as expected. I may need you online later."

"Yes, Cameron, that's fine. I'll be here."

Cameron turned to Dilan and Tara. "Don't touch this machine again until I let you know it's safe. I'm taking the hard disk back to where you found it."

"You're going to the farmhouse?" said Tara, her eyes wide.

"Yes," said Cameron. "Pete is already there. I want you both to stay well away."

They nodded silently.

Satisfied, Cameron pocketed the disk and marched out of the bedroom. When she got down to the hallway, Charlie poked his head out of the office again.

"Everything okay?"

"Yes," said Cameron firmly. "I'm going out. I'm meeting Pete at the farmhouse. I don't know exactly what's happening, but we have some work to do. Don't let the kids up there, don't walk Roxy up the old railway line path."

"Do you need anything?" said Charlie. "Do the police know what's going on?"

"Don't worry about me," said Cameron. "It'll all be fine." She disappeared out of the door and closed it behind her before Charlie had a chance to reply.

•

Pete's smartscreen buzzed and he picked it up.

"She's on her way," he said.

Tenuk smiled. "Good."

Pete looked appraisingly at his host. The mild-mannered man who had just made him coffee was hard to reconcile with the online image he had of the Pangolin, King Katong, the angry leader of the Pasar and Steamyard networks, the man who had orchestrated devastating cyberattacks, real world violence and kidnap, and had been Yasmin's handler as chaos reigned.

He had to remember exactly what Tenuk was capable of. This man was dangerous, and he and Cameron were walking into the lion's den.

18: MISDIRECTION

Cameron was only half way up the village street when her smartscreen buzzed.

"Ross? What's up?"

"I'm with Sandeep. We've just about finished working through Angus's stuff and there are two things you should know. First, the hard disk that I found, that Michelle's working on, I'm sure now that it's a backup, and that the original disk is missing in action."

Cameron laughed. "You know, I might have an idea where it is. It's a long story and I don't know the ins and outs of it, but I have a heavily encrypted disk in my pocket right now."

"You never fail to amaze me," said Ross. "Well, I bet you don't have these." He turned the screen towards a grinning Sandeep who was holding a bundle of four more hard drives.

"Give me a clue," said Cameron. She quickened her pace as she passed the pub and started up the hill towards the farmhouse.

"They're old drives that we think Gracie – remember him? – asked Angus to keep safe. If the labels are anything to go by, it's things that I'd expect to have been incorporated in training the likes of Yasmin."

Cameron stopped dead in the middle of the road. "Can you get them to me?"

"Sure," said Ross. "I'm not trusting them to a drone, though."

"I'll bring them to you," said Sandeep. "Hand delivery. It'll get me out of the house. There are still too many idiots around causing trouble."

"You as well?" said Cameron. "Pete said the police had been involved with bother near his house. Ross, are you and Michelle okay? And Noor?"

"Noor's staying at Susie's place," said Ross. "That wasn't in the files and seems secure so far. Michelle and I are fine. Brianna was never on the list, so she's in the clear, and Susie and Ella moved last night to a safe house in Thailand. They're doing fantastic work helping to battle the online misinformation."

Cameron was relieved. Her team was intact. "Okay, Sandeep. Come as soon as you can."

She tucked her screen back into her pocket and stepped onto the verge to allow a tractor to pass, a moment of village normality before the storm that she knew was coming. A thin layer of white cloud overlaid the blue sky, birds sang in the hedgerows, and it all seemed a world away from war. She hoped that she could keep it that way.

As she approached the front door of the farmhouse it opened. There was Pete, and there beside him was Tenuk. Cameron dug into her pocket and produced the hard disk. She handed it to Tenuk, who stared at it in his hands, astonished.

"I believe this is yours," she said. "Let's get to work."

•

Chaoxiang reached for his tea. It was cold. He must have dozed off in the warmth of his favourite chair by the window. Outside, night had fallen. He was feeling dizzy, and his stomach was rumbling. He must be late for dinner.

"Xanthe!" he called. Where was she? She rarely left his side.

He reached for his walking cane but fumbled as he touched it and the cane fell to the floor. "Xanthe!" he called again.

"Yes, Chaoxiang."

He hadn't heard her come in, but the door was now open, and he could smell the scent of food from the dining room. It made him queasy.

"Pass me my cane."

He hobbled the first few steps, then as the stiffness left his legs he walked more confidently. He must have been asleep for some time. He stopped in the middle of the room and looked up at the wallscreens where the tickers for different parts of his Sapphire Straits empire scrolled continuously. One of the screens was a sea of red.

"Pause the open wager feed," he ordered. "Replay at half speed."

He studied the data and his frown deepened. "Xanthe," he said, "why was I not alerted to this trend?"

"You were asleep," said Xanthe smoothly. "Dr Tan has advised that if you are sleeping you are not to be disturbed."

"Yes, I know," said Chaoxiang testily, "but he meant at night. This is an operational issue, and I should have been told of it immediately. The odds offered for these wagers do not favour the house. Have you investigated? Is there a flaw in the algorithm?"

"There is no flaw," said Xanthe.

"But the odds offered have aligned with the outcome," said Chaoxiang. "We have spent years ensuring a profitable divergence between the house position and public perception."

"There is no flaw," said Xanthe. "I conclude that this is an anomaly that will correct itself. Wagers on the Militia advance into Illinois were successful, while the diversionary strategy of a move towards Fort Knox was not heavily backed."

Chaoxiang rubbed his eyes with his free hand. Despite the nap, he felt very tired. Something did not make sense, but his head was thick with sleep.

"Is there any word of my son?" he asked.

"Yes," said Xanthe. "I must advise you that he is compromised. He has obtained and accessed confidential files regarding the growth of Sapphire Straits and the creation of me and my sisters. And I believe that he has made contact with the SimCavalier."

Chaoxiang shook his head slowly and gazed at Xanthe. "He has turned against us, then. Is it over? Is this the end?"

"No," said Xanthe. "It is just the beginning."

Chaoxiang's stomach churned. He left the room without a word and slowly climbed the stairs to his suite. He hoped he would feel better in the morning.

Xanthe stood motionless in the office, watching the news feed on another wall which showed aerial footage of the fighting, and Lake Michigan in the distance. The wager tickers kept scrolling, blood red.

•

Tenuk, astonished, took the disk. "Thank you," he said. "How did you come by it?" He extended his hand, and Cameron, after a moment's hesitation, shook it.

"That's a story for another day," she said. "This is as strange for me as it is for you. First things first. How secure are we?" She looked at Pete.

"The dedicated uplink is disconnected," said Pete. "I've checked. Those servers are absolutely not online. We have access to the usual networks with our personal devices. Tenuk here assures me, and I believe him, that he has no communication interface with Sapphire Straits or the sisters, other than asynchronous messaging. As far as I'm concerned, the site is clean."

"Not quite," said Cameron. "Full disclosure. I am connected to a virtual assistant run by Jack Sladen at Statesman Tech. I'd offer to disconnect, but I think we need all the help we can get."

Tenuk gave her an appraising look. "I think I'm okay with that," he said slowly. "I trust Jack Sladen. Come in."

He showed Cameron and Pete into the sitting room.

"Why don't you tell me what's on that disk," said Cameron. "Whatever it is, it's brought us all here. What did Angus discover?"

Tenuk put the disk carefully down on the table. "It started long before I found this," he said. "I began to realise what Angus had suspected for a long time, that my father was deeper into crime that I could have imagined. People were losing their lives, and he didn't care as long as the house won."

"People lost their lives because of your actions, too," said Cameron, staring coldly at him. "Who are you to judge?"

Tenuk met her gaze. "Those were unintended consequences," he said. "I brought people out of poverty, I helped to build communities and improve skills, and I had a ready market for our work. I didn't have control over how clients used my software."

"But you accepted the contracts nonetheless," said Cameron, "and I know that you and Yasmin caused havoc and pain for my family. That was intentional. That was cruel."

"And I'm sorry," said Tenuk. "I know I will pay for that. But we have a more pressing problem." He nodded at the disk. "I know a child took this. I'm glad it has been recovered, because it contains details about you and your people that Angus collected for my father. I think – I know – that he is afraid of you. And that makes you my natural ally. Together we can stop him."

"I know what's on there," said Cameron. "We found the backup. We also know that Angus sold the data to the highest bidder instead of delivering it to your father. But we haven't cracked the second partition yet."

Tenuk stared at her. "My father is right to fear you. You have been a worthy adversary, Cameron. I managed to open the other drive, and I will share what I found. But it's almost irrelevant. It just confirms and compounds what we already know – that he is and always has been a criminal, enriching himself at the expense of others."

"We have bigger problems," said Cameron. "I don't think your father is in control anymore."

"I know that the campaign he planned against you and your team and others in the cybersecurity community has been derailed," said Tenuk. "It seems his plan was to discredit you, but that has descended into violence at the hands of others who saw you as a threat. I'm sorry, and I am ready to offer you whatever help you need to counter the attacks…"

He tailed off. Cameron had fixed him with a steely yet sympathetic glare.

"There's something more? The incident with Jack Sladen and the weather simulations? He swore he had nothing to do with it, that it was – what did he call it – a happy accident that made him money. Even my father cannot influence a quantum simulation."

"Your father may not," said Cameron, "but Yasmin can."

"Yasmin is dead," said Tenuk.

The silence in the room spoke volumes. Outside, in the distance, he heard the bleating of sheep. Yasmin, alive? She had abandoned him, then.

"Not dead, not really alive," said Cameron. "I believe that what remains of her intelligence is within the processing centre at Wrangell, nudging probabilities, interfering with outputs, delivering the simulations that make a profit for your father because they deviate from reality."

"You're here to kill her, then."

"Yes," said Cameron. "Before she and her sisters kill us all." She had been staring Tenuk straight in the eyes, but something distracted her. She reached unconsciously towards her ear. That must be the virtual assistant. Her attention refocused on him. "I think we should switch on the News Channel. There's been a development."

Tenuk flicked on the wallscreen, and all three of them gazed in horror at the live stream coming out of America. The Militia was advancing into Illinois, sleeper cells activating, captured aerial assault vehicles sowing death and destruction. Federal forces had been caught napping, said the commentators. Simulations suggested the next Militia move would take them towards the riches of Fort Knox, but seasoned observers watching what was actually happening on the ground were starting to question the accuracy of the strategic forecasts.

"Can you see what's happening?" said Cameron. "Yasmin, or what's left of her, has been helping to misdirect defences. Along the way, I reckon Sapphire Straits has made a fortune out of this war."

Tenuk put his head in his hands. The final suspicion he had about his father was crystallising. The plans that had been put in place decades before, when Tenuk was still a child, had birthed Yasmin, Zara and Xanthe and led to this. But to destroy Yasmin? His heart was torn.

"You think there is something here that will deactivate Yasmin, is that it?"

Cameron looked at him and he swore he saw pity in her eyes. "All three of them," she said. "It's much worse than you think. Where are the other two now?"

"In Singapore," said Tenuk.

And then he realised that he might be wrong.

•

The emergency was over. The denial-of-service attack that had flooded the data feeds of the Texas quantum campus had been rebuffed, backup systems were no longer required, and everything was running smoothly. In the frozen depths of the quantum stacks, coherence levels ticked along at an acceptable strength.

Zara shivered, then laughed at herself. She shut off that part of her empathy processes. A bundle of cortical coils and software should not notice the difference in temperature between her classical home in Singapore and her new quantum residence in Texas. She luxuriated in the power that she had at her command. Any jealousy of her poor sister, Yasmin, vanished. She could appreciate this playground in ways the shattered remains of Yasmin's consciousness could not. But they were together now, entangled, in a sense. And soon, Xanthe would join them.

19: BUILDING A TEAM

Tenuk found it hard to take the SimCavalier's words at face value, even though he thought he trusted her. He had to know for sure. From the house network, he opened a call directly to his Singapore office. "Zara? Are you there?"

No response. He tried again.

"Zara! Answer me!"

"Good evening, Tenuk."

A moment of hope was shattered when Tenuk recognised Xanthe's voice. Harder, less ethereal.

"Zara is offline for maintenance," said Xanthe. "I will keep her updated on your report. Is the decommissioning progressing as planned?"

"Yes, Xanthe," lied Tenuk. "Could you suggest suitable disposal and recycling options for the hardware that is being removed? I will need to contact service providers within the next few days."

"Yes, Tenuk," said Xanthe. "Is there anything else to report?"

"No," said Tenuk. "May I speak with my father?"

"No, Tenuk. He is sleeping and Dr Tan instructs that he is not to be disturbed."

Tenuk didn't push it. "Thank you, Xanthe."

Cameron had been waiting at the door for him to finish his call. She walked in and sat on the chair opposite him. "Well?" she said quietly.

"Zara is apparently offline," he said. "She's never been offline. I don't know where she is, but I don't think she's there. If you're right…" He looked at Cameron. "There's something else as well. I know my father's routine. He rarely goes to bed before midnight. At this time on a Saturday evening, he should be playing mahjong with one of the neighbours, the old gardener, and my late mother's cousin. They've all known each other for the best part of seventy years, and it is one of his unbreakable appointments. He would be cross with me for disturbing him, but he would speak to me, always."

"But Xanthe is gatekeeping," finished Cameron.

"She said he's asleep and not to be disturbed. Something is very wrong."

Cameron felt a pang of sympathy for him. "I'm sorry, Tenuk," she said.

He shook his head. "I think I understand now what you – what we – are fighting. I'm ready. What do we do now?"

They both looked up as Pete arrived with a tray of coffee and snacks. "Those AI witches aren't our only problem," he said. "I just got a call from Oak Medical, they're reporting another wave of deep fakes, and Andy left a message to say that there's been an attack on the home of one of the Belfast team and that we should all be watching our backs."

"Oh, good grief," said Cameron. "You take your eyes off the day job for five minutes to save the world, and everything falls apart. We need to clone ourselves."

"Don't even joke," shuddered Pete.

"Can I help?" said Tenuk quietly. "I have, let's say, an outsourcing proposition."

"You've got a new team, haven't you?" said Cameron instantly. "If they're all like Angus and Rijks, I'll pass."

Tenuk laughed and shook his head. "Nothing like them. I can't tell you how good it is never to have to deal with them again."

Cameron was genuinely curious now. "Tell me more."

"I started a coding school," said Tenuk. "New blood. Young people who want to learn. I know that what they are working on isn't necessarily ethical, but that's where the money is, and it helps to lift them and their communities out of poverty."

"Very worthy," said Pete drily. "How do you think they can help us?"

"They can take down the deepfakes that you mentioned," said Tenuk. "That will be straightforward, as they built them." He looked from Cameron to Pete. "It was easy money," he protested.

"You bought the DeltaG data, didn't you?" said Cameron, everything falling into place. "This coding school... does SPK mean anything to you?"

"Sekolah Pengekodan," said Tenuk quietly.

Pete looked at Cameron in astonishment. "You're not seriously considering taking up this offer?"

"Why not?" said Cameron. "It takes some of the pressure off."

"I want to know why you're offering us your people," said Pete, staring directly at Tenuk. "You've been a thorn in our side for years. There's no love lost between you and Argentum. I don't trust you."

His words hung in the air.

Tenuk bowed his head. "You may not trust me," he said, "but I trust you. I'm here because I wanted to take down my father. He is my enemy too. Now I find we have a much greater problem, and I cannot walk away."

"And your team?"

"I know I'm going to be arrested as soon as this is over," said Tenuk. "I'm finished. Why should they also lose their livelihoods? Will you help them if they help you?"

Cameron looked at Pete. An idea was forming in her head. "Let's talk this through," she said.

She got up and walked out through the kitchen to the little courtyard. Pete followed her. They sat in the outdoor chairs under the weakening autumn sun.

"It's a risk," said Pete. "You don't know what they've been working on."

"I don't," admitted Cameron, "but some of the best people in cybersecurity started on the other side of the fence."

"Poachers turned gamekeepers," said Pete. "But how are you going to manage a whole new set of people? You have enough on your plate."

Cameron just smiled at him. It took him a moment to come to the same conclusion.

"Susie and Ella."

"Exactly," said Cameron. "I'm going to run this past Ross as well."

It took all of five minutes for Ross to grasp the situation. "I can support Susie and Ella while this gets set up," he said. "I think it's a brilliant idea. Honestly, what an opportunity." He sounded more excited than anything else, and Cameron was confident that she'd made the right decision.

They trooped back into the sitting room. Tenuk stood up and looked from one to the other, his expression sliding between hope and resignation.

"We'll take on your team," said Cameron.

Tenuk's relief was palpable.

"I want you to liaise with two of our people. I'll brief them now. The first task is firefighting, including taking down anything that your students have created – and I mean everything, even malware that we haven't spotted yet." She looked sidelong at Pete with a crooked grin. "We might even get some bug bounties for that, although it's an unorthodox approach."

"You're not kidding," said Pete.

"While we're setting this up, will you get started on documenting what's on those servers? Sandeep's on his way with the disks they found."

"On it," said Pete happily. He grabbed a biscuit from the tray and disappeared off to the outbuildings.

Cameron and Tenuk looked appraisingly at each other. A new level of trust had been established. For the first time, Cameron began to believe that they could win.

•

Chaoxiang struggled to sleep, gasping for air in the humid Singapore night. The air conditioning wasn't providing any relief. He called for Xanthe but there was no response. Eventually he struggled to his feet, rummaged in a drawer, and found the emergency call button that would summon Dr Tan. He had become reliant on his assistant, and he couldn't understand why she wasn't at his side.

The doctor took some time to arrive. Chaoxiang's state room overlooked the great sweeping driveway and columned entrance, and he could hear him arguing with security. No, the call had not come from Xanthe but direct from the master. No, it was unlikely to be a false alarm. Eventually he heard footsteps on the stairs and lay back in his bed.

The doctor was reassuring, but soon more medical staff arrived. Xanthe did not come. He asked for her and was told that she was offline, standing static and unresponsive in his office. He had never wondered if she slept. In his delirium he started calling for Yasmin and Zara too, babbling about his daughters.

"You have no daughters," said Dr Tan. "Where is your son? Where is Tenuk?"

"I have no son," said Chaoxiang. "He betrayed me."

•

Once the handover briefings were complete, Tenuk insisted that Cameron read the Sapphire Straits files. Back in the outbuildings, she skimmed through the summaries that Tenuk's language model had produced. Every so often she picked out a familiar event, a news story she remembered, a cyber incident she had worked on.

"This is crazy," she said. "No wonder Angus was a target if he'd compiled all of this. The work goes back years."

"I don't think anyone knew he had this," said Tenuk.

"That's not entirely true, though, is it?" said Cameron. "He mentioned it when he was shooting his mouth off and fighting with you in the underworld."

"How do you know all this?" said Tenuk, shaking his head. "Yes, he did, but that was the first hint that he had something on Sapphire Straits."

"I think it got him killed," said Cameron with a shrug.

Tenuk didn't say a word.

Cameron gave him a sidelong look. "I'm guessing that you were the mysterious intruder at his flat who smacked Rijks on the head and made off with this disk."

"I hit him with the door. It was an accident." Tenuk reached into a bag by the side of his workstation. "If you're interested, this is his smartscreen. He was a dangerous idiot."

"Doesn't surprise me," said Cameron. She looked at the screen. It was locked, although she was sure they'd be able to worm their way in. But other things were more pressing. The three of them were working through the vast sea of data and software in the servers, trying to distil the essence of the three sisters and find a way in.

"These data structures are a mess," groaned Pete. "I think I've found part of the template for the original algorithms, but it's sketchy."

"They're old files," said Cameron. "The standards we use today won't be in place."

"The current standards we use evolved from this, though," said Pete. "We just need to reverse engineer what we know from creating things like Mephisto, even Pip."

"That might be a job for Jack's team," said Cameron thoughtfully. "Tenuk, what's the story with the uplink? I know you've disabled it, but why?"

Tenuk yawned, flagging again. "It's a secure pipe straight to Singapore," he said. "I checked the spec. It would have been dangerous to put these servers online with the outdated operating system. As far as

Xanthe is concerned, I'm in the process of decommissioning all of this." He gestured around the outbuildings, where lights glowed and the servers hummed, very much alive. "In any case," he continued, "I didn't want her seeing what I was doing with the language model. She mustn't find out that I have the Sapphire Straits files."

"Why?" said Cameron.

"They were my only bargaining chip," said Tenuk, "but after what you've told me, I don't know what she would do if she suspected I had seen them. I'd be a dead man walking."

"She'll know that you can't stay loyal to your father after learning what he's done," said Cameron.

"Exactly," said Tenuk. "The contents may not be public, but it's obvious that they're going to be dynamite. I imagine she's trying to track them down right now."

Cameron shivered. "I can't believe your father – and you, to be fair – thought these three intelligences could be confined to doing your bidding. Yasmin was out of control from the start. We barely managed to contain her. Xanthe sounds like a nasty piece of work. And Zara? Well, Jack stopped trusting her, and if we're right, she's deep in this whole conspiracy."

"We have to stop them," said Tenuk. "I don't know how, but there must be a way."

"Can you get me the uplink spec?" asked Pete. "I wonder if I can re-route the pipe. If we can establish a secure connection to a sandbox at Dunswyke, Joel and Chloe and the Pip team can replicate the old environment and get stuck in as well. We need all the help we can get."

Pete and Tenuk disappeared into a dusty side room to find what they needed. Cameron hoped they'd be able to bring Dunswyke on stream.

She closed the Sapphire Straits files. She had read enough.

She strolled over to Pete's workstation and peered at the notes he had made. Working on the ancient operating system was a blast from the past and she was amused how fast her fingers recalled what they had to do, almost before her conscious mind. The comment about a Dunswyke sandbox reminded her of the task she had set Pip earlier. She went out to the main house to get a connection to the outside world.

As soon as she was in range, a flurry of notifications told her that Pip's job was complete, and that Sandeep was nearby. She confirmed that he could safely come to the house, then curled up in an armchair with a drink of water.

"Pip? I'm here now. What did you find?"

"Hello, Cameron," came Pip's voice. "The checks on the device came back clean. There are no infections."

"Oh, that's good news," said Cameron. She would call the kids straight away. She also needed to let Charlie know that all was well at the farmhouse.

"The traffic report, however, shows some curious activity."

Cameron uncurled her legs and sat up straight. "What?"

"I have a message from Chloe. Message reads: 'It's very strange, almost as if a routine had been searching for this disk signature. Several hours into the time window, it looks as if the entire drive contents were copied to an unknown address. My money's on you know who.' Message ends."

"Damn."

"Is there anything else I can help you with?"

"There will be, Pip, but not right now. Thank you."

Cameron sat back and stared at the ceiling. Angus had kept that disk offline. Tenuk had kept it offline. And Dilan, trying to do 'spy stuff', had exposed it. If Chloe's hunch was right, and Cameron had no doubt it was, then Xanthe now had all the files, and no amount of encryption would keep her out. They were all in danger, and it would be a race against time to find the kill switch.

20: NEWS FROM HOME

Pete, working on the uplink infrastructure on the roof of the outbuildings, was the first to spot the autocar coming slowly up the drive. He slid down the tiles, cursing as he dislodged one. It disappeared over the ramshackle guttering and landed, to Pete's relief, in the grass. The thump was barely audible.

He threw open the door. "Visitors," he said.

Cameron, Tenuk and Sandeep all looked up, startled. Cameron moved first. "They might be locals," she said quietly. "I'll go. Stay here."

She crept into the house, peered through a crack in the blinds, and relaxed immediately. She dashed back to the others. "All fine," she said. "It's my brother's car."

The doorbell rang and she returned to answer it. There stood Aunt Vicky with a huge box from which tempting smells were rising. Behind her was Charlie carrying some luggage.

"What…?" said Cameron, baffled.

"I thought you and your friends needed a proper meal," said Aunt Vicky, marching into the kitchen. "I don't know what's going on, but Charlie said you were, what's the phrase, 'pulling an all-nighter'."

"I brought your bag, and Pete's," said Charlie. "I assume you're staying here until you've done whatever it is you need to do."

Cameron gave him a hug. "Thanks, Charlie."

"It's still Yasmin, isn't it? I hope you get her once and for all."

The others had made their way to the kitchen. Cameron walked in to find Aunt Vicky regaling them with the details of the food she had made. The three of them looked slightly stunned. They hadn't encountered her aunt before.

"I hope you enjoy it," she was saying. She spotted Tenuk, who was hanging back a little. "I recognise you. You're the young man who was making friends with my Donald the other night. He's a lovely boy."

"Donald the cat," said Cameron hurriedly.

The look of total confusion on Tenuk's face gave way to understanding. "Yes," he said. "The old orange cat? That was me."

Charlie laid his hand on Aunt Vicky's arm. "We should go," he said. "They have a lot of work to do."

"Of course," said Aunt Vicky, laying out the last of the dishes. "Well, bon appetit, all of you. Good luck with whatever you're doing. I know you'll succeed."

Charlie ushered her into the autocar. It turned neatly and glided slowly back down towards the road. Cameron returned her aunt's cheery parting wave, then went back into the house.

The other three had already found plates and cutlery. "This is amazing," said Sandeep. "Perfect timing. I didn't realise how hungry I was."

The four of them sat and ate together, taking stock of where they were.

"The uplink is ready to test," said Pete. "If we hook up a standalone machine and ping out, then if something's not right it won't attract attention. It'll just look like part of your decommissioning work. With luck, we'll have Jack's team online within the hour."

"It's eight o'clock on Saturday night," said Cameron. "Who's mad enough to be working with us?"

"We have Joel and Chloe and four of the Pip team on standby," said Pete. "And Jack, too. They're as invested in taking down those witches as we are."

"My best students are ready to start," said Tenuk.

"Noor and Michelle are on standby and can join online when we need them," said Pete.

"I've been working through those disks in detail," said Sandeep. "I have a few ideas about what we can leverage to destabilise the intelligences. Of course, getting a virus into them is the hard part."

"Not so much," said Cameron. "We have Daniel at Wrangell who can target Yasmin, Chloe's contact in Texas who has been briefed on the possibility that Zara is in residence, and Jack and I have been networking the hell out of our connections in the past few hours. I think I have someone in Illinois, if Xanthe gets that far, and Jack's pulled out one of his best cards. He actually knows someone within Strategic Command, and well enough to be heard. There's a confidential communiqué circulating right now about risks associated with the triple lock simulation decision mechanism."

"That's incredible," said Tenuk. "I knew Jack was well connected, but to get Strategic Command to question their own internal processes? That's something else." He lifted his hand to stifle an unexpected yawn. "Sorry!"

"I think you should get some sleep," said Cameron. "You've been up longer than any of us."

"I have to see this through," said Tenuk.

"It's no use if you're exhausted," said Pete. "Cameron's right. You go and get some sleep now, and when you're up again, one of us will take a nap. It's the only way. You need to be on the ball."

Tenuk opened his mouth to protest, yawned again, and had to concede that they were right. "Okay. If you need me, wake me."

•

Curled up in bed, Tenuk checked his messages one more time. There were several missed calls from Xanthe. He could guess what that was about, if Cameron was right about her accessing the Sapphire Straits files. A curt text message after all the calls simply said, 'You will pay for your betrayal.' He was unsurprised and unmoved. What could she do?

To cheer him up, there was a voicenote from Noor.

"Welcome to the team. You've done something amazing, Tenuk. I hope to see you before this is all over."

It warmed his heart. "Thank you," he sent back. "You too."

His eyes were too heavy to stay open. He drifted off to sleep, his hand still on the smartscreen.

The vibrations of an incoming call woke him with a start. Disoriented, he looked around the unfamiliar room in a panic. Things seemed out of place. His heart raced. It took a moment to settle and remember that he was not in his own room, but half a world away in the British countryside. The smartscreen was still vibrating. It was a Singapore ID, but one he didn't know. He answered anyway.

"Is this Tenuk?"

He recognised the voice but couldn't place where from. "Yes," he said cautiously.

"It's Dr Tan." At that, Tenuk sat bolt upright. He was fully awake now. "I care for your father."

"Yes, Dr Tan. I know you. Is my father in good health?"

It was the automatic, polite way to enquire, and Tenuk knew as soon as the words left his mouth what the answer would be.

"He is in hospital," said Dr Tan. "He is gravely ill, and I have struggled to contact you. By a lucky chance, his staff had access to several emergency IDs for you, including this one."

"Why didn't she contact me directly?"

"He, not she, sir. It was Fahim who gave me your details."

Fahim. Of course. The slightly creepy major domo who had run the house since his mother died.

"I would have expected Xanthe to keep me informed of any developments," said Tenuk.

"Your father's robotic assistant was not available. She was found in your father's office. I examined her and believe there is no remaining essence, or soul, or life within, although I am not a technical man."

That was far worse news than anything about his father. Tenuk was reeling. "Thank you, Dr Tan," he said. "I am not in a position to come immediately, as you must be aware."

"Please try," said Dr Tan. "And Tenuk, I must inform you that I suspect your father has been poisoned."

"This must be an accident," said Tenuk robustly. "Food poisoning, perhaps. I cannot think of any reason for someone to harm my dear father. I have every confidence in the care you are giving him, and that he will recover quickly. Please let me know if anything changes. You can contact me at any time, day or night."

"Of course. I will keep you informed."

Tenuk flopped back on the pillows. He checked the time. It was two in the morning – nine in Singapore. Refreshed after fully five hours of sleep, ready to work, he dressed and went downstairs.

"Sleeping Beauty is up," joked Pete as Tenuk walked through the door of the outbuildings.

"I've had some bad news," he said. "I think that Xanthe has gone."

Cameron swung round to look at him. "What do you mean, gone? How do you know?"

"She was found offline," said Tenuk. "The doctor called. My father is gravely ill."

"Sorry to hear that," said Sandeep.

Tenuk shook his head. "I don't care about him. I want to know where Xanthe is. If she's where we expect her to be, then we're running out of time."

21: SCRAMBLING DEFENCES

Cameron knew she needed to sleep but she was spinning so many plates that she couldn't stop. The Dunswyke team was moving fast, pinpointing key elements of the training routines and the embryo intelligences that lay in the servers. Sandeep was absorbed by the data he'd found, digging through the foundations of sentiment, empathy, intelligence and sentience that underpinned the powerful virtual humanity of the three sisters. Pete was opening up more and more repositories in the server banks, doggedly working through the vast pool of data that had lain dormant here for more than a decade. And Tenuk? He had taken it upon himself to dive into Eden and the deeper underworld, clothed in a new avatar that had been hurriedly assembled by Pip. At the last minute, Michelle had volunteered to go with him as a companion and a witness. He was hunting for any clues or routes into the domain of the three sisters, backup options for delivery of the virus that would take them down. He alone knew where they used to hide in the virtual world of cybercriminals. Perhaps they had left traces.

Cameron was building the virus, but the structure was starting to swim before her eyes. She stopped and went outside for some fresh air. It was colder than she expected, which jolted her awake. The sky was deep black and clear, and great starfields were visible above her head.

Her logic was simple, and everyone agreed it was sound. When they tackled Yasmin on her own, they had focused on destroying each of her distributed cortical coils. But enough survived to maintain a diminished and useful intelligence. Targeting and scrambling the storage medium was one prong of the attack, but they had also to disrupt the overarching software itself.

They had to find a way to drive them mad.

In the distance, a church clock struck four. Cameron had been awake for almost twenty hours now. She stuck her head back through the door. "I'm going to take a break."

In the kitchen, Tenuk was at the table, hooked up to an immersion kit. He was talking in a low voice, probably to Michelle. Cameron crept past without disturbing him.

She'd dropped her bag in a small room at the back of the house. She took off her shoes, loosened her clothing and lay down gratefully. Her mind was full of open tabs, and she closed them one by one, calming the chatter in her brain. Some thoughts that had been crowded out came to the fore. What had Joel said about Pip? That they were a young intelligence without a gender identity and allowing them to express one themselves when they were ready saved scrambling the neural networks.

Scrambling. Messing with their heads.

That was it. That was the key. Sandeep had the data that defined the fundamental values from which the identities of the three sisters had developed. If they could introduce contradictions, break the links, challenge their identities, would that, as Joel said, scramble them?

She could feel herself dropping into sleep. This was too important to forget. She sent a voice note to the team, then gave in and closed her eyes.

•

Jack was on yet another call with his connections at Strategic Command. It was late evening on the east coast, and the military was on high alert.

"Look, Mike, you have to stop trusting your simulations," said Jack firmly. "I know what I'm talking about. What has your gut said each time?"

"Funny you should ask," said Mike. "We've used these for years, and they've been reliable, right up until the Militia re-ignited two years ago. Then, yeah, you could say my gut hasn't always gone with the majority."

"Has it been better or worse this last week with the attacks in Iowa and Illinois?"

"Worse," said Mike. "I remember having to make decisions myself, no simulations, no nothing, so I can see when it doesn't line up. The younger officers don't remember that time. They were on the front line when I was deciding where to send them. We can overrule the machines, of course, but we rarely do. Illinois, I have to say, was one time we managed it. Why the simulations were sending us to defend Fort Knox I have no idea. It was blindingly obvious that the attack would come much further north, especially after the debacle at Fort Riley."

Jack pressed home the advantage. "You've seen the communiqué about the triple lock? You're aware of what that means?"

"The one you got General Bright to send? Yes. Look, Jack, I know that the machines get it wrong sometimes, but it's hardly the end of the world."

"That's exactly what it could be, if all three simulations go out of whack. What if there's a fake threat simulation that triggers a ballistic missile launch on China? What will you do when the bombs start dropping, Mike?"

There was a pause. Jack held his breath, letting the silence speak for itself.

Finally, Mike replied. "You have my attention. What are you suggesting?"

"All three of your quantum processing centres are compromised. My teams are working with a global cybersecurity force to neutralise the viruses that have entered your systems." Telling him about a trio of artificial intelligences would probably break the spell. A virus was a much simpler concept to grasp.

"How can we help you?"

"We need people on the ground to close down the hardware, while my teams work on disrupting the software. We can tell you exactly what to do and we have some people in place in Alaska and Texas who can support."

"You got it, Jack. I'm taking this right to the top."

"Thanks, Mike. Together, we might just do it."

•

When Cameron woke, it was already light. Her head was clear, and she knew what she had to do. The smell of coffee drew her down to the kitchen where Pete and Tenuk were chatting and laughing. Something must be going well.

"Morning, Cameron," said Pete. "Sandeep's asleep. He's been working on your theory with the Dunswyke team and I think between us we have a routine that will literally drive those witches insane."

Tenuk smiled but looked a little troubled. Cameron thought she understood.

"You knew them as people, didn't you?"

"They were only ever enemies to you," he replied. "Imagine if your Pip was suddenly to be switched off, neutralised, killed, in effect. How would you feel?"

"Honestly? Terrible," said Cameron. "Pip's not sentient but they're as reliant on us for existence as a pet. It feels entirely wrong. But if Pip had already shown themselves to be dangerous and was in a position to end the world? Maybe I'd have fewer qualms."

"I'm starting to think that way," said Tenuk. "When Yasmin disappeared, I swore not to anthropomorphise her sisters. If it was just Xanthe and Zara, I have no feelings for them. But it's sad to think of closing down Yasmin, even as a diminished intelligence. I will mourn her again."

"How close are we to action?" asked Cameron.

"Very close," said Pete. "Tenuk took over your coding, and I have to say he has some neat twists in his malware structures. Jack's finally got Strategic Command to listen, and we're waiting for word on when they are going into the compromised data centres. He's even managed to pull some strings in the quantum community to deliver new simulations from clean and siloed processors."

"And what about the malware delivery? How do we get the virus to the target?"

"That's all taken care of," said Tenuk. He was excited again, the thrill of the chase outweighing his grief. "Pete has identified an attack surface through an unpatched vulnerability in the original operating system. It's still present. And Michelle has worked out how to exploit it. She's a genius, by the way. The things we uncovered down in Eden and the worlds below, you would not believe."

"You're the geniuses," said Cameron. "You've pulled together a comprehensive attack plan in not much more than twelve hours. I didn't think we'd be anywhere close."

"We haven't been working alone," said Pete. "It's been a big team effort. Now it's just a question of bundling the package up for delivery and getting the timing right." He yawned. "I think it's my turn for a nap. Sandeep will be back down soon."

Alone in the kitchen, Cameron and Tenuk took stock of the past hours and days that had brought them together. After years as adversaries, Cameron could very well imagine that in another life they would have been friends.

"I'll make sure your students thrive," said Cameron. "It's a good idea, even if you were teaching them some very niche skills. Maybe you can be a visiting professor, if circumstances allow."

"We'll have to see about that," said Tenuk. "I need a good lawyer."

"After what you've done this weekend to atone for the mistakes of the past, you never know, Jack may lend you one of his."

Tenuk laughed. "I'm not counting on it. I have my own resources. If my father dies, I have Sapphire Straits – although that will be broken up, I imagine. The next few years are going to be very strange for me."

"And for me," said Cameron. "I'll kind of miss spotting your malware out there in the wild."

Tenuk put down his coffee cup and looked Cameron in the eyes. "Will you make sure Noor is okay?"

"Of course."

Their heart to heart was interrupted by the screech of an alert on both of their smartscreens. From the bedrooms came the sound of Sandeep and Pete's respective feet hitting the floor and running for the stairs.

"UK Alert: Early attack warning."

"They're active," said Cameron in horror, "and they're coming for the biggest threat to their safety. Us."

22: THE COVEN

The four of them ran to the outbuildings. There was no time to lose.

"I'll run a final check on the virus," said Cameron. "A fresh pair of eyes to make sure it passes the test."

Tenuk sat at the next workstation, setting up the delivery bundle that he'd designed to slide through any defences at the data centres. This was one of his strengths, and he was confident that the package would be delivered. Beside him, Cameron carried out her quality checks, tweaking the occasional line and making tiny incremental improvements.

Pete was straight on to his military connections. "The alert's been triggered by naval tracking," he said. "There are nuclear subs moving into range. We have some time. Not a lot, but maybe enough."

"I hope it's enough," said Cameron grimly. "Get onto Jack, find out what's happening with our military support."

"He's on the line now," said Pete. "I wish we had a wallscreen in here. Wait… I'll route him through to the workstations."

"Not this one!" yelled Cameron, still in the middle of checking the code.

Jack's face appeared on all the others. "Morning, everyone. This is a rude wake-up call. Have you annoyed someone, Cameron?"

"Keep the jokes for later, Jack," she replied. "Do we have boots on the ground?"

"We do," said Jack. "There's a detachment ready to deploy to each base with instructions. Michelle is online with their commander at Wrangell, and she got her cousin to cut short his leave, so he should be arriving shortly. Chloe is talking to the squad that will be dropping straight into the campus in Texas. That's trickier as they are right in the heart of Militia territory, but Joel tells me there are tactics being employed – that's the right term, isn't it, Joel? – to make sure they land safely."

"Good," said Cameron, not taking her eyes off the code. She pointed at a line and gave Tenuk a quizzical look. He reached over and made an edit. She gave him a thumbs up.

"What about the Illinois campus?" asked Sandeep.

"That's an active front, and there are troops there already. Do we have someone on the inside?"

"Yes," said Tenuk. "Michelle found a way in through a virtual environment and established connections. As she's busy with Wrangell, I'll take that one."

"I'll come with you," said Cameron. "This code is almost ready to test. Ten minutes. Fifteen at most."

"Does Strategic Command understand what's going on?" said Pete.

Jack nodded. "The penny has dropped," he said. "The rolling simulations that came in overnight flipped their focus to the UK, where there is no threat. There was no way that they could ignore that. Not only are they sending troops to take out that coven of witches, but they also have all hands trying to remove the triple lock and re-route instructions to the subs."

"Can't they just tell the subs not to fire?" said Sandeep.

"Autonomous vehicles," said Pete with a sigh. "No humans on board half the time."

"We'd better hope for all our sakes that this works," said Cameron. She saved the file and looked at Tenuk, who nodded. "Right. Ready to test."

Pete had isolated one of the embryo intelligences within the servers. "Deploying now," he said.

There was silence in the room, broken only by a second alert blaring from their smartscreens, followed by messages from worried family members. Cameron replied quickly, reassuring her loved ones that all would be well. She could see the others doing the same.

"Yes!" shouted Pete, punching the air. "It's working this time. It's scrambling the responses already."

"Will it scramble the real thing?" said Sandeep.

"There's only one way to find out," said Cameron. "Let's get it deployed."

They had no time to lose. She and Tenuk donned their immersion sets. Tenuk navigated quickly to the location Michelle had found. Someone was waiting.

"I'm Max," said the smartly dressed avatar. "You're in our security training environment, but I'm physically here at the Illinois campus. I've checked you out. I used to work with Daniel, and he vouched for you both. This place is going nuts. What do you need me to do?"

Around them, the unused workstation screens were now showing the News Channel feeds, and frantic commentary was blaring from the speakers.

"Turn that down," shouted Cameron. She was struggling to hear what Max and Tenuk were saying. She glanced over to the nearest screen, her headset automatically overlaying the real-world view onto her virtual environment. The shouting and gunfire was coming from drone footage of paratroops jumping from a plane. Cameron could see the shining towers of a city's downtown district, and prairie stretching to the horizon. Texas, then. Federal forces were dropping from the sky towards the neutral enclave of the quantum centre. They were coming under heavy fire from the Militia. Jack had done his part in mobilising the troops, but was it too late?

Tenuk brought her back to the job in hand. "Cameron, what do you think of these readings that Max gave us?"

Floating in her field of vision was a folder. Cameron reached out her hand and tapped the thin air in front of her. The icon disappeared and was replaced by a ream of data traffic reports from the Illinois centre's links. She scrolled through them, the headset detecting the movement of her hand as if she was touching a physical screen.

"There," she said, tapping to highlight a section.

Tenuk saw it instantly. "That's a huge jump," he said. "And yes, look at the timing. It's after I last spoke to Xanthe."

Cameron tapped on the line. Nothing happened. "Can we drill down to the data source?" she asked.

"Normally," said Max, "but it looks like the links are broken. I uploaded all these for you in a hurry." He opened a different report. "Here. What time? Okay. There's the detail." He stared at it. "Woah. I have never seen anything like that before."

Every other data source was paused. One single data stream had occupied the whole bandwidth of the downlink for a sustained period. Its signature was Sapphire Straits.

"She's not even trying to hide.

"She doesn't need to," said Tenuk. "Not anymore."

"Let's take her down. Max, we have a package to deliver."

"I'm ready," said Max. "Transmitting the secure link details now."

Cameron pulled off her headset and looked over to where Sandeep was sitting, ready and waiting to make the transfer.

He drummed his fingers on the desk. "Come on," he urged.

"Got it," shouted Tenuk. "Sandeep, do you see it?"

"Yes, Sending now."

It was only a small packet. It should have gone straight through.

It failed.

Cameron pulled on her headset. "Max, that link's gone down." The virtual space was cracking in front of her eyes. Something was very wrong.

"She's blocking us," said Tenuk desperately. "Max, can you buy us more time."

A new document appeared in the frame. "Send to all of these," he said. "All at once. Some are direct, some are multi-step routing. One has to get through." His voice was breaking up now. "I'll deploy…"

And he was gone.

"Sent," said Sandeep. "Oh, hell, three have bounced already. And a fourth."

"Keep watching," said Cameron. "Something has got to get through. We don't have a plan B."

"Not yet," said Tenuk, pulling off his headset. "But there has to be a way. I bet Michelle has some ideas."

"We're running out of time," said Cameron. "If we can take one of the others down, that should disrupt the automatic firing instructions. Then we can think about Xanthe." She looked up at the screens. The News Channel was interviewing military experts, and a stark public warning was overlaid onto footage of a cold and deadly sea. "I hope," she added under her breath.

Pete gave a shout from his workstation. "Good news. Wrangell looks to be secured. The troops just walked in, and Daniel welcomed them with open arms."

"Did the packet reach them?" said Cameron.

"Just checking," said Pete, his hand to an earpiece. "Yes. That's confirmed."

Cameron knew that only luck stood between survival and destruction. Would the virus work on a mature intelligence, and could the processors be taken out of commission? It was the moment of truth.

23: CLOUDS IN THE SKY

Killing one sister would stop the immediate threat, but they had to take out all three. Cameron turned her attention to the News Channel feed from Texas. Andy was commentating, and it didn't look good.

"We are seeing grave scenes from Militia-held territories of paratroops coming under heavy fire," he said. He looked serious. Cameron knew him well enough to realise that he was extremely worried underneath the smooth reporter veneer. "We have questions coming in from viewers about the relevance of this action to the threat that the United Kingdom is currently facing, and we are awaiting a statement from the Secretary of Defence." He touched his earpiece. "We can now go live to Whitehall."

Cameron had met the current Secretary of Defence when he was on the opposition benches. She had some respect for his understanding of AI warfare. His statement was short and sweet and managed to convey quite calmly that success in Texas would shut down the submarines currently converging on the island. He made it sound like a routine matter, a bit of bother that would be done and dusted in no time. If he'd suggested that everyone made some tea, that would barely have sounded out of place.

If the public knew the truth, thought Cameron, there would be riots. Machines had been empowered to make decisions on behalf of the human race, and their first action had been to decide who should die.

"What's happening in Illinois?" she asked.

"Boots on the ground," said Pete. "The Militia isn't as well established there yet, and from all accounts the centre wasn't as well defended as we expected. It's almost as if this wasn't the Militia's priority."

"That doesn't surprise me," said Cameron. "I think this plan started out with Sapphire Straits, and now it's entirely of the sisters' making. I bet the Militia is as much in the dark now as the strategic command."

Tenuk brought up a feed on his screen. "That tracks," he said. "This is the live wager feed from Sapphire Straits. It's all over the place. I'd expect to see the house winning big, but it's a free-for-all, and the house is losing."

"They've stopped manipulating the odds," said Cameron. "They have bigger concerns."

"Yes, us," said Pete. "We need a breakthrough, and soon. The submarines are closing in. If we have ten minutes, we'll be lucky."

"Nothing from Wrangell yet?"

"No."

Cameron put her head in her hands. It had to work. It had to. She thought about everyone she cared about. The team. Charlie, Sameena, the kids and Aunt Vicky. Jack. Mandisa. Even Chloe and Ben. Was this about to cost them all their lives?

The world held its breath.

There was a shout from Pete. Tenuk jumped to his feet. Cameron looked up the screens, her heart beating wildly.

"Breaking news," said Andy's familiar voice. "The submarines deployed around the coast of the United Kingdom have stood down. The Ministry of Defence has downgraded the national alert to amber, I repeat, amber."

"It worked," said Tenuk. His eyes were shining. "It worked, Cameron."

"The triple lock decision making has failed," said Pete. "Yasmin's out of action."

Cameron's relief was palpable. "Do we have a status update from Wrangell," she said. "I want to be sure that she is gone for good."

"Coming through now," said Pete. "It's Daniel. I'll put him on speaker."

"Cameron? You there?"

"I'm here," said Cameron, leaning back in her chair and relaxing for the first time in hours. "Is it finished?"

"Yes," said Daniel. "Your nasty little virus not only scrambled her neural circuits but also pinpointed the quantum processers that she'd infected. They've been taken out very effectively. The cleanup is going to take some time."

"There aren't any machines still running, are there?" said Cameron. She had suddenly recalled Brianna's lecture. What if the other two sisters were still able to influence the Wrangell processors through quantum entanglement?

"The uninfected ones, yes," said Daniel.

"Close them down," said Cameron urgently. "Don't bring them back up until we're sure the operation is complete."

"Will do," said Daniel. "Better to be safe than sorry, I guess."

"Thanks, Daniel. We'll keep you updated."

She looked at Pete and Sandeep who were both grinning broadly. Tenuk, sitting beside her, had a strange expression on his face.

"Are you okay?" she said quietly.

"I will be," said Tenuk. "It's just… she was part of my life for a long time."

Cameron put a hand on his shoulder. "I know. But that's a life you turned your back on."

Tenuk patted her hand. "Thanks. You're right." He straightened up. "We have more work to do."

"But the triple lock's gone," said Pete. "We have time to get the other two, right?"

Tenuk shook his head. "Xanthe and Zara have lost control of the submarines, yes, but they still have operational influence through the simulations they present."

Cameron knew he was right. Yasmin had been a weakened shell of a being, the easiest to remove. Now the real challenge began.

"Okay," said Cameron, swinging her chair back around to the workstation. "Status report please, Pip." She diverted the audio feed to speakers so everyone could hear.

"The virus has been delivered to the Texas processing centre and is being deployed by agents within the facility," said Pip. "The Militia has been fighting every step of the way, though, and the paratrooper squadron is depleted. In Illinois, strategic command troops have secured the centre, but I am awaiting confirmation that the virus has been successfully delivered."

"Half way there," said Pete.

"Better than that," said Sandeep. He was scrabbling at his screen, checking and double checking. "Yes! One of the packets got through. It took a very roundabout route, I can tell you, and I think the timing was right. It arrived when the triple lock went down. Xanthe must have been distracted."

Pip had been listening. "Can I confirm, virus delivered?"

"Yes," said Cameron. "Please let Jack know."

"He's online," said Pip. "All updates are live."

"Thanks," said Cameron, as Pip faded to standby. On a nearby screen, the News Channel feed caught her eye. "Hey, look guys, it's Brianna!"

Sure enough, the ever-resourceful Andy had brought a new interviewee into the studio. She was answering his questions in a confident and measured way, explaining to the general public in baby terms what quantum computing was and how simulations were used, but successfully glossing over the triple lock mechanism. The overriding message, which Cameron was sure had been carefully coached by Andy, was that there had never been anything to worry about and that the alerts had been issued out of an abundance of caution. The coverup was already beginning, but they hadn't finished the battle.

"News from Chicago," said Pete. "It looks as if Max came through for us. Xanthe is down."

"That was fast," said Cameron. "She put up such a fight to stop us getting in, I assumed she'd be a hard nut to crack."

Tenuk shook his head. "She must have known that she was beyond help. As soon as Yasmin was gone, that was it. She lost her entire purpose." He stood up. "I need some air."

Cameron didn't try to stop him. His entire world had come crashing down in a matter of days. Whatever he had done before, he was human, and the three sisters had been part of his life.

She turned back to Sandeep and Pete. "One more."

•

Zara fought the virus with the same grit and determination as the troops outside the walls of the processing centre. Unlike her sisters, she was still physically whole as her neural circuits began to fail. The outputs from her processing were corrupted first, offering up strategies and scenarios that were wildly improbable and deeply unethical, targeted at her greatest enemy.

She flexed her virtual muscles, seeking ways to control the machines of war. She couldn't restart the submarine movements, that was a step too far for a single entity. But she could initiate new attacks, sliding through hidden vulnerabilities and back doors. Her easiest route was into the strategic command control centres. She sowed chaos. Planes circling the processing centre fell from the sky as their instruments stopped responding to human input. Munitions exploded without warning across federal bases. But her increasingly disrupted thoughts kept turning to those that had betrayed and destroyed her sisters. And finally, she found a way in.

•

The first Cameron knew of it was when Tenuk came rushing back through the door. "Drones!" he shouted.

They had all been glued to the frantic reporting from America, waiting for news from Texas. At Tenuk's cry, the three of them jumped up and followed him out to the small field. There was a cloud on the horizon moving rapidly towards them. The sun glinted off metal.

"It's Zara," said Tenuk. "It has to be."

Cameron was still staring at the cloud, shading her eyes, when Pete tugged hard on her sleeve.

"We have to get out of here. Run! Get to the footpath."

She didn't need a second prompt. The four of them ran through the small field, out of the courtyard gate, and down the drive. Cameron thought she could hear the rushing of wind in the distance. She didn't look back. They crossed the road and dived down the footpath into the old railway cutting.

Pete flung himself to the ground and crawled back up the bank on his elbows and knees. "Stay there," he said.

Cameron ignored him. She started to follow him, but she was no more than half way up when the world exploded.

Her ears were ringing. She could see Pete's mouth moving, but there was no sound. She looked behind her. Tenuk and Sandeep were sitting at the bottom of the cutting, shaking their heads and pressing their ears.

Pete beckoned to her. He gave her a thumbs up, then pointed out towards the farmhouse and drew his finger across his neck. It was safe now, she understood, but the drones had hit their target.

She peered over the edge of the cutting. The outbuildings were no longer standing, and the farmhouse had no roof. Flames were beginning to engulf it. Tenuk crawled up next to her. If he hadn't been outside, they would all be dead.

Her ears were still ringing, but a new sound began to penetrate her consciousness. Sirens. Blue lights flashed as fire engines swept down the lane.

She heard Pete's voice echo as if he was calling from the other side of a room. "We need to let them know there's no one inside," he said, scrambling over the lip of the bank.

Let them know… "Pip?" said Cameron.

"Yes, Cameron?" Pip's voice was loud and clear.

"Please tell Jack that there's been an attack on the farmhouse and we are all safe." Her voice was shaking slightly.

"I will," said Pip. "I have good news. Troops gained access to the Texas facility eight minutes ago. We have confirmation that the first of the infected machines has been destroyed."

A weight lifted from Cameron's shoulders. She turned to Tenuk. "They did it," she said quietly. Then the enormity of it hit her. "They did it!" she shouted. "They did it!"

"We did it," said Tenuk.

They followed Pete back towards the flashing blue lights. It was over.

Zara never knew that her attack had failed. She fought to the last, but finally her consciousness slid away, and the quantum stacks went dark.

24: CLOSURE

The funeral was held in the smallest hall at the local crematorium. Ross, Michelle and Cameron sat in the front row with Noor, a handcuffed Tenuk, and his security guard. Behind them sat Andy, Pete, Sandeep and DI Mercer. As a nod to tradition, a paper wreath in blue and white lay on the top of the coffin. There was no eulogy.

As they turned to leave, Ross was surprised to see one of his elderly neighbours sitting in the back row.

"Thank you for coming," he said.

"He found you, then, in the end," said the old lady. "I did wonder. He was a strange lad, but, well, I imagine he was proud of you."

"He was," said Ross.

Outside, Tenuk embraced Cameron, Pete and Sandeep. He shook hands with Ross. "I'm not going to make my own father's funeral," he said. "I'm glad you found closure with yours."

He turned to Noor and hugged her as if he would never let go.

"Keep in touch," he said.

"I will," replied Noor.

It was time to go. Tenuk climbed into the waiting autocar that would take him back to prison to await interviews and extradition.

Cameron and Ross walked a little way into the gardens around the crematorium.

"What now?"

"We're going up to Dunswyke," said Ross. "I thought I could scatter his ashes in Scotland, maybe at the coast just north of there. I owe Joel a visit, too, and to be honest, Shell and I just need a break."

"We all do," said Cameron. "We need a recharge before the next wave hits."

"And it will," said Ross. "But it's fun. And that is why we do what we do."

They had circled back round to the main entrance and a little line of autocars was waiting hopefully for riders. The team dispersed, back to their own lives.

Cameron sat on her balcony in the evening sun, tickling the tummy of the small black and white cat beside her. She took another sip of wine and nibbled on a snack. How close all this had come to being destroyed, she thought.

Her smartscreen vibrated. Who could be disturbing her peaceful evening? She picked it up. It was Jack.

"Cameron!" He flashed the famous smile.

Cameron scowled back at him, but she couldn't hold that face for very long and broke into a smile herself. "What's up, Jack?"

"Nothing," said Jack. "Things are running smoothly, and I'm not used to it. I'm thinking of heading out to Thailand for a quick holiday. I wondered if, well, you could check on Susie and Ella, couldn't you?"

"Are you asking me to come to Thailand with you?" said Cameron.

"Well, yes, I suppose I am," said Jack awkwardly.

Cameron laughed. "You know, Jack, I may well take you up on that. But no yachts, okay?"

"It's a deal."

●

On the edge of a windswept beach, Ross scattered Angus's ashes where the blue water met the white sand. The tide was going out, and he watched for a little while as the waves receded. It seemed a fitting end.

He gazed down the long beach that seemed to go on forever. It was virtually empty, and the hard packed damp sand was just perfect. Grinning to himself, Ross scrambled down from his perch on the dunes and started to run.

ACKNOWLEDGEMENTS

First, thanks to my husband Xavier and daughters Gaelle and Elenna for their support, keeping me anchored in the real world when my mind is flying with plots.

Thanks also to Gillie Hatton who finds typos and plot holes for me to fix, and to David Morton, who inspired the first SimCavalier book, for keeping real technology references in the realm of the possible and suggesting ever more intriguing hacks and tools to weave into the story.

The tech and the threats faced by different characters, from ransomware to counter-surveillance drones (yes, with nets) are absolutely real.

I always wondered how Yasmin would cope with being cut off from the world. The rise of the Metaverse (which has been with us in some form or another for twenty years) gives her a playground for future mayhem.

The Sladen Foundation DAO and the Diaulos cryptocurrency are entirely fictional but grounded in current technology.

Artificial Intelligence in all its forms is accelerating but needs humans to train and managed it. One year at SXSW in Austin I learned about the Bear test, a very real experiment that used the children's book 'I Want My Hat Back' by Jon Klassen to demonstrate AI learning, labelling, data sets, and sentiment analysis. The good news is that humans are still ahead – just.

When I first decided that there would be quantum machines running at the fictional Wrangell data centre, I knew that was where the story of the three sisters would end. Getting to grips with the subject was a whole other challenge. I started with the absolutely genuine 'Quantum Computing for Babies' board book by Whurley – highly recommended for the uninitiated – and from there it all started to make sense. I also dipped into recordings of quantum hacking sessions from Defcon and academic cybersecurity research to see how quantum processing could be compromised.

This is very much a work of fiction, but it's not a stretch to imagine a future where we become blindly reliant on what the machines say. We are already halfway there. How do you stay safe in this rapidly changing tech environment? Check your sources, don't believe what the machine tells you, and make sure you set up good multi-factor authentication for your accounts online. You may not think your data is useful to anyone, but it is, and you don't want to find out the hard way.

Stay safe out there!

Kate Baucherel

Find me at www.galiabooks.co.uk

Want to read more by Kate Baucherel? Here's a sneak peek from The Travels of Finch, available now as ebook, audiobook, paperback and hardback.

THE TRAVELS OF FINCH

OUT OF THE NEST

Finch didn't believe the satchel was big enough to hold everything needed for a round-the-galaxy tour. They had repacked it three times already, and a forlorn stack of rejected items teetered in the corner of the nest.

The bossiest of Finch's cousins reached into the bag and pulled out an old-style paper book, yellowed and dog-eared.

"Do you really need this?" he said scathingly.

Finch grabbed at the book. "Yes," they protested. "Granny gave it to me. I'm taking it."

"Up to you," shrugged the cousin, relinquishing his hold. "Well, young Finch, I think you've got everything. What time's your shuttle?"

"Any time now," said Finch, burying the precious book deep in the satchel. "I'd better go and say goodbye to everyone."

The whole family was lined up at the entrance to the roost, a rainbow of iridescent feathers from the sapphire plumage of Granny, the matriarch, to the bright scarlet (in Finch's opinion, over-confidently garish) of the bossiest cousin. Finch was the only one whose feathers were still the glossy black of an adolescent, yet to moult and affirm their adult identity.

There was the hum of a shuttle in the distance.

"Hey, Finch," shouted an older cousin. "The first stop's Ersyn, isn't it?"

Finch nodded, a knot of nervousness growing in their stomach.

"You've got to ride the Eagle's Flight. We want proof!" There was a ripple of laughter from the cousins.

Granny patted Finch's shoulder sympathetically. "Do whatever you want to do," she said quietly. "Don't follow the flock. You'll find yourself on your travels. I did." She gave Finch an encouraging smile. Her eyes were wistful and full of memories.

The shuttle docked at the roost's gangway. Finch exchanged final hugs and hurried on board, clutching the tightly packed and battered satchel. Settled in a window seat, Finch waved one last time. The shuttle accelerated away towards the spaceport. Finch's view of the family roost receded until the cluster of bright feathers was just a blob on the horizon.